GEMINI MAN TRILOGY

The Complete Series

JD Cowan
&
Thomas Plutarch

Dedicated to Phyllis Pascas Goodwyn

Book Cover Art and Design by Manuel Guzman, LolosArt.com
Illustrations by Pencilmania

Table of Contents

GEMINI WARRIOR...............................1
Prologue...1
Chapter 1: MATTHEW & JASON................................2
Chapter 2: NEXT PHASE...6
Chapter 3: CASTOR & POLLUX.................................9
Chapter 4: MAGIC CITY MAGEUOPOLIS..............12
Chapter 5: ESCAPE FROM THE MIST PRISON......17
Chapter 6: BIG WRECK...23
Chapter 7: BETWEEN DEATH AND DREAMS.......28
Chapter 8: DUEL ON MIST MOUNTAIN.................32
Chapter 9: BATTLE ON FROG MOUNTAIN............35
Chapter 10: EMPIRE OF GOLD................................40
Chapter 11: IN A STRANGE LAND...........................43
Chapter 12: INTO TYNDARUS.................................46
Chapter 13: FIRE LIZARD INVASION.....................53
Chapter 14: THIEVES' TOWN...................................58
Chapter 15: PHANTOM STAB...................................64
Chapter 16: WHAT LIES IN THE DEEP WOODS....68
Chapter 17: THE ONE WHO WILL SAVE................71
Chapter 18: LAST VILLAGE.....................................75
Chapter 19: INTO THE TRAP....................................82
Chapter 20: STONE MOUNTAIN CASTLE..............84
Chapter 21: EDGING TOWARD CAVERN'S END. .87
Chapter 22: SERENITY...91
Chapter 23: END OF THE ROAD.............................95
Epilogue...97
GEMINI DRIFTER............................100
Prologue...101
Chapter 1: CROSS COUNTRY................................102
Chapter 2: A RUN THROUGH ROANOKE............107
Chapter 3: THE RAIN POURS................................110
Chapter 4: LITTLE WINTER...................................112
Chapter 5: SUMMER MORNING IN WINTER......116
Chapter 6: BLOODEATER......................................121
Chapter 7: STREETS OF ALBION..........................124
Chapter 8: UNDER THE SURFACE........................129
Chapter 9: FIRE IN THE NIGHT............................134
Chapter 10: A TREACHEROUS PATH....................140
Chapter 11: CHAMELEONS...................................144
Chapter 12: REAL MAGIC.....................................148
Chapter 13: WHAT HIDES IN THE SHADE...........152
Chapter 14: DYING FOR IT...................................157
Chapter 15: DEEP DOWN IN THE DARK..............162
Chapter 16: RAGING THROUGH THE VOID........168
Chapter 17: MIRROR DANCE................................172
Chapter 18: DOWN TO THE GROUND..................178
Chapter 19: RISE OF THE GEMINI MAN..............182
Chapter 20: SUNSHINE...186
Epilogue...192
GEMINI OUTSIDER.........................194
Prologue...195
Chapter 1: OUTSIDERS..197
Chapter 2: BURNING TOWN.................................202
Chapter 3: KNOW YOUR ENEMY..........................208
Chapter 4: WELCOME TO RIVERVIEW................213
Chapter 5: THE HARBINGER APPROACHES......219
Chapter 6: NIGHT STALKERS...............................228
Chapter 7: AT THE WATER'S EDGE......................237
Chapter 8: DARK STARS OF TWILIGHT..............244
Chapter 9: SUICIDE...247
Chapter 10: NEW DAWN...252
Chapter 11: SUMMER STORM...............................260
Chapter 12: MIDNIGHT LIGHTNING....................264
Chapter 13: MORNING THUNDER........................274
Chapter 14: THE GIANTS ATTACK.......................280
Chapter 15: PANIC ON THE WATER......................286
Chapter 16: RIVER MASSACRE............................290
Chapter 17: MASS SUICIDE..................................294
Chapter 18: END OF THE OUTSIDERS..................299
Epilogue...302
CODA...304
GEMINI DREAMER..........................305
Chapter 1: EVERY NIGHT......................................305
Chapter 2: MAN OF STONE...................................309
Chapter 3: THE DREAMING CITY.........................311
Chapter 4: GLASS ASSASSIN................................316
Chapter 5: THE DREAMER'S PRISON..................319
Chapter 6: SECOND SON..321
Chapter 7: TOMORROW'S KINGDOM..................324
Chapter 8: DREAM'S END.....................................327
Chapter 9: GEMINI DREAMER..............................332
GEMINI DESTROYER.....................334
Prologue...334
Chapter 1: DEAD & ALIVE.....................................335
Chapter 2: THE GIRL IN THE MIRROR.................337
Chapter 3: THE FALL OF MAGEUOPOLIS...........340
Chapter 4: GEMINI HARBINGER..........................343
Chapter 5: THE GREAT SORCERER KING...........346
Chapter 6: FINAL MEETINGS...............................350
Chapter 7: LAST PIECE..354
Chapter 8: GEMINI DESTROYER..........................357
Chapter 9: THE ENDLESS PLAINS........................360
Chapter 10: END OF THE GEMINI MAN...............363
Epilogue...364

FOREWORD

IT HAS BEEN A LONG TIME since I set out on this journey. My ability has let me see the stories of so many from all sorts of places and from people of all shapes and sizes. We all bleed the same, but some bleed more than others.

And some never truly stop until the last drop drains from them.

This is a story I thought long lost, a tale of two who united as one to stand against forces far beyond known time and space. Before I set out to chronicle the tales of the world that fell between the cracks, I would never have imagined there was so much about this crazy existence we just could not understand. Even I don't always believe it.

The author whose words you are currently reading has caught a glimpse into this, and I helped steady his mind to process it, just as I have others before.

Not all those stories will be told, some simply cannot, but once you know exactly how far out existence stretches—how many lives, how much magic, and how much mystery, can be found out beyond the everyday grind we all face, you will understand just why I am called to share it all with you. It is only through worlds of imagination filtered through reality (or is it the other way around?) that we can truly see ourselves from a new angle and understand our place in it all.

But enough of my interference.

I will now let the author of this story take over and let you in to a tale that exists on the fringes of your perception: a place you might know but have never lived yourself.

Well, now you will.

Enjoy the true story of a pair of heroes who fell into the margins themselves, and learn just what they found there. In a world where heroes, villains, and the supernatural itself, is everywhere, you might be surprised at how much awaits you out there.

It is waiting for all of us!

Welcome to the world of heroes.

~ *THOMAS PLUTARCH*

Gemini Man

A Heroes Unleashed Tale

JD Cowan
&
Thomas Plutarch

BOOK ONE

GEMINI WARRIOR

JASON VERMILION

PROLOGUE

Matthew White walked the length of the narrow hall with his mind moving faster than his legs. He'd heard stories about Williams' Tech Corp, but he never imagined they would send their employees to meetings so far out of the way in Greycoast. This slummier area of Serenity City had a reputation, and this building upheld it well. Painted grey halls, old hokey pictures of abandoned country-sides, and faded carpets swallowed him whole and assaulted his allergies.

Dust choked the stifling heat. A sneeze caught in his nostrils. Even with summer blazing outside, these jokers still put the heating on. A job was a job, and this was no different, but an eerie feeling clung to his nerves. Two looming men in grey suits led him onward through the humming fluorescent lighting while Matthew fought against his gut.

"Have either of you ever been to Cavern Cove?" he asked them. The silence was too much. He straightened his cheap tie. He wore an ugly lavender suit, all that he could afford from the Salvation Army. Richie wouldn't take any more credit from him. Not that he could blame the poor guy. "It's no Serenity City, but it sure is a nice place to hang your hat. No Primes, city lights, or chaos there. Good vacation spot."

His two sentries continued on in silence. Footsteps glided across the carpet. He cleared his throat.

"I've only heard rumors about this place. Do you guys research superhero—I mean *Prime* powers here? I can't imagine why you would want to. They're not going anywhere."

A large wooden door swung open at the end of the long, winding hall. Matthew moved into the small room with two chairs in the center. A woman in a blue suit, glasses, and her platinum hair in buns sat in the one facing him. She held a tablet on her lap and smiled towards his entrance. Before Matthew could say anything, the door shut behind him. Pale light from the fluorescents buzzed above, emphasizing the emptiness and reminding him that the two of them were alone. He grabbed at his collar, hoping his sweat wasn't showing through.

The woman gestured to the chair in front of him, and he sat down.

"Mr. Matthew White," she said in a honeyed tone. Her lips lingered on every word. "I am Marguerite Stohl. Thank you for applying to Williams' Tech. You are an interesting individual. I have been looking into your application, and must say I'm mystified."

He was more confused at the fact that this wasn't the Williams' Tech building but didn't bring it up. "I'm pretty mystified, myself. I thought I applied for a general security position at a warehouse down by the bus depot. How did my application get to Williams' Tech?"

"We have a lot of friends. Do you mind if I ask some personal questions?"

Sweat ran down his back, causing him to shift. "It's your position. Ask away."

"You are twenty-two years old, have no formal education, have worked many menial jobs, and yet you also do not have any references. Is there a particular reason for this?"

Matthew bit his lip. "I . . . made a lot of mistakes when I was younger. You probably won't find my name anywhere online or in any files. There's no big secret—I just keep to myself. I don't have any family left, and I've never had much in the way of friends."

"That is a shame. No children? I have one little girl I constantly worry about. Surely you hope to one day have young ones?"

"Money is about all I need. If that's a problem, I'm sorry. I'd rather keep to myself and away from that kinda thing. That's why I applied for a job in such an out of the way place. I didn't expect someone like you would take my application."

"You do not have to sell yourself short, Mr. White. My sources say your work ethic is admirable. Very good. Apparently, you worked as a dishwasher for a Chinese restaurant for two years and were well regarded there. I do like what I've heard."

"Thank you. The Rustik was a good place. Friendly folk; paid well."

"But this job is not for a security position. I want you for a product tester. You will work on your own, and keep to yourself. Mostly. This is why I sought out someone with your personality."

"How do you mean?"

"You will be required to move into an apartment of our choosing and be monitored for all hours of the day for at least a month. You can sign for an extension when your time is up if you wish to go longer. It is challenging, but I feel you are perfect for the position."

Matthew scratched his carefully shaved chin. "I don't know. I prefer privacy."

"One look at the contract and you will change your mind. The amount paid is far more than what that security position would earn you."

She showed him the tablet with an estimated number staring back in his face. For a second he couldn't tell if he imagined it, or if these people were just *that* crazy. With this amount, he could live high off the hog between jobs for years. Resisting this would be hard.

"I still have one question," he said, keeping a stony expression.

"You can ask whatever you like."

"What exactly am I testing? Food? Drugs? Tech?"

"It's a bit more complicated than that, but I can assure you that you will not have to ingest anything unnatural." Her smile broke into a line of bright white teeth. "In fact, there is a strong possibility that you will not have to do anything at all. It depends on how you work out."

It would have been a lie to say that this job didn't pique his interest. But he'd been around this block before. Work that didn't involve work was too good to be true. There must be a catch.

Still, it didn't matter. He didn't care how real it was. In a city of superheroes where he could be wiped out at any moment, he had long since given up on expecting a long life. All he wanted was a place to work, and a way to live for the moment before the end arrived. He wanted what he could scrape together. Whatever this place offered was already more than he expected.

Even though she went on with her sales pitch, Matthew had already made his decision. When she wrapped up, he would sign on the dotted line. He had made that call when he walked in the front door. This was exactly what he needed—a place to forget the chaotic world outside.

He just wished he could figure out why it was so hot inside.

CHAPTER 1
MATTHEW & JASON

HEAVY SWEAT RAN down Matthew's back as he watched the clear blue sky from the inside of his new apartment. Ever since he had moved to this place a month ago, it rubbed him wrong. The cameras in the corners of the rooms watched his every move, and no one ever came by. Even the view through his window was a forgery—a wall-length video screen constructed to give him the false impression of a world outside his door. But there was no outside. Matthew had been left alone.

He wouldn't complain even if there were someone else to tell it to. This was the job, and he took it, warts and all. But that didn't mean sitting around in a fake apartment doing nothing was a healthy way to spend a month. He wore old black sweatpants that clashed with his blonde hair and pink skin and had nothing else on to fight the heat. It was just too hot; there was no air conditioning, and he hadn't packed any shorts. He couldn't imagine walking around in his underwear with those cameras on him. They could already see the abs on his shirtless body. The first thing he would buy with his pay for this job would be a decent set of clothes.

Matthew fell back in the faux-leather couch and yawned. Only two more days until his contract ran out and he could leave. Then he could pocket the money and get a *real* apartment with a *real* view. Dreams of real furniture filled his every thought. He'd kill to have proper hardwood floors. Heck, he could even live off the extra money for a year without needing to get another job. It was perfect.

But also not his style.

The sofa leather squeaked under Matthew's weight as he sat up. He slammed his fist against the armrest.

"I can't just sit around," he whispered to himself. He found himself saying that a lot. Matthew didn't like to talk to himself, but there weren't many other options to keep his voice fresh. "I can't do this."

Yet he did. This was the twenty-ninth day of May, and freedom was close.

A sharp voice squeaked out from the speaker in the corner of the ceiling like a wooden chair against a bare floor. The intercom system. He hadn't heard it since his first day. He crinkled his brow.

"Mr. White," Marguerite Stohl said. Her voice crackled inside the tiny space. "You are doing quite well. It is time for the second phase of the project."

"I hope it doesn't take as long as the first."

"Please open your front door, and we will begin the true test."

He did not have to be asked twice. Matthew bounded off the couch.

The front door was usually locked, but he distinctly remembered a small narrow metal hall outside that led back the way he entered from. Matthew relished seeing it again.

If he were honest with himself, he would have admitted that he didn't remember much about coming here. The building he had his job interview in was just a random warehouse. After accepting the offer, Matthew packed clothes like the sweats he currently wore. He didn't have much else. Then they loaded him into a van and brought him to this building. He exited into a parking garage and took an elevator to a floor of metal halls. He saw a nice atrium of stone pillars on the way up, but little else.

But it did make sense to bring him here like that. With superheroes and villains in the world, there was no telling who was watching. If their work was that important, then they clearly didn't need Primes getting in the way.

What didn't make sense was what he found on the other side of the front door. A boy stood in front of him.

"Hello, sir, I'm Jason."

Jason looked no older than fifteen and wore a green hooded shirt with jeans and sneakers. His blond hair, blue eyes, and general demeanor eerily reminded Matthew of his own. This boy was his doppelganger. Unlike Matthew, however, he was slightly shorter and looked dead tired.

Beside Jason stood Marguerite Stohl again. This time she wore a green dress and had her long platinum hair down. Matthew found himself staring at her until she spoke.

"Do you find this sort of wear appropriate, Mr. White?"

"You're a bit overdressed."

"I mean you."

Matthew glanced at his bare chest, and his cheeks reddened. He ran back toward his tiny bedroom. He could hear that woman laughing to the boy as he dug through his clothes.

As Matthew shuffled through his small closet for a shirt, a sinkhole spread in his stomach. Jason was the first non-employee Matthew had seen in nearly a month, and he looked so much like him. This boy gave him a bad feeling. No one had said anything about children being involved when he signed up.

When he returned to the living room, he found both of his visitors sitting at the small kitchen table across from the couch. They didn't talk. The boy had his arms folded and looked down at his shoes. Only the woman stood to greet Matthew.

"You really must invest in a new wardrobe, Mr. White."

"I haven't seen another body in a month, and this is all you have to say? I sure hope the second phase is more involved than the first." Spending all his time doing push-ups and sit-ups exhausted his energy and his patience. The only other thing he could do was think about old times, and he had no interest in that. "This whole project has been a massive disappointment."

"Oh, I promise you that you will enjoy what is to come. I certainly will."

He joined them at the table. The two males sat across from each other and didn't so much as look each other in the face. The woman watched with a smile. Finally, Matthew broke the silence.

"Is awkward silence part of the project?"

"No. There are three parts. Phase one was getting you acclimated to these surroundings and weeding out the other candidates. Only you two remain."

"*Weeding out*," he repeated. "You mean I could have been fired at any moment?"

"You would have simply reached the end of the testing period and then been sent on your way. But the two of you have passed, so you both move on."

"I hope phase two has more than health food and water in the fridge. I'm dying here."

"It is simple, Mr. White. For the next forty-eight hours the two of you are to stay in this apartment and learn as much about each other as you can. And you will be wearing these."

The woman lifted a hand from her side and placed it in the middle of the table. Her slim fingers opened, and two round objects fell free from her grip, bouncing against the cheap wood. Bracelets. The circular trinkets rolled to a stop in the center. She laughed at their confused stares.

The accessories were perfectly circular bands without any engraved words or jewels to be found on them. Other than the bright yellow color, they looked like normal bracelets one could see at a jeweler or a pawn shop.

One of them caught Matthew's eye. The pair looked precisely the same, no difference whatsoever in their simple shape, and yet the one on the right had a distinctive vibe to it. It whispered for him to reach out. Before he even realized it, he did exactly that. The boy did the same to the opposite bracelet, spinning it in his fingers. They glanced at each other in bewilderment before the celebratory shouts of Ms. Stohl broke their confusion.

"Put them on," she said. "This is part of phase two."

The two males scanned the bracelets then glanced at each other. Matthew could not get over how much this kid looked like him. Maybe this was also part of the experiment.

"If you say so," Matthew said.

He placed it on his left wrist and showed it to the woman. She nodded her approval. The boy followed a second later.

"Good," she said with a bright smile. "Leave those on for forty-eight hours, and we will continue on to phase three, and you will be paid. You are almost there!"

"This is it?" Matthew looked over the bracelet once more. "What's the gimmick?"

"The *gimmick* is that we need two subjects perfectly in sync with each other. Having the bracelets helps. It would also aid us if you knew more about each other. If there are no further questions, I will take my leave."

Marguerite Stohl bid the two of them goodbye and strode to the exit, her slim form gracefully sliding like a swan through a calm lake. Matthew did want to ask questions, but couldn't muster them up. A dull pain formed in the back of his brain. He decided to ignore it. He was so close to being paid. He wouldn't risk it now.

She grinned. "The two of you have forty-eight hours to spend together. I suggest getting started."

With that, she closed the door behind her and left the two alone. The view screen where the windows should be now displayed a hard orange sunset. The stifling heat continued unabated. Jason faced Matthew, his serious expression as irritating as ever.

"You're Matthew?" he asked. "Good to meet you."

"I'm Matthew White. What's with your clothes? You look like you fell into a clothesline. That's weird for a serious looking kid like you."

The boy blinked and looked Matthew over.

"You're one to talk, Mr. White. You look like you just rolled out of bed."

"Don't call me *Mr. White*. It's *Matthew*. I'm not that much older than you are. And of course, I'm wearing this. It's boiling in here. I forgot to tell that woman to turn down the heat."

"Mrs. Stohl told me that it's high because it is part of the stress test."

"Trying to see how quick they can cook us, I'd say." Matthew thought for a second then jumped from his seat. "Wait, Stohl is married?"

"Of course she's married." The boy looked genuinely confused. "Didn't you talk to her before the experiment started? It was one of the first things she told me about her. She's happily married to a great man with a daughter of her own."

"I don't pry into other people's lives. I have my own crap to worry about."

"Is that why you're here? To avoid other people?"

"I'm here because it was a job with good pay. Why else would I be locked in a room with a nosey stone-faced kid like you? Why are *you* here, smart guy? Aren't your parents worried about you?"

"Me?" Once again it appeared the boy did not expect questions directed at him. "My parents don't mind. Money is money."

"So we do have that in common."

"Unfortunately."

"If you have a problem with me, Jason, then tell me now. I don't deal with snide punks."

"I don't know you well enough to tell you my problem, *Matthew*. But you are rude, and I don't like that."

"Kids really are clueless."

Matthew fell into the couch and cupped his head in his hands. The earlier headache ratcheted up. It thumped his skull like a hammer on steel. Where did this pain come from? He bit his lip and fought it off.

"You can sleep in the spare room at the back," he said. "I wondered why it was there, but I guess this is the reason. There are ready-made meals in the fridge, but I suppose you had those in your apartment. There's about five left."

"Whatever."

"Oh, I hate kids."

Hours passed. Matthew kept his distance from Jason. Having no internet or television in the apartment only made things worse. Normally he would just do some exercises to pass the time, but Jason's presence made that awkward. He sat on his bed and counted the ceiling tiles instead. The orange sun on the screen had nearly set, so he turned on the light.

A sound stirred in the hall outside his room.

He sat up and sighed. "What are you doing out there?"

"Going to sleep."

"Isn't it a bit early for that?"

Jason paused as if in thought. "How can you even tell what time it is?"

"Good point. Well, at least let's do what Marguerite asked us to do."

Matthew crossed the hallway and leaned against the door-frame to the spare room. Jason already sat facing him on the bed.

The boy rolled his eyes. "You mean we should talk?"

"What else? We're going to be here for a bit. Might as well do something. What's your last name?"

Jason stared at the wall. "I'd rather not tell you."

"Then let's talk about something else. Where are you from?"

"Not saying. This conversation must be unpleasant for you, Mr. White."

This was one smug punk. "Actually, I don't want to know. But I'm bored and sick of doing nothing around here. What do you like to do?"

"I like to keep up with Primes."

"You're a hero nut?" Matthew cut off a groan. "I guess that's a kid thing to do."

"I'm not a kid. I'm fifteen. And yes, I like to think about them. They showed up one day and ended up changing the world overnight. Don't you think that makes them a big deal?"

"No, that makes them annoying. I was only a squirt at the time, but haven't you heard of the rampage Achilles went on? How about the Highway War? Did you never hear about how the Ionic Man magnetized everything he touched before Pendragon somehow slipped through to take him out? Even that guy is a piece of work. Too squeaky clean, and he always manages to say the right thing to make everyone fall all over him. Can't stand his type. We'd be better off without all of them. Life is tough enough without the whole hero and villain shebang."

"Oh, what do you know? You're just a normal human."

"And thank God for that. I was born with nothing, and I'll die with nothing. There's no better way to go out than even and square. I pay my dues, and I get left alone to do what I want. Prying into other people's business is a waste of time."

"Well, it can't *totally* be a waste of time." Jason suddenly cracked a grin. "Mrs. Stohl told me they were in the business of looking into powers themselves. Maybe they'll find the secret to them. Maybe everyone can get abilities."

"Or maybe they'll find a way to wipe them out. Why do you like these Primes so much anyway? You wanna be one? Why? It looks like a lot of hassle for no reward. Two of the most popular heroes are dead or in jail. Just jump off a roof or rob a bank if that's the ending you want. It takes a lot of arrogance to put on a mask and decide you're going to change everything. Some of us like the way things are."

Jason jumped up. He marched over to Matthew with clenched teeth. He met the older man nearly face to face. "How could you possibly like the way things are? Crime rules the city, and people get stepped on every day. If we had more heroes, we wouldn't have those problems!"

"I hate to break it to you, but yes. Yes, we would absolutely still have those problems. We had monsters long before Primes showed up, and we'll have them long after they're gone. It's only a matter of time. We're only lucky it hasn't happened yet."

"Because we have heroes to stop them. We just need more of them."

"Until they turn into Achilles and wipe out half the city."

"That wouldn't happen again if we had more heroes to stop him!"

"Crime doesn't stop just because heroes exist."

"I never said it did! I said it can be stopped if more good people stood up against it."

"You are surprisingly naive, Jason. I bet you also think all those arrogant fame-grabbers care one whit if you or I get stepped on. Here's a clue: they don't. You have no idea what you're talking about."

Jason leaned forward and jabbed a finger into Matthew's chest. Matthew stood his ground, but something strange happened. Dizziness gripped his skull, and queasiness stuck in his gut.

Matthew floated off the ground, lifted by an invisible force and was thrown forward—into Jason!

The boy put his arms up, but there was no impact. Matthew flew forward into Jason and melted into him. Darkness overtook Matthew momentarily.

Hard breaths fell and tension pooled in his blood.

"What happened?" Jason asked. "Where are you?"

"*I'm here*," Matthew said.

"Where's here? Why are you speaking like you're inside my head?"

Matthew looked around. He had lost some height and now stood where Jason had just been. But the boy's voice spoke from his mouth. The revelation hit Matthew like a cold flash: it wasn't his mouth. He was inside Jason.

"*Because I think that's where I am.*" A sting of panic settled both inside of Matthew and around him—Jason flipped out. "*Calm down and look at a mirror.*"

Jason ran across the hall into the bathroom. He looked straight into the mirror and patted himself all over. Nothing was different on the outside. Matthew saw all of this as if he was in the boy's body. They had somehow merged together.

"*Look at your hand*," Matthew stated as calmly as he could. "*Your bracelet's gone.*"

Jason instantly looked at his left hand. His breath pumped out in spurts.

The bracelet had indeed vanished. The boy trembled. Matthew couldn't blame him; he barely held back his own panic. Sweat covered goosebumps grew all over the boy. Jason fell back against the wall as Matthew tried thinking this through.

This was the experiment? The bracelets merged two people together? That couldn't be it. Some level of compatibility had to be needed. This had to be why they were chosen to pair up.

Any hope that this project was just a lark, or for some good cause, faded at that moment. All Matthew could see was that smile on Marguerite's face as they put on the bracelets. She knew this would happen.

Jason breathed deeply as he leaned against the wall and clutched the hand where his bracelet should have been. Matthew said nothing. Fear held him back. He didn't know what to say, but he knew what they had to do.

They needed to get out of this place, and fast.

CHAPTER 2
NEXT PHASE

PANIC OVERWHELMED JASON'S SENSES. He touched Matthew, and now Matthew was in his head! And where was the bracelet?

Pure madness.

Jason only agreed to this whole thing because of Mrs. Stohl. She couldn't have known this would happen . . . could she? She had been so kind when she found him sleeping in the alley. She fed him and kept him warm.

He stumbled out of the bathroom and towards the living room. This had to be a mistake. Maybe he could convince Mrs. Stohl to open the door and let them out. Maybe this whole thing was a misunderstanding.

"Where are you going?" Matthew's voice said inside his head. *"I can't even tell what you're thinking in here. Damn, this is crazy. But you need to calm down."*

"Calm down?" Jason replied in his mind. *"You were just absorbed into my head, and I can't get you out!"*

"Listen to me. Don't freak out. We need to address this rationally, even if it is mental."

Matthew's eerie cool succeeded in simmering Jason's frantic mood. The boy paced behind the living room couch. Matthew was right. There had to be a reason for all this.

"Think about it," Matthew stated. *"Why would they create bracelets that randomly merge two people?"*

Relief smashed against Jason's nerves. That was true. There must be a way for them to split apart again. The bracelets had to have some rationality behind them.

"You understand, then? There has to be a way to separate again. Concentrate. If physical contact got us here, maybe mental force will get us out."

"Alright. I'll try."

Jason took a deep breath and closed his eyes. He couldn't push Matthew out of his head, but he could try to isolate and separate the two of them mentally.

An outline of Matthew floated in the depths of Jason's mind. With a thought, he imagined removing the older figure like a needle from a haystack. An odd weight stuck inside him like a splinter slowly being pulled free from his head. It was Matthew!

"I feel that," Matthew said. *"We're almost there."*

Stars shot across Jason's vision, and a sudden queasiness came and left in an instant. It was like losing a good deal of weight and regaining it again. Jason fell against the back of the couch in the middle of the open room. A shape formed before him.

To his right stood Matthew, whole again. The bracelets returned to both their wrists.

"Good job, Jason. Not sure how you managed, but we're back to normal. Looks like the bracelets are back, too."

Jason wiped the sweat from his brow and took notice of his left hand. "What are these things?"

"Part of the experiment. These psychos knew this would happen, and they didn't say anything. Do you still think these people are going to help heroes?"

It took Jason a moment to realize what Matthew had just said. He was right. This project was a sham. He tried to think it through, but his legs trembled violently, and it took too much concentration to keep them still.

A sharp odor Jason couldn't place wafted in the air. It reminded him of a skunk, but less pungent. Had the air changed, or did the bracelet do something? Whichever it was, he wouldn't risk it further.

"Do you smell that?" he asked Matthew.

"Smell what?"

"Take the bracelet off!" Jason yelled.

He reached for his wrist, but his balance was still off. Jason's hands slid against the sweat on his fingers, and his arms flailed. His left arm crashed against the couch. The resulting bang sent it soaring into the kitchen, denting the wall. Plaster sprinkled from the broken spot as the couch crashed down.

Familiar fear crept back into Jason's thoughts. What had this bracelet done to him?

Matthew looked at him sideways. "You did that."

"I did." Jason looked at his hands and then Matthew. "Did the bracelet let me do that?"

"Let me try."

Matthew lined himself up against the smashed couch and pulled. The furniture budged, but he struggled. After a pause, Matthew looked at Jason then at the bracelet. He closed his eyes in concentration and threw his arm out like Jason did earlier.

But he didn't strike the couch. Matthew's body turned to mist and ran up against the furniture.

He had become intangible.

Matthew reformed whole again and patted himself down. His face shone sheet white. "Different powers."

Jason nodded with widened eyes.

Matthew sunk back and his whole body misted into an ethereal form. A cloud of fog spun across the floor. He instantaneously re-emerged beside Jason.

"You can turn into air? That's weird."

"Hang on," Matthew said. He smiled. "Let me try something else."

Instead of mist, Matthew melted down into a puddle of water. He moved and swirled about the floor, a living liquid.

Jason watched as Matthew pulled himself back together again. Several times he tried transforming into other shapes, but nothing else worked. Apparently, air and water were his limits.

"Liquid and mist." Matthew scanned the band around his wrist. "Your physical traits are enhanced, and mine changes shape. What exactly are these things?"

But instead of answering, Jason thought. For as long as he could remember he had been trapped in dreams involving a mountain range. A golden light pierced the towering ridges from somewhere deep within. He had to find it, wherever it was. The distinctive vibe from the dream felt exactly like what he got from these bracelets.

A pang of fear shot through his heart. He told Mrs. Stohl about those dreams when he met her.

He groaned over his stupidity. This must be why she chose him for this project.

"So you have super strength, and I have transforming powers," Matthew said. He laughed. "So that's what this is all about!"

"Take it off."

Matthew stared at him again. "Why? This is amazing."

"You're crazy, man."

"I'm just blown away. Aren't you?"

"Forget it," Jason replied, reaching for his bracelet. "I'm done."

Jason pulled against the bracelet, but it wouldn't budge. He thrashed against the accessory. It was no use: the bracelet was stuck to him.

"Why can't I take it off?"

"*Calm down.*" Matthew said into his head.

Jason looked up. Matthew stared at him. Their mental link remained even though they were separated.

Matthew nodded. *"We're being watched, remember? Don't tell them what you're planning."*

"What do we do?"

"Wait until we have an opportunity to get outside this apartment and learn where we are being held. Then we make a run for it."

Jason disagreed. They couldn't just run away. Whoever Mrs. Stohl really was, she wanted these bracelets. She wouldn't just let them leave.

Matthew took one step forward and wobbled. He put a hand up against the wall to steady himself.

"Hey, what's wrong?" Jason asked.

"I don't know." He slid against the wall to the floor. "I'm feeling tired."

Jason approached, and a weight crashed down upon him. Fatigue dropped him to his hands and knees.

Matthew fell across the floor, unconscious and unmoving.

Jason tried to get up to reach him, but his muscles cried against him. His cheek kissed the carpet as his muscles gave out.

"I'm sorry, Mom. I'm sorry, Dad."

He remembered his dreams. After running away, they became vivid and more frequent. They were just dreams, but they always had messages. A woman he could never remember after waking whispered to him constantly. What did she say about this place? He couldn't remember. Mrs. Stohl had a way about her. And she reeled him in like a trout.

The front door slid open. Mrs. Stohl entered with a sextet of men in dark suits with skin even paler than the two sick figures on the carpet. The six converged on them.

"What did you do?" Jason rasped out.

She took a knee beside him, a beatific smile upon her thin cheeks. "It isn't what *I* did. It's what *you've* done."

"You better hope he's alive."

"More than that, Jason. You are both a part of a much Greater Kingdom than this one. You have passed."

Before he could argue the point, darkness overwhelmed him, and the suits fell upon the fallen pair as his last thoughts died out. Mrs. Stohl whispered in the corners of his thoughts.

"Welcome to Phase Three."

CHAPTER 3
CASTOR & POLLUX

PALE LIGHT FLASHED in Matthew's eyes, awakening him from slumber. Groans escaped his sore throat. He shook the sleep from his thoughts and awoke in the dark.

The metal room held little light beyond small streaks dancing against the steel ceiling and tall walls. Despite the deep darkness, he spotted nine other figures hidden in the enclosure. They could only be more men in suits.

He couldn't see Jason anywhere.

"You're awake," Jason said through his thoughts. *"Took you long enough. They've got you tied pretty well. I'm stuck. I can't get out like you did earlier."*

Matthew blinked. *"You're in my head now?"*

"I guess. Don't know when that happened since I only woke up a few minutes ago. None of them can hear me in here, though."

"Wait for it. We need an opening."

"Mr. White," Marguerite said. She held a tiny light in her hand. A lighter? He couldn't see it. But he knew she was grinning. She had to be. "Congratulations."

"You." Rough ropes burned the arms tied behind Matthew's back. Even the bracelet on his wrist was gone, the most obvious sign that they were not separated. He groaned as he sat up. "Is this any way to treat the two idiots who completed your tests?"

"You're staying still for now. I'm only doing this because I know your character, Mr. White."

"You think you do."

"No, I do know. You planned to take the Gemini Bracelets and run. You were thinking about how you could profit from their power. You think you haven't left a paper trail, and you haven't; however, you do have people who can attest to your disappointing character. Lazy, unfocused, unambitious, and unreliable. Why do you think you were chosen? No one is going to miss you when you fall into the Mirror Gate. But that doesn't mean you won't run anyway, which is why I placed a bomb against your heart."

"You what?"

"Relax. It is timed, not set by detonator. You're too valuable for that. It is set for a week. Long enough to do what we need. If you live, we will return here, deactivate it, and you will be rewarded for your efforts. Be obedient, and you'll live. Simple."

He placed his hand against his heart. His beats were the same as ever, but a small scar ran along his skin. She didn't lie. She didn't need to.

"What about the boy?"

"Yes, him as well. You are a team now, after all."

"Crazy witch!" he shouted.

"What does it matter, Mr. White? You're both still being paid. No one will miss you should you expire. But enough. Now we will take our trip through the Mirror Gate and begin the final phase."

Matthew winced at her words. No one would notice if he disappeared. But Jason had been chosen as well, and that didn't sit right. No kid should be pulled into this—whatever *this* was.

"*Mirror Gate*?" Jason whispered.

"What's this mirror thing, Marguerite?"

"Look around you, Mr. White."

He peered into the dark, the shadowy shroud momentarily letting him see through.

Each of the walls, except the one with the large door behind him, had full-length mirrors covering them. Eerie reflections danced against their surfaces, masked by the black sweeping the room. Shards of glass glinted against the floor. That was all he could see, but he couldn't help but feel that something else was in there with him.

After a pause, Matthew leaned his wrists against the rope. It felt like a Prusik knot against his back, though there was no way to tell. He needed to get the rope around his shoulders off. As Marguerite Stohl went on, he used the darkness to flip his hands out from behind his back and under his legs to his chest. He pulled backwards with his elbows out. None of the suits noticed.

It wasn't tied as tight as he thought it would be.

"The Mirror Gate," she said. "This is the way to the kingdom, Mr. White. This is the final test. This is where we separate the men from the boys. Now, have you gotten those ropes off yet?"

He blinked. The ropes around his wrists slid free.

"She's trying to lure you in," Jason said. *"Just get out of it!"*

Matthew pushed down against the ropes around his shoulders and forced his arms up. He'd been in tighter spots before. He fell loose and threw the bondage off his shoulders.

Almost immediately, a stream of mist swirled out of his body. It was the boy. Matthew leaped back up as Jason now appeared at his side.

"I expected you to be faster," Marguerite said with a heavy sigh.

Jason raised his fists. "Now you're going to tell us what these things are."

"Please, Jason." She waved one delicate wrist and the light dissipated from it. "There is no need to be uncouth."

"He's right," Matthew interjected. "We're going to find out what these are, and she's taking these bombs out. Now."

"I already told you! You are wearing the Gemini Bracelets. You, Mr. White, are wearing Castor. It allows you to transform your form to air or liquid. There may be more than that, but I do not know. I have never seen its full potential."

Matthew mouthed his confusion. "What do you mean you don't know?"

"I mean that you are the first to use them in my lifetime." She nodded to the boy. "It is the same with yours, Jason. That one is Pollux. It allows you to enhance your physical capabilities beyond your limits. But it *is* based on your limits."

"My limits," Jason mumbled to himself.

"Stuff it," Matthew interrupted. "That doesn't explain why you're doing all this. What happened to the other people you gave these bracelets to?"

"At your feet."

She raised a hand, and a new small flame erupted out of the tips, illuminating the room. Stained white and yellowing slabs like stones painted the dimly lit room. Jason recoiled at the sight. Bones.

"God help us," the kid whispered.

"A small price to gather the relics. I will take you back to my home where we will find yet another of them. Jason will lead me straight to it. His dreams are the key."

"What is all this, Mrs. Stohl? You know what those dreams are?"

"Not only do I know, but I finally have a guide who will lead me to the seed: You. The Great Sorcerer King truly smiles upon me."

At the front of the room, Marguerite threw her hand against the mirror behind her. A purple glow shone from the solid surface. Small ripples ran across the large slab, running from the floor to the ceiling like fuchsia waves. Before Matthew could react, a weight crashed against his back.

The group of men fell upon them, punching and pushing them forward. Matthew tried to change his body, but couldn't concentrate. A guard flew past his face and slammed into the mirror on the wall to his right. The surface fractured with the impact. Jason punched away as they pushed and grabbed him. The guards herded the pair toward the large mirror.

"Welcome to the greater world," she said.

Marguerite's men shoved Jason and Matthew into the Mirror Gate, following after. The group whipped through a wind tunnel into the narrow space. Stars streaked by their path at an insane velocity. The men around him screamed.

Their suits burned to cinders. A few caught ablaze at a deeper level—their skin and bones crisped. Their screams were the worst. Flecks of ash sprinkled into the tight tunnel as the flames incinerated them.

Matthew's skin burned too. He held to the bracelet, its cool sensation cutting through the ripping heat. His clothes burned to ash off his back, and his skin curled as if on fire. Beside him, Jason yelled. The boy also held fast to his bracelet. The two of them were going to cook alive.

Marguerite, however, merely watched them from the front. She giggled over the mayhem behind her, unaffected by it all.

"In seconds we shall be home!" she shouted over her shoulder. Her voice sounded strangely metallic and muffled in the small space. "Here we are!"

The flashing tunnel illuminated pulsing plum darkness in their path. It started as a pinprick and grew within half a second to the size of a humpback whale readying to swallow its next meal. It consumed them just as fast.

The force of a brick wall hit Matthew. The wall wrapped him in a coat of purple fog. Then it simply evaporated.

He kissed night air, and it burned against his steaming skin. They had reached the other side.

Matthew struck the tiled stone floor with a dead weight, screaming the whole way. His lobster red skin laid naked for all to see, his clothes charred away to ash. The boy lay still a few feet from him.

The last thing he needed to see was another corpse. This world killed enough: it didn't need to take more kids. Not like this, alone and scared. He wouldn't let it.

Matthew ignored his pain and climbed along the stone floor on his elbows. Jason didn't move. His red skin smoked.

"Jason!" Matthew forced out through the pain. "You're still in one piece."

Matthew shook Jason's shoulder. The boy became intangible and dragged forward as if magnetized. He disappeared again. Stunned, Matthew stared a second before remembering this was part of the bracelets' abilities. They worked here, too. Wherever *here* was.

Most of the men that had followed them through became little more than ash and bones. The harsh air was black and thick. However, some were not dead. In fact, they were no longer men at all.

Where Matthew and Jason lost their clothes, these men lost their skin. Without it, they also lost their humanity. Flesh had burned away, revealing green skin and flashing narrow eyes like . . . a lizard. They stood tall and muscular with scaly faces, long noses, and lashing tongues. Their tails were long, with man-shaped hands and scaled feet with claws far sharper than nails. Hunched backs and long limbs told him that they were probably never humans to begin with.

Lavender mist smoked from their skin, and their lungs breathed deep. Their scales shifted with every hard breath. The lizardmen looked down on him with hunger in their grins.

The journey left only one individual untouched. Marguerite still wore the same dress with the same perfect face. But her eyes had changed. A mad reflection glinted off the moonlight from the open balcony before her. The monstrous snarling smile she showed him was worse than anything he had experienced so far.

"Mr. White," she said. "You have passed Phase Three."

"We're not in the building anymore, are we?"

"Thank the Great Sorcerer King, we are not."

They were in a similar set up to the small room from earlier. Three mirrors lined the long wall behind him, but they were decorated far fancier than the previous chamber. They looked almost medieval, these walls. The stone craftsmanship, the weaved tapestries, the long carpets, and the musty paintings on the walls, revealed a place entirely different than Serenity City.

He wanted to ask so many questions. A large ship like those he had seen in old storybooks passed by the balcony behind Marguerite. It sailed not on water, but flying up in the air. His questions caught in his throat.

Larger sights lay beyond the ship and into the night. Mountains spiraled into misty tops, and bright lights slipped through the sheet of white fog below the beaming moon. Buildings and towers lined the ridges ahead. A city.

He tried to speak but his words caught on his trembling lips. How could any of this exist?

Above the distant mountain range, the black shape of a fortress climbed hundreds of feet into the raven capped night. Dozens of deeply embedded square and round towers, echaugettes, and turrets had been grafted onto the monstrosity. A large barbican marked the front, but the Gothic-like height of the fortress itself caught his attention, stretching into a faintly purple abyss of a cloudy sky. A presence in that place sent chills down his spine. Try as he might, Matthew struggled for the words.

He opened his mouth wide before he spoke. "This is—"

The lizardmen seized his arms and legs. Their grip crushed him as he thrashed against their hold.

"Quiet, meat!" one of them hissed in his ear

Marguerite waved to him as they dragged him down the dark hallway. The woman blew Matthew a kiss.

"Welcome to Tyndarus, Mr. White. You are now a member of the Greater Kingdom."

CHAPTER 4
MAGIC CITY MAGEUOPOLIS

THE RAGS on Matthew's body itched. He had been given a ratty shirt and pants to wear over his naked form after he was thrown in a cell. Their captors gave the boy the same. The cramped area was no bigger than a bedroom. The stone walls and floor and the complete lack of natural light assaulted his senses. Dampness ran through his bones and caused a chill that went beyond simple weather.

Torches burned on the wall outside his prison cell. Orange outlines of armored lizardmen shifted back and forth down the thin hall. Matthew was made to wait in this cell for the entire night. Tomorrow one of those flying ships would take them to the leader of this place: the Great Sorcerer King. Matthew sat on the bench and watched the long shapes of the lizardmen pass him by. They had not said a single word since throwing him in here.

He was more concerned about Jason. He *knew* that Jason was okay, the bracelets had formed a link between them, but they both had those bombs inside of them. The kid had to be terrified.

Matthew held Jason's clothes between clenched fists. What kind of monster dragged helpless teenage boys into her messes? He didn't even know where they had been taken to. Tyndarus did not exist on Earth. It was no historical location he could think of, either. But he still had to get the boy back home and get that bomb out of him.

Flying ships, a mountain mist city, and man-shaped lizards combined to make this a sick fever dream. The lizards especially attracted his attention. Now he knew why the heat had been so high in the facility. A harsh purple air hovered across the armor and bracers of the lizards. That must have been why the damp mountain air did not harm them. That fuchsia mist had opened the Mirror Gate back in Serenity City. Marguerite used it. If anyone could explain all this, it was her.

He clutched the spare clothes tight. They needed a plan to get out of this place.

The glistening, wet stones of the cell stifled his thoughts. They must be underground. The lashings of the torchlight made it appear like the flames moved on their own. He flinched and looked again. They *were* moving.

In the left-hand corner of the cell, two small stones in the corner of the wall slid backwards. A pair of eyes poked through the abyss.

"Ay!" the voice whispered.

Matthew tilted his head. A guard passed the front of the cell, oblivious to any noise. This intruder had clearly done this before. Matthew kneeled down beside the opening with his back to the wall. He caught a closer glimpse of smoky grey eyes and long hair through the small opening. The visitor was a woman.

"Hello," he said plainly. "Come here much?"

"Are you from the other world?" the woman asked.

Her silky voice slunk through his thoughts like a strong drink. He resisted the urge to look into her eyes. He had more to worry about than getting a date. Thankfully the guard was halfway down the hall now. No one could see her except him.

"I suppose I am. My name is Matthew. What is yours?"

"Ordopha," she replied. "Do you wield the Gemini Bracelets?"

"We do have the bracelets. Are you with these lizards?"

"Hardly." She pushed back a few more stones to allow more room for her to fit through. "I'm here for you."

Her long platinum blonde hair fell from her shoulders and down past her filthy shirt. Long lashes and soft lips scanned him over, oblivious of his eyes running across her slight form. How long had he been alone in the fake apartment? Finally, she broke the quiet.

"Is your partner injured?"

Matthew waited for the lizardman to pass before he spoke again. "No. The problem is that the trip through the mirror really hurts. It burned off all our clothes and quite nearly our skin. Many guards didn't make it through."

"Oh my. I hope he is well."

"He's a tough boy. He'll be fine."

"A child?"

"He's fifteen. He can handle it. How come I can understand you? Do you speak English?"

"English? No. I am speaking Neronian. Is that what you call it? English?"

He dodged the language question. There were more important concerns. "What do you know about those Mirror Gates? We need to get back through."

"All the magic in Tyndarus comes from the Great Sorcerer King himself. He's the reason those gates work. To get through you need his magic to activate them."

"*Where do we get magic?*" the voice in Matthew's head asked.

"Jason?" Matthew inquired. The woman was about to question his sudden exclamation, but he put a hand up. "You're awake? How do you feel?"

"I feel like I fell through a paper shredder. But I heard your conversation. What should we do?"

Matthew pursed his lips. The girl had come from somewhere close by, and he needed to have a conversation with her. But he also had to worry about the lizardmen noticing his departure. The boy probably wouldn't like he what he had to do.

"Get out there, Jason. I'm going to follow her and gather info. You need to stay in my place."

The boy thought on it. He groaned and sighed. "*Okay. I'd prefer not moving anyway.*"

Jason drifted like smoke out of Matthew's head and solidified at his side. He was totally nude.

"Oh my!" Ordopha said, turning away.

"Whoa, where are my clothes?"

"Here." Matthew thrust the prison garb the lizards gave him into Jason's chest. "Your old ones burned up. It doesn't look like much survives a trip through the Mirror Gates."

As Jason changed, Matthew explained his idea to follow Ordopha. Jason looked so much like him in the dark that it was doubtful the guards would notice the change. The boy agreed.

"Go ahead," he said. "I need a few more winks anyway."

Ordopha leaned in again. "You are so much alike. Are you brothers?"

"*No,*" they said at once.

Matthew watched the bars. "Alright, the lizard is coming back. Show me the way, Ordopha."

The two disappeared into the tight tunnel, leaving Jason behind. Shallow pathways barely bigger than the span of Matthew's shoulders twisted on like a labyrinth. The winding tunnels led downward and splintered off in many directions through the dark. Ordopha climbed onward without pause as if she knew this place far too well.

"Where exactly is this prison?" he asked. "Is it above us? Below? I have no idea where we are. I saw mountains and a large castle outside earlier."

"That is because we are in Mageuopolis, located in the northern mountains. No one can enter this place without magic. The Great Sorcerer King's power prevents it. Here he hides and builds his forces for his eventual conquest of Tyndarus."

"Tyndarus is a land?"

"It is the name of our world."

His lip twitched at the knowledge. That crazy woman brought the two of them to a whole new planet. He didn't want to believe it, but nothing else explained all the insanity. Ordopha kept speaking as he pondered their situation.

"All magic flows from Nieto himself. He is called the Great Sorcerer King because it is his life-force. He is like a god. Magic comes from his very bones."

"Magic being real aside, I always thought it came from spells or enchantments. Fairy tale stuff. I've never heard of it originating from one being."

"That depends on what you believe Nieto is. He comes from the stars themselves. We had no magic before he arrived thousands of years ago. This city, those ships, and the relics would not exist if not for him."

"You mean he invented the Gemini Bracelets?"

"No. But he did bring them to Tyndarus. Please stay still."

Matthew stopped. He couldn't see Ordopha, but a hard slapping sound pounded ahead. Torchlight burst into the tiny crevice and bathed over the girl and nearly blinded him. She climbed forward and disappeared into the light.

Outside the tunnel was another cell. Damp and wet stone tunnels went on through hallways on his left side. Triple the size of his cell, this one also contained more prisoners. The sleeping figures wore cloaks, ratty shirts and pants no different from him or Ordopha.

"None of those lizards will see you. They do not patrol here so late. Most of us don't see a point of escape, and those monsters know it."

Around a dozen other young people, no older than Matthew and no younger than Jason, slept on the floor. All of them had the same platinum hair color Ordopha and Marguerite had, both men and women. Did everyone on Tyndarus have the same hair and pale skin color? But they looked just like ordinary people otherwise. A few were tall and muscled men, and some were slim women with longer hair. They didn't look like criminals, but neither did he.

"Is there no one in the city below to help you?" he asked. "How could friends or family just leave someone in a place like this?"

"We don't come from Mageuopolis. We descend from a line that was taken from the land beyond the mountains. We are the current and last generation here. Only the fourteen of us remain."

At the opposite end of the open cell emerged a figure clad in a cloak. He lowered his hood to reveal short platinum hair and a sharp nose. This man had the same grey eyes as Ordopha only with a strong jaw and clean-limbed look. He did appear underfed, but the tenacious glare of his gaze betrayed a man Matthew would not want to be left alone with. Ordopha shrunk back when the stranger approached. A few of those pretending to sleep held their breaths.

"I am Alain," he said, simply. He took Matthew's hand in a vice grip. "I am Ord's brother. We heard talk of someone arriving through the Mirror Gate from the other world."

"Yeah, me and the boy. I'm Matthew."

"A child?"

Matthew laughed at Alain's identical reaction. "Your sister said the same thing. No, he's fifteen. He's resting upstairs. But we have the Gemini Bracelets."

"You feel endangering a child is a joke? You helped bring him here? I see Shaula has chosen her victims well."

"What?" Matthew stuttered. "I think that came out wrong."

"Alain, you're twisting his words!"

"I will seek no help from vermin. We have enough troubles without relying on a rat."

Matthew thought quickly to avoid the mood turning further south. There was only one way to set it right, and words wouldn't do it. A display of power.

He lifted his left hand and showed off the gold band adorning his wrist. The dim orange light glittered hard against it. Matthew concentrated. He lifted up and transformed into mist.

Both Alain and Ordopha recoiled at the sight. They stared at him floating in the ether until he changed back into a human once more. It took moments for them to speak.

Ordopha beamed at her brother. "I told you he could help!"

"Then we can escape!" Alain whispered.

"I'm not so sure," Matthew replied. "We've barely used these things before, and we don't even know where we are."

Alain grimaced. "A coward? My sister and I have traveled these catacombs our entire lives. The tunnels were formed by us. We know the way to the ships and escape; we merely lack the numbers to fight through. Ordopha has observed how to fly the ships. Do you have a plan?"

Truthfully, Matthew hadn't thought one up. He worried more about Jason and the strange new world they were in. To get back to Earth they needed a source of magic and a Mirror Gate. He told Alain as much. If they were taken to the castle tomorrow, there would be no guarantee any chance of escape would remain once they got there.

"That is simple enough," the cloaked man replied. "When they bring you to the airship, we will attack and take them by surprise. With your added strength we would easily overwhelm them. We will take the ship into the mountains, and you will escape through the Mirror Gate on the upper level. Does that not sound enticing to you? Perhaps it is too much for a coward."

"That's not it. I'm just not sure what the limits to our powers are. We've barely used them."

"Combat is the best way to learn anything, coward. You worry for nothing. We will cover for your lack of skill. Those of us here have experience with fighting. Will you join us or not?"

Alain's crudeness did little to convince Matthew of anything. However, he did need to disarm those bombs. The faster, the better. If he could help these people escape, and give Marguerite a black eye, then so much the better. But could he trust someone like Alain?

"I don't know," he muttered.

"This all hinges on you, Matthew. Are you a woman, or a warrior? Will you fight, or flee? If you will not partake then make certain I never see your face again."

There was a spark to Alain that reminded Matthew of someone. The sister was more reserved, but the brother gave off the vibe of a man of his word. It had been a long time since Matthew had met anyone like that. He had certainly never *been* like that. But this was a new place, and he needed all the help he could find, especially for Jason.

"I'm in." Matthew offered his hand. "Count on Castor."

Alain flatly observed the outstretched appendage. He sized Matthew up. Finally, a grin formed on the corners of his tight mouth. He clapped his hand against Matthew's and shook it.

"It's good to see that the wielder of the Gemini Bracelet is no coward after all."

"That reminds me." Matthew nodded to the girl. "You were going to tell me more about the magic and these bracelets, right? Who is the Great Sorcerer King?"

Her lip trembled but for an instant before she bit down on it. Matthew tried not to let it bother him, but it was difficult to put her clear discomfort aside.

"My brother and I have been here for near twenty years. We have learned much through these walls, and much we were never meant to learn in the tunnels. However, there is still that which we do not know. The Great Sorcerer King has never left his mountain castle, and we have never learned anything of his true origins. His secrets remain. However, we do know of certain relics that many of his pets still speak of and puzzle over even so many years later."

"Relics other than the bracelets?"

"There is one in these mountains that they have been seeking for centuries. All the relics bestow great abilities, much like the one you hold."

"How does that bracelet work, Matthew?" Alain asked.

"I can become mist or water with Castor. The boy's is Pollux. He has strength to spare."

Ordopha chimed in. "I have heard that the bracelets were meant to combine two warriors into one unstoppable force. It is meant to create the ultimate man. Surely they can be mastered to give you each greater control."

"Wow," Matthew replied. "You sure know a lot about this."

Alain nodded. "Ord has a much better memory than I do. That is why she travels the tunnels while I focus on fighting in the pits."

"What are those lizardmen?"

"An ancient race that swore fealty to Nieto." Alain huffed. "We are their entertainment."

That word filled in any gaps Matthew could imagine. No wonder they needed his help to escape.

But could they? Even if these people could take a ship and escape into the mountains he doubted they would get far.

"You have a place to go?" he asked.

Alain sighed. "We have few options. I have heard whispers of a golden shrine in the mountains, but I do not pretend that we will find it. Should we make it beyond the mountains then we can find a new place to call our home. However, if we have the wielders of Castor and Pollux on our side, escape will be much simpler. If you can get us to the ship, we can do the rest."

Matthew thought on it. He could help the lot escape to the ship and turn back to find the Mirror Gate, but he knew it wouldn't be enough. There was a good chance they knew that, too. This kingdom extended far along this entire mountain range. Surviving out in the wilds did not sound probable. Then again, this was none of his business. All he had to do was get them to the ships as part of the deal. He would worry about the rest later.

"I already said I'll help. But I should let Jason in on this. Can you point me back, Ordopha?"

She consented, and they left back the way they came. Matthew was less than enthused with crawling back into the claustrophobic darkness. Ordopha took Matthew back through the tight tunnels where he let his mind run wild. She said nothing as they went on.

But there were a few things he had to know.

"Your brother never really answered. Who is Nieto exactly?"

"I have never seen him. Many think the monster God Himself."

He suddenly thought of that castle behind the mountain city. He did get a chill when he looked upon it. "This guy sounds screwy. What do you think of him?"

"I've seen what he has created." Her dour yet sharp words hit him as hard and bitter. "You have seen the air around the lizardmen? That's magic Nieto embeds in their flesh to give increased vitality and body warmth. His servants are a superstitious lot. They do believe he is God."

"That must be why they don't question anything he says."

"Yes, it is because of the King's magic. It flows through these mountains and powers all from the flight crystals in the airships to the mist that hides his kingdom from the world."

"I don't understand why he wouldn't just take over everything," Matthew replied. His head bumped against the ceiling and pebbles crumbled over his brow. He wiped it clean. "With power like that, he doesn't even need the bracelets."

"Long ago he used a tremendous amount of his life force and fled to these mountains. He only ventures out via his pawns to collect prizes and food for his kingdom. It is only a matter of time before he expends his remaining life."

Matthew wasn't convinced. It certainly appeared that Nieto had sent Marguerite and her men to Earth to find a suitable candidate for the Gemini Bracelets, but it didn't explain why he needed to find them in the first place. Could he not use the people of this world? Matthew thought long and hard about this so-called Great Sorcerer King. There was more to this Ordopha didn't know. He decided to change the subject.

"I don't think your brother likes me."

"He only trusts those around him. We have been surrounded by enemies for our entire lives. The reason he is using you is because you have Castor and Pollux—and because he is desperate."

Silence filled in the conversation gap. As someone who had spent most his time in voluntary solitude, Matthew just didn't understand. A boring life meant little in the way of enemies.

The two continued in quiet and reached the small cell once more. Jason still leaned against the wall. Matthew waited for the guard to pass before the pair slid out of the tunnel. The males sat on either side of the hole as the woman waited.

"Took your time," Jason whispered. "So what happened?"

Matthew explained everything from the brother and sister to Nieto himself. Eventually, he came around to the escape plan. Ordopha broke in to let them know what their idea had been for years now. They were simply waiting to use it at the right moment.

"Are you fine with just leaving?" Jason asked Matthew.

The older one blinked. "Yes. We can't let this Sorcerer get the bracelets. Plus, there's the bombs to worry about. No telling how much time we have left."

The boy gave the strangest expression Matthew had ever seen. It wasn't anger or disappointment. His mouth was a line, but his iced eyes were sharper than daggers.

It only lasted for a second, and Jason turned away. "Just take me through the plan."

Castor beamed like a beacon into Matthew's mind. A low voice, unlike a person, more like an idea, hung in the back of his thoughts. The nearly inaudible and impossible to comprehend whisper remained in his head.

He went on to discuss with Ordopha and Jason their idea for escape, but still it spoke. His back stiffened and sweat grew on his brow. This intangible thing inside of him hid at the bottom of his soul. Castor melded into him. Regardless, he continued to discuss the plan.

Then, his skin particles slowly burst like bubbles and his muscles and skin liquefied before evaporating. Was it the bomb? He couldn't tell.

Ordopha held in a gasp and Jason gaped as Matthew faded away into the darkness.

CHAPTER 5
ESCAPE FROM THE MIST PRISON

HARSH POUNDING BANGED in the back of Jason's brain. Sleep had not come, and one of the passing lizardmen made a reference to the coming morning. Matthew's body had rippled like the surface of water. Particles mixed and twisted in the air like the atoms were confused about their proper place. The mist reformed and the atmosphere shifted.

The twisting specks snapped back into place. Skin solidified, and blood flowed in through veins again. No more queasiness or illness remained. But something had changed. The older bracelet holder absorbed into Jason's head. The two switched places, and he became the main body again. Jason just couldn't figure this out.

"Wait," Jason had said, out loud. "Why am I the body again? We switched?"

Matthew groaned. *"Morning, I take it. I had a feeling. Once the sun rises, we change. You're the pilot now."*

"Oh right, we landed here at night, didn't we?" His breaths calmed. "And it was day when we first wore these things. So that's it."

Day for Jason; night for Matthew. They switched bodies depending on the time of day. This would get old fast.

But Matthew instantly seized on this and adjusted the path forward accordingly. After Jason calmed her down, Ordopha departed. As the boy sat on the bench, he left his hands to his sides and drummed his fingers on the wood. He just wanted this over with.

All he ever wanted was for it to be over with. Waiting never ceased being difficult.

Long ago he heard about how his parents left Serenity City because a former hero went on a rampage and destroyed a large chunk of the place, killing many. Jason's mom would always say there was a chance any of the heroes could lose their minds and do the same. She wanted Jason far away from superheroes and villains. She meant well, but it never stuck with him. He didn't want to hide—he wanted to be there, to cheer them on, and to reassure them that they really were the good guys. They needed support, and she didn't get it.

But his dad told him differently.

"This world is like nightfall that never ends," he had said. *"Some of us will never make it to the sunrise, some of us by choice and some by luck. The night isn't forever, though. Eventually, the sun has to rise."*

Jason clutched the bench with the memory, splinters breaking against his palms. Now he had a power of his own, and he squandered it waiting in a jail cell for certain death. He wouldn't let it end like this.

While he was unconscious, that dream returned to him. A shining light of gold buried in distant mountain stone. It beckoned him closer. He could almost see it—almost touch it. All he needed was one more inch . . .

He blinked awake.

A voice overtook his meandering thoughts. The woman on the other side of the bars waved to him. Marguerite wore light purple robes, her hair in neat buns. A mysterious aura wafted from her and the six lizards surrounding her. Jason kept his left wrist hidden from them.

"You used me," he said. "Liar."

"I am sorry to deceive a child," Marguerite replied. "Please believe me, Jason. It was a risk using you, but the King needs the bracelets. It is why we built this kingdom in the first place. But I did not wish for you to be the one to wear Pollux."

"But if I were Matthew's age it would be okay? You put a bomb in me, in him. You're sick."

"You have no bomb in you, Jason. Check your chest. No marks."

He checked. She was right. He blinked several times before speaking again. "But you told us before that you put them inside us."

"Only *him*. Mr. White had to be tamed. I am no savage, Jason. I don't hurt children, especially not you. You have a very important job outside of your bracelet. You've seen it, correct? The prize in the mountains?

There we will find a relic of great importance. It is why my Lord chose this world so long ago in the first place."

"You're out of your mind. Take the explosive out of Matthew's chest."

"Not until the task is complete. Calm yourself, Jason. You will be unharmed. I told you that we are not a violent people."

"How many bones were in that mirror room? How many corpses were there?"

"What does it matter? Your own Serenity City has heroes and villains battling to kill each other every single day. What we take from Earth is nothing compared to their disgusting war."

"I came to you because you said we were going to help the heroes. All those bones . . ." His teeth ground together. Veins showed through clenched fists. "You won't walk away from that."

She smiled as if remembering a long lost memory. "You remind me of my little girl. So much potential. With the bracelet and your dream, we can change both Tyndarus and Earth. The more relics we have, the more power we will wield. You won't need your heroes any longer."

"Is that why you almost killed Matthew and me? Is that why you killed all those people? You're a disease. All you villains are."

"Me?" She asked, perplexed. "Certainly I am no hero, but I am not a villain. What must be done must be done. If I must stomp a promising pup like you in order to bring about the kingdom, then I will not hesitate."

"I knew you would say something like that. You just don't get it.. Your time is up."

"Surely you don't think the two of you can escape. I was impressed that neither of you was stupid enough to try last night, but that is very unlike you to wait. Has Mr. White's influence rubbed off on you already? I'm sure he figured it out. Only the magic of Lord Nieto can open the way back through the Mirror Gates. You will never return to your humdrum existence. You are now part of the Greater Kingdom."

At first, Jason objected to Matthew's decision to stay and help the prisoners escape. He only thought of escape from this insane world. But then he remembered all those bones in that chamber. How long had Marguerite been doing this? Never before had another being imbued him with such disgust. He would stop her.

"There's nothing greater about this hell," he said.

The floor trembled. Stone shook, and the bars rattled. A quake rocked the very foundations of the fortress. Marguerite and the cadre of guards tumbled to the floor. Jason watched as they gathered their wits.

"What was that noise?" she asked. Two of the lizardmen ran down the hall shouting for others. "Did the frogs get in?"

"No," Jason answered. He stood up and faced her. "That would be the prisoners."

"Impossible!"

Jason showed her the bracelet on his formerly hidden left wrist. It flashed against the torches. She paled as she realized what it meant: Matthew was not fused with him. The remaining four lizardmen raised their spears and swords.

"Nothing is," he said with a smile.

THE FOURTEEN PRISONERS surrounded Matthew by the cell door when Castor trembled. An unbridled rage beat through him like a pumping heart. Where did this come from? It had to be the boy. Jason's anger boiled over inside Matthew. Their emotions, as well as their minds, were linked. The boy had to be talking with Marguerite.

He scanned the empty hallways. No guards, just as Alain and Ordopha said.

"Can you do it?" the bulky man named Case asked.

"I can."

"Keep your wits about you. The lizards are fierce opponents."

Other than Ordopha and Alain, the other twelve shared similar platinum blonde hair but had little else in common. Some were short, some had long faces or their hair cut short, but they were all lined up behind him and ready. Only two other women aside from Ordopha were among their number. After years of waiting they had to act now.

Matthew took a hard breath and concentrated. The bars gripped before him, he closed his eyes. Flesh rippled and broke as the wind rushed between skin cells and disintegrated blood and bone. His new form splashed to the floor in a puddle. His watery figure flowed through the tunnel.

The winding paths splintered off around him. Pairs of large lizard men clutching spears marched side by side everywhere. They blocked the paths, their beefy frames nearly touching the arched ceilings. He slid underneath and followed the directions Alain had given him.

An untold number of large wooden doors blocked off every room, but he remembered the directions. When he turned down the proper hall, he made a right and emerged in the cold gust of the yellow early morning daylight.

The mountainside blew wind around him. The hall led outside.

A lone pathway connected the castle between this side and the other. Harsh wind whistled through the silence. The carved path lined with ramparts extended over the void below. No wonder Alain had wanted him to come this way. No one would expect him here.

Low sunlight cast harsh beams through serrated mountain peaks and against the grey stone archways dangling above him. The castle hanging above the fog shone brighter than anything inside its dreary interior or the muted brown of the mountains. He slid along the floor toward the jutting walkway that led to the next section of the castle and hid in the shadow of the ramparts, his form quivering in the cold. Now, to wait for his targets.

Unfortunately, he didn't have much time. Marguerite would soon catch on that they were separated.

His form began to tremble. He wouldn't be able to keep this up forever. An intangible muscle would give at any moment, and he would be thrown back into his normal body. He clenched himself.

Up ahead, a pair of lizardmen marched out from the inner hall of the castle. Tongues lashed against the breeze. The cold wind blew across their slouched forms, but they did not even flinch, their jerkin and armor rattling in the breeze. They stomped side by side in lockstep, their short tails swaying with timed steps. They each had spare swords around their waists on top of the spears they carried. A rusty key hung around the left one's neck.

Matthew moved along the shadow of the ramparts. Heavy, bare claws slapped against the stone and passed him by. He carefully flowed after them.

Matthew formed up between the pair, becoming whole. Skin solidified as he advanced. He drew both swords from each lizard's scabbards. They turned at the sudden interruption.

He stabbed both blades forward. The lizard on the right pivoted. He pierced the other through its chest. The left lizard fell sideways against the ramparts, gasping its last. The remaining lizardman hissed and lunged at Matthew.

The spear prodded him as he fell back. Matthew's legs wobbled. Was it because he had just reformed? One slash cut his right arm, drawing blood. Matthew cried out, and the weapon thrust forward. The bladed tip glided along his side. A thin line of blood formed under his slit shirt. The lizard licked its lips and dove for him.

Matthew only had one option left: mist. As the lizard came down on him, he moved in.

The blade flew to his neck. Air sliced apart as the weapon met his skin . . . and flew through his mist form! The lizardman hissed and tripped forward.

Matthew reformed behind the creature and ran the sword through its back. The lizard let out a horrid cry before joining its compatriot in death.

A wave of emotion consumed him, and he kneeled to it. It wasn't just his fading energy—he also hadn't used a sword before. He managed to survive against two opponents. They were only felled by his powers, not his skill. He was lucky, and his trembling bones knew it.

Yet their deaths shook him. His stare refused to leave the corpses he had just made. They might not have been human, but they were living things.

"When you have slain them and taken the key," Alain had said, *"throw them to the mountain mist. Can you do that much, Matthew?"*

It would be simple. He just had to move past this. Matthew hoisted the first slain foe up on the ramparts. He left it propped up as he regained his breath. The heat from the bracelet cooled. His fingers shook. He took deep breaths to calm his nerves and his power.

A raspy voice cut the mountain air. "Break out!"

A lizardman screeched from the opposite end of the bridge. Its partner ran off, most likely to sound an alarm.

Matthew cursed and abandoned the plan. He had wasted too much time here.

He put the key around his neck and ran back toward the fortress with both swords in his hands.

He rounded the corner into the dark of the castle halls again. This shade allowed him to turn back into water undetected. The swords came with him, proving his theory that his power spread to what he directly touched. Matthew glided back along the rock floors toward to the cells.

Alarms sounded, and lizardmen ran past him toward the bridge.

Now for the flight crystals and the explosives.

THE TREMOR SHOOK the entire hall. Stones kicked spores into the air when the jail bars hit the wall across from Jason, nailing the lizardmen and sending them prone and unconscious. Pebbles crumbled from the dented rock wall and onto their bodies. Only Marguerite Stohl remained standing, staring at him with unchecked rage. She had been smart enough to duck.

Jason held one of the guard's swords to her throat. Blood dripped in a thin streak down her neck.

"What did Mr. White do?" She asked.

"They got into one of your flight crystal storage areas—whatever *that* is. I heard they can't stop gathering heat from the atmosphere if their shells are cracked too deeply."

"As if the prisoners could get in there."

"I know one of them could, and I think you know who, too."

She bit her lip, and her glare narrowed. After a pause, she let a smile show.

"I did not take Mr. White as brave. Wandering off into an unknown place and finding new allies does not suit his temperament."

"I agree." He watched his back. Several of the lizards groaned and sat up. "Tell your pets to back off. The two of us are going for a walk."

"Are we?"

"Yes. You're going to see something really cool."

After a pause, she finally waved the guards aside. That smile remained.

"As you wish," she replied. "You all! Stand down."

The lizardmen that weren't unconscious froze. They watched Jason with sideways glances and flailing tongues. Listening to their master, they backed against the wall.

A horn blared through the dark halls. The prisoners moved toward the skydeck. Now it was Jason's turn.

He brought the woman by the arm, the sword still at her throat. None of the lizardmen budged.

The pair arrived at a set of stairs and Jason took her up, just as Ordopha had suggested. Winding steps carried them up in a cradle of stone and dusty air.

"Now how did you know about this way, I wonder?" Marguerite said.

"Quiet," he whispered.

"You were far more polite in Serenity City, Jason. Did coming here turn you rotten? You had nothing on Earth. That was why you came with us to begin with. Why do you wish to return?"

"You just never stop, do you?"

She giggled. "I suppose I do not."

The pair pulled out of the stairs and out into a new set of ramparts. The castle loomed down on the mist-masked mountain where stone structures, hovels, spires, and keeps, lay far below, just above the fog. There were clearly hundreds of homes across the range. How many lizardmen were there, anyway?

Airships cut above the mist. None of them appeared to notice the pair as they kept a steady pattern across to the city like a ferry service.

Jason led his captive across the ramparts, occasionally glancing back for potential pursuers. No one was on their tail. That didn't alleviate his fears. Why weren't they coming for her?

"Is there a problem, Jason?"

"You feel strangely warm for someone out in the cold like this. Did he use his magic on you like he did the lizardmen?"

"No," she said with another laugh. "I'm just a naturally warm woman. There is much about me you wouldn't understand. Why don't we go back and I will explain it to you?"

He ignored her and moved into the castle hall ahead of them. Stairs led back down into another narrow walkway over a high, hundred foot drop. They entered a large cavernous room where darkness reigned. Boxes and bladed weapons littered the floor. Torches hung on wet walls and the skydeck poked out through the walkway ahead. He had made it.

Lizardmen flooded out from the archway before him. Jason turned back to see them also lining the other side.

They'd trapped him.

"Oh, this is unexpected," she said with a chuckle.

"I'm sure. Was this your whole plan to stop me?"

"Where did you think you were going, Jason? I planned to lead you two here from your cell. If you had just taken me straight to the Mirror Gate, I might have just brought you back to Earth out of respect. Why did you come here on your own? For prisoners you don't even know? I would really like understand."

"So would I."

She was supposed to be their hostage, a bargaining chip to help the prisoners board a ship while the two of them took her back to the Mirror Gate, but he never bet on the lizards not caring if she lived or died. Nor did he imagine she would be fine with being thrown away. Did that Sorcerer King really care so little for his underlings?

Jason watched his surroundings. He could charge through and reach the docked ships, or turn back and find another way around to the skydeck. He could also take the hundred-foot drop down. Would Pollux hold out after a fall that far?

Voices clamored below. At the bottom of the drop waited fifteen figures bathed in torchlight, all brandishing swords, round shields, spears, and axes. He instantly recognized the one at the front.

"Matthew!" he called out.

The man in the lead looked from left to right, and then up. He tried to project his thoughts into Matthew, but it wouldn't take. They were too far apart.

"What's the holdup, Jason?" he shouted back.

"Surrounded. Move back!"

The guards on either side of the walkway swooped in. There remained only one option for escape.

"What?" Matthew called back.

"I said move out of the way."

Marguerite paled. "You're not—"

He lifted her into his arms. Without waiting, Jason ran forward and jumped over the side.

Gravity forced him downward. The breeze slashed through his thin clothing. All the figures at the bottom backed out of the way as he rocketed toward the floor. A nasty landing awaited his bones below.

Pollux changed that. Jason put all his energy and concentration into the bracelet. Unlike how he held back against the cell door to avoid killing Marguerite, Jason let Pollux loose. Warm heat cut through his muscles and marrow while he tucked his body for impact.

Wind cut around him, he could hardly hear the woman's screams as he held her tight. When he was twenty feet away from touching down, he focused his power. White heat filled his vision. Then he hit the ground.

The floor quaked and shattered under his weight. Stone splintered and shifted with the impact.

But he was fine. He looked up and saw the gap of dead space above him. The bracelet allowed him to do all that. He tried to find the words to speak but only one thought broke through: he was alive!

Jason looked up, still clutching Marguerite tight. Matthew stood amidst a crowd of platinum-haired prisoners, all of whom watched the event with stunned expressions. Jason uselessly shuffled his feet against the stone. The broken slabs sunk deeper into the floor with every movement he made.

Matthew marched up to him. "Are you insane, Jason?"

"If I'm going to die, I'm going to do it on my own terms. Take her."

Two prisoners took Marguerite from his arms, and Jason slid his legs free from the floor. Dizziness stirred his vision, and a bout of fatigue overwhelmed his mind. Pollux was already running dry.

"There's no time for this," one of the men said. "The ships are just ahead."

The world spun under Jason's feet.

"Shut it, Alain," Matthew snapped back. He caught Jason by the arm. "Not now, kid. We're not done here."

Shouts called from above. The lizards on the walkway let arrows loose.

Projectiles clattered against the floor around them. One bounced off Jason's bicep. He winced. How much longer could he keep drawing his bracelet's power?

The group charged through the hallway ahead. Alain shouted directions. The shipyard waited just ahead. An ajar gate guarded the path. A crack of sunlight pried through. Alain led the charge through the opening.

They arrived in a wide open shipyard skydeck with fleets of ships lined for miles down. Some vessels reminded him of cogs and hulks with their bulky and round size and sails that stretched dozens of feet high. Large wooden arms elevated all the ships, lifting them up to large stone docks that allowed easy entrance. The wide open air of the mountain lay to his left with its death drop below. In the city across the range was yet another shipyard. This one had about half as many ships as the one here, but it had also been built several thousand feet lower. This whole complex had been built to ship between the two sides.

The prisoners ran onward toward one of the nearby cogs, and Jason followed behind.

The cog was not all that different from the pictures he had seen on that museum field trip years ago. It was twenty-five meters long with sides of lapstrake planking and a big stern post with both the tall sail and mast traveling up tall. He couldn't believe that these things *flew*.

As the group of prisoners boarded the ship, arrows soared once more in their direction. Large clumps of lizards charged the docks towards their position. Wood creaked, and shouts erupted as they poured down the hard decks.

"We have your mistress!" Jason called out. "Stop firing!"

A shot thumped into the mast beside his head. He swore.

"You're wasting your breath," one of the women said from across the deck. "They don't care."

Several of the prisoners ran down to the hatch and to the bulkhead and cabin. Two escapees took Marguerite with them. Matthew threw Jason a sword.

"This one has blood on it!" the boy said.

"It's about to collect a whole lot more."

More arrows flew towards their newly claimed ship. He caught a thrown spear and hurled it back, narrowly missing one of the pack members. Still, they scampered and bounded on.

Objects ceased firing as the lizards came aboard. Jason took a shaky breath. Time to fight. At his side were five others including Matthew and Alain.

"Ready to do this?" he asked them.

"I have been waiting years for this moment!" Alain roared. "To arms!"

The one called Case cheered, and the others followed suit.

Lizards screeched, coming upon the quintet with swords, axes, and spears flashing. Grunts and clangs sang out as the prisoners danced and dodged through the strikes. Alain ran his blade through a scaly gut while he spoke to Jason.

"Ordopha is readying the flight crystal right now. It needs time to gather air. The others are arming themselves for the fight. We will be taking off within moments."

"We need it to be seconds," Matthew retorted.

"She will get it," a tall warrior said with a smirk. "Don't worry, Alain. The others will watch your flank."

Alain laughed heartily. "Thank you, Bran. But be sure to aid Matthew. His experience is lacking. We can't have him dying on us now."

"What about the child?"

"Didn't you see him crush stone earlier? He needs none of our help."

Jason played it off with a laugh. He would not be able to keep this up forever. Already his fatigue caused a sword to cleave into his blonde hair. Blood trickled down his earlobe.

As he slashed back, he asked the other question on his mind. "Where's the prisoner?"

"Down in the hold," Case answered with a thick voice. His beard nearly muffled his voice. "Focus on the fight!"

Another roar sounded. Six men brandishing spears and bows swooped in beside Jason and his comrades.

More guards raced down the skydeck. They would be overwhelmed soon.

Case slashed a lizardman that nearly fell on Jason.

"Keep alive!" Case shouted. "It does not take more than one foolish move to lose your head."

A spear drove for Jason's eye. The boy twisted and stabbed, piercing the chest of his aggressor. The enemy howled and dropped.

"Thanks for the advice."

Case smirked. "You can thank me once we escape this place."

"What is taking them so long?" Matthew asked Alain.

"Patience," Alain said.

As if the universe heard his question, a harsh hum burst from below the deck. Purple smog-like steam billowed out from under the airship like a train whistle. The ship shifted and rumbled, lifting from the dock. The entire body of fighters slid as the airship rose up from the arm. The vessel floated in the air and turned towards the opening.

They shot forward. Several of the lizardmen lost their footing and fell to the docks and over the railing. The airship drifted out of the skydeck and towards the open sky. Alain and his men charged the three remaining lizards and easily slew them.

The men on the deck shouted victory as the ship flew over the mountain range into the burgeoning daylight. But Jason didn't join in. A high-pitched alarm sounded over the skydeck.

Jason caught sight of the opposite mountain range. The large castle at the peak loomed over them all. A sudden chill bolted through his blood. A dark force awaited up there.

Down in the port across the range several larger ships lifted from their arms. He counted at least five below in addition to the ones coming out of the skydeck behind them.

A pit grew in Jason's gut. The pursuit began, and they were totally outnumbered.

CHAPTER 6
BIG WRECK

Cannon fire sprayed over their ship and across the harsh yellow sky. Matthew ducked for cover, and the vessel shook with the force. Missiles shot up from the ships rising out of the mist. The airship turned to port and away from their attackers. Ordopha clung to the wheel and steered towards the mountain range.

Matthew put his sword away and let out a hard breath. It took a moment for him to realize that both he and Jason were not supposed to be there. But that ship had, quite literally, sailed. He would just have to make the best of it and hope they would live through this bad choice.

Jason gestured toward the airships rising out of the city's skydeck. They weren't out of this yet.

"Why are you here?" Bran asked. He scratched the back of his square head. "I thought you were to make your way to the Mirror Gates?"

"When was I supposed to do that?" Matthew replied. The two of them were in this now, for better and for worse. "Enough of that. How far can those things follow us?"

Case growled. "They are leading us away from the city. I don't understand why."

"Maybe they're leading us somewhere," Jason said. "Should we fire back?"

"No point wasting what little ammunition we have down below." Case instantly dropped his cold grimace. "You have potential, boy. Sloppy swordsmanship, yes, but you have a fire only matched by Alain."

"It wasn't that good."

"It was not," Alain agreed. "Hold your tongues. They are gaining."

"Keep moving!" one of the men exclaimed. "We are almost out of these mountains."

Cannon fire exploded above their heads. The vibrations caused several of them to hit the deck.

"Keep your tongue still," Alain barked. "We don't need more bad luck drawn to us."

The ship picked up speed toward the horizon, sailing across the jagged mountain range and the wool blanket of fog. Yet the ships did not speed up in pursuit. They slowed.

Matthew shouted, "Something's wrong!"

Black smoke steamed in place of the formerly purple energy. The ship shook and rumbled down below in the engine area. Clouds rushed up to meet them.

"Inside the hatch!" Alain yelled back. "We're falling!"

The lot piled inside except for Alain and Matthew. The two hovered by Ordopha as she twisted the wheel. The ship barely budged under her direction. It darted in a straight path towards the black rock ridges below the mist.

"I'm going to land it as best as I can," she said, her knuckles white. "We have lost the power in the flight crystal."

Alain swore. "Why?"

"I don't know. Get underground!"

"We're not leaving," Matthew replied.

Alain braced himself against the wheel as they dipped lower. "Ordopha, leave this to me. I'll make sure we make it safely."

"Not on your life!" Her fiery glare flashed at her brother and Matthew. "*You* go with the others. I will make sure we land. I learned to fly this behemoth! This is my mission. You will not take this from me."

Alain threw up his hands. "If you will not be moved then I will stay by your side."

"Just leave."

This time Matthew swore. "You're both idiots."

Wind screamed past them in their descent. Ordopha repeatedly pulled back on the lever beside the wheel, but nothing changed. The angle of descent steepened. She aimed their ship between the rising peaks ahead. Tall rock bases whipped by them. Wood screeched as the mountain stone scraped against the sides of the ship. She slammed the same lever repeatedly. The ship groaned. It slowed slightly, but not nearly enough.

Finally, Matthew could wait no longer. When it was clear she made no further change to their velocity, the two of them jumped forward to drag her away. The ship rocked, Alain stumbled, and Matthew seized his wrist. As the mist swallowed them, only the vague view of a quickly approaching rock bed remained. Within seconds they would crash. Before she could protest, Matthew took Ordopha by the waist and drew her close.

If the bracelet worked on the swords earlier, it should work on them. He used his power, and Castor screamed in his mind while his flesh burned.

The impact shook the foundations of the deck. Rumbling boards broke underneath them.

The airship split into stone as it smashed into the mountain below, wood spraying everywhere. The mast cracked and toppled over, and the wheel tore free of Ordopha's grip. Pieces of the ship broke off, grinding into the ground and flinging boulders upon the deck. Matthew let Castor roar as falling rocks buried them completely.

THE WOOD BENT AND SHATTERED. Shouts rocketed around Jason's ears. Groans creaked in every direction. One of the women lost her grip on the post and tumbled through the twisting ship. He reached out and clasped her close. Pollux raged as boards slammed against his body.

The large vessel shook, throwing everybody about like spare change in the washer. Some of the swords and spears stored below flew loose and crashed into wood and bodies. The bottom of the ship squeaked, sending stone up from the opening below.

Finally, their momentum gave, and they stopped. The sudden change in speed caused everyone in the hold to fall over each other.

Jason landed on top of the girl, his arms on either side of her head and his knees just missing striking her. She looked up at him. He let out a breath as Pollux's power faded.

"Are you alright?" he asked.

She looked at him with watering brown eyes and nodded.

He helped her up and scanned the ship interior. A large hole punctured the rear and mist flooded the insides. They were all lucky to be alive. Ordopha had saved them.

Realization dawned on him—where *was* Ordopha? Matthew and Alain were also gone.

Jason ran out of the open hole in the ship, stumbling over the destroyed ship parts every third step or so. He could see no signs of anyone in the fog.

Bangs like hammers against steel rang off miles behind them. Just as quickly as the pounding arrived, it ceased. Was it something hitting the ground? Was it Matthew?

"Hey!" he yelled out into the wide expanse. "Matthew! Are you there?"

His voice bounced around the jagged coves and sloping ledges of the gorge. No matter how many times he called out the mist absorbed his exclamations. Had he lost his last link to Earth?

A soft airy patch of wind floated twenty feet above him and swam downward. It drifted toward him like smoke from an upside down flame. The intangible form broke up and solidified into three solid shapes inches from the ground. The trio gasped for air.

Matthew and Alain landed feet first on the dirt. The latter's bulging eyes and hard breathing betrayed his attempt at a cool posture. Ordopha clung to Matthew's shoulder, shivering.

"I—what," she stuttered. "Matthew, was that Castor?"

She stared him in the eyes a moment too long before glancing away. Alain coughed and groaned, shaking his head. Matthew let the two of them pull away before he answered.

"It was the only way to be sure the two of you weren't smashed into pieces." He gestured to the broken remains of the vessel behind Jason. "Turns out that it was a good decision."

Alain rubbed his watering eyes. "How did you transform with us?"

"I don't know, but it works with my clothes and weapons so I thought it would work here. But if you two went down to the hold, I might not have needed to do it at all. Is everyone okay, Jason?"

The boy slowly began to speak, but Alain ignored him.

"Someone had to make sure we landed safely," Ordopha's brother replied. "None of us understood how to use the ship."

"Ordopha, when did you learn that the magic was going to leave the flight crystal? That's what happened, isn't it?"

Her attention focused on the ship behind Jason, she took a moment to reply.

"I apologize, Matthew. I only suspected it when we began to lose height. We were told Lord Nieto's magic covered these entire mountains. It appears that is a lie."

"You are the only one of us that learned to pilot one of these," Alain said. "How did you not know the limitations of the craft?"

"I have never once heard of any!"

"That might be why they let us take it," Matthew mumbled.

"Why are you here?" she asked. "You were to return home. This is not your concern."

He grunted. "And yet, here we are. Now we need to find a new way back to get the bombs out of the both of us."

"Just you. There is no bomb in me." They stared blankly at him as he explained what Marguerite had said. "We have her in the ship, though. We can make her tell us anything."

"That witch." Matthew rubbed his knuckles. "What's her game?"

Alain shrugged. "A monster is a monster."

"Do you suppose she let us take that ship?" Ordopha asked. "But then, why take us out of her comfort zone?"

"Are you three done yet?" Jason interrupted. "Either way, we're out of the city. Drop it."

"You're right." Matthew clapped a hand on Ordopha's shoulder. "Good flying. Just be sure to work on your landings for next time."

The four returned to the ship where two of the prisoners met them at the opening.

"Case is dead," one of the men said. "Rubble buried him while he tried to protect Jules. Please help me bury him."

Jason's throat dried instantly. Case? The large warrior who saved his life? He didn't even stop to consider Case as they crashed. Now all he could see in his mind was the goofy grin on the bearded man's face. And he was gone.

"I'll help."

Matthew yelped. His body became smoke and snapped forward. His smoky form blew into Jason, making them one being again.

"Sorry," he said. *"I guess there's a time limit to being separated."*

"That's not good."

Alain jumped. "What happened to Matthew?"

"Inside my head," Jason replied. He put up a hand for concentration. They apparently couldn't hear Matthew inside his mind. "You're scaring them, Matthew."

"I can't get out again. Looks like it takes energy to be separate. I'm tapped out."

"Forget it. Alright, I'm ready."

The two younger warriors entered the broken ship where the survivors all crowded around Case. He lay face up with a flat expression. Broken barrels and shattered blades lay all around the split floor, some stained with Case's blood. Jason had not even seen the carnage inside before running out to find Matthew. They truly were all lucky to be alive. All except for Case.

The mangled look on the larger warrior's face drove a knife into his heart. Jason held back his grimace as he watched the corpse. Not only did they have to bury him, but they also had to leave as soon as possible. He could not rest. He could not reflect on his deeds.

Did they come so far from the castle to die before nightfall? Perhaps Case was the lucky one after all. Jason fought off the notion as he moved to bury the dead.

THEY SCROUNGED AROUND for supplies in total silence for nearly an hour. Matthew tried not to think about the reason, though he could figure it out even inside Jason's head.

The diggers piled rocks and loose dirt on Case. The prisoners said a few prayers to the God of the Land Beyond Sunsets. They mentioned something offhand about the body crumbling back into the Earth. Did their corpses not rot? He couldn't find a way to ask. Not one of them had a bad word to say about their fallen friend and a few let tears flow. Matthew had never understood this sort of thing.

Matthew had left home long ago. He'd been alone since. No one ever bothered him, and he had no inclination to bother them. He lived in a city where his life could end at any moment, so why worry about it? But as he looked at Bran and Jules pile dirt onto Case's body, he began to do just that. Eventually, he would be just like Case. He might even be there before sunset. Without knowing why he suddenly had the urge to see his parents again.

But that could never happen.

When they finished and too much time had passed he decided to cut in on the awkward quiet. Something lurked nearby. What it was he couldn't be sure, but a vague feeling swelled inside him. He whispered his concern into Jason's mind.

"What was that?" the boy mumbled.

"You haven't noticed it? The atmosphere is heavy."

"It's pretty foggy."

"No, I mean that the longer we've been here, the more I'm sure something's approaching. Don't you feel it?"

"No," Jason replied. "But I also haven't been listening. Bit busy here."

"Ask Marguerite if she knows anything about what's out here."

Marguerite sat beside her guards, bound with chains. The prisoner kept an eye on the grievers. She remained quiet the entire service, not even shivering from the cold.

She looked up from her torn dress at Jason's approach. The corners of her mouth began to upturn.

"What's out there, Marguerite?"

"Why should I say? That silly girl brought us out of the range of Lord Nieto's magic and nearly killed me. Whatever is out here is beyond His power."

"I didn't ask that." Jason concealed his disgust behind his warbling voice. The anger shook Matthew from inside the boy's head. "I asked what you left out here to catch people like us."

"We *left* nothing in this wasteland. There is plenty ways to catch mice without the need of cats."

"Lying isn't doing you any favors. Spill what you know."

"I owe you nothing, Jason. You owe me some respect, even if I am your prisoner. I am still a lady, and I gave you that bracelet you currently threaten me with."

"You also put a bomb in Matthew. Tell us how to disarm it."

"He has about a week left. Do not worry. Might I remind you that I didn't put one in you?"

"What else is out here that would stop us? Didn't you say something earlier in the castle about frogs getting in?"

Her lip trembled for only a second. Jason seized on the pause.

"Are there frogmen out here? Are they working for your king? Come on. This Nieto can't be worth dying for."

He bit the inside of his cheek as his fists balled. Matthew understood his anger. She was responsible for this entire situation and still insisted on messing with them. Jason's trembling arm pulled back.

Before he did something stupid, hands grabbed his shoulder.

Alain's eyebrow raised as his hold tightened. "Are you aware of whom this woman is?"

"Marguerite Stohl," he growled out. "One of the pawns who brought us here."

"No. This is Queen Shaula, wife of the Great Sorcerer King. We require her alive in case of bargaining, but that is all she is worth to us, and she knows it. Do not expect to get any worthwhile answers from her."

Jason stuttered. Matthew also found it difficult to fully comprehend. Why was she on Earth if she was more than a mere secretary? He asked Jason to ask his question.

She answered with a shrug. "This is a project I have more than a little investment in. And I am one of the few with enough power to keep even holders of the Gemini Bracelets at bay."

"Not without your magic," Jason said. "You're as weak as a newborn pup."

"I suppose I am." Her smile remained.

"Forget her, Jason. I saw ridges above this embankment when we fell from the ship. We should look for shelter before dark. If there is something out here, we don't want to meet it."

"I don't know, Matthew. Everyone's still out of it from Case's funeral."

"We're pretty dry on energy right now. Getting into a scuffle now is a bad idea."

Jason thought for a minute then nodded. "What's your suggestion?"

"There's a better path some ways back. Less chance of being found."

"That's as good a plan as any."

"Are you speaking to Mr. White?" Queen Shaula asked. "Can you ask him how he escaped the cell? I am curious about that."

"I'm sure you are. Get up."

He lifted her by the arm and marched toward the group. Jason called out to the remaining prisoners, and they converged on them. He asked for an inventory of supplies which turned out to be a stockpile of bread and cheese in their sacks. Each carried a sword or ax except for Bran who held a spear. The women carried bows. Some brought shields.

He explained Matthew's simple plan, and they all talked amongst themselves about it.

"We had no reason to think we would survive out here," Bran said. He kept stealing a glance at Case's grave. "Our only plan was to take what we could and run as far as our legs could take us."

That was all they could hope for, especially now.

They had little choice. The escapees could either die in the wilderness or rot in the dark of the dungeons. Matthew would have made the same decision.

After enough discussion, Alain led the charge south for shelter in the direction Matthew had indicated. Nieto's men normally wouldn't follow them out of the range of his magic, but the tyrant might send them to rescue his wife.

"You won't make it far," Shaula interjected.

Jason glared at her, and she returned his look with a blank expression. Matthew believed he had her pegged. Shaula only ever aimed for what she wanted, and never more than that. She lived to pull men's strings. The boy had clearly never dealt with a woman like her. But Matthew had.

Alain led the group on into the thick mountain mist with Jason hanging near the back. Matthew, still trapped inside Jason, hoped they would hear nothing in their journey but the echoes of their footsteps. No one spoke as they moved on from the grave site.

"You're awfully quiet, Jason."

"*Trying to listen,*" he replied to the man in his head. Matthew could only hear the thoughts directed to him. "*Just keep an eye out. I doubt they'll let us leave that easy.*"

Shaula hummed to herself, even as they led her on in chains. "I wonder what will come out tonight."

CHAPTER 7
BETWEEN DEATH AND DREAMS

THE EARTH MEN and the escapees traveled forty feet up the ridge and several miles from where they crashed. The mountain mist grew thinner the higher they climbed. It faded more as the night came on.

They found a cavern with enough space to fit the lot inside. Alain and Bran made a fire near the entrance, and the group settled in the best they could. Nightfall gave Matthew control of his body once more. He sat with his back to the rear wall and his eyes on the black night outside.

Just before him and in front of the blaze lay Shaula, formerly known as Marguerite, watching the fire. The rest of the men lay around her in a ring. One of the warriors choked back snores, and Shaula pouted to herself. Ordopha finished checking on her brother and noticed Matthew. She silently strode over, her hips swaying in time with the dancing fire. The girl pretended not to see Shaula as she approached.

Ordopha dropped down beside him with her back to the wall. He nodded without looking over.

"It is far too cold out there," she said. "No one has ever frozen to death in Mageuopolis. Lord Nieto willed it to be so. Every resident of the town and the castle is bathed in his magic. We are all warmed and kept alive by his will. He knows if anyone has leaves his realm or enters into it. That is the price of risking escape." She bit her lip. "Case would have told us it was inevitable."

"You did what you had to." Matthew tried to sound confident, but he didn't know if he had the energy in him to puff his chest up. "At least no one else died."

Ordopha let out a small choking noise. Her slender hand ran across her cheek and hair, wiping away a tear. He pretended to stare into the fire when she looked up again.

"It's going to be rough tomorrow," he said.

She took a hard breath before she spoke again. "Yes. We have a long journey ahead of us."

"So, tell me about Case. Was he a good man?"

"There was no man braver or with a faster blade. Next to Alain, he had the most victories in the arena. It is because of those two that we are still alive."

"So they made you fight in an arena. They looked callus enough to enjoy that sort of thing. Why not just kill you?"

"I don't know. I would suggest asking *her*. We were used as entertainment and food for the lizards. Now that we've escaped they will certainly look for replacements."

"Not at all," Shaula interrupted. Ordopha jumped at her low and sultry tone. The dignified prisoner sat up from the fire to face them. Her shadow framed, by the flames, danced like a mad piper's puppet. She looked strangely at ease beside the blaze, as a demon would. "Do you wish to know the truth, little girl? You were distractions to keep the beasts entertained. Nothing more. Whether you die out here or not is of no consequence to your Lord. The only disappointment is that you have managed to drag these two into the filth with you."

"Shut your mouth," Ordopha said with bared teeth. "Never address me again, you hag. Even the lizardmen speak of your deceptions."

"There are no deceptions. There only truths properly expressed. The Great Sorcerer King created me. He created this land. He created every bit of you, silly girl. He will reclaim his creation. If Mr. White and the lad would put aside their pride, we could avoid far worse casualties than that fool at the crash site."

Ordopha sprung from the wall, chipping stone from the rock behind her. Her fury reflected the blaze of the fire. She leapt at Shaula with the force of a bear. Matthew reached out and caught her in his arms. Ordopha thrashed against him.

"Let me go, Matthew! She will die by my hands."

"No, idiot," he growled. "She wants you to do that! This is what she does."

Shaula winked at him, flicking long hair from her shoulder.

A few of the others turned to watch them before he waved them away. Finally, Ordopha took a breath and ceased struggling.

"I apologize, Matthew. Alain might want her alive, but I do not agree with him. She should die."

"Believe me, I get it," he replied. "I think Jason should have just thrown her over the ramparts instead of taking her, but there's nothing to be done about it now. Just take a rest."

"I will." She paused and looked up at him. "You can . . . let go of me now."

The two glanced at each other for a second before he complied. He could have sworn her cheeks reddened for an instant.

"Sorry," he said. "I guess I didn't get as much rest as I thought."

"Thank you for stopping me." She gave a small bow. "We will need all the strength we can muster tomorrow."

"Sleep well."

As he watched Ordopha settle down beside her sleeping brother, Matthew thought about her last words. Tomorrow would be treacherous. If it got any colder, they would freeze long before they made any headway out of these mountains. But there had to be an escape. Nieto wouldn't set up his operation if he didn't have a back door.

"Speaking of Jason," Shaula said. She faced the fire instead of him. "How is he faring? I know he speaks into your mind. This place must be terrifying for the poor dear."

"He's sleeping. Don't bother trying to mess with his head. You've done enough to the kid."

"You mistake me, Matthew. You don't mind me calling you that, do you? Jason reminds me of my daughter. Zelana was truly special. A darling girl with the world in her eyes. Jason is full of promise, just like any child is. It is a shame they are all so timid."

"If you were my mother I'd probably run the other way, too. You better get some sleep, Shaula. You've got a whole lot of walking to do. Don't think I won't hesitate to run you through and throw your carcass over the side of the cliff."

"Such violence. You would fit well in with your villains back on Earth."

"Maybe I would," he answered her. "What do you know about Castor and Pollux? Tell me the truth so I can adapt faster."

She sighed and shook the long strands of locks from her shoulders. "They come from the stars, same as my love. Far away on a long-dead star were Castor and Pollux forged. Whoever made them, and why they did so, is unknown. Since my love found the relics abandoned, it is safe to say they failed. How do you feel being the first successful results of their experiment?"

"Great," he lied.

They fell quiet, and Matthew went back to watching the opening. The night went on, the dead air droning outside. No birds, no crickets, no car horns, or any sounds of life. It reminded him of a graveyard.

THEY WOKE UP EARLY. Jason regretted sleeping and leaving Matthew alone all night to watch over Shaula and the perimeter. Pollux had worn him down. But even though he slept without a physical form, he could still feel Matthew's doubts. Apparently, emotions worked differently than thoughts in that he could feel them all when combined. Waking up to his mumbling was not a pleasant experience.

Daylight transformed Matthew's body into Jason again. They quickly broke camp and set out into the morning light of the mountains.

Jason's dream told him the direction forward. It was that same vision of the mountain he had seen a hundred times before. But it was closer, more vivid.

"It's a dream, boy," Alain said. "It's foolish to pin our hopes on such frivolous things."

"It may be," Ordopha mumbled. "However, we do not have any other clear direction to go. He bears Pollux, and he was instrumental in our escape. Honor dictates we give him room to make his case."

Shaula laughed. "I agree. Jason is a natural born talent. He is much too modest."

Bran pulled on the ropes around her, and she quieted up. The rest, however, now spoke amongst themselves about Jason's ability.

The vision of the golden light had only strengthened since their escape. But Jason was convinced it was their best shot at finding a way out. He just didn't want Shaula to know. She wanted to bring him out here to find it, after all. Thankfully her magic had vanished with her connection to Nieto, but his stomach still twisted. The way she watched them talk amongst themselves with her grating smile stuck to his last nerve.

The lot argued for some time before Alain interrupted. His teeth bared, they all fell silent. Even with his own people he had little patience.

"Ord was right," Alain said. "We have no clear direction. We are stranded in the mountains. We have no protection against the cold. If it weren't for Jason and Matthew, we would not be out of imprisonment now. I vote to follow him. What say all of you?"

There was little disagreement after that, but Jason didn't like being a leader. He did not choose to have these dreams. The gold light loomed closer than ever before. If only Matthew weren't dead asleep.

Onward they went. The daylight could not pierce the beige blanket over the cliffs, steep drops, and bladed crags. Midnight black chasms awaited below the narrowing trails ahead.

It must have been at least an hour they traveled. The pathways dipped down lower into the mist again and around tight bends above the sharp drop. Jason peered into its depths and thought he saw the fog thickening and taking a greener tint. He was thankful they were not going down that way.

Alain tapped him on the shoulder. "How long have you had these visions?"

"As long as I can remember. I get a picture of this bright gold light in the cracks of some great rock wall. A woman is talking, but I always wake up and forget her."

"Couldn't it be a trap?"

"I have this feeling deep inside that it's not. Someone is giving me these visions. I just have to trust her."

The day passed on like this. His concentration remained on the road ahead, and the others talked amongst each other. Alain shared old stories with his friends, Ordopha kept quiet, and Matthew slept. Only two of the others, Jules and Tess, would sometimes interrupt his concentration.

Finally, after what felt like half a lifetime, a familiar voice whispered in his head.

"What's bothering you, boy?" Matthew asked.

"Nothing," Jason replied with his mind. *"Listen, I have something to tell you."*

He relayed his tale about the dream. To his surprise, Matthew did not act concerned.

"That's all well and good, but I think we need to find a Mirror Gate sooner than later."

"I thought that was what we were doing," he accidentally said out loud. Tess and Jules asked what he was doing. Jason explained it best he could before going back to Matthew. "*Now you're making me look crazy.*"

"If it weren't for these people, I would have gone straight back to that damn fortress. The longer I've been here, the more I've been thinking about that magic. Did you feel it? It's like poison."

Jason thought of that green fog deep below them. "*You been having bad dreams?*"

"I don't dream. Think about it, Jason. They can go between worlds and take whatever they want. You've seen all that magic can do—all that one freak can do. Can you imagine Nieto getting loose again? If you think Serenity City is a hellhole, you haven't seen anything."

"This gold light will give us what we're looking for. I know it."

"I still think we're being followed."

"Alain says we're not. The others agree. But I don't know. I think I hear something far off."

"Might be Pollux. If your physical state is heightened, wouldn't your eyes and ears be, too?"

"Wait, Matthew."

Jason stopped in his tracks and listened. The longer he waited, the more it came into focus: the light rustling of pebbles. A slight tapping echoed into the wide canyons. More than one figure moved out there somewhere.

Howling wind snapped about, and stone crumbled from cliffs. But what was it?

Then he heard it: a footstep. Then another. Jason focused on it, his ears cocked. One lone trickle of boots became a flood of them. They were miles behind and gushing forward.

"Alain!" he called out.

Shouts sounded from the crags around the group. Masked faces attached to men wrapped in black rags and armor emerged from the fog like shadows forming from the stone of the mountain. The men held bows in their arms with spears and swordsmen at their side.

Alain ordered his group to raise their hands and not touch their weapons. For one so prideful, Jason half-expected it was a ruse. But Alain refused to allow them to attack.

One of the black-clad men stepped forward. He removed the dark mask that covered his mouth. The same bright and familiar hair color and skin of every one of the prisoners showed through. Scars ran along his face.

Jason whispered to Shaula. "Friends of yours?"

"Hardly," she replied.

"Travelers," the man announced with a joyous expression. "I am Richter, leader of the Vultures. Tell me the names you would like marked on your graves."

"It's a trap," Alain mumbled. "He wants to see where our allegiance lies. He believes we are part of Nieto's forces. Having the witch with us does not help our cause."

Shaula threw him a glare but said nothing.

"We escaped from Mageuopolis," Jason shouted back. "We only mean to pass. I am Jason, wielder of Pollux."

"You fool!" Shaula hissed.

"Pollux?" Richter asked. "Do you mean that old legend? Preposterous!"

"That's what this band on my wrist says."

Ordopha clapped onto his shoulders. "Quiet! You are playing into his hands."

"We can't afford to wait around." Jason shrugged her off. "If this group is not with Nieto, then we need to let them know who we are. There's something else in these mountains. I heard a heavy crowd approaching in the distance. It wasn't these guys."

"I don't understand."

"I'll tell you when this is settled."

Richter had already begun discussing the situation with his allies. Finally, he addressed Jason once more.

"That could be any cheap trinket. I am more concerned with that woman. I can sense heavy darkness in her. She stinks of magic."

"She's our prisoner."

"This could be a ruse to trap my men. I do not tarry with magic. I should plunge blades into your stomachs."

"Whether you believe me or not means little," Jason snapped. "There are bigger things to worry about. Something in the mountains is getting closer. We need to pass before they find us."

"What is it that you heard?" Matthew asked.

Jason ignored him. "What will it take for you to let us live?"

"How about a test of strength? If you best me in battle, I will let you all go. I might keep your women, though."

"Funny." Jason grinned. He nodded to Alain. "I might have to use Pollux here."

"If he has been living in these mountains then he must be tenacious. A warrior with your skill has no chance even with Pollux. I should take this duel."

"He already knows I have the bracelet. He isn't going to let me go without a fight first."

"Precisely!" Ordopha hissed. "Why didn't you listen to me?"

"Let him alone, Ord. Should he fall like a fool, then I will step in. If he is a man, he will fix his own problems."

"Alain's right. You're being stupid."

Jason growled. "Everybody shut up! This is my fight."

No longer would he sit by and let others fight for him. They needed to get out of this place, and he could help them do it.

Half of the three dozen men including Richter slid down the embankment toward the escapees. Richter approached with his blade in hand. Without looking, he threw his longsword to the men behind him. They tossed him back a short blade and shield.

The remainder perched above with arrows trained on their targets. Running would not be an option.

Richter stood before Jason with the short sword and round shield by his side. He gestured for the boy to come forward.

"A test," he said. "Should you break my shield, I will believe your claim. If not, you die."

Jason drew his sword. He had cleaned it the night before, but it never felt right. The blade had been made for lizards, and not men.

"Don't kill him," Matthew chimed in. *"Hold back."*

"Didn't think I'd hear that from you."

"If you kill Richter, it might cause a bigger scene: we don't know these people. Act smart. Just beat him."

"You have to be kidding me."

Richter nodded to the boy. "Are you talking to devils, little man?"

"You wouldn't believe me if I told you."

That much was definitely true. But now as the two warriors, one clearly with a bigger advantage, circled each other, the silence became deafening. Except for the noise miles away that only Jason could hear.

The clatter gathered closer. It could be lizards or more of Richter's men. Maybe it was an entirely different group. Unless he beat Richter, he wouldn't be able to tell.

Jason stabbed, and the sword struck the shield and slid off. Richter closed the gap instantaneously. He brought his blade up. Blood flew from a graze on Jason's cheek.

The sword snaked for his chest. He pivoted. His arm stung as blood dripped from his bicep.

This man was fast, and he was good.

"Is that all, boy? I must say, I expected more from the great Pollux!"

Richter's men laughed. Alain and the others grew grimaces as wicked as death. They all knew what he had already realized. This battle was Richter's to lose.

Thunder rolled like drums in the distance. The pounding beats rolled inside Jason's mind. The storm or the mystery men: which would arrive first?

Jason dodged another attack as a raindrop slapped against his cheek. Pollux begged to be let loose. But could he trust it? Richter lunged forward, and Jason swung, cutting air instead. The enemy ducked back.

Chills like cold fingers ran across his spine.

He was going to lose.

CHAPTER 8
DUEL ON MIST MOUNTAIN

JASON COULD DO little to strike Richter. He tried to use Pollux, but couldn't portion out the power properly. Every strike he made had to be pulled back to avoid killing the opposing warrior. He had to hold back on speed for the same reason. This gave Richter a clear advantage over him.

Jason tried to get in closer but his efforts were in vain. Richter did not allow him any momentum. With every shortened gap, the more experienced warrior glided out of the way. Richter's reprisal lashed against Jason's cheek.

The boy wiped his wound with the back of his hand before lunging in again.

"I hate to tell you this," Matthew chimed in. *"It's almost sunset."*

"*This isn't helping*," he thought back.

"You're using Pollux like a light switch. It's not off or on, Jason. Look at his speed and try to match it. You can see the intensity in his swings. The cut you got on your arm was pretty good. Give it back."

"I will."

The sky rumbled, and another heavy drop splashed against the mountain stone. The storm would arrive shortly.

Jason concentrated on Pollux and parsed it out with his thoughts. The sword strikes beat against his blade like a drum, but he kept his head on the task at hand.

Pollux had chosen him—or was it the other way around? They fit each other like a revolver and a bullet. Pollux was not just a tool; it was a part of him. It burned inside him like a desert sun.

He thought only of Pollux. Like a muscle it pumped when he moved and like a muscle it grew tired with him. It had molded into him. He just needed to train it right.

As Richter fought with him, Jason reined in Pollux as if he were doing a push up with a hand behind his back. His movements tightened as the bracelet adapted.

"Slightly sharper, lad," Richter shouted. "But I am still waiting for this Pollux of yours."

Jason's muscles tore against him with every move. His sword reflected Richter's blow.

One good hit would be enough, but Richter was too good to jump in.

They exchanged swings a few more times before he saw his opening. The boy pulled back with his blade ready. As if he saw Jason's intent, Richter froze.

He nodded to the younger fighter. "Do you have a plan?"

"Not particularly. I think I have you pegged now."

"Put those words into action. Break my shield. Or are you a child pretending to be a man?"

"I have nothing to prove to a scoundrel who robs corpses for a living."

"Very good, boy." Richter's expression did not change, but swirling darkness welled in his eyes. "If that is what you believe, then you can die with those thoughts on your feeble mind."

"Sore spot?"

But Richter didn't answer. Instead, he moved in. His sword struck out like a cobra.

Pollux had never been more difficult to wield. Jason could not gauge when to use it for offense or defense, and ended up with cuts and loosed blood. Richter's speed was no joke. But the warrior's rage did help, and let Jason calmly assess the situation. His sight now felt the strength of Pollux, allowing his eyes to follow the quick movements.

The sword came down on his neck, but he saw it coming. Jason slashed at the shield guarding Richter's chest. Pollux and his legs burned as one, allowing speedy movement. Every breath was like a heartbeat, steady and predictable in an easy to understand pattern. Richter's blade may have been quick, but Pollux allowed Jason to be quicker.

Richter's sword came down and parted the boy's blonde hair. In a flash, Jason whipped out his blade and shifted Pollux into his arms. His weapon smashed into Richter's sword and the attacker shook from the force. Both blades broke in the impact, spraying metal splinters sideways.

Richter grasped Jason by the shirt, but the boy was already moving. Jason tackled Richter to the dirt and pointed the broken sword in his face. Richter could only concede. The battle was over.

"You failed to break my shield, but you did far better than I thought."

Jason's eyebrow slanted. "Then you believe this is Pollux?"

"My sword's destruction is proof of that. But don't give yourself credit. You're far too sloppy to have beaten me otherwise."

He couldn't deny it. Pollux was the only reason Jason had accomplished anything.

"Call your friends off, Richter."

"As you wish," Richter shouted for his men to stand down. No longer did arrows or blade tips point towards Alain's group. "This would the perfect time to explain who you are."

Jason told the fallen leader a condensed version of all that had happened since they first arrived in Tyndarus. As he went on to explain it, Richter only blankly nodded back.

When the tale was finished, Jason got to the point.

"My senses are improved with Pollux. It isn't as direct an improvement as my muscles or bones, but my sight, hearing, and smell are also stronger. I can hear something in the distance. I've been trying to tell you."

"From where?"

"I don't know. Sometime during our fight it stopped."

"Then it was only rock-slide somewhere out there. May I sit up now? I don't like women seeing me like this, you understand."

Jason rolled his eyes. He allowed Richter to his feet and discarded his broken weapon.

The leader of the Vultures addressed the entire crowd. "You are welcome to travel with my men to our village. I have no doubt that you would rest well there."

The reaction to his invitation was much arguing, though mostly among his own men.

"Preposterous!"

"We know nothing of them."

"Exactly!" Richter answered. "They have escaped from the Great Sorcerer King and found their way through the mountains without succumbing to the elements. In addition, they have Pollux among their number. Do you not think they would be an asset to us?"

This time even Alain and the other ex-prisoners argued with him. No one would ever convince Ordopha's brother to trust anyone. But as they continued arguing, Jason's uneasy feeling returned.

Sunset was coming, bathing the mist in a fuzzy orange light through the thickening clouds. Jason smelled wet sewage as the sun dropped lower and thunder grumbled. He couldn't make out what the scent was from.

Ordopha crossed through the chattering groups toward him. "Are you hurt?"

"Only my pride. That was the most embarrassing thing I've ever done."

"It was . . . not pleasant to watch."

"Not to fight, either," he agreed. "What do you think of his offer?"

She scanned over Richter from his thick black boots to the scars on his sharp cheeks. He was a man who had been through many worse battles than this one. And yet he lived through them all.

"Alain will argue because that's his way," she said. "But Richter makes a good point. I don't entirely trust him, but we have little choice."

"The weather?"

She nodded. "We also do not know where we are. The others are tired, and Case is still on their minds. This man could have easily killed us all, but he didn't."

"I'm not sure if Alain will accept. His pride even outdoes mine."

"That's not entirely true. Alain only does what he must for the others. That requires shrewdness and cleverness."

"You're just like him, though."

"If you compare our accomplishments then there's no competition. Now I only want to get them all to safety. You too, you stupid boy."

She ruffled his hair, and he tried not to blush. Matthew laughed in his mind.

Clouds gathered in and blocked the orange beams in the sky. Soon only muted light shone through the gathering clumps of nimbus. Drops fell from the clouds.

The thunder cracked from above, and the rain poured down. Alain came running over to the pair with Shaula in tow. The droplets plastered down their hair, and their soaked clothing made them look like drowned animals. Ordopha's brother shouted to them.

"We've agreed to go with them!"

"What was that?" Ordopha answered. The shrieking wind made hearing difficult.

"Jason! Look up!"

As if falling from the storm clouds, stocky and long-legged men with flashing swords and helms dropped from the nearby ridges. Dozens flowed from nowhere.

Frogmen.

"Everyone, attack!" Jason pointed to the plunging attackers.

The large group shouted at their oncoming enemies. They brought out their blades and bows as the attackers fell upon them. Clashing steel erupted with rolling thunder booms and the dancing rain under their feet. Frogmen bounced everywhere. Visibility faded with the downpour.

Ordopha drew her bow and fired, catching an enemy in the throat. Alain shouted to Matthew to come out. They needed as many men as they could get.

Matthew obliged, joining them in battle.

"We need to stick close," Matthew said to Jason. A large tongue lashed like a whip, smacking against his sword. His hands shook. "We need to keep Shaula close and our backs covered. You and Ordopha stay with her. We can't tell if they're here for her, On the other hand, she could use the chance to run."

She laughed. "And where would I go, you imbecile?"

"Quiet, woman."

Matthew and Alain struck out at the frog men that dove upon them. Alain took one head, and Matthew cut another. Jason took up a fallen spear from the dead and joined in. Ordopha flung arrows from her quiver, striking several amphibians as they leaped. The quintet soon found themselves backed up to the sheer mountain wall. They would be surrounded quickly.

"Jason!" Matthew yelled. "Give me a boost!"

Jason looked at him. "Why?"

"If I can get higher I can see where they're coming from. It's about fifty feet up. Can you do it?"

The steep wall went up far, but it only meant that Matthew would be a sitting duck ready for slaughter up there. The frogmen would easily surround him on his own.

"I can, but I think you should take Ordopha with you." There was only one way out of this corner and anyone left alone was at a massive disadvantage. "We should stick together."

"Fine," Matthew agreed. "But make it quick. I'm not sure how much energy Pollux has left."

"It has plenty!"

Matthew and Ordopha stood together, and Jason used Pollux to lift them up in each arm. Power burned in his muscles causing them to shiver. He shifted Pollux's energy through him evenly, peaking with his arms. With carefully managed strength, he tossed the pair. They soared through the air and passed the downpour and above the target. Jason cursed his aim.

Matthew clutched Ordopha close as they flew. They transformed into mist in the rain and slowly drifted down to the top of the wall.

When he was sure they were fine, Jason turned to Alain. The boy seized Shaula by the waist and then Alain.

"What are you doing?" he asked.

"Watch yourselves," Jason said. "This is going to be a mess."

Using all the strength he felt in Pollux, Jason jumped into the rain-soaked sky, breaking stone underneath his shoes. He flew thirty feet above target before kicking downward towards Matthew and Ordopha on the ridge.

He slammed shoes first into the stone. His legs let out cracks and pops. Both Alain and Shaula were held high at his side and missed suffering the impact.

Jason yelled as he let Shaula and Alain go, stumbling over his own feet and falling on his face. Pollux ran out of energy at the last possible moment. His muscles numbed as the power cut out. The backlash gripped him hard, seizing his body. Jason's vision blurred.

The frogs landed on the stone, surrounding the group. He couldn't stay lying down.

However, that was when he felt it. The vision. He was close. Gold waited close by, brighter than any sun that might hide behind this storm. It was their best way out of this mess.

Alain and Matthew still fought the frogs while Jason slowly crawled back to the stunned Shaula. She watched him with an open-mouthed stare as she sat against another flat rock wall. He needed to prevent her from getting away.

That was when he realized: the others were all gone. He couldn't even hear their blades banging against frog flesh in the distance anymore. His enhanced senses had been lost. The five were alone in this mess.

Jason crawled up and realized he had lost his weapon. He lifted a sword from a dead frogman, his muscles burning. He ran through a leaping enemy and backed up against Shaula. Rain dashed on his stained blade. Jason shook off a groan as the storm, and fatigue beat against him.

They needed to find the gold before either the frogmen or the storm finished them.

CHAPTER 9
BATTLE ON FROG MOUNTAIN

THE RAIN STREAKED Matthew's vision as he guarded against the leaping frogmen. With Jason falling all over himself to guard the witch, Matthew could only hack the enemies pouncing upon him. He kept glancing over his shoulder and around the rain-slicked mountain for any sign of the separated escapees. The frogs were all he saw, and they only grew in number. He couldn't fight them off alone forever.

His control of Castor was also weakened. Rain made the enemy's weapons hard to gauge, and misting and solidifying became difficult because of it. They slashed at him as he struggled to track their movements.

"We need to find cover from this blasted storm," he said to Alain.

"And these monsters." The other warrior downed one foe before two more fell from the dark sky toward him. "We could use an extra sword or two. Where is Jason?"

Matthew glanced back. Jason leaned against a nearby rock wall with Ordopha and Shaula at each side. He was breathing hard. The boy had taken a bad spill. "What happened?"

"Pollux cut out." Jason drew in a ragged breath. "Never mind it. I think I can find the golden light."

"We can't go. I'm not leaving the others."

"What others, Matthew? I can't see or hear them. Can you?"

No, he couldn't. There was no sign of any life in the storm. Thunder growled, and lightning kicked, but only the rain kept them and the attackers company. He feared the worst.

"We must get to shelter!" Alain yelled. "When this storm clears we can return to find Bran and the others. We are easy prey right now."

Matthew's sword flashed against the spear of an attacker. He became fog and flew through the weapon, and ran the frogman through.

Sharp pain spiked through Matthew's ribs. Castor throbbed inside of him. Low energy.

"Okay, you're right," Matthew replied. "I don't know about your gold, but we can't stay here."

An arrow whizzed past Matthew and struck an oncoming frogman. Ordopha signed to him. He returned the gesture and decapitated another aggressor.

"I've got the path in my head," Jason called out. He pointed to a shallow crevice in the rock wall to his left. It burrowed deep into the mountainside. "It's far, but we can make it from here."

"If I didn't know you were crazy," Matthew responded, "I would commit you for this."

Matthew clapped the boy on the shoulder. The two merged together leaving Matthew as the host body. The remaining four barreled through the crevice. Frogmen screeched after them.

"Good thing the sun went down during that mess," the kid said.

"Not that you can tell with the rain. So tell me which way to go."

The rain kicked dust into the air making visibility even worse. Matthew swirled down winding paths with Jason yelling the directions in his brain. Alain and Ordopha followed after, holding onto Shaula. The rumbling behind them told him that their enemies still pursued them.

Sharp drops awaited in every turn through the thick mist. One slip and they would be done. Yet cautiousness could not be afforded. They kept on through the darkening skies, spray beating them down from above.

A small gap in the path waited ahead. Ten feet wide or so, Jason pushed him through it. Matthew leaped over the death drop and kept running.

"Wait!"

Behind him, the other three remained on the opposite side.

"Why are you guys just standing there?"

Ordopha pointed to the pit. "You don't hear that?"

"Hear what?"

"Listen!"

He glanced down into the void below. It was impossible to see anything through the downpour and thick wall of white mist and distant green fog, and the hard raindrops and thunder didn't help. But he caught a subtle sound in the abyss. The rustling of footsteps and breaking stone crumbled from far below. The blasted frogs had followed them from underneath.

"These things don't give up," he mused.

"Forget them! The gold is just ahead!"

"Hey! Jason says we're close."

The brother and sister made Shaula go first. After some pouting she obliged them. When she made it across, the witch wiped the hem of her robe.

"I hope for your sake that Jason is correct."

"I thought you trusted him?"

"Jason is an honest boy, not a smart one."

"She's right. I trusted her, after all. Ugly witch."

Matthew nodded. "You can say that again."

Both Shaula and Jason agreed without knowing who he actually referred to. Ordopha and Alain soon joined them on the other side. The mountains shook around them.

Alain let his breath catch up with him. "Where is the boy taking us, Matthew?"

"He thinks we're close to that place in his dreams."

"Those visions were enough to run us out in the rain with those things on our backs?" Alain grumbled. "You had me abandon my kin for this? I was fine following him before, but not after we found those who could help."

"What do you expect, Alain? There's nowhere else to run. We don't know where the others are, and we're being swarmed by those frog freaks. If you have a better idea, I'd like to hear it."

"I'd much rather be slain in battle than run from them."

"You and me both. But it's not just us, is it? You have to think of Jason . . . and your sister." He pointed to Ordopha. "Do you want to see her die in a place like this? I sure as hell don't."

"Please, you two." Ordopha piped up. "For now we should trust Jason. We will find the others when the storm clears."

"I am only asking for an explanation," her brother answered. "I deserve that much."

She rubbed her eyes free of rain. "Do you want to end up like Case? Jason is injured, and our enemies are still in pursuit. No more death. Stop arguing and let's go!"

For the first time since this whole mess started, Matthew really looked at her. When he lived in the city, he met many women. None of them did much more than offer momentary entertainment. Ordopha had no filter. He didn't even know if she did it on purpose or if she was just that trusting. Her clear eyes always locked onto his, her graceful hands always ready for the bow, and her thoughts always on those around her. She reminded him of a world he had thought he long ago abandoned. He'd forgotten there were people like that.

"What are you staring at, man?"

Dumb kid.

He ignored Jason. "Alain. Ordopha. I'm moving on. Are you coming?"

"Of course," Alain replied. "Who do you think I am?"

The group glided down rock paths and fought against the blowing storm. They followed the roads down into a closed cavern embedded in the mountainside.

The way was at least forty feet long and only six or so wide. The narrow crevice allowed shelter from the rain but little room. At the end remained a tall flat wall that stretched on at twice Matthew's height. Matthew led with Ordopha, Shaula, and Alain in the rear.

Jason exited Matthew's head. He reformed in time for Shaula to call out from behind them.

"Finally you return, Jason. Now maybe you can explain where we are. All I see is another dirty cave for the filth out here. Will you be sleeping in the trash once more?"

Alain seized her by the arm and lead her deeper inside. "You know much of filth, witch. Keep your lips fastened. Explain, Jason."

"Give me a second," he responded.

Ordopha's brother faced the cave opening where the downpour continued unabated. He tightened his hold on Shaula's shoulder and pushed her toward the cave entrance. Alain kept watch on the opening with her at his side.

Matthew leaned against the cave wall, and Ordopha joined him. They watched Jason stare at the flat surface mumbling to no one in particular. He ran his hand against the solid stone wall at the end of the path. Matthew and Ordopha remained alone together in the center.

Outside the rain poured harder. Any sound of the frogmen had been lost to the storm. Matthew breathed a sigh of relief.

"How long have you been doing this?" he asked Ordopha.

"Excuse me?"

"Taking care of your brother and the others. You've been doing it for long?"

She laughed nervously. "I hope this is not an indirect way to ask my age."

"I may be insensitive, but I'm not that dumb. I'm asking because you're shaking a lot."

"That would be the cold."

"Not shivering. Your hands have been twitching. You weren't doing that before those frogmen showed up. You miss your friends."

"This is unlike you. Normally I would expect this from Jason."

"I'm just curious. We have some time to kill, so give me a hint. What did you do in that prison?"

Ordopha took a moment to think before she locked her stare with his. Those grey eyes betrayed a depth within them that hid a world from him. Finally, she bit her lip.

"Our father and mother died three years ago. They were the last to be slain in the Trial Bridge. When we get to a certain age, we are sent to the arena and fight against impossible odds. We don't always return—they didn't. The ones you met? We are all that is left."

Matthew shook the dampness from his hair. Water drops leaped off. He needed a moment to tackle this revelation.

"I'm not privy to Shaula's master or his plans," he replied, "but I'm sure he thinks everything is born to be a sacrifice to him. Did your parents ever say anything of the outside world?"

"They were raised here, too. Their ancestors, as well. All we learned about the outside was of the God Beyond Sunsets. He is the one that waits for us to reach Him and the end of our long day."

"So you don't know anything about Tyndarus."

She blinked and laughed softly in a gentle whisper. "You make me sound as if I were an automaton with no thoughts of my own, Matthew."

"I just meant that you haven't seen or heard anything beyond Nieto's city."

"Truth be told, I'm a bit afraid of what lies outside. I never expected we would get this far. Is there anything out there? I have spent late nights worrying about it."

He held back a laugh. "I'm sure it can't be as bad as all this. I'm more worried about whatever it is that is messing with Jason's head. He's losing it."

She sighed as if a weight had lifted from her. "Of all of us, I worry about his head the least. It's his body that needs training."

"That goes for both of us. Tell me, Ordopha. You must have heard a story or some speculation from the lizards about Tyndarus."

"I've learned only what I've learned by deception or thievery, and only in that cramped castle. All I know is that the Great Sorcerer King fled the outer world of Tyndarus ages ago. Why he left is a mystery no one ever talks about. It is almost as mysterious as you."

"Me?" Matthew recoiled. "I'm mysterious? How so?"

"We helped each other escape, and you know more of us than we of you." She winked. "That isn't quite fair, is it?"

His mouth opened but no words escaped. He finally coughed them out. "There's nothing to tell. I don't mean that cryptically. I mean that there's nothing to me. I'm just a man who was chosen for a simple job. But if you want to know more then, we should save it for when we're out of here."

She outstretched her hand. "Promise?"

"Promise."

They shook their hands and shared a small laugh.

"Hey!" Jason called out. "I think I've figured it out."

The boy crouched by the flat wall and dug deep into the dirt. When he finally spoke up, Alain nearly jumped out of his skin.

Matthew stepped up behind him with Ordopha in tow. After a few more moments Alain and Shaula also crossed over from the entrance. Still, the boy plunged his fingers deeper into the dirt and dug furiously.

"Well?" Matthew broke the silence. "What exactly is this, Jason?"

"I can't get under."

"It's a solid wall. Why are you trying to get under it?"

Jason slammed a fist on the dirt and stood up before the group. "This is a door. We need to get on the other side. I can't figure out how to open it. See the crease right here? But there's nothing to grab onto, so I can't pull it."

"Why not use Pollux?" Alain suggested. "Surely it has recovered some strength by now."

"It doesn't work that way. Pollux is part of me. We share the same energy. We're both spent."

"Fascinating," Shaula whispered. She watched him intently.

Alain ignored her. "In other words, the reason you were hurt earlier is because you are not strong enough to use it?"

"Alain!" Ordopha exclaimed.

"What did I say, Ord? It wasn't a lie, was it?"

"No," Jason interrupted. "You're right. I'm learning to parse it out. I got through Richter without losing control, but I used too much getting us out of that dead end. Anyway, that's not the point. Even if I could smash it, there's no guarantee it won't come down on us. We need a way in."

"How about Matthew?" Ordopha asked. "Castor still has strength, yes?"

"It does." Matthew thought on it a second. There was a chance he could get through. He placed his hand on the small crease at the base. "I'm not sure if I can get in. It's a tight fit, and I can't see any light at all. How thick is this gate? If I run out of power getting through I'm dead."

"That's why I was digging. See? There's less than half an inch of space. You can turn into water and go under to the other side."

"Not that I don't trust you, Jason, but this whole gold thing has been weird from the get-go. If you've seen this place in your dream then don't you have any hint on getting in?"

"I told you that I only ever saw gold through the cracks. I don't know what's in there at all."

"Then this *is* a gamble."

Alain sighed. "Leaving the others was already a risk. They will never forgive us if we return with nothing."

"That's easy for you to say, Alain," Ordopha cut in. "You are not the one who has to risk his life going inside. We should wait for the storm to pass and return to the others."

"No way," Matthew answered. "I'm not going to waste this chance. Sure, the kid might be wrong, but there's a chance he's right." He took a hard breath. Putting all his chips on Jason was not a plan he wanted to rely on. "Just step back in case I open this thing."

Before anyone could respond, Matthew let Castor loose. His body sunk into the ground with a splash, and he squeezed into the crack. It was a tight fit, but not as difficult as he expected.

He slipped out the other end after only a foot in pitch darkness. Dust motes and thin ash streaked the empty stone carved hall. He did not transform back for the simple reason that he couldn't see anything ahead.

Matthew streaked forward, sliding against the gravel floor. He felt around the edges. The pathway stretched easily twenty feet wide which meant the outer tunnels blocked the door. A switch or lever should be on this side.

Onward he traveled, but the floor shifted underneath him. Before he could gather his bearings, gravel broke open, and he fell through into black darkness.

A trap!

Long spikes stabbed through him. Red streaks of pain reverberated through his watery form. Thankfully the holes gouged out instantly refilled but the burn split through him like a needle injection of fire. He hit the jagged ground of the pit with a splash.

He landed in a narrow crevice with no way out. Stone spikes littered the small pit. He would have to transform to escape.

However, the spikes were too close together. He didn't know what would happen if he reformed, but he would have to risk it. Castor slipped a little, and the pain lit his soul on fire. He couldn't leave the others stranded out there.

Matthew reformed in the pit, his body growing and solidifying back into shape. As he pulled himself together, the stone spikes buckled and shifted, breaking under his weight. His skin was harder than rock. The trap shattered against him, laying several of the spikes to pieces. He was whole again, as was his skin. It solidified hard for the brief moment he transformed back.

After slowly climbing out, his reddened vision allowed him a momentary glance of the surrounding darkness. The narrow path from the door stretched onward, but ahead of him, a small groove in the wall waited. There he spotted a lever.

Matthew used Castor again, this time for mist. He floated forward over any possible pits. Thankfully, concentration came easier this time.

He reached the lever and became normal again. Up the slope to his left he spotted a hallway that went on for twice the length of this one. At the very end was a sharp turn to the right with a glowing light.

The pale light shone of gold. Jason's dream was right.

Matthew hit the switch. Stones and tightening gears shifted behind him in the walls. The large door opened. Stone and rock slid apart as the outside wind blew in.

The spikes made him think twice about the whole expedition. Whoever built this place did not want them there, and if it held a relic like the Gemini Bracelets then maybe they had a point.

As the door swung open, he thought he saw Shaula's toothy grin flashing with the lightning. Whatever happened he would make sure she got nothing.

Even if it cost him everything.

CHAPTER 10
EMPIRE OF GOLD

MATTHEW WARNED the group about the spikes before they entered. Thankfully the faded light from the outside storm gave some visibility to the tunnel. Falling on those spikes had sent pitchforks of pain into his chest, and without his powers, he'd be dead. The others wouldn't be so lucky.

Alain checked the floor for any further traps. Several pokes of his sword revealed false coverings carefully laid out over more pitfalls. The holes were arranged in a jagged diagonal pattern from the left wall back to the right. The only other sights were grooves in the walls and ceiling, but nothing came from them. This setup was almost *too* elaborate.

No one had been in this place in ages.

When the others made it to the branching pathway, he plainly asked Shaula what she knew.

"I'm sorry, Matthew. Not everything in this world is related to me or my love."

"You wanted Jason to find this place, and you don't know what's here?"

"I'm here for a relic left here thousands of years before my birth. How could I possibly know what was hidden here? And before you ask, no, my love did not put it here. Every world has its own relic, and they are all as potentially powerful as yours. It is no wonder this hideous place has been left so well guarded."

"Nobody has been in here in years. The torches are extinguished. You're telling me this isn't magic? This is the relic you've been looking for?"

She scanned the light with a furtive glance. "That is an excellent query. What say we find out?"

"You're crazier than I thought if you think I'm just going to let you lead. Magic or not, I'm not trusting you. I'm going first again to see if there are any more traps."

"I'm not convinced there are any," Alain interrupted. "The ground had been softened and dug up with the stones plainly sticking out. The floor ahead is stable and solid. But check regardless."

"Sure. Anything I should look for?"

Alain scanned the dark through slitted eyes. "Off-center plates or grooves on any solid surface. Don't trust anything that can be pushed. This witch had traps all over the castle like those."

"It keeps rats out," she sneered. "And in."

Alain grumbled. "I would remove your tongue if we had the moment to spare."

"Alright, I'm going," Matthew said.

He transformed into mist and flew toward the light. In this form he had a total three-dimensional view around him. It would also be harder to fall into any more pits this way. But there were no spots like the previous path—no badly placed false floors or grooves along the walls. It appeared Alain was right and the traps were finished.

Around the corner, he found another lever in a wall groove. Before he could figure its purpose out, he glimpsed what was beyond it. Gold light beamed through the jamb of the great gates. The relic had to be the source.

If he hit the lever, it might set off another trap. He would have to gamble.

He carried Ordopha and Alain before the crash. Could he carry them all again?

Making sure there was nothing to land on, he reformed beside the lever.

"You guys should all go back outside," he called around the corner.

Eerie vibrations ran along his spine. No matter how he tried to rationalize it away, he couldn't do it. Some seedier presence hid nearby, watching and waiting.

They assented to his request and disappeared back the way they came. After waiting few moments, Alain yelled that they were outside the door again.

Matthew took the metal lever between sweating palms. There would be only a split second to transform when he pulled it, and he needed to be sure he could. He prayed that it would hold a bit longer. They were so close.

Goose-flesh prickled his skin as he threw the lever. The ceiling rumbled above him as did the hallway behind. He transformed—but it wasn't fast enough.

Stones in the ceiling slammed down upon him. Pain flashed as the rocks broke apart and the rubble dug into his back, but they didn't break anything. His body hardened just before transformation, just as it had when he was in the pit. He became fog, and the stones fell through his form. Metal tinged in his chest—the bomb? The rest of the rocks fell through his ethereal body. Crimson lights surged through him.

He drifted above the rubble to get a sense of what happened. The large metal door cracked open. Matthew focused on his lack of crippling wounds. It meant his transformation was not instantaneous, and that his whole body changed as one monolithic form. With some training, he might figure out how to force different parts to morph independently, but not yet.

Fallen and shattered stone littered the floor around the corner. Upturned tiles and switches hid buried under the fallen rocks. The lever dumped everything in the ceiling like a baby thrown from the dirtiest bathtub in existence. As far as a fail-safe went, he couldn't imagine much better. Now only the open, cracked door remained.

"At least we know the floor's safe."

He drifted over the rubble back to the first hallway and saw the same sight there. Piles of crumbled rocks everywhere—the stones had even crushed the spike pits.

His four traveling companions waited by the gate. Their stares darted around the wrecked tunnel.

"You said the door opened?" Shaula asked. "What is inside?"

"I don't know, I came here first."

They traversed the way back, stepping on the dispensed remainders of the loosed traps. When they reached the slightly cracked open gate the lot of them looked on in awe.

The thick solid metal door spanned twenty feet in length.

Ordopha watched over Shaula as the three men pulled at the gate. Matthew and Alain strained, but without Pollux, Jason was weak as a kitten. But still, he pried with the two of them, panting. Sweat covered his reddened cheeks.

They pushed, creaking the jamb, and finally shoved it open. They grunted as they used their full weight against it.

They all stared into the now uninterrupted golden light. The hot glow shone upon them. No one spoke. Matthew didn't have to ask why as he felt it himself. Even Shaula fell silent, the unutterable beauty piercing her black heart. Nothing could describe the warm sensation in Matthew's blood swimming inside his tired wounds. There was never anything so radiant.

The large golden shrine was held up by towering marble pillars, and an over-sized flashing altar lay at the opposite end of the chamber. A wall-length mirror hung on the opposite side. Long rotten pews littered the gigantic space, and the musty smell crinkled his nose, but it couldn't deter him from what he saw ahead. A nearly invisible chalice sat perfectly in the center of the altar. The ancient holy place gained its light from what beamed from the cup. His prize awaited inside of it.

"Is that a seed?" he asked. No one responded.

The door behind them slammed shut as if a magnetic force had kicked in. Matthew and Ordopha jumped.

Jason made it halfway across the shrine's open floor space before anyone noticed he had moved. Alain remained transfixed on the gold glittering against the gaudy walls and didn't notice Shaula crossing the rows after the boy. Ordopha shook her brother while Matthew followed after the witch.

Shaula's robes hissed against the floor like a cobra. Matthew passed in front of her. She stopped and watched him with a blank expression.

"Did you forget that you're our prisoner?" he asked. "You have no magic."

"I forgot nothing, fool. I am more than just magic."

Shaula outstretched both hands and nodded. A bright red fire lit across her forehead like a torch and rolled down to her palms. Flames burst out from her, burning against her exposed skin. A cyclone of heat lashed across the chamber.

Sweat streaked across walls, and the floor warped. Pressure pumped from her as if a steam valve had been thrown loose. It would only be a matter of time before she consumed everything.

Matthew backed up as the fire swirled across the ground. He tried to process it. She had powers.

"You're a Prime," he whispered.

"Very smart, Matthew." White teeth smiled. "Now stand aside or become cinder."

Flames snaked around her, slithering to and fro like ripples on the waves of her curves. She could easily roast him.

"No, you won't do that," he replied.

"I won't?"

"You need Castor."

"I need more relics. My love will become the ultimate being."

"Can't do that if you destroy the bracelets."

A twang sounded, and she grimaced. Shaula cried out. An arrow sunk into her shoulder.

Ordopha and Alain stood beside Matthew. They had their bow and sword drawn, respectively.

Shaula crouched and launched upwards in one fluid motion. Fire exploded from her like a geyser. Crimson red and orange light enveloped the ceiling. Gold leaf dripped like rain from a leaking roof. How powerful were her flames?

The trio dove sideways into the rotting pews. Fire streamed across the open room after them, burrowing into the floor. Matthew slid forward as several pews burned around him. Alain and Ordopha dashed behind marble pillars. The wielder of Castor stood alone in the center of the room with only Shaula between him and Jason.

But the boy still stood before the altar, unmoving. Matthew called out, but the raging flames silenced his voice.

Shaula remained still in the burning pyre. "Jason! Give me the Kharis Seed!"

"So you *do* know what it is!" Matthew said.

"Of course I do! It will parse out unbelievable power and strength but at the cost of lifespan. However, how do you think an immortal would be affected by such limitations? He would not."

Over by the altar, Jason touched the cup. The chalice crumbled at his fingertips. Any semblance of gold light faded, now consumed by the flashing flames around Shaula. He took the seed.

"Give it here!" she shouted.

Matthew watched this play out with increasing terror. The thousand-yard stare on Jason's face showed a boy losing his grip on reality. The queen took one step towards him, and Matthew transformed. He became water and slunk along the floor as the woman was distracted. Neither Jason nor the witch paid him any mind.

Shaula shouted at the boy, "What are you doing?"

As if it were the most normal thing in the world, Jason swallowed the Kharis Seed with a single gulp. He blinked, and his vision became refocused.

"Did I just do what I think I did?"

"You stupid boy!"

"At least you can't get it now," he replied.

"Oh, I still can retrieve it."

Matthew slithered along the floor. An incredible heat burned into him as he passed her. His form steamed, evaporating into the ether. He would melt to nothing before he made it to the boy. Matthew sprang up between them and held his sword out towards Shaula. Pure heat pressed against him.

"I've had more than I can stand of you!"

"My feelings are the same, Matthew!"

Alain and Ordopha ran to his side, rounding the witch with their weapons ready. They shook nearly as much as he was sweating.

"You used us, witch," Alain said. "Why did you not attack when we first took the ship?"

"The seed is all I desire. I knew the mountains Jason spoke of in his visions. I knew he could take me to the prize—the one my love has sought since first coming to this cursed world. But why would I waste my time forcing you here when you fools could bring me here of your own volition? Give it here, Jason."

"Stay away from him!" Ordopha yelled. "Enough madness. Do not think I will fail to put an arrow in your eye. You cannot burn them all."

"Can't I?" Veins pulsed on Shaula's fiery forehead and delicate pale neck. "You two fools are nothing but simple entertainment for my pets. But Castor and Pollux are another thing entirely. And the Kharis Seed is an even greater find. I'm sorry to say, Matthew, but the two of you are expendable. We can always find other candidates for Castor and Pollux. We cannot find another Kharis Seed. Give it to me, or I will burn it out."

She hungrily licked her lips. Her eyes blazed hotter than the flames. Her playful edge vanished with wrath.

"I choose neither," Jason said.

Shaula's rage grew as her gaze widened. "Come back here!"

Jason leaped the altar and pressed hands against it. Gold light flooded out of his palms. His reflection enveloped him and threw light across the room.

"*Holder of the Seed,*" a voice echoed through the cavernous place. "*Where do you wish to travel?*"

Jason spoke up without pause, his tone subdued. "Take my friends and me out of the mountains to the closest Mirror Gate."

"Stop!" Shaula screamed.

The bright light clashed against her wild flames and sent her stumbling. Matthew, Ordopha, and Alain lifted from the floor and were pulled backwards toward Jason. All four slammed into the mirror.

Shaula whipped a fiery bolt at Jason. The fireball crashed into the mirror, shattering it into thousands of pieces. Her targets vanished.

The woman wailed as they disappeared into the darkness.

Matthew watched as the shrine faded. White shapes soared under the quartet in large rows blown by the wind. Clouds! The night sky surrounded him. Cold air rushed by as they soared through.

Gravity dropped them like a heavy stone. They plummeted downward through the sky. But no matter how far they fell, the clouds never broke.

Matthew held on to both Alain and Ordopha. There was nothing else he could do.

Jason dropped lower and lower. The boy disappeared below the void of clouds and disappeared from the endless white.

Only the three of them remained.

But the world began to sink away from them, and clouds swallowed the trio. Matthew could no longer even see his own hands.

And even with the universe disappearing around him, Matthew could still hear the rage of the Queen of Mageuopolis howling uselessly into the void.

CHAPTER 11
IN A STRANGE LAND

DARK SKIES AWAITED his aching head when Matthew blinked awake. Spotlights of stars beamed down in a pattern completely unrecognizable to him. Two decades alive and he had never seen these skies before. No Big Dipper, no Orion—the patterns were completely foreign.

Never in his short life did Matthew imagine he would step foot on another planet. But he still breathed the air and walked the dirt just as if it were Earth. Would he ever return home? He grabbed the grass under his fingers and relished how soft it felt.

That was when Matthew realized that he was awake. His hands batted about all over his sore skin. No broken bones, no bruises. Somehow, he'd lived.

"*You're awake, Matthew?*" Jason asked in his head.

"So you're alive!"

"*That voice in the mirror almost got us killed. Why did I listen to it? My head's still ringing.*"

Tall trees loomed down, and thick bushes littered the spaces around Matthew. They had landed in some kind of forest.

"Where are we? Where are Ordopha and Alain?"

Before the boy could answer, the siblings stepped out of the nearby black brush. Matthew breathed a quick sigh. They both noticed him and instantly flashed grins. Alain put his away instantly. The girl crouched beside Matthew and felt his forehead.

"Alive, are we?"

"I'm breathing and not bleeding. You two?"

She nodded.

"Good," he said.

Ordopha interrupted. "More importantly, is Jason there with you?"

"He is. Just a bit stunned."

"Good," Alain spoke. "Now you can have him come out here so I can crush his throat."

Matthew winced. Of all the times to be a jerk, Alain did not have to pick now.

Ordopha ignored her brother. "We found a disheveled hovel further ahead. There was a man named Sai—he looked like a hermit. We asked if he could point us towards the mountains, or a Mirror Gate, and he supplied us directions to an abbey at the end of these woods. That was all he would say."

"I'll go talk to him."

"Do not bother," Alain answered. "He wouldn't open the door again. Useless."

"Did he look like you? Same color hair and everything?"

He shook his head. "We couldn't tell. He wore a heavy hood and hid behind the door. Enough, Matthew. If you are well, then we should leave. There is no telling what lurks in this place."

Alain walked off, leaving the two behind. Ordopha looked after him, saying nothing. His rotten demeanor remained unchanged. A delicate white hand reached for Matthew as he sat up. She helped steady him. His calves trembled, nearly buckling. Before she could say anything, he straightened up. Alain had already vanished into the brush.

"Thanks," he said to her. "Did I do something to set off your brother again?"

"Alain will always be Alain. Let's make certain he doesn't do something foolish."

The shady haze of moonlight bathed them as outstretched branches and brush rubbed against their torn clothes. Ordopha led Matthew on in silence. Only the distant hoots of owls kept them company.

The scent of honey and wilderness clung to the night breeze. Thinning grass ran off in every direction. All of this continued to remind Matthew that the dead mountains of Mageuopolis were now far away.

Why else would Alain be annoyed? They had abandoned his friends on the mountain and simultaneously left Shaula alive to hunt them down. And there was little they could do about it.

Alain had a way of letting others know how he felt, whether they wanted to or not. But this was more than that. Why else would he just walk away from them like this?

They all failed against Shaula, but neither Alain nor his sister could have known about Primes. These super-powered beings first started showing up decades ago on Earth when Matthew was only a rug rat. He had no idea they'd show up here on another planet.

But Primes weren't magical. Prime powers extended from inside their bodies. Tyndarus' magic was purely external, created by Nieto. But his bride could unleash both pyrokinetic Prime powers as well as magic. She had both—and she was still out there.

Matthew knew Shaula would be back. They needed to find a way out and back to Serenity City before anyone else got hurt. As he mulled this over, he thought he caught Ordopha glancing at him several times. The last thing he wanted was for her to worry about him.

"To be honest," Ordopha began. "I had never given much thought to what I would do when I finally escaped the mountains. What do you do in your world?"

"Not much, really."

"You always say that. Do you really not trust me, Matthew?"

There was more than a little playfulness in her tone, but she was right. He just had nothing to tell. A red blush filled his cheeks.

"Where I live is a city with tall buildings, many people, and a lot of monsters running around. There are some good people and some bad. Heroes and villains, cops and criminals, doves and dogs. Not all heroes are all that great, despite what Jason thinks. Most of them are just looking out for themselves. We can all be blown up at any moment, and all they care about is good press. How can you trust your life to people like that? Just walking out your door some days is a risk. You might be killed before you even hit morning traffic. I just scrape by and hope no one notices me. A meager existence, sure, but it was something. That's why there isn't much to tell."

She said nothing for a long time, so he let it go. They crossed a path to the left that led up a small dirt road. The way connected to an old stone structure covered in leaves and cracks along its door-frame. There were no windows or any flickering of light squeezing out into the bleak night. Matthew had seen designs like this in old Middle Age history books. This must have been that hermit's residence. Even in other worlds, there were still those who kept to themselves. Perhaps he belonged in a place like this, after all. Ordopha pushed him on.

"Where you come from sounds similar to Mageuopolis," she said. "I suppose I can understand your way. All I wished was for my friends to be left alone."

"It *was* my way of living. Things change. I have Castor now, and I have to look after the idiot in my head. Being left alone isn't an option."

"No, I understand, Matthew. I held Alain back from any attempt at escape because of a selfish worry that we would die in the mountains. I was fine with dying in that horrid prison as long as I had those I loved by my side. Pathetic."

"There's nothing wrong with being scared of death."

"Isn't there?"

Perhaps it beat cowering in a corner and begging for scraps. "I can't say I gave it much thought. You're pretty good with a bow, by the way. Much practice?"

"Far too much." She shifted the quiver on her back. Arrows were low. "Combat is not for me. It would be nice to have something a bit less . . . *mannish* to engage in."

"Well, sorry." He couldn't manage to fight off a grin. "Can't help you there."

"You're smiling. Are you feeling better now?"

He had almost forgotten his sore muscles and spent energy. "A little. Oh, wait, there's Alain. What's he looking at?"

The two of them stepped out of the brush and into short grass. Alain stared up the front of a tall stone wall that traveled several miles left and right and went up at least fifty feet. Soldiers in armor patrolled the top. The three of them had found a small fortress.

Alain grimaced, highlighting his disheveled look even further. Torn and bloody prison clothes would easily stand out. Matthew debated running until Alain made a blunder. He called up the wall.

"Hello! My friends and I are lost," Alain shouted. "Are we near the mountains?"

The two armored men on top brandished bows toward at Alain. One blew a horn.

"Are you from Thieves' Forest?" the other guard shouted. Loud voices erupted from the other side of the wall. "Your name or we will open fire."

Matthew took Ordopha by the wrist and fell back into the brush. She landed beside him in the grass. Before she could speak, he pointed to her brother's right. A gate opened, and three men on horses bolted out. Except that they weren't horses.

The beasts had four legs and were built like horses, but their manes were of fire red and their long faces each had long whiskers and cat-like ears. Their bodies were not as lean as equines either. These were built to be more agile—something between a jungle cat and a horse.

Ordopha also watched those alien animals. Her reaction was less horrified and more amused.

"What are they, Matthew? Do you have them in your world?"

"We have horses. This isn't anything like them. But forget about that. Wait here. I'm going out to meet Alain and talk our way through this. I know that's not his thing."

"I apologize. I forgot myself." She readied her bow and retrieved one of the few arrows remaining in her quiver. "Give me one word, and I will strike the commander in front."

He put a hand on her raised arm. "It won't come to that. I'll handle this. Trust me."

The three men on the cat-beasts held spears and swords in scabbards. Close helms adorned their heads. Moonlight glinted against their shining armor, casting beams against the dark brush and dilapidated intruders. These men were soldiers.

Alain had no sense about him for picking a fight here. Matthew ran out to meet him.

The three of them rode up to Alain just as he waved them down.

"What are you doing?" Alain hissed. "This is my fight, Matthew."

"The hell it is."

The leader of the group, a man with a stoic, granite face nodded in his direction. He thought quick to get out of this.

"I am Matthew," he said. "I wield the bracelet Castor, and this is my guard, Alain. We escaped through a gateway in the magic city in the mountains. Could you please tell us where we are?"

The two men behind the leader spoke with each other in hushed tones. They also spoke English, just as the people in the mountain did. The man in the front put up a hand in greeting.

"You are two days and nights from Nerono, the city of slayers. This is a place for holy men." The leader's voice was sharp and cold with precision. "I do wonder how you got through without succumbing to the poisonous air. We of the Knights of the Plain require a show of strength. Prove you are as hard as these hills and as swift as the wind. He Who Watches From On High observes and will tell who has the honor and the guile to be allowed victory. How you duel proves what you are."

Alain shoved Matthew aside and put his arm out before the holder of Castor. His fingers danced upon the hilt of his weapon.

"I have had enough of this," Alain said. "Get off that sad beast and take your blade. I will be enough for you."

"Alain!" Matthew exclaimed. "He asked to fight me."

"I let the boy fight a battle for me before. Look what that did to us. I will not make the same mistake twice."

The large man did not stop to consult his men nor did he pause to reflect on the young man's words. He leaped off his cat and clanked against the ground. With his sword at his side, he met Alain in the open grass. Guards above aimed their arrows towards the newcomers. Was dueling really so important to these people?

"*Jason!*" he yelled into his head. He used every force to push at the boy and get him up again. "*Get up. We have to stop this!*"

But before anything else could be done, the two warriors bowed to each other. The large man's size advantage and armor looked disproportionate to Alain's beaten down and bloody form. But despite this, Ordopha's brother only tightened his trembling grip on his sword. Alain was in a hurry to die, and Matthew could do little about it.

Their blades clashed. Alain yelled as blood slashed loose from his shoulder. At this rate, the warrior would not last much longer.

CHAPTER 12
INTO TYNDARUS

ALAIN'S FURY rose with each slash he made. Their swords reverberated with such force that their bones rattled. Matthew swore to himself. This had to stop.

A man in grey robes emerged from behind the soldiers. His average height and slight build didn't stick out, but his platinum hair and pale skin did. The newcomer stopped before the dueling pair.

"Your friend is sick. He should surrender. There is no honor in this."

"You overestimate my influence," Matthew said. "Only one person can stop him now."

Matthew called out into the brush, and Ordopha emerged from the shadows. She dropped her bow to her side and raised her hands. The bowmen above trained their arrows on her, but the girl paid them no mind. She kept her focus on her brother. The man in the robes bowed at her approach.

"Milady," he said with a bow. "I am Abbott Granzer. I apologize for Sir Orach's violence. This is far too savage an introduction."

"My brother is out of sorts. We have been through much. Please call your knight off, sir."

"Sir Orach!" Abbot Granzer yelled. "Yield! These are our guests."

"Alain!" Ordopha also called out. "Stop this! We have no reason to fight."

Both men stopped momentarily. They stared at each other, blades still bared. Breaths grew harsh. They remained at odds for what felt like hours.

Matthew stepped between them. "This can wait. We have other problems to deal with."

"I should slay you for this," Sir Orach said.

Alain nodded, saliva pooling in the corners of his mouth. "Matthew, stand down."

"It's late, and we're tired," Matthew interrupted. "Your sister is scared, and the Abbott has invited us in. This is a waste of time, Alain."

They both glared at Matthew. Another moment passed before they consented.

The pair put their swords away. Ordopha embraced her brother as Sir Orach removed his helmet and begged her for an apology. He had the same color hair as those in the mountain did, though his hair was closer to the scalp. His sharp brown eyes pierced Matthew before settling on the Abbott.

"I apologize. My blade hungers for the blood of tigers. I have been here too long."

"Intactilis is at sunrise, sir knight," the Abbott replied. He then smiled at Matthew. "Your words were well-meaning but rather foolish. This is a land of honor and sturdy men. Do not step in between such a battle again, for your sake."

Matthew thought about arguing but quickly decided against it. All he had to do was see the expression of contorted rage on Alain's face to know that this went beyond a battle. There were still things he didn't understand about this world.

The soldiers led the group back through the gates of this strange place. The Abbott walked beside Matthew, observing him.

"Who are you, friend?"

Matthew gave his name and a general summary of where he was from. "What do you know about Castor and Pollux?"

"I wonder. If you are truly who you say you are, then there is much to discuss."

"Do you know where I can find a Mirror Gate? I need to return home as soon as possible. People are after us."

"Rest first, friend. Tell me about your journey."

The door slammed shut behind them. Alain still refused to look at him, and Ordopha slowly dragged her feet onward. Of the four escapees, only Jason rested.

"Aren't you tired?" he asked the Abbott. "This is late to be receiving guests."

"Very much so. Do you wish to sleep before we discuss things?"

With the way the bracelets worked, he didn't need to. Matthew would simply swap bodies with Jason at daybreak. But that would take time to explain.

"If you want to know about us, Abbott, I'll tell you. Just let me start from the beginning."

☠

THE VISION of the girl filled Jason's dreams. A feminine teenage figure floating in the void replaced the gold in the mountain. She called his name constantly, whispering into his mind's eye. The closer he moved to reach her the further she disappeared into the oncoming light shining out from behind her. She yelled her name as the brightness overcame Jason like a tidal wave.

Both the sun slapping him in the face and the crunch of a rake against gravel woke Jason dead out of his sleep. His eyes hurt almost as bad as his brain. The sun sluggishly climbed the sky with its orange beams pummeling his consciousness. It was daylight.

He sat up from his bed. It *was* daylight!

The long building had simple beds like his scattered around with thin blankets on top. It had all been so well organized. But the place was barren. The crafted wooden walls and vaulted ceiling gave the impression of some sort of monastery. That might explain the raking he heard outside.

"You are awake," a man said. The source of the statement wore grey robes with carefully embroidered black and white lines which formed patterns of clashing shapes similar to waves in the surf. They each formed an image of two faces that blended into one like a silhouette. "Matthew has told me all about you, Jason. You are in an abbey on the outskirts of the Thieves' Forest. The Black Mountains you escaped from are beyond them. I'm amazed that you four made it so far."

"This is the Abbot," Matthew interrupted. *"He's on the level. Alain is sleeping in the knight's quarters, and Ordopha is with the servants. You've been out for two days. Well rested yet?"*

Jason blushed. "Hello, Abbot. I'm Jason. I guess you know about Pollux and everything else."

"I do. Matthew also told me about a *bomb* in his chest. Something like a curse?"

"That's right!" Jason threw his cramped legs over the bed and stretched. "If I've been out for two days then that means it's been four days since he had that thing put in. We've got to get going."

The Abbot smiled. "Matthew should be able to tell you what you need. Do you mind? I have my duties to perform, and he can speak inside your head, correct?"

"Please go on with your day. I'll listen to the jerk say what he has to say."

The Abbot bowed and disappeared into the burgeoning day. Jason groaned at the pain. Even with all that rest, his muscles hurt.

"So, boy. Where do you want to start? Have any dreams?"

Jason thought on it, but nothing came to mind. "No, I can't remember. It doesn't matter anyway, we got that seed. Anyway, I'm going to find Alain and Ordopha. Has Shaula contacted you?"

"No. I understand you're worried about the bomb, but she wouldn't set it off. Not as long as you have the seed and she needs these bracelets. Besides, she said there's a time limit."

"If it's a week then we have three days left. We can't just sit around here."

"A lot's been happening, you know. No need to fly off the handle."

As Matthew began to go on, Jason stood up and stretched again. Sore muscles and bones beat with his headache. It was going to be awhile before they could get back out on the road to . . . wherever they were going. Nonetheless, he needed to find the others.

He noticed a pile of clothes on his bed. The well-tanned shirt and pants fit far better than the old prison rags. The green tunic simply slid over his new wear. Jason grunted as he dressed.

That was when he spotted his bandages and the lack of dirt on his skin. They had cleaned him.

"The Abbot received a message via hawk days ago. It was from the Misery Mists in the Black Mountains."

"What does that have to do with us?"

"It was from the Vultures. Richter specifically."

Jason perked up. "Continue."

"They escaped the frogs back to their village, but they kept looking out for us. They thought we died in the storm. The Abbot sent them a response last night that we made it here."

Jason let the weight slide from his shoulders. "Alain and Ordopha should be ecstatic."

"Yeah, they should."

"We got away, at least."

"I'm still not sure how. Apparently, that green fog is poisonous to Earthwalkers. It's all over the forest, too. That's why no one makes it through. Whatever that mirror was, it really saved us."

There were boots on the floor that might as well have been pillows for his feet. He slid them on his sore toes. Those old prison shoes would not be missed.

Jason stepped out into the day with a yawn. The morning sun beat down on his fresh wear.

Before him, men tilled small fields. Strange cat-like horse creatures pulled carts. The men wore brown robes, and the beasts obeyed their every word. Beyond those working were knights on the ramparts and gates surrounding the area. Buildings littered this abbey, mostly smaller than the one Jason had left, built with wood and housed cruck roofs, though there was what looked like a barn made of timber with a roof that was thatched. The place was a bit too small to be a village.

The abbey centered on a medium-sized, weather-beaten stone church. The moss on the blocks looked as though it had been allowed to grow for ages. Chanting floated out from the interior of the over-sized place.

"I don't get it," Jason said. "What's an Earthwalker?"

"These people are known as Earthwalkers. Legend is that thousands of years ago the Great Sorcerer King created them out of the very dirt of Tyndarus."

"So he's their God? Does that mean they worship Nieto?"

"Not at all. Listen to the rest."

Matthew went on. When Nieto arrived from beyond the sky, he created the Earthwalkers from the very dirt under his feet. For centuries they lived as little more than drones and puppets.

But then a man on wings of light flew down from the heavens and fought the Great Sorcerer King to a standstill, sending life essence down onto the people. The Earthwalkers absorbed the strange light, and it freed them from servitude. The battle ended, and the warrior of the sky disappeared, but Nieto had been left close to death. His former subjects chased him into the mountains where he hid ever since.

"Okay," Jason said. "That explains this place. I get that. But who is Nieto?"

"No one knows. No one has even seen him in centuries."

"Probably because he's been busy on Earth."

Jason pushed open the large door to the church. Creaking pews filled with men awaited inside. They all kneeled in prayer. The empty embroidered chair at the front glistened with plated gold. The freshly picked flowers tickled at his nostrils. The Abbot himself kneeled before it all with his face flat against the floor. Jason sidled into an empty pew as the prayers continued.

"Do you see Alain or Ordopha?" he whispered.

"Near the front."

Sure enough through the rows of people, he spotted the backs of his friends' heads where they kneeled. They took part in this strange service.

Matthew said that the Abbot called it Intactilis. This was their way to give thanks to the one who saved them from their enslavement so long ago . . . whoever that was. Jason scanned the carved stone and wood. The patterns of flying men in the walls were hard to ignore.

Stained glass with large white wings over an orange sunset showed the hope these people had taken from the defeat of Nieto. Little wonder the Great Sorcerer King used what life remained in him to take back what he had lost. His world, Tyndarus, had changed overnight, and all he built had been ripped from his control.

No wonder he even looked to Earth. Jason thought of the service where they kneeled to a god that freed them from a poisonous hold. Men outside carried small boulders on their backs as they did their work and the women bruised their knees and shins on the paths as they crawled across them in prayer. How bad was Nieto's control over these people that this could be seen as an improvement?

"You probably think they're crazy," Matthew interrupted. *"But they have stories of their own. I heard the books of their prophets contain insanity beyond even what we went through. Not to mention they have heard of Mirror Gates."*

"How many are there?"

"The Abbot guesses that Nieto has four from the legends, but he doesn't know. Nieto didn't create the Mirror Gates: he took them from another world and warped them with his magic. They could be anywhere on Tyndarus."

Jason stared at the painting of winged warriors assaulting a mountain covered in purple mist. "I'm sure that Shaula hid them well if the two of them are as hated as it appears they are."

"The king has a Mirror Gate. It's been locked up for centuries. That's our best bet. Since you're up and feeling better, we'll leave tomorrow."

"If it's not Nieto's it might not head to Earth."

"Got any better ideas? We could go back through the forest."

"Quiet."

Earthwalkers lined up before the empty seat. The Abbot sat in the chair and said a few words in a language Jason didn't understand. The line moved forward, and the first man kneeled before the Abbot. The robed man put out his hand and asked the kneeling figure a question. After the response, he slowly slid his hand into the man's chest as if it were sinking into water. The strange smell of rotting flesh filled the air. The Abbot removed his hand, and the man bowed and returned to his pew. He looked perfectly fine. Jason clenched his stomach at the stink and backed out of the pew.

"*Something wrong?*" Matthew asked.

"Didn't you see what he did?"

"Yes. And?"

"We're leaving here as soon as possible. This place is screwy."

A few minutes later the service ended. Alain and Ordopha met them outside, and Matthew left Jason's head. Alain beamed. He looked the best Jason had ever seen him with fresh clothes with a new sword that glinted against the sunlight. Matthew stared at Ordopha, and Jason couldn't blame him. She cleaned up well. Her hair was done up, and her simple green dress brought attention to her glowing smoky eyes. That extra day of rest did them well.

Matthew started talking to the pair as the rest of the church emptied, but Jason blew past them. He couldn't stand the church any longer, and he found himself swearing under his breath about the place. His breaths sharpened, and nostrils flared.

Between the oblivious worshipers of a god that left them and a demon that still lived to terrorize a whole other world, Jason couldn't decide which he detested more. Nieto should have been hunted down and destroyed.

But it still stuck in his mind. If that god had abandoned them then what was this service for? Were they calling upon some deity's power? If that essence that nearly killed Nieto remained inside them then maybe these people weren't so crazy after all.

Jason crossed the pathway toward the ramparts. He couldn't blame the Earthwalkers of this place for how they lived, but his allies were a whole other matter. It was as if Matthew and the other two thought all their problems were solved. Did they forget Shaula was still out there?

He stood atop the ramparts and looked far into the distance back the way they came. There the dark clouds swirled about the mountains like a permanent black mark on its existence. Between them lay untold miles of misty green-hued forests. His stomach curled scanning over it. The memories of Mageuopolis would stay in his thoughts until his death.

"Duel!" a man yelled from behind him. "Sir Orach is about to duel the newcomer!"

A crowd of knights swirled around the large square stone building down the road from the church. Jason assumed this was the barracks. Men from all over ran toward it, including Matthew.

The blacksmith was located beside the barracks. The smithy leaned against a post, ignoring the chaos. The barrel-chest man grinned straight at Jason.

The boy leaped down from the stone steps into the grass and passed the crowd. He ignored the hooting and hollering as they shouted in a circle.

"Jason, eh?" the man barked. "I have a present for you and your brother."

A cheer shouted from the crowd beside them. Swords clanged from within their circle.

"Abbot Granzer told me you could use some armor for your trek. I have it for you whenever you wish it. You're well built for a boy."

"I'm fifteen. You're making me armor? I don't even know you."

"Even if the Abbot and Sir Orach didn't ask me, I still would have done it. There are some strange tales of Pollux. I've forgotten so many of them, though. Age is a fickle mistress."

One of the duelers in the center of the crowd shouted. A blade reverberated against a hard object: probably a shield.

"What do you know about Pollux?" he asked the blacksmith.

"The wielder is destined to be a god. Strength and immortality, the stuff of legends. You should be grateful that Pollux has chosen you, eh?"

Jason thought of Case's buried body. He suppressed a shiver. "I'm not so sure about that. Does anyone come out of the forest often? I'm half-expecting a witch to come flying out of it."

The blacksmith grinned. "We sometimes get stragglers, but they have already gone mad from the fog by the time they reach here. You won't meet any witches out here!"

The crowd gave a disappointed sigh. Jason could no longer ignore the interruption. He said his goodbye to the blacksmith and pushed through the gaggle to the center. He would put an end to this distraction. When he finally slipped inside, he found two familiar warriors.

Alain stood breathing hard and triumphant with light cuts across him. Matthew lay splayed out on the grass with his sword two feet from him. Bruises covered him. The fallen man gave Jason a thumbs up as he sat forward. At the edge of the crowd stood Sir Orach, arms folded. None of them wore much in the way of armor.

"Matthew?" Jason asked. "You're fighting Alain?"

"He's showing me some tricks. Apparently, I hold the grip too tight and have bad footwork. I'm also too slow."

Sir Orach nodded. "You have work to do. For now, Castor will cover for your amateur movements."

Matthew listened intently as he gathered his breaths. It was unlike him to seriously take advice. When Sir Orach finished, Matthew stood back up and hobbled over to the fallen sword.

"For a beginner, it's not so bad." Sir Orach clapped Alain on the shoulder. "However, your fury overwhelms you and dulls your movements. A foe can easily steer you how they wish. Be more aware of your surroundings, Alain."

Alain looked down at his battered blade. It had taken more of a beating than Matthew did. The victorious warrior said nothing as he let Sir Orach continue his lecture.

Jason could not tear his attention from Alain. For someone who had won, he sure grimaced a lot. The warrior had lived his whole life fighting and protecting those he loved, but he had never considered how he would battle in a different landscape from his former prison. Now the rules had changed. Maybe Jason had more in common with him than he first thought.

And that was when it hit Jason. He had held them all back since the two landed on Tyndarus. Matthew led, Alain and the others fought, but Jason had been a tag-along that would have been dead ten times over if he didn't have Pollux. He couldn't get by on luck forever.

"Finally, he walks," Sir Orach said to Jason. "You are due for your lesson."

"Me?"

Matthew handed his sword and shield to Jason. "Good luck. Alain doesn't play nice."

"He *what*?"

But Matthew passed into the crowd without saying anything. Several soldiers clapped his shoulder as he passed. In front of Jason, Alain grew a grin that was as sinister as it was joyous.

"Now this," Alain said, "*this* is what I want."

Jason gulped and stepped into the center of the grass.

"Remember," the boy said. "I'm new at this."

"That hermit left something for me while you slept. Would you like to see it?"

"I guess."

"Beat me, and it's yours."

Before Jason could reply, Alain charged him. The boy's arms trembled with each sword strike. This would not end well.

They spent the rest of the day in training with their swords. Alain thrashed Jason handily, but the boy did pick up a few tricks for handling his blade. Matthew couldn't help but admire the kid's fire and refusal to stay down. His spirits rose abnormally high.

At sunset, the two of them and the siblings gathered on the ramparts. Matthew traced the path they would be using in the morning for the boy. He'd gone over it in his mind many times while Jason slept without dreams.

There they saw the road that went miles into the distance. Halfway up the path waited a destroyed town that had been raided by lizard men decades ago. Far beyond it and over rolling hills sat the last town before Nerono. After that was a two-day journey to the city.

"I still wish to see the others," Alain said. "But I will offer you two my sword."

"Can you at least tell me what the hermit gave you?"

"It's this." Alain removed a tiny slab of a mirror. The shard glinted sunlight across their faces. "He said it was a piece of a Mirror Gate, but it doesn't do anything at all. I kept it as a gift, but it appears quite useless. I would offer it to you, but I plan on traveling with you regardless."

Matthew scanned the horizon, tracing their possible path. "You two don't have to follow us. I'm still not sure how exactly we're going to handle this. Shaula will probably find us soon."

"We cannot leave until I properly defeat you in a duel, Matthew."

"What?" He asked, incredulous at the idea. "Why?"

"You interfered with *my* duel. You should be grateful it is not Sir Orach. I will only crush you—he would take your head."

Matthew laughed to himself. "You Earthwalkers are something else. Honor is everything, huh? Me? I would have just kicked you in the throat and called it a day."

"I would expect that from you."

Ordopha sighed. "Men. Can you two think of nothing else but violence?"

"I guess I just don't get it," Matthew said.

"Well, you are human. I'm sure there are many things you do that we cannot understand."

"The Abbot is lending us three cat-trals for the journey," Alain replied. "We'll be in the village in half a day. Compared to the mountains, this is nothing."

Unless Matthew's bomb went off. But he didn't need to mention that. They had enough worries without him adding his own. Shaula would be crazy enough to set it off, if she could, but he had to hope she wouldn't. Otherwise, he would ever be able to relax.

Crows squawked from the branches of nearby trees and chatter from soldiers erupted from below. The slow descent of the orange horizon darkened blue. Night arrived.

Soon enough Alain and Jason left them alone. The boy was tired and unwilling to talk about the seed and Alain wanted to attend Intactilis one more time. Matthew waited with Ordopha for what felt like hours as the remaining curve of the sun seemed stuck in the sky. He wanted to thank her.

After they found the Mirror Gate and figured out how to open it, Matthew would never see either sibling again. If it weren't for them he would be a puppet of Shaula. There was nothing he could do to thank them. But as he struggled to think of the words to say, Ordopha laughed.

Her shining platinum hair ruffled in the light breeze. She brushed a strand from her face, and her lips curled into a smile. Peace flowed across her. In a universe full of decay, she had only become more radiant.

"Is there something wrong?" she asked, looking up at him.

Blood rushed to his cheeks and glanced ahead once more. "No, I was just thinking."

"You do that a lot. About your home?"

"You could tell?"

She laughed softly into the wind again. "You aren't difficult to puzzle out, Matthew."

"I'm just trying to figure out what I'll do when I get back. If I even do destroy this bomb and the Mirror Gates, I'm still at a loss. Do I become a hero? But then I have to get in with *that* crowd, and I can't do that. But Castor is incredible, and I can't just get rid of it."

"So use it. Use it like you used it to save us from Shaula. There must be many on your world in need of saving. You've mentioned there are many like you with odd abilities."

"Sort of." Of course, there were superheroes and villains where he came from, they were what Serenity City was known for. But he just couldn't see himself with them. He couldn't put on a face. "Jason loves them. Maybe he'll become one when he gets back."

"And you?"

"I don't know. There are still things I have to do." Her fragrance caused him to lean in closer. He paused, shaking his head. What was he doing? Women always did this to him. He leaned back. "But what about you? You're free now. You can do anything."

She hummed and looked up to the sky again. "What do you think of this dress?"

Ordopha wore a simple green number that could not have been made for anyone but a peasant. The material bunched as she showed it off. But it worked on her. Then again, he wasn't sure there was anything she could wear and not look good. He had never seen her more dignified in the short time he had known her than in that moment.

"I'm a man. You're asking a member of the wrong sex."

"No," she said with a smirk. "I mean that I have never worn clothes like this in that prison. Very fetching. I was told this is merely common garb for women, but I feel as regal as a queen."

"Not sure how you can tell the difference. You look good in anything."

She locked eyes with him after a short pause. His cheeks reddened. He tried to laugh it off. When she looked away again, he thought he saw red in her soft cheeks. Now he felt even worse.

"I'm going to hit the sack early," he said. "Jason's tired, and I don't want him to transform while we're standing out here. I'd never hear the end of it. Besides, maybe he'll finally spill about the seed."

She nodded, still focused on the distance. "I understand."

"Are you going to be okay out here? It's getting cold."

"Thank you, but I will be fine. The mountains were far worse than this."

"But you don't have magic protecting you here."

"No," she said with a smile. "I do not."

Matthew marched to the sleeping quarters. Knights continued their practicing outside with swords clashing, and monks kept up their chores, but they began to thin out. Soon enough only the guards would be left.

Inside monks prayed by their beds while some slept. Jason lay in his bed with his hands under his head. Matthew sat beside him. The boy hummed a song from some old cartoon.

"How is Ord taking it?" Jason asked. "You leaving Tyndarus, I mean?"

"About as well as Alain, I guess. That's a dumb question."

Jason laughed. "Right, *I'm* dumb. Anyway, I think I'm getting the hang of that sword. Alain beat me a few times, but . . . hey, are you listening?"

"I am." But that was a lie. He kept watch on the window and the large moon that had just lit the sky. Earth's moon was not so different from this one. "Tyndarus really is a lot like home."

"What does that have to do with anything?"

"Never mind."

The night fell fast. A dog howled miles off. Jason slept inside Matthew's head as the latter lay awake on the bed. What was this sick feeling he kept having? Something here wasn't quite right. Hopefully, when they left in the morning, he would regain his senses again. Soon enough his eyes became heavy like weights, and his thoughts petered out. Sleep won over him.

The ground trembled. He shook in his bed as a horn bellowed outside. An earthquake raged.

Guards bellowed outside. Matthew jumped from his bed half-asleep with Jason stirring inside his mind. The other monks sat up. While they mumbled, he ran out into the night still in his shirt and pants.

Flaming arrows arched over ramparts and into the grass. Several struck the buildings, including the church. The guards ran about flinging arrows outwards to their attackers. Shouts screamed into the night.

"What's happening?" Jason mumbled.

A horrendous sight climbed the ramparts towards the inside. Red lizardmen screeched and slashed at the guards as they landed on the inside of the walls. Soldiers ran out to meet the beasts.

"We're being invaded."

Chapter 13
FIRE LIZARD INVASION

Swords flashed and fires burned across the abbey buildings. Jason and Matthew ran into the barracks for weapons while the madness exploded around them. There they found the blacksmith who led them to their new armor. The silver shone brightly as did the close helms and sturdy looking swords. Jason clutched his new blade close. Matthew then guided him back out where the battle raged on.

Chaos ruled the outside. Red lizards burned anything they could get a hold of. Swords clanged, and axes split skulls, but the monstrous beasts simply kept coming in over the walls. First a dozen, then another dozen, and yet another.

Alain fought by the front gate surrounded by several men, including Sir Orach. Their swords slashed the invading lizardmen apart. Jason and Matthew joined them in a circular pattern to help with defense.

But as the beasts swarmed the soldiers, Jason quickly noticed an abnormality. The lizards centered their attention on the two of them over anyone else. The monsters ducked and weaved around most other soldiers purely to assault Castor and Pollux. Shaula had sent these things for them.

That was when Jason got an idea. He deflected a sword swing and yelled out to Matthew. "Find Ord. These things are coming for us. We should get out of here before this place is razed."

Matthew paused as if considering Jason's words. His shield slammed against the helmeted head of a lizardman.

"You're right," he replied. He waved to Alain. "You guard him, and I'll find her."

"As if I can guard that monster."

Matthew took off towards the servant's quarters, slashing anything that came near him. The lizards slunk back as he passed and soon followed after him. They swarmed in a crowd, sweeping across the ground. A blade caught one in the back as they gave chase.

It was Alain. He waved Matthew off, and the wielder of Castor vanished into the flames.

"Where did they come from?" Jason yelled to his friend's savior.

"Out of the forest fog! Shaula's puppets appear to desire you above all else. We need to leave this place now."

Jason grinned. Lizardman blood being spilled sounded good to him at that moment.

Sir Orach ascended the ramparts, and his men followed, cutting any who dared get close. The lizards hissed and swore as they fell upon their enemies. Sir Orach barked orders to Alain and Jason to get going. The soldiers all slashed like mad, downing lizardmen in waves of pure carnage. Alain used the moment to run, with Jason right behind.

"To the barn," he told the boy.

They ran towards the barn and found two cat-trals that had been set aside for them. The Abbot waited for them inside. He handed them their supply sacks for the journey filled with wrapped and salted foods. It was time to leave, but neither Matthew nor Ordopha had returned yet.

"It is a madhouse outside," the Abbot said to the pair.

"They're coming for us," Jason replied. "The faster we leave, the faster they'll stop."

"Jason!" one of the soldiers from outside was calling for him. "Hurry!"

Alain growled as they returned to the carnage. "What is the problem now?"

"It is Matthew. Hurry and come with me."

Alain and Jason glanced at each other and then at the soldier. Matthew was supposed to be getting Ordopha. Before either could answer, there was a loud voice booming above like a muffled megaphone. Her regal tone could never be mistaken for anyone else.

"Castor and Pollux! Please come outside quietly, or everyone and everything burns."

Jason instinctively flinched, and Alain tensed. They both knew the voice of Queen Shaula of Mageuopolis quite well by now.

MATTHEW STOOD at the door to the servant's quarters with goosebumps growing on his skin and fire in his blood. The large lizardman looked down on him with smoldering eyes. This one was different from the others. This one had a round head, stood seven feet tall, and wore silver armor, not unlike his. The red beast held two women, one under each of his massive arms. They were half-conscious. One was Chel, the servant girl, and the other, Ordopha.

Heat burned in his blood as he gripped his sword tighter.

"I watched these two for a while now," the lizard boomed. "They're mine."

"You were hiding here." Of course Shaula had agents outside the mountains, but he didn't expect them this far out. "What took you so long to make your move?"

"I only had to take the place of one of the guards." The large beast squinted. "You are Castor or Pollux I take it. Is one of these your woman? I certainly hope so."

Matthew sprang for the lizardman. As if he set off a trap, three smaller enemy warriors darted for him from the corners of the room. Blades barreled at him.

A sword sliced his helmet, and an ax slashed his shoulder. Pain burst through his rage, and he cried out. But the giant lizard had already leapt past him. Matthew ran one enemy through and charged after the escaping monster.

Other soldiers poured in to assist Matthew, but he left them to their work.

The giant leaped up upon the ramparts, crushing stone under his massive feet, and bounded over the wall in one easy motion. Matthew rushed as fast as his legs could carry him, parrying whatever strikes came his way. He followed the giant enemy over the side.

Split earth and upturned stone awaited around the perimeter of the defensive wall. Lizardmen burst out from the fissures and slung themselves up the vertical surface like spiders. He fell between them into the pit below where the ground itself swallowed him inside of it. Broken rock and earth closed in around him like a closing maw.

Matthew morphed into water, and let his form sink down into the shrinking gap. The earth absorbed him as his form stuck into it. The world became black as his existence evaporated.

Indistinct cold air crashed against him from below. With as much force as he could muster, he willed his very atoms to press downward toward it.

He splashed against the stone ground, his form raining through like a sudden downpour. Red sparks of pain ran through his being—he needed to pull himself back together again. With Castor on his mind, he reformed to whole human in an instant.

Matthew landed with his back against a rock wall. A faint light beamed through a crack. His breaths fell hard, his bones rattling, but he held his groans in despite his throbbing muscles. Voices echoed against the darkness through the opening.

"Take the girls to the Thief Town," a woman's voice said. It wasn't Shaula, but it sounded suspiciously like it.

The giant lizard man grunted. "I don't take orders from you, Camille. The Queen is the only one I listen to, aside from the Master."

"That's irrelevant, Rantan," she replied. "The Salamanders will give you cover for your escape. The Queen wants Castor and Pollux, and they are sure to come for this girl."

She had her platinum hair in braids and wore light armor from head to toe across her well-toned form. Matthew tried to see her face, but it was next to impossible in the flickering torch she held. There was an air about her that reminded him of Shaula. A large group of red salamanders stood behind her, waiting for her word to strike.

"Then let us be moving, girl." The lizard's tongue slurped air. "If the Queen doesn't need them both then I will quite enjoy the useless one."

"That's disgusting. But very much like you."

"I was the one who had to slip in and live among these weaklings. I deserve a reward for having to wait for you to finally make a move."

Matthew sunk into a puddle, his form allowing him through the crack in the stone. He slid forward in the obscure shadows that dipped in and out with the torchlight. The pair of villains continued arguing.

The one called Rantan took a massive step forward toward Camille. Matthew slunk under it and plunged upward. He solidified whole and brought his sword upward in a vertical arc. The slash glided through flesh, and Rantan yelled.

A massive scaly arm flew from the enemy's body, dashing against the rocks. Matthew caught the loosed woman who fell into his arm. Rantan moved back to where Camille stood watching.

Matthew could barely make out who he caught but instinctively knew that it was not Ordopha. Not the right proportions. Chel moaned and shook her head.

"Matthew?" she mumbled.

"Don't worry, you're fine. I'll get you out of here in a minute."

"Castor!" Camille shouted. "I thought Pollux was the bull. The Queen said you were the snake."

"The Queen doesn't know much of anything. Give back Ordopha and call off your Salamanders. If you're lucky I won't decide to cut you like I did your goon."

"You bastard," the lizard man hissed. He held Ordopha tighter in his remaining arm. She let out a soft cry. "You are in no position for demands."

"Then tell me what you want!"

The woman laughed. "We will return with our queen by the next moon fall. You and Pollux are to meet us at the gate to that monastery when she arrives. If you do not, this one will die, and everyone inside will be put to the sword and burned. Is that simple enough for you, sir?"

"Why not just take me now?" He glanced at the red lizards. Many fled down the tunnels. They clearly did not have the numbers left for a full assault. But Shaula would be able to defeat the two of them, as she had almost done in the mountains. "Or can you?"

"I might convince you to throw down your arms, but what about Pollux? Where is he?"

"Probably cutting your pets apart. Bring Ordopha back, and I will go quietly. She has nothing to do with this."

Camille paused and looked over her shoulder as if she were being talked to. Her fingers trembled and dried dirt fell from them. How long had she spent making these tunnels and how many more could she make in her tired state? Before he could puzzle it out, she turned back to him. "We have no more time to play these childish games."

She crouched and slammed her hands down. Tremors ran from her fingers along the ground towards the walls and then the ceiling. The stone above them broke open like God ripping open the universe itself. Rubble formed from the crags. A trail of rock forty feet tall lead back up to the surface. Stone stairs split into steps from his feet.

"Go and tell them," she said. "I do not know how you found us down here so fast, but you will not be following further."

Once more she clapped down. The ground before her lifted up then slammed into the stone ceiling like a sliding door. The solid surface had to be several feet thick. He saw no way through.

From the opening above chimed familiar voices. Several soldiers peeked through the gap and called down into the dark.

"We're down here!" he yelled.

"Is that you, Matthew?" one asked.

"Chel is with me," he replied. "She's coming up."

She looked at him sideways. "You're not coming?"

"No. I have to get Ordopha back. You heard what they said, right?"

She nodded. "Yes, but how can you—"

"Be sure to tell everyone what these guys are up to."

Matthew sunk back into water and pushed himself to soak through the stone just as he did in the mountains. His atoms ached as they were torn apart in his squeeze through the cracks. Castor held tight through the red flashes before him.

When he kissed air, he reformed back into the dark again. His brain swirled as his matter reconstructed. His vision focusing on the black atmosphere, he spotted the low flicker of torchlight far ahead. Matthew took off through the tunnels in a mad dash.

"WHAT DO you mean that Matthew left?" Jason asked. "Why would he just run off?"

The soldier mentioned Ordopha being taken and all of a sudden everything made sense. One of the lizards had gone for her. Matthew chased it out of the abbey.

A crowd of soldiers led by Sir Orach fought beside the burning remains of the servant quarters. The number of lizards had thinned, but plenty still remained. Alain made a move toward the wall and the ramparts. Jason seized his shoulder.

"Leave it to Matthew," Jason told the warrior. "We need to help Sir Orach."

"I will never abandon anyone again."

"You aren't. I'm telling you that we need to help the people here first. Matthew can find her. We can help here."

"But can you?" a new voice said.

Jason and Alain spotted a warrior emerge from one of the burnt out stables. He wore a large helmet over his oval head and large black eyes peering through. This warrior dressed in heavy dark armor and stood half a foot taller than Alain. He carried a large ax and shield.

"Are you with them?" Jason asked.

"Come and see."

"Forget the boy," Alain growled. He shook with every word. "I'll be the one to end you."

Alain crossed blades with newcomer. Their swords crashed against each other.

A hand clamped on Jason's shoulder. He turned to see the same man who just challenged Alain to a battle. A twin? Had he been hiding in the shadows to strike the boy from behind? The clone grinned sorrowfully.

"Pollux, I presume," the duplicate knight said. "I hope you do not mind sharing a piece of yourself!"

The strange knight jerked his hand back, and Jason's soul rattled inside his skin. The boy saw double for a moment. A sharp pain like a bone being ripped from his skeleton ran through his shoulder. He struggled back and saw exactly what his attacker was doing. The knight pulled a whole body free from Jason's shoulder like a rabbit from a hat.

The removed body was, in fact, a whole human being. Jason looked it over, mouth agape. It was another Jason. The doppelganger wore the same clothes and held the same sword. He wore a blank expression as he stared at Jason with dead saucer eyes. A clone!

"You're a Prime," Jason said to the knight. "How is that possible?"

"You will find us three more than common fodder. I am Oronidamus the Cutter. I apologize for stealing a piece of you, Pollux."

Jason did feel lighter, and his posture had been thrown off kilter. He could not seem to remain calm as if his emotions became unbalanced. His clone clashed blades with him, flat expression and all. The fake breathed and moved as if it were the real Jason. Sharp pain rolled inside Jason like shattered glass. The boy yelled as he pushed back against his doppelganger.

"What did you do to me?" His breaths were almost choking him.

"I cut out a piece of the subject to create more of them. I only needed to hold you off but mere moments. Since we have achieved what we came for, I believe I can leave you with a few words."

Pollux thumped in Jason's bones as he slashed the sword. The clone Jason moved with him, deflecting his blows as if it also had Pollux to rely on.

But his thoughts were off. Bloody visions of the clone before him began to flood his mind. There were so many ways to kill this beast and then the Cutter right after him. Deflect the blow, wait for the moment, and dive in with teeth bared and—

"I'm going to eat your heart," Jason growled. He leaped in on the clone with his sword dancing. The deflection and his heavy stomps on the earth shook the ground itself. "Stop running!"

Pollux had energy to spare, and Jason was willing to burn through it all. He would push it to the wall. All he needed was the right moment and the right chance. Then the blade would come down and the blood would—

"Jason!" Alain yelled.

Jason stalled in mid-swing, and his copy moved in. When their swords bounced, a third party had attacked. Alain stabbed through the clone Jason. The doppelganger hardened and turned to ash, blowing away in the wind.

Jason blinked. Bloodlust pulsed through his veins. He wanted to kill, and wanted to do so very badly. Was it so wrong? Even if killing this thing wasn't enough, there would be other targets. Meat hung all over this place.

Before these thoughts could continue, a tremor rumbled inside his stomach. It took a moment for his senses to return to normal. He had been punched in the gut. His lungs seized with the impact as he doubled over. Alain had been the one to strike him.

"Jason!" Alain repeated. "Regain your composure! We are not done."

Jason's heart burned like a spear had been lodged inside. Was this the missing piece? Was it coming back? His face fell against the grass as he clutched his heart. A short vision passed before his eyes—a girl with platinum hair suspended in a cocoon of light. A name beat up against him. He could almost remember it. Was this a forgotten dream? Tears welled in his eyes.

"I will be your opponent," Alain said to the Cutter.

"Was it really proper for you to jump into the boy's fight? That is not the way a man of honor should act."

"Some things are beyond honor, knave. You tore out a piece of his soul and forced him to fight it. There is nothing honorable about that."

"I suppose not," the Cutter said with his usual sad tone. He paused as if he were listening to someone else speak. "But it does not matter. We are done."

"We agree on that!"

Alain rushed in and slashed. Their blades beat and Alain grunted as the skin on his forehead sliced open. The Cutter ducked his reprisal swing. Alain screamed the most intense battle cry Jason had ever heard and parried the attack. The enemy wobbled as his weapon bounced back and armor cracked. Blood flew from light slashes not quite reaching their mark, but one man just would not relent. Alain leaped in and ran the enemy through, and then swung for the neck. The Cutter's head rolled across the grass, turning to dust. Alain let out a hard breath and dropped to one knee.

"You did it!" Jason shouted. He slowly climbed back up. "It feels like he split something off of me, and then it snapped back after. What was that guy?"

Alain gazed at where the body had fallen. "Something foul is afoot."

"What do you mean?"

"I don't know. My gut tells me this is not as it should be."

Jason struggled back up to his feet, his chest still aflame. The battlefield was emptying. Lizard corpses, soldiers, and ashes were strewn about all over. At least this mess had ended.

"Look here!" Sir Orach yelled from nearby. He guided what looked to be Chel. She was shaking. Her dress had been torn. "Please tell them what it was you told me, Chel."

Chel could not look either Alain or Jason in the eyes. "They have Ordopha. You have one full day to surrender Castor and Pollux, or they will kill her and raze the abbey."

"This is impossible," Alain said. He gripped her shoulders and scanned her over. "Is she hurt?"

"No," she said, quietly. "I was to be bait for Castor and Pollux, just as Ordopha."

"Who led the attack?" Sir Orach asked.

"One was the giant lizard who did not act like a lizard, and the other was a beautiful woman wearing armor. She controlled the earth and sealed off her escape with it. That was how they arrived so close to the wall without us knowing."

"And where is Matthew? I thought he went after my sister?"

"He is still following her. He turned to water and chased her through the earthen wall underground. I do not know where he went after that."

"Get her inside!" Sir Orach told the others.

The other soldiers led her away. On the field, the remaining enemies had been slain, and the fires put out. The battle had come to an end. But many were still wondering about Matthew.

"You ride to the next town," Sir Orach said to Alain. "We need aid to mount our defenses. Hurry."

"We should follow Matthew," Alain grumbled. "But I understand that it would do no good now. There is little chance of any of us catching him. Jason, come with me. We will ride to find the Count."

Few things were stranger than Alain not being the one to rush into battle. The older warrior's fists still trembled, but Jason wouldn't argue with him. He felt much the same.

Jason's throat seized. An odd spark flashed through him like lightning. Invisible hooks penetrated his soul and dragged him back. He first thought the Cutter was responsible until he realized this sensation pumped inside like blood. His muscles stiffened.

He transformed into mist. An intangible force roped him backwards and out of reality. He flew through the wall of the abbey and down into the earth. Sir Orach and Alain yelled after him, but it was of no use. He vanished before they could do anything.

Jason launched through down black tunnels and solid rock and dirt like a missile. He could no longer control his own body.

CHAPTER 14
THIEVES' TOWN

A FORCE from behind Matthew shot toward him at blinding speed. He didn't let it stop him from sprinting through the pitch black tunnel. Regardless of his pursuer, he couldn't let Ordopha get any further ahead. He would deal with it when it reached him.

The tunnel lightly vibrated around him and began to shrink. The woman had begun sealing it up.

The heavy weight crashed into his back. Matthew tripped before slamming against the side of the tunnel. But there was nothing there. Whatever hit him had to be no heavier than air.

That was when he realized just what it had to have been.

"Jason?"

"*Is that you, Matthew?*" Jason's familiar voice bounced around the inside of Matthew's skull. "*Why am I here? Our time limit isn't up yet.*"

"I guess there's a distance we can't cross. Sorry about that." Matthew grunted as he stood back up from the shaking wall. Dirt bounced off his boots as he continued on. "I didn't mean to take you out of the battle."

"The fight was over. The bigger problem is that we have one day until they return to attack the abbey. Unless we give up. Damn, I can't get out of here. I guess we need to wait a bit. Where are you going, anyway? Is Ordopha down this way?"

"I guess Chel told you. There's two of them. One is a giant lizard, and the other has control over rock. I think they're Primes."

"No way. We fought one up top who could create clones. Alain killed him, but I dunno. He thought it smelled fishy."

Now Matthew's anger cooled towards confusion. There were three Primes on top of

Shaula's pyrokinetic abilities, and they now had Ordopha. Where they really going so far out just for Castor and Pollux, or was that seed really so valuable? "I think it's time you came clean about the seed. You saw something in your dreams again, right?"

"That's . . . hard to say. I don't know, man."

"Don't give me that." The shaking walls rumbled his words. "You're not a good liar. Just say it, Jason. At this point, it could be the key to what Shaula and her followers want."

"I didn't remember anything until my last fight but never mind that right now. All I saw in my dreams was a cute girl."

"A girl?"

"A teenage girl just floated there in this void. It didn't mean anything."

"And that's all you saw? Nothing about the seed?"

"Just . . . a name. Zelana."

That name sounded familiar. "Zelana?"

"Look out!"

The contracting walls suddenly sped up. Dirt chunks fell from the ceiling, and the ground broke up into jagged pieces.

"Looks like we're about to see how well I can transform with you inside."

Even the thoughts in Matthew's heads were shaking as Jason replied. *"I fought Richter with Pollux while you were inside. It should work."*

"Maybe, maybe not. I suggest you pray."

He kept an eye on the shrinking tunnel. The space once wide enough to fit a large fighting force now only spanned the width of a narrow walkway. Stone tore against the elbows of his armor.

"Hold your breath, Jason."

Matthew leaped up and the stone crushed in. His puddle form splashed between squeezed plates that ground into each other. He sunk into the earth, allowing him no recourse but to push upward. Red flashes of pain erupted through his vibrating molecules. It wouldn't throw him out of the form—not yet, anyway—but Castor didn't like being used this way. He had to fight gravity and nature itself with its power.

Unlike his mist form which allowed him to fly, his water transformation allowed him to be absorbed into other materials. The stealth and speed it gave him were invaluable, but it offered nothing in the way of defense. He could very well break apart.

The earth crushing in gave him a compressed and heavy feeling in his atoms. It was as if the dirt were pushing him out like water in a flooded garden.

"*Can you move?*" Jason asked.

Despite extra weight from Jason, the strain did not fully grind him to a halt. He concentrated, keeping his form in one piece. This wouldn't be enough to stop him.

"*I can move,*" he replied in his head. That was true, he could move. Even though he shouldn't have been able to. Did Castor just allow him to become water and air, or did it become one with *him*? These bracelets were about pushing the limits of physicality. A simple transformation wasn't all they were. They merged two things together that were never meant to be one in the first place. "*It's not just a question of moving. It's about becoming my surroundings.*"

"I thought you were water. Isn't that like being one with everything?"

"More than that, Jason," he thought back. "Castor melds me with the elements. I just have to learn how to make it work."

If he could smile, Matthew would have done so. He understood it now! Just as Castor could let him become air and water, Matthew could, in turn, become other forms of each. Changing his properties sent lightning flashes of red pain, and winded Castor as much as him, but it could be done.

Humidity heated his very being, pushing him through the earth. Within seconds he steamed up into the dark night, his mass crying out to be reformed. It began to drift apart.

Matthew reconstituted and landed on his hands and boots. Hard breaths rocked through him and his pounding headache as sweat poured from him. His heart beat against the inside of his armor.

At the same moment, Jason stepped outside. He leaned against one of the many knotted trees surrounding them, his face pale.

"Those freaks led us backwards," he said. "We're in that forest at the base of the mountain. I can't see anything through this fog."

"Don't care where we are." Matthew gulped down his breaths and stood tall again. "The tunnel leads this way, so we keep going."

"Not that I don't want to help Ordopha, but we should go back and get Sir Orach and Alain. They can only help."

"We only have a night, Jason. Not only that, but Shaula's lackeys don't know how close we are. Going back now lowers our chances of surprise. And if this forest is as poisonous as I've heard, then we can't wait any longer. She's in trouble now."

Matthew traced the path. Dark trees cluttered the green fog surrounding them. If that tunnel only just closed, it meant they were near the end. But before he could make any further plan, Jason shoved him.

"Don't be so reckless," the boy barked. "I knew you wanted to get home as soon as possible, but this is ridiculous and brash. It's like you want us to die."

Matthew shoved him aside. "Stop being stupid. Ordopha and the others are the only reason we're still alive. We owe them."

The forest encroached on him the further Matthew went. The fogged green air was not like that in the mountains. This atmosphere contained a sharp material that felt like breathing in tacks.

"You're doing this because you owe them one? Boy, Alain has been quite a bad influence."

"We can't all rush into battle as blindly as you. I saw them take her, and I followed them. Running away now would only let the trail grow cold."

"Yeah, I'm sure that's why you're doing this."

Matthew spun around and grabbed Jason by the shoulders. He slammed the boy into a nearby tree, pinning him. The trunk shook, and several birds scattered from the branches.

"Are you getting stupid on me?" Matthew asked. "Someone was taken, and I went after them. That's it. You're getting on my damn nerves with your self-righteous crap. You couldn't even tell me about that dream and you think you can question my honesty?"

"Because it meant nothing!"

"How do you know? You don't get to make that call. Do something like that again, and I'll put you back in the ground."

"Then do it," Jason snapped. "If you think you did this for any other reason than your own wants then you're lying to yourself."

"I don't care what you think my motives are. I *do* care that you're wasting my time. Is preaching embedded into your tiny brain or are you going out of your way to annoy me?"

"Don't act like I don't want to help her, Matthew. You know I do."

"Then shut up and help me, or turn around and go back. Your choice."

"You know very well that it's not. The bracelets won't let us go separate ways. Since we're here, I'm fully willing to go with you. But I'm telling you to think this through. You nearly got us both crushed to death!"

Matthew let the boy go and retraced his path. The longer they argued, the further away Shaula's goons got. They had already wasted enough time. But tracking the thugs would not be simple.

The dark green mist threatened to choke the breath right out of him. Heavy knots of trees outstretched over the dark sky above them, keeping the air stagnant. The humidity pushed down against the cramped forest.

"This way," Jason said. He pointed through the thick brush to his left. "There's a lot of people gathering over there."

"And you know this."

The boy tapped his ears. That was right, Matthew had nearly forgotten about Jason's physical enhancements. The boy led him onward.

Crows called off in the distance and the musty smell ground into his nostrils. Nature's graveyard could not be too different from this place. The pair plodded through it in silence.

The treeline ended where fog flowed freely over a dark grass grove. Across it lay a town of broken down houses, empty fields, and a road that split the entire area in two. Men in dark clothes walked beside and rode cat-trals toward a few brightly lit buildings. They traced the vague size of the village the size of a city block. However, three-quarters of it had been destroyed. The homes crumbled and the dirt upturned, it looked as if twelve landslides had their way with it.

Matthew mused it over. Shaula would definitely be comfortable in a place like this.

"I'm going to go check it out," Matthew said.

"Me, too."

"No, you're not. In case you haven't realized, or perhaps have the memory of a mentally deficient goldfish, powers are harder to use if we're joined together. The last thing we need is to show up in the middle of enemy territory with nowhere to run and no energy. I'll do reconnaissance and see what I can find. In the meantime, you keep an eye out if anyone comes by."

"Are you really still going with this John Wayne crap?"

"You know John Wayne?" Matthew couldn't hide his curiosity. "Your parents taught you well."

"It's nothing to do with that. I just like Westerns."

"That's the first thing you've actually told me without being coaxed."

"Can't whine about things forever, can I?"

Matthew smiled. "Guess not!"

He transformed to water and splashed into the grass, whipping along at a breakneck speed. Matthew sped through the taller grove and slid out under a broken fence which bent out over the dug up street. He skidded over fissures and passed laughing drunks and wandering cat-trals too busy being steered to bother with him. Eventually, he reached the noisy inn and tavern where the light spilled out into the street. He slid inside the same moment a beaten-up looking passerby crossed the threshold.

The place boomed with song, drink, and loud bodies at every table. It had a feel like a funeral for an enemy. The songs were bitter, and the laughs scornful. This was not his sort of bar.

But at the back of the tavern there sat one man with an honest laugh. He laughed from the gut and bellowed songs with gusto. The voice reminded Matthew of someone. He slid under the table. Several minutes passed before the drunk finally calmed and began speaking normally.

"Many good thanks for the drink, Reg. A fantastic warrior deserves a fantastic bounty!"

The man beside him laughed. "Oh, come now, Rantan, tell me more about the beauty you acquired. Who is the lucky one that takes her?"

The name was familiar to Matthew, but not the face attached to it. This man's thick beard and weather-beaten features held no similarity to the lizard that attacked the abbey. Not to mention that Matthew had severed its arm clean off. He kept listening as the oaf went on.

"She's too small for my tastes," Rantan said. "I prefer women with more meat on their bones. But, aye, she is not unpleasant to look at. I suppose she's pretty if you like scrawny women."

"Perhaps I do. Is there a chance I can have this one?"

"No one will have this one, Reg. The Queen wants her as a trade."

"Hopefully you will then allow me a chance afterwards. It's cruel that you magic-born can be awarded such prizes. We all support the Great Sorcerer King here."

Heat grew inside Matthew. It took all his willpower to resist transforming and begin cracking skulls. But not yet.

"Aye, I understand, Reg. You are not like the riffraff in the Deep Woods. But the Queen wanted her taken to the caves."

The large man sighed. Rantan downed a glass.

"Was she so easy to take?" Reg asked.

"Yes, I expected more from the Gemini Bracelets. Castor especially was a disappointment. I took his woman, and all he could do was take my arm. Laughable."

"All Earthwalkers outside the mountains are weaklings. I am more surprised that the two fools escaped the mountains in the first place, never mind reached an abbey. Your mother must be beside herself."

"Do not presume to understand her, Reg. Being in the company of filth has turned her livid."

"Was she really captured by those prisoners? I find that hard to believe."

"She used them to find some trinket. They stole it from under her nose before escaping. But regardless of all that, today was a success. What say we have another round?"

That was half of what Matthew needed. Shaula's men were here, but he still had no direction to search. This whole village gave a mood of a people infected with mad fever. None of them would jump at the chance to help a stranger. Had this town been abandoned and taken over by Shaula's agents, or were these travelers and passersby? He couldn't confirm either.

Matthew listened longer. The two of them talked about all sorts of asinine things, but finally, the subject came up of where the big idiot lived.

"I am not carrying you home this time, Rantan."

"Then be sure to have one of the wenches get another. I am not leaving until I have my fill."

"They won't carry you that far. You outweigh everyone here. Wouldn't you rather sleep in that large mansion of yours?"

"A mansion?" Rantan cackled. "Please. It's a poor place to hang one's hat. The Queen insisted I sleep somewhere that would do her proud. She built that hoary hovel which smells of old things and death. It is like living on a graveyard. You must not judge how impressive a home is on its size, Reg. This shambling tavern is more of a home."

"Was that supposed to be a compliment? It did not feel like one."

"Aye, I'm only being truthful. That sort of things I find in my home after being away so long would surprise you. Some of those bandits really believe those rumors of treasure. My maps lead to nothing they want, I'll tell you that much."

Reg groaned. "There is not enough gold in all of Tyndarus to convince me to go inside. I've heard tales of what lurks in your halls."

"Oh, have you?" He laughed. "But enough about me. Tell me about your cousin. Did he solve that problem with his neighbor yet? I say just steal the chicken back."

"That is your solution for just about every problem, Rantan. Steal this, steal that. We do not all have the power to do what we want."

Matthew's form quivered. The bit of knowledge gained would have to be enough. Matthew had at least something to go on. He couldn't wait in this place forever, not with Castor fading on him. He zipped back out under the table and towards the exit. Stomping drunks obliviously thumped the boards around him.

He swam back along the ground. A cat-tral paw slammed down beside him. It hissed as he swirled along. The rider swore at the creature, thankfully unaware of him.

Matthew slipped back into the tall grass and toward where he last left Jason.

The idea of leaving that scumbag Rantan alone did not sit well, but Matthew had no choice. If he caused a scene, it would alert the other criminals and possibly Shaula herself. At that point, Ordopha would certainly be dead. Where would he find those caves? That was the reigning question.

Matthew arrived back at the treeline and morphed back to normal. He called into the brush and Jason emerged. Matthew told him all he had heard, and the boy nodded along.

"So we go to Rantan's place and see if we can find anything," Jason said. "He has to have something, maps, notes, or clues of some kind. Shaula built that place, after all."

"We're not both going. I already told you it takes more effort to carry other people when transformed and we can't walk in there wearing armor like this."

"That's why we wear these." Jason brought forth two heavy cloaks from behind his back. They were big enough that they should cover even the tall pair. "I filched them from that house over there while you were gone. Had to look around a bit, but I don't think anyone will miss 'em."

"Stealing, boy scout?"

"You really don't know much about me."

"And whose fault is that? Are you dumb enough to not know what they'll do to Ordopha if they know we're here?"

"They won't do anything. They need her alive. But, yes, yes, I get it. As long as I'm not seen it shouldn't matter, right? Well, I wasn't seen."

Matthew tried to make heads or tails of the idiot. He sighed and shook his head. As long as Jason wasn't seen, there was no sense harping on it.

They threw the cloaks on over their armor. The rough visibility around the perimeter of the village meant they should be fine, but Matthew could not escape the feeling that they should avoid it. A distinct rotting stink wafted around this dead space. It didn't appear like this fog would poison them, as it hadn't hurt any of those here. However, Matthew felt like they should leave soon. Some presence remaining in the fog froze the pumping blood in his heart.

The pair moved at a decent pace through the broken hovels surrounding the main road. The drunks avoided them as did most of the passersby. Every now and then one or two leaning against the ancient stone would watch them but only for a moment. None in this place wanted to cause a scene.

But that did not mean the two of them would be left alone.

"Keep close," Matthew whispered.

"I can handle myself."

"If they think we're together they are less likely to try anything. Criminals aren't the bravest."

"You used to things like this?"

Matthew grinned. "You really don't know much about me."

"I guess that's my fault."

No one had followed them, not yet, but there was no sense waiting to see if any dregs were trying to catch up. Up ahead and across the field lay a large wooden structure masked by the green air.

He turned a corner around a shattered building and kept moving. They weren't any different from common scum. Nothing other than thieves, drunkards, and murderers roamed this place.

Finally the two arrived at the front of the mansion, or at least what those goons called a mansion. It went up three stories, with round stone towers in each corner. Tall grass stretched along the length of the property. The surrounding buildings were broken and abandoned like everything else in this town. This mansion looked impressive compared to its neighbors, but it was just as empty as the hovels. The over-sized structure loomed like a gargoyle over the pair.

"Multiple ways in," Jason mumbled more to himself than Matthew. "I could break down the door, or you could slip in and find what we need while I wait out here. Obviously, it would be smarter for you to go, but it would be faster if I went."

"We're both going."

Jason blinked at him and glanced around the barren area illuminated by muted green light. "I'm not sure about that. Isn't it better to be separate?"

"There's no argument about this. Whoever stays out here is a sitting duck for the guys following us—and don't think one or two aren't following us. They're probably still unsure of what we are. We need to go before they figure it out. Splitting up is silly."

"So you have done this before."

"Breaking into places?" Matthew replied with an acidic edge. "Not one of my proudest moments, but yes, I have. The important thing here is to find a spot that gives you a better vantage point than those who might stumble upon you. Wide open areas are a no-no."

"It's not that I want to fight those guys, you know. The last thing I want to do is get Alain even madder at me."

"He's probably mad enough that he's not here with us. Get over here. We're going in."

Jason merged with Matthew. Light footsteps slowly pressed against dirt in the green light behind them. Thieves would be upon them soon. Matthew moved to the door.

He became a puddle and slid through the jamb. The steps stomped further and further away until they disappeared. When he was certain they were gone Matthew solidified into a human again.

The dark mansion overwhelmed his senses. Eyes focusing in the dark, he got word of where he was from Jason before he could see anything. Matthew rubbed his brow to focus.

"This is worse than outside. We shouldn't be here."

"Because it smells like death?"

It certainly did stink of corpses and ash, but the stench of alcohol and an unrecognizable aridic fragrance also lingered.

"Not just that. Look over there."

Matthew bumped into a small table and fought off a swear. At the end of a scuffed up and dusty red carpet, he spotted a limp figure lying against the stone wall. The green fog from the window sent a lime tint across the inside. It shone across a chalk white object that looked like a bone.

"You know what that is, right?"

Matthew swallowed his nerves. The round object gained an extra dimension in the shadows as he leaned closer. He crouched down, dust attacking his nerves and tickling his nose. His fingers ran along the dark figure, and his spine tingled. He pushed it back, and a head rolled back against the wall. Dead eyes stared past him into infinity.

"A body," Matthew whispered.

Somewhere on the floor above him, boots scuffled on wood. They weren't alone in the house.

CHAPTER 15
PHANTOM STAB

JASON WINCED when he heard the movement from upstairs. The boy quickly left Matthew's head and kept his fingers near his scabbard.

He wanted to split up, but Matthew shot that idea down.

"Not yet," he whispered. "It's easier to hide if there's one of us, and I'm the better one at it. Sit silent here until you see something. For now, we just need to look for a clue."

An unspoken tension lingered in the room even with the revelation that they weren't alone. The corpse at Matthew's feet disturbed Jason more. Its face stretched out and gasping for air that would not come, and hands gripped like claws along the cold stone floor where scratches remained. The corpse had greying hair with a long face and beard, and underweight. His dress of finer silk and jewels betrayed any sense of belonging to this town. One single stab wound pierced the victim's throat, but he could see no blood on the floor around the body. A black, solid mass like dried blood remained inside the puncture. Jason paid special attention to the empty eyes, the only clue that this shell had once been a real person. Whatever lay upstairs killed him.

"There's no time for this, Jason. He's dead. Sticking around here isn't going to help us."

"It's hard to explain to someone that should have a better sixth sense than I do, but this body is giving me a bad feeling. I'm going to wait here for you."

"Of course I'm getting a bad feeling, but I've gotten that since getting into this town. The whole place is *wrong*."

"Just go upstairs. I'm not going anywhere."

Matthew sighed and rotated his shoulder. "Then I guess I should find that idiot's room. If he has maps like he said then hopefully one will lead to Ordopha."

The stairs to the left of them were made of a solid stone that spiraled upwards. Despite outside appearances, the inside of this place didn't look like any mansion Jason had ever seen. It had been left to crumble, just like everything else in this town.

Matthew slowly ascended the stairs with his sword drawn at his side and his steps light. He soon disappeared from sight, leaving the teenager on his own.

Jason's skin stood on end in that place. He watched the corners of the cavernous rooms adorned with tapestries, candles, and paintings. It took a few seconds for him to realize the shape of the place reminded him of modern Earth. The ground floor specifically had an open concept floor plan with oddly placed thin pillars and a smaller table with chairs sitting around it ahead of him. The carpet placement, as well as the modern fireplace, made this look like an apartment.

Jason had been in a mansion before. Despite that, he hadn't been in one in a dog's age. Not since . . . well, he didn't need to think about it now. He wouldn't be going back there again. Now he had powers, and he would become someone else—a hero. Jason McCrae was dead: now he was a whole new man. When he got back to Serenity City, he would be that hero he always wanted to be.

As he stood there in the dark remembering old times, an intense heat grew in his chest. It prickled like heartburn. His mind turned and knew it was the Kharis Seed before he understood it himself. An outside force connected through him and to the seed itself. The seed wanted to go somewhere—somewhere close. For a second he saw the face of the girl from his dreams. Was she nearby?

Before he could react, a dark light reflected off the dead man's eye. Jason leaned in closer, the Kharis Seed burning against him. He closed the eyes of the corpse, and a shock surged in him. The world in his eyes warped out of shape like a bad camera lens and then refocused again.

Thick carpets of mist flowed out of the hole in the corpse's throat like black soot in a chimney. A vague floating darkness wafted inside of the dead man. Jason placed his palm out instinctively and the black heat danced. Smoke swirled into his hand as if magnetized.

He blinked and the world cleared. The corpse at his feet crumbled into dust. At the same moment, a scene played in his head.

Matthew was in danger.

SO FAR THE going had been good for Matthew. The tight hall on the second floor led him beyond small empty stone rooms. Inside the spaces he caught tiny beds and tables decorating the otherwise bare places. But he met no one. Perhaps a book fell from a desk to make the earlier noise.

Eventually, he reached a larger room which opened up from the hall. Dusty shelves and parchment strewn about the tall surfaces awaited him. Moldy tables braced against walls, and broken chairs littered the room. Judging by the way he acted at the tavern, there was doubt that Rantan had ever even looked at any of the tomes or used any of the ink left lying about. This room looked as if it had not been lived in for years.

Matthew ran his hand along the book spines. They were ancient, despite not being treated as such. Slashed covers, torn pages, and stained ink littered the shelves. Insults had been scrawled inside covers and on loose parchment, probably by Rantan himself.

Moonlight made it easier to scan the spines against the dark backdrop, but it didn't help lead him towards anything. Random ramblings and mystic junk filled the pages. He still needed that one hint.

But he soon spotted one book that caught his attention. Other than being covered by dust, it lay undisturbed. The title was *The Book of Aster,* a rather thin volume that hadn't been vandalized. Perhaps Rantan hid one of his maps inside. He flipped through it with the moonlight shining on his back.

Aster spoke of awakening in the plains of Trafarenka and recounted his journey from the wilderness. He mentioned the battle the Great Sorcerer King had with a being of pure light in the sky. The resulting chaos set sparks and lightning off across the land, creating canyons and gorges with their blasts. Every Earthwalker had woken to explosions of light. While the battle raged on, the Earthwalkers fled in confusion. Many had visions of a world far off from theirs—a place not so different from Tyndarus. A world run by what were known as Humans where those like Nieto could never defile.

Matthew skimmed stories, visions, and historical accounts before reaching the back cover. In the rear was a folded parchment that had only a few words. An arrow led from a crude drawing of Rantan's mansion which traced down a path through the village toward the deeper forest. Twists and turns ended in a giant circle with no defined shape in the scribbles. At the target were two words: *The End*.

This was it. Matthew had found it.

But was it a trap, or was Rantan just that easy to read? Perhaps he thought Aster's predictions and stories led to whatever was in the forest, or maybe he enjoyed this one book over the others. It was also possible more than just the Abbot took this Earthwalker religion thing seriously. Either way, it was the only real clue. He couldn't spend all day searching for other ones.

A tingle danced down his spine. Matthew perked up. Was something coming?

"Matthew!"

He twisted at Jason's voice. The boy ran into the room, frantically pointing at the wall behind Matthew. Matthew pocketed the parchment and threw the book on the nearby table.

"What are you doing up here? I thought you wanted to stay downstairs?"

"That thing killed the guy downstairs!"

"You saw it?" Matthew scanned the circumference of the room. "Is the killer here?"

"It's a long story, but yes."

"Stand back to back with me."

Jason ran up behind Matthew, and faced the opposite wall. They both took their swords from their scabbards. The creeping silence brought sweat down Matthew's back.

"Who is the murderer?"

"The dead guy was a caretaker. But he kept pilfering little things from this place. He came here when Rantan left on a mission weeks back, and a shadow attacked him. I think Rantan found him out."

"I'd ask how you know this, but I'm going to guess it's that seed again."

"Earthwalker corpses don't rot, they crumble." That would explain the ceremony for burying Case. "But only when the soul leaves the body. Sir Orach told me that was why they said Intactilis—to free them from the bodies Nieto made for them. It's the only way they can ascend. The thing that killed him poisons and locks their souls to the mortal plain for eternity."

Shivers slipped up Matthew's spine. "Did this corpse tell you himself?"

"Yes, actually. When I touched the body, light shone, and he broke free. I think that was the Kharis Seed. I saw what offed him before his remains disappeared."

"Okay, but where is this enemy? What is it exactly?"

"It sneaks in from behind and stabs the throat of the victim with the sharp edges in its palms. I don't know what it looks like because he didn't see it before it got him. If we keep back to back like this until we get out, we should be fine."

"Can we kill it?"

"Matthew, I don't even know what it is! If we get out of this house, we won't have to worry about that. Did you get what you came for?"

"Yes." He edged forward. Jason followed at his back, bumping into him. "This isn't going to work."

"We can't risk a fight, Matthew. You said it yourself."

"I'm not saying it because I want to fight. I'm saying it because we have no way of knowing what this thing is. Does it hunt the prey until it leaves this house or when the victim dies? Is it a monster or a magical being? Is it a Prime? Will it follow us out of here? We can't risk *that.*"

"How do we trick it out then?"

"Merge," Matthew replied. "Watch my back from inside. When it comes out, let me know, and I'll attack."

"The old man had a sword, you know. It still got him."

"The old man didn't have Castor. Hurry it up."

Jason backed up and fell into Matthew. Instantly, a heavy shift in the atmosphere punched down on the room. The humidity grew heavier. But Matthew didn't see anything, and Jason said nothing.

The mansion creaked and settled as his eyes darted through the darkness. Outside the chirps of crickets and an owl broke the air, but his heavy breathing filled the empty spaces inside. Would the shadow make the first move?

"Nothing, Matthew."

Matthew edged toward the hall. Maybe he could bait it out.

"There it is!"

A rough boot step broke out behind him. Matthew twisted and cut the air at his back—and air was all he cut. The darkness remained undisturbed. Nobody was there.

"What the—"

"Behind you, Matthew!"

Matthew ducked. A heavy and hot breeze blew over his helmet and cloak. He sprang forward into a roll. When he landed he turned around. There was still nothing behind him.

"You saw it, right? Tell me what it was."

"I wish I could! I only saw the outline of a grey shadow. It looked about as big as you, but it had something on its palms that looked like pincers."

"Do you see it now?"

"It's gone."

Matthew tightened the hold on his sword. Of all the things that could have happened in this thief town, fighting a phantom was not something he expected. Its presence made no sense. Rantan had been here mere weeks ago. This mansion wasn't abandoned. So then, he owned this stray monster. The headache pounding in his skull slightly lifted when he realized it.

This was Rantan's guard. Why else would he have no fears about leaving the place unguarded in a thief town? That psychotic monster must have loved the idea of people breaking in and getting themselves killed. He probably stayed away on purpose on the off chance that someone would come and do just this. Why else didn't he speak about it in the tavern?

"Behind!"

Matthew stayed perfectly still. He stabbed his blade backwards along his side. No sound erupted when it hit its mark. But he trembled with the strike. It was like hitting stone. The rear force continued to push forward. He bent and brought his stance backwards. However, there was nothing to strike—the enemy had vanished again.

Instantly, Matthew turned to mist. He fell downward and drifted through the floorboards and stone. He came through the ceiling and landed in a wide open room. The layout looked conspicuously like an apartment in Serenity City. Matthew reformed and scanned the strange sights.

"Did I hit it?"

"Your hit didn't go through. Actually, that's not true. It went through, but the thing solidified, and it pushed the sword out like the thing was rubber."

"It felt like rock."

"For all I know, that's what it is."

Not good enough. Matthew remembered what it was like when he transformed into mist and water and reformed. This shadow was like that: just like him. If this thing could fade away and reform as easily as he could, then he would outdo it at its own game.

"Let me know when it's about to grab me," he whispered.

"What? Why would I do that?"

"Just do it. I have one move left."

The moon shone through the emptiness. A dog howled somewhere in the distance. After a few moments, Jason whispered what he'd been waiting for.

"It's here."

"Let me know when it's close."

Jason paused.

Matthew's heart plunged into his throat. Sweat ran down his neck into his arms under his armor. There would only be one shot at this. He had to hit it just right, or they were dead.

"Now!"

Blurred ethereal arms drifted before Matthew's eyes, nearly invisible. Faded grey palms closed in on his face. He wouldn't be able to dodge. The shadow brushed his neck before hitting skin.

Matthew activated Castor as he fell back. The large grey body fell forward as its arms enclosed over nothing. Matthew let his airy form fall inside the phantom's inexplicable figure.

The shadow's faded grey skin and lack facial features caused him to retch. Its wiry limbs jutted out at angles no normal human skeleton could allow. Overlong spider length arms and legs and eyeless oval face completed the picture. Matthew sunk into its hardening form. He guessed correctly at how it worked. It was typically intangible before hardening when it struck. But it didn't count on Castor. The monster turned on its thin heel back to the wall when the thing realized Matthew was inside of it.

Now to act before it turned back.

Matthew became normal again. Just as in the mountains, his skin and muscles became rock hard for the first few moments of transforming.

Instantly, the enemy snapped apart. The phantom's physical form cracked open and dashed bloodlessly along the walls as it let out a high-pitch squeal. The limbs and parts puffed into ash as they slapped down. The atmosphere changed as it faded. It wouldn't be coming back.

He leaned against a table and caught his breath.

The mansion settled and the outside crickets returned to capture his attention. The peaceful night reigned once more.

"Is it dead?"

"I don't even know if it was alive to begin with. But no, it's not coming back."

"You sure?"

"I think my sixth sense is. There might be another one on standby for all we know. I'm not sticking around to find out."

"Slow down, Matthew. Take a breath."

"Not worth the risk."

Matthew's lungs burned, and his heart pounded. Rest could wait until they were out of this town. Jason left their merged state and followed after him.

"See," Jason said. "The body's gone."

And it was. No trace of the earlier corpse remained.

Matthew grimaced. "What did the Kharis Seed do to him?"

"I think it freed him from his prison. This relic is wild. Much different than ours."

Matthew led the boy back out into the fogged night of the thief town the same way they came in. No one was around: that crowd following them had long since vanished, and only the hoot of a distant owl haunted him. His fists trembled at his side. He took a breath to calm his nerves.

All he wanted to do was get that mansion out of his mind and out of sight. He removed the map from his pocket and carefully traced his path into the night.

If that lone phantom had been guarding the mansion, he couldn't help but imagine what wandered in the Deep Woods, waiting for them.

As they crossed the lonely road, wind blew in the distance. Jason glanced around wildly.

"Are you sure we're not walking into a trap?" the boy asked. "They might've planted that map."

"It's the only lead we've got. We're going to have to take them on regardless of what they have. Keep Pollux ready. You're gonna need it."

The two crossed a small wooden bridge over a thin, black creek. The green brush covered forest led into even thicker fog. Even if they were out of that house, Matthew couldn't breathe easy yet. Shaula was somewhere on the road ahead.

CHAPTER 16
WHAT LIES IN THE DEEP WOODS

JASON MIGHT NOT HAVE HAD Matthew's heightened sixth sense, but he also wasn't stupid. The quiet won in the mansion battle had already begun to fade the further they traveled from the town. The trees became even more knotted and warped and not a single bird chirped through the green mist. This made it harder for Jason to tell Matthew his thoughts.

But maybe that was for the best. Matthew had been acting odd since the attack on the abbey. The two of them had not been on the best terms since they met, but there was always a bit of detached feeling from their situation. They wouldn't be here forever: they would be going home eventually. Assuming they got that bomb out of him.

Meanwhile, the older warrior continued to trace the map in silence and Jason followed.

Wind blew from every direction and without any consistency in force. The muggy atmosphere persisted despite the gust, and the fog refused to part. The hard earth and rock made leaving a trail impossible. The weather worked against them the whole way.

They walked for what felt like hours with familiar rock formations and long branches passing them by multiple times. Jason knew they had to be going in circles, but Matthew wouldn't have it. The map had to be going in the right direction, according to him.

"It's a fake, Matthew," Jason hissed. "Rantan left it there on purpose."

"That's a lot of work for a forgery, especially when he had that Phantom that would kill intruders. Keep close. We're almost there."

"Let me see it."

Matthew shoved the parchment into Jason's chest and kept walking. "Do what you want."

"No need to be angry. I just wanted to confirm."

"I'm telling you what my sixth sense already knows. Dead ahead. If you don't trust me then you can turn back."

Then why did it feel like they saw the same sights? Was it merely some trick of the forest? Did Nieto's magic reach out here? He couldn't deny that he was out of his depth.

He handed back the map. Matthew took it, wide-eyed at the move.

"Done already?" he asked.

Jason blandly looked to the masked sky. "Nothing to be done. Just do what you have to."

"Thanks for the vote of confidence, but I think we've got a bigger problem to worry about."

The further they traveled the more Jason began to see what he meant. The heavy humidity lifted and the wind died. Eventually, the fog lightened, but that same feeling Jason had back in the house wouldn't shake. They closed in on a darker force.

Then the mist split and fall away toward an outer ring on an invisible border. They crossed through the green tint and into the open area. This was once a town. Once. But unlike the one they had just left, there was no tavern or street full of hollering criminals.

Broken buildings and wooden houses were crushed and battered, emptied for miles. In the very center, a large towering tree like a mighty oak twisted into the sky with branches as big as a flying ship. Its roots twisted and traveled down through the buildings and had been embedded there for a long time. Familiar purple mist wafted from the foliage into the capped sky of the dead town. The two of them needed to get there. A voice whispered and told him to run.

The pair crossed into the middle of the street and realized the presence of something other than people. Growling wolves emerged from the alleys and roofs.

Howls cut the cool air of the starless sky. Stone wolves near his height stood in the streets and on the rooftops. Snarls broke from the pack.

"We should go," Matthew said.

"No, we shouldn't. We need to get to that tree." Jason's heart beat like a jackhammer on six times the speed. The Kharis Seed wanted him here.

"You've come," the cloaked man said. He emerged from the broken doorway. "Good night."

"Rantan," Matthew replied. "I see why you didn't worry about anyone finding the map."

"I certainly didn't think I would find you here tonight," Rantan said. "You appear surprised to see me. That must mean you ran across me in town. But that wasn't who you think. It was a copy created from that man over there."

The familiar lanky figure of the man in black armor leaned against the opposite house. The Cutter nodded blandly to both warriors. He crossed through the wolves toward Rantan.

"What do we do?" Jason whispered. "Do we take them on or run for it?"

"You say there's something in that tree and I believe it. That magic pouring off it is a bad sign."

Two enemy warriors and enough stone wolves to be a big problem moved in on them. Matthew and Jason took hold of their swords and shields.

"Go for the roofs," Matthew whispered. "Head for the tree. I'll try to distract them by going for the homes. They'll be after me."

"Why?"

He smiled at the boy. "I'm the weaker one. You make a run, get what you need over there, and I'll be behind you."

Jason shifted his attention from Matthew to the approaching horde. He couldn't think of a better plan. Perhaps they would even chase him instead. But that was wishful thinking. He would just have to hope Matthew had a plan.

Without looking his friend in the eyes, Jason crouched low, felt the dirt buckle under his boots, and jumped. He soared upwards into the night air and landed on a nearby thatched roof. The straw surface buckled under his weight, leading him to leap to the next and then the one after. Behind him, teeth snapped and growls echoed in the dark.

The thatch roof splintered under the pressure of his weight as he moved forward, but a new sight appeared at his side. On the house across the row to his left, a shape sped towards him. A large lizard-like man with fire red scales for skin leaped across the road. This was the Rantan that Matthew had told him about.

"Did you think I'd be letting you go, boy?" the lizard hissed. "No chance of that."

A heavy queasiness overcame Jason for a moment. The boy flinched and missed Rantan bounding directly for him.

Before Jason could react, the large beast brought its sword down on his head.

MATTHEW MADE it across the street and barreled into the busted door. The snapping of teeth blew hot air against the back of his helmet. He turned and slammed his blade down. The first wolf through the door had its rock head cleaved in two. Two more burrowed into the room while the first wolf crumbled. All he could do was move backwards through the shambling structure.

He found a large open hole near the top of the crumbled wall by the rotting bed. The wolves dove into the cramped space after him. He slipped into mist and poured through the opening. Barks echoed after him as he reformed on the other side.

The scratching of claws slapped up against the broken wall behind him. He caught his breath and his bearings. One problem solved.

But a heavy weight suddenly crashed inside his chest. His head swam, sweating profusely. He ran a hand across his brow, and the sudden illness faded.

"What was—"

An ax flashed for his head. Matthew ducked, and the weapon beat into the stone. The one called The Cutter now stood before him with blank eyes watching him without expression.

"You move well, Castor."

"I've had practice." The scratching behind him ceased, and the padding of claws retreated. The wolves were coming around. "That's one thing about Tyndarus: you're always trying to avoid a blade getting buried into your neck."

"I understand you better than you know. But you are not ready for the three of us."

The dead village lingered like stained ash on Matthew's thoughts. This place wasn't like the Thieves' Town. This area had been destroyed. Burned rock and wood, bones, and slash marks adorned every building and alley crevice. It had to have something to do with that dark tree.

Across the way was a tavern, two floors with only the front wall smashed open. He would need to funnel the pack in behind him to allow himself a quick escape route. The other hovels were little more than glorified grave markers with only a wall or two to remind passersby that people once lived here. The tavern was his best bet for shelter.

That heavy weight grew inside his chest again. Matthew bit his lip and tried to fight it off with some speech. "Why do they call you The Cutter?"

"I would think that was self-evident. Why do they call you Matthew?"

The wolves tumbled around the corners of the house toward him, biting and howling. Their large paws clawed and tore into the earth.

"Follow me to find out."

Matthew ran across the open road. He leaped through the broken wall, and several wolves charged in after him. With a bang he hit the floor and waited for the first wolf to come upon him. The beating of paws grew louder outside towards the narrow opening.

The first large wolf body blasted into him with a heavy weight, smashing against his armor. He bounced against the floor in time to see the paw slash his face. His helmet rang with the hit, barely protecting him from the blow. Jaws dug for his throat. Matthew slashed, striking and fracturing the stone neck. The beast whined and fell back. Matthew rolled back up in time for a second wolf to dive in from the side. He batted it to the side with his shield.

The two stone wolves circled him, and more converged on the entrance outside. His thoughts began to drift. This strange feeling kept coming and going like a breeze. Still, he kept his sword swinging.

"Do you want the woman that much, Castor? She is just like every other Earthwalker on Tyndarus: destined to blow away in the very dust we were created from. What use is a puppet that won't dance for her master? You are not like us. You are destined for greater things."

The first wolf sprang from behind Matthew. He ducked and stabbed upward, piercing its rock gut. The stone broke open with its cry. The cracked corpse touched down and shattered into thousands of pieces. He rounded on the second wolf before it could also join the fray.

"Are you still attempting to return to your world? What use is that? You will become one of us eventually. Throw down your arms before the bracelet is damaged."

Matthew backed up towards the stairs as the growling wolf slunk towards him. It moved at a glacial pace, its solid form rumbling. He ascended the steps one foot at a time with the beast snapping at him. Wood creaked and crunched as pieces broke out from under them. The stone wolf bit his right arm and grinded into the armor. He slammed his shield against its nose and set it back.

The beast moved, and he leaped backwards up the steps. The floor gave slightly under him. The wolf landed with its full weight and broke through. Wood splintered around it. The wolf dropped to the first floor. A whine escaped the monster as it crashed down. Matthew let the stairs fall under him, smashing against the bottom, and jumped for the second floor.

His only chance at escape lay here. Matthew ran to the window at the end of the hall. Before he could reach it, the figure of the Cutter kicked it open and bounded into the abandoned place. The pair became trapped together in the thin hallway outside burnt rooms with a sea of wolves waiting below.

"You puzzle me, Castor. Nothing you attempt to do is rational."

The arching ax screamed for Matthew's head. His shield angled the strike away from him. Matthew swiped his sword at the attacker. The Cutter dodged and retreated a step. Their blades clashed again and again.

Matthew couldn't rely on Castor. There was no telling what lay ahead and Castor was too valuable to waste on a guess. Ordopha and Jason also still needed him.

They exchanged blows, and the floor creaked and cracked under their boots. The Cutter quickly anticipated Matthew's attacks and effortlessly evaded them. Wolves howled from the floor below. Time ticked against them.

"The Queen will be sad to know that I had to kill you, Castor." His tone kept its dead level. "But she knows I get carried away ending your kind."

"You can't kill me."

"Surely you are joking. I can, and *will*."

That overconfidence was Matthew's only chance to end this quick. He charged forward with the bracelet before him. The board under him gave way. Scraps of wood tumbled down to the floor below. Wolves dove on the tiny pieces. Heat glowed through Castor as the Cutter watched the bracelet and brought his ax back. Matthew turned to mist in his leap.

He streamed toward the Cutter. Matthew would have misted through and stabbed his opponent in the back, but the Cutter would expect that. Matthew counted on it. The enemy watched the mist as it fell upon him.

"I am no amateur!" the Cutter shouted. He brought his ax down behind him, slashing nothing. "What?"

Matthew had stopped short at the Cutter's now exposed back. He became human once more and plunged his blade in the enemy's back. The Cutter's confused grimace traveled from where he thought Matthew was going to go to where he actually reappeared. Blood trickled from his lips at the moment he realized he had been tricked.

"Very good," the enemy said at length. "You cast aside honor to beat me."

"I'm not dying here. I'll throw away my honor for them."

"Your tenacious nature is in vain. The girl is already dead, as your friend will also soon be. Defeating me will not change that."

Matthew removed his sword, and the corpse dropped lifelessly to the crumbling floor. The body fell through the broken boards and landed with a dead weight between the wolves. They ignored the remains and instead snapped and leaped at Matthew. The floor shook under him.

He backed up towards the broken window as the bottom of the floor broke apart. Out on the roof he looked out towards the towering tree looming over the dead place. The large shape of a giant emerged from between the buildings. A twenty-foot monstrosity of a golem bellowed into the night.

Blurriness fought against him. He blinked, hoping this sickness would pass. For a moment Matthew believed the dead man's words. This night would ever end.

CHAPTER 17
THE ONE WHO WILL SAVE

JASON LIFTED his shield in time for the blow to miss his neck. The impact shook him, sending Jason careening downward from the rooftop. He broke through boards and stone and the house around him crumbled into naught but ash on the wind. Stars crossed his eyes. He rolled sideways without thinking. A sword stuck into the dust where he had just been. Jason regained his breath, and he glimpsed the giant lizard before him.

This was the one called Rantan that Matthew had met in the underground cavern. Somehow his severed arm had grown back again.

None of the other lizards Jason had fought had regained their limbs during a battle, and none of them had grown to the size of this one. If Rantan really had a Prime power, it was not one of simple transformation.

Ashen and broken boards crumbled around the duo. Jason retraced his path. He needed to zigzag between the hovels north to reach the tree.

Jason bolted forward and smashed against wood which shattered in his wake. He streaked through the dirt, kicking it up around him. Heavy steps followed behind, but he kept moving.

At the edge of town, the massive tree stood beside a dried up river and water wheel. The redwood-like monstrosity towered hundreds of feet high. He placed a hand on the trunk, feeling heat against his skin. Rantan skidded to a stop behind him.

No longer a lizard, but the figure of the tall man in a purple robe from earlier, he all but strutted down the road towards Jason.

"Where is Shaula?" Jason asked.

"Your queen is currently indisposed. I will bring you to her."

"Because you're her servants or because you're all Primes?"

"Primes? Is this a term where you come from? We're not from your world."

Jason grimaced before he spoke. "You're children of someone who is a Prime, and there was only one Earthwalker back home when they first appeared. You are children of Queen Shaula."

"We are servants. The Great Sorcerer King deigns us suitable to serve. We are lucky that the one who gave birth to us let us keep our lives, and the rewards we get are more than worth it."

"That's a horrible way to live. Your lives don't have to be disposable."

"But they are, Pollux. Mine is. Yours is. Those on Tyndarus, and on Earth. There is only one place left for us, and that is at the feet of the Great Sorcerer King. Our only choice is whether we are alive or dead when we bend. It's inevitable. Let's just enjoy ourselves in the meantime."

"Fat chance of that." Jason ran his fingers across the tree bark of the roots around him. The Kharis Seed called him forward through the rising headache breaking into his thoughts. He was so close. "You give up too easily."

"Give up what? I live for my King and Queen, and I will do so to my dying breath. What do you hope to accomplish fighting a god?"

"I've never had any aspirations except wanting to help others take down villains like you. But that was before. Now I'm going to be the one to stop you." A light burst forth from Jason's chest as he spoke, illuminating the darkness and driving Rantan back.

Jason blinked to find a small seed bathed in golden light floating before his chest. He snatched it, and the warmth heated his hand. The Kharis Seed wanted the tree. That had to be why he was called there. Jason placed the seed in the dirt beside the outstretched roots of the tall monstrous trunk. The tiny object dug down through the dirt like a mole. Light shone through the wood as it flowed up the trunk like a reverse waterfall. It disappeared up the base and into the branches, letting the light bathe out into the night. The Kharis Seed left him behind.

"What did you do, Pollux? You were to bring that seed to the Queen."

"In case you still haven't figured it out, I don't like being told what to do by your kind. It was never her seed."

"You've lost me my reward feast. Fool! You know nothing about what you are trifling with. I will not say it again. Throw down your arms."

Jason brought forth his sword and shield, the latter heavily dented. "And if I don't?"

"Then I will do to you what the Great Sorcerer King has done to this town."

"You're going to need more than a weak lizard transformation to beat me, Rantan. You couldn't even take down Matthew one on one, and he didn't have Pollux. You've got nothing."

The earth rumbled, shaking them off balance. To his right, upturned dirt moved like a sentient earthquake in a beeline of broken stone and ash towards them.

Rantan smiled. "My sister's pet returns."

Out of the ground burst a looming figure, a hulking brute with overlong, wide arms and giant feet. Its bulky frame made of the earth itself formed into a distorted giant facsimile of a human being. Where its eyes should be were two empty sockets of black ash. The golem howled mindlessly toward him.

This was the work of the woman who created the tunnels back at the tunnel. Matthew called her Camille.

Rantan clapped. "Camille left her pets to guard the way from intruders, but I never thought we would have to resort to the golem."

"Your whole family is disturbed. I'm going to enjoy using Pollux to stop you."

"Stop me? You're just another slab of meat for the tray, boy."

The large man placed one large palm on the giant and closed his eyes. His bones bent and warped and his height grew in a sudden spurt. Rantan's body stretched and shot up twenty feet and his skin thickened and darkened to dirt. He had become the golem, and now two stood before Jason.

The behemoth beside Rantan slammed a Buick-sized fist down. Jason leaped as it dropped and landed on the limb. He slashed it, but to no effect. Only small pebbles dislodged from the arm.

The second limb swiped out. Jason guarded with the shield, and the attack knocked his feet loose with the impact. He bounced against the earth with a crunch and rolled to his feet. The monster dove upon him again.

Jason raised the shield and heard it crack. The blow lifted him from the ground, and the shield broke apart with the strike. Rantan elbowed him in the back. A sharp pain ran along the boy's spine. Jason coughed up saliva.

The two were much too fast and strong for their size. Jason's measured strikes with his sword did little, and his shield had been shattered. If he wanted to survive this, he needed a distraction.

"Whatever is the matter?" the Rantan beast roared. "Surely you have not given up so soon!"

"Not yet. I've got a good one coming your way."

They exchanged blows, but Jason couldn't get a good cut in on either of them. Pollux did not have an unlimited supply of power. Jason sheathed his blade and readied his fists.

Howls cut through the heat of battle. Across the torn up road tumbled a pack of stone wolves towards him. A bead of sweat ran down his neck. Where was Matthew?

As if answering his question, Rantan let out a shout. A man leaped on his back and brought down his sword with the force of a sledgehammer. Matthew had arrived. The second golem made a run for him, giving Jason his opportunity.

Jason's thunderous steps shook the very forest around them. The enemy golem turned to meet him just as he jumped. Jason threw his fist forward, punching through stone and flying through the open wound. The golem whined as its stomach burst open. Earth crumbled, and the monster shattered. Jason's muscles seized as he landed.

Matthew rolled in the dirt beside him.

"Looks like you didn't need me on that one," Matthew said.

"I take it you got the Cutter. Why are the wolves here?"

"I can't kill everything."

The pack of wolves fell in beside Rantan, leading to a veritable wall of enemies. With the tree behind the two warriors, they had no way out. Jason's muscles burned, and Matthew coughed up a storm. Rantan swore at the two of them.

"Where is my brother, Castor?"

Matthew wiped his bloodied mouth. "Hell."

The giant screeched so terribly that Jason believed he might smash the sound barrier. The wolves encroached on the trapped pair. The battle would soon be over.

Bark crunched behind the pair. Jason turned around first.

"Who is that?" Matthew asked.

Jason's mouth fell open. "That girl!"

Out of the tree emerged a girl bathed in golden light. She walked from the trunk, crossing an invisible threshold into the tangible plane. Dark brown eyes as hard as the earth itself watched him. She wore a simple white robe with curled hair and stepped with a graceful glide that almost made him forget they were in a battle. This was that girl he saw in the dream back in the abbey. Did she lead him here?

She placed a hand against his cheek, and the growing heat in his body died off. She was over a foot shorter than he was, but a strange sense of intimidation permeated her existence. He knew her. And now she had the Kharis Seed.

"She's Zelana," he said to Matthew. "She was the girl in my dream."

The older warrior cleared his throat. "Shaula's daughter was in that tree? You've met before?"

"We have," she answered with her eyes still on Jason. A beatific smile shone from her fading light. "Only in dreams. I'm not like my mother."

"She's on our side, Matthew. Trust me."

"You little idiot. How do you know she's not screwing with you like Shaula did?"

"You saved me," she interrupted. "Why would I betray your graciousness?"

"No, I—" Jason began. She pressed two fingers against his lips, and the golden light shining off her skin faded with it. All his exhaustion vanished completely. He felt as if he could crack the sky itself. "I'm better?"

She giggled lightly. "The seed told me you needed it. Will this prove my loyalty to you?"

"You!" Rantan boomed behind him. Jason had almost forgotten that he was still there. "Were you hiding in the enchanted blackwood tree? Who are you, girl? Are you—"

"Me?" Zelana asked. "I am no one. Just know that I owe these two my life."

"All three of you are about to lose them."

The pack of wolves sprinted across the broken field. Matthew had his weapons ready, and the girl stood back. The beasts would be upon them in seconds.

"Matthew, watch her. I'm ending this now."

Before Matthew could argue, Jason kicked off in a run. Pollux burned hard with a heat stronger than any he ever grasped before. Wind split around his boots and the earth itself trembled. He was back to full strength.

Rantan bounded in his direction. The false golem's hoarse cry could cut through glass.

They both punched. Rantan's large fist and Jason's collided, and the earth shook. Jason pushed back and swung with his left into the golem's punching arm. Rantan's stone limb crunched and crumbled. Before the enemy could make a reprisal, Jason jabbed again and again. Rantan's right arm broke with the impact, scattering dust and pebbles to the wind.

The body broke off pieces as each strike landed. Rantan wailed and dove on him. Jason put everything into Pollux and jumped upward.

His fists crashed through the golem's head. Earth and stone shattered. Rantan crumbled.

Just like the first golem, the enemy shook apart until nothing remained. Rantan cried out as his remains blew away.

Behind him, Matthew ran his sword through the last stone wolf. Ruined earth and pebbles ruled the battlefield now.

"That was crazy," Jason said to the girl. "How did you supercharge Pollux like that?"

She blanched before looking down at her feet. "That was the seed. Not me."

"That can't be true." A twinge of pain split into his head. It vanished just as soon as it arrived. "You're Shaula's daughter. Don't you have magic of your own? You have to know about her magic, right?"

"Ease up," Matthew said. "You're scaring her."

"Scaring her? She just walked out of that tree like a ghost and gave me the power to finally stop that bastard. Now isn't the time to be scared of me!"

"Oh, shut up, stupid. You said her name was Zelana. How did you even know that? That's something you could have told me earlier."

"It only came to me later. I didn't hide anything. I only saw her there in the dream, nothing else happened. Besides, she saved us. She's gotta be on our side, right?"

"And that leads me to my next question. Why did Shaula leave her there? If you saw this girl in your empty head, then it had to have meant something."

Jason didn't have an answer. Why would the seed choose to bring him here to the daughter of their enemy? The teenage girl even had trouble meeting his eyes. There was always the chance that she knew more about him than she let on.

"Could you not stand so close?" the girl asked.

A blush ran over him, and he backed up. Despite Matthew's laughing, he kept his tone level.

"Sorry, I know we haven't met before, and you did help us out of that jam, but I still don't know about dealing with Shaula's daughter."

"I don't really know myself," she nearly whispered. "A long time ago they put me in that tree and left me there. It's been . . . I think it has been decades. At least that is what the seed told me."

"It spoke to you?" Matthew groaned. "One of you needs to explain what this Kharis Seed is, but we need to find Ordopha first. Rantan was with that Camille woman earlier—"

Earth bubbled and formed into a dozen figures that pushed out of the dirt like swimmers from a lake. The wolves were coming back.

"Run!" Matthew shouted.

He directed the boy forward past the tree and bolted. Jason clasped Zelana's wrist and followed.

They whipped through brush and tall grass, the howling and snapping of rock teeth growing louder. Would these beasts ever stop?

Green sickness shot through Jason's bloodstream. He narrowly avoided falling and kept pace. Up ahead Matthew was doing the same, although he was tough to see in the haze. Jason growled and dragged Zelana forward. She screamed about the wolves getting closer.

Jason called to the man in front. "Where are we going, Matthew?"

"Shut up!" he shouted. "I can't think straight. My sixth sense is telling me this way, but I just don't know."

A thin shaft whizzed past Jason's shoulder, sinking into a wolf. It whined and crumbled. A cavalcade of arrows sunk into the ground mere feet behind the trio. Archers emerged from the fog and brush around them. Men with spears and swords appeared, leaping at the beasts. Jason, Zelana, and Matthew stopped.

The attackers all wore heavy vermilion cloaks over their armor and strange looking face-coverings that reminded Jason of old kabuki masks. They were not dissimilar from the Vultures.

Before Jason could say anything, Matthew slumped to the ground. He lay still in the fog, and the boy couldn't see if he was still breathing. Jason took a step and found himself also falling to his knees. His headache screeched, causing his stomach to flip. The sickness had caught up with them.

The last thing Jason saw was a stocky man with bulging muscles at the front of the group. He held an ax in each hand but kept them steady by his sides. The leader. His mask blocked his eyes and expression.

Jason opened his mouth to speak, but the fog enclosed on him, and he knew no more.

CHAPTER 18
LAST VILLAGE

CONSCIOUSNESS SPLASHED over Matthew like cold water. He sat up and wiped the wet cloth from his forehead, tossing it to the stone floor. The wooden pew he sat in dug into his spine. He had been brought into a church.

"Jason!" he whispered roughly. He stood up, and his leg muscles cried out. "Jason?"

The boy's head shot up from the pew in front of his. A cloth also fell from his forehead. "What's going on?"

"We're in a church. How did we get here?"

Jason jumped up. "I lost consciousness after you. I don't know who brought us here."

"Kydil did," a man said.

A priest crossed over from the rear of the church and Matthew could see familiar sights. It reminded him of the monastery. The size was at least half of the other location but remained packed with pews and candles perched precariously about. The priest wore black robes and was totally alone. He sat beside Matthew on the bench.

"Please sit," he said. "You are not yet well."

"Where is Zelana?" Jason asked.

Matthew nodded. "We also have a friend in the forest we need to find. We have no time for this."

"The girl is well, Jason. Yes, she told me your names. Do not worry, you are safe here. But you mustn't stand so readily. The fog is still in your system. Zelana is currently washing herself clean of its influence."

Matthew swayed and slumped into the pew. "Its influence? Is that what was messing with us?"

"It poisons the mind and floods the soul. I am surprised you weathered so well inside of it. Your dedication, and your bracelets, truly proves you are Castor and Pollux."

Jason dropped back into his seat facing forward. He rubbed his brow. "I don't think the fog can explain what I did."

"You mean Rantan?" Matthew flatly asked. "It had to be done. We need to get out of here and find Ord. We can't sit and mope about this sort of thing."

"I still killed him without thinking about it."

Matthew blinked. The boy had to get beyond this fast. Regrets were luxuries they could not afford. "How did you think that was going to end, Jason?"

"I know, I know. There wasn't another choice. But I felt nothing when I did it. It was like punching cardboard. I didn't even realize what I had done until . . . just now. I woke up ready to move onto the next thing. What is wrong with me?"

"Well . . ." Matthew stopped short of being honest. The boy became too thoughtful when he did anything other than jump into a fight. This was no different, but they were no longer the same ignorant saps Shaula had tricked into coming here. Jason had changed, though he didn't realize it. "This is just how it works here. Maybe it works like this back home, too. I don't know. Good people are threatened, and you move to save them. You do what you need to, and that doesn't mean holding back. Rantan was a vicious scumbag who reveled in death and destruction."

"But shouldn't I feel something? Anything?"

"No," the priest said. "I apologize for interrupting your conversation, but I can't sit still."

"Yes," Jason paused on his words. "Do I call you *Father* here?"

He cocked his head. "My title is Hodegeo. I am Hodegeo Himmello."

Jason had learned little from the Abbot, though Matthew expected it. The kid didn't make any attempt to learn anything since they came to Tyndarus. He wanted to put this world out of his thoughts. His desperation to return home was obvious. Did he care that much about the bomb in Matthew or was something else there waiting for him?

"That aside, you must understand how the Deeper Woods functions, young man. The fog warps and distorts the mind, and it causes one to lose control of their baser impulses. Those inside do not often think twice about their decisions."

"You said something like that before," Matthew said. "Do you mean it made Jason do what he did?" He did not find that thought as relieving as the priest probably expected it to be.

"No, young one. The fog heightens and twists thoughts, but only with prolonged exposure, and only through months or years will one truly lose their way. With less than a day, all one can do is forfeit control of urges they already bore. That fierceness was inside of him, though he would have normally kept such violence at bay."

Jason shivered and gripped his arms.

There was nothing further to discuss, as far as Matthew believed. Jason did what he had to in order to save others and survive. But Matthew wasn't Jason, and he wasn't a teenage boy. Killing could never be a pleasant thing, but it would be necessary here. Even if they got back to Serenity City, he might have had to make a similar choice against a villain someday. Jason was simply lucky to have to make it here first. But Matthew didn't mention those thoughts. They would have to wait. The pair still had someone to rescue.

"Do those masks block the fog?" he asked the priest. "The ones the men who found us wore?"

"It is not so much the masks, but the water. The river in Fortuna runs deep under the earth and splits the village in two. But it offers protection when any material is soaked in it—even when dried. Poisons and the elements will not pierce or bend the target. The benefit lasts half a day, enough for hunting, but that's all we need. Hunters return here for Intactilis before any permanent damage can be done to them. You two shall wash in the water to clean yourself of any of the fog's influence when we are finished here. You require it."

"So why not stock up and leave this village? Staying here looks like a deathtrap."

"The benefits wear away the further one walks from the stream, and lasts no longer than half a day. That is why it is used for hunting. It also keeps invaders out."

"I don't get why you would form a village in here in the first place. These woods are a horror show. It can't be worth it just to hide from Shaula's goons."

"We were an outpost for travelers long, long ago. The village's old location might be familiar to you as the sight of that garish blackwood tree. Our ancestors were chased out when the fog fell and nearly drove them mad. Many left the Deeper Woods in time, and some formed Fortuna out of the fog's reach. Those of us that stay here choose it."

Jason broke his silence. "You choose it?"

"Yes, young man. It strengthens one's resolve to live surrounded by darkness without bathing in it. Your guard can never falter, and your trust in God must remain absolute. It's not simple, or altogether pleasant, but it is our village."

A gruff cough broke their conversation. A tall man entered the church and introduced himself as Kydil. The leader let them know that it was their turn for the bath. They said their goodbyes to the priest and followed Kydil out of the rear of the church.

Zelana passed them on the way in. She wore an old white gown and nodded towards them. Jason waved back, but Matthew kept his focus on what awaited outside.

Kydil led them to a small pool of water surrounded by a tall fence. Steam wafted from the open-air bath and brushed against the overhanging branches of the trees. Matthew found himself oddly anticipating it. It wasn't a hot tub, but it would do. The two stripped away their sweat-drenched clothes and climbed inside.

The water soothed his aches. His muscles instantly clenched and released as if a steam valve had been turned in his bones. The steam lifted his cares and allowed him to lay back against the carved edges of the pool as his nerves relaxed. The priest's earlier words still rang through him as he splashed his face. This was no normal water, though it very much looked and otherwise felt like it. The intangible knot in his stomach loosened and he breathed comfortably again. His rage melted into the night.

Jason sat across from him at the other end of the pool. His attention focused on the steeple of the small church.

But Matthew didn't worry about him. It had been too long since he had the opportunity to get clean, and he would enjoy every moment. His throbbing head settled, and he slid into slumber.

"If I killed a villain in Serenity City, what would have happened?"

Matthew jumped and rubbed his eyes awake. He coughed his surprise away. "You would be arrested. You're a hero freak, so you should remember what happened with Achilles. He was a good guy for years and loved by everyone. Then he changed. Now he's in solitary. Big difference between him and you: he lost his mind, and you didn't."

"I know. But it came so easy. If Mom and Dad could see me now, they'd—"

"They'd *what*?"

The boy clammed up. Matthew expected a flash of rage that never arrived. The bath was apparently working. If Jason still didn't trust him after all this, then there was nothing to be done.

"You can keep your secrets. It's hard to give advice if you can't tell me anything."

"That's not it," Jason said with a sigh. "It's hard to explain. Forget about that. Even if we get to the place they're holding Ordopha, how are we supposed to get her out and go through the Mirror Gate at the same time? She'll die on the way through. Will we leave her stranded here?"

"We're just going to have to worry about the bridge when we cross and blow it up behind us. The important part is getting her out."

"She's changed a lot since she left the mountains. So has Alain. Does Intactilis have anything to do with it or is that whole story the Abbot told us a load of manure?"

Matthew chuckled. The boy really didn't have a head for people. "I remember that presence when we escaped on the airship more than any other magic we've faced so far. That was *him*. I know you felt it too. But we know Nieto isn't invincible. Things can change in our favor. Shaula is still the key. If we can crack her, their whole operation gets crippled."

"That's right!" Jason exclaimed. "They were her children, and she just tossed them aside like they were nothing. I bet she doesn't even care that they're dead."

"She left one of them imprisoned in that tree. And, if I remember right, that's the one she's actually proud of."

"Damn witch."

Matthew dropped the subject. Shaula didn't care about anything but the artifacts to help revive her husband. They needed to get off Tyndarus, and stop Shaula. But first came Ord before anything else.

They left the bath and changed into the simple blue tunics and pants left for them. It was hard to not feel refreshed outside of the armor after that long night.

The pair returned to the church where they were directed to a back room behind the altar. There a large table had been set up with six men sitting around it. Zelana sat facing them in a lone chair. Her hair had been done up, and she now wore a fresh blue dress. Jason pulled a chair beside her and Matthew stayed by the doorframe, leaning.

Kydil sat at the head and called for silence to the meeting. The mustached man greeted Castor and Pollux and introduced them to the village council. After quick introductions, they got to business. These elders were gathered together to discuss everything from hunting schedules to managing court hearings and dealt with problems caused by Nieto's magic flooding the woods. The meeting eventually got to discussing Zelana.

"Frankly, this girl is more of a concern for us than you two are. While it is good to see capable young men wielding the legendary Gemini Bracelets, it is not enough to assuage our fears that the blackwood tree is dead after this one walked out of it. What was she doing in it to begin with? The Deeper Woods are filled with enough monstrous creatures to make us think twice about what her appearance portends."

"I told you," Zelana said. "I was put in the tree long ago. I do not know what my purpose was."

One of the older men cleared his throat. "Be that as it may, girl, it does not explain how you are capable of using the Kharis Seed? Most who use relics die to them. What are you, exactly?"

"Calm yourself," Kydil warned. "She is still a child."

Zelana winced at the word. "The Kharis Seed brought me out of the blackwood tree. It infused me with new life. But it wasn't until I left the tree that I learned the truth. You see, the seed transferred knowledge from its previous host into my mind. I live because of Jason."

Despite her impressive story, she still wouldn't look the boy in the eye. She was probably telling most of the truth, at least what she knew. Matthew did believe her. Were he trapped for years and emerged with brand new memories he would express just as much confusion.

"There's more to it than that, isn't there?" Jason said. "When you touched me it recharged Pollux, and there was a flash of strange memories that went through my head—they were things I hadn't thought of in years. I thought I finally recognized that woman, too. Did you do something to me?"

"That was the seed telling me what you needed. But I did not affect your memories." She still refused to look him in the face. "I promise you."

"Then what did you do?"

"I saw *them*."

He laughed to himself. "No, you didn't. That's not possible."

She nodded to herself. "Not here then."

Matthew blinked. Jason's cryptic nature aside, they were getting off track. "Can we get a move on here? We have things to do."

"I agree," Kydil said.

One of the other men broke in. "This still does not explain who you really are, girl."

"That," she said, "is not a question I can answer. You may imprison or cast me out if you wish, but you will not call me a liar. Jason can prove I am not one."

"We'll take responsibility for her," Matthew said. He would not reveal her parentage. It would only cause chaos. "If she causes any problems, it's on us. She won't though because she helped save us. Now I'm sorry to ask you all this favor, but we're going to need you to take her in when we leave. We can't bring a girl to a battlefield."

"I am not a girl!" she shouted with a stomp of her foot. "My age might have slowed while in that tree, but I was as old as Jason when put in there. He knows it's true, too! Do I look like just a girl to you, Jason?"

Jason shook his head, still in thought. "You don't look like a kid to me."

"See?"

Matthew laughed to himself. Kids had a way of getting bothered by the dumbest of things.

"We're not getting anyone else involved in this. I appreciate your enthusiasm, but you have nothing to do with our mission. Jason and I will handle this one alone."

More back and forth occurred, but Matthew would not budge on the issue, and the old men agreed. Jason even piped in to confirm his feelings. Eventually, that was enough to shoot Zelana down and allowed them to move on to other topics like what Castor and Pollux were doing in Tyndarus to begin with. However, Matthew couldn't tell them much.

He still didn't know anything about Castor or Pollux or why the bracelets chose them. The men soon clued him in on more legends. Earthwalkers had never been able to use the bracelets. That would explain why Shaula brought them to Earth. It was as if they were made for human biological systems.

Though Matthew desired to go after Ordopha as soon as possible, he still couldn't quite walk straight. Apparently, according to the villagers, a short rest would finally clear out the remaining effects of fog. He finally assented to taking a small nap before setting out.

Eventually, the meeting ended, and the pair departed the church. Cheers erupted from townspeople loitering about outside. They chanted for Castor and Pollux and patted the two of them on their backs. Questions about their identities and powers washed over the pair.

Their chipper attitude was entirely unlike anything Matthew had encountered in this forest. There was no fog in this village, but the distraction in his head remained. Until his sixth sense stopped spinning in his mind there was little he could do.

Kydil pointed them to the tavern across the way, parting the encroaching group.

The owner of the place allowed the three to stay in two rooms on the second floor. The girl vanished inside the room next to theirs, unwilling to talk. Matthew tried to avoid having any flashbacks to the last time he had been in a place like this and passed into his bed without a second thought. Jason sat on Matthew's bed a little longer, staring out into the night.

They would have to leave this place early in the morning before the sun hit the sky—even though it was rather difficult to see sky in this place—and they would have to make it quick. The two were still on a time limit before Shaula made good on her threat to attack the abbey, and Ordopha remained out there. Any rest he could get would be absolutely necessary to survive.

Before sleep overtook him, he heard Jason lie back in the bed and reform into Matthew's head. The last thing Matthew heard was the boy whispering into his thoughts.

"I'm sorry I got you into this, Matthew."

"Shut up and go to sleep," he mumbled.

"It won't ever happen again."

An edge stuck to that statement, but Matthew didn't have the chance to question it. Slumber smothered him into a deep sleep. A few hours were all he needed. The boy could wait that long.

Jason tried sleeping, but his nerves repeatedly shook him awake. Time passed, and he could only stare at the moonlight's shadow dancing on the wall.

The door knocked, and Jason almost jumped out of his skin. Matthew remained in his unconscious slumber, oblivious. Before he could be awakened, Jason flung himself up and made a line for the door, leaving Matthew slumbering in the room.

"Who is it?" Jason whispered.

"Me," Zelana answered.

Jason flung open the door and followed her out into the hall. Her platinum hair had been ruffled, but she otherwise looked just fine. She must have been having a bad sleep like him.

"Something wrong?" he asked.

"I apologize for almost sharing your secret."

Now she no longer glanced away. Even though the girl blushed like mad, Zelana stared Jason right in the face. Her fierceness reminded him of Alain. Why was everyone here so motivated compared to him?

"So you know," he said. "That's not a big deal."

"But does Matthew know?"

"No."

The girl put her hands on her hips and let a hard breath out through her nostrils. "I do wish I could say I understand what it is like to have gone through what you have, Jason. But Matthew is the first friend you have made since *that* time. You might not like each other, but he has been by your side since you have come here. Why don't you tell him?"

"I didn't think I would have to," he whispered. "But I'll tell him. When we get back. He has enough to worry about right now. Your mother currently has someone important to him, and she's threatening to attack others. His chest is also a literal ticking clock. My problems are nothing compared to that. For now, we have to keep focused."

"My mother," she said, staring at the floor. "I don't remember her, even though I've seen her through your eyes."

"She's not worth thinking about. Just like my past." He'd never even told Shaula about his old life when they met. He was Pollux now, and that made a world of difference. "You can tell that much by what she did to us."

"Well, if you say so," she said with a hint of indignation. "I don't know what to think of her. I was just used to help fertilize that tree. I was of no concern to her."

"You were left there for a reason, and I'd like to know why. After all, you know everything about *me*."

"That is not by my choice. I don't have anyone to return to, or anywhere to go. You are the only one I know anything about which is why I desire to stay with you. Can you not understand that?"

Her voice had heightened and strained with each passing sentence. By the time she finished talking, she had nearly shouted. However long she was in that tree was far too long. Jason put a hand to his lips and another to her shoulder to calm her down.

"I do understand what that's like," he said. "You very well know I do. But you also know why I can't take you with me. You saw Mageuopolis in my head. You saw Shaula hunting us for these bracelets and that seed. You'll be a target if you come with us. You should stay here where it's safe."

"But that's . . ." she trailed off trying to get her bearings straight.

Jason used this pause as a moment to break in. "We don't really know each other yet, but I'd like to get the chance. Once we rescue Ordopha, we'll come back here again, and we can talk. Just give me some time. Please."

He was not just puffing up his chest. There was a place for her in Tyndarus, just as there was a place for him on Earth. He'd wasted so much time hiding from the world and waiting for someone else to save him that he never did anything for himself. Now Pollux was his, and he *could* do anything.

She nodded. "You have to find *them*, don't you? The ones who killed your parents."

He froze. "I do."

"I'm not certain how to access the seed's power fully, but I think I can give you a bit of it for the journey ahead. Can you give me your armor and weapons?"

Jason disappeared into his room. He retrieved the armor, sword and shield sitting by the window and brought them into the hall. They weighed next to nothing with Pollux, so he also brought Matthew's as well. He placed them before Zelana, and she crouched down.

She outstretched both arms and showed her bare hands, revealing a fine purple mist floating from them. She scrunched her fists and groaned, muttering for under her breath. The purple then warped into a dark blue before lightening to a white tint. Zelana presented her palms once more, her lips mashed by her clenched teeth. She shook as the energy flashed in her open fingers.

"It hurts," she said through gritted teeth. "I can purify the magic inside me, but I can't hold it for long. This is all I can do for the two of you."

Zelana placed her hands on each of the chest pieces. Energy flowed off of her fingertips and into the armor, bathing it in a warm white glow. Jason felt the heat from where he stood. The light spread down to the rest of the armor and into the new swords and shields Kydil had given them. Within a minute the glow faded, but the warmth remained. She let out a breath and removed her shaking hands.

"Your armor is infused with my magic. It should protect you as long as the power lasts. I apologize that I could not do the same with your bodies. Magic shouldn't be used on living beings for corruption is always possible—you might not be the same man you were before.

He opened his mouth to reply, to say anything, but the words would not come.

But he didn't have to. The screech of a hawk cut the night air outside the tavern. It started low and slowly rose higher than a harsh whistle. Volcanoes erupted in Jason's skull.

Jason and Zelana fell against the wall, clutching their ears. Inside the room behind them, Matthew swore. He quickly barreled out of the room.

"What's this armor doing here?"

Before he could continue, the sound suddenly cut out. The ringing in Jason's ears ceased.

A voice sliced through the air outside the tavern.

"Castor and Pollux!" Shaula screamed through the night. *"Come out, you cowards!"*

Matthew and Jason ran down the stairs and into the night. Out on the streets, the townspeople milled about, clearly dressed for bed and stunned. But Shaula was nowhere to be seen.

The voice cut in once more and the town fell quiet. They all looked to the sky where the harsh sound blasted in from. She must not have known their location to communicate this way.

"First you spurn my generous invitation. Then you steal our property. Then you take my treasure. Finally, you dare to attack my men and steal my prize! Who do you think you are? I am the Queen of Mageuopolis, wife of Great Sorcerer King Nieto. You are nothing."

Jason's breaths stiffened. She knew they had left the abbey. Should she do anything, they could do little to stop her.

"I not only have the girl, but I have caught more flies in our web. I believe this one is named Alain. The fool stumbled into our hands."

"He went off on his own," Matthew muttered. "The idiot."

"The deal is simple, fools. Bring me both Castor and Pollux and the Kharis Seed, and I will let the prisoners go. Bring them to the tree. You have until sunrise. I will tolerate no more games."

The voice echoed away into the night and died. The peace was short lived. Soon the people began to argue with each other, and the subject of their discussion was obvious.

Kydil and the priest attempted to calm the crowd down.

Jason interrupted their back and forth. "We're leaving, Matthew. Get the armor on."

Matthew looked at him with a flat stare, but he nodded nonetheless. "I wasn't planning on staying." He pointed to Zelana. "But we're not taking her. *She's* staying."

Kydil broke their silence. "You men are leaving alone?"

Matthew answered in the affirmative, and a weight lifted from the crowd. Jason couldn't blame them; these people had no reason to be loyal to the two wanderers. Still, Jason wanted to be very clear on the subject of Zelana.

"I understand," Kydil replied. "We would never willingly deliver a child over to those monsters. We will keep her safe here."

Matthew shook his hand. "I don't doubt it."

These people had done nothing but help. This was not much like the city Jason knew on Earth. He liked Fortuna, and yet they would already have to leave it behind for the wilds. Perhaps this was the way they would have to live their lives from now on. He didn't want to imagine that as their future.

"Thanks for everything," Jason told them. He put his hand out, and Kydil shook it. The boy smiled. "We'll be moving on now."

"Do you not need a guide?"

"No, I've got a dog for that." He pointed his thumb at Matthew.

"What's that mean?" the Castor-user asked.

"You know the way, don't you?"

"I can figure it out, but I'm not a dog. I'm also still not at one hundred percent yet."

"We'll just have to hope for the best. Do you all have any of those masks to spare?"

Jason and Matthew said their goodbyes to the crowd and the few warriors that had helped them to Fortuna in the first place. They went back into the tavern and recollected their armor and weapons. Matthew asked why it all felt so much lighter, but Jason said nothing. He would explain it later.

They were given masks and placed them across their helmets. It was an awkward fit, but it would do for now. It wasn't as if they would keep out the fog forever.

The pair traveled to the fissure in the large stone hole at the edge of Fortuna. Behind them, Zelana waved from the back of the crowd. Pangs of guilt attacked Jason, and his stomach sank. If there was anything he regretted about coming to this world, it was how he found that girl and then stranded her among strangers. She trusted him, and he left her there alone.

Then again, this was all the more reason for him to return here.

The pair disappeared into the crevice. Jason choked his fear down into his gut. They walked the winding path through the rock and into the Deep Woods, back into enemy territory.

But this would be the last time. When he told himself that, the pit in his gut died. This was because he knew that it was true. Whether it killed him or not, he would face Shaula down and end this tonight.

CHAPTER 19
INTO THE TRAP

"YOU FEEL THAT?" Matthew asked the boy. Jason had transferred into his head for easier travel, but it didn't take too long for them to come across trouble. After several hours traveling the forest, their silence had been interrupted. "Listen carefully."

Bodies moved miles away in the brush and only crept closer. He couldn't actually tell if they were Shaula's men or just some other abomination hiding in the night's green mist. At least his sixth sense seemed to be recovering. Steps softly pattered against the grass.

"I don't hear anything. It might be because I'm in here, you know."

"Stay put," Matthew whispered. "We don't want our time limit to run out in a fight, and it is harder for them to sneak up on one of us. Especially me. No offense, but you're the clumsiest person I have ever met."

"Ha ha, you're a real comedian," the boy mocked. He paused as if mulling over his next words. *"Tell me something."*

"If I want to tell you, I will."

"Back at the abbey, why did you just jump over that wall? You could have found me yourself. Did you really think Ord was in that much trouble?"

Matthew had not put one ounce of energy thinking about it. "Just instinct. Why you asking?"

"Because you usually think before you do things."

"We can't all be mopey impulsive teenagers, Jason. Sometimes you have to move whether it makes sense or not."

"I'm not mopey!" the boy argued. Once more he fell silent as Matthew brushed aside a low hanging branch from a sycamore-like tree. *"Am I?"*

"The fact that you have to ask tells me everything."

"We have been through hell, you know. Sure I might have whined . . . once or twice. But I stopped. You could cut me a little slack."

"What did I say before about you not really knowing me? When we get back to Serenity City, I'll teach you something fun, like counting cards."

"Should we really be going back? I know we need to get the bomb out, but after that . . ."

Matthew's spine let out a small tremor. Those footsteps were getting closer.

"We have to go back, Jason. This isn't our world, and as long as we're here those like the people of Fortuna are at risk. It's pretty clear Shaula won't stop until she gets these bracelets, and we aren't going to let her take the stupid things. The only way to do that is to go back to Earth and seal the way between worlds. We can't help these people any other way."

"We could come back and fight."

"At risk to people who have done right by us. You've heard the legends about Nieto. Think about it. Ever since that being came from the sky and did battle with him, his magic waned tremendously. His power no longer extends beyond the mountains, and it shrinks over time.

Leaving is the best way to make sure he can never gain that power again. What's the deal, anyway? I thought you wanted to go back."

Jason didn't answer right away. Matthew had thought of the boy as a bit of a whiner, but he wasn't stupid. He had been tricked by Shaula into the experiment and struggled to make up for his failings since. Staying here in a world of warriors when he was still such an amateur was not good for him. There had to be some family left back home. The boy couldn't stay here.

"I don't want to stick around. But I think we should."

"We can't. I already told you why."

"Why do you even want to go back, Matthew? Forget Castor and Pollux and Ord and Alain for a second, and tell me. Is there even anything left for you?"

He had nothing. That was why he had taken that job at what he thought was Williams' Tech Corp. He needed a fresh start and a reason to get back into the working game shed that loser image and become something better. Never did he think that would lead to this.

Then there was Serenity City itself. He was only a tiny rug rat when Achilles went ballistic and leveled whole blocks, but he had somehow remembered that feeling ever since—that feeling of emptiness adults had when looking at heroes. They were waiting for them to fall. Those fake celebrities didn't help. It was a horrible place, and he only stayed because of the opportunities.

But was that all? He hadn't given it much thought before. There might have been another reason he had stuck around that place despite nothing tying him there. It could have been the hope that things would change, that they would get better, and that someone like Achilles, or Pendragon, or the Banshee, might rise again from the darkness. What would the world be like if there really were heroes worth looking up to? He had never known that world.

And he probably wouldn't.

"I'm going back because I have to. No other reason."

"Suit yourself."

He cocked his head. "Did you hear that?"

The branches above the mist shook as an owl flew by. He couldn't tell if the rest of the trees around them swayed because of the slight wind, passing birds, or something else. The footsteps rumbled closer and closer.

He crouched under a branch, and Jason spoke into his head. "*There's something in the trees.*"

Leaves rustled above. A thin shaft whizzed for his eye. Matthew ducked, and the projectile slammed against the trunk. Salamander lizard men dropped from the trees. The same red species from the attack on the monastery.

"Impressive, Man of Earth. Our Lady will be so delighted to have you with her."

"I thought she wanted us alive," Matthew said. Jason exited his head, ready for a fight.

Now the approaching footsteps rumbled harder and heavier. They would be here in seconds, and there were a lot of them. Matthew kept his sword ready.

"Where are Ordopha and Alain?"

One smirked. "Where is the prize?"

"She isn't coming."

"Our Lady will not like to hear that. Put away your blade. It will do you no good here."

The other lizard man hissed. "We should take them!"

"You are aware they are Castor and Pollux, correct? Whether they have a sword or not makes no difference. They know their struggles are meaningless. Kneel and surrender, dogs."

Matthew really wanted to do otherwise, but even if they killed these enemies, they would have nowhere to go. They would still be stranded. Ordopha and Alain would still be in trouble.

"Put it away, Jason. We don't need to fight here."

Matthew slid his sword back in his scabbard and kneeled on the ground. Jason slowly followed after him as the lizard men cackled. The pounding of steps was closer than ever.

The large group of salamanders jumped out of the brush and seized them, binding their arms and legs. The lizards threw their masks aside and sang a horrendous victory chant that scraped against eardrums. Shaula had finally gotten her prisoners back. As they were carried away, Matthew winked to Jason.

The boy nodded back. He had to know what Matthew had already figured out. These fools would bring them right to Shaula. When they did, this mess would finally be over.

The lizards led them through the green mist and into the rising sun of the morning. Matthew hoped this wouldn't be the last sunrise he ever saw.

CHAPTER 20
STONE MOUNTAIN CASTLE

THEIR ENEMIES TOOK the Gemini Men deeper into the forest. They eventually poured out into a wide open field before what looked like a mountain. The giant fortress had been carved into the large stone base of a crater. Rocks led up through the wall of green fog making Jason think they were near the mountain range they had first escaped from. The bad vibes he received from this place made him doubly sure of his belief.

The carved in fortress wasn't as big as the castle in Mageuopolis, but retained all the menace. The place stretched as tall as a twenty story building with spiraling pillars and a large barbican before the gate to keep out any intruders. Bartizan turrets spied down, ready for any incoming threat. Circling crows cawed over the fogged fortress.

The group guided them inside the front gate where the cavernous hall crumpled down into thin stone paths. The clearly carved tunnels descended into the dark. Small grooves on the sides led out into nests where lizards slept and patrolled. Most here were red—the Salamanders.

But the lizards dragged them deeper. Heat built up the further they went. The very air rippled as they exited into an open cavern with a hard drop below into a good hundred feet into magma. The harsh orange light nearly blinded Jason. Only the large platforms bridged with thin walkways held up by columns prevented them from falling to a scalding death. Sweat poured down Jason's neck as he passed through yet more tunnels.

Then the path opened up into the largest cavernous area yet which went on two hundred feet in every direction. Even more death drops and suspended platforms awaited them. In the center was an over-sized circus cage suspended over the open lava via a pulley system. The ropes led down to a crank on the rock edge. Shaula, queen of Mageuopolis, and yet more salamanders crowded the ropes. Inside the floating prison, Jason and Matthew finally found Ordopha and Alain.

The queen nodded, and the Salamanders shoved Jason and Matthew forward. Shaula wore a long red dress that hugged her hips and breasts, showing off her busty and well-toned figure. Her piled up platinum hair gleamed harshly against the orange light. The only thing that burned brighter was the snarl on her lips. Her long nails pressed into her thin arms.

"Where is my prize?" she asked the salamanders.

They cringed and slunk at her tone. Instantly, she turned on Jason.

"You will tell me where she is."

He growled back. "You aren't getting anything out of me, *Marguerite*."

"This is how you reward saving you from poverty and giving you power? I give you purpose, and you do this to me. It already took much too long for my injuries to heal after our last encounter. Magic takes time and energy, you know, and my time is valuable. Horrible boy."

"You lied to me. All you've done since we met is lie. I didn't ask for any of this, and I'm going to be damned if I let you do it to anyone else. Let them down."

Jason eyeballed the cage shifting in the heavy heat. Fifty or so feet spread the distance between the steel trap and him. He wouldn't be able to make it before the pulley turned.

Shaula laughed without merriment. "I did not touch them. I made a promise, Jason. I understand Mr. White being a pain in my side, but not you."

"Stop calling me *Mr. White*. I'm not going to say it again. We're not giving you an innocent girl to prey on, witch. We've seen what you do to those you *want*."

"She is above even you, *Matthew*." She sneered at him, her white teeth bared. "You had no right to remove her, just as you had no right to take my Kharis Seed. Do you know how long I searched for it?"

"Me, me, me," Jason interrupted. "Everything is about you, isn't it? Aside from the seed, don't you care about your men?"

Shaula furrowed a brow and glanced to the crowd of salamanders. "The lizards?"

Now it was Jason who was losing his patience. "No, not them. The Cutter and Rantan. Your children. Don't you remember them?"

Slowly her eyes widened and her mouth opened in realization. Then a laugh broke her confusion. "Of course I don't worry about them. You should worry more about Camille."

Shaula whistled, and the mountain trembled. Giant shapes formed from the earth. Large stone gargoyles tore their way up from the rock bed, letting loose stone fall from them like a rain shower. The gargoyles grew at least thirty feet tall and morphed to the vague shape of Rantan and the Cutter. The salamanders joined the monstrosities, trapping Jason and Matthew between them and Shaula.

"Thank you, my dear," she called out to the invisible Camille. "Such a good girl."

"You really are scum," Matthew said.

Jason concurred. "I can't believe I ever trusted you. What are you even doing all this for? Fun?"

"Fun? I would never do anything for such a base reason. And before you ask, no it is not because of the King. My husband asks this, yes, but I do it because it needs to be done. This is required for both Earthwalkers and humans. You have seen this world, divided by a false god that gave us a taste of freedom. They rejected the Great Sorcerer King after he gave them life, and for what? They are fragmented and frightened, hiding in their little kingdoms and villages from the overwhelming world. They are just like those on Earth."

Matthew groaned. "And now you're babbling."

"No, Matthew, you are simply stupid. You live where heroes roam and yet you hide in fear. That is why you both came to me, remember? You realized what Our King already knows. The false heroes of your world failed time and time again to change anything, and now you see the world for what it is. You know there are no heroes left. They are only mortal. They cannot save you from the sword hanging above your head. But I can."

"Wrong again," Matthew answered. "These bracelets saved us. If it weren't for them, I would have been another failed experiment like every other one of your castoffs. And thank God for that! I only made it this far because of Castor, this idiot, and the two people behind you. All you have done, Shaula, is destroy."

"And all you have done is disappoint me. Fine. You can have it your way." She snapped her fingers. "Kill them."

Matthew pointed his blade to her. "Why don't you do it?"

"Because I do not wish to damage my precious bracelets." She paused and cocked her head to the side as if hearing a distant call. "But perhaps we will meet again sooner than I first thought. I'll set your room up just how you like it, should you make it back."

Shaula strode along the stalactite bridge towards the rear tunnel. Jason contemplated making a run for her but thought better of it. She expected it. She had to. Behind him, her lackeys advanced on them. Now he had to choose one of three paths: go for the siblings, go for Shaula, or go for her men. One had to have priority. As if sensing his thoughts, Shaula lifted a hand of purple mist and snapped her fingers once more. A floating line of magic zipped toward the pulley and poured inside. The device strained and squeaked.

"That bitch," Matthew muttered.

"Forget her and come here."

Matthew took one look at Jason and told him his choice. They were going for the cage.

Jason lifted Matthew with one arm, Pollux holding steady, and threw him toward the squeaking cage. He had learned from his last try. The boy parceled Pollux out just enough: not too much strength, but enough to adjust to Matthew's weight. At least, he hoped.

Rocks broke behind Jason. He went for his scabbard and shield.

The lizards dove upon him. Swords, spears, and axes flashed, and he slashed his weapon in defense, clanking against blades. The cavalcade of lizard men quickly encircled him. The two gargoyle golems stomped toward him, shaking the entire world with each step.

The floor shifted and slanted. Several of the lizard men tripped as the ground slid to the right and sank like a sand pit. The funnel pulled hard at the men on the battlefield.

Jason scanned for the source and found it in the tunnel forty feet ahead. He squinted and saw the figure of a woman embedded in the same stone pathway Shaula escaped through. The earth trembled around her indentation.

Around him, the enemies still slunk towards him even as they slid backwards into the center of the pit. They wanted him dead more than they wanted to live. Then he remembered that they were stone monsters and fire lizards. A fall into the trap might not hurt them even though it would kill him. Still, the floor slowly sank like sand as they pressed him.

"Hurry up, Matthew," he whispered.

Soon enough there wouldn't be any place to escape to.

MATTHEW KNEW Jason would throw him before the dumb kid did it. He couldn't help being predictable. But Matthew welcomed it. They needed to get Ordopha and Alain out before the cage fell into the lava. This was the fastest way.

He made a beeline directly for the cage at what felt like the speed of a Mack truck. The bars whipped close as the humid air pushed against him. His face brushed against the steel.

Matthew morphed into fog and whipped through the bars. Both Ordopha and Alain moved to the sides as the mist darted past. He solidified and slammed face first into the bars at the rear end. The cage rocked back and forth, and the chains squeaked and creaked. The three stumbled as the floating prison bobbed.

Alain clapped his back. "As crazed as ever, Matthew."

"You'd know. How you doing, Ord?"

Her trembling lips curved into a grin. "Well."

"Sounds good to me. You two, grab on," Jason said. "We're gonna do this like the airship."

Ordopha outstretched her hand just as the chain above whined, and broke. Matthew darted for her, with Alain at his side and they both clasped her wrists. The ceiling of the cage hit Matthew, and he turned to mist, taking the two with him. The bars of the falling prison battered his incorporeal form. Hot pain spread inside him into particles of dust.

Slowly, his molecules reformed into the ethereal mist again. Red aches stabbed his senses. Whether air or liquid form, disturbances could break him apart and changing his basic structure caused tremendous discomfort. Using Castor to its full extent still stayed outside of his grasp, but one thing he could still do was hold together. Keeping three different bodies inside his transformation took concentration. Tears raked across the inside of his soul threatening to split him to pieces.

The steel trap spun all the way down into the magma below. He drifted forward, battered about by the humidity and hot air. There was still a twenty-foot drop to get back to the ground.

"Matthew, you fool," Alain yelled in his mind. *"We are falling. Transform back!"*

"I can't do that."

Ordopha whispered from inside him. *"Yes, you can. It is right there. We can touch it."*

His sight through the mist returned as he focused, and he saw what she meant. The broken chain for the cage hung above him, swinging back and forth. He reached for it.

"When we reform we'll be in the same position we went in on. Hold on to me."

Matthew transformed to normal again and found himself falling. He reached out and took hold of the chain with his free hand, and weight pulled against his muscles. Underneath, Alain and Ordopha let go of him and also grabbed the chain. Matthew's concentration and breath returned.

"So," he said to the woman below him. "Still doing well?"

"I cannot say that I am." Her breaths were rushing hard. "Now what do we do? We're trapped."

"No, we're good." Matthew's second wind returned. "We just climb back up and over down the chain. The pulley's holding out."

"You are endlessly positive," she said. "It is nearly endearing."

"Nearly?"

"Yes, every time I am with you our lives are in constant peril."

"Come on," he said with a laugh. "You love it."

She giggled. "I cannot say it is altogether unpleasant."

"Will you two shut up?" Alain asked. "You may reconvene your idle chatter when we're not suspended above certain death. Can you move yet, Matthew?"

"I sure can spoil sport." He took a breath and began climbing upwards. The other two followed. "We'll talk later, Ord, when your brother isn't in such a prickly mood."

"But then we will never speak again."

Alain sighed. "Very amusing."

The entire cavern shook. On the platform below Jason fought the oncoming swarm. The platform sank in the center.

Off to the right that woman, Camille, hid herself inside an entrance with her hands buried into the cavern. She was destroying the platform with her power, and none of her cronies care.

He helped the siblings down onto the stone floor and removed his sword. Alain came to his side.

"I'm going after the witch," Matthew said. "Can you help the boy out?"

Alain held a wolfish grin. He found an abandoned blade among the lizard corpses. "You don't have to ask me. I was not planning on leaving yet."

"I'll go with you," Ordopha said to Matthew.

"We won't be gone for long."

Matthew sprinted down the thin pathway to the left as Alain drove toward Jason. The platform slowly sank behind them. The woman in the stone ahead leaped out into the tunnel as Matthew and Ordopha got closer. She raised one palm towards them. Large stone projectiles broke free from the surrounding floor and soared forward. The size of beach balls, the slabs also flew like baseballs.

He slashed the first one out of the air and misted through the second which flew off into the lava. But the third made a beeline for Ordopha.

Matthew dove and seized her by the waist, knocking her to the ground. The stone flew directly overhead. Matthew straddled her with his arms and legs on either side.

"You alright?" he asked.

"Above you!"

Three stone balls merged into one and careened downward like a guillotine.

After a solid deep breath, he took her shoulders. "Are you ready for this?"

She nodded. "Always."

The large boulder slammed into the earth and sent shattered stone firing out in every direction. Thankfully he had turned to mist once more, but the aches flowed through him regardless as he floated out of the way of the rubble. He transformed solid again, wincing at the remaining pain. She stared at him as if nothing happened.

Camille ran away and disappeared into the tunnel. He helped Ordopha up and followed after her.

For a moment, the platform behind them stopped sinking.

The stone walls bent and jumped out around them as they followed. Camille could have sealed the paths off, but she needed concentration to do it. With enemies in pursuit, there was little chance she would risk it. The two had the edge on her.

"We got her on the ropes," he said under his breath.

"Unless she is leading us somewhere."

"Maybe she's leading us where we need to go."

"I wouldn't trust a snake like her. Stop! Let me look in here."

Ordopha broke off into a nearby carved room where weapon racks lay on the wall. Swords, shields, and spears propped up next to arrows and bows. Quite the arsenal had been set up. She took a bow and a quiver full of arrows from among them.

She nodded approvingly as she inspected the bowstring. "Now I no longer feel quite so naked."

"And that's why I like you so much."

She laughed. "I will miss this."

Shortly, they continued on. Camille, and Shaula by extension had to be close by. Hopefully, Jason and Alain could hold their own until they made it to the witch.

CHAPTER 21
EDGING TOWARD CAVERN'S END

THE GOLEM'S large fingers slammed against Jason's shoulder and sent him spinning. The massive trunk of an arm swung sideways and successfully swept several salamanders from their feet and down into the magma below. The golem brought its arm back for a second hit. Jason's shield rang, and his knees shook.

A spear thrust in on his left. He brought the shield up to deflect it, and another stab came from his right. His blade blocked the point of the spear and guided it to the side. A lizardman sprinted to his unguarded front during the madness. He kicked out with a Pollux powered leg. The hit sent the salamander soaring into one of the golems, crunching rock and lizard. Jason rolled backward.

His sword clashed against armor, blade, and shield. Every attack he made spun like a whirlwind. Jason's shield guarded and pushed potential blows away. His reflexes had never had quite this much of a workout. He silently thanked Alain and Sir Orach for teaching him pacing. Despite it all he kept measured breaths.

Slashes nicked his armor and shield. The metal slowly reformed as if it were hard plastic springing back to its original shape. Zelana's gift to him held out. He could last forever at the rate her magic covered him.

The golems leaped over the crowd toward him. He braced Pollux and his shield. Then, just as they were about to land, the monsters broke. A rain of boulders poured down on him, pelting and crushing lizards. Before he could tell if that was the monsters' intention, he also realized the floor was no longer sinking.

The lot of surviving lizards let out guttural howls and rushed him. He could not tell if it was due to fear or stupidity, but this desperation struck him as odd. He met them in the shifting sands of the platform.

But a cry cut through.

The lizard to his left fell dead to the dirt. Two more beside it spun around and lost a head and right arm. The rest of the pack backed away at Alain holding a bloodstained blade.

Jason smiled, unable to hide his excitement. "I could really use a hand."

"Of course you could," he replied with a grin. "I have seen you swing a sword before."

Alain took to his side, and the formation of the enemy momentarily faltered. But they quickly regained their courage and hissed out a battle cry.

Metal collided against metal, and skin slashed open. Alain laughed like a madman. Jason darted his blade from enemy to enemy. The sealed exit where they had first entered quaked. Rocks along the red walls broke and dislodged. Stone split and burst open like a dam, revealing two dozen men in armor and masks led by Zelana. She had her arms held out where the wall had just crumbled.

Without a wasted second, the men from Fortuna all shouted and charged with their weapons out, and poured down into the open cavern onto the lizards.

"Now this is what I live for!" Alain roared. "Show some fire, Jason!"

For once, Jason understood Alain completely. The two fought their way into the thick of it as the salamanders shrieked and shouted a tsunami of battle-cries against them. Blood and steel flew all over. His adrenaline only climbed as the skirmish raged on.

Still he could not help but think about his other friends. Where were Ord and Matthew?

"DID YOU HEAR THAT?" Ordopha asked with her bow raised. "Shouts."

Matthew nodded but did not stop moving. That woman had to be nearby, but she had not used her power once since the two of them had followed after her. Either she didn't know they were behind her, or she led them into a trap. But the two of them couldn't stop.

Salamanders crawled about the tunnels. The narrow space made dodging difficult for the larger groups which made them easy targets for Ordopha's arrows and his sword. Corpses fell as they ran past.

Finally, they reached a throne room. There he saw a towering regal chair of polished oak and flowing weaved red tapestries. A large mirror lined the rear wall. He recognized that glint shining from the last one. Despite the gold and gems adorning the room in tapestries of colors and crimson beauty, that mirror drew him in. The Mirror Gate. This was their ticket back to Serenity City. Shaula must have gone through there, but what about Camille?

Ordopha checked the corners of the room and found no one. Camille had vanished. Before he could make a guess, the ceiling above him creaked.

By instinct, he tackled Ordopha to the ground. Her bow twanged as she dropped before him. The cavern shook, and a large boulder struck the floor where he had stood seconds ago.

"Look!" Ordopha yelled. She pointed to a spot in the wall where her arrow lodged in. Blood streaked from it. "The stone was moving so I fired. Rock doesn't bleed."

The two approached the thin stream of blood. The rocks crumbled out to reveal the body of a young woman with an arrow in her chest. Camille fell listlessly to the floor, groaning.

Ordopha raised her bow to finish her when Matthew brought a hand up.

"We should end her now," Ord argued.

"Answers first. She apparently needs to touch the earth with her skin to move it, so cover her hands and get her up."

The pair removed a blood red tapestry and wrapped Camille in it. When she was held tight, he let Ord do her work. She slapped the unconscious girl.

"Wake up, witch."

"What are you doing to me?" Camille mumbled. Her eyes opened after a few seconds. She thrashed and bit at the air.

"Asking some questions," Matthew replied. "Where did Shaula go?"

"I have no cause to tell you, especially after what you did to my brothers. I will return that tenfold!"

"Do you think I wanted to fight them, Camille? It was either them or me. You made your choice working for a woman who doesn't care if you live or die."

"It is because of her that we not only have life but these powers at all, imbecile. We wouldn't exist without the queen. But I suppose you know little of loyalty."

"You got me there. I don't know much about being loyal. But I also don't steal young girls to siphon life force from them. I don't sacrifice people to test my magical bracelets. I don't imprison innocents to provide entertainment for my slave soldiers. But I know who does. All you have to do is tell us how to get through that mirror, and I can show you."

"Only those with the blood of the King may open it. And you are no royalty."

"No," Zelana said. "But I may be able to help."

Jason and Alain, as well as the men from the village, including Kydil, ran through the hall behind them. Zelana led the pack to Matthew and Ord. She rushed to the Mirror Gate as greetings were exchanged.

"What does she mean?" Ordopha asked Alain.

He gestured to Matthew. "She was able to lead Kydil's men here because of the magic she planted in their armor. Her awakened abilities are tied to magic."

"*You*," Camille simply stated.

Several of the men seized the fallen villain and placed her on her feet between two of them.

"She's bleeding," Jason said. He meant Zelana. A thin stream of blood dripped from her lips. "We can't ask her to do any more than this, Matthew."

"Any more than what?" Ordopha asked. "Don't talk around me."

Zelana let out a cry as she slammed her palms on the tall mirror. Clear white energy flowed like steam from her into the gate, rushing like a small typhoon. The large mirror flashed gold.

"Impossible," Camille whispered.

"Time to go," Matthew said. Jason didn't argue. The crowd watched the mirror before noticing the pair moving toward it. "It's been fun, everyone, but we have a witch to stop."

Alain threw out his hand and gave both warriors a shake. "I only regret that we never had a proper duel. Keep practicing, Matthew. Don't become sloppy. Pay attention to your surroundings. Jason, simply stop being a fool."

"Thanks, man," Jason replied, oddly serious. "You too, Ord."

Ordopha embraced the boy in a hug. He squeezed back. "Alain is right. You have Pollux now, and Matthew. You can trust them both."

Jason blushed and slowly nodded back. He left them for the mirror by Zelana.

"Matthew," Ordopha said. "Thank you."

He rubbed the back of his neck. "Please don't do that. I'm not good at this sort of thing."

"Fine, you don't have to say it. Not now. How about when next we meet, then?"

Matthew laughed. "Something to look forward to."

She giggled back. "Precisely!"

"I will be glad to be rid of all this foolishness," Alain grumbled.

Matthew joined Jason by the Mirror Gate. The flashing lights and swirling dots like dust mites inside nearly hypnotized him. Before he could say anything to the boy, Zelana squeezed Matthew in a hug. The move threw him off balance, and he stiffly patted her shoulder back. Finally, she gave him a wide smile. Jason laughed.

"Jason told me you like hugs."

"Jason is a liar." Before she could react, he added, "But they're not always so bad."

"Alain told me he was given a small piece of a mirror from that hermit," she said. "I inspected it, and I feel faint traces of magic in it. The shard doesn't work, not now, but perhaps we can use it to see through the other side to your world."

"I wouldn't put much stock into it. The corresponding mirror was probably destroyed long ago."

"Perhaps," she said with an upturned grin. "But it does not hurt to hope."

Matthew laughed to himself. Maybe it didn't. She bowed to the two of them.

"Goodbye, Matthew."

"See you next time, Zelana."

Matthew looked back one last time and saw a strange sight. Camille split open the tapestry, covered in a thin layer of earth. The guards saw her a second too late. She tackled Matthew and Jason, knocking them backwards into the Mirror Gate.

Jason was thrown further into the funnel as the villain stuck to Matthew.

Camille screamed as she flew through space grappling against Matthew. The wielder of Castor drew his sword, but she was too close. Camille shaped her thin layer of earth into hard rocks on her knuckles and slammed it into his face. Before he could regain his senses, she struck again and again. They pushed against each other in the drifting void.

"What are you doing?" he shouted.

"I'm stopping you! This is the least I can do for my queen and my brothers."

"The least you can do is to get lost." They spun out of control through the tunnel. He had to get her off before he rammed the sides at the edge of this funnel of light. He figured out one way to do it.

Matthew transformed into mist and let her fly forward through him. There was no way for her momentum to stop now. He flew back towards Jason, but even in his mist form, the force of the tunnel pulled against him. The invisible wind sucked him forward once more once he reached the center again.

But Camille wasn't so lucky. The momentum from Matthew's move sent her into the side of the black tunnel where the light died. The spinning darkness reminded of the sides of a tornado. Her shrieks instantly silenced as she was ripped through it and she vanished from sight.

The two remaining figures soared onward at faster and faster velocities. Just as before their clothes sizzled and Matthew's skin burned.

But their armor shined regardless. Jason even pumped his fist and laughed. "We'll be okay!"

"What were you talking to Zelana about, anyway?"

"Just saying I was sorry I couldn't keep my promise."

"We owe her a lot more than we can pay back."

Zelana's magic held out. They would make it after all. The light ahead grew from a pinprick as they were launched onward into a veritable sun.

The force shoved both warriors outside the gate and into the light. The brightness momentarily disoriented Matthew as he stood back up. Behind him, the shine of the Mirror Gate died out. That was fine as they would not be using it again. The pair were back in Serenity City.

However, his mood soon changed when Matthew realized just where they were. They landed in a large dark room with fluorescent lights hanging overhead. Men in black suits lined the metal room before them. They had returned to Serenity City, alright—in the William's Tech building. Shaula headed the men, wearing another fancy red dress. A familiar smile glistened on her lips as she grinned at their appearance. It was almost as if they had never left the building to begin with. Her men blocked the door.

"Shaula," Matthew said. "It's like we never left."

"You may call me Marguerite here, Mr. White. But I am confused. You still wear your armor?" she asked with a raised brow. "How is this possible?"

Matthew and Jason drew their blades from their scabbards, and the men in suits raised their firearms. Shaula's uncovered arms sprouted flames that waved around like loose fur on a beast. The lights above her flickered violently.

"I'll show you what's possible," Jason mumbled.

The pair charged forward and shots fired upon them. The heat from the woman's blaze rose as they closed the gap. Matthew charged regardless. He thought briefly about the bomb in his chest but put it to the back of his mind immediately. First, Shaula had to be stopped.

CHAPTER 22
SERENITY

BULLETS SLAMMED against Jason's armor. Beside him, the shots tumbled off of Matthew just as easily as they did him. Zelana's magic clung to their armor, swallowing the speed of all the coming projectiles milliseconds before they hit their mark. But the magic could not protect them forever.

There were also no bones on the floor, and the other mirrors were nowhere to be seen. This Mirror Gate had clearly been moved to another room. Shaula—or Marguerite—had set them up to be trapped.

"I'll get out of here and find the controls for the bomb," Matthew said to him. "While they're distracted with me, you break this mirror. I'll see if I can find the other ones outside."

Jason had nearly forgotten they needed to destroy the other Mirror Gates. While he slashed at the men in suits, Matthew transformed and flew toward the crowd. They continued firing on him, hitting nothing but air. Jason used the moment to turn around and punch the mirror. Pollux gave him that extra kick he needed.

The glass webbed with the strike and shattered a second later. Pieces sprinkled to the metal floor.

On the other side of the crowd, Matthew's mist slammed against the sealed metal door and pushed through the cracks into the other side. Several of Shaula's thugs opened the door, followed him outside and down the hall. The majority trained their firearms on Jason.

Shaula screamed at her men to chase Matthew. They complied, bolting back out into the hall with the others. She gathered a handful of fire in her palm and threw it toward the boy.

Jason dodged, and the flames slammed against the wall where the gate had been. Shards of the metal melted into an orange slag puddle on the floor. A cavalcade of red streaks flashed toward his chest. Three of the balls struck him dead on. The fire's hiss burst like a grenade and threw out heavy pressure, flinging him backwards. He regained his footing, his armor smoking.

Sweat dripped down Shaula's face as she flung fire. He began to understand her pattern. Her power turned on and off like a light switch. She couldn't avoid destroying everything.

"Do I amuse you, Jason? Whatever your armor is made of, it will not protect you forever."

"It was a gift from your daughter. You threw her away, and she gave me the key to beat you. What do you think of that?"

"I knew she would open the gate for you. I sensed her coming in the caves. However, your armor and weapons remaining unharmed? That was unexpected."

"You had more than one. Camille, the Cutter, and Rantan were real pieces of work."

"Those failures?" She snarled. Her disgust was palpable. "They are excellent soldiers, yes. But they inherited nothing of the blood. I respect their allegiance, but they are nothing compared to Zelana. She is the future of the kingdom, and what my love has lived so long for."

He smirked at her. "And we took her from you, huh?"

"She was our prize, all that we worked so hard for. The king and I have had many failures over the centuries, but none were more than mortals no different than those you helped escape. They inherited nothing. She was different—she had the magic burned into her bones. All I needed was the Kharis Seed to complete her growth. But we could never find it . . . until you came along."

"It's gone, Shaula. Your daughter is free from you now. All that's left is to put you away, and your husband will rot away to nothing."

Fire flashed around her skin and against her clothes. The fiery red marker on her forehead grew as she furrowed her brow. Heat hammered against him like a charging bull.

Pyrokinetic abilities could be used several ways. But her Prime power in addition to the magic Nieto imbued in her with made it worse. Her magic allowed the fire to spread further and faster than normal pyrokinetics.

She lifted both hands perpendicular to her shoulders and bit her lip. Flames completely engulfed her, swirling out in a twister. And they were growing by the second. The metal floor, ceiling, and walls, melted as the heat intensity pressed against Jason. The blaze crept closer.

He scanned the room for ideas. Holes were melting open in the metal wall behind him. Jason decided to make a play for it.

The boy beat against the melting metal as the heat built on his back, but he paid it little mind. The steel bent and crunched with every punch. No matter how many times he hit, it didn't look like he would reach the other side. Sweat poured down his neck while he burrowed further into the metal hole.

Sizzled steel burned as he pressed on. He grimaced and pushed his muscles and the bracelet to give their all. Pollux let out its full energy, and he crashed his fist forward.

An explosion of metal shards erupted. Thick darkness awaited him ahead, and he dashed for it. Jason leaped and fell flat down, clanging on steel. Orange light flashed through the hole. Fire lit the darkness and showed him the door ahead. He charged through the new steel room. Slag melted around him. He kicked open the heavy door to reveal a long steel hall with dim fluorescents. Some of them flickered, but most lighting remained normal. Thankfully none had burst yet. The last thing he wanted was mercury filling the air. Unfortunately he saw no windows so he could not even tell what floor they were on. The metal melted around the hole behind him. She was coming.

Jason made a sharp right down the hall, his footsteps clanging with each press. Now to find Matthew.

CASTOR WAS FAR TRICKIER to use than Pollux. Matthew didn't exactly know how to use his powers while fighting. Of course, he could just disappear in a battle. That was always an option. However, he didn't like to make that choice.

Even if his body did harden for a few seconds after he solidified again, there were a few things he didn't want to risk. His insides could be pierced by whatever passed through him at the same moment he transformed back. While his skin became tougher for those few moments, he didn't know if the same applied to his organs, bones, veins, muscles, or brain. A single stray slice, gunshot, or poorly timed solidification could end him. He decided to stay a human for now.

He ran from the men in black suits chasing him through the halls. There were at least ten lizardmen in disguise among them. The flashing alarm pulsing red in the corners of the steel ceiling meant more were on the way. He could lose more than a few by zipping in and out of the labyrinth of halls ahead. Matthew had the energy to spare.

His sixth sense was all that lead him on. The more he turned down the halls, the more he recognized the layout. He reached that false apartment complex he had lived in before this whole mess began. They had originally taken an elevator to reach this floor. He now gathered an inkling of their location. They had to be very high up. But what mattered was that the mirror room had to be close by.

Matthew made a sharp turn around one of the corners and transformed into water. He slid under the door to his left and into the office. The empty meeting room only contained one lone wooden table in the center and some potted plants around the perimeter. Six guards stomped down the hall past him and toward the next room. Matthew slid behind the pot. One of his pursuers threw open the door and scanned the room. After one second he left. Matthew streaked back out into the hallway and became whole. He continued in his original direction.

He traveled down a few hallways to meet a familiar metal door. Bones lay on the floor inside, and that musty stink reminded him of their last visit here. The remaining Mirror Gates plastered against the walls sparkled against the dark of the room.

A spark glittered on one of the broken shards lying in the corner. His sixth sense pulled him towards one piece in particular. A low heat warmed him as he picked it up. He pocketed the scrap behind his back before bringing his attention back to the three remaining Mirror Gates.

Now the question about breaking these things arose. Matthew's strength was nowhere near Jason's with Pollux. But he did have one advantage—the magic Zelana put not only into his armor but his shield and his sword.

The three tall mirrors perched precariously on each wall watched him. Despite the lack of light in the room, speckles of some other starlight millions of miles away reflected in their glass. A distinctly alien vibe stuck to them.

As he thought about what distant world these unholy objects came from, the blade in his hand grew hot. A faint white glow rang against the edges. It wanted him to act.

Before Matthew could make a decision, the rough sound of a bursting bonfire blasted down the hall and shouts followed. The cold voices of the disguised lizardmen remained harsh even in death. Thankfully he didn't hear Jason among their symphonic screams.

Not yet.

Matthew slashed his sword against the mirror with as much strength as he could muster.

JASON TOOK a turn down the hall too fast and skidded over onto his side around the corner. A gust of fire flew over his head and scorched the potted plant where he had just been standing. The melted slag pooled while he regained his footing. Shaula had already found him.

Around that corner she flew, her pyrokinetic abilities sending fire downward from her dress and legs in streams. Fluorescents cracked above her. She threw a football-sized blaze at him.

He brought his shield up to guard. The power shot pounded against it. The force pushed him backwards to the metal floor. He tumbled, and his back hit the wall, stunning him. But there was a worse problem: the glow in his shield faded to nothing. After a few seconds, it warped and bent under the heat. The magic was dying.

"That explains how you are so strong. My daughter's magic aided you. It has already begun to leave you."

"Zelana saps her life every time she uses magic. She's done enough. I'm not going to let you kill her any more than you already have!"

The fireball whipped across Jason's face, singing his helmet. The wall behind him erupted in flames.

More fire exploded from her skin. "Why do you all insist on foolish posturing? My beloved does not have all the time in the universe to achieve his unified kingdom. You are all parasites."

"That's a funny way of looking at things."

"I'm glad you think so. Now give me Pollux before I take it from your charred remains."

As she lifted her hand and the flames smoldered, Jason turned to the wall behind him. The fire swirled towards him, licking against the sides of the narrow hall. He punctured a hole through the metal layer. The heat brushed up against his armor and agony melted into him. Jason burrowed into the room through the new opening, armor smoking. Flames scorched out the hall. The blaze still burned while he ran through the empty room. He smashed open a hole into the next one. Soon enough he landed back in the hallway.

Before she could notice, he moved. Jason dashed down the complex and circled around the block to Shaula's back. He watched her from a distance as her wall of flames died.

"It is a shame that I must kill you, Jason. Pollux is quite useful, and I wish I didn't have to find another to use it."

"It's not just Pollux," Matthew whispered.

Jason flinched when he noticed Matthew at his side. The bearer of Castor held a small piece of mirror wrapped in cloth. He handed it to the boy.

"Keep this safe. I think there's something about this particular piece. It had a weird tint to it."

Jason placed the shard behind his back and his armor. "You destroyed the Mirror Gates?"

"They're gone. The stairs are all blocked, though. Guards are in all the staircases, and the elevators are down. I found the apartment we were kept in when I was looking for the mirror. If I recall, it was high up in this building. In other words, we can't just jump out the window and hope for the best. If we want out, we have to get through the witch. There's no other way."

"I can't get close enough to hit her. Zelana's magic is wearing off. We're only going to get one more shot at her before she can scorch us away. We need a plan."

Matthew scratched his chin in thought. "There's one thing I can try. I can't promise it will work, but it's all I've got. If you distract her, I'll get behind her in puddle form, then I'll—"

"You'll get her in the back!" Jason glanced around the corner. The woman waited in the hall, perfectly aware that they had nowhere to run. They would have to face her again to escape. "If that fails I'll hit her with everything Pollux has. Either way, I'm dead getting in that close."

"No, you're not. But we don't have that much time if we want to do this before the magic is gone for good. I'm heading in."

"Wait, what about the bomb? Did you find a way to stop it?"

His grin faltered for a moment. "Long story. I checked around. I can't disarm it, but I can use it."

"I don't understand. What are you going to do?"

"Stay safe, Jason. Use Pollux to find an escape."

Matthew melted into the floor and zipped back around the hallway that Jason had come from earlier. He quickly slid out of sight.

Jason took a deep breath and moved out. The boy turned the corner in time to see Shaula raising each of her hands in a different direction. Orange light flashed, and pyrokinetic streams flowed in flamethrower waves along the halls. He slid on his knees, and the fire flew over his helmet, sizzling the metal.

But the rooms on the floor suffered. Hot orange puddles of slag filled the space where the metal walls had been. Rooms melted to nothing. The wide open area trembled and groaned under the heavy weight of the weakened ceiling.

One stream of fire crashed against his sword, his last guard. Sweat splashed his skin. His last weapon had been destroyed.

The armor warped and the fire beat against him. His consciousness faded. Just before the air left him, a flash snapped out behind Shaula.

Matthew sprang up and rammed his sword into her back. The blade stuck out through her chest. She howled as flames gushed from the wound, knocking Matthew down and backwards. His blade melted away into the pyre.

Shaula turned toward Matthew, her injury instantly cauterized. Their plan had failed.

What Jason did next was not what he expected to do—he ran towards her.

The witch breathed hard, purple fog slowly drifting from her mouth. Perhaps her internal injuries ran deeper than the boy thought. He could not let her have the opportunity to slink away.

Jason brought his fist back when he reached her. She turned back on him with her raised hand, ablaze . . . and in his face! The fire flickered as she grinned. Jason was dead.

Matthew leaped upon her back, throwing her shot off its mark. Jason skidded to stop under a pyro blast. The flame shot lashed into trembling ceiling, shattering whatever fluorescents might be left. Puddles of metal splashed out from her shots. Matthew's armor smoked, and the shield on his back dripped to useless soup on the floor. He yelled in pain while he held her tight.

"Matthew!" Jason shouted. "What are you doing?"

"My trump card. Use Pollux and go down! At least one of us should get out."

Jason shouted back, but it was no use. Matthew misted and the air changed around Shaula. His typical white mist form started to morph. The air became wavy and started to smell.

It was gas.

Jason wasted no time punching the floor, bursting out the metal below. The metal floor gave under him, and he jumped through.

But the gas was not enough. Through Matthew's haze, Jason glimpsed a small metal object where his heart should be. He had used Castor to leave the bomb exposed.

Shaula realized it much too late.

"Get off of me, worm!" Shaula flashed and let her body burst with even more flame.

"Not a chance."

"Matthew, release me!"

A chain reaction of explosions rocked the building. The floor rocked. Large blasts consumed the entire area in a fireball. The ceiling above Shaula trembled and broke under the heavy weight. Melting steel splashed and crashed against her flailing form.

Her bones bent and snapped. The rush of fire and crushing metal consumed her screams as she was torn and ripped apart. Plumes of purple air puffed and expelled from her before evaporating into thin air.

Jason watched her scorch away to ash under the blaze as he fell through the floor, her body incinerating, and Matthew's ethereal form with her. The life of Queen Shaula of Mageuopolis had finally ended in the blaze she had set herself.

Not a single thing remained on that burning floor but cinders, liquid metal, and ash. The quaking from the ceiling continued.

The entire building was about to come down on Jason's head.

CHAPTER 23
END OF THE ROAD

THE VERY FOUNDATIONS of the building shook, shedding metal, stone, and drywall as Jason's dropped through them. Everything around him imploded.

One floor, two floors, three floors . . . just how high up he was he couldn't tell. And above the ceilings continued coming down. The floors above were nothing but rubble now.

He saw no one in any of the rooms or offices on his way down.

Jason dropped out thirty feet into the tiled atrium area. Daylight bathed the carved marble and large water fountain in the center. Security guards stood outside the front doors. Civilians wandered out there with them. Red and blue lights flashed around the corner of the large doors. The police must have evacuated everyone on the lower floors. No one else was left inside.

But he had no time to think about it. Ceiling tiles fell around him, breaking against the floor. Soon a building would fall on his head. Jason punched the floor again and fell through, just as the ceiling gave in. He landed in a maintenance area. Tight tunnels and the pungent smell of cleaning products assaulted him. Another hit sent him twenty feet downward into the parking lot. The quaking concrete threatened to toss him aside. Abandoned cars laid about everywhere, but he found something nearby that could help him: a manhole cover.

He threw it open and jumped down into the dark. His boots splashed in pungent water. A long sewer tunnel stretched on in both directions. He went right in the opposite direction of the police. The parking lot cracked apart above him, sending stone into the small tunnel.

Pollux fired on all cylinders as he cut it loose. The ceiling crumbled in and the broken building crashed into the sewer with him. Rocks cut at his cheek as a piece of cement knocked the broken helmet from his head. Each hit against his armor broke off more metal pieces, slicing into his tunic and pants and drawing blood. Fatigue slammed into his insides like a jackhammer. Pollux was running out.

A large pile of stone fell through the ceiling. He swung his fist and shattered it instantly. A manhole cover smashed into his back as he slid forward and—landed in a pile of garbage. Jason rolled over and slammed into the side of the tunnel when he finally realized that the ceiling had ceased collapsing. The ground still quaked, and shouts roared far behind and above, but the wall of destroyed concrete and road sat motionless in the tunnel behind him.

Jason took a hard breath. He had outrun the destruction.

After several minutes taking hard breaths, he looked at his hands. The bracelet was gone. He then realized the weight that hit him was Matthew. But was he alive or . . .

Jason tried to stand, but his legs seized, stranding him in the tunnel where sirens whined in the city above. Pollux ran out of energy.

"Are you there, Matthew?"

But Matthew didn't answer.

No choice. He had to do it himself.

Jason crawled along the bottom of the sewer on his elbows, knees dragging. Inch by inch he pushed as his muscles cried and jerked against him. His fingers spasmed. Blood from his forehead obscured his vision. Each push brought blinding pain.

But he did push. Jason dragged his legs for what felt like years as the city erupted in chaos above. He climbed onward, the destruction raging behind him. His goal was the end of this tunnel.

Sickness swirled in his head. A blackout almost consumed him. Jason smacked himself awake.

He remembered what Matthew had given him. He reached behind his back and pulled out the mirror. Miraculously, it was still in one piece, but he couldn't see anything through it. Why exactly did Matthew bother with this?

He stared into it, and a strange sense of nostalgia blanketed him. He remembered the mountains, Alain and Ordopha, the abbey, the forest, and Zelana. Sure he had only ended up in Tyndarus because of Shaula, but it felt like an eternity ago. He bit his lip, and his fingers tightened. He couldn't just to die here.

Jason put the mirror away again and crawled onward. He had nowhere to go, but he could not stop now.

Light burst in from the ceiling. His blurring vision made it difficult to see just what it came from. Suddenly he caught a figure in knight armor standing before him. The man kneeled down in front of him.

"Are you okay? Your clothes are all torn. How did you get down here?"

Jason blinked. He knew that voice. "I'm fine. Just really tired."

"I can imagine. I'll get you out, so just keep calm."

The knight lifted Jason in both arms, and finally, he realized just who this was. Pendragon! The most famous hero there was. And he was saving Jason.

"It's been a bit hectic up above," the hero said. "I'm going to put you down outside, and you wait for the ambulance to come by, okay? Don't move."

Sleep consumed Jason before he could respond. He had so many things he wanted to ask Pendragon about heroes and villains, but he didn't get to ask them.

"Jason, get up!"

"Matthew?" he mumbled

"No one is looking. Now is your chance. Get up!"

Jason's eyes flew open, and he sat up. People were flying about all over in the medical tent around him. How long had he been out?

Thankfully with so many people hanging around, he could easily slip between them and back outside. He dipped around the doctor checking the broken arm of a college girl. Orange sunset beat down on him when he stepped out. Crumbled stone and broken roads lay several streets away, and sirens blazed unabated. They were coming this way.

Jason slid through the crowds and towards the shelter of the alley. No one noticed as they were busy dealing with the other wounded in the tents. But he kept his distance, hiding around vehicles and scattered people as he moved. It would only be moments until he switched bodies. The boy ducked down between dumpsters as the sun vanished from the skies. Thankfully the alley was vacant.

The transformation kicked in within seconds, and the boy found himself without control of his physical form again. Instead, there was Matthew in the empty alley where he had been.

Matthew's armor had been blown to bits leaving him with a scorched shirt and torn up pants just like Jason. He limped while he walked, yet he retained more energy than Jason had. But at least he was alive.

Matthew tripped and leaned against the side of the brick. "I know a guy at a Salvation Army on 103rd that can hand us some fresh threads. He can give us a few bucks to get out of town and lay low for a while. If any of Shaula's goons are still alive, then we don't want them to find us."

"I was there when the whole building came down. Trust me, there's nothing left of them."

"We should still be careful."

"Are you sure we can just walk away, Matthew?"

"I'm not walking away. We've got Castor and Pollux. We're going to do something with them."

"And what's that?"

Matthew groaned. "What do you think?"

"I think I met Pendragon. He's just as cool in person. I mean, he was helping people. He even got me out of the sewer. We can do that."

"That's his job. But maybe he isn't so bad after all. It's better than what I'd use his powers for."

"You're not any different than he is."

"Don't be stupid. Just wait until I get out of here. Heck, maybe I'll use Castor to make some extra money. You don't know me that well. Either way, we have to keep this out of the wrong hands."

Before Jason could question it, Matthew left the alley out into the night. He didn't believe Matthew would use Castor for anything like that. Matthew wasn't that guy anymore, just like Jason wasn't that same scared kid wandering around the city looking for revenge. They were Castor and Pollux now.

And Earth would know it just as Tyndarus did.

EPILOGUE

MATTHEW ENTERED the motel room with his paycheck in hand. The sun would be rising soon, and the boy would be in charge again. Matthew yawned as he flicked on the old light.

He sat down on the squeaking bed and peered at the red sunrise peeking through the trees on the opposite side of the highway. It was going to be a long day.

The bag on his lap, Matthew removed the mirror piece once again. Even now when it had been a few weeks since he took the thing from Shaula's long destroyed hideout, he couldn't understand why he felt the compulsion to take it. He kept looking at the useless scrap at ever spare moment. Leaving Serenity City and Greycoast for the outskirts of town wasn't enough to break his roaming thoughts. He didn't think he would ever fully escape that world.

But his security job at the warehouse gave him too much time to think. He had saved up some money over the last few weeks, but what would they even do with it? Where would they go? Recently he had even thought he was being watched, but nothing ever came of it. Perhaps he was just getting stir-crazy. July was already here. The summer marched on.

"We could go back to Serenity City and become heroes," the boy had said.

Matthew only shook his head. *"And make ourselves targets? That's no plan."*

"Then what do you suggest? We can't run forever."

And Matthew had been trying to figure out the plan ever since. There wasn't one. Of all things, getting into the hero crowd was not at the top of his list. But he would do it if he had to. He just needed some direction, some clue.

"*We're back?*" Jason asked. He stepped out of Matthew's head into the real world again. "That was a long night. I fell asleep earlier than usual. Sorry about that!"

"Just gave me more time to think. The mess in Serenity City seems to have blown over. They think it was some sort of gas leak even after the investigation. Pendragon also caught a gang of car thieves a few days later. Big bust. We're in the clear. But I think we're missing something."

"I keep telling you about my idea, but you don't want to do anything about it."

"Get real," Matthew grunted. "I'm responsible for you now. There's no way I'm traveling west just because you think there *might* be something there. For now, we have a solid thing going."

"And you're okay with a solid thing? You might think you're cool and collected, but I see the way you look at the sky at night and hate that you can't see the stars. The news reports about villains have you double checking before changing the channel. You don't like it here any more than I do."

"It's irrelevant, Jason. What I want and what I have to do are two separate things. You'll understand when you're older. For now, we have to do this."

"And if I get another dream?"

Matthew lay back on the bed and felt the rock hard pillow turn into a marshmallow against his skin. Heavy eyelids signaled the oncoming dreams that awaited him.

"Good question," he said with a yawn. "I'll think about it."

Matthew closed his eyes and let fatigue win. There he saw the cavernous mountains, wide blue skies, and lush forests of a distant world. He traveled windswept plains with wildflowers whipping in the breeze, and up ahead he met the figure of a woman with familiar white hair and a welcoming smile. He would dream of Tyndarus again: a faraway world where dreams were reality and the intangible was always just within his grasp. One day he would return.

The creak of a door opening let in a burst of light to momentarily distract him. Jason had run outside again. He was probably going to the bus station. Maybe this time the stubborn kid would buy the tickets to go out west. Matthew almost wished he would.

As the daylight was cut off by the door, Matthew turned over and fell back into the world of slumber. His eyelids slid shut.

Just one more dream. That's all he needed. One more and he might reach home again.

BOOK TWO

GEMINI DRIFTER

PROLOGUE

THE TWO BOUNTY hunters were ready for anything. The silence of the dimly lit parking lot matched the midnight hour just fine. Distant traffic and sirens screamed in in the depths of Serenity City far away from this dark place. A pipe in the ceiling dripped water atop a Toyota truck, and a rat screeched close by as it ran under a nearby jeep. The lack of vehicles in the lot emphasized the lonely atmosphere the muscular man felt. Not the best spot for a meeting, but it would do. The pair could handle whatever would come their way.

Hammersmith straightened the tie on his suit and tugged on his too-short cuffs. Nothing was more humiliating than a barrel-chested man in a suit. Sure, it was for a job, but it didn't make it any more comfortable or natural. The former boxer crossed broken pavement towards the single white limo parked in the north end.

"Here we go," he whispered.

The man walking beside the young man clapped a meaty hand on his shoulder. Hammersmith smiled halfheartedly at his superior.

"Problem?" Roadbuster asked him.

"Did we have to wear suits? I know this guy works for the mayor, but it isn't as if anyone else is going to be here. We look like trained monkeys."

"There's no shortage of guns for sale in the wild west. He came to us, and that is worth taking seriously. Beats another trip to the job board, no? Be grateful they didn't hire Sonlight for this."

"Would be better if we didn't have to meet alone in the dark."

"Wrong on that one. We've got company." Roadbuster nodded to one pillar far to the right. "Keep your eye out."

A woman stepped out of the shade as the pair approached the car. Hammersmith didn't have any reason to suspect shifty dealing, but he had heard the two of them would have competition for the job. This must have been one of their rivals.

The woman wore a long grey coat and matching wide-brim hat, making it difficult to see much beyond her sharp cheeks and blue eyes glinting in the dark. She winked at Hammersmith, even though the two parties kept their distance. Trusting other bounty hunters was a good way to get yourself offed.

The door to the limousine opened to reveal an older man wearing a brown suit and matching overcoat. He looked different here than when he appeared on television. The smell of expensive cologne filled the air around the assistant mayor. He gestured to the three bounty hunters with a wave.

"Good evening, everyone," the assistant mayor said. "As you can tell, I have chosen you three from out of all our other potential candidates for this mission. Your files impressed me greatly. Now, before I get to the finer details of your work, are there questions?"

The woman pointed a thumb at the duo. "You want me to work with the gorillas?"

"No," he replied, ignoring Hammersmith's grunt. "I would prefer you spread out for this job, which is why I hired two separate parties. I'm uncertain what you will find on your little journey, but it is sure to be interesting."

"Is it a retrieval?" she asked. "Are we not after a person?"

"Calm down, my dear. Your mare is rather far ahead of the carriage. I shall start with the simple part of the mission. The Williams' Tech building that went down two weeks ago. I'm certain you remember it. But you probably also remember that they have found no culprit. There's a good reason for that."

"Because it was some sort of gas leak, if I'm not mistaken," Roadbuster interrupted. "Some hapless jerk lit the wrong light on one of the top floors, and it ended up bringing the rest down. The shockwaves were so bad they spider-webbed underground. There were rumors that maybe a piece of work like Thanatos was involved, but nobody buys that, right? He hasn't been around in years. And, also, there's been no news since the cleanup started. Why no arrests? All we got was PR from the acting CEO about some poor soul who fried himself. There's no way that was just an accident."

The suit nodded. "Very good, sir. You were well chosen."

"I agree," the woman said, chuckling to herself. "I've been waiting for an arrest since it happened. When it never did, I kept an eye on the phone. I'm glad you called, Mr. Assistant Mayor."

His smile twitched. "Don't call me that, please. Officially, the case is closed. There is no evidence of foul play or any possible motive, there are no witnesses, and the police are shutting the book on this one. The whole affair is dead in the water. We have real villains to deal with, or so they say."

"However," Roadbuster continued for him. Hammersmith couldn't help smirking at that. The guy really knew how to get to the point. "You don't believe them."

The suit whipped his hand around in a circular gesture. "I'm getting to the crux of it. *However*, we have received security photos from inside the scene as the building fell during the explosion. Most show nothing, but one is bizarre. It's a shot of a man dressed in half-destroyed medieval armor falling through the floor. But we can't get any more information than that. He was in frame for less than a second."

Hammersmith rubbed his chin. "Pendragon?"

"Not likely. His alibi is rock solid."

The assistant of the mayor handed the three of them a printed photo. Hammersmith made sure to give it the once over twice. A figure shot from the back wore warped old medieval-style armor. Was it damaged by heat? The subject appeared to be punching through the floor.

"I've sent the pictures to your designated inboxes. It should be enough to help you find this suspect. How many men in knight armor are there in Serenity City? Williams' Tech Corp. has no record of anyone such as this matching a Prime with super strength. But we do have the names of two employees from the logs that haven't been accounted for. One of them must be the target."

"You want him alive," Roadbuster stated. It wasn't a question.

"Of course I do. I need to know just who this is, where he came from, and why he was there, causing chaos in my city. You can't get all that from a corpse."

The woman raised a hand. "I'm fine with all this, but if the police aren't interested, then why are you? Did you even show them this photo? Are they even aware of it? I like to know all the angles when I go into a job, and you're not sharing them."

"I like to keep my city safe, believe it or not. But I also want to know what's going on it. Why was that knight up there, and what was he doing? Why are there no records of this Prime, and why have no investigations into Williams' Tech Corp. revealed anything relating to him. His power alone did not bring the building down. So what did? Something is missing, and I bet our mystery man will lead me to the answers."

"This sounds like it'll be a hassle." Roadbuster handed the photo back to the suit. "What if we step in something above our pay-grade?"

The assistant mayor nodded to himself before smiling wide. "Then we can add an extra zero to the end of your pay."

Roadbuster and the woman shared a look. Hammersmith had been in the business long to know what that meant. He rolled his eyes when Roadbuster spoke his mind.

"So what are we waiting for?"

CHAPTER 1
CROSS COUNTRY

IT WASN'T EVERYDAY Jason got kicked off a bus for talking to himself, looking like a mental case in the process, but these last few weeks contained a lot of firsts for the perturbed teenager. Not only did he find himself with newly acquired powers from a bracelet, he had also fallen into a whole other world and fought to escape it. As far as summers went, this was a crazy one. Now he traveled the highways in the blistering Virginia heat with the voice in his head —the voice that happened to be his friend with powers of his own.

All that considered, getting thrown from a bus wasn't all too out there.

Jason shielded his eyes from the beaming sun. The bus barreled out of sight from the rest stop, and now he had to walk. He shifted the bag on his shoulder and pulled the collar of his lime tank top. It was too hot for this. The boy sighed.

"That was embarrassing."

"I was trying to get some shut-eye," Matthew said from inside his head. *"It's an eight-hour drive to Roanoke, and I didn't get much sleep last night. Did you really have to choose that moment to talk about the bracelets? It could have waited until lunch."*

"Well, maybe if you didn't start yelling in my ear."

"Please. I did nothing of the sort."

"Yes, you did!" Jason glanced over his shoulder to make sure no one was watching. Thankfully, the area was vacant. "Just because we switch bodies at sunrise and again at sunset doesn't mean you have carte blanche to distract me like that. Do I talk in my sleep when I'm in your head at night? No, I don't. You're supposed to be the adult here, Matthew."

"Oh, shut up. Are you ever not whining? What's done is done. Where are we, anyway?"

The summer sun beat down on the highway. Traffic blitzed by, cars, vans, and trucks, all heading to and from Roanoke. Summer vacation was an exciting time for normal people. The two of them were definitely anything but normal.

Jason pulled at his pant leg, wishing he hadn't chosen to wear blue jeans. This heat was murder. He continued his walk down the shoulder of the road as the sweat pooled on his skin. For early August, it was far too hot.

The route led from highway 460 straight from Serenity City. Until this point, it had been going well. A low profile was the best way to get to their destination, especially when enemies could still be chasing after them. The Mirror Gates to the other world of Tyndarus should have been closed off by now, and with the Williams' Tech Corp. building down, their primary base on Earth was smashed. It *should* be clear sailing from this point.

"We're a few miles away from Roanoke," Jason said. "It's half-past two, and I'm feeling beat."

"I told you to exercise more."

"That's easy for you to say. Why don't you come out here and join me?"

"I could," Matthew teased, *"but I like hearing you whine. Anyway, there should be a motel just outside of the city. Bonsack is about three hours away on foot. Hey, maybe if you run through the trees and hills, you'll beat that stupid bus to the next rest stop. It must bore you taking it slow all the time. Use Pollux and really let it out."*

Jason hesitated. He hadn't used the power of the gold bracelet on his left wrist since escaping that collapsing building weeks back. The super-strength power he gained was tough to control. At least he covered his wrists with sweat bands to make sure no one could see the bracelet magically glued to him, but he couldn't hide it forever. With an ability like this in a world of other powers, he would eventually have to use them again.

"What if they see us?"

"That's why I told you not to do it on the road. You don't need to run at full speed, either. Use the opportunity to distribute the bracelet's power sparingly without running out of energy. You're out of practice, right?"

True enough, it had been a while since Jason had used Pollux properly, and his muscles shook at the opportunity. His body was more used to it than his head was. He couldn't go all out, but he didn't need to. It was just like riding that bike he lost in the fire last year for the first time in ages.

Jason took off at a run, his legs thundering into the humidity of the roadside brush. He climbed over the hills and through the trees, his heart shouting for joy. His muscles moved, and his blood boiled, carrying him like a sprinter.

Within half a minute, he dashed two hundred meters. And he kept going through trees and over hills. The heat in Pollux lit his limbs ablaze. Up ahead, the next rest stop waited for them.

"You were supposed to take it steady," Matthew barked. *"I know it's been a while, but we don't want to draw attention."*

"Sorry, I know. By the way, these wristbands chafe. Can we get better ones?"

"Well, if Pollux and Castor didn't show on our wrists when we separated, it wouldn't be a problem. For now, you'll just have to deal until we get to Roanoke. Have you had any more dreams? The last big one saved our butts in Tyndarus, so I'm hoping this one is worth it."

"These dreams aren't like the ones I've had before. It's like a phone line connected directly into my brain with heavy static on the other end. Whoever is calling is vague about what they want."

"So it could be a Prime just trying to mess with us."

"I don't think so. No one knows about the bracelets on Earth except Nieto's men. But that's not it. What I mean is that I remember these dreams. I see the city of Roanoke, and I see Little Winter on the outskirts. An old woman is talking. We have a connection."

"You know her?"

"No, but I get a vibe that we're similar somehow."

"Well, that's nice, I suppose. But I'm the one with the sharpened sixth sense, and I'm not getting any vibe at all. Watch where you're going."

Jason dashed across a hill over a shallow drop. He slid on the grass and rolled down, pushing up dirt. The ground met his cheek and his bag smacked against the back of his head. He groaned and rubbed his chin.

"You alright?"

"Yeah, looks like I still got to practice."

Jason emerged out of the trees into a wide-open lot where cars and pavement joined together in a hodgepodge of boisterous families and lone travelers. It had been a while since he'd seen so many people in one spot. Cars, vans, and trucks, littered the rest stop, as did the overpowering sunshine. He sauntered past the rushing children and chattering teenagers. Adults made plans with each other and called to their kids. No one thought twice about a random teen like him passing through.

At the edge of the lot, he spotted the bus pull in. The 1511 from Serenity City parked by the entrance, just on schedule.

He ducked behind a van. At some point, he really had gotten in front of the bus.

"Last thing I need is for someone to ask how I got ahead of a bus. Maybe we should have taken one that requires transfers. We're going to be ducking these guys until we get into Roanoke."

But they had to get to Roanoke. They had to get to Little Winter. His dreams had never steered him wrong before. Because of them, he had Pollux and with it, the power of super strength, speed, and endurance. He had also met Matthew and his allies from the other world of Tyndarus. If anything, he owed it to them to see this through.

"Speaking of my sixth sense . . . I'm getting something here."

Jason turned his head and raked his eyes over the crowded stop. No lizardmen, obvious Primes, or silver-haired brigands, were to be seen. It was odd to think about, but who else would be after them? How would they know the two of them were even out here?

He thought he saw a pretty woman with blue eyes winking at him from one of the blue cars in the lot, but he shook it off. No time for romance.

"It's just families."

"We need to leave. Now."

Jason dashed around the lot and back out onto the highway. Maybe he should have stayed on that other planet. Hopefully, he would be able to take a breath one day. Today wouldn't be that day.

THE FORESTS of Tyndarus were quiet when the men weren't out hunting. Zelana sat alone by the stone bank hiding the entranceway to the village. Fog filled every space around her, as it always did, but she enjoyed being in this place. It allowed her to think and enjoy the silence.

She sat among the rocks and squeezed the mirror shard in her small hands. A sigh escaped her. The teenage girl brushed some of her platinum hair from her eyes.

Ever since Jason and Matthew had left through the Mirror Gate, she expected them to return. They didn't have any reason to, but she kept hoping they would. It had been far too many days since they departed.

Recently strange thoughts and notions whispered to her in her dreams, as if someone were brushing her shoulder and asking a question. But when she awoke, it vanished, and she could remember nothing else.

The chance it could be her mother—that somehow she survived and came back after so long was a reality she did not wish to face. Besides, Jason had surely defeated her. Surely.

That evil woman would never return to Tyndarus.

Zelana squeezed the hem of her dress and breathed out her anger. She had no idea where she would go from here.

"There you are," Koa said. The young man hopped rocks towards her.

"This is where I usually am," she replied in her dreamy haze.

"Are you still waiting for them to return? The mirror was smashed. Should they return to Tyndarus they will not be near here. Besides, I'm certain they have families of their own to care for."

Zelana smiled at Koa. They were probably near the same age, around fifteen years, though he tried to act as if he were experienced with his attempt to wear leather armor and carry a sword at all times, even when there was no reason to do so. He had his long platinum hair in a braid, and his lean form crouched low as he peered around the rocks and into the forest before them. He meant well, but he always gave the impression to her he was trying too hard.

"They do not," she answered him. "But I have the impression, a feeling that something is close by. I cannot shake it."

"Just be wary out in the mist. You might have immunity to the polluted air, but there is more to fret over. You never know when a lizardman might find his way around. The bastards think they own Tyndarus."

"They more or less did before my father arrived. Now they are slaves to him. I do not fear them."

"Nonetheless, should you see one? You call for Koa, and I will slay it. What are you looking at?"

"Flowers," she said simply. The forest lilies had a delightful fragrance she had never caught before. "I don't suppose you know anything about them?"

He shook his head. "My apologies. Regardless, do be careful out here, Zelana."

"Thank you, Koa."

The young man wandered off, his grip around his hilt so tight she thought his fingers would break it. He had been through a lot from what she had heard. Most people in this forest village of Fortuna did. She didn't pry. Zelana related to that rage he hid just underneath the surface.

But she worried more about the recent strange feelings stirring within. Something was about to happen, and she couldn't tell what.

Zelana looked once more at the mirror piece she had been given. "I hope you're well, Jason."

A chill ran across her spine, and so did the accompanying doubt. What she was worried about wasn't here on Tyndarus. It was on Earth. Trouble was coming for her friends.

MATTHEW ALLOWED Jason to sleep in the motel while he went out alone into Roanoke. The kid had knocked himself out running around all day, and now it was Matthew's turn to do his part.

They still had to reach the other end of the city and pass Alpine Hills into the trails, but that could wait for tomorrow. Now sunset had come and gone, and he wandered around Williamson Road just outside their motel. If Matthew was lucky, he could run into the criminals he was looking for.

Across the street from the nearby auto-part shop was the convenience store he spotted when they first arrived in town. As Matthew passed it, the two men casually loitering in front made his sixth sense power go crazy. Matthew didn't tell Jason about it. The kid didn't need more to worry about. Matthew instead made a note to check it out on his own later. This area of Roanoke was not known to be particularly safe, and that is why he chose to come through here. Not just because he was broke, although that was certainly part of it, but because this would be a good chance to cut loose with Castor. While Jason slept on the ratty mattress underneath the dirty sheet and torn lampshade, Matthew would scope out the street for himself and have some fun. It looked like he wouldn't have to go very far for some action.

He strolled down the street in the dark, vehicles blowing past him. Heat built in the bracelet hidden underneath Matthew's cheap wristband. The night air weighed down every step he made.

This wasn't where he was supposed to be. No, Cavern Cove was the place. His dream retirement town far away from the chaos of places like Serenity City and Roanoke. Away from this hero mess. Where everyone kept to themselves and the weather would always be comfortable, and he could grow old and die in peace.

That would never happen.

Jason was another story. The fifteen-year-old needed stability and a real home. Matthew wasn't that much older at twenty-two, but someone needed to be responsible for the kid. In a world of super-powered monsters running amok, stability was necessary. Jason deserved better than to end up like Matthew. If it meant giving up any chance at normalcy, then Matthew would just have to work harder.

To do that, he had to learn to use these powers better.

Through the store window, a glint off the freezer jabbed into his retinas. Two figures in heavy black coats milled about the rear of the store. They were the same ones he had spotted outside earlier. One moved sideways and, for a second, revealed the object hidden inside his zipper: the butt of a handgun.

Matthew took a breath and walked into the sliding door entrance. His earlier hunch was correct—these two were trouble. Time to work.

THE CHILL CRAWLING up Jason's spine set him awake instantly. The dream returned. Not the one that led him to Roanoke but the one he had not had since returning from Tyndarus. The woman he could never remember had pried into his thoughts to warn him of impending danger yet again. But what it meant he didn't know.

Jason sat on the edge of the bed and rubbed his eyes with his knuckles. Even with the cheap air conditioner rattling, it was still too hot. He pulled on the collar to his second-hand shirt and pushed the sticky sheets off. Comfort couldn't be had on the road like this. But he wasn't here for that. He was here for answers.

At some point, Matthew had left the room, possibly for fresh air. Jason couldn't blame him. He needed to shake this humidity off too.

The teenager pushed open the squeaking bathroom door and tried not to look at the grimy tiles. He splashed sink water on his cheeks and across his blond hair. It really was eerie how much Matthew and Jason looked alike despite not being related. But they weren't family. Jason didn't have any left.

"Is this really okay?" he mumbled into the mirror.

His parents had been gone over a year, and here he was nowhere near finding out who had done it. A woman promising great things had taken him in off the streets of Serenity City and led him into worse trouble. But now, he had powers. If he couldn't do anything for his parents, he could make sure no one else went through what he did. Perhaps he could help heroes save the city, one person at a time.

Marguerite promised the world to him without directly saying so, but that was all a crock. Instead, he was just a guinea pig for her and her husband's experiments. Jason now wore a bracelet that gave both him and his friend Matthew incredible powers, though it quite nearly killed the pair to get them. Now they were wielders of ancient relics from another planet somewhere off in space. Life takes sharp turns, and he was lucky enough not to run off the mountain road. Now he had the chance to use this bracelet, Pollux, to do what he wanted. But what exactly did he want?

His bloodshot blue eyes scanned his sunken cheeks. A moan fought its way out of him. Pollux must have really taken its toll. How long did he run today?

The front door thumped. He flew out of the bathroom towards the banging. Did Matthew forget the key? The door jumped open to reveal a muscular young man in a blue jacket and jeans with short cut brown hair and green eyes like daggers. He was built like a wrestler with old cuts across his white skin. The stranger pointed a firearm at Jason.

"Bounty hunter," the intruder said. "We've been looking all over for you, boy. Now, how about you tell us just what you did to murder those good people back home."

"Get out of my room. You don't know what you're doing. You better leave before I get mad."

"No dice. You're under arrest. Where is Matthew White?"

"Who?"

The bounty hunter flashed handcuffs in his free hand and approached him. No more talking. Jason put up his hands.

So much for a quiet trip.

CHAPTER 2
A RUN THROUGH ROANOKE

THANKFULLY MATTHEW WAS the only one in the store, aside from the cashier and the two aspiring criminals, that is. No one could have suspected his identity with the bandanna around his mouth anyway, but one could never be too careful. He ducked around the shelves of salted snack treats and canned food towards the frozen goods. The two criminals conversed among each other, unaware of his approach.

"You ready?" the man with the mustache said.

His friend with the coal-black eyes nodded. "Let's clean house."

Each man drew a silver-metal handgun and spun around towards the cashier. Unfortunately, neither expected Matthew standing in their way. They both jumped backwards.

"Evening, fellas. Mind putting away the pieces?"

"Alright," the mustached man said. "You first."

Coal eyes fired, and the bullet smashed into Matthew's chest; or it would have if he were still solid mass. Matthew's mist form swirled from human into intangible air. The criminals shot wildly into his ethereal body, but the bullets blew past him and embedded into shelves and ceiling tiles. Shards of shattered plaster and metal shook loose.

"What was that?" the shooter queried.

Mustache gritted his teeth. "He's a damn Prime!"

Matthew flew between the pair and solidified. He threw his forearm around Mustache's neck and choked him, bracing the criminal in front of his ally. Coal eyes ducked back around the shelves towards the front of the store and left his friend to the wolves. Mustache gagged and slowly sunk to the laminate floor, where he fell into slumber.

A click sounded from the other side of the shelf. The manager had his handgun trained on Coal eyes. The would-be villain lifted his arms and let his weapon clatter down. The middle-aged manager in the smock and grey shirt smiled as the villain laid down on his stomach.

"Ey, man, thanks!" the manager said. He jutted his chin toward Matthew. "You a new hero or something? Never seen you around here before?"

"Just passing through."

"I called the cops, so you best be headin' out, then. They don't take too kindly to us civilians doing their job for 'em."

Matthew wouldn't argue with that. The last thing he wanted was attention from the authorities.

He ran out the door into the warm night and back down the street. Cars still shot past him, unaware of what had transpired mere moments ago. Up ahead in the motel parking lot, he sighted a strange black car parked out front. Before he could speculate on the inhabitants, a bang sang out of a motel room across the lot. Gang business, or Jason: what could it be?

Matthew dodged the few cars passing by and reached the lot. His sixth sense cranked mercilessly inside his brain. That had to be Jason.

"Don't move, vigilante."

A hard piece of metal jabbed into Matthew's spine.

"I watched you in there, Mr. White," the burly voice said. "Since when are you a Prime? There's nothing about that in your records."

Matthew let out a small breath. At least this guy wasn't from Tyndarus. But it still didn't add up. Who else would chase the two of them? How would they have known they were here?

"I'm sorry," Matthew replied. "Am I under arrest? What law did I break?"

"Williams' Tech. You were there when it went down."

"You're babbling, buddy."

"And you're used to lying. Makes sense; I've seen your record. You worked security at half a dozen poker places in Serenity City and even spent a few months hanging around Greycoast. That must have been awful. But you never stood out, did you? No complaints against you anywhere. I can't even find anyone that remembers your face. You must be a real weasel, White."

The motel door whipped open, and a body tumbled out of it as if thrown from a moving vehicle. Jason rolled over and up to his knees, facing the now ajar room. A large man emerged with a gun trained on the boy. These guys were good.

"There's no escape, boy," the big man yelled. "On your knees!"

A crowd formed around them, including the manager of the motel. The man by Jason flashed them a badge, and the gaggle silenced. Matthew clicked his tongue and pursed his lips. Roanoke must have been used to bounty hunters.

"Easy, Hammersmith," the voice behind Matthew said. "He's not going anywhere. Tell him we've got White."

Hammersmith glanced at Matthew and then back to Jason. "Are you going to abandon your friend, kid? He's not going anywhere, so you might as well give it up. I'm ready for round two if you're not."

The guy behind Matthew growled. "Hammersmith!"

"Just joking, Roadbuster."

"Damn rookies."

Jason scratched his ruffled blond hair and grunted. He placed his hands behind his head and moved to his knees.

Hammersmith clapped the handcuffs behind Jason and Matthew and pushed them into the car. The crowd dispersed, sparing careful glances at the group. Roadbuster moved to the driver's seat and started the engine. Hammersmith made sure to sit between the prisoner pair, and informed Jason that his cuffs were reinforced. It didn't matter much since the boy didn't fight back.

They pulled out onto the street south, back towards Serenity City and away from Little Winter. Matthew swore under his breath. He needed a plan quick.

"Who hired you?" he asked.

"You don't need to know, White," the driver said. The big bulky man wore a simple white shirt with his hair combed back. His flat tone betrayed what a man of his size should sound like. "You're not supposed to be a Prime. Where did those powers come from?"

"I'm just a late bloomer."

"You really think that's going to fly, huh?" The car dragged to a stop at a red light. "You're either born with powers, or you're not. Your record is unbelievably dull, with only a few small crimes from when you were sixteen, including petty theft and breaking and entering. If you had those powers back then, why didn't you use them? What were you doing at Williams' Tech?"

Matthew leaned forward slightly to look at his friend. Jason slowly jutted his chin at the man sitting between them. They would need to get past Hammersmith without revealing themselves.

"Why do you keep assuming I was at William's Tech? You haven't explained that part yet."

"We found want ads; we looked at online applications and questioned those involved. One name that came up was Matthew White. Looking into your pathetic background and suspicious movements over the past few weeks led us to seek you out. And lo-and-behold you're running with this kid. He must have been the one to wreck the building. Little surviving security footage remains, but we can guess what happened inside before the building fell. You might as well tell us why you are running."

"You don't know what you're talking about."

"Quiet, moron," Hammersmith said. He jabbed his weapon into Matthew's chest. "You don't have any place to talk."

"Forget it, Hammersmith. We don't need to hear anymore. The client can deal with that."

Matthew sat back and thought. There was no way he could explain their situation to these bounty hunters. They wouldn't understand any of it, especially the revelation of a whole other world out there filled with magic, monsters, and an entire race of people birthed from the dirt itself. Then there remained the question of the bracelets.

"*How was Tyndarus?*" A gravelly voice spoke in his mind.

Matthew froze up. The only one who could share his thoughts was Jason, and that wasn't Jason. The boy was still silently sitting in his seat. Quiet dread filled the corners of

Matthew's mind. He swallowed his amassing fears.

"Are you one of Shaula's lapdogs?" Matthew answered back. *"How did you find us out here?"*

"How can I be the lapdog of a dead woman, Castor?"

Matthew snarled at the name of his bracelet. No one should have known that unless they were on Tyndarus, or in Williams' Tech. He watched the dark buildings and passing cars. Matthew watched the window while he concentrated his thoughts on the voice.

"*Good to hear you survived your ordeal at the building.*" This voice had to be with the enemy. There remained little chance that Shaula's operation centered on one business in one city, and Matthew always had the feeling that someone would eventually find him out. "*Ready to talk business?*"

"How many of you are left?"

"From the building you two wrecked? Pawns and small fish. They scattered to the wind. But more are out there. Now how about I get you out of this place?"

"Excuse me?"

"You heard what I said."

Matthew did hear it, but he didn't understand it. For what reason would an agent of Williams' Tech want anything to do with him? Unless they wanted to drag the pair back to Tyndarus.

"*I'm not giving you back the bracelets,*" Matthew replied. Should Great Sorcerer King Nieto reclaim the bracelets, Earth would be in grave danger. The two of them might have sealed the way off to his kingdom by destroying the Mirror Gates and finishing off Queen Shaula, but that didn't mean they were out of the woods yet. Psychos like this were still running around on Earth. "*I'd just as soon stay with the bounty hunters.*"

"Then you're a fool. Listen, I'm right beside you. When I blink twice, you will have three seconds to get through the door. You'll thank me later."

Hammersmith was with Nieto's forces? Matthew stole a glance at the big man. He stared directly ahead as he sat between Matthew and Jason. This voice had to be bluffing.

Slowly, the car pulled out of the red light when a siren screeched past them. The police were finally on the way to the store. Rain beat on the roof of the car. This day just couldn't get more frustrating. But then, as if he read Matthew's thoughts, Hammersmith blinked twice.

Being his only chance, Matthew went for it. He leaned forward and turned to mist for less than a moment. The cuffs slid off his wrists. He leaped sideways and touched Jason's shoulder. The boy blinked as he was sucked into Matthew's head like a magnet pulled to the right polarity. When he was absorbed, Matthew became mist once more. The wielder of Castor slipped through the crack in the window.

It happened in less than a few seconds, but Hammersmith didn't budge an inch the entire time.

"What are you doing, rookie?" Roadbuster yelled. "Get them!"

Matthew solidified outside the window and the moving car swept around to a stop in the middle of the busy road. Horns honked, and tires screeched, but he weaved through them into the humid night where heavy rain drops beat across his bruised skin.

At the side of the road, he approached a sewer grate. The stink caused his stomach to twist like a juiced orange. Would he really have to go in there to escape? The bounty hunters barreled towards them through the rain. It wasn't the way Matthew wanted to go, but there were no other options.

Summoning his courage, Matthew transformed into water. He splashed into a puddle on the road and slid through the grating and into the sewers. His liquid form plopped down into the water like a bucket dumped in a trough. The current dragged him away, and his pursuers dropped out of sight.

All he heard above him were the curses of Hammersmith: the man who had let him get away.

"What was all that about?" Jason asked from inside his head. *"Why did he do nothing when you moved to escape?"*

"Not now. I need to concentrate so we don't get swept away."

At night, Matthew regained control of the body, though there was no way Roadbuster or Hammersmith could have known that. Why did Hammersmith bother to chase them down if he was just going to let them free?

Matthew's form barely held together as the raging river of rainwater rushed them onward through the sewers. They only had to get a good distance away before he could get to the side and climb back out. He did not relish looking for a place to get a good shower next.

"I knew we should have gone to Cavern Cove."

CHAPTER 3
THE RAIN POURS

HAMMERSMITH FELL against the pavement and clutched his wounded cheek. The punch and resulting fall added to the grinding sensation in his brain. Rain doused his slumped form as Roadbuster stood over him.

The two were out of the public's sight in the alley, but it didn't matter to his superior. Roadbuster looked down at him with a scowl. A flash of shame ran through the rookie bounty hunter. He slowly stood back up.

"Rookie!" Roadbuster yelled. "What is wrong with you?"

"I just froze. It was a mistake."

"That's an understatement. They're the only witnesses to what happened in that building. We need them to get paid. Unless you don't think it's important to keep rogue Primes in custody. Why are you even here?"

"I apologize," Hammersmith forced out. The downpour caused him to wipe his brows, though it was hardly as frustrating as losing their two bounties. "I don't know what else to say."

"You don't? How about if they had been villains? Criminals? Killers? What if they attacked bystanders when they escaped? You massive moron!"

"They're harmless. Two schmucks in far over their heads. They don't know anything."

"The info we have is straightforward. Matthew White was obscure enough—some dumb kid who signed up for the wrong job. How could the boy be any different? Is he White's brother? They do look alike."

"No relation." Hammersmith's head buzzed like a train whistle blasted inside of it. He paused as if the words had wrapped themselves in her tongue and refused to leave. "McCrae is wanted for questioning regarding his parents' deaths, and White had nothing to do with them —his parents are also dead."

Roadbuster's hold on Hammersmith loosened. "So you do take this seriously. At least a little. They couldn't have gotten out of the city yet. Keep up this time."

A heavy clamping feeling crushed into Hammersmith's mind. It had flared up ever since they visited the site where the building fell in Serenity City, but it was never this bad. He winced and held back a scream. He couldn't fight through the growing fog filling his mind.

"Problem, Rookie?"

"There's . . . one place around here they might be," Hammersmith choked out. "Little Winter."

"I've heard of it. Never been there."

"Has anyone?"

"It's past Highway 81 and Alpine Hills into the trails of Carvins Cove. It's that area where it's always snowing and freezing. No one likes to go in there because there's no guarantee you'll come out whole, and no one knows why it snows even in the summer. Probably some sort of obscure Prime thing. If they're heading in there, then they've either got a suicide mission planned, or there's something going on here deeper than we know."

Hammersmith pinched the bridge of his nose as hard as he could. "That can't be. It's like I said: they're just two schmucks in over their head."

"Either way, we should ask around first before heading there half-cocked. Are you feeling better now, Hammersmith?"

"Yes," he lied. Hammersmith glanced up into the downpour jack-hammering his skull. Finally, his thoughts had smoothed out. "Sorry. I screwed up. It will never happen again. Next time I'll get them both."

He meant every word he said.

"THESE CLOTHES ARE AWKWARD," Jason said. "I'd ask how you keep getting so many clothes for such low prices, but I think the answer would disturb me."

They had escaped the sewers and get back into the alleys of Roanoke. Jason was grateful for the opportunity to take a break. They entered the Salvation Army and got new clothes including winter jackets, which was more than a little embarrassing. Now they were back on the streets again and heading north. At the very least, the rain had ceased.

"You know how I can tell you're a rich kid?" Matthew chided. "You completely misunderstand the price of clothes. You probably think a pair of pants costs fifty bucks. I have no idea how you survived on the streets for as long as you did."

"It wasn't long. Shaula found me soon after I got into the city and took me in. She was scanning the streets looking for subjects. No Primes, though. She was adamant about it."

"Might have to do with the way these relics work. Maybe Primes can't use them."

"Would there be any way to know?" Jason asked. "We're the first people who have been able to use these bracelets without dying in centuries. That's way before Primes existed. Anyway, it's ridiculously hot out. Should we be dressed like this?"

The humid night made visibility difficult. They both wore winter jackets on top of their light sweaters and jeans as they walked through the rain. Jason already felt dumb carrying an umbrella on top of it. They would have been committed to an asylum if anyone was watching them.

Because of an attempted home invasion five blocks away, the police kept their distance from the path Matthew traced for the pair. In the sky, they both spotted what looked to be a hero in a multicolored uniform flying to the top of a building. This town was mental. Serenity City was still worse, but this one could be runner-up to worst city on Earth. No wonder Matthew wanted to go someplace like Cavern Cove. Too much chaos played with the nerves.

Across the highway, they slipped between cars in the rain and arrived at a tall metal fence. Jason used his power to leap over it while Matthew misted inside of the thing. Despite their similar names, from what Jason had seen in pictures, Cavern Cove couldn't have been any different from this Carvins Cove. The rest of the trails looked to be welcoming to visitors with rolling dusty trails and overhanging brush, but a bad cloud hung over this area. The further the two bracelet wielders marched, the darker the sky became. This had to be the infamous Little Winter.

The mountainous area contained many trails for hikers and various other sorts to trek through, but Little Winter was a bit of an urban legend. People lived there, but privacy was enforced, and no one knew just what caused the strange weather inside its borders. Matthew's plan to storm it unannounced wasn't the best idea.

The terrain turned rough and uneven, and pathways narrowed between the seas of trees. Jason felt the awkward stones underneath pushing into his boots. Eventually, they had to put the umbrellas away as any trace of rain tapered off the further they trekked. Soon enough, the drizzle completely vanished—and snow replaced it.

"We're close," Matthew muttered. "Stay near."

"Do you know anything about the family that owns this place?"

"Not much to learn. They keep to themselves. The only reason I agreed to take you here is because of that dream. It better be accurate, or we're going to have problems."

Snow banks rose from dirt-covered mounds into towering ridges, coating the thin trees and masking the sky like a heavy fog. The chill bit harder with every trudge they made through the path.

Matthew grumbled with every step but never said why. It couldn't have been fatigue since he never wore his problems on his face. This only left one possibility.

"There's someone out there," Matthew said. "My sixth sense is shouting at me. How about you?"

"I don't have a sixth sense like you."

"I meant your hearing."

"Let me concentrate first."

Jason focused on the world around him where thunder, rain, snow, and the cacophony of the highway raged on. They all merged as one glorious symphony of nature playing on key and in perfect time. But one piece grew out of sync with the rest. The more he concentrated, the more sure he became that his hunch was correct. Many pairs of boots were approaching.

"There are at least eight," Jason said. "We're surrounded."

"Just like Tyndarus. We have nothing to barter with this time. No Zelana, either."

"If they know we're here, then they have to be watching somehow. But I don't see any cameras."

Matthew shouldered a nearby tree and nearly swore at it. "They have the territorial advantage, too. We better hope they're friendly."

But despite the horde stealthily encircling them, the two continued forward. The terrain grew sharper, with blind drops and rolling hills aplenty. Any second, they could be attacked by their pursuers, and they would be left helpless to do anything about it. And yet, those hidden in the growing snow never appeared.

Jason and Matthew broke through the trees into a large open snowfield with a house in the center. White paint to match the drifting snowbanks and black shutters to stand out from them met the travelers. The place measured three stories tall, with over-sized white curtains masking the sweeping windows. A figure waited on the porch through the squall, but it was impossible to tell for sure.

"I might have spotted someone," Jason said.

"Good. Because there's someone else here."

Behind them waited five men dressed in white snowsuits. In the trees, Jason spotted three more keeping their distance. They aimed their rifles toward the intrusive pair.

"Hello, strangers," the man in the lead said. "Don't move. You're expected, not welcome."

Jason and Matthew put their hands up, dropping the useless umbrellas in the snow. A fight at this point wouldn't get them anywhere except dead.

The boy looked at the house one more time and thought he saw someone on the porch once more—an older woman. That was when it came to him. She was the one who sent him that message in the dream. This was the woman they were looking for.

"Hello, Jason," the woman's voice said in his head. *"It's about time. Welcome to Little Winter."*

CHAPTER 4
LITTLE WINTER

IT WAS ENOUGH to trust the boy's dream—after all, dreams had saved them from the mountains back on Tyndarus—but Matthew could do without busting into other people's property. Even when he was a brat sneaking around in the city, it was only to mess with adults. But if these men in the snow wanted to take a chunk out of his head with a clean shot, he couldn't blame them for doing so. The two of them didn't have any right to be in Little Winter.

And yet, he was supposed to be protecting the boy. Jason had no one else to turn to. The kid had little space to be a normal teenager with all these crazed zealots, bounty hunters, and strange dreams. Matthew needed to be the adult here.

"My name is Matthew White," he said. "Normally, I would have called, but we just had a fight with some bounty hunters, fell into a sewer, and got rained on before ending up here stuck in a snow storm. Crazy weather you've got in this place. We're not looking to start anything."

"We know who you are, son." The large man in front dropped his rifle to his side. He gestured to the pair of intruders to follow him, though none of the other armed men dropped their sights. "Don't mind us. We don't trust anyone, even folks we expect seeing."

Matthew forced a smile through the cold. "I get it. There are a lot of weirdos out there."

"If what Ma has said about you two is true, then I would have to believe it."

"She knows who we are?" Matthew pulled back the collar on his jacket. Sweat from some rising heat had irritated his skin. Something was off about this weather.

"You'll be finding out shortly. Still feel cold?"

"This town is going to kill me. What's in the air in Roanoke?"

"Nothing to do with the air, son. At least, not fully. You probably guessed that it has to do with Primes. That's how we keep so many people out. You should have called ahead."

"Well, we don't have any phones on us. And I was going to do it at the motel until those hunters showed up. Then we had to run through the streets. Tonight hasn't been working out."

"At least you've got those bracelets."

The hairs on the back of Matthew's neck stood up. "Who are you people?"

"The Carter family, Mr. White," a woman answered from the front door. She wore a night robe that matched her silver eyes, and her white hair was perfectly curled. "And you are Castor and Pollux, wielders of the Gemini Bracelets. Good to finally meet you. I have been waiting to bring you here ever since you escaped Tyndarus. We have much in common, us three."

The pair traversed the porch with the men following behind. Heat pummeled against Matthew, forcing him to take off his coat. His skin had turned red and itched. The other men filed into the house, leaving the three of them alone outside. She didn't react at all to the wind blowing snow across the porch.

"Are you the one giving this kid nightmares for God knows how long?" Matthew asked. He needed some angle to assess her true identity. She couldn't just be some grandmother out in the woods. Why else would she have sought out two total strangers? "Are you an Earthwalker?"

"I'm a human, just like you. And I've never sent any dreams before, just messages. It is because we're related, you understand. Jason told me everything about you after you returned to Earth. I didn't know there was a planet like that out there."

"He told you?"

"He did not do it knowingly," she said, raising a hand. "It is part of our connection. Come in, and I can explain it to you."

Jason looked back and forth between the two of them, clearly lost in the moment. "You said you needed our help, but you never told me how you even found us."

"The relics are linked. Those who wear them can communicate with each other through their unconscious thoughts. This is new to me as I've never met another one with a relic before."

"Another?" Jason asked. "You have a relic?"

"Before that, please come inside. We need to have a conversation about more important topics."

"It can't be more important than rare relics from other planets."

"You would be surprised."

Old woman Carter exited the porch into the house. The area around the remaining pair cooled considerably. Jason huddled at the snapping cold.

Matthew grunted. "How did she get a relic? Aren't they so rare there's only one per planet with life on it? I don't buy this. She's using a power to screw around with our heads."

"Little Winter's been around since heroes and villains started popping up. At least, that's what I heard. She seems to be the oldest person here. So is she the source of this weather?"

"She wasn't wearing anything like a bracelet, though. It doesn't add up."

"Well, ask her."

"I knew this was a bad idea. I should have made plans to go to Cavern Cove instead."

"Come on, Matthew. We can't hide out while the rest of the world crumbles around us. The Great Sorcerer King wants any relics he can get a hold of. Do you think destroying the Mirror Gates will stop him? He'll find another way to Earth. Until then, we should learn everything we can about these bracelets and other relics."

"I'm not stupid. I know we can't cower from reality. But we also shouldn't be searching for trouble like this. I wont pretend she isn't an interesting old bird and probably is genuine in seeking us out. Just keep in mind she *did* seek us out. She wants something. Making ourselves targets for Primes and bounty hunters when there are already agents from Tyndarus after us? *That's* stupid."

Jason threw up his hands. "Fine, fine! Just hear her out for now. We can argue more after."

This woman came charging into Jason's dreams for a reason. She and her family were clearly private people who wanted nothing to do with the outside world, yet she still sought them out. Not only that—she apparently had a relic of her own. With a madman from another world seeking them out to rule over everything, he could not just walk away.

The two of them entered the cabin where the eight men and the old woman waited for them. The large man from earlier stood at the kitchen table while the other seven sat around the living room area on old leather couches where they chatted about some baseball game in Roanoke. None wore their jackets and instead held plenty of sweat upon their brows. The heat was stifling. The old woman led the pair to the kitchen, where they all slid into chairs.

Thick wooden walls, long black rugs, and the scent of pine hung in the air. Matthew hadn't seen such good décor in ages. There was no heating system. The fireplace remained unlit, and yet the heat stayed high. Jason removed his jacket and took one more glance out one window. He nodded for Matthew to look. The snow had ceased falling.

"You must have figured it out," she said. "What the relic does."

Matthew rotated his wrist at her words. "Right now, I want to know what you want. You can give me that song and dance later. Why do you need us here?"

"I don't need you *here*. I need you to help me find someone and bring them back."

"Wait, Ma," the large man said. "Before you do all that, I want to see what Castor here is made of. You said he destroyed the building in Serenity City. He has to be a tough one."

"That is a long story," Matthew said. "I don't want to get into it."

The large man sat across from Matthew and extended his arm. He was a well-toned man, not too much taller than Matthew, but wider in the gut. "The name is Franklin. Put 'er there."

Matthew reciprocated after a moment's hesitation, and Franklin clasped his right hand. The two locked gazes. Matthew sat forward, and Franklin grinned at his approach. He wanted an arm-wrestling match.

"I want to trust you, Castor. Ma says you played the hero, but that was just for show, right? You're just some unemployed loser from Serenity City. Why should I trust you with anything?"

Matthew's voice stayed flat. "You shouldn't. We don't know each other, and I've got nothing to prove to you. But if you want to test me, I'll be glad to wipe that grin off your face."

The two shifted in their seats and placed their arms in the center of the table. Matthew hadn't arm-wrestled in a while, but he wouldn't back down when challenged. They stared at each other for a few seconds before anyone spoke again.

"Count to three, Ma."

She did so, and both men's elbows banged against the table.

Matthew grunted, and Franklin clenched his jaw as their forearms pressed against each other, and their muscles bulged. Their arms shook at that starting angle for what felt like hours.

Sweat formed on Matthew's brow, and Franklin's cheeks reddened. Their arms trembled with the pressure. Matthew's elbow ached. It had been ages since he last did something like this.

He gritted his teeth and pushed forward. His upper arm folded down onto his opponent, but Franklin forced him back. Their breaths fell hard.

"Is he used to this?" the old woman asked Jason.

The teenager nodded. "I think he's taking it seriously."

Matthew roared, and his arm plunged downward. The back of Franklin's hand slammed against the table, knuckles first. He blinked twice as if attempting to figure out what happened. Matthew dropped back into his seat. Both parties struggled to bring their breathing back to normal. The loser rubbed his red knuckles.

"So you can be serious," Franklin noted with a smirk. "I just had to be sure."

Matthew wiped his forehead. "I'm always serious."

"Maybe, but I was told you needed to be prodded. If you're going to do what we're asking, I need to see if you're going all in. Weren't you a lowlife before you got Castor?"

"You've got a real mouth, man." Matthew's teeth flashed in a grin. "Do you think I would have come here if I wasn't serious? Get real. We came through blistering heat, a rainstorm, and all this snow. I'm fortunate enough not to have caught a fever. At this point, I'm half expecting to be struck by lightning. What relic does the woman over there have?"

"Relic?"

"Stand aside, Franklin," she interrupted. "As you two have probably already noted, we're a close-knit bunch. We don't do well with outsiders. But recently, we've been in contact with someone who took an important person from me right out from under our noses. I need some information from you two. But not now—it's late. You two get some rest, and we'll discuss it in the morning."

Matthew folded his arms and sat back, quiet as a mute church mouse. He didn't want to trust her, but since she knew so much about them, he could hardly brush aside her offer. The old woman could have done them in by now if she wanted. He leaned forward, elbows on the table.

"Give me something. Why did you call us here? Who took the person you're looking for?"

"A man who said he believes in magic."

The damp air made Hammersmith's shoulder throb. After spending the last hour running the streets searching for the suspects in this humidity, he was exhausted. None of the people out so late had seen anything (that they would tell him) and the rain only poured in more random spurts the longer he searched.

Finally, he returned to the car and tumbled into the passenger seat. His superior was already smoking and did not acknowledge his return.

"Nothing out there," Hammersmith said. "They're back in hiding."

"I told you to wait in the car," Roadbuster spoke between drags on his cigarette. "I'll check the street when the damn storm lightens up. We found them the last time, and I can do it again. You've got a shortage of newspaper in that birdhouse you call a brain."

"I don't know what happened before. You didn't feel it, but I'm telling you there was a heavy weight crushing down. Whatever powers they have, it must involve some sort of mind control."

"Don't use an excuse, Rookie. I saw White turn into mist, and we both saw him become water. You said the boy had super strength. We know their powers. While you were running around like a headless turkey, I heard some guys in heavy gear were headed to Little Winter."

"Do they think White is headed there?"

"We have no idea what their motives are, but I doubt it. Even cops can barely get in without trouble. Those jokers aren't going to have the door opened for them. I just can't quite nail down what they're planning on doing. None of this makes sense. They get drafted into Williams' Tech, blow the building, then run? I don't see the point. We're missing a piece of the puzzle."

"Next time I'll definitely make them spill."

"You've been acting strange since we met with the assistant mayor. Tell me what's going on."

Hammersmith let out a heavy breath. The words to describe his feelings came so slow that he spoke at a similar glacial pace. "Mind control is a lot like being poisoned. Something slips inside of you and slowly drains the life out. When a Prime uses a power, it's like breathing. Just comes naturally. Boxers are all about breaths. It's how they flow when we fight. This was entirely different. I'm telling you that those two weren't Primes."

"Then what were they, Hammersmith, some kind of magicians?"

"They're going to Little Winter," the voice slurred into Hammersmith's mind. *"They'll certainly be leaving in the morning. You can catch them before they get away."*

Hammersmith clutched his temples and doubled over in his seat. Searing heat burrowed into his brain. The compulsion to scream out loud was cut short by his superior shouting at him. He fought off the creeping smile forcing its way onto his dry lips and sat back up.

The rain danced against the roof like the jumbled thoughts tumbling deep into his mind.

"Those two are freaks of nature," Hammersmith said. "And I think I know where they're going."

"And how do you know that, Rookie? Voices in your head? More magic?"

"Common sense," he said slowly. "Little Winter has something in it that no one has found thanks to the unnatural weather and residents keeping it safe. Those two went into Williams' Tech, came out with powers they never had before, and leveled the place on the way out. And what does Roanoke have that is similar to that building? Little Winter. They're after what is inside."

Roadbuster looked him over and flicked his spent cigarette out of the window. "Your voice sounds off. Are you sure you don't need rest?"

"I'm not joking here. We can't get into Little Winter, but your power will make sure we know if they've got in, and where they're going when they leave. We can cut them off again."

"Fine. It's a better lead than anything we've got now, and I can't do anything in this weather, so we'll give your plan a try. It'll help make up for your flub."

There would be no way Hammersmith could ever explain he knew White's destination. That would play his hand too early. First, this bounty hunter had to be taken care of. Just a little more time, and both Castor and Pollux would be in Albion with the girl, and the trap would be closed. All aces.

The Great Sorcerer King awaited in the cleansing fires of purgatory for his return. They were so close.

Hammersmith smiled at his ally.

Paradise was a stone throw away.

CHAPTER 5
SUMMER MORNING IN WINTER

JASON DIDN'T SLEEP WELL on the freshly prepared guest bed. It didn't look like Matthew did either. The older traveler sat in the chair across from the second bed, hunched over his knees and staring at the hardwood floor. During the day, Jason had control of the main body when they merged, while Matthew had it at night. Matthew didn't like daylight much, so it worked out for both of them. But now, he sat in that chair under the low lamplight as if he wanted to drink it in. He had to be thinking about the old woman.

Rachel Carter had been a courteous host, but she wasn't ready to hear about magic. Nobody could be. How could you tell someone about a powerful evil energy created by a being millions of light-years away?

And Jason couldn't quite bring himself to trust her. Despite Matthew's posturing, he probably believed her more than Jason did. Her straightforward warmth was nice, but the last time Jason let someone like her in, he ended up fighting for his life in another world. Shaula also pretended to be welcoming. Rachel Carter reminded him too much of the now-deceased queen of Tyndarus.

At five in the morning, a big man wearing a flannel shirt and jeans and finely combed hair leaned into the room. The open door let in the strong scent of maple syrup. Franklin called them to follow, and led them out into the kitchen in silence.

The kitchen appeared larger in the day, with not only a baker's dozen of children and adults sitting around the table but with the hard morning sun casting red inside the panes in bright streaks. Jason and Matthew joined the group, as did Franklin. The chattering mass devoured grits, toast, eggs, and bacon at a rate Jason had never seen. The younger children mentioned returning home to their houses as soon as they finished, but Rachel coaxed them into staying longer. A younger teenager named Davey chided them for being babies.

"Aunt Marge doesn't like when you guys come over here and stay all day without telling her."

"Ah, Mom's fine. I like it better here. It's louder."

"You would," he slapped the boy on the back. "Weren't you, Phil, and Ronnie, playing war yesterday? You yell loud when you die. I heard you from the field. You got a mouth on you."

"At least I'm no Steph. She used to blow us up with nukes. Cheater."

"Don't bring her up."

"But I haven't seen her in weeks. Where did she go?"

"Drop it," Franklin interrupted.

The table fell silent, leaving a weight on the room. Every party continued eating in silence. Jason tried to enjoy the food, but the tension made it difficult.

Afterwards, they finished up and cleaned the dishes. The children, teenagers, and adults filed out of the house. Only Rachel and the boy, Davey, remained with the two visitors. The boy sat beside his grandmother and folded his arms to inspect the pair.

The old woman smiled at their silence. "I don't have to tell you about how things fell apart when Primes suddenly began appearing decades ago, do I? Men and women everywhere receiving powers, and on top of it, many died of cancer. Their cells couldn't handle the change. A lot of chaos emerged from this disturbance."

"I'm aware," Matthew suddenly said. His icy tone caused Jason to flinch. "I appreciate you housing us, but what does any of that have to do with you and why we're here?"

"We've been living on this land for generations, and we were on good terms with our neighbors, but the Primes changed that. People we thought were friends committed the vilest of acts, we lost others close to us in random violence, and this city tore itself apart. You were there; you saw how bad it still is even now. Who knows how many heroes and villains the city has now. I had to protect my family from that. I used the earrings passed down my husband's family line to do it."

"So they're earrings, then." Matthew gestured to the window. "And they affect the weather."

"I didn't believe they were what my husband said they were—until I used them."

"Doing is believing."

"When I first married Ed, I was strictly told never to use them. We were to pass them on in quiet. I obliged. Until this Prime business happened. I'll be damned if I'm just going to twiddle my thumbs when my family is in danger. So, yes, I used them."

"But you aren't wearing them," Jason interrupted. "I didn't think you could take a relic off."

"One day, they came off on their own. When I first wore them, I could only do simple things like affect the weather directly around me, but the longer I kept at it, the more I could achieve. I could create weather for multiple areas. I can make cold and heat share space beside each other without causing a storm. I could have taken the air out of your lungs when you entered my area, or struck you dead with lightning. Would you like to know why we get no visitors in here? No one dares to make their way through that. But I don't need the earrings anymore to do it. It is as if they are a permanent part of me. Others have tried to put them on, and they couldn't do anything. I believe the power has become part of me and will stay there until I die. Then the earrings can be passed on to someone else. Would you like to see them? Davey, go get them for our guests."

Jason watched Matthew's face turn green, and the boy felt no different from him. He now understood why they couldn't remove the bracelets. They were permanently joined. It was no wonder the burning sensation from Pollux felt less foreign the more he used it. His fate was sealed: Jason would be Pollux until he died. His fingers trembled involuntarily.

Davey returned to the kitchen with a small wooden box tucked under his rolled-up sleeve. He removed a small black key from his pocket and used it to open the lock. Jason recognized the gold shining out from inside the shallow container. Davey placed the box on the table before them.

Rachel Carter removed the two golden earrings and showed them to her guests. They were like small pearl earrings, no bigger than his pinkie thumbnail. He held it beside their bracelets. All three were constructed of the same gold material and, despite having to be at least thousands of years old, did not appear any older than the cheap trinkets Jason's mom wore to parties years ago. But these had a foreign, indescribable energy inside of them. They were not natural.

"How long has your family had these?" Matthew asked. "They brought them from overseas?"

"Apparently not. I heard my husband's great-great-grandfather might have found them searching for gold over in Arizona long after the Civil War. He gave them to his wife, and she developed strange abilities. However, she took them off as soon as possible and never used the power again. He squirreled it away for generations, and the story spread inside the family. And that rumor somehow got out. It is why they targeted my granddaughter."

Matthew tapped his fingers on the table. "There are people who know about these relics aside from your family? There's only supposed to be one of these on every planet, and the one who told me that isn't even from Earth. Who here could possibly know?"

"The same people after you. No one can get in here, but I can't stop my family from leaving. They do. They work, shop, meet friends, marry, but they always return. We don't fit in very well with the outside world. There are already many rumors about us since we put up the barrier, but most assume it is a Prime power. They don't have any idea about the truth. However, someone seems to. We've been watched for years."

Jason couldn't help himself. "It has to be Nieto's men."

"When we first met in the dream, and you told me about your adventure, I assumed they had to be related. This Great Sorcerer King has traveled the stars for millennia, searching for the artifacts. Only he understands what Little Winter truly is. But his men have never been able to find a way in here. My power is too great. You two have the bracelets, and you found that seed on Tyndarus you gave to that girl. Because he lost you two, I assume he has gone all-in trying to get mine. That's why he went for Stephanie."

"So this is what you took your time getting to," Matthew said. He sighed. "That girl the kid mentioned before. They took her, hoping to ransom her for the earrings, and you want us to go get her back. Correct?"

"It isn't safe around the area she's in. There have been stories of kidnapped young ones."

Jason leaned forward. "Is she one of them?"

"My granddaughter wasn't kidnapped. Nothing of the sort. She fell in love with a piece of trash and ran away from home. Stephanie is a stubborn brat. She's nineteen, but I swear she acts like she's nine."

"Steph is an idiot," Davey said. "But the kids like her."

Matthew snorted. "And you aren't a kid? You can't be any older than twelve."

"I'm thirteen. She used to babysit most of us. Showed us some good hiding places in the woods and was always with us when Granddad died. She might be dumb, but I like her just fine."

"You sound like Matthew," Jason said. He kept talking over his friend's protestations. "But I don't have any problem helping you find her. I just don't see why you can't get her yourself."

Rachel's eyes darkened. "I don't want to send a child out among the wolves to help me, but I don't have any other options. Stephanie is at risk, as much as she pretends she isn't, and I can't tell anyone why she would be targeted. The only one who can help me is someone who knows what they want. I can offer you some money, but that's all."

"First of all," Matthew began. Jason cringed, expecting the worst. "He's fifteen and not a kid. Second, we already have a beef with Nieto. If he has agents still left on Earth, we're going to meet them anyway. But we'll get your granddaughter back. If you want a price, then how about the earrings?"

Jason craned his neck toward Matthew. "And what would we do with those?"

"Nothing. But if we bring them to the stupid girl, then she'll know we're serious."

"Don't call Steph stupid," Davey barked.

"She sounds plenty stupid to me, running off with some idiot she barely knows."

Jason held back a grin. "You like her, huh, Davey?"

"Well, yeah." He pretended to look out the window. "She's family, you know?"

"I get it," Matthew said. "You have to hold on to what you've got."

"They didn't already ransom her yet?" Jason asked. If they had her granddaughter, why weren't they making demands? "What are they waiting for?"

"That's because she chose to go with them," Davey said. "She's probably sold Grandma and the rest of us out."

Jason grimaced. "Don't say that about family."

"I admit it's a possibility," Rachel said. "Maybe he really did convince her, I don't know. She hasn't contacted us since leaving. She never liked staying here to begin with."

Matthew shrugged. "We all want privacy sometimes. But I'm curious. Where is she now?"

"In Albion, near New York."

"That's fairly far. Why did she go there?"

"Why indeed. That's what I want you two to find out. Take the earrings, just get her home again. Please."

Matthew laughed. "It's not like we've got anywhere else to go."

The two visitors made travel arrangements with the old woman. They would take a charter bus up north and transfer over to Albion. The trip would take seven hours. She agreed to pay for their entire way, but a worry crept in the back of Jason's mind. Her motives remained strange.

The last woman he trusted had nearly led to their deaths. Would this one be so different?

But he wanted to let the thought go. Their quest remained unfulfilled, and the last woman who had helped them wasn't Shaula, now deceased wife of Nieto, but Zelana, the girl they had rescued from the Thieves' Forest. She had entrusted them to return to Earth to stop her mother, and they succeeded.

But now, she lay defenseless against her father back on Tyndarus. She needed him to go back.

Perhaps Matthew thought the same, and perhaps not. But if these were agents of Nieto, and if they were from Tyndarus, then perhaps he could find a way back there. He owed Zelana that.

He thought back to the mirror fragment he kept in his bag. Not even the girl's magic could speak to them through it on Earth. If they kept on this path, would that change?

Jason would help Rachel and her granddaughter, but there remained more to this. They had to get off this planet and go back to where this all started. They needed to leave Earth again.

"His name is Jason McCrae," Roadbuster said after hanging up his phone. Hammersmith sat on the motel bed opposite his and waited for his superior to continue. "Your guess was right again. He was a suspect for his parents' murders. He's listed as dead now."

The morning sun peaked through the blinds and draped across the otherwise barren space. They ate take-out pancakes in small Styrofoam boxes. Hammersmith yawned through a bite of toast. He'd tasted better.

"They were planning quite the project at Williams' Tech," Hammersmith said. "First get a goon like White, then a psycho like McCrae, and give them powers. What were they doing there?"

"Info about CEO Arlen Williams and his wife is straightforward. Williams' Tech specialized in creating support gear for Prime powers. Williams has taken ill over the last few years, and his wife took charge. No one's seen her in weeks, even before that building went down. I'm thinking there was a disagreement over pay, and White and McCrae got testy. Their desire for a bigger cut leveled the place. I can guess, but there's no proof. Problem is, we've got nobody, and they're listed as dead. The top floors were all scorched ash . . . and that is before you add in the explosion that took it all down. The lower floor staff was evacuated with minor injuries before it got too crazy, but no one knows what happened up top. Not high enough security clearance."

"Still doubting my powers of deduction?"

"I'm doubting something, all right."

Hammersmith's lip twitched. "Fine. You want to check if I'm right about Little Winter, too?"

"Lead the way," Roadbuster said. He massaged his tiny pancake with his plastic fork. "I have to say that your new initiative is shocking. And in between those massive migraines, too."

"You trying to say something?"

"I just want you to be well, Rookie. We'll see just how much you learned over the past few days."

They slowly finished up their food and departed back into the orange glow of the morning sun. Roadbuster drove them out back down the streets towards the infamous Little Winter. Even in the daylight unraveling over the trees and mountains of Roanoke became interrupted the closer they got towards the patch of trees down the trail. Wind storms raged, and snow blew out into the summer weather surrounding them, melting instantly once they floated past the invisible barrier. Little Winter awaited on the other side of the nearby metal fence.

Roadbuster parked on the shoulder of the road, and the two approached the main snowed-in and narrow road into the place. Many routes led inside; however, this was the one most city residents told them about. The two stopped short of walking into the blizzard, awaiting them inside the fence.

Roadbuster crouched down and laid both hands on the cold road, his palms flat down. Shoulders slumped; he stared down into the solid dirt. He closed his eyes and muttered under his breath.

"This might take a while," Roadbuster said. "Can you call Diamond and let her know where we are?"

"Last time you were in and out."

"We were both at an abandoned warehouse last time. No one had been there in months. I don't have to trace nearly as many paths when most of the activity is recent. There's less to sort through."

"As long as you realize I'm right."

"Just call my wife, alright?"

Hammersmith groaned and slipped the phone out from his pocket. He quickly found Diamond's number and rang her up.

"Hey, Diamond, we're in Roanoke going after that bounty. We should be done soon."

"It's about time. Billy's birthday party is coming up next week. It would be nice if his father didn't miss it *again*. That clown husband of mine never stops working."

"He'll make it. We're close to wrapping this up. Once we get these guys in cuffs, we'll be on our way back home. These villains are going down."

"Since when did you care about villains? I thought you were in this for the pay?"

"I am, but sometimes it's nice to see bad people take a fall. Gets the blood pumping. Everyone wants to play the hero now and then."

"Are you alright?"

"Why wouldn't I be?"

"You don't sound like you."

"Alright, alright. Your husband is finishing up the scan. We're going to wrap this up, and we'll be back soon. Satisfied? Bye."

Hammersmith hung up and put the phone away as his superior stood up to meet him. Roadbuster watched him with a curious expression before repeating his wife's question as if he heard it.

"Are you alright, Rookie?"

"Yes, why does everyone keep asking me that? I may be new, but I'm not dumb. I'm just trying to do my job. If these two are as dangerous as we think, shouldn't we be doing everything we can to get them?"

"If they're guilty of what we think they are, then I agree with you."

He laughed to himself. "And you doubt that? You think they're innocent?"

"Innocent of *what*, Hammersmith? We still don't have any evidence outside of a paper trail, a hunch, and sketchy camera footage. We know they were there at the building, but that's all. They still have no motive or defined goal. Will our employer even care about any of this? We should be approaching this with cool heads or we'll end up making everything go south fast."

"Last I checked, you aren't employed by a reputable organization like Hound Dog, Sonlight, Parvati, or Aegis. Why do you act like you are?"

"Watch it, Rookie." Roadbuster suddenly rounded on Hammersmith, jamming his finger into the younger man's bulky chest. "I work alone because that's where you get the best results. Independent means fewer fingers in the pie. The only reason I hired you is because you told me your powers make fighting fair impossible, and you wanted honest pay. This is honest work, and I take it seriously. If you want to be a cog in some big-shot's machine, then send your application at one of those places. You work for me, then you do what I say. Got it?"

The two watched each other for what felt like hours. That odd irritation set in on Hammersmith, and he saw red for a split second. The former fighter smiled and let it fall away.

"My bad, sir. Did you find what I was talking about?"

"You were right. Again." Roadbuster looked him up and down. "I traced the road and found many family members traveling the road over the last couple of decades, but the two we want were only here the once. Last night. They left through one of the western trails this morning. I don't know how they managed to get in and be welcomed by that family. Nobody gets into Little Winter outside the Carter family. Everyone around here kept emphasizing that point over and over."

"How long ago did they leave?"

"About an hour."

"Then shouldn't we go?"

"Who do you think you're talking to? I'm not stupid, Rookie."

They piled back into the vehicle and drove back out onto the highway, following Roadbuster's directions. Hammersmith had always admired his superior's power to track. It was unrivaled, despite its clear drawbacks of sifting through so much junk and noise, which was why he worked alone before Hammersmith joined him. Roadbuster had never found the right partner. But now, they were a team, and Hammersmith could be useful to the experienced hunter as the muscle.

Silence soon followed minutes after pulling back onto the highway. A voice whispered in Hammersmith's ear about the heavy humidity. He ignored it. They passed waves of mountains and pockets of hills and tree brush, only stopping for gas. The car barreled onward for hours as the sun lifted the humidity in its climb through the day.

But still, he couldn't escape the awkward irritation spreading inside his head.

"You alright, Rookie? You're sweating up a storm."

He shrugged. "I could use a storm right now."

"No kidding. This humidity is killing me."

The air conditioning never turned on in this rust bucket, but neither of the two complained about the weather before today. Roadbuster refused to fix it. He was a total masochist. Hammersmith cracked the window, but the passing breeze was not enough.

The car pulled off the highway and down a thin side road into a brush of tall trees with branches blocking not only the sky but the road before and behind them. They pulled to a stop in the barren place, and Roadbuster shifted into park. He got out and lit a cigarette as he paced back and forth beside the car.

Hammersmith blinked, unsure of what to do, and then followed his boss outside. Sweat instantly pooled on the back of his neck, and he swore. This heat only irritated the shadow in his brain.

Roadbuster drew his gun on Hammersmith. "Okay, Rookie. It's time to sing."

Hammersmith put up both hands. "Mind telling me what you're doing?"

"You missed the code word."

Cold goose-flesh ran down the rookie's arms. What did he miss? He straightened up. "Sorry, I wasn't paying attention."

"Who are you? Why do you know so much about White and McCrae?"

"You're making a mistake."

Hammersmith made as if he were nodding his head and then dashed forward. The gun fired, bouncing a bullet from his chest against Hammersmith's momentum. The shot landed in the dirt.

He knocked Roadbuster down and pinned his shoulders. "What did I tell you?"

Two hands clasped Hammersmith's neck, and a surge of cold pumped into his thoughts. Random pathways and visions of countless people filled his mind. It was as if clutter had filled his brain to the brim. Hammersmith tried to fight it off, but Roadbuster jumped back up, seized his wrists, and rammed his forehead into Hammersmith's nose. The younger hunter dropped.

As consciousness faded from Hammersmith, a hard voice hissed in his head. He couldn't lose yet. Not when he was so close to the two of them. The presence needed to leave Hammersmith behind.

He leaped forward and out of Hammersmith's body.

The rookie slumped to the pavement and left the blood man standing in his place.

Bloodeater cringed as thin beams of sunlight punctured his throbbing thoughts and blood-soaked form. Roadbuster blinked at the liquid form solidifying before him. The man made of red and black blood rolled the kink out of his neck and stared at the skin threatening to reform on his exposed body. It had been too long since he had been outside.

"I wanted this to be simple, but you just insisted on pushing, so I suppose I will push back."

Bloodeater flexed his muscles, and the energy flowed through him like hot lava down a mountain. Hammersmith's power remained inside for now. Before he heard the gun bark, the blood man dashed forward for the kill. The bullets splashed through his liquid form like shots into the ocean.

There was no way he would be stopped here. The blood man had a schedule to keep, and the fires of purgatory awaited him.

CHAPTER 6
BLOODEATER

THAT ICY FEELING lashed itself around Bloodeater's thoughts yet again. The shell of Hammersmith fell under him to the shoulder as he lurched forward across the empty road. Bloodeater crouched and clenched his oily fingers around Hammersmith's neck and held his unconscious form before the armed man. Roadbuster froze.

However, the black shape could not shake the cold nipping at his brain. That man's power was still doing whatever it did to his target. Bloodeater's brain twisted inside his skull.

"What is your power?" Bloodeater asked.

"Put him down."

"I'll do just that if you do not answer my question. Your power. Tell me."

"I can peer through time through objects I touch."

"This works on people?"

"Put him down, and I will tell you."

"Drop your weapon, and that can be arranged."

Roadbuster wavered. The fool had to know he could never shoot his own partner, even if he didn't know Hammersmith's role was only as a mere puppet in Bloodeater's plan. After another pause, Roadbuster tossed his gun down.

Bloodeater closed the gap and tossed Hammersmith aside. The unconscious idiot landed in the dirt on the shoulder of the road, groaning. Bloodeater stepped on the fallen firearm and plunged his dark mass of an arm toward Roadbuster's chest. The large man raised his hands in defense, allowing Bloodeater's nails to stick into his forearm instead.

Bloodeater's form blackened and liquefied and broke down into a thin stream of dark liquid. He swirled downward into the freshly opened wound. His victim cried out as he sunk inside.

He flooded inside the large man's bloodstream and insides, seizing control of his organs. He made Roadbuster crouch down and pick up the fallen gun. The fingers twitched until he could move them like they were his own.

"You're mine," Bloodeater whispered in Roadbuster's voice. "Stop struggling."

A tiny voice inside the depths of Bloodeater's thoughts cried out and went dead. He clenched his stolen jaw and grinned. A car engine blared down the road on their rear. It would be here in seconds. The struggle flared in his brain again. His concentration wavered for only a moment, but it would be enough for a more seasoned opponent. He couldn't stay here and risk another encounter.

Pitter-patters of rain drop popped against the surrounding leaves and pavement. If only *he* were here now he could change this weather at a single word. Thunder cracked miles away.

Bloodeater, still inhabiting Roadbuster's body, entered the car. Behind him, an engine roared as the small rust bucket of a vehicle rolled to a stop behind them. He leaned out the window.

The front door of the new vehicle slammed. A woman in an unseasonably long coat walked towards him, her brunette hair tied behind her and thin cheeks spread in a welcoming smile. Sunglasses adorned the brow underneath her wide forehead. She waved two fingers in a salute towards him.

"Car trouble?" she asked in a chipper voice. "Do you need some help?"

"No," he replied with as much venom as the fool's vocal chords would allow. "You can go."

She pointed a thin finger at Hammersmith. "What about him?"

Bloodeater could not hold back his growl. She had him trapped. Her honeyed tone betrayed the glare he knew she sent out from behind those sunglasses. He would have to dispose of her.

She pursed her lips. "Are you going to shoot me or use your mind control power instead? Decisions, decisions. I'd try the one that leaves a smaller mess, personally."

"I remember you." He recognized her as the one at the assistant mayor's meeting back in Serenity City. He had hired her just as he had these two. "Keep walking. This has nothing to do with you."

"I considered. But right after I pulled over, I saw you standing there, and I saw your real face. What did you do to him?"

"A bounty hunter would have to be a royal pain." He drew Roadbuster's gun. "Oh well."

He fired. The bullet streaked toward her chest—and whizzed into the trees. She dodged the shot completely. She moved just as he pulled the trigger, as if she saw it coming. Another Prime. Her power was not a good match for him. He shot again and again, and the same result occurred.

The woman rolled sideways, fired her gun, and leaned up behind her car. Rain leaped off the pavement, obscuring his line of sight. He wouldn't be able to get her easily.

Bloodeater shifted into drive and stomped the gas. At this rate, he would attract the attention of local law enforcement. Shots careened past him as the wheels tore up the road leaving tire tracks behind.

Roadbuster's voice whispered inside his mind. "*Who are you?*"

He glanced into the rear window and saw the woman vanish from view. For some reason, she wasn't pursuing. He allowed his relief to shine through in his sigh before addressing Roadbuster's pathetic query.

"You'll see soon enough."

KNUCKLES LIGHTLY RAPPED Hammersmith's forehead. The ache in his skull drilled deeper into his brain. Heavy dabs of rainwater doused his brow to help him force his eyes open. He instantly felt the storm falling down on him and over the road.

A woman with tied-back brunette hair stared back at him. She wore a beige coat and held a gun in her right hand. She crouched beside Hammersmith and looked him over.

"What am I doing here?" he asked.

She shrugged. "I should ask you that. Last time I met the two of you was at the parking lot back in Serenity City. I heard police reports last night and have been tailing you from a distance since. I was watching you with my binoculars. But then I saw that blood man jump out of you. Who was that?"

"The blood man?"

"Your boss's power is to track, right? Why didn't he see the guy? Heck, why didn't he see me?"

"It doesn't work that way. He has to know who he's searching for to find them. It's not like some trump card in a fight. Ouch."

"You okay?"

A rush of memories blasted through with blood rush in his head. Fog inside dissipated, and his thoughts returned. That blood man had been inside him for days, slipping in after following Hammersmith to the hotel room in Serenity City when Roadbuster was out. He had masked himself inside and wreaked havoc on Hammersmith's mind. Slowly, his thoughts cleared again.

But the rain dropped harder with every passing moment. The woman bounty hunter led him down the shoulder of the road towards a parked car. It was almost comically small, just like a Beetle. They buckled in, and she tore off down the empty back road.

"Wait, where's my phone?" He patted himself down and found dashed plastic and split wires in his pocket. His phone had been broken apart. "He thought ahead."

"You can use my phone."

He could have, but he still didn't trust her just yet. "It isn't like the police would believe me if I told them what happened. I've got no proof. Besides, I don't even know who you are."

"That's fair. However, we've both got the same goal, so we should help each other. Once we get to Albion all should be clear."

"How long were you listening in?"

She smiled. "Those pancakes sure where awful, huh?"

"Thanks for reminding me. Now I can remember even the taste of that. The blood man's powers sure are something."

The wheels threw up rain across the barren road as they blasted forward. Through the increasing downpour, Hammersmith spotted Roadbuster's car a ways down. They weaved through the back road, the encroaching trees thickening as the distance was slowly being closed. However, the bad weather had slowly blocked their vision of the road ahead. The woman muttered under her breath.

"We're being led into a trap."

He nodded. "Not like we have a choice."

They drove on in the downpour, visibility decreasing with every moment. She mentioned simply leaving him behind to catch up faster, but he didn't put stock in it. Despite her words, she did not so much as slow down.

He thought back to the dark presence haunting his mind. It had already faded, but one name remained like a chant floating above the rest. Who was Nieto and what was Tyndarus?

They drove on in the silence of the surrounding rain, Hammersmith's skin crawling more by the second. Whoever this Great Sorcerer King was, his influence went to the darkest and strangest places. And now he had Hammersmith's partner.

He sighed and sat back in his seat. What exactly did White and McCrae do to get these psychotics after them?

Suddenly the woman slammed on the brakes. The wheels skidded in the mud and screeched.

"What are you doing?" he yelled. "There's nothing there!"

"Look out!"

A large sphere glinted at the top of the windshield. The boulder tumbled down through the branches towards them. It crashed down into the dirt-stained road, kicking up mud against the windshield. The vehicle spun, nearly taking his breakfast.

The crunch shook the car, and the driver's door dented. The woman moaned as she massaged her forehead. Hammersmith threw his door open and stepped out into the rain. He crossed around to the opposite side and found the boulder. It had embedded itself into the shattered pavement with the remains of what looked like bits of frayed cords in its crevices. Behind them lay a long rope that had extended the length of the road before being tripped. A trap. He put his hands on the massive stone and pulled it back.

His strength budged the fallen rock, but not by much. He groaned and gripped harder, his fingers digging deeper into the stone. Between the rain and the mud at his feet, he couldn't keep his hold. Had his power been super strength, this would be easy, but momentum powers were not as useful in this sort of situation. The metal of the door popped as the boulder creaked loose. His muscles bulged, but his shoes sank into the mud as it he rolled it aside.

Hammersmith leaned against the driver's side of the door and threw it open. The metal cracked, and the woman looked up at him with confusion dawning on her brow. A small trickle of blood ran down her forehead. She gestured to the road ahead.

"They're gone," she said.

"But we know where they're going. Engine working?"

"No. Mud in the engine. Needs to be drained and flushed. They did a number on this road. How did he set that up? You sure you don't know him?"

"He led us this way before he met you. He knew what was down here. That bastard was hoping for this result."

She fumbled a phone in her fingers, and he ripped it from her hands. He called an ambulance before calling Roadbuster's phone. No answer. He gave it back to her.

"I don't know who he is, but he's got something to do with those two bounties we were after."

"White and McCrae? What could they have done to warrant this much attention? I spotted them outside Roanoke, but they ran before I could get to them. They're too clean. We both know they couldn't have destroyed that building."

"I'm going to find out when I get to Albion."

It took far too long for the ambulance to reach them in the storm, but Hammersmith hardly cared at that point. All he knew was what he would do when he finally got his hands around the blood man's neck. That freak job would regret ever crossing a bounty hunter again.

The sirens went off as the ambulance carried the two of them into the setting sun behind the storm clouds. He bit his lip and hoped it wouldn't be too late for his partner.

Thunder rumbled above, and the woman shouted in surprise. This storm wasn't finished yet.

CHAPTER 7
STREETS OF ALBION

THE RAIN BLEW walls of water across the bus stop, souring Jason's mood. The bus pulled out as the former passengers loaded both inside the station and sprinted to their cars, families packed under waves of umbrellas. Jason crossed the lot with the cheap umbrella Matthew bought back in Roanoke, and cringed as he uselessly angled it against the wind. No headlights peeked through the brutal storm raging around them, aside from those leaving the lot. For a summer afternoon, it was surprisingly quiet outside.

He turned into the sidewalk towards Albion. It was only a short walk away through some drenched roads and lots. He wished they could have taken a bus straight into town.

"I wouldn't be a drowned cat if I took the right bus." He stepped along the shoulder of the road, careful to watch for oncoming traffic. The darkening skies made it tough to see the thinning passersby as the headlights beamed streets ahead. "You really think they know what bus we would have been on?"

"One of those hunters knew where we were back in Roanoke. They're definitely watching the busses. We should stay away from larger groups."

Matthew had shared worse ideas, and Jason couldn't fault him for this one. The bounty hunters and the people harassing the Carter family were two separate issues. Throwing both off their trail was the best idea, and sneaking into Albion by a back road into an obscure motel would give them a better opportunity to set up shop here. They could also focus on the real issue at hand.

He gripped the mirror piece in his pocket. Zelana had given it to him before leaving Tyndarus weeks ago. It helped calm his nerves when he held it.

Jason crossed the shoulder of the road by a line of trees. He tightened his fingers on the handle as the wind threatened to take his umbrella from him. Rows of faded gray suburban homes with ancient and bending metal fences and freshly cut dark green lawns stared at him. He trudged onward through the empty rain-soaked streets, his thoughts on the destination ahead. The motel was only a block away, and he relished getting inside and dry.

"I've been getting weird vibes," Matthew interjected.

"That's normal for you."

"This town is messing with my sixth sense. The closer we get, the more this force pushes back. There's a wall keeping it out."

"Anything like when we walked into those woods?"

"Yes. Funny you should say that, because this foreign presence reminds me of Tyndarus."

Jason stopped at the crosswalk and waited for the light to change. A father and his son ran by in matching yellow raincoats. A sedan of towheaded children shepherded by a young married couple rolled to a stop. The wife was laughing at some joke her husband made. Jason crossed the intersection with a crinkled brow.

"Not seeing it, Matthew."

"Neither am I. It's like my head is full of static. Just get to the motel, and I'll handle the rest."

Soon enough, they stepped into the lobby of the Albion Rest-Stop Motel, a small and awkward square building planted in the middle of a parking lot. An L-shape structure where the rooms were clearly located surrounded the business. Matthew reminded Jason what to say when he got inside. They would decide what to do next after getting the room. Right now, getting out of this storm was the priority.

A fat man with a tan and a red Hawaiian shirt sat in a rolling chair at the front desk. He had both hands behind his short black hair and his feet on the table. Jason rang the bell extra hard as he pushed open the door. The man behind the desk nearly fell over himself when he saw Jason stroll through the door.

"Good afternoon," the man said in a hurry.

"Hey," Jason squinted at the name-tag, "*Vincent*."

"Are you here alone?"

"No, my brother's dealing with luggage. He sent me in. I'm Alan Simonson. My bro is Ted. I think our grandmother called to reserve a room?"

"Sorry for asking. There have been a rash of disappearances of kids around your age recently. Not just in Albion, but even in New York. We have to ask these questions."

"I understand. But we should have reservations. Please check."

Jason trusted that Mrs. Carter called ahead for a reservation like she said she would, but he didn't quite see why they needed such odd names. The man behind the desk scanned the soaked guest over before finally nodding.

"One second." Vincent leaned over his nearby computer screen and scrolled through. A few clicks later, he nodded. "I have you marked but unpaid. You gonna do that now or wait for your bro to get here?"

"I was put in charge of the money. My brother's got a bit of a gambling problem."

"It's nice to see a responsible younger brother take charge."

"One of us has gotta be."

Matthew whispered in his brain. "*You're pushing it, Jason.*"

After paying, the boy took the key to the room, a magnetic card, and exited back into the rain. He made strides across the drenched and almost empty parking lot and into the entrance of the actual block of motel rooms. The barren halls were silent aside from the heaving, beating raindrops from the storm. The sky was so dark that he needed the faded orange hallway lights to see.

"You know why she told us to take those dumb names, right?"

Jason didn't reply. He was too busy watching the room numbers. Room 513 had to be close.

"We don't know who we're up against here. We don't know if they're expecting us."

"Found it!" Jason chirped. He ran his card through the lock, and the door clicked. He charged into the room and a tight weight lifted from his chest. "Finally!"

Matthew jumped out of Jason's head and landed on the bed closest to the door. He took the bag from the boy and threw it down, digging into it.

While he did that, Jason walked into the bathroom and snapped on the lights. He tossed the wet umbrella into the bathtub and lingered a second on the face staring back at him in the mirror. His eyes had grown bloodshot red, and his headache had flared again.

"I got a question," Matthew asked from outside the door. "Are you still carrying that mirror shard?"

Jason couldn't deny he kept the shard around for selfish reasons. They had limited space to carry things due to constantly having to transform, and a single bag to carry their clothes meant trinkets would have to be left behind. But Jason stared at that mirror shard every night and kept it close. He didn't know if it was in the hope that it would activate and he would see Tyndarus again, or if he just kept it as a reminder. Either way, Matthew probably didn't like having it around. He never wanted to talk about that place.

"I'm keeping it," Jason said. He ran his fingers through his drenched blond hair and plastered it down. A shower would have been nice. "Do you think Vincent is in with Nieto?"

"Vincent? That clerk? No. Rachel sent us to this place because it's out of the way. Albion looks normal to me. Whoever is in charge is hiding. I'm sure of it."

Jason splashed his face, his pores relaxing with the douse. He dried his face and marched out of the bathroom. "How do we figure that out?"

"Easy." Matthew tucked the bag under the bed. He had removed two pairs of fresh clothes and tossed one to Jason. "Put 'em on. We've got the girl's name, and we know she's here. Rachel gave us that phone, so I'm gonna look around for some addresses. Then we'll get her."

Jason ran his palms along the dark blue shorts and gray t-shirt Rachel had given him from her grandchildren's wardrobe. It had been a long time since he wore clothes he had purchased himself, and it never ceased being embarrassing. Jason took them back into the bathroom and put them on, amazed at their perfect fit.

"Rain's already tapering off," Matthew muttered. "We'll wait for sunset. The quicker we get in, the quicker we can get out. The vibe in this town is making me sick. We shouldn't stick around long."

Matthew scanned the screen of the phone they received from Rachel and talked about the humidity. He planned where they would be going after this.

But Jason didn't understand what he was thinking. Didn't they have to go back to Tyndarus? Sure they were hiding out on Earth so Nieto couldn't get a hold of them, though that didn't mean he didn't have ways of reaching them here. The danger of being found remained.

"This is off-topic," Jason said, "but I just want to know. How come you never ask about the mirror shard? Ever since we got back from Tyndarus you haven't said anything about it."

"We have more important concerns than worrying about Ordopha and Alain. I'm sure they're better off than us."

"So you *do* think about them."

Matthew groaned. "Just get ready. We have a job to do."

"Do you always avoid subjects that make you uncomfortable? We should talk about Tyndarus."

"Fine. After this. I want to know more about who on Earth knows about the relics."

But Jason still thought Matthew wasn't being fully honest. They were doing this job to make sure Nieto had no other way to come to Earth, but what after that? They couldn't keep drifting like this forever.

"Okay," Jason said. "I can wait. For now."

The rain and wind outside had softened to a light drizzle. Relief washed over him. The last thing he wanted was to be wet again.

Sudden warmth emanated from Pollux. Was it his imagination, or was it matching his emotions? He felt along his wrist and remembered Rachel Carter's words. Eventually, this power would be a permanent part of him. Would they be running for the rest of his life?

The warmth vanished, and a harsh chill slipped through him instead. He put his dirty clothes away in silence and forbade himself from thinking about it again.

For now, he needed to be Pollux, the hero from Tyndarus. Jason McCrae—no— Jason *Vermilion* could wait for later.

If any part of him remained by then, that is.

MATTHEW LET the kid sleep a few hours in the motel room. Unlike last time, he didn't wander out into the rain alone. He wouldn't make that mistake again. Instead, Jason snored as the sunlight masked behind the dark clouds faded into black, and Matthew peeked at the mirror shard the boy had carried close. It wasn't as if he could do much else.

"Stupid kid," Matthew whispered to himself.

He didn't like to think about Tyndarus. He could never go back there, not with Nieto still alive. It was difficult to believe that place ever actually existed. They were taken into another world with magic and a whole alien race of other people. Even just that was hard to believe. He would never have believed it if he had never ended up there.

The rain outside his window had all but vanished, and pale white moonlight replaced the dying orange from behind the clouds. Matthew shook Jason's shoulder, and the boy vanished into his head as if he was a loose piece of dust being vacuumed up. The boy could rest safely there.

Matthew left the motel with only the room key in his pocket and wandered out into the town of Albion.

There wasn't much to see for a Friday evening, though he deliberately walked through smaller neighborhoods and away from main roads. Rusted and old cars full of teenagers heading out into town and older adults in minivans returning from a long day of work were the majority of what he met. However, he spotted a few dog walkers passing through and kids chasing each other around. A small laugh escaped him. Summer would always be summer, no matter where he was.

"What was that?" Jason mumbled. *"Oh, you jerk. Did you leave without telling me?"*

"The apartment complex is behind the park. Go back to sleep. I can handle it alone."

"Stop avoiding me. We're a team. Besides, you might need Pollux if things get hairy."

"I'm just going to talk to the girl and say her grandmother wants her back. She doesn't know anything about the bracelets, Tyndarus, Nieto, or any of that stuff. It'll be simple. For all she knows, I'm just a glorified messenger boy."

Jason sighed. "*If you say so.*"

The building only went three floors up and with length enough to fit four different residences inside per floor. The red brick pattern and freshly painted brown balconies each apartment dotted with sliding doors to the outside. For a smaller town, it was remarkably well maintained. The people in charge must have actually cared about it.

Hopefully, the people were as accommodating.

Matthew slipped into the foyer and pushed the intercom. A burst of fuzz responded.

"*Hello?*"

"Ms. Carter?" he said in his best-behaved voice. "My name is Ted Simonson, and I've come a long way to speak with you. It's related to your grandmother."

A pause followed. Matthew glanced around the cheap grey carpet of the foyer. One potted plant sat in the corner of the very sterile area. The inside was nowhere near as nice looking as the outside. The chipped cheap white paint didn't help his impression.

"Okay," she replied. *"But this is the last time. I'll explain it again so you can tell her to her face."*

The door buzzed, and Matthew threw it open. So far, things were looking up. He climbed the stairs thinking of the words he would use next.

"Someone already talked to her?" Jason interrupted.

"I'm sure one of Rachel's kids called. They know she's here, after all. But I don't think anyone came to get her. We're probably the first."

"It's a bit weird none of them came."

"Family business is a minefield I don't even want to think about. But a lot of Rachel's issue here is that she thinks the guy Stephanie came with is a scumbag. A hunch isn't enough to go on. But ever since we arrived, I've had a feeling that there's something else hidden here."

"Your sixth sense?"

"Whether she's involved or not, I don't know. Maybe it's just a coincidence. But Rachel has a relic, and so do we. Nieto wants them both. The best thing we can do is convince her to go home. We don't have time to fool around with those bounty hunters on our tails. Here's hoping this is as simple as it should be."

Matthew reached the top of the stairway and mindlessly shoved open the door to the hallway. Two small bodies jumped back from the swinging slab. The pair of boys, probably no older than eight, looked up at him with their mouths agape. Quickly, they circled around him and bolted down the staircase.

Jason laughed. *"Still great with kids."*

"Shut up. It's not them we have to deal with."

He thumped his knuckles on the right apartment. After a beat, it creaked open, and a set of blue eyes stared back at him. This time, unlike with the children, he tried to force a smile. She didn't say anything, and her flat expression didn't change.

"Stephanie Carter," Matthew said.

"You're Ted?" she asked with a yawn. The young woman threw a hand over her mouth before she continued. "You're not from Roanoke."

"You would know. No, I'm not."

"So then tell me why you're here, Ted."

"I'm a private investigator your grandmother hired. I'm here to bring you back home. This shouldn't take a lot of your time. Why did you come out here, Ms. Carter?"

"That's none of your business, or my grandmother's, is it? Look. I'm not leaving. I was stuck in that freezer for nineteen years. I looked after those kids and did what I was told, and when I finally found someone who gets me, they all tried to chase him off. It's my life, Ted. Who do they think they are?"

"Worried, as far as I can tell. Who did you come here with? I know he's not local to Roanoke."

"You're a piece of work. I'm not telling you anything. All I'm going to say is that I'm home here, and I have no interest in hearing what any of them have to say about it. You can bring that back to them. Goodbye, Ted."

The door swung shut, echoing the slam throughout the empty hall. Matthew stood at the door, blinking for a few additional seconds before he finally turned on his heel and left the way he came. Jason already complained in his ear as he reached the bottom of the stairs. Matthew ignored him and walked back out into the night.

"You just gave up?"

"There's nothing I can do tonight. We know where she is, and we've got her reasoning. We'll wait until the morning to see what to do next."

They would rendezvous at the motel and figure out a plan going forward. Matthew couldn't let it end here. She was hiding something. Or someone.

This was what Matthew expected to happen. She had no reason to listen to him, after all. But a strange sight outside the building caused him to double-take. He spotted several men walking down the sidewalk giving sidelong glances towards him. A man in a jean jacket and scar across his forehead sat on a bench in the park, watching him pass by. He tossed back his brown hair as Matthew passed him.

"Who are they?"

"Not friends," he whispered back.

After careful surveillance of the people passing them on the street, he returned to the room at the motel. No one followed him back. Jason instantly exited his head and sat on his bed.

The boy looked up and presented the mirror. "It's hot. I couldn't notice it in your mind."

Matthew squinted at the brilliant light springing from the slab. "This is weird. It didn't do that when we got here."

"Your sixth sense has been going haywire, too. Maybe they're related."

"Maybe," Matthew agreed. "But the Mirror Gates only react to magic. The shards from them should be the same. Nieto is also the only one who can activate them."

"Meaning?"

"There's a Mirror Gate in Albion that leads to Tyndarus." He thought on it a second and hoped his hunch was wrong. "That's why they lead that girl here. They want her grandmother's artifact, and they're going to use her as bait to get it."

"That doesn't make sense. They should have made their demands by now."

"Unless she made a deal to trade the Gemini Bracelets for her granddaughter."

Jason didn't reply. He watched the mirror. It was just as well since Matthew didn't want to discuss it any longer.

He stared at the window, the beginnings of a plan forming in his mind. Whether or not these people knew who they were was irrelevant. The two of them couldn't just leave. Not now. That stupid girl wouldn't listen to reason, either. They needed some way to move forward.

"You don't believe she'd do that, do you?"

"The last woman we trusted did. It's not crazy to expect the same again."

"Then Nieto knows we're here. We should consider calling the police."

"And tell them what? This is our best chance to investigate before anything crazy happens. If Stephanie isn't going to help us, we've got to show her why she should. Let's wait for midnight and go out on the town until we find that Mirror Gate and whoever's got it. We can plan from there."

Jason pocketed the mirror shard and sighed. It looked as if the mirror's light was already beginning to dim. "They'll see us leave this room if they're watching us. I doubt they'd stop at midnight."

Matthew pointed to the window. "We've got more advantages than we know what to do with."

He didn't want to make this gamble, but he couldn't just leave here empty-handed. Not when he had so many questions about what this town was hiding. Matthew played around with his borrowed phone, and Jason went back to looking at the mirror between bouts of glancing at the television. Time passed far too slow as Matthew poured over maps of Albion. Thankfully, he didn't have that long to wait.

He thought up a general idea of where to go, then noticed it was getting close to the hour.

Jason hopped back inside his head, and Matthew took a deep breath before turning into mist.

The outside of the motel remained just as quiet as the inside when Matthew became whole at the base of the rear window. Thankfully a thick line of brush between the back of the building and the mini-mart across the street sheltered him from any potential passersby seeing him. Hard moonlight beat down as the sweat formed on his brow. Humidity ruled the town.

Bounty hunters on his tail, a stubborn woman that wouldn't listen to reason, and enemies potentially watching their every move made Matthew question what he was doing in that town. But Nieto's cronies had left behind many filled graves and grieving victims. If that monster had a way into this world then chaos would only continue.

Matthew turned into water and streaked along the dirty ground and sidewalks into Albion. Nieto would never see him coming.

CHAPTER 8
UNDER THE SURFACE

SHADE from two tall trees in the park blocked the streetlight beams and allowed the two a hiding place. Aside from a minuscule breeze, no one walked the streets so late at night. Matthew and Jason made sure to keep quiet regardless. The boy removed the mirror shard from his pocket. It glowed bright white again.

Jason instinctively crouched deeper into the bushes. Someone might have seen, even at this hour.

"Ease up, Jason. There aren't even any bars nearby. This area is dead."

"The mirror's getting hot. What's near the park that would be a good place to hide a Mirror Gate?"

Matthew pointed across the park to the medium-sized rectangle brick building. The parking lot was empty, and the lights were all off. Albion's library was an otherwise harmless-looking giant shoe-box with square windows. He cleared his throat.

"It's got to be in the library. Nothing else stands out to me. You wait out here in case anything happens or someone shows up. I'm going to check inside to see what I can find."

"It's not like I can do anything else. But one thing before you go, Matthew. I have to know. If you find a Mirror Gate, what will you do with it?"

The older figure paused for a second. "You think I'll break it."

"Won't you?"

"I was thinking about it. We'll see. Stay put."

Once more, Matthew changed into his watery form and slipped into the dark grass ahead of Jason. He disappeared towards the library in the dark, leaving the boy alone.

Then a twig snapped. Jason crouched lower into the brush. The sound vanished, leaving only the barren streets and light rustle of leaves in the breeze.

Someone was nearby.

MATTHEW SQUEEZED through the cracks in the over-sized wooden door. His liquid form pressed thin as he pushed his way into the dark on the other side. Black shadows and old carpet awaited him in the vacant space. He transformed into a human again and regained his bearings.

A twinge of pain caused his eye to twitch. He still couldn't concentrate his sixth sense. Whatever was in this town had to be big to do that. His eyes focused in the darkness and scanned the empty space of the empty library. Slowly he crossed the entranceway, his steps light.

Tall bookshelves loomed over the empty tables. The longer he stayed here, the louder his skull screamed. The cause of his misery had to be somewhere in here.

The mirror in his pocket grew hotter with every step he made. He unwrapped the shard, and white luminescence blasted him in the face.

He weaved through the bookshelves and toward the western wall, the growing heat in the mirror piece only increasing. As it reached its fever pitch, he met the edge of the library where a large shelf lay covering nearly the whole wall surface before him.

Matthew brushed aside books on Irish topography and leaned forward. Large and ugly chunks of grey plastic blocked the wall. But a faint scent of ash tickled his nostrils through the floor cleaner smell. He moved up and down the shelf, examining the area.

A small light peered through a set of heavy books. He squinted at the pinhole crack hidden at the back of the shelf. Tiny pockets of musty air pushed through to kiss his cheek.

He turned into mist and drifted into the opening. Red streaks of pain flashed inside his contracting form. Shockwaves shot through him when he slipped through to the other side.

Thankfully he became human again when he came out on the opposite end. The small stone cobwebbed room was barely bigger than a closet. Low light pressed through the cracks in the thick door before him. He was alone aside from an empty metal shelf bolted to the wall on his right. The space clearly hadn't been used in years.

The burning sensation in his pocket burned to his touch. He wrapped it again as he reached a wide-open hall on the other side of the door. The path was also dark, but torchlight shone through the open doorway at the end of the pathway ahead. How old was this place?

Without warning, a voice played through the covered shard in his hand.

"*Matthew?*" Zelana asked.

He partially unwrapped the piece again. The small shard revealed the corner of the teenager's young face. She pulled the shard back to reveal her platinum hair, wide brown eyes, and furrowed brow, staring at him. The girl stood in a dark forest of green mist.

"Zelana?" he said. "Did you turn this on somehow? Where are you?"

"*I'm just outside Fortuna. The mirror's heat suddenly grew intense, so I thought something must be amiss on your side. Where is Jason?*"

"He's waiting outside the library."

"*Library? Is it large? Are you in the capital?*"

"I'm not sure what you know about libraries on Earth, but I'd guess not much. Let me just say that we got to this town and both this shard and my sixth sense went wild. I think there's a Mirror Gate nearby. I'm looking for it now."

She nodded and glanced around her into the black forest. "*I will go find Ordopha and Alain. They should know about this.*"

"That's fine," he said. "But I'm going to need more than that. If I can find a Mirror Gate, it will lead somewhere in Tyndarus. If I can activate it, I can see where it's located in your world. Then you all can find it, and maybe we can learn about what's going on here."

"*You won't simply destroy it like you did the others?*"

He wanted to explain the whole situation involving Rachel Carter's granddaughter and the possibility of Nieto supporters in this town, but he couldn't leave Jason outside forever. "Not yet. It might be a part of a bigger scheme. Until I figure it out, I don't want to risk setting something off I don't understand. Keep quiet for a bit until I re-establish contact with you."

Zelana moved, and the forest behind her swayed through the frame of the mirror. "*Keep safe, Matthew.*"

He pocketed the shard. The heat remained, but the warmth steadied instead of growing even hotter. Matthew reached the end of the hall and peered out into the torchlight.

A winding set of stone stairs lead downwards with old torches plastered on the walls shining like a spotlight down into the pit. His shuffling steps were the only sound he heard. The stairway was vacant aside from the torches' fire.

The tall metal door at the bottom blocked his way forward. He placed a hand on it, and warmth flowed into his fingertips. He was close. Matthew became water to avoid making noise and reformed on the other side of the door. Still no sign of life.

New darkness enveloped him, as did a branching path. A dimly lit room casting a soft purple hue lay to his right while a whole other hall led to another metal door on the left. He took the way to the right where the open stone area's light momentarily blinded him.

Matthew threw up an arm over his squinting blue eyes. A man-sized mirror lay propped against the edge of the circular room. It glowed harshly at his approach.

He had found the Mirror Gate. It was much smaller than the wall-length ones he had seen before.

The heavy air in the round room gave him a feeling of trepidation. Matthew stood before the large mirror and took the shard from his pocket once more.

"Zelana?" he whispered. "I'm here."

The piece in his hands lit up, spilling heat into the air. He blinked, and a face appeared on the shard. However, it wasn't Zelana. The familiar female on the opposite end frantically searched the length of the small mirror as the overbearing light dissipated. When she noticed him, her expression flattened. It had been awhile since Matthew had seen Ordopha.

"Hi there," he said.

"*Hello.*"

"Is everything okay over there?"

"*Yes.*"

An awkward pause followed as he fumbled for words to say. Thankfully two other faces appeared behind her. Alain and Zelana greeted him in a far livelier manner.

"*Matthew!*" Alain boomed. The usually stiff-necked swordsman grinned wide. "*It has been far too long. Where are you? Where's Jason?*"

"Keep it down!" he whispered harshly. "The sound in this thing carries, and I don't know who else is down here. Jason is outside waiting for me."

"*Is the Mirror Gate you were searching for close by?*" Zelana interrupted. "*Let me see it.*"

Matthew turned the shard toward the Mirror Gate. The voices of his friends mumbled through. The black edges and solid surface of the Mirror Gate reflected a Matthew back at him that looked the same but tinted in purple. The subtle voice in the back of his head growled at the sight. He needed to leave this place, his body wanted him to, but he couldn't go just yet.

"*Put the piece on the gate, Matthew.*" Zelana's soft voice drifted like a delicate dream through his thoughts. It calmed his nerves. "*I will try to put my magic through it.*"

Matthew placed the mirror shard on the gate without asking if it could be done. After a moment, the fragment glowed bright hot white and spread out into the tall reflective relic. The black edges pulsed dark purple, and a matching fog poured out of the surface, rippling like a small pebble thrown into distilled water. He winced as the shard's heat burned into his palm.

The sinister reflection dissipated, and the purple mist parted to reveal a new sight in the Mirror Gate. Rock surfaces and flickering torchlight shone through the frame.

He could make out the faint outline of a cave.

"*Do you know where this is, Zelana?*" Alain said.

Zelana raised her voice a bit. "*Hold it still, Matthew. I'm going to send magic.*"

A burst of white light squeezed through the mirrors and fell into the cave opening at the other end of the wall gate. Just as soon as it flashed out, it muted and died in the dark. But Matthew flinched against what he saw in the moment.

Two lizardmen slept on the floor. They wore leather armor, and each held spears by their sides.

That meant this Mirror Gate had a specific purpose. The Great Sorcerer King Nieto had a base of operations under Albion to specifically connect with someplace in Tyndarus. But where? And what reason did he place this Mirror Gate in the town for?

"*Remove the piece,*" Zelana said.

He did as she told him, and the world inside the mirror faded away once more. The white light receded from the gate, and the purple mist evaporated.

"I take it you saw the lizards on the floor," he whispered. "That's not good."

She waved a hand dismissively. "*It's fine. I know the general location. I can go and find it.*"

"*Not alone,*" Alain said with a growl. "*I will gather a group of villagers together, and we will form a party in the morning. In fact, I'll go inform Kydil now. Keep safe, Matthew.*"

Alain stormed off and left the two women behind.

"*Wait,*" Zelana called out. "*Sorry, Matthew. It might take some time for us to find our side of the Mirror Gate.*" She paused. "*Tell Jason that I am still waiting for him to uphold his promise.*"

Though he had no idea what promise the boy had made Matthew nodded regardless. "Sure."

Zelana ran off shouting toward Alain, leaving Ordopha alone with the mirror shard and Matthew. Neither of them spoke. An uncomfortable silence settled again.

"So," he said. "You stayed in Fortuna instead of leaving the forest. Any particular reason?"

"*Zelana wanted to make it up to the villagers for dragging them into our fight, and she thought the two of you would return. I have to admit, I didn't think you would.*"

"It wasn't at the forefront of my mind, especially considering only those with Nieto's blood or magic can open the Mirror Gates. And even if we went through, without protection from the relics, we'd burn up. But if we can secure a Mirror Gate for ourselves, who knows what can happen? Either way, we'd be taking a weapon away from Nieto."

"*I understand, but I still question why you are in harm's way yet again. Are Nieto's minions really still a threat in your world?*"

"That's a long story. A girl in this town appears to be involved in something deeper than we first thought. This Mirror Gate underground is proof of that. Some group in this town is related to Nieto, and we need to find them. But I also think they know we're here."

A cold shot blasted through him. His sixth sense was warning him. He glanced around in the dark, but nothing was there. He soon realized that his ability wasn't signaling danger for him. Jason was in trouble outside.

"Matth—"

"Ord?" he asked.

But the light in the shard faded, and the girl vanished from sight. Zelana's lingering power inside of the piece must have run out. He pocketed it.

Whatever could be done about this Mirror Gate would have to be done later. He couldn't carry the object out right now, and if he destroyed it, that would give away their position to whoever their enemy was. Even if the two of them were being watched Matthew was not convinced that their identities were known.

Not yet, anyway. When those bounty hunters showed up and started firing half-cocked, it would be trouble for everyone. Matthew only had about a day before that became a mess itself.

Matthew sprinted back into the empty dark pathways of the underground corridors. He thought he heard a voice and paused.

"—nyone?"

He traveled back down the hall towards that second door. He shoved it open and found a small stone room inside with a matching altar. On top of it was a young boy wearing jeans and a polo shirt with a blindfold over him. He couldn't have been any older than ten. The gag around his mouth had been bitten into and torn. Matthew tore the ropes holding him down.

"Are you okay? Hurt anywhere? What are you doing here?"

"I . . . thirsty. Water?"

Before Matthew could respond, the boy passed out. How long he had been here, Matthew couldn't tell. The altar gave him a clue as to what they might have planned to do to him.

But Jason still awaited outside.

Matthew lifted the child in both arms and headed back through the dark hallways to the winding stairs. A weird cult, Nieto, and a spoiled girl, were all related to this whole thing somehow. Hopefully, Jason didn't do anything stupid until they met up again.

"Fat chance of that," Matthew muttered.

This town was going to be the death of them all.

Jason remained still in his position hiding by the bushes in the park in front of the library. He scanned the area and soon found he wasn't alone.

Across the street, a window on the second-floor slammed shut at the pawnshop. A short man wearing large glasses stared out towards the library. His mouth moved as if he was talking to someone.

Jason shifted to his knees, keeping low in the brush. Did this guy see Matthew go in the library, or did he expect the two of them to show up there?

Down the street, a greasy-looking man in far too baggy clothes hid in an alley. This large fellow also had his eyes on the library.

In the parking lot outside the laundromat two men lay back in their car seats. Jason didn't have to question what they were there for. Not anymore.

"They're *everywhere*," he whispered.

A twig crunched and he stiffened as his ears perked. Six men wearing heavy boots traversed the sidewalk to his left. Most wore casual clothes for the summer as if they just came from bar hopping. The lot of them marched past him toward the library.

"You think those two are going to show up?" one asked.

The lead man, a fellow with his dark hair in a ponytail, nodded. "Bryan reported two young blond guys checking into a motel. One of the bounty hunters chasing them was found on the back road outside of town earlier. That means they should be here."

"Then we should meet that guy and ask. Nicely, of course."

"Men are on it."

Jason choked back a reaction. Those two bounty hunters following them were attacked? Then they weren't involved in whatever was going on in Albion. They were just doing their job.

And it was because of Jason and Matthew that they were in danger.

The group approached the library, and Jason could only tighten his fists in response. If Matthew left the building now, he would be ambushed before knowing what was going on.

There was also no telling where he was inside or if he'd found anything while in there. It was up to Jason to make a decision.

Pollux burned on his wrist, the power holding tight. He lifted the wristband and watched the smooth gold surface glisten in the moonlight. They had gone through so much to protect these things from Nieto and his underlings. Even though Jason was putting himself at risk charging in, he couldn't leave Matthew alone. They were both in this together.

Jason stepped out from the bushes and trudged toward the library. Pollux would get a workout tonight.

CHAPTER 9
FIRE IN THE NIGHT

HAMMERSMITH BLINKED awake to a raging headache. He sleepily glanced around the empty emergency room where only a group of nurses passed between the outpatient desk and into the surrounding halls. It was late. Pitch black night awaited outside the emergency doors. He swore with the realization he had been asleep for hours.

His neck creaked, and he sat forward, holding back a moan. He scratched the hours-old bandage on his palm and stared at it. Where did he get that?

"Oh, right," he mumbled to himself. The nurse had taken the woman in to look after her while he had his wounds looked at. Some aspirin and light bandages were the worst he got, though it wasn't as if anyone knew he was a Prime in this place. "Where am I?"

"Albion," the woman from the car said, sitting down beside him. She handed him a can of iced coffee. "Feeling better? I thought about just leaving you here and going after the bounty myself."

She was tall for a woman at near five foot ten, though still nothing on him. She sat with her long legs folded and her mud-stained coat on her lap. Her shirt revealed muscles on her arms that told him she must have been a hunter for a while now.

"Why didn't you leave, then?" he asked.

She took a long drink before responding. "I guess I'm just not that mean. I wonder how much of a head start that blood man got on us."

He popped open the lid and devoured the contents. The thirst in his throat became quenched but only momentarily. He licked his lips when he downed it all. "Well, we know he was following us because of the two targets, and he's no bounty hunter. If we're in Albion then we should ask around."

"Ix-nay on that. When I went out to get some fresh air, several plainclothes men were watching."

"You're a woman that is pleasant to look at. What's weird about that?"

"They were talking into their phones when they thought I wasn't looking. We're being watched. At least, I am."

"Not a problem. We split up and slip out. The only question is where do we spread out to?"

"I overheard some of their whispering about the eastern area by the library. They were going to meet up with their buds. That's probably the best bet if we want answers."

"You think?" He didn't. Even if they were ostensibly on the same side in this situation, she still wasn't with him. If the downtown area was the busy spot, then White and McCrae were unlikely to be there. They weren't that dumb, and she had to know that. "Don't look now, but you have an admirer."

At the edge of the waiting room, a trio of men in loose clothing pointed to the pair of them. They tore across the room towards them. One called out, and the woman leaped from her seat.

"Good luck, Rookie," she said.

The woman whipped down the hallway behind him and swerved around a nurse. Two of the men blew past Hammersmith and also nearly body-checked the same nurse on their way after their prey. Another quartet of poorly dressed men entered in from the sliding exit door. They all sat down in the seats surrounding him. None of the nurses or doctors passing by paid them any mind.

"Thanks for showing yourselves," he chirped. "Now, maybe I'll get some answers."

One of the men slid into the seat beside him, and the remaining encircled

Hammersmith. The leader had messy black hair to match his eyes and a round face to go with his bowling shirt. "Ray Hammersmith. I've heard of you. You could have been a pro boxer, but you stopped when you realized it would be too easy. You're not even running because you think you can take us all on, am I right?"

"You know my name. Should I be impressed? There are deadbeat drunks in Greycoast that know it."

"Are you going to come quietly? There's no need to make a scene. You know we have your partner. Who is that woman, anyway?"

"Someone who helped me out of a jam. She's got nothing to do with us. How do I know Roadbuster is still in one piece?"

"Come with me, and I will show you."

"Are you trying to muscle in on the bounty? That's an aggressive move for such a basic job."

"You don't even know who you're after, do you?" The man laughed and rubbed the black circles under his eyes. "I can't blame you. It isn't as if everyone can know about the purging flames."

"Some of us have better things to do than craft a hat from foil, pal. Make your point."

"It's simple. The two of them were given marvelous gifts. You dealt with their powers; you should know. That isn't all they can do. No, that's just the tip of the spear. Our master wants them both returned. All you need to do is step aside and let us do what we need to. You will be rewarded handsomely."

"Is that why you're telling me all this nonsense?"

"I'm telling you this *nonsense* so you will get context to what we are trying to accomplish. If you walk away we will return your partner to you. If you don't leave, well, have you ever seen those news reports about the corpses they find in drums in the Hudson Bay?"

"You guys really are righteous bastards, aren't you?" Hammersmith remembered the tips he learned from Roadbuster in a situation like this. He hadn't practiced them long enough, but it didn't matter now. "Prove to me that he's still alive. You only get one chance."

The man smirked and shrugged. He removed the phone from his pocket and called a number. "I need to speak with—*Hey*, calm down. What do you mean he was spotted going inside? Well, send someone in!"

Those sitting around the pair sat forward. Hammersmith cocked his ears.

"What time did he go in?" the man asked.

Hammersmith jumped up and snatched the phone. He sprinted for the exit. The doors slid shut behind him. He spotted several of the men stumbling after him. Unless they had super strength or speed they wouldn't be catching up.

"I'll come and help," Hammersmith said into the phone. "Where are they?"

"*Who is this?*" the voice crackled back.

"Do you want help or not?"

"The library! Just get here ASAP!"

Hammersmith threw the phone aside, letting it clatter on the pavement, and thundered through the parking lot. Two men sat on the hood of a blue car, puffing smoke into the air. They noticed him coming, and one went for the holster in his jacket pocket.

"Oh boy," Hammersmith whispered.

This night just kept getting better and better.

Jason stepped low through the brush, the leaves lightly crumpling against his boots. The six men walking the path towards the library remained oblivious to his existence. Slowly he followed after them.

"Excuse me," he said in his best meek tone.

All six turned around. The man in the front of the group pushed through his friends toward Jason and stood at the rear. He wore a simple black shirt with baggy shorts, looking like just another young guy going out on the town. The only thing that set Jason edge was the way his brow furrowed when he scanned the boy over.

"Name," the man said.

"No way. Strangers are strangers. Why are you hanging around out here so late? You guys some kind of vandals?"

"Go home. Now." His tone indicated that he wasn't asking. "Stick around, and you'll regret it."

"Oh, no. I'll just use my phone and—" Jason pretended to reach for his pocket and found his hand locked. Someone had seized his wrist. "I can't move."

One of the men had grabbed him. This one wore a striped shirt and a cap over his coal black locks. The furthest man on the right had somehow gotten around to Jason's back. Had he teleported? Were these thugs Primes?

The capped man searched Jason's pockets with his free hand. "He's got no phone, Kyle. He doesn't even have a wallet."

"Oh!" The interest in the leader's voice made Jason's skin crawled. "Lucky, lucky, lucky! The little runaway has come to us. You must be Jason, then. So where is your buddy?"

"I just forgot my phone at home. What are you ta—"

"Shut up with the lying, Jason. I know it's you. Williams' Tech's files might have got obliterated, but we still got your names. There's someone who wants to see you. Hold him down, Snake."

"Will do," the man holding Jason said. Snake tightened his fingers on Jason's wrist. "We should take him inside."

The energy inside Pollux and the boy's bones lashed out inside him like a violent tornado. Jason roared and whipped his left arm out, throwing Snake across the grass. The flying man rolled forty feet into the side of a tree with a violent crunch.

The five others surrounded Jason, with Kyle at the front. None of them acted even the least bit surprised to see his strength. Were they also bounty hunters?

"Easy now, Jason," Kyle said. He put both hands up. "We don't need to make a scene. But if you want to be a brat and get bruised and broken then that's your call. Just tell us where Matthew is. Is he inside the library? No, he wouldn't leave a kid out here alone. Is he hiding nearby? Naw, he would be out here with you. Did you come out here alone?"

"I'm not telling you a single thing. But *you* can tell me who is in charge of your operation."

Kyle stood right before him. The muscled man breathed hard. His frown broke into a grin, and he smacked Jason across the face with the back of his hand. The group chuckled.

It wasn't much in the way of strength, but the jerk did laugh when he saw Jason's confused face. "You aren't in any position to make demands, junior."

"Fine," Jason muttered. "You asked for it."

The boy delivered a swift gut punch. The fist slammed against Kyle's stomach, bringing the opponent to his knees. Thankfully he had held back on Pollux's strength. Jason brought his index figure up and pointed to the rest of them.

"Anyone else?"

But none of them so much as blinked at what had befallen their leader. The one wearing a mesh hat on top of his rusty blonde hair even laughed.

"Your power is strength, right? Oh, that was a bad luck of the draw, kid."

The boy shrugged. "Doesn't look like it to m—"

A punch beat into Jason's chest. He slid backwards in the grass with as he choked out a breath. Hot licks of pain coursed through his ribs. He fell to one knee.

Kyle waved his hand as if putting out a pretend fire on his stomach. "That's not much you've got in the way of strength. I thought it'd be more than that if the boss was worried about ya."

Jason groaned. "How would you know my strength?"

"I use force thrown at me and send it back at twice the power. Not that it would do you any good. Your kind has no chance against me."

"My kind, eh?" He stood back up, rubbing his burning chest. This group wasn't told about Castor and Pollux. They thought he was a Prime. "I guess you would know all about my kind."

"Got that right. You were chosen to be warriors for the cause, forged in the fires beyond the mirror. But you ran. I can see why with powers like that. This is such a disappointment."

A pair of arms crushed Jason into a bear hug from behind. Cold spikes of pain skewered into his bones from invisible locations. He threw his arms up, broke out of the hold, and spun around. The large man in the muscle shirt behind him instinctively jumped back.

The cold feeling exited Jason as quickly as it had entered. That man didn't have freezing powers—this was a different sort of cold. A sudden twinge of tiredness attacked Jason. Energy draining had to be this one's power.

"Get it yet?" Kyle said. "We're your worst matches. Why else do you think we were sent to find you? All Primes have their own counters. Bloodeater has you all figured out."

They didn't appear to know about the bracelets, which was Jason's lone edge. Nieto did not tell them everything. These guys were only pawns used to block the bishop's advance.

The gang of five advanced on him, and he raised his fists. He hoped Matthew would use the chance to escape if he was still inside. Things were about to get messy out here.

But weren't there six enemies? Before he could spot Snake, the other five closed in.

The moonlight squeezing through the closed curtains at the entrance to the library was the only thing guiding Matthew on. He carried the unconscious boy in his arms, careful not to drop him as he weaved through bookcases. But he soon realized his exit would not be so straightforward.

Small wriggling creatures reminding him of a pile of worms or small snakes slipped under the jamb of the front entrance. They made a beeline for him as if of one uniform mind.

This odd wave of dark creatures masked by the shadow of the library had to mean a Prime was here, and he had no way to get by this one without risking the kid in his arms. And where was Jason?

Matthew did all that he could do—he turned and ran. The deluge of small creatures followed.

He turned down the narrow hall to the right beyond the bookcases where the emergency exit sign lay. Bathrooms and old beige paint awaited him ahead, but he kept moving. Matthew ran into the exit door with his shoulder out, and it swung open. Behind him, he made out the tiny creatures following him. They *were* tiny snakes. The wriggling mass formed into the shape of a man. Matthew backed up into the parking lot away from the Prime that had become a human again.

"Found you!" the big man said. "Now, what were you doing in the library of all places?"

"Looking for the bathroom. What are you, security? I wasn't expecting a Prime that could turn into worms. Disgusting."

"They're snakes, and I can become any one I want. I can even combine different species if I want. Ever see a cow crushed by an anaconda or a dog poisoned by a cobra? Or how about a baby water snake slip across a kitchen floor. I'm all of 'em at once."

"They sure don't skimp on security, do they? What do you say I just head over to the cop shop and hand myself in and get this kid back to his parents?"

"Matthew White. You're a long way from Serenity City. The Master needs to talk with you. Come with me. You know what I'll do if you don't."

Matthew hoped the sweat forming on his forehead was not as obvious as it felt. Castor could help him escape, but this Prime would easily follow. Not to mention, getting into a fight with this boy was out of the question. He would just have to buy time until Jason got there.

"Now that's no fair," Matthew said. "You know everything about me, but all I know is that you're a Prime. Why don't you tell me all about what you're planning to do in this town?"

"I'm sure you've got an idea."

Headlights raked white beams across the parking lot, but Matthew only spared it half a glance. Dealing with this punk's backup on top of him would be a pain.

The car braked hard behind Matthew, and a familiar voice called out from the window.

"Get in, White!" Hammersmith shouted.

"What are you doing here?"

He had almost forgotten about the bounty hunters on his tail. Was this snake guy with them? But Hammersmith's words quickly shattered that impression.

"These guys took my partner, and they want you for some crazy ritual."

The small bit of doubt eroded when Matthew noticed that Hammersmith's partner really was not in the car. Matthew decided to trust him. At least he knew this one didn't want to send him and the boy to Nieto's cult.

Matthew hopped in the passenger seat. "Go!"

"Where's McCrae?"

"He's fine, don't worry."

As long as they had the bracelets, the two could never be far apart, and if Hammersmith drove far enough, Jason would come to them, whether he wanted to or not. Right now, they needed to escape.

"I don't think I gave you permission to leave," the snake man said. "And you, Ray Hammersmith. You're supposed to be at the hospital. What are you doing out here?"

Hammersmith slammed on the gas and spun the driver's wheel, taking the car back around the way it came. "Tell your boss that I'm coming back, and next time it'll be for his head."

The vehicle barreled out of the parking lot, hopping the curb and flying out into the night. It banged down on the road and threw Matthew against the seat before he even found the seat-belt. The kid slept silently in his grip.

The enemy in the parking lot didn't bother following. Instead, his body transformed back into snakes and slithered back into the grass of the thick brush surrounding the library.

Matthew could only speculate as t just how many of these creeps there were. What was it that Nieto wanted with Albion, anyway? He had an inkling that they would soon find out.

JASON HUGGED HIS RIBS. They weren't bruised yet, but his inability to use his full strength while fighting off a mob simultaneously stressed Pollux out. He had never fought a group of Primes like this before. If he didn't have the enhanced endurance of Pollux, he would have been laid out ten times by now. But his greater concern was that one of the six men was missing—the one called Snake.

He rubbed his sore chest and stood tall. The five men still surrounded him. The one named Kyle still stood at the forefront. While the others had simpler powers such as telekinesis over small objects or improved agility, making it harder for him to hit them, their leader merely watched him take the beating. His cockiness strangely faded with each strike Jason received.

"You have more than this, don't you, Jason?" Kyle asked. "I know you're holding back, but why? You do understand what will happen to you if we get you, yet you act as if you are above us. Are you stalling for Matthew White? You do know he won't be able to do much more to help you, so that can't be it. Help me out, Jason. Why are you acting like such a fool?"

"You don't want what I've got," Jason whispered. Snake had probably gone after Matthew. Jason couldn't afford to hold back anymore. "I'm giving you a chance to back off. If I get serious, it will be bad for you."

"Doubtful. You know what my power can do, and I know yours. You have no ace in the hole against me."

A cold hand slapped Jason's wrist and frost formed on his skin. He broke free, and the chill receded. At the same time stones the size of baseballs whizzed past Jason's head. Before he could assess it, a kick caught him in the stomach. He coughed out saliva. Attacks soared at him from every angle.

The boy fell backwards into the grass. He covered his head just as a stone smacked against his skull. Four of the men closed their circle on him, but Kyle remained watching.

"I've been wondering why you haven't tried calling the cops or yelling out."

"You want it?" Jason couldn't play around anymore. "Fine."

Jason jumped up and ran forward. The man with the ice touch closed in, and Jason backhanded the thug. The second man approached and ducked under his punch when the wide-eyed enemy hit the grass. Jason felt the enemy's kick meet his face but kept charging through regardless. Pollux surged through his legs and he leaped at the last two attackers. Jason landed before Kyle and seized him by the shirt collar.

"Pretty fast!" The absorber tilted his head at the boy. "What are you gonna do, big man?"

"You wanted it."

Jason lifted Kyle with his spare hand just as a surge of cold went through the other and a pair of arms wrapped around his neck. The others had piled on him, feebly attempting to stop his attack.

Kyle wouldn't be able to absorb this. The growing weight on his body dragged Jason downwards, and it would be seconds before they dropped him. But at least he could bring the leader out. All he had to do was put Kyle into the ground.

Jason gripped his prisoner's collar, spun around, and swung downward with both hands as if he were throwing down a sack of potatoes. Kyle whipped down with the toss, but the momentum broke as Jason's body rippled into intangibility. The enemy hit the ground lightly. However, the boy could do nothing about it.

Jason's ephemeral form was thrown backwards into the night. The men that had piled on him dropped to the grass as if they had fallen through the air. Before Jason could figure out what happened, he watched passing trees and the road underneath him.

His body snapped into place, and he blinked himself back to consciousness. He was inside a car.

"Am I in your head again, Matthew?"

"You got it."

Suddenly he understood. Matthew had gotten a ride from whoever was in the front seat. They had driven blocks away from the library. The invisible border that allowed the pair to be separated had been passed. They were brought together just by the fact that Castor and Pollux had rules neither Jason nor Matthew could break. Relief washed through the boy. He noticed the unconscious kid sitting in the seat beside him but had other concerns to express first.

"Who saved us?"

"You'll never believe it."

"Who are you talking to?" Hammersmith asked from the front. "Hit your head?"

Jason wanted to ask Matthew if he was insane but thought against it. Getting arrested by a bounty hunter was preferable to being crushed by a gang of Primes.

"Hammersmith? Where's his partner?"

"Your other bounty is in my head now, Hammersmith. I'll tell you how that happened later. But first I—we want to know where your partner is. Where is Roadbuster?"

"I'm surprised you remember his name. But if you want to know, he was taken."

Hammersmith explained what he meant in far too few words, but Jason pieced it together regardless. The two of them chased Matthew and Jason from Roanoke to Albion when a mysterious figure emerged out of Hammersmith's head and escaped with their car, taking Roadbuster with him. A woman bounty hunter rescued him, and they ended up in an accident, and now she was also somewhere in town. All these separate parties made Jason's head spin.

But it did clear a few things up. The hooligans sent by this Bloodeater character were connected with Nieto and Tyndarus. It didn't explain why these punks didn't know about the bracelets, but when it came to Nieto, Jason could hazard a guess as to why. He didn't want his men to know the entire truth.

"Should we go grab Stephanie now? We need to get her out of this town. She's in danger."

"She sure is," Matthew agreed. "But we're being pursued. I think waiting for daylight when all these agents aren't sneaking around town would be our best bet. It'll be easier to hide among normal people and in crowds. Besides, she won't listen to us at this hour. Pull over, Hammersmith. We're taking the kid to the police station."

"One second. I'm going to take a side road to get there."

The drive back went fairly quickly. They made a quick stop at the station, Hammersmith dropping the kid off at the front desk before tearing back out into the night. The bounty hunter volunteered to do it since he would be the one least likely to be recognized, especially if Bloodeater had men in the department. Soon enough, they were back on the road heading for the shopping district.

Lines of empty stores and shining streetlights waited on every street. Hammersmith pulled into an empty lot where the tall brick wall of an alley shielded the view from the main road. The pharmacy wouldn't be opened for hours, so the car being found wouldn't matter much by then.

Hammersmith threw the keys into the seat before closing the door. They made sure the alley hid them before finally loosening up and talking.

"Now what?" Hammersmith asked. "We hoof it to some motel? They've got eyes everywhere."

Matthew shook his head. "We sneak back to our room. Nobody will ever know we left if we're quick enough. Come here, I'll use my power to bring you back with us."

"You're just going to trust this guy?"

"No choice. We need more information, and he needs to know why he has to stop chasing us."

"Okay," Hammersmith said with a deadpan tone. "You're going to have to explain why he's in your head."

Matthew took Hammersmith's shoulder and the pair sunk to a puddle into the cement. Matthew ignored the shocked protests rattling around inside his form and bolted through the dark streets at top speed. Storm clouds rumbled miles away, as did engines crying blocks in the distance. Matthew seemed to ignore it all, slipping through fences and along strangers' lawns. It wasn't as if anyone would see him anyway.

Before Jason knew it, they swam across a backyard and arrived out onto the sidewalk. The motel was just ahead up the hill, dark brush waiting on either side of the street.

And police sirens.

A cop car sat parked by the motel's main office, and an officer stood smoking a cigarette by the entrance to the rooms.

Matthew sunk under a car by the sidewalk and plotted for a moment.

"Hold still," he said. *"We're going to have to do this smooth."*

The watery form slipped out onto the parking lot and moved towards the side of the building.

Jason bundled his nerves together. *"Now to make our way through this without getting shot."*

CHAPTER 10
A TREACHEROUS PATH

OTHER THAN THE lone police car in the lot, Matthew couldn't spot any other signs of life. The sirens were not even flashing. This gave Matthew a chance to relax as he approached the one cop by the motel entrance.

"Hello, officer," he said with a pleasant smile. "What are you doing out so late?"

The officer, a slouching man with sandy brown hair and a matching mustache, scratched his chin with his thumb. "I could ask you the same thing, sir. You two are out rather late."

"We're night owls, officer," Matthew quickly replied. "It's too far from New York to have any fun. Are you waiting for someone?"

"You're the man who rented the room this afternoon, right? You can do me the favor of answering some questions."

"Fire away."

"Where have you been tonight, sir?"

Matthew shrugged. "Walking around trying to figure out where things are. I lost my phone, and my brother won't let me use his. Kids, right?"

The officer rolled his eyes from Matthew to Jason. "And you?"

"He's not lying; my bro is a jerk. Is it safe to go in?"

"The suspect was spotted two hours ago hanging around the trees behind the building. We haven't found any trace of any suspect yet. It's been quite a night. A kid missing from New York just showed up randomly at the station from some bruiser. We also just got reports of suspicious activity near the hospital and the library on top of it. No suspects for those either, but the night is young."

"You don't say," Matthew mused. "I didn't picture this place as a crime capital."

"It's not. I already got your info from the front desk. Now, if you're done, you two can head inside. If we need more, we will be in touch."

"Thank you, officer. Don't worry; we'll be good boys."

The two slunk by the officer into the halls of the motel. A different clerk from the one who had checked them in stood before their door. This one was rail thin and wore a black polo shirt and matching slacks. He introduced himself as Cedric and told them what the officer had already said.

Before letting them go, he put up a finger to indicate he had more to say.

"You had a message. I was going to slide it under your door, but I didn't know you were out. Crazy night this has been. Vincent sure lucked out with his shift."

"It just keeps getting weirder," Jason muttered behind Matthew.

"Who is the message from? A family member?"

"No, actually. It's from the mayor of Albion. He wants you to call him back in the morning."

"You can't be serious," Jason said. "We've never even been in this town before."

"I'm just giving you the message, boyo."

Matthew put up a hand between the two speakers. "And you know this is real?"

"It's no crank call. I've met the mayor before, and I know what his aide sounds like. He didn't say what his message was about, but I'd recommend getting back to him ASAP. It's certainly important. He's a good man. Voted for him for a reason."

The clerk handed them the phone number on a small piece of paper. After a few more words about the mayor, he stepped back out into the night. The exit door gently shut behind him.

When Matthew and Jason finally returned to their room, the latter fell on the bed and let out a yawn. While he did so, Matthew approached the window at the rear of the room. He jostled it open, and the warm wind blew inside. Hammersmith emerged from the trees behind the motel to peak through the opening.

Matthew became mist and floated out of the window. He reformed whole and grabbed Hammersmith. The two became intangible, and Matthew took Hammersmith back inside with him again. When they both became whole once more, Matthew finally let his nerves settle and shut the window with a heavy breath.

After Hammersmith regained his bearings, he did the same. "We've got a lot to tell each other."

"Unfortunately." Matthew closed the curtains over the window. Jason had begun to nod off, which told him they shouldn't waffle. "I'll give you the cheat sheet version of the story."

"Shoot."

"Okay, then." Matthew cleared his throat. "We interviewed at Williams' Tech for a job, and a woman named Marguerite Stohl hired us, but she lied. It was anything but a simple testing gig. Anyway, she died in the building explosion you're chasing us down for causing. If you knew what she did, you would get why I'm not exactly broken up about what happened."

"The cops have been going hard into that," Hammersmith said. He pulled up the collar on his shirt and leaned against the wall. "They couldn't find any evidence of either of you in their systems, and that Stohl woman had a shady trail behind her. The founder and CEO of the company collapsed in his home around the same time the building went down. He's been in the hospital since, in and out of comas, but no one knows exactly what is going on. So, you see why when our employer found that small piece of evidence pointing to you that we were hired."

"I get that, but tell me about Mr. Williams. You don't think he has anything to do with this?"

"So far, it's looking as if Stohl used this guy. She was some kind of Prime; I don't know. I'm inclined to believe what little police investigation there was, especially after everything I've seen recently. That isn't even going into what that blood freak did to me."

"Catch me up."

Hammersmith folded his arms. With a sigh he told a story as strange as anything Matthew had experienced since becoming Castor. A man who could enter others through the bloodstream. Why not?

Over by the bed, Jason had already fallen into deep sleep. Matthew did not anticipate telling him he had been in contact with Zelana, especially considering that he didn't know if they would ever see her again. The kid already put himself out there deciding to help the old lady. Now the mess from Tyndarus had followed them here to Earth.

What exactly had Nieto started on Earth, and how deep did it go?

The fight that started in Serenity City wasn't over yet.

ALAIN VIOLENTLY SLASHED APART the overhanging growth and kicked a large rock out of the pathway. Zelana followed after him, grateful for his presence. What they were doing was imbecilic to the highest degree, and Alain let her know it. He kept to himself as the group of four marched through the fogged trail in the Thieves' Forest, but he certainly had to dislike that he had to keep company with a party of four.

"I apologize for making you all a part of this," she said to the rest.

The entire group wore masks to escape the poisonous air of the forest. It had to be just as uncomfortable for them as it was for her. Carrying armor and weapons was hard enough without having to worry about the weather.

"Nothing to be done," the old man behind her barked. "Kydil is not about to let his best hunters and fighters away from the village. Fortuna needs all the defense it can get. Even if the Queen is dead, there is no telling what else she might have been left behind in these woods. We could not let a girl travel alone. If anyone it is Alain that appears upset."

"I do not blame anyone, Dyne." Alain kept moving without looking back even once. "Neither do I blame Koa or you. I would much prefer to move with the two of us. I understand Kydil's concern since he is worried about Nieto's lizards still roaming these woods, but I am warrior enough for whatever we might meet."

Dyne laughed. "I cannot decide if you and the girl are brave or simply inept."

Not once had Zelana ever thought of herself as brave. Her blood came from those who had no qualms about killing innocents and corrupting the land. She could have been just like them. Zelana thought of her mother far too much. That witch was dead. She had no more influence over her daughter's life. Zelana was free now. "We should keep our spirits up. The four of us should be enough to find a simple Mirror Gate."

"We should be," Alain said. "So enough of this foolish talk."

Sweat rolled from under his helmet as he gestured for them to keep their pace. Alain walked at the front and the younger warrior, Koa, kept to the rear. The group traveled close together, not straying too far due to the fog. They wore their simple leather armor and helmets, with swords and shields ready. The old man, Dyne, had his blade at his side, and Zelana could not help staring at it.

"Is there a problem?" Dyne asked.

"Nothing." She sighed. She missed her dress and didn't want to imagine how she looked in mannish armor. A sword was so awkward to hold. She was not built for such things.

"I would rather not travel with a girl who has no experience with a weapon."

"I repay my debts. Of course, if my father has planned something, then I will also be there to stop it. I do appreciate your assistance, but I would attempt this alone if I were able."

"No, I wouldn't allow it," Alain said. "Neither would Ordopha. She had to stay behind simply to assuage Kydil's guilt about letting two women wander off alone. We do not need more of us running off chasing the passing dreams of a mere girl."

Zelana glared at his back. "I am not a child, Alain."

"So you say. I wouldn't have come if it wasn't to pay a debt to Jason and Matthew. You have every right to make this journey, but not without my assistance."

Cold air slid through the humid night and wrapped itself around her shoulders. She clutched her elbows, holding back a shiver. Her innate magic could keep her warm, but not forever. By noon their masks would no longer be capable of filtering out the poisonous forest fog, and she would need to focus on that as well. Her leadership had led them on a seemingly aimless path through the woods, and all she could guess was they were approaching a cave. Her magic was not enough for the others to rely on, and the others had to know it. Nonetheless, she led them on.

"May I ask a question?" Koa asked. The younger man kept his gloved hand wrapped on his hilt. Despite his gangly frame, patches of muscles betrayed him as a fighter to be feared. He hadn't said much since Kydil ordered him and his master to go along with Alain and Zelana, so his sudden speech surprised her. "This has been on my mind since we departed Fortuna."

"Speak up, Koa," Dyne said.

"What shall we do with this Mirror Gate when we find it?"

"Smash it," Alain said without pause. "It is the only way to prevent Nieto's reach from expanding outside of the mountains again."

Zelana disagreed but wanted to keep them focused. "For now, we would be better served watching our surroundings."

"Do you see something with your third eye?" the old man asked.

"It is not a third eye. The magic is an extension of my being, and I sent a segment through Matthew's mirror and back into our world. I can sense we are growing closer to it."

"My blade hopes you are right," Alain said.

The quartet moved through the fog and into a grove of overgrown grass. With every step, the mirror piece shone brighter from the small bag hanging at her hip. How much farther could it be?

Alain slashed at the tall growth and stopped dead. He gestured to the others to join him upfront.

Stone walls traveled up a gravely rocky base into the green fog above and stretched off into the distance on either side. They had reached the mountains. Was this where the mirror was located?

Koa shook his head slowly. "I was not expecting to reach the mountains."

"Always expect the worst and prepare accordingly," Dyne responded. "None of our kin have made it such a distance since the days of the first forest settlers. If it wasn't for the lass here, I would have gone what little time I have remaining never seeing this sight."

"I apologize," Zelana said, feeling her cheeks redden. "I had hoped it would be a simple cave."

"What does it matter?" This time it was Alain who broke the sour mood. He waved his growth-covered sword along the mountain base. "We promised we would find that Mirror Gate, and we still will. Are you all going to stand around mewling like shrews, or are you going to find it?"

"Easy for you to say, lad. You aren't old as me or as unused to travel as these two are. You're just a brash idiot looking for death."

"Master!" Koa broke in. "Must we squabble here, of all places?"

Alain chuckled softly. "The lot of you are welcome to turn back. I will not shirk from my duty so easily. Besides, I have been through similar caves before. Zelana, tell me where to go next."

The girl nodded and led the group along the base of the mountain, her fingertips gliding along the hard surface as she followed it through the thick green haze. The mirror heated the further she traveled.

"Are there any flowers out here that catch your interest, Zelana?" Koa asked.

"I'm afraid I haven't been paying too careful attention." That was true; her nerves prevented her from paying too much attention to her surroundings. All she could do was question if she was doing the right thing. "I could certainly use one now."

Koa seized her shoulder. "Wait! Do you see that?"

He pointed into the fog along the rock base. A cave opening! Maybe they were closer than even she thought. The girl tore off towards the opening, her clunky armor weighing her down. The three companions joined her at the entrance.

Cold terror frosted Zelana's heart when she spotted the corpse. The dead lizardman lay against the stone wall. Its neck broken with no blood to be seen, the thing had a hole through its throat the size of a smaller spear shaft.

The old man crouched beside the corpse and inspected the wound. He sighed, wiping his glove against its torn rags and pierced leather armor. "This is unfortunate, to say the least."

"What—what is it?" she squeaked out through the pounding in her ears.

"The armor is relatively clean, and there are fresh footprints around the dead. This one died recently."

Zelana swallowed her breath. "Do you know what could have attacked it?"

"I've never been this far out in the forest, girl. Its predator must be near."

"What do you say?" Alain asked. He stepped past them into the dark of the cave. "This is the last chance for any of you to quit."

The quiet cavern broke in on her thoughts. Everyone watched the dead body for a moment before Zelana trailed after Alain, followed by the old man and his apprentice. Zelana couldn't deny the relief she felt in her heart that they chose to continue past it. No one would be quitting this journey now.

"Good," Alain said under his breath.

Zelana steeled her nerves. No more doubts could shake her from this quest. It was just as Alain had said: there was no turning back from this. Now it was time to focus on what lay ahead in the dark.

The mirror piece in her pocket lit ablaze once more for but an instant and died out again. The next time she would look at it would be to tell Jason good news.

Her father's quest would end here, and so would his rotten legacy. Zelana would make sure of that.

CHAPTER 11
CHAMELEONS

THE MORNING SUN raged against Jason's tired eyes, clashing violently against his growing headache. Despite the sleep he had managed to squeeze in over the past few days, his tired bones still weighed him down. After a long yawn, he stumbled out of the motel, into the parking lot, and down the sidewalk. They had an appointment to make.

"How's Hammersmith doing?" Matthew asked.

Jason nearly jumped at the voice in his head. He still couldn't quite get used to that part of their power. "Sleeping better than I did. He's in the bathtub. Why not just take a bed?"

"That's in case someone breaks in. The cops have seen his face. Besides, remember the supposed prowler? There's a good chance they were after information on newcomers like us. If they break in while we're gone, he probably doesn't want to be caught unaware."

"I don't see how the bathroom would make that any easier for him."

"Do I look like a sleep doctor? He says he's a lighter sleeper when he's on a hard surface. Forget about him. Why does the mayor want to talk to us?"

That was a question Jason hadn't spent much time thinking on for the simple reason that there was no answer aside from two possibilities. Either the mayor was involved with this Bloodeater character, or he heard about what happened at the library and knew about the attackers. He could also have talked to that kid Matthew found in that basement. They would soon learn the answer regardless.

Jason's left wrist tingled as if it were stung by an ornery hornet. He rubbed the skin around Pollux.

"Throw a bad punch last night?" Matthew asked.

"Pollux is acting up. What Mrs. Carter said has been getting to me."

"About the relic becoming part of us?"

"I asked her about that before we left, and she wouldn't give me a straight answer. Eventually, the relic will merge totally with us. We're supposed to be two halves of a whole. What if it forces us into one person permanently? We might never be able to separate again."

"Then you can have the resulting body to yourself. I could use a vacation."

"This isn't funny, Matthew."

"Stop being you for five seconds and focus. The mayor wants to meet us, so we're going to do that. Your problem isn't a priority. Are you always thinking of yourself? How come you didn't ask about how Zelana is doing when I told you about her this morning?"

Jason didn't bother answering. He still owed Zelana for getting them out of Tyndarus, and still she gave them aid on the other side now. Of all the people he didn't deserve to face, she was top of the list.

The Sunny Side restaurant on the east side stood out over the otherwise drab brown buildings. The dark brick reflected the rising orange light of the day, and the eggs and bacon cartoon characters dancing with each other on the sign clashed against the drab candle shop and brick bank across the street. A line of four older vehicles parked on each side of the street, with a larger black car slightly to the restaurant's left. The mayor had to be there among the packed patrons inside.

Jason moved to the alley beside the restaurant and made sure nobody saw him. He then allowed Matthew to leave his head, and the slightly taller man stood before him once again. Matthew reminded the boy once more of their goal here, and the boy rolled his eyes. This guy would never trust him.

The bell on the door rang as Jason walked in with Matthew trailing behind. None of the chattering patrons noticed as waitresses moved through the space, taking orders and delivering heated food with pleasant breakfast smells such as ham, sausage, and coffee. Two men sat at the rear booth in the corner, and the chubby well-coiffed one sat up and greeted the pair.

"Welcome, youngsters!" He grasped Jason's and then Matthew's hands for a vigorous shake. "I have heard so much about you."

Matthew cocked a brow. "We've never met before."

"You were sent here by Rachel, were you not? We've talked several times about her granddaughter Stephanie. She's a firecracker. Glad to have her in Albion. Please sit and order something. I recommend the pancakes."

The pair reluctantly assented to join them. Jason and Matthew were seated opposite the wall across from the mayor and his assistant when the waitress came to take their orders.

The heavyset mayor had his grey coat jacket hanging on the rack beside him and his red tie loosened on his neck. A grey streak hung down the center of his combed hair and a matching mustache stretched across his wide mouth. In contrast, his skinny assistant nervously scanned the pair and straightened his blue tie from his seat.

The two new arrivals gave their orders, even though Jason's appetite had already begun to fade. Mayor Sandburg waved away the waitress and winked at his visitors.

"I take it you understand Mrs. Carter's situation," he whispered.

"We do, Mayor Sandburg," Matthew said. "But do you understand her granddaughter's situation? Because if you do, we are going to have a problem."

The assistant snarled. "You don't have any idea what we've been putting up with in this town."

"Does it involve doing nothing while a bunch of cultist punks run free kidnapping children? These psychos are involved with someone much worse than you think."

"And how would you know?"

"Easy, Marvin!" the Mayor said. He raised a hand, and it trembled slightly under his cool demeanor. "We don't need to antagonize each other. We have the same goals in wanting to bring these criminals to justice. Do we not, Mr. White?"

Matthew couldn't resist his stupid smile. "Should I be flattered that the mayor of this place knows my name, or was that meant as intimidation? I'm not here for you or your voters. I'm not even here for that old woman."

"Then why are you here, Mr. White? You have to have drifted very far to get here, but for what gain? A romantic interest in the young woman? Were I a few years younger . . ."

"Don't be a moron."

"The language is uncalled for."

"We don't all live off emotions, Sandburg. You are sitting here getting fat in a diner while letting them roam free, like leaving a viper in a baby crib. I'm here because I know what these people can do, and I know what they are capable of. If you think I'm being harsh now, then you should have seen me before I made this trip."

"It's true; he was meaner," Jason said with a nod.

Mayor Sandburg grinned. "So you are here to play the hero. That is very endearing. You should have gotten a costume, hero name, and a fan club to hype up your arrival. Heroics don't go too far these days without the right sponsors and backing."

"I'll bet," Matthew said. "Hero junk aside, I'm going to give you a tip. These men worship a . . . *Prime* . . . who can warp reality with his purple mist. They think of him as a god, and with his power, he is close to it."

Jason didn't try to question why Matthew described Nieto as a Prime. Mentioning Tyndarus would be a quick way of being dismissed out of hand. This needed to stay simple.

"What Matthew is trying to say is that we found a chamber under the library that had some strange things inside. When we went to investigate, we were attacked."

"And what did you find in there? Does it have anything to do with the boy dropped off at the police station? He was reported missing in NYC three weeks ago."

" . . . I wish I could say what we saw down there," Jason said. He had no idea if that boy told them anything, and he wouldn't be the one to involve him further.

"I called you here because I wanted to help. I can't do that if you're unwilling to talk."

Matthew locked his glare on the mayor. "We don't need you. Stay out of my way, and no one needs to get hurt. I work better alone. The last thing I need is a suit getting in my way."

"Sir!" Jason decided to jump in. "He's not saying that to be a jerk, even if he's very good at it. You don't want to get involved with these people."

"Then you tell me, son. Why should I let you run around my town, putting my people at risk? What do I gain by doing that? Why should I trust you? I do like Rachel, but we are not friends. It is you who owe me an explanation, gentlemen. What happened last night in my town?"

No description they could give would satisfy this man, and neither would he believe them. All Jason could do was what Matthew couldn't—he would talk around the subject. They wouldn't have another shot to get the mayor on their side if they blew this.

Jason cleared his throat. "We signed up for a job back in Serenity City. You might have heard about the William's Tech building falling down. We were there at the time."

"Jason!" Matthew hissed.

"He won't trust us if we don't give him something." Despite his partner's protestations, he went on. "What happened here last night is related to what brought the building down over there."

"That seems like a stretch, son. That's down south, and we're near Canada."

"It's a cult, sir." He avoided mentioning anything about the bracelets. Instead, Jason thought up an explanation that had relation to the truth, even if tenuous. "They find people like us, catch us unaware and try to . . . put us through their rituals. Thankfully for us, they didn't know we had powers and it ended blowing up in their faces. Now we're trying to stop them before they hurt anyone else. We don't want to get you any more involved in this than you have to be."

"He doesn't have to be involved at all," Matthew said.

"Just let me do this, Matthew. Mr. Sandburg, we saw a shrine in the library basement similar to the one we were taken to in that building. We were overwhelmed down there and had to escape, but I'm certain they're going to take Stephanie there. They want Primes."

"Take who?" a woman asked.

Jason and Matthew snapped around in their seats. A couple approached them through the crowded restaurant. The woman, Stephanie Carter, wore her hair in curls over her slim shoulders and atop her plain white t-shirt. She had her hands in the pockets of her jeans. The man had a hand on her shoulder. He wore a tank-top and had the dark hair on his bulldog face spiked up. Jason recognized him as Kyle from the park. Jason hid his grimace before the thug noticed.

"You've seen this guy before?" Matthew whispered.

"Oh, yes," Jason said. Kyle's grinned crack underneath his smooth facade.

Matthew ignored him. "What are you doing here, Stephanie?"

Her hands flew to her hips. "What are you still doing here? What did my grandmother pay you, and can I double it to get you out of town? How many of you did she send, anyway?"

"Now, now, Steph," Kyle said with a grin. "Don't be too harsh. Your family just cares. But I would have sent someone other than these two. It's a long way from the city, boys."

Matthew smiled back. "How did you know we were from the city?"

"Steph told me about you. Look, I get that you were hired to find her and all, but there's nothing to worry about. She's in good hands. You should just go home."

Matthew leaned back in his seat. "What if I decide I like it here?"

The front door to the restaurant slammed. A middle-aged man dashed to the cashier, his red-faced panted with sweat. His breaths came heavy as he bent over and clutched his knees.

"Theresa, you got to see this!" he said.

The pudgy middle-aged woman behind the cash register frowned. "What's that?"

"Someone slashed the mayor's tires. The knife is still there in the rubber. Call the police."

"They did *what*?" the mayor said, jumping from his seat.

He slipped through the crowd, and his assistant followed. Raucous chatter filled the restaurant, and patrons flocked to the window. Matthew and Jason waited inside as the mayor checked on the claims.

"What did the knife look like?" Jason asked the sweating man. "Did you see the guy?"

"The knife had a strange snake pattern on the bottom with a blood stain along the edge. I didn't think much of the guy who did it. Just a man in slacks and a matching blue shirt. He looked normal until he rammed the knife in the tire and then ran off. What the heck was that about?"

"Tell me everything," the cashier said.

The witness retraced his morning walk to her. The mundane story failed to attract Matthew's interest, and the two slowly backed away. The rest of the crowd circled around the storyteller.

Matthew and Jason met Kyle and Stephanie in the middle of the floor, away from the crowd. The wide-eyed woman gaped out the window toward the mayor and his assistant. But her boyfriend watched the pair with a triumphant grin. He winked at Jason. The boy bit his lip and felt his fists tighten.

"What is going on in this town?" Kyle said to no one in particular, but his eyes locked on the two before him. "We might have to move up our plan to get out of this place, after all."

"No kidding!" Stephanie whispered. She still had her attention on the window. "I can't believe it. The mayor, of all people."

The thug took his girlfriend by the shoulder out the front door at the exact moment the manager reached the police on the phone. Chaos erupted inside as whispers spread through the rest of the patrons of this knowledge.

Jason and Matthew remained at the back of the crowd. They stood stupefied and unable to decide their next move. Jason pounded the table with a fist, somehow holding Pollux back from breaking it in two. No one else in the place appeared to notice the resulting clatter.

"I should have stopped him last night."

"Forget that. He's moving up the plan. We're going to have to beat them to the punch."

The noise in the establishment overwhelmed Jason. All he could do was stand there and admit that he missed his chance. Jason would make that sociopath suffer, and Nieto would regret ever screwing with Earth in the first place.

Now the two just needed to figure out how to rescue this dumb girl before getting killed, arrested, or captured by a cult. And who knew how much time they had left.

Matthew nodded as if he understood Jason's thoughts.

The two slipped through the crowded restaurant and back out into the brightening day.

It was time to get rough.

The knock on the window caused Hammersmith to jump up and bang his head on the bathtub edge. Flashes of light danced across his vision. He groaned and rubbed his sore skull, slowly waking up to the harsh daylight reflecting off the bathroom mirror through the crack in the door. The dark in the bathroom made it difficult to find the doorknob, but he still managed to peek out the frame. There he spotted her.

The woman from last night stared in through the screen and waved when she noticed him. He tried not to breathe a sigh of relief at the sight of her.

"Were you asleep in there?" she asked.

"Sleeping in a bathtub does wonders for your back, but I was just resting my eyes." He coughed to cover his obvious lie. "It's harder to sneak up on someone with their back to the wall or a bathtub. How did you find me?"

"I'm good at hiding . . . and that hound at the front desk will talk to anything in a skirt. I knew you'd track those two down, and I knew you would team up with them."

"Were you the one sneaking around out here last night?"

"I'm not that fast. Hey, I need to show you something."

"You never even gave me your name. Why are you so eager to trust me?"

The woman sighed and twisted a strand of her blonde wig around an index finger. "I'm Annette Kline, bounty hunter. You should always ask a lady for her name before speaking so casually to her, you know."

"Ray Hammersmith," he said. He nodded at his own name. He'd always liked it. "I figure if we're going to work together, then we should know each other's names."

"How quaint. I want to show you something, so shake the sleep out. Have you heard about the scuffle at the library last night?"

He already knew where this was going. "Yes. The police were asking questions outside the motel last night. I was even at the station last night, and I would like to keep my distance from it."

"Well, while you were playing around with other boys, I found your partner. Come with me."

"What about the two bounties?"

"No time. We'll pick them up after."

Hammersmith barely stifled a laugh. "You're still worried about them running?"

"I'm worried about what's going on in this town. We walked into something bad, Ray. Once you see your partner, you will understand."

"Alright. Meet me out front in the parking lot."

Hammersmith stretched his hamstrings and found the boots he left by the tub. He splashed cold sink water on his face.

The last thing he wanted to do was leave Jason and Matthew alone, but Hammersmith couldn't leave Roadbuster on his own. He couldn't stand by and hope for the best. That tough hunter had taught him so much in such a short time of Hammersmith getting the job. Heading out with a pretty woman didn't seem like such a bad move, either.

After making sure he was finally awake, Hammersmith left the motel room behind for the hallway. The lock clicked shut behind his exit. There was no turning back now. She met him outside in the sunlit parking lot and shook his hand vociferously.

"This is going to sound strange," she said, "but hear me out. Do you believe in magic, Ray?"

CHAPTER 12
REAL MAGIC

ZELANA HAD A GOOD FEELING, despite the darkness surrounding them. They were close to reaching daylight. She might not have had Matthew's sixth sense, but she was certain they were close to escaping. Although she would have felt better about it if there were less dead bodies in this place.

"Another one," Alain said. He kicked the dead lizardman propped up against the side of the pathway. The group carefully stepped around the corpse. "That makes six."

They'd been climbing the twisting paths upward through the mountain stone for what felt like ages, with only torches to keep them safe. Not one other creature had they met. There were no animals, monsters, or Earthwalkers here, nor were there any other corpses beyond the six the group had found. That left the question of what exactly killed these lizards. Zelana didn't want to know.

None of the others spoke. Koa's mood had darkened with Dyne keeping close to the boy. This left Zelana alone with Alain, who kept peeking ahead. Zelana could do little but follow along. Thankfully the shadows lengthened, and light peeked through the cave path ahead of them. She could hardly contain her excitement.

"Look! Daylight!"

Sun sprayed through the opening, and wind whined against the jutting rock. Alain led the four out into the brightness, putting the torch out as they reached the outside. A sudden chill crashed against Zelana.

She surveyed the mountain around them. An ocean of white mist lay around the drop below them, and a carved gutter of a trail lay ahead. Wind whistled and carried the scent of blood across the rocks.

The group moved through the tight corners of the mountain trail, the slight warmth of the air clinging to the skin under Zelana's leather. At least they no longer had to wear the masks outside since the poisonous fog didn't exist in the mountains.

"Not a soul to be seen," Zelana said. "The killers of those lizards should be close by."

The old man snorted. "You can track so easily? You have not been out of your tree that long, lass."

"I haven't, but I did see into Jason's memories when he freed me from it. I saw a situation similar to this. I'm trying to remember where. Most of those memories have all but faded away."

"They saw something such as that?" Alain asked. "I didn't hear anything of this. It had to have been after they left me in the monastery and before they found my sister in the forest. Does that help?"

"I'm not certain. Let me think."

Alain gestured to the road ahead. "Be quick about it. I do not wish to be left unaware when those killers reappear."

When Jason and Matthew freed her from that tree, she had seen into the soul of the one who shared the Kharis Seed with her. It brought her back to the living from a state she could no longer remember and endowed the magic embedded in her bones with a purifying agent. After awakening, she had many of Jason's memories lodged within her own, leaving her disoriented. Even still, she couldn't be sure why she was imprisoned. But now, with her magic settling in, she could think clearly and scan those slowly fading memories like dusty old books on a shelf. It took a moment for her to find what she needed.

"They hide in the shadows. Jason and Matthew met one deep in the Thieves' Forest before they found me. This is a monster that moves behind its prey before stabbing the throat. It nearly killed Matthew."

"What?" Alain said. "To think they met one of these things."

The old man cleared his throat. "Phantom Claws. You can find them in marshes down south and in the northern mountains now and again. They can only eat meat with poisonous blood like vipers or scorpion-runners, and they hunt at night and sleep during the day. I have never seen one in our woods. Why are they in this place?"

"We should move," Alain said. He rushed down the pathway. "If they attack at night, then we must reach our destination before the sun sets. Tell us what they look like, sir."

Zelana pursed her lips. "I believe the killer was not a normal Phantom Claw. This one was as tall as a man and remained stationed in a mansion. My mother must have kept them as pets."

"Impossible, lass. I've never seen such things, even in Tiger territory. You must be mistaken."

"I know my mother, sir. I may not remember her from before I was found, but I have seen what she did to both my friends and others. She knows—*knew*—secrets we couldn't know. Nieto is that way."

"Be that as it may—"

But before he could continue, they turned another corner, and their conversation ceased. The mouth of a giant cave waited ahead of them. There the purple mist rolled out in waves like a tide at one of the beaches Zelana had seen in Jason's memories. Stalactites like fangs snarled at the jagged edges making the opening appear as the mouth of a beast. Koa and Dyne hesitated at the sight. Alain and Zelana moved toward the mist, Alain drawing his sword.

She understood at that moment—the Mirror Gate waited inside. Their trek was finally near the end.

"It's in there?" the boy nearly shouted. "But surely you all feel the pure menace pouring from inside. Master, what should we do?"

"We should enter, of course. What else do you think we're here for, lad?"

"I'm beginning to question that."

"Then you can leave."

Alain nodded. "That is fine with me."

"Okay," the boy said with a sigh. "I will help for the chance of slaying lizards, but I worry about those Phantom Claws." He pointed to the line of stone to the left of the opening.

"Oh, spare me." The old man waved a hand dismissively and drew his short sword. "Be worried for what the Great Sorcerer King hides in places such as this, not very mere misplaced swamp beasts. You know the stories, and his creations are more vile than simple Phantom Claws."

No one spoke as the four of them moved into the mouth of the cave. But Zelana did not appreciate the old man's words, and they remained on her mind. Jason wasn't lying—he couldn't lie to her since these were his memories she had to parse through. He was not imagining things.

A weight crashed on her heart, and her head pounded. Perhaps the old man was right. Her father had far worse at his disposal than any mere Phantom Claw. This Mirror Gate connected to Earth, and who knew what was over there—perhaps what Jason and Matthew were currently dealing with.

She held her mirror fragment tight at her side and pushed deeper into the shadows with her companions at her side. The shard was only getting hotter.

"WHERE THE HECK did that moron go?" Matthew shouted. He pinched the bridge of his nose.

"Your brother?" the man behind the desk said. Vincent was eating takeout Chinese takeout from a container. "He just went to the bathroom."

Matthew forced a smile and held the phone tighter to his ear. The clerk had lent him his phone, so he couldn't afford to be rude to the idiot. Instead, he sat down across from the desk and waited for someone to pick up. The old lady was taking her time.

"*There you are, Matthew,*" Mrs. Carter said. "*Any news?*"

"It's a bit complicated." Matthew smiled at the man behind the desk, who finally got the hint and backed away from him. Matthew lowered his voice. "This town is hiding a secret, and your granddaughter is involved. One bounty hunter has gone missing, and I'm dealing with his sidekick. A kidnapped kid was being held underground. On top of that, I found something unsettling in the library's basement. I'd head back there, but the cops are all over it now."

"*You can't think she's one of these people. She only knew that Kyle character for a few months before running off. Please just confront her about it and let her know how ridiculous she is being. After that, you can do what you want, but I don't believe she is a part of this.*"

Matthew rubbed the bridge of his nose again. Families were rarely anything but pains in the neck. They always wanted more of you. Not that he knew much about them, to be fair.

"Okay. I'm giving her one last chance tonight. If she's covering for them, I will take her down."

"*Do what you must. You can't go now?*"

"The mayor said he is coming by right now. He wants to talk about the library and what they found inside. I'll deal with Stephanie after that."

"*Thank you once again for your help, Matthew.*"

"One last thing. You said it takes time for the relics to merge with the user. But what happens when it becomes part of you? Do you feel it, or is it a subtle thing?"

"*That is hard to say.*" She went silent for a few seconds before speaking again. "*Imagine a broken bone on anesthetic. Your body knows something is wrong, and you know it too, and yet nothing feels out of order even though it is. However, a fracture heals with the right treatment, and you will eventually not even remember it was ever broken. Do you understand?*"

"As best as I ever will. Thanks again, Mrs. Carter. We'll be in touch."

Matthew hung up and sunk into the chair opposite the desk and beside the window across the lobby. The clerk shuffled back to his desk as Matthew stared up at the popcorn ceiling.

The prickling in his wrist had been occurring more and more recently, but nothing compared to when he escaped from that snake man last night. He scratched the wristband where Castor lay hidden underneath. This would be a permanent part of him. But hadn't he already accepted it? Jason had. Heck, the boy still wanted to go back to Tyndarus.

The difference between the two of them and the old woman was that the bracelets were not the same as the earrings. These two relics affected both of them and allowed transformations and abilities far different from each other—not to mention that it made two bodies combine into one. Would they still be able to do that, or would something else happen when this power fully-formed?

Matthew rubbed a palm across his forehead and sat forward. That could be dealt with later. For now, he needed to deal with the cult. That mayor didn't give them anything to work with, and now they had a target on their backs. Matthew stretched and stood up, groaning as his knees cracked.

Jason crossed the lobby with large strides. "Did the mayor show up?"

"He's already fifteen minutes late. You going to the little boy's room was great timing. It's a good thing our limit for being separated increased, or else we'd have a real problem." Perhaps it was another sign that their powers were morphing. Matthew didn't want to think about it. "What is it up to, an hour now?"

"Oh, we still have a problem. You didn't tell me what Zelana said to you last night."

"One thing at a time, Jason. Once the mayor tells us what he found at the library, we can finally have some leverage to either get him off our backs or to offer us help. At this point, I don't care which. I want to find these cultists and the missing people before we worry about Tyndarus problems."

"But Tyndarus has everything to do with this. That's why it's happening. Nieto created this cult. You sent Zelana after the Mirror Gate in her world even though we don't know where the thing is located. Now the mirror piece she gave us doesn't even work. So how do we help her?"

"Have faith that she's fine. We can only deal with what we can do here, Jason. Speaking of which—there's the mayor now."

Matthew led Jason outside the office where the car pulled up. The same black vehicle, with fresh tires, rolled to a stop at the door. The mayor leaned outside his window. A cloud spread across the middle-aged man's uneasy visage.

"I need to see you both back at the office."

"Can I ask why, sir?" Jason asked.

"We didn't find anything in the library basement, but there was a message scrawled on the floor in blood-red ink. It said *Castor and Pollux will burn in the cleansing fire*. Can you explain that?"

Matthew shook his head. A tingle ran up his wrist from Castor. "It means they saw you coming. These guys got eyes everywhere."

"Come on, then. You've both got some explaining to do."

"Matthew," Jason whispered. "You feel it, right? We're hitting the limit."

"We are." Matthew looked over the mayor and the empty lot. There was nothing else to be done about it. "It's okay if he knows."

"Why?"

"You'll see."

The mayor sighed. "Are you two coming?"

Matthew fell into the back seat, and Jason followed, shutting the door behind him. Just as the door closed, Matthew rippled into fog. The resulting mist zipped into Jason's head.

The mayor glanced at Jason with a slightly open maw. "And you're Primes on top of all this."

There was no sense making this worse than it already was. Matthew told Jason what to say to the chubby politician. "You might as well let the cat out of the bag. You're a Prime, too."

"Balderdash. If I were a Prime, I would admit it. We've had Primes as mayors before."

"That's not why you hide it. I saw your hands shaking in the restaurant. Not withdrawal symptoms, either. The air moved around your palms."

"What are you getting at, son?"

"You keep our secret; we keep yours."

The mayor paused, scanning the faces of the younger man in the overhead mirror. Finally, he let out a sigh and slouched back in his chair. He gestured, and the car drove off out of the parking lot.

"I suppose I better tell you then."

"Tell us what? We don't need to know about your powers."

"Wait until we get to the office. You don't know where there might be ears waiting to hear."

Matthew remained quiet in Jason's head as they turned down Main Street and passed the library where cop cars sat parked around the lot. Already there were almost none left. It looked like there wasn't much in the way of an investigation going on.

Jason spoke inside his mind to him. *"I'm not sure about this guy, Matthew. I don't trust him."*

The car kept on. Eventually, they reached their destination, or so Mathew thought. The two-floor mayor's office was sandwiched between a real estate office and a small law firm —but the vehicle moved past it. Neither of the two in the front seat said anything.

"Should we say anything?" Jason asked.

They slammed their breaks at the red stoplight, and the mayor leaned over the seat.

"What do you boys think of magic?"

"QUIET!" Alain whispered harshly. "Do you hear that?"

Zelana, Koa, and the old man, paused in their steps. The smell of ash had grown more pungent for quite some time, but the torchlight revealed nothing new.

"What is it?" she asked. These mountains would be the death of her yet. "I hear nothing."

"Listen more closely."

She did, but the only sound she could decipher was the distant howl of the wind. Slowly she scanned the darkness ahead, and as she did so, a subtle tapping played in her ear and then vanished as suddenly as it came. It did not play again.

"It's gone away," the old man said.

Alain nodded in the direction Zelana was staring. "You both heard it, yes?"

She froze. Was that a Phantom Claw? A chill ran through her.

"Judging by the girl's expression, I would say so. We should depart from this place. Now."

"If you must, you can take Zelana and the boy with you. I will continue onward. Simply tell me how close we are, Zelana."

"You fool!" the old man rasped. "I am telling you this for your own good. That was the sound a Phantom Claw makes when it has disposed of its prey. But this one sounds much larger than any I know of. We are close to one."

"You told me there is nothing to be afraid of."

"I did. However, that is also not what the girl said is waiting for us. If this is a different breed that hunts larger prey, then we are at a severe disadvantage. They are prime hunters that travel in clusters. The wielders of Castor and Pollux could not easily defeat one such as this. How do we stand a chance?"

Zelana inched forward in the darkness as they argued. The small scratching sound had vanished, but a heavy weight slapped against the ground. The other two behind her were too busy talking to notice. Koa exclaimed and pointed it out in the pitch black ahead.

A body. But not just any body. She searched her mind and the fading memories from Jason and recognized it. He had seen this man before.

"Alain!" Zelana harshly whispered. She gestured with the torch. "You know this man."

Alain came forward and bent over, the torch bathing the body in orange light. He stifled a gasp.

The corpse lying against the cavern wall stared empty-eyed back at them. Its garb consisted of a black cloak and armor. The hole in his throat was the same as the one from Jason's memories. More than that, she also recognized this Earthwalker from her friend's experiences.

"This man was with Richter," Alain said. "He was one of the Vultures, the bandits we met when escaping Mageuopolis. What is one of them doing so far afield?"

Scratching from the rocks ahead interrupted them. Alain shot up and pointed the torch toward the sound. But nothing moved. The scratching never repeated.

"We should go before they attack," he said.

The old man glanced over his shoulder. "Phantom Claws don't hunt when outnumbered."

"How close are we to that Mirror Gate, Zelana?"

"Very close. We only have to make a few more turns."

"Old timer, stick close to her and the boy. I will keep to the point. Watch the edges of the torchlight for any suspicious movement."

Zelana's two protectors kept close. Her attention stayed on the torchlight shadows dancing against the walls. The fading vision of Jason and Matthew fighting one of these monsters kept her heart in her throat.

Pebbles crumbled in the rock walls around them, dropping small stones against the ground. The three men raised their blades and kept alert as they slowly trudged into the darkness. She trembled involuntarily.

The Phantom Claws were already here.

CHAPTER 13
WHAT HIDES IN THE SHADE

Matthew perceived the desk as something of an eyesore. It smelled of far too much of wood polish with a hint of disinfectant. He couldn't articulate why the polished redwood rectangle was as fat as a freezer and gave him just as many chills.

Jason sat beside him at the desk with the mayor and his crony opposite them. Matthew studied the bookshelf as they spoke. Nothing there was to his taste, mostly law and travel books littered the length of it. Matthew couldn't make out any suspicious texts such as magic or occult books.

After repeating his sales pitch for the greatness of Albion, the mayor finally came around to why he asked them there, keeping it as vague as possible.

"We found nothing under the library. Our fine officers questioned the boy and he didn't remember anything aside from being brought there, so there is little to follow up on. He wouldn't even say who rescued him, though I can't tell if it's because he didn't remember or decided to cover for his Good Samaritans. However, we did find those tunnels. They were vacant. The reality that there were tunnels at all has me concerned. So, I require you good gentlemen to fill in the gaps for me. How did you both know to go there? Who was down in that basement with the boy? Were the other missing children there? Where did they go? You must have these answers, and I need you to give them to me. I would use the police to question you if I had anything to tie you there, but since I can't, I'm just going to ask you *mano y mano*. While we're at it, I would like to know your powers, too."

"I'd be appreciative," Jason said, "if you told us what yours were, sir."

"That hardly seems like it matters since I do not use them, but I suppose I am asking a lot and giving very little. How much would you be willing to accept to part with the information?"

"We're not here for money. We're here to help someone."

Matthew sighed at the boy's words. Jason's sentimentality never failed to irk him. The mayor wasn't being forthcoming as it was, and Matthew didn't need this on top of it.

"Okay," Jason said. "Just between us, we think Stephanie Carter is involved with a cult. We're not sure if she even knows it, but her boyfriend—the one she ran away from home with—definitely is. We think the cult wants her to blackmail her grandmother. But we can't get any closer to her without setting off alarm bells. As for the library, we saw some suspicious figures hanging around during the day and decided to investigate. Turns out it was a good call!"

"Undoubtedly," the mayor said with a nod. "I'd say you boys have done a lot to confirm my growing suspicions. It wasn't until you both came to Albion that I became convinced that there was something worse than a kidnapper at play."

"That kidnapper, sir, if you don't mind me asking: how long has he been active?"

"There have been a dozen children missing over the past year fitting a specific profile, all from New York City and the surrounding areas. Until now, there hasn't appeared to be any rhyme, reason, or lead, on where they are being taken. But we have only found one, and he won't talk, so there remains little proof this is a larger conspiracy."

Jason pursed his lips. "They must not have been here that long if they only got a foothold a year ago. Can't you do some investigating?"

"I don't even know who they are, son. That man we met at the diner? I have nothing on him except his name. Nothing is tying him to what happened to my car or to the library last night. I need more information before I can look into this."

"That's nice," Matthew interrupted. "We were just going to talk to his girlfriend this afternoon before you called us up."

The mayor's dry lips cracked into a wide grin. "That is perfect. Perfect! Whatever you can get out of them would help me out tremendously. Tremendously! Try to get names before all else."

"I'm more interested in motivation, but I'll see what I can do. Is there a bathroom around here? I need to make a pit-stop before we leave."

"Yes, yes. Down the hall and to the left. It was at the top of the stairs when you came in. You can't miss it. While you're gone, I'll ask your brother a few questions. I hope you don't mind."

"I prefer it when he shuts up, but as long as I don't have to hear it, I'm good."

Jason stuck out his tongue at Matthew. "Jerk."

"Wonderful!" the Mayor said.

Matthew left the hall and lightly closed the door behind him. Jason could keep that old man busy for at least a little while. They had no reason trust this mayor, and Matthew would confirm his feeling.

Matthew had never been in a mayor's home before but this was close to what he imagined. The immaculately clean hall impressed as much as the rest of the house with polished wood paneling and bright red carpets strewn about the recently cleaned floors. Striped wallpaper plastered the wall, and framed photos of the mayor with everyone from children to the elderly and groups such as scouts and sports teams had been placed strategically around.

He threw himself in the bathroom at the end of the hall, locked the door, turned on the light, and transformed into mist. He squeezed through the cracks and floated back down the hall the way he came. Even though he kept low, however, no one else exited into the hall.

Jason would definitely keep them busy while Matthew floated to the office at the end of the floor.

The mist form glided under the office jamb, and he solidified whole on the inside of the room. The black curtains had been drawn, and the door behind him was locked, but the computer light illuminated the small space in a harsh white glow.

"No screensaver?" he whispered.

He glanced at the screen and saw it locked with a password. He wouldn't be able to guess it, so instead, he approached the cabinets. Oddly enough, he found they were not locked but contained nothing in them besides receipts, permits, and forms. However, the desk drawers were another story. Locked.

Without the key, he would either have to break it or stretch his power to try something new, and he didn't know if he could. He tried once more searching for some sort of key or password in the cabinets and even under the carpet to no avail. Only one choice left.

Castor burned as he focused his power into his right arm. He concentrated energy into his fist and let it crawl along his limb into his shoulder joint. Castor tingled and flared, threatening to tear him apart. Pricks pierced along his limb. With one last thought, he willed the transformation.

Bones and muscles tickled and skin itched, but Castor obeyed his will. Matthew's arm broke apart into a stream of mist. Where his shoulder met the body was a steaming mess like a train stack pumping smoke. His energy and concentration were quickly being sapped. It reminded him of a leak in a dam—if he left it unchecked, it would break and flood the lands below. Aches consumed him.

The mist rolled off his invisible limb as he foisted it against the crease of the drawer and allowed his ephemeral form inside of it. He solidified fingertips as he blindly felt around. The rough texture lightly scraped at his formed skin. Soon he touched a small metal object inside. The tiny shape and jagged edge could only be a key. He clasped it with his fingers and turned it into mist with his hand before yanking the entire thing free of the desk.

Matthew's arm became normal again, and the key lay in his reformed palm. But what was the key for? He checked the few filing cabinets that were locked but found it didn't fit in any of them. The key rolled around in his hand as he watched the room for some clue.

Nothing else stood out around him. The hardwood under the carpet was solid, with no loose boards to be found. He could move the filing cabinets, but that would make too much noise and take too much time. Instead, he looked over the picture frames on the wall.

The smaller frames held images of the Mayor posing with several charities, children, and the elderly. A few had to be taken with family members as he wore more casual sweaters and slacks in those—nothing abnormal here. But two paintings, each sitting on the opposite walls from each other made him think twice about giving up.

One was a picture of a neon-lit cityscape in the rain, and the other was of a plain where a lone man threw a disk, and a Labrador retriever leaped through the air to catch it. The first had nothing behind it, but the second showed him what he'd been hoping for—a safe with a lock on it.

"Are you okay in there, sir?"

Matthew froze at the voice of the assistant. Had he already figured out the game?

Knocking echoed in from the outside hall. It wasn't on this door. No, he was knocking on the bathroom. Matthew felt the pressure to move faster.

The safe let the key into it, and he unlocked it quickly. A piece of paper lay inside, and he pocketed it. Matthew shut the safe, put the painting back, and returned to the desk where he had first gotten the key. He placed the key back in the desk with his power and approached the door.

"What was that?" the assistant asked.

Footsteps pounded against the hardwood. They rushed closer and closer to the room.

Matthew transformed to mist and wafted to the wall where the door would meet it when opened. His fog form flattened against it. The lock clicked open outside in the hall.

The door swung open, and Matthew slipped through the jamb as the assistant rushed in. Matthew sped through the hall and into the bathroom again. The assistant did not turn around. He instead made his way to the closet.

Matthew became whole inside the bathroom and removed the paper from his pocket. He slammed it on the counter beside the sink. It was hard to parse in the low lighting, but Matthew tried regardless. He flushed the toilet and turned on the tap before glancing back to the paper.

"What am I even looking at?" he muttered.

They were a set of instructions. He read it over three times, trying to understand it, to no avail.

Three on the left

Wait one second

Two on the right

Wait one second

Four in the center

"We are the One and Only."

And that was all. He turned it around and upside down, but there was no more information.

He pocketed the paper, washed his hands, and left the bathroom. He would have to transcribe it with Jason later. For now, he needed to get the kid.

"You sure were quiet in there," the assistant called. He locked the office door behind him. "Are you fine, sir?"

"I would hope so. Is there a reason you need to lock up your room so tight? There can't be that much interest in raiding a mayor's home office."

"Normally, no. This isn't a normal town. It hasn't been for a while. Some would say it hasn't been since Primes started showing up."

"Some would say things have never been normal. God just hit the fast-forward button with Primes. Is there something about this whole thing your boss isn't telling us? He didn't look like he was taking this situation seriously until we showed up in town. Was he that desperate to keep the illusion of normalcy in Albion?"

The assistant approached Matthew with a long stride and clapped the younger man on his shoulder. "You shouldn't speak about things you don't understand, young man. Being a mayor—guiding the people, is not so simple. Could you imagine what it would be like if the town realized there was a cult of Primes running around after dark while they were in bed? Handling it discreetly is the only way to approach this situation."

"But how discreetly? He won't even tell us what his Prime ability is."

"That is your problem. Not his."

"It won't be just my problem if I don't know everything I can know to fix this."

"If you have anything to ask, then you can ask. Don't let me stop you."

"Spare me the vague politician talk."

The assistant shrugged and opened the office where the mayor and Jason awaited them. Whatever he was hiding would stay there for now.

Matthew reached into his pocket and felt the paper. There were still secrets here, and he would find them. After he found that girl and talked to her one last time, he would return and learn the truth. Until then, he would keep quiet for once, just as Jason had suggested.

Matthew stepped into the office, where Jason flicked a wink back at him.

"Ready to go?" the boy asked.

"As I'll ever be. Let's end this."

HAMMERSMITH DIDN'T like watching from a distance. The woman nudged him after he spent far too long watching the cops milling about. The pair had crouched behind a group of trash cans in one of the alleys across from the park.

She whispered low. "They showed up this morning, after everything had already been moved."

"You know that?"

"I doubled back here last night after I escaped the hospital. The cops were swarming around that library looking for prowlers after you split. The thing is that they only came back this morning after the mayor called them up. I can't imagine what could have happened."

The most likely possibility would have been his meeting with Matthew and Jason, but Hammersmith didn't bring that up. He was more concerned with the current problem.

"Are you going to tell me why we're here yet, Kline? We could have waited to bring those two with us for extra security."

"No time. Come on. I found your boss *and* an interesting treat. We need to go get them before they move 'em out."

She led him back into the alley and to a warehouse at the rear end. The large, badly rusted door looked as if it hadn't been used in a dog's age. It squeaked far too loudly when she pried it open, and the two pushed their way in.

The dusty abandoned storefront contained badly painted white walls and a stench of wet fur. She hopped the crumbling wood of the counter and brought him to the back room. On the floor sat a metal trap door with a patch of rust dead in the center. How old was this place?

"Did no one bother to clean this store?" he asked. "Here, let me give you a hand."

Hammersmith helped her pry the trap open and revealed a wooden staircase that dropped down into the darkness. A gust of humidity punched him in the teeth. Before he could ask any questions, she disappeared down into the ground without looking back.

He followed her into the stone tunnels with the lousy lighting hanging above them. The twists and turns appeared random as they fell deeper and deeper into darkness. No sound could be heard aside from their footsteps and a distant water drip that threatened to drive him mad with constant tapping. Time dragged on, and Hammersmith began to believe they would never reach their destination. Annette Kline charged ahead of him without once looking back or saying a word.

"Where are we?" he asked. Someone had to break the silence.

"Under the town. There are a series of tunnels from a long time ago. This is how they moved everything in the library."

He could only guess at how she could know that. "And you saw this."

"I certainly did. Did you not notice the strange amount of people watching the streets from the windows last night? They get back out onto the street and back in places like that bakery down the road without using the doors. How else could they have managed that? I thought you were a bounty hunter. You're supposed to have some skills of observance and pattern recognition."

He let that one roll off his back. The strange humidity under here was far more concerning. "My partner was always better at that part of the job. Are we close?"

"We are."

She took off down a narrow hall where a steel door like a vault awaited them. Before he could raise a question as to how they would open it, she gave it a push to reveal it was already ajar. He shouldered it, and the steel slab opened.

The dark room stretched on for a length he could not see due to the lack of a light source aside from that from the hallway behind him. However, one object ahead of him produced a faint glow of its own.

A full-length mirror no bigger than him stared back at Hammersmith. Sparkles of purple flickered against its surface, and a sinister sickness in his gut drew him toward it. The closer he got, the more the creeping disgust strengthened.

He put a hand along the serrated edge. This had been cut out of some bigger piece. A burning sensation in his fingers caused him to recede.

Slowly he began to make out a figure inside the mirror. It looked to be curled up on the floor, and it wasn't human.

"What is that thing?"

Scales, a tail, and leather armor fitted the taller shape. The figure slept unaware as Hammersmith's focus became clear. A man . . . shaped like a lizard?

Hammersmith's tongue lashed across his dry lips, and he instinctively wretched. "What is going on in this town?"

Two arms wrapped around his shoulders from behind, caressing his neck. A small metal knife licked at his throat.

"So you're with them," he whispered.

Annette Kline sighed. "You don't recognize your old friend, Hammersmith? Even after all we've been through?"

Black smoke floated from her lips and tickled his ear. Bile rose in his throat. He would recognize that cold sensation nipping at his spine from anywhere.

"When did you get her, Bloodeater?"

"She didn't make it very far out of the hospital last night. Here's what we'll do. Do what I say, or you are both dead. It's so simple even a moron like you can understand it. Touch the mirror."

The dark air smoked under Hammersmith's nostrils, and his gag reflex kicked in. The memories he spent under its control were not ones he wanted to relive. Kline had to be suffering under that same control.

"Before I do anything, Bloodeater, I need you to tell me where my partner is."

"He's with the others—and where this woman is going. If you do what I say. Now put your hand on the mirror. It's a righteous pain cleaning blood up down here in the dark."

The knife pressed tighter against Hammersmith's throat. The blade burned in his neck.

Hammersmith reached out and touched the mirror. A ripple of cold energy ran through his fingertips, and the hair on his arms stood on end. This wasn't a power—it was something else.

"This mirror is yours," Hammersmith said. He glanced over his shoulder without turning his head. "What even are you?"

"I'm flattered you think me so grand, but that is not the case. This is a gift. This mirror is a gate to the fires of purification. All you need to do is step inside to meet it, and nobody need die."

"You really are insane."

"Can you feel the energy? The life force seeping into you is *The Essence of Everything*. You should be grateful you are allowed in its presence. We have still not been judged ready."

"You won't hurt them if I go in this mirror? What about the other two?"

"Your bounty? Off the table. But if you want to see what awaits them then here's a preview."

Bloodeater shoved Hammersmith forward. The taller man lost his balance, and his right hand plunged into the mirror. The strange force dragged him through, and the darkness devoured him. Bloodeater waved with Annette's body before the lone light vanished from sight.

A tunnel flashed into existence when Hammersmith pried his eyes open again. Purple energy swirled about him in a funnel that carried on into infinity before and behind him. Pitch black waited everywhere else. His heart leaped into his throat. This whole thing was impossible.

His skin burned as if on fire and he howled into the void. His epidermis boiled red like a lobster, sizzling under invisible heat. Hammersmith was not put here to go anywhere—he was put here to die.

He burned in agony as he tumbled through the abyss. White heat scalded his brain and scrambled his thoughts.

The next thing he saw was the smirking face of Bloodeater in his mind's eye.

Then that disappeared with everything else.

Chapter 14
Dying for It

"I wish I knew where Hammersmith went," Jason said. "Why did he run off like that?"

Matthew shrugged. "Do I look like his mother? He's probably looking for his boss, or that woman that helped him. Either way, the more chaos he causes out there, the more heat we lose."

The pair entered the motel lobby and greeted the clerk. Thankfully he didn't ask how the meeting with the mayor went. The two exited out into the street again, making their way to their next destination. This time they would convince Stephanie of her ignorance in this situation.

Jason had been replaying the last meeting here in his head since they left the mayor's place. He would have given anything to go home again, but that could never happen.

This Stephanie girl was way too stubborn. That anyone could have a family waiting for them back home and refuse to see them made no sense. Meanwhile, Stephanie had stumbled into this mess with Primes, Nieto, and a whole other world, and didn't understand what she was in for. No one in this town did.

"*Isn't it tough?*" the mayor had asked him.

Matthew had gone to the bathroom and left Jason alone with their host. He needed to stall to allow Matthew time to do what he needed to do.

"*Sir?*"

"*Being so far from home with only your brother and in this mess. That's a lot to ask of a boy.*"

"*I'm fifteen, sir. I've seen my share of . . . bad. Don't think anyone twisted my arm to be out here. The two of us? We work well together. Even if he's a piece of work.*"

"*It's good to see someone of your age with so much fire in their blood. But what does your mother think about her teenage son doing all this? She must have reservations.*"

Jason took a breath. "*My mother is gone, sir.*"

"*Oh.*" He coughed into his fist. "*I'm sorry. In that case, I can see why this would be so important to you. Family is a precious thing, and once you lose someone important, you realize how hard it is to be without them, and how important they truly were. And how hard it is to know you can never have them back.*"

The mayor's right hand trembled, and he shoved it under his desk. Jason said nothing and glanced at the pictures on the wall. Many smiling faces of children and the elderly met him. Any number of these could have been the mayor's relatives, but the boy wouldn't ask. He had no right to do that. It was best to let sleeping dogs alone in their yards.

"*Well, sir, all I can say is that you never know what tomorrow will be like.*"

"*Good for you, son. It might be hard, but I think you and your brother can handle it. If you ever need anything, you can always come back to Albion. We're working on making this town a real powerhouse. New businesses, new tourist attractions. Once this matter is settled, you will really see a difference!*"

Jason had smiled at the mayor's suggestion, even if he wasn't sure he believed it at the time. Now, as he walked through this strange town with his only remaining friend to convince an idiot of the trap she had fallen into, a growing fire kindled in his stomach. Perhaps this really would work out.

They knocked on the apartment door, the orange light of the afternoon burning against the dirty hallway carpet from the outside. No other soul seemed to be around. It was just as well since he didn't want to deal with any kids this time.

After a brief pause, the two knocked again, and finally, the door creaked open.

Stephanie stared at the pair and sighed. "Come in."

Neither questioned the unexpected invitation. At this point, he would take whatever he could get. Matthew nodded to Jason and then to the apartment interior.

The inside was nicer than Jason expected. Nicely dusted and recently vacuumed, the distinct odor of a stew lingered inside the entrance. She directed them to the floral-patterned couch in the adjoining living room as she returned to the stove.

"I have some stew cooking. You boys interested?"

Matthew grumbled. "*Boys*? I'm older than you, girl."

"That doesn't mean you can't enjoy a good meal. Give me a few seconds here, and I'll join you."

Before returning to the small living room, Stephanie stirred the pot and turned the heat down on the stove. She sat in the matching chair across from the couch beside the balcony window and leaned forward. Her thin arms trembled as if a sudden cold attacked, and she hugged them.

"Problem?" Jason asked.

"As weird as it is to say, yes. Ever since I made Kyle go home, there's been this chill I can't quite shake. It's been happening more and more this week. I might be coming down with something."

Matthew put up a finger. "Home? He doesn't live here? But you both ran away together."

"I told him we'd move in together when we tie the knot, but he's been stalling and making excuses. He's not as cool as he thinks. So he can stay with his roommate if that's what he wants."

"I didn't expect an old-fashioned girl, especially since you're a runaway and all."

"Look, I don't even know your names. But since Grandma sent you, and I've been rude, I'll be upfront. I'm sorry for my attitude. I thought you were just private eyes or bounty hunters or whatever you hire to find people. When I saw you with the mayor, I got to thinking that maybe there's more to this for you two than a paycheck from my nosy family. So, let's talk."

"I'm Matthew, and the dumb one is Jason. We came from Serenity City."

"That far? How did my grandmother find you?"

"We found her. We were out on other business, and she enlisted our services."

"If you got into Little Winter then you must be the real deal. The easy way to know if you did is to ask if you know where the weather comes from."

Matthew tapped his earlobes. "Did you tell your boyfriend or his stooges anything about it?"

"Nope, and he's never asked."

Jason doubted that part, but the girl had no reason to lie. On the other hand, it was clear Nieto wanted the relics like the Gemini Bracelets and Mrs. Carter's earrings and that these thugs were sent to retrieve them. So why didn't they question this girl about them? Why did they take her out here in the first place? It wasn't because that Kyle jerk loved her. Jason had only fought him once but still knew he was a monster.

"Do you mind if I take a look around?" Jason suddenly asked, both to his and the other two's surprise. "It's a nice place."

"Sure thing," she replied. "There's not much to see. Just stay out of my room, if you wouldn't mind. Not that I'm hiding anything, but you know . . ."

"Understood." There were some places men didn't dare go uninvited. "I'll be quick."

Matthew made more small talk as Jason wandered down the hall beyond the kitchen. There were only two other rooms aside from the bathroom, and only one was left open. The open one was clearly her bedroom with a carefully made bed with frilly sheets and a small polished dresser. He passed that room and touched the handle of the locked one.

An illness washed over him. A black feeling filled his insides. Magic from Tyndarus.

Pumping a light touch of Pollux's power into his arm, Jason shoved the handle, and quietly popped it loose. He didn't waste any time thinking this over. He would explain it to Stephanie later.

"Everything alright down there?" she called.

He stepped backwards and flicked on the bathroom light before him at the same time. "Yeah, I just gotta use the washroom for a moment."

"Okay."

He stayed out in the hall and closed the bathroom door. The boy listened to see if Matthew had bothered covering for him. Their voices drifted out of the living room.

"Why are you with that Kyle thug, anyway?" Matthew asked. "You could do a lot better."

"Are you offering?"

"Drifters don't get into romances, but I'm definitely a better man than him. No doubt about that."

She laughed. "You just don't know him."

"I know he's full of himself."

"He's just confident, like you. He knows what he wants and how to get it. Once we save up enough, we're going to the city itself to make a name for ourselves. We even have the apartment lined up. It's just . . ." She paused. "I don't know."

"Something's off."

"Yes. No. I don't know. It's like there's a nagging doubt in the back of my head telling me to be careful, but I don't know what it is about. Paranoia, I guess."

Jason had heard enough of their conversation. Matthew could handle the rest.

The boy pushed open the busted door of the mystery room. The shades had been drawn in the dark space. Boxes filled the area, all covered by dust-covered sheets. He stepped into the thick of it.

At the rear, a long plank-like object leaned against the curtained window draped in a white sheet. It wasn't caked in dust, unlike the rest, but a strange sensation drew him towards it. A dark feeling swam through his head as he inched towards the sheet, fingers trembling. Jason opened it up and found a locked crate. He lightly hammered it open with Pollux and glanced inside. There sat a pile of knives inside, all with a snake insignia—the same one that was left in the mayor's tire. Could this be the—

"Hey!" Matthew yelled. "Are you alright? Hey, get up!"

Jason paused. Matthew wasn't yelling at him. He ran out of the room and bolted down the hall.

The girl was slumped in the chair, and Matthew shook her shoulders. She was out of it.

The front door to the apartment flew open, and a man dressed in slacks and a polo shirt stepped inside. He had a pointed chin, a small beard, and eyes blacker than the darkest coal. Three other men, one of which was Kyle, followed him in.

"Declare was quick as usual," the front-man with the beard said. "I'll have to give him a bigger piece of the pie. Kyle, you can collect her now."

"Who are you?" Jason asked. "Get out of here before I make you get out."

"She won't be waking up for a while. In fact, she won't be waking up at all unless you both come quietly. Declare can do anything to someone once his parasite has been ingested."

Matthew spoke softly under his breath. "So you did do something to her."

"Just enough to make sure she wouldn't run away. But you two are wedging yourselves into this situation far too well. Now that I know exactly who you are, I can no longer have you lingering around town. You could have heeded Kyle's warnings and left, but you did not. That is all the time you both get. The Master will see you now."

"Are you the one who attacked Hammersmith and his partner?" Matthew asked.

"Those two won't be a problem anymore. All that awaits you is the Master." The three men swarmed Stephanie and Matthew. Jason remained frozen in the hall with his fists tightened. The leader didn't even look in his direction. "As for me? I'm the one that will lead the Master's arrival. I am the Bloodeater."

"So you're Nieto's underling," Jason said. "Do you understand what he is? Do you know what you're asking for by giving him what he wants?"

"What he wants is to bestow us all to the purifying flame. You, your friend, and that girl's grandmother are the ones the Master requires before we can meet it. It's not much of a price to pay when you understand what he is capable of."

"I know what he's capable of, and so does Matthew. I've been on the other side of the Mirror Gate. I saw the kingdom he kept, the ones he stepped on, and the world he wanted to destroy. He didn't even tell you why he wants us."

"It doesn't matter why, junior. What matters is what he will do. He has only ever asked for loyalty, and in exchange, he will show us how to reach the Higher State. Master Nieto is a god."

Jason flinched at the word. Not only did Nieto avoid telling this cult about the artifacts, but he had utterly convinced them he would bring Earth to some greater era. What he had done to the bounty hunters, to this girl, and to those kids they had kidnapped, would happen again again unless he made the first move.

"Not a god," Jason said. "Just a devil."

Pollux's power burst loose from Jason's wrist. A strange sharp sensation stabbed inside his bones and muscles when he did so, but he forced himself forward through it.

Bloodeater blinked in surprise as Jason reached him in a flash, but didn't move as the attacking fist plunged towards his face. In an instant, Bloodeater's eyes flashed white.

Then the villain dropped to the ground as if he fell through a trapdoor.

Jason paused as a swirl of black mist spun across the floor. The man with the beard lay unmoving on the carpet as if he had decided to suddenly fall asleep.

"What did he do?"

"Jason!" Matthew shouted. "Turn around!"

A heavy weight crashed against the back of Jason's neck, and the resulting pain sent him downward. As he fell, he glanced up to see a man covered in some black liquid standing behind him with an outstretched hand.

Jason lost his consciousness, his questions unanswered, and knew no more.

AN ECHO like the rolling of distant thunder ran inside Zelana's thoughts. Other than the stray Earthwalker, they had not met any obstacles, so what distressed her thoughts? Was it the Phantom Claws hiding in these tunnels, or was it something else? Could Jason be in trouble on Earth?

She immediately ruled out her last thought. Jason wouldn't allow himself to die. He had promised to see her again. No, clearly, she was projecting her fears on someone else.

"Are you well, Zelana?" Koa asked.

"Yes, thank you."

The young warrior flashed an uncertain smile and turned from her. "I was hoping you could tell me more about those flowers. I've lived here my whole life but have never paid much attention to such things before. I suppose I never will now."

"Don't talk like that, Koa."

Koa stayed in the rear, away from the group. The boy muttered more and more to himself the longer they moved through these paths. Had he begun to lose his mind?

Eventually, Dyne whispered to her. "I took Koa in because he wanted to know how to kill lizards. Only lizards. He has never had any interest in dueling or hunting, though he could do either if pressed. He got it into his fat head that lizards are the reason Tyndarus is the way it is."

"Isn't it?" she asked. "Certainly my fath—*Nieto* is to blame, but the lizardmen were the ones who sided with him when he arrived here."

"Aye, I don't care to know why they betrayed their land and their lives to such evil. However, the boy is more obsessed with collecting their hides than the Great Sorcerer King himself. I didn't bring him here for petty grudges but because I thought he could grow beyond them. Do you understand me?"

She licked her lips in thought. "Are you insinuating that I am like him?"

"There is nothing wrong with revenge as far as justice goes. Or repaying a debt owed. But neither will amount to much if you are dead. I learned that on the seas. Don't heedlessly leap into danger."

"I am not, Dyne. It is good to have you with me. I'm all too aware of my limits."

"Everyone," Alain whispered from the front. "Quickly, stand at my back. Come over here, Koa. A figure melted into the wall just ahead. I'm certain of it."

Neither Zelana nor the old man wasted time obliging his request. Alain held the torch out and waved it about, the light not covering as much space as it should. The four packed in tighter.

"Now what are we to do?" the old man asked. "Wait patiently for one to attack?"

Alain laughed. "No need. Zelana can tell us what we need to know."

"I can?"

"You gave both Jason and Matthew an armor of magic over them when you helped them through the Mirror Gate. Surely you can do similar for us. A brighter light? Perhaps a way to sense where they are in the walls? You have powers, Zelana."

Alain had not spoken a lie. She did have abilities. But ever since she had used her power to send Jason and Matthew back to their home world, her magic had been limited, only coming in spurts. Other than purifying the masks for travel, she had not been able to summon anymore. But there always remained the possibility that she had been looking at her abilities wrong. They were embedded in her being, not a foreign object she could tear off and ignore. She only had one other she could look to for advice, even if he was far away.

Jason had activated Pollux through force of will and connecting his mind with the bracelet's energy. She couldn't know if those artifacts worked the same as her father's magic did, but there were no other options. Zelana had to start somewhere. The seed was embedded in her soul, after all.

She searched her thoughts, scratching around for anything. The Kharis Seed lay still deep inside, waiting for her to call upon it once more. Pollux gave Jason great strength, and this seed filtered her magic from her father's poisonous power. At the bottom of her thoughts, she touched a floor of cold steel: the seed. Zelana scratched down, and pulsating warmth began to beat from below. The heat grew in her palms.

"I have it!" she suddenly shouted.

Dyne kept his blade close, scanning the dark. "Have what, lass?"

The golden heat slowly dripped from her soul like tree sap, flowing where she needed it. Her sight burned for but a moment as she blinked in the black space of the cave. The tunnel no longer held any secrets from her glowing eyes, at least not in her direct range of sight.

"You told us Phantom Claws only attack from behind, sir. They're hiding in the walls around us. There are exactly five. If one of you would expose your back, I can tell where they will attack."

Alain scoffed. "This is quite the plan, girl. Has the magic made your head soft?"

"Easy, lad. Chances are they will attack us at once if we move from here regardless."

"Zelana, share your vision with us. The old man knows how to kill them, and the boy and I can learn, but you are still no fighter."

As crude as Alain could be, he was correct. They were at a disadvantage in the dark, and only she could see. But if her powers could also enhance eyesight, what else could they improve? She remembered when she charged Pollux's energy, and it ended up saving them.

"I will try," she said.

Zelana put each hand against Alain and Koa's eyes and concentrated. An intangible mass shifted in her soul. She pulled the power like a thread through a needle from the depths of her insides and out of her hands. A golden light slipped down her fingers and into her ally's eyes. After a moment, the two of them gaped.

"I can see them!" Koa remarked. "Master, I can win against these creatures."

"I am not yet finished," she said. Zelana repeated the process on Dyne. "Hold still, please!"

Sharp black blades flashed deep in her soul as she sent the energy out. Her insides tore, and she choked back a scream. The girl stumbled backwards, and Koa caught her by the wrist. He shouted something she could not hear. A black fog rolled across her vision. She slapped her cheeks, and the world came into focus. Her powers had momentarily failed her and left her back in the dark.

"Move!" the old man shouted, taking Zelana from Koa. He put her at his side. "I will watch her. You two use what you were given."

"Watch out!" she shouted.

Zelana instinctively ducked, pulling Dyne down, and a hard strike smashed her helmet. It flew from her head, smacking against the dirt. She dipped down, and a streak zipped over her platinum hair. Dyne clutched her close and fell back. Shriveled black arms slipped through the shadows just in time for the old man's sword to sever them. A horrible bellow echoed throughout the tunnel.

Alain cleaved the shambling monster in twain with his blade.

"Are you alright, Zelana? Did it get you?"

She blinked. "You killed it."

"I certainly did. Keep awake!"

Alain twisted, and his blade caught against another beast reforming from the smoke behind him. The sword slashed it apart, and the Phantom Claw howled. Both Alain and Koa darted back and forth at a speed that amazed her, and their strength was twice what she had seen earlier. Had she given them this power?

But a storm raged inside her mind and brought her to her knees. The light in her vision faded before extinguishing fully. She struck the dirt with nothing but the sounds of shuffling feet against the dust behind her. Big arms wrapped her shoulders.

The light inside died, and the darkness swallowed her whole. Even the constant shouting and cries of pain behind her could not get Zelana to awaken.

The emptiness inside drifted away, as did her thoughts and consciousness.

CHAPTER 15
DEEP DOWN IN THE DARK

"ZELANA!" Alain shouted.

Zelana jerked awake, slamming her forehead against a solid surface. She winced, and another voice whined in response.

"Land's sake," Alain moaned. He sat beside her rubbing his right eye with one hand and reaching for his fallen helmet. "What is your skull made of?"

"Serves you right," Dyne said. "You shouldn't remove your helmet. Even to check on her."

"That hardly matters now, old-timer. Zel, are you awake? You fainted when they attacked."

She felt for her helmet on the ground. The leather hadn't been cut, and no gashes were to be seen. Luck and craftsmanship had saved her this time. She put it back on and rubbed her fresh bruise.

"You defeated them?"

Koa held a torch over them. The golden glow in their eyes had dissipated. "You fainted just as we managed to frighten the final two off. What is wrong?"

"I am fine. *Now*. Every time I think of using more power, my head aches. It will take some time before I can do more with it. Will you all be alright without me?"

"Certainly," Alain said with a grin. "It held long enough for us to beat them, but it wouldn't do much in a bigger skirmish. For now, we should hurry before they regroup."

"They won't, lad. Phantom Claws, once scared off, will not reengage the same prey. Nevertheless, I agree with your greater point. Let us keep on, lass."

Dyne and Alain hoisted her back up so quickly and easily that she hardly noticed they had done so. She tripped a step before regaining balance. The pain in her head had vanished, but just thinking about magic would bring it back again. This was the cost of the Kharis Seed, after all. It exchanged life force for power. She would need to take it slower, or it could drain her dry.

Before they left, Koa approached. He rubbed the back of his neck, and she thought she saw him blush. "Thank you for your help. I apologize for my earlier cowardice."

"You did all the work, Koa. I just gave you what you required to do it."

"Are you two finished?" Alain asked. "We cannot keep dawdling like this."

The quartet continued through the tunnels but didn't have much further to travel. Without lizards or Phantom Claws in the way, they soon crossed out into a large cavern lit by dozens of torches.

Below lay a drop that had to have been as high as three fully grown black birches. The surrounding swirl of steps around the outside rim ran down to the floor far below, where at least a dozen lizardmen lined up in two rows. Against the wall opposite the group sat a long flat object glowing with purple energy.

Zelana recognized this antique. They had found the Mirror Gate.

"Who is that?" Alain whispered. He pointed to a figure lying on the ground between the two rows of lizardmen. "Is that Matthew or Jason?"

It was difficult to see from high above the ground, and traveling lower would be risky. Instead, she concentrated, and the intense cutting sensation inside her chest slashed throughout her mind. Zelana stared down into the dark and into their ring of torches, where a naked man lay with chains around his arms and legs. The lizards waited around him as if ordered to.

"I cannot see who it is," she admitted. "We must get closer."

The trio extinguished their torch and descended the winding pathway. A handful of side passages led back out into the caverns, but they appeared vacant. The only remaining occupants of this cave lay below.

The men made short strides down the winding ledge. Zelana attempted to drag energy from within her, but she received only jagged pinpricks of agony. She bit her lip. The last thing she wanted was to leave her friends outnumbered.

"Did you hear that?" a cold voice called out from below.

The group paused, and Alain's fingers went to his hilt. The enemies remained still far below, but he didn't appear to notice what Zelana had. Koa laid a hand on his shoulder, and he slackened.

"That's not a lizard," he whispered.

Alain cocked an eyebrow. "What?"

"How much longer do we have to wait?" a different man said.

The original voice scoffed. "Let us leave now. I was expecting another message from Bloodeater first. He has yet to explain why this one was sent to us and not the two requested."

"The light in the gate has faded. We've waited long enough, Ioseph. We should bring him to the fortress before it gets dark. The last thing we want to run into besides frogmen would be more of those troublesome Vultures.

We do not have an unlimited supply of Phantom Claws."

"I understand your concern, Gido. Alright, we shall take him now."

The two rows of lizardmen bound together and took hold of the unconscious man. Gido moved to the front of the pack and gestured to one of the tunnels. The group, as well as Iospeh, shortly joined him. They quickly vanished into the darkness.

The two remaining lizards left to guard the Mirror Gate quickly curled up before it. Were they attempting to sleep? Soon enough, the bottom floor had fallen completely silent.

Alain guided the others down to the bottom. He checked every corner he could, but they did appear to be alone. Koa muttered under his breath. The closer he and Alain inched to the sleeping guards, the more he visibly trembled as if in excitement.

Swords found the necks of the lizards, and both winced before tumbling over dead in the dirt.

"We have our prize," Alain said, sheathing his blade. "This gate is different from the one I've seen before. Far smaller. This could fit in one of the homes back in Fortuna. Is it a remnant of a larger piece?"

Zelana ran her fingers around the smooth edge. "Why would they leave it in a place such as this?"

"Orders from Nieto, I would think. They must be bringing it through the mountains back to the Magic City."

"No," the old man replied. "There are probably Mirror Gates like this one scattered throughout these mountains. It would make his espionage easier if his trinkets are spread out."

Alain nodded. "To avoid what happened to his gates in Mageuopolis. I cannot think of a better choice. We should smash this one before it gets reactivated."

Zelana placed her palm on the surface. She felt nothing inside, as if it were just another ordinary mirror. Not just anyone could use them. But she had something most others didn't —her father's life force.

"We cannot destroy this," she said. "That man was brought through, and we must send him back. This object can be useful, as well. We could use these Mirror Gates against my father."

"Ridiculous." Koa sighed, kicking the corpse of the lizard. "That man is most likely dead, and Nieto cannot be allowed a path into Earth. It should be destroyed, and we should leave."

"Please, Koa. It does not have to be this way. What if I can usurp his control and make it so that he cannot use *any* Mirror Gates instead of just this singular one? We can cut off his pathways to Earth completely. All I need to do is understand how they work. We should take this with us."

Koa scoffed and wandered off towards one of the tunnels. A weight lifted as he left. His dismissive attitude had begun to bother her.

"Can you not activate it now?" Dyne asked. "What is on the other side?"

She concentrated, and finally, a scrap of power burst through her thoughts. Her magic flowed into the Mirror Gate, and the warm sensation bubbled out of her fingers and into the slab. Bright white light flooded the room for a moment before quickly dying out. There was a wall of darkness on the other end of the mirror. She removed her palm when it became clear her attempt was a waste of time.

"I can't see through. There must be an obstruction on the opposite end. Wrap it in cloth so they cannot see through our side, and we will take it with us."

"And where will we go?" Alain interrupted. "We can't turn back with this mirror and chase the captive simultaneously. It is one or the other."

"Alain!" Koa called. He pointed to the tunnel ahead of him. "You should see this."

"Who goes?" a voice said from the tunnel. "Are you Earthwalkers?"

"We are," Dyne said. "I was unaware there were more of us down here."

Over inside the tunnel, they found two men housed in a cage of large bones from ancient birds, all dressed in black clothing. The pair leaned against the bars and waved out at them through the torchlight. Piles of ashes littered the floor.

"You are with the Vultures," Alain stated. "And how is Richter doing these days?"

One creased an eyebrow. "You know Richter?"

"The last time we met was when we were assaulted by frogmen. I had heard he survived, as did my friends, but I had no idea what chaos he trafficked out here. Hold still while we free you."

The boy and old man retrieved keys hanging on the wall and used them to unlock the hastily constructed jail. The prisoners muttered their thanks.

Zelana moved to the front of the group. "Are there any other prisoners in this place?"

"No. We're the only ones remaining. The others were either incinerated on their way through the Mirror Gate, or their remains were fed to wolves."

"What were they doing here?" she asked. "This is a strange place to set up such an elaborate working. It isn't like my fath—*Nieto* to work so far from the magic city."

"He has his followers through that gate that believe he is a god delivering them to a promised land beyond the fires. They send sacrifices through, and the lizardmen send trinkets back to make them appear to be rewarded. Nieto does this to gain their trust, and then he can have them do whatever he wants. He lends his magic to those two traitors to use the gate."

Zelana thought for a moment. "Do not objects burn when taken through it?"

"Not if they are soaked in enough of his life. It is living beings that are a gamble to send through. Anything tied to them will burn as easily as they will."

"That aside," she interrupted. "Where are they taking that man that came through?"

"A fortress. That is where they took a few of our comrades. We can bring you there though it will not be a pleasant visit. It is not that far from here."

Dyne cut in. "Should we go, Alain?"

Alain stared at the Mirror Gate and nodded to Zelana. "Zelana is the leader of this expedition. I'm only a guard. She will decide our course."

Zelana forced a smile at his words. Alain had to have questions about his friends lost in the mountains, yet he still ceded the decision. The easiest choice would be to take the Mirror Gate and return to Fortuna. The simplest route is the quickest—her mother would agree.

"We will rescue that man," Zelana said. She knew it was the right choice. It had to be. "Please help me to bring the Mirror Gate with us."

"Are you prepared, miss?" one of them said. "Lizardmen are no simple opponent, especially when there is a fortress of them. We will have to intercept the lot before they reach it. Carrying this slab with us might slow the group down."

"Please help me, gentlemen. We cannot leave this behind."

"And you also wish to rescue that human? Are you certain? This is asking much."

A warm glow heated up within Zelana like boiling water. The pain in her mind subsided, and the magic in her soul flowed again. The magic's effect on her body must have depended on how she used it in succession. Giving it to others must take more than using it on herself. She needed to learn to use it correctly before the next encounter.

"We will rescue him. You two are free to escape. Does anyone disagree with my choice?"

The group stared back at her without so much as a shared glance between them.

Alain laughed. "Who do you think you are talking to, woman? Follow me into battle, and I will show you just how a sword is meant to be used."

They wrapped the Mirror Gate in some spare cloth left lying around the cell. The two surviving Vultures agreed to carry it so the others could ready their weapons. Zelana regretted using them like this but had little choice. They needed to move before that man was killed.

She couldn't escape the dark thoughts creeping into her mind. Was it a premonition of something odious or just her nervous disposition catching up with her?

"Coming, Zelana?" Koa asked. "We might get to slay more lizards, so I would like to hurry."

She quickly joined the group and they traveled back through the tunnels. They moved surprisingly quickly with the Vultures carrying the Mirror Gate between them. Eventually they reached the outside and the setting sun prying into their subterranean world. Now they had a man to save.

THE MIDNIGHT BLACK of the cell stared back at Matthew when he awoke. His eyes couldn't focus on anything but a pure void; the complete vacuum of sound allowed nothing through. The stink of dirty water, along with the incessant dripping from a pipe nearby, distracted him. He had ended up underground somehow.

Everything ached as he felt himself over. He remembered it—the group had taken him down in Stephanie's apartment. If only he could remember what happened after that.

"Are you okay, Jason?" he said with a rasp. He felt his sore throat. "Jason? Wake up in there."

No answer. The boy must have been knocked out, and it must be night outside if Matthew was in charge of the body. He also couldn't tell how long he was out for.

"*I'm up*," Jason mumbled.

"You don't sound like it."

"*. . . It hurts.*"

"What hurts? Do you remember what happened?"

"You were already out like a light . . . tried to fight them all off. Then Pollux ran out . . . ouch."

"Come on out, Jason. Hey. Hey!"

No response. Matthew felt along the floor to get a gauge their location. If Jason couldn't help, Matthew would have to find the exit on his own.

Aside from the vague smell of water dripping from pipes, the rest of his senses might as well be blind. No matter how he struck out an arm, he never met any wall. A creeping chill ran like cold fingers along his skin.

Matthew's palm reached a solid surface, and momentary relief washed over him. He wasn't as lost as he originally thought.

At least, he thought so at first.

The momentary relief died away as the thought entered his head that he was imagining what he was touching in here. But that couldn't be. Was his body playing tricks on him?

He felt his face to wipe what he thought was sweat from his brow. His fingers—were they his fingers?—touched what could have been sweat. Was that real? The hand before his face was completely invisible as far as he could tell.

"Anybody out there?" he shouted. Perhaps some guard or passerby would hear him. "What's going on? Where am I?"

No answer.

Matthew fell with his back against the wall—or what he thought was a wall. Perhaps his brain had tricked into thinking it was there—he couldn't tell anymore. The silence swallowed his thoughts.

He sat in the void with his head in what he believed were his hands and tried to shut his eyes.

Time passed slowly with every moment he wasted. The still air nipped at his mind, and the lax humidity was unpleasant enough to make him pant. He had no way out. Without any clear exit, he was at their mercy.

Sure he could wait for one of Bloodeater's men to come barreling in, but how long would that take? His legs were already cramping. What if they had left them in there to die?

"Jason," he said. At least, he thought he said it. "Jason!"

But no response arrived.

The abyss hugged Matthew's thoughts and made him try to think of other things. Cavern Cove, paradise. He imagined lying in the sun. He was somewhere where life made sense. Why couldn't he stay there forever? But reality returned to destroy his fantasy. His back irritated him, as did his thought that the wall he had touched wasn't actually there.

"Am I dead?" he finally asked.

"That is the dream, Castor."

The voice hit like a sledgehammer to the skull. Shots of pain reverberated through Matthew's bones. His eyes blurred, or he thought they did. That wasn't Jason's voice.

"I don't know you," Matthew said.

"We've never yet met, though we came close."

The acidic tone of the disembodied voice hung in Matthew's ears against the silence of the blackened space. He remembered it from somewhere despite not recognizing it.

"Are you going to tell me why I'm here?"

"Originally, it was to make you suffer while preparations were completed, but since I enjoy watching you lose your mind, it is now mostly for my joy."

"Preparations? What are you going to do, cook me? From the sound of your voice, I'd say ants and boll weevils might be more to your tastes."

"Very droll. I will enjoy this memory when I'm peeling the soul from your broiling bones."

Cold air ran across the back of Matthew's neck. Why did this voice disturb him on a visceral level? "You're not Bloodeater, but you bear his stink . . . or perhaps I have that backwards."

"You do."

Slowly the voice in the void melded with a memory from Matthew's time in the other world. This chill was the same he felt in the mountains of Tyndarus. He was the presence from the fortress that bore down on Matthew when they escaped on the airship.

"Nieto," Matthew said.

"I'm pleased you remember despite us not meeting face to face. I never imagined you would unleash the chaos you have upon my planet. Now you must pay the toll before I can let you meet oblivion. It is simply justice as it were."

"This is about killing your wife? I'm not going to apologize for burning her up like rotting firewood. I can fix that mistake and make it better. The two of you can burn together in Hell instead. Would you like that?"

"You are as I expected. Childish and stupid."

"You don't know anything about me."

"I know you are a coward, and I know when next we meet, you will be begging for your life. Enjoy the darkness. It enjoys you."

"Call me that to my face." Matthew waited for a reply. "Now who's the coward?"

Nieto never replied. His presence had disappeared from the void and left Matthew alone again.

Time passed by unabated inside the dark. Matthew groped around but found no door or exit. All he touched included the floor under his feet and the walls sealing him in—and his mind doubted those were even real.

Finally, after what felt like an eternity and throwing caution to the wind, Matthew dug at the solid and unbending floor. Steel? Maybe he was imagining it.

He transformed into water and ran along what little he could. There wasn't even the slightest bit of a crease or hole out of his cell. What kind of prison was this?

There remained only one option, though he did not know if it would be worth trying. His trembling muscles and racing mind led him to believe he would have to try.

Matthew thought hard and became mist. Instead of looking for openings that weren't there, he tried a similar tact to what he did before. Back when he killed Queen Shaula at the Williams' Tech Corp. building, he used his form to mix with the air. He would try that again.

But his attempt to merge into the dark speared through his ephemeral body and sent sparks through his form. This room had a strange effect on him.

Castor screamed through him every moment he reached out inside the darkness. It was as if the bracelet had turned on him. It burned and twisted, fighting against his very being.

He couldn't do it. He wasn't ready for it.

Castor deactivated, and Matthew's normal body slammed down as dead weight. Exhaustion won out. His mind slid back into the abyss surrounding the emptiness.

Before he lost sight, he thought he saw a spark emit from what he thought was his wrist. Castor? No, his head had to have been playing tricks on him.

Matthew lost himself to the endless dark, unsure if he had even been awake in the first place. Death was tapping his shoulder and showing him another way out. Perhaps he would take it.

THE GROUP of six reached the mountain crevice where the two rescued captives had directed them to go. They made good time, even with a mirror in tow and running across unfamiliar territory.

The moon beamed down as the party cut through shortcuts the two Vultures pointed out to them. This rocky road was barely wider than the size of a wagon, with jutting tall stones and overhanging ledges dangling above the sharp drops that spun upwards hundreds of feet. It would be dangerous were it not it so clearly barren.

Zelana perched on a ledge near the bottom of the trail and watched as the others took to their spots along the ridge. They drew their bows, aiming from their hidden spots between the jagged rocks. They had beaten the enemy here, thanks to the shortcuts the Vultures with them had given, and would use this to their advantage. They would attack, and then she would rescue that prisoner.

Alain and one of the Vultures took the highest ground on each side of the trail. Meanwhile, Dyne and the other new addition took a lower spot behind jutting boulders, positioned at sharp angles. Koa stayed near the front of where the lizards would march from, obscured enough to avoid sight-lines. Heavy steps reverberated a few turns and stone throws away.

Zelana crouched low with what magic she had left pooling into her fingertips. She would put it all into this next attack.

Her right eye twitched, and a headache washed over her thoughts before dissipating again. She felt this once before when she last heard her mother's voice. But Shaula was dead now.

"Father," she whispered. Who else could it be?

Zelana felt the rough stones and damp dirt under her fingers. The night came on hard, as did the beating of the lizardmen claws ahead of them. The troop soon rounded the bend as a stampede would.

"*Now*," Alain mouthed to the man beside him.

The first bowstring sang, arrows flew, and the battle began. Zelana's palms glowed as the lizardmen screamed their battle chants. This time she was ready for them.

CHAPTER 16
RAGING THROUGH THE VOID

JASON'S WRIST sizzled as if a furnace scorched it. He couldn't shout, he couldn't move, and he couldn't understand anything happening. What he thought might have been Matthew's voice vanished as if caught in a breeze, leaving him alone in the black emptiness engulfing him. Jason's consciousness lost to the pain, and he drifted further from reality. Was he dead?

The dark presence washed over him, and his breaths came harder. Fear seized him in a way he had never felt before. This evil would swallow him, turning Jason into nothing but a memory. There was nothing he could do.

He would die in this void.

Then he thought of Matthew—the man he owed his life to. He remembered Zelana —the girl who saved them both. That wasn't everything. Jason also couldn't forget about Mrs. Carter's Granddaughter.

He couldn't stop here. Not now.

Jason raged, biting what he thought was his lip and focusing on Pollux. As Pollux burned, so did his thoughts lighten. Even if it tore his soul apart, he would break free of this.

"You're doing well," a woman said.

The voice vanished, and he continued. Pollux flared inside the dark corners of his thoughts.

"I don't have much left to give you, Jason. My time is running out."

Jason tried to ignore the distraction. The black whitened, filling the emptiness with light from Pollux.

"Once more, I will show you the way. You won't remember me this time, just as you didn't the others, but I understand. As long as you remember the way. Goodbye, Jason. I don't think we will meet again. Not until it is your time."

Pollux scorched out, and Jason shouted as he threw off the shackles in his mind. This time his voice did cry out. The darkness broke for but a second as he charged his way forward into the void. His senses burned, ignoring everything around him except his rage.

Jason charged, shoulder first, and a solid metal weight gave under his speed. He rammed through and fluorescent lighting instantly bathed him. The boy couldn't avoid flinching as both his mental and physical states merged once again. The weight on his shoulders lightened.

Finally, he could see the room he had been imprisoned in. Jason turned and scanned the wide metal box with a flat sliding surface as a door about the size of an apartment. Outside the cage was braced by stone, and a musty smell choked him. Wide rock hallways shot off in every direction. Pipes dripped somewhere nearby. They had been taken underground.

A stampede of bodies fast approached their location. Their shouts echoed through the tunnels.

"Matthew!" Jason said. Where was he? He glanced around. If Matthew wasn't in his head—and he couldn't sense him there—then he had to be nearby. Jason headed back into the now bright cell. "Are you in one piece?"

Matthew's limp body lay in the center of the steel room, slightly twitching. His lips and eyelids trembled and he was completely out of it. Jason crouched beside his fallen friend and shook his shoulder. Castor felt hot to his touch, just as the bracelet on Jason's wrist had. Pollux's energy was unreal—as if it had been supercharged.

"Come on, Matthew. We can't fool around. You need to get to the surface and call the cops."

"What?" Matthew slurred, slowly blinking. He groaned. "What do you mean?"

"I remember my dream, and in it, I saw this whole place. We're under Albion, and there are prisoners even deeper down than us. I can make it to them, but I don't know what's on the surface. You can get there faster. Plus, you look half dead."

"Half alive is better than nothing." He touched his bracelet and flinched. "Castor is killing me, but I can make it to the surface. You sure you can handle it alone?"

"I could tear through one hundred of those stone golems from Tyndarus right about now."

Matthew smirked. "Don't get in over your head. Remember how easy it is to run out of juice."

"You watch yourself, too."

Matthew moaned as he stood and shuffled out of the dark room. He stared up into the ceiling, eyeballing the cracks in the stone. With Castor, he could mist through and find his way up. So what was he waiting for?

"Guys are coming," Jason said. "Don't know how many. You better hurry."

"Remember what I said about that note I found at the mayor's place. If you find a weird door: Three on the left, wait a second, then two on the right. Wait another second, then knock four in the center. Then say *We are the One and Only*. Don't forget it."

"I'll try not to."

Matthew nodded and leaped up. His transformed body blew like a gust up through the cracks in the ceiling. He had left Jason alone in the tunnel.

"One of them is out!" Snake shouted. He was soon joined by two other dirty-clothed men Jason had never seen before. "Stop him before Bloodeater finds out."

Jason laughed. He'd been waiting for this moment. The energy poured through him as the men charged towards his position.

Suddenly the whispers of a forgotten dream flooded back into him. He remembered a peculiar thing he didn't understand. The voice of the woman. She was the one who showed him the map of this place and had visited him in dreams before—and he knew her. Her face cleared in his mind as Pollux surged through him.

"Mom?" he said.

His eyes involuntarily watered as the cultists swarmed in on his position. Jason let out a primal scream with Pollux and they collided against their enemies in battle.

CASTOR COULDN'T HAVE BEEN A BETTER fit for him. All of Matthew's aches vanished as his mist form slipped through the cracks in the tunnel ceiling floor by floor. He still didn't know where in town they were, but he had an idea. The further he traveled, the more he confirmed his assumption.

Matthew reached the top level, where the stone ended and he solidified. Above him, the fluorescents covered a solid ceiling of much tougher material. He wouldn't be able to go higher.

The stone hall ducked down into a steel door. It led toward some stairs in a cylindrical room that spiraled down into the earth. However, he followed another flight that climbed up towards a heavy wooden door on the opposite side. That had to be his way out.

Matthew pried it open and stepped out into a dusty basement with stained white sheets covering old furniture and boxes. At the edge of the room, he reached yet more stairs. A locked door lay at the top.

At this point, he couldn't risk making a scene that would attract unwanted attention to himself. Matthew morphed into water and slid under the door.

He came out into a vastly different place. The wide-open kitchen area glistened with a polished marble island and smelled of freshly cooked steak and mushrooms. Moonlight bathed the barren space meaning that it had been hours since they had been taken underground. Matthew exited towards the archway to his left and into a waiting room.

Floral wallpaper and the scent of pine-scented cleanser distracted. Then he saw those stairs, and he knew where he had to be.

Matthew passed by a phone on an end table and grabbed it. He called 911 and gave the location. Before they could keep him too long, he reiterated his location and left it on the table.

Voices from the top of the stairs pressed him to move in. He slowly stepped up the stairs and across the hardwood floors. His light movements made sure he wasn't heard. Matthew peeked around the door-frame to where two people sat at a desk surrounded by papers. His earlier intuition was right.

Matthew crossed the threshold and knocked on the wall. The two figures looked up from their work.

"Mr. Mayor," Matthew said. "Working late?"

The Mayor blanched. "What are you doing here? Do you have any idea what time it is?"

"Time to turn you black and blue, I reckon. Think you could leave me in a box and not face any consequences?"

"Now calm down, Matthew," the assistant said. He outstretched one hand out as if to ward the intruder away. "Have you been drinking?"

"Your home is on top of the very tunnel system where I was held prisoner. Don't think you can talk your way out of this one. No wonder Rachel sent us here. You were working with Nieto the whole time."

"Wait just a second!" the Mayor bellowed. He slammed his meaty fists on the desk and launched himself up. The wood quaked as if in distress. He passed to the center of the room and pointed a trembling finger towards Matthew. "Have you lost any bit of sense that God gave you?"

"Right now, I'm not even sure if I'm still sane, friend. Before the cops get here, you might want to tell me what you know about Nieto. I'll make it easier for them to identify the dental records."

"Am I supposed to know who that is? Marvin, can you please talk some sanity to him?"

"Without fail, sir."

The assistant slid his hand out from behind the desk and fired the pistol at his boss. Matthew launched himself sideways, taking the Mayor with him. Two shots struck the Mayor in the back, and the third buried itself in Matthew's left forearm. Both men landed on the carpet, and the assistant traced their path with his weapon. He aimed carefully at Matthew and shot again.

But Matthew was already moving. He rolled backwards, and the bullet punctured the floorboards. Pieces of wood splashed outwards. Matthew ducked another shot and ran out into the hallway. He shouldered himself through the door across from the office. Shots careened off the wallpaper. The hallway light smashed and dumped shards across the upstairs floor.

Matthew felt his wounded flesh and flinched. He thought about transforming to get the bullet out, but he couldn't muster the concentration. He also knew that Castor was an all-or-nothing thing—choosing to make the bullet the only thing solid was too tricky for him. How much concentration would he need?

"So it was you?" Matthew asked. He called through the hall between shots. "You wrote that note and hid it in the office."

"You were the one who took my note. I figured. Damn, this is a mess. Looks as if we'll have to abandon this town and start fresh somewhere else. Things were just getting interesting, too."

"Ha! You're just going to cut and run. That sounds like your crowd."

"You have a lot of nerve saying that after killing our Queen. I'll just have to throw your corpse into the purifying fire after her. Then Bloodeater will gather a flood of lizardmen through to wipe this town off the map. This is all your doing."

The mayor's breaths were coming deep from the office. "You did all this, Marvin?"

"I apologize, sir. But it was necessary. I wanted to bring you through the fire first. But that opportunity was lost."

"It certainly was," the Mayor said.

The sound of scuffling shoes pricked up Matthew's ears. A lamp shattered.

"Get off!" Marvin shouted.

Matthew leaned around the corner in time to see the mayor grappling with his assistant. The older man was sweating up a storm. "You told me never to use my power, and that was wise, Marvin. Now I will show you what it can do. Get out of here, Matthew!"

The floor shook with an incredible force. The earthquake rumbled through the entirety of the house, rattling windows and knocking picture frames from the walls. The assistant scrambled against the mayor's grip and even lost his gun in the struggle, but still, the trembling ground caused them unbalance. But the old man's pale face told Matthew that he didn't have much time left to continue doing this.

"You used me, used my town, and my people. No more. You will die here with me, Marvin!"

"Take your hands off of me!"

Matthew tilted and weaved as he moved through the doorway, but he still lost his balance. He fell over as a filing cabinet, and the paintings on the wall dropped beside him. Matthew rolled to his knees in time to see a cabinet crush the floor before his flailing legs. Plaster from the ceiling dropped down, and before he could make sense of it the entire floor went out from under him.

Matthew plummeted down through the crumbling house. The last thing he saw was the ceiling falling with him.

COLD WIND SMACKED Matthew's face and brought him back to consciousness. Harsh moonlight bathed the rubble of the house. Crumbled wood and furniture were sprinkled among the beams and boards. He couldn't move. The remains of the trashed roof covered his cut-up body.

He pushed the beam pinning him against the beaten in floor. His muscles cried out, but the large slab of wood would not budge. He was stuck. Police sirens blared in the distance. Matthew knew he couldn't stay here, especially with Jason and the prisoners still down below.

Ripples of agony flowed through his wounded left arm. Now the rest of him hurt as much as that bullet wound did. He needed to concentrate. Matthew forced his eyes shut and focused his wandering thoughts on transformation.

His body burst into a gust of thick smoke, wafting over the rubble and toward a patch of flat ground. He turned human again, his knees buckling when he touched the smashed hardwood.

"You idiot!" the assistant shouted.

Matthew twisted towards the source. The man who had shot both Matthew and the missing mayor lay on the ground. His bloody body lay mangled by beams and oblong bits of rubble that twisted his legs in the wrong direction. Guttural growls expelled from the dying man.

"He made me the arbiter between Paradise and Purgatory. You left them all trapped here, you halfwit. I could have saved us all. Now you will feel the wrath of the harbinger."

"Save your tongue before I rip it out."

"You made me kill him, and then you kill me, but now Justice comes for you. You will burn with the ones whose salvation you stole."

"I can live with that."

The light died from the assistant's eyes, but his awkwardly bent right arm lifted, and slits like a knife wound cut open from his palm. Purple mist swirled out of the enemy's skin and smothered against Matthew's nose.

The agony ripped through him like a whirlwind. Purple blotches painted his vision.

Pictures of dark mountains from another world flashed before him. A subtle outline of a nearly invisible man stared with white eyes from the shadows, boring a hole through Matthew.

"He is mine, Castor. They all are."

"You will never have them again, Nieto."

"Your mind is as small as your ambitions. There are more Mirror Gates than you possibly can know. Once Bloodeater sends the little fool to me the game will be won. My lizards will swallow this city whole just because of your persistent interference."

"Send them over. I'll kill them all. You have no idea what you're in for."

"Do you, Castor? The boy is certainly dead by now. If only you hadn't abandoned him to his fate."

"Just rot away and die already."

"You first."

The haze squeezed Matthew's mind like a vise. He could swear his skull cracked under the pressure. Breaths choked out of him. Only one thing could be done to escape it.

Matthew twisted himself into fog, and the attacks on his mind snapped off. He spun through the air, and the remaining purple magic broke apart and faded into the night's air.

"This will not stop me for long."

Matthew kept spinning, knocking away what remained of the haze.

"Get off from my planet and die, already."

The fog dissipated, leaving only the corpse of the assistant behind. Still transformed, the Castor wielder shot forward and down toward the ruins of the basement and barreled through the tunnels into the dark. Red splotches of pain rippled through him in his descent.

Even if Marvin had been stopped, there were still others below to deal with. Others had to die before Nieto sent those lizards through the Mirror Gate to attack the town. This time there would be no mercy for these wretches. This time Nieto would lose everything.

CHAPTER 17
MIRROR DANCE

ARROWS LEAPED across the stone-strewn pathway, jabbing into lizard men left and right. Their stiff formation made their ranks easy to spot in the tight space. The survivors took cover behind the large boulders and jutting walls. Several enemy lizardmen pointed towards the locations of the attacking archers. Zelana used this moment to act.

She placed her hands on the rough dirt, and magic flowed into the ground. The carpet of energy slipped along a path stretching as a net over a hundred feet, covering the earth around the claws of the lizardmen trapped in the pathway. The magic morphed the dirt under them.

The rocks leaped up as dozens of dusty limbs poked through, clasping the knees of the lizards and the two Earthwalkers with them. In their confusion, they dropped the prisoner, and he flopped against the ground. He groaned as he shook himself awake through the chaos.

The prisoner slowly stood with a tattered cloak wrapped around him. The two Earthwalker enemies pried their feet free of their sunken boots and brandished their blades towards him.

"Stop!" Ioseph shouted.

The former prisoner charged at their approach, both arms swinging for his lizardmen attackers. The resulting crack was enough to cause Zelana to utter under her breath.

The enemy's swords broke against his swinging arms. As the shattered blades still spun in the air, he slipped in through their opening. Fists furiously slammed against armor and their helmets dented with his attacking force. Both enemy Earthwalkers met the ground and didn't get up again.

Around their prone bodies, lizardmen hissed and bellowed. Arrows and blades from Zelana's descending allies skewered what remained of them. Within moments, corpses blanketed the mountain pathway.

Zelana approached the freed prisoner. His dark hair and pinkish skin betrayed him as a human like Jason or Matthew. He staggered before reaching a knee. She crouched beside him to allow the poor man balance.

"Are you hurt?"

He wheezed and choked. For a moment, it looked as if he might vomit, but only saliva ejected from him. However, he continued coughing until a small round object spilled out of his mouth. The gold surface glistened underneath the moon. She dared not touch but inspected it from over his shoulder. An earring?

"Where did you find that relic?" she asked.

"It's what saved me," he said at length. The former prisoner wiped his mouth clean with the back of his large hand. "Everything burned in that mirror, even my clothes. This thing was all that didn't burn. Without even thinking, I swallowed it, and it stopped the burning. Where am I, anyway? Were those giant chameleons?"

"You're in Tyndarus," Alain said. He cut down a still-thrashing lizard. "From what I've been told, it is a whole different world than your Earth. Your name?"

"Name's Ray Hammersmith. I'm on another planet? That mirror sent me through space and time?"

Alain waved dismissively. "I suppose. But only those doused with Nieto's magic or carrying a relic can pass through it and live. That trinket of yours must be one. I am Alain, the girl is Zelana."

"That earring," Zelana said. "Where did you get it?"

"Matthew White and Jason McCrae. The kid told me to hold onto it as collateral to prove they wouldn't run. Said it had some kind of dormant power. If this is an alien world, then I guess they weren't trying to get one by me."

"You are familiar Jason and Matthew?" She couldn't help but grin. "Are they well? Last we heard, they were investigating a village that might involve Nieto."

"That's right!" He shot up. "Damn! I have to get back there. The town is in trouble. Those cultists have my partner, and a bunch of other people are also in danger. Things are going to hell. But can I make another trip through that mirror?"

"No worries, friend. I can help." Zelana showed her palms which glowed bright white. She wasn't sure when her power had changed color turned from gold to white, but it hardly mattered now. The stranger flinched before she interrupted his incoming protestations. "I am Zelana, the daughter of Nieto. But I am no monster. My magic can purify you and your relic long enough to allow you return passage. That is how Jason and Matthew left this place, after all."

The former prisoner looked her up and down and then scanned the dead lizardmen and the remains of their armor blowing under the night wind. "I suppose I have little choice."

"We should hurry," Dyne interrupted. "We don't know if reinforcements are on the way."

"Get the mirror, please," Zelana said. "I will send you home right away."

The two Vultures unwrapped the cloth around the Mirror Gate and placed it face up in the dirt. Moonlight glinted harshly off the surface. Tiny plumes of purple smoke slipped out into the night air from the void trapped inside of the mirror.

Zelana placed both palms down on the Mirror Gate and willed her magic through the surface. White heat bolted it through it like lightning. The purple mist soon cleared, and the surface heated.

She did the same to both the earring and to the cloak the stranger wore. It was all she could do for him. Her power should work long enough to let him through the new opening. The white glow broke the darkness of the mirror.

"Hurry through. Please give aide to Jason and give him the mirror you find on the other side of this gate. He can keep it safe."

"Girl, I'll do anything you want if I live through this."

"Move, fool!" Alain interrupted. "We have to leave this place and take this mirror back to Fortuna."

"Okay, okay, I'm going." He waved to the girl. "Thanks, Zelana."

"Have good fortune, Ray Hammersmith."

The stranger jumped into the mirror, sinking through it like it was water. After a moment, the light faded from the Mirror Gate, and the Vultures placed the cloth back over it.

"We can only hope he made it," Koa said.

Dyne laughed. "Unfortunately, we might not."

Shadows moved along the sides of the crags surrounding the trail. Alain drew his blade and the others did the same. They had no way out of this predicament.

The magic slowly heated up in Zelana's fingertips. She wouldn't have enough to do that trick again, but she would do what she could. Her friends, and the mirror, must be kept safe.

Koa stood tall before them. "Forget the lizards. We need to take this mirror home."

"Are you feeling well?" Dyne asked. "I thought you were here to kill them."

"I was. But this mirror is more important than any of them. If it can bring us Castor and Pollux to our world again then it is invaluable. Zelana, please, lead us home."

Scraping stone sounded above the ridge, and boulders broke loose under quick footsteps. Enemies were pouring through the trail far ahead.

"Quickly now," the girl said. "It is time to return home."

Zelana led the group back through the crags away from them. They would live to fight another day. For now, surviving was all that mattered. Hopefully, Jason and Matthew would make it through their predicament, too.

SHARP SNAKE FANGS stabbed through Jason's arm. He cried out and reached for the culprit. However, the giant snake had already slithered away into the dark of the hallway. With his improved vision from Pollux, he managed to see the enemy slink back into a large hole in the stone wall.

Were he anyone else, he would be a sitting duck. Scrapes and hisses echoed as the snake slithered behind the wall. Jason stood in the center of the shabby stone hallway, his arms outstretched and his ears open.

The earlier earthquake had shaken his enemy quite a bit, making the attacks come frantic and vicious. Jason questioned just what Matthew did up on the surface to frighten his foes so much.

The football-sized holes in the side of the tunnel wall extended the one hundred feet it took to get to the barricaded door at the end of the hall. Jason considered running and leaving this thing behind, but that would allow his foe the chance to escape.

That wasn't an option. None of these scumbags were getting away. Not this time.

"Come out," Jason said. "Don't think I won't find a way to break you in two."

Snapping jaws lunged out of the dark. Jason punched, but its fat head swerved out of range. Before he could clasp its hide, burning pain cascaded through his legs. Two more snakes had sunk their fangs into his flesh.

He swore and stumbled back. The serpents tore away before he could react. How could he catch what he couldn't touch?

The snakes jumped in and out of the holes in the wall like a warped whack-a-mole game. Jason struggled to strike a single one of the set.

His vision blurred. Was it poison? Pollux might have had energy to spare—but Jason did not.

A spiral of smoke spewed out of the hallway behind Jason and twisted into the shape of a man. Matthew had finally made it back. His breaths were heavy, his clothes slashed and stained, and he held his bloody left arm. It looked like he'd lived through a napalm strike.

"Get moving," Matthew said. "I'll take this thing. You know where to go and who to hurt."

"I can't turn tail. You look half dead!"

"I'm better than those other guys you beat the brains out of back there. You've gone down three floors, and yet you're still going this strong? Use that energy for someone other than yourself. There are people waiting for you. Move it!"

Jason thought against it for but a moment. The glare in Matthew's stare told him the subject was closed. However, Jason couldn't help being wary.

"What about you?"

"There's more important things at stake here than how pretty I look. Am I going to have to tell you again to go, or do you want those snakes to tear you apart?"

Jason scratched his head with both hands then smacked his cheeks. Matthew was right.

"Okay!" Jason said. "Just make it quick."

"Don't I always?"

Jason's quickened pace blitzed through the hall. He twisted through stone catacombs and down spiraling stairs. The light bulbs hanging on the ceiling flickered more the deeper he went. As he ran, he struck at any passing guard in his way. They dropped like swatted flies. He felt invincible.

Pollux flickered for nearly inconsequential periods as he ran, but those dead spaces slowly became more and more common. He probably had around twenty minutes of full power left at this rate, and he could not afford to fool around up here.

Each flight of stairs only led down one level, which left him to run the length of the floor to reach the next set. Jason considered punching his way down but couldn't risk another Williams' Tech situation or burying the prisoners alive. After too much time, he reached a metal hallway with a matching giant reinforced fire door in the center. This blockade sealed the way forward with a large five-prong handle poking out like one of those submarine hatches he'd seen in movies. This had to be the spot.

Light bulbs above flickered dead as he approached the metal obstruction. No voices could be heard from the other side, but there were heavy breaths.

Matthew had already told him what to do here. Smashing the door would take some effort, but he needed to store his energy. The metal shook with his taps.

Jason knocked on the door with the specific pattern Matthew had told him to use. Three on the left, wait a second, then two on the right. After a second, he rapped four in the center. He then said the password.

There was a brief pause where he thought he might have been found out. Thankfully clicks and moving gears finally erupted from inside the solid object. It slowly swung open to reveal a pair of men on the opposite side.

"Hurry up and get in before those freaks get here."

"The freaks are already inside," Jason said.

The duo swore, but Jason rushed them. His fists crashed against their faces, sending them spinning off their feet.

He threw the giant door open, and it smashed against the wall.

The large cavernous space reminded him he was deep underground. A steel walkway suspended over a carved-out rock bed was not too dissimilar to some metal egg's interior. The walkway went around the length of the round hundred-foot area, housing dozens of men of all shapes and sizes staring him down with hunger in their eyes. Bloodeater's men. At the edges, he took note of cells with children inside. There were a few more than the eleven he had been told about. But Jason was more distracted by what lay in the center of the oval room.

At the bottom of the pit, an altar of stone had been built with various long glinting objects surrounding it like petals on a sunflower. A boy with his legs folded on the stone slab sat as he stared down into the Mirror Gates surrounding him. Jason called out to him.

"He can't hear you," a woman said. "He's drugged."

Amid the dozen men encroaching on him, and the dozen more keeping their distance, was a woman with tied-back brunette hair and a sharp face with a small nose. Her lips curved in a smile, but no joy showed from her expression. Black ink dripped from her thin fingertips.

"He will be my gift to the quenching fires."

"Who are you?" Jason asked. "I mean the *real you*, Bloodeater."

"You recognize my voice even inside this shell? Very impressive, Pollux."

"This is the woman that was with Hammersmith, isn't it? Get out of her so we can do this right. I've had my fill of you."

"Oh, Hammersmith. I had almost forgotten. He was fortunate enough to meet the fires first."

One of the jailed men yelled out. "What about Hammersmith?"

"You need not concern yourself with the past. He is with the purgatory flames now."

The man in the cage slammed a fist against the bar.

"Get out of the woman, Bloodeater," Jason said. "Face me like a man."

"You sound like Castor," the woman said with a laugh. "First, come to me."

Bloodeater's group swarmed Jason, who remained unmoving. He did not relish beating every single one of these acolytes down, but if that's what it took . . .

Jason squeezed his fists so tight he thought Pollux would pop a knuckle.

"Then I'll cut through you."

He charged through the group, his fists, and feet flying at every opponent that dove upon him. Men shouted and groaned as flesh smashed against flesh. Blood and saliva splashed about with every strike. One attacker after another was knocked aside as he stomped through them.

Flying bits of metal and blasts of electricity tore past him. Jason repelled them with one crushing punch after another. A Prime kept sending one large brute of a clone after him over and over. One of the large clones felt a crushing kick and soared backwards towards the woman possessed by Bloodeater. She ducked the body and made a beeline towards Jason.

The woman bent and twisted around every strike the boy made. Her speed wasn't impressive, but her predictive abilities were. She knew where he was punching before he did. Finally, Jason took hold of her jacket collar. He raised a trembling fist.

"That's right," she said. "I know you won't hit me."

"Get out and fight me."

"I'd rather you hit her. But you can't. Not unless I let you."

Stray electricity streaked around the metal grating, nearly scorching Jason. He turned his head and caught a shoddily constructed steel dagger in mid-air with a free hand. Without a second thought, he whipped it back and nailed a telekinetic user through the shoulder. The attacker cried out and stumbled backwards over the steel railing. Jason's heart jumped into his throat. The woman he held tight laughed.

"You are out of your depth here, Pollux. Without Castor you are a child. Can't hit a woman, can't kill a murderer, can't save a town, can't stop your power from overpowering you . . . this is perfect. Perhaps a life as a hero would suit you well. You certainly are weak enough."

Jason held back vomit. His head pounded like a jackhammer. The woman watched him, not even bothering to struggle. Was the snake's poison getting to him?

His field of view narrowed. Unless he ended this quick, he wouldn't be able to end it at all.

"I can't imagine why the Master wants the likes of you. You will not last five more minutes."

Jason's footing stumbled. Streaks of volts fired towards him bounced off the wall. The bolts sent shock-wave ripples into the atmosphere. They avoided hitting the steel walkway again, refraining from striking Bloodeater. The Primes continued to throw their elements out. Another surge streaked over the air, and Jason got an idea. He would flush Bloodeater out of the woman.

"You see what I'm going to do before I do it," Jason said. "But what about what you can't see?"

"What are you—"

Jason lifted her and the minion's electricity beamed into her back. The woman writhed and screamed as smoke trailed from her jacket. Black smoke poured out of her skin and plumed into a whole man behind her limp body. Jason caught her as she slumped.

"I told you to get out of her," he said. The boy checked her breathing. "No more holding back."

"You brat." A tall, imposing figure made of shadows with slits for eyes, Bloodeater had no distinguishing marks to separate him from the dark aside. "You really don't understand your position. My power steals. The amount of blood I take allows me to control more. All you've done is delayed her death and yours. Now I also have no reason to hold back."

The enemy numbers closed in on Jason. Twenty more, including five hulking clones, remained. His situation had not changed, but at least he had freed the woman.

"Then how about we make it a one on one. You and me."

"A duel? How antiquated. But I will oblige. I want to be the one to choke the life from you."

Jason took the woman back to the door and placed her behind a set of crates. She moaned softly before blinking awake. Words formed soundlessly on her lips, but he only hushed her. She mumbled incoherently.

Jason crossed to the center of the steel grating, and so did Bloodeater. Black sparks of energy popped against the enemy's hands. Barely visible liquid dripped down his corded arm muscles.

"I'll only need one second to take you apart, boy. It'll take me much less to do the same to this town."

"Then you better make that second count."

Pollux burst with energy as Jason moved. The grating directly under his feet shattered with each quick step. Bloodeater's men shouted and stumbled with the shaking ground and fell to the bottom floor.

The pair howled as they crashed into each other, sending white and black lights streaking in a horrible monotone rainbow into the empty oval cavern. The force sent blood streaking from Jason's mouth. Bloodeater howled. Jason saw spots in his vision. Pollux was running out.

At least the boy could take Bloodeater with him. In mere moments they would both be dead. Jason hoped he wouldn't be the first to fall.

Yet his failing vision and rickety steps almost made him miss something. Bloodeater was howling with laughter—not pain.

"That was fun, Pollux. Now, how about that quick death I promised?"

Bloodeater's heavy punch struck the back of Jason's neck like a sledgehammer. There was some sort of a crack, and Jason slumped over.

He had lost.

THE BURNING SENSATION on the way back through the mirror was nowhere near as bad as it was the first time. Hammersmith swiped the cloth blocking his way out from the opening, and he tumbled through and landed on the dusty grey carpet. The heat around his bones faded quickly.

The white light around the earring in his palm died with the warmth.

This dusty dark room had a bed in the corner with a suitcase stacked on two boxes. The only other objects were boxes with white sheets over them and a suitcase propped against the windowsill. The window behind him let moonlight peek inside. He had landed in an apartment.

Hammersmith shuffled through the suitcase and found a pair of slacks. He slid them on his naked form. It was a bit tight, but it would do. He pocketed the earring and slunk towards the door.

He tripped and quickly regained his footing. His senses hadn't quite come back yet. After a second, his breath caught up with him. Hopefully, whomever's apartment this was didn't understand what they had here. Mirrors that led into other worlds! He still didn't believe it, and he lived it.

"Is she going to get up?" a male voice said. "I don't want her to know we just moved the mirror here, but I can't make an excuse as long as she's out of it."

Another voice grunted. "For the one-hundredth time, Kyle, no. My power is hooked too deep into her now. Even if I'm napping, it will stay active. She's going to be out until Bloodeater wants her."

"Sure it will, but why doesn't he just have her swan dive off the balcony already."

"My power doesn't work that way. It just lowers inhibitions; makes people tired or more awake. Besides, didn't Bloodeater want her alive? He kept her around to lure out that old woman. We got Castor and Pollux instead. I'd say that was a step up."

"Who cares?" Kyle said with an acidic tinge. "We were using her to get that weather witch out of Roanoke, but she won't leave her coven regardless. She might finally act if we cut up her stupid girl."

"I don't know why the Master wants them, but I will not decide what to do with his pawns for him. You might want to cool it."

"Sure, sure . . ."

Hammersmith leaned around the corner. In the center of the living room lay a young woman on the couch, unmoving. Two men sat on each side of her, one with his arms folded on the sofa and the other leaning back in the chair. Both of them mumbled in conversation.

The one with the so-called dream power was a fat man with a bushy beard, and the other man was toned well enough to fight. Hammersmith couldn't get an angle on him from here. The couch and the corner of the living room blocked him from a stealthy approach.

Across from him, he spotted the kitchen and scanned for appliances. Something heavy would do the job.

"You know what?" Kyle said. "Forget it. I'm just gonna finish her here."

"Kyle!"

"I've had enough of dealing with her, Shade. Either get out of the way, or you can join her."

"Hey, I'm not going to stop you. Just be sure to tell Bloodeater I tried to."

Hammersmith swore under his breath. He crouched into the kitchen and searched for anything heavy. A large pan sat on the top of the stack beside the stove. Hammersmith swiped it and doubled back to the hallway.

He jumped out and flung the pan, his power enforcing its momentum. Kyle noticed and ducked. The hard surface crashed against Shade's face—his nose bending and a couple of teeth lost in the process. The enemy whined and slumped back in his seat. The chair fell over with the unconscious body.

"How did you get in here?" Kyle said, scanning Hammersmith's odd garb of slacks and nothing else. Kyle rounded him towards the center of the living room. "Where did you come from?"

"I'm not sure I can answer that."

On the couch, the woman stirred. Shade's hold appeared to be broken, despite his earlier words. She groaned.

Kyle grimaced. "Great, now I gotta do it the hard way."

"Well—"

A fist crashing into his face cut Hammersmith's words off. The strike reverberated through his brain and nearly sent him falling. He swung back with a cross, and the enemy dodged. The two backed off from each other.

Blood leaked from Hammersmith's cheek, and he wiped it clean. He put up both fists.

"Not much for talking, are you?" he said.

"You won't even be breathing in a few seconds."

Hammersmith still felt a bit off from his trip through the mirror. He flinched and instantly regretted it. A wide kick crashed into Hammersmith's chest, sending him flying backwards.

His power halted the momentum, but it couldn't stop his back from striking into the side of the kitchen counter. His spine cried out. His power could only weaken the force of the initial hit—it couldn't stop the force itself.

Kyle spat on the carpet and took several strides towards Hammersmith. He knew a few fighting moves himself.

This was going to be a rough one. Hammersmith felt the dented counter crack and break under him as he sat up. His back ached, and he knew it was bleeding. This fight wouldn't be that simple—this Kyle character wouldn't let it. Roadbuster would have to wait. Hammersmith braced himself for the next barrage about to come down on him and hoped he could find an opening.

CHAPTER 18
DOWN TO THE GROUND

"WHAT'S GOING ON?" the girl asked. She jumped up on the couch. "Who is that, Kyle?"

"I'm Hammersmith. This guy and his partner over there were going to kill you."

The woman stared at the unconscious man on the floor. Her eyes lit up before her mouth slid open. She looked between the two parties, her confused frown slowly fracturing to pure hatred. Somehow she understood what had occurred here.

"I've never seen you before, but I remember *him*. He was in my head. Why, Kyle? Why did you let him do that to me?"

"Oh, shut up, Steph," he barked back at her. "I've had it up to my neck with your whining and pouting. You wanted out of that cramped hovel and away from the cold, and I gave it to you. I gave it to you so well you took it for granted and gave me nothing in exchange. As if I were a wallet with legs. Ungrateful."

She rubbed her temples. "Kyle, you . . . I thought we were . . . why?"

"Because it was easy. Maybe it could have been more pleasant for the both of us if you weren't a total cold fish. Now you get to die not knowing what you missed. No offense, but you're expendable."

"Okay," Hammersmith said. "That's enough, you pathetic ogre. Whatever happened between the two of you doesn't matter. I want you, lover boy, to answer my questions. The random missing people: my partner, the girl who helped me, Matthew White, and Jason McCrae. What are you using them for?"

"Using them?" Kyle slapped his forehead and wiped the lone strand of hair from his sweating face. He covered up a grin that had begun to poke through his anger. "Sacrifices are inevitable. When we reach Paradise through the flames, we won't have need of emotions such as regret."

"Paradise? Is that what you call that other world? I've been there. It was only for a short while, but it's horrific. Lizard people, weird folk with white hair, and strange powers . . . it's not too different from here, actually."

"You went through the Mirror Gate? Did you come through the one we took from the library?"

"Are you kidding? Your boss threw me into it. The folk there were nice enough to help me get back. Your Master is some kind of demon to those people. What are you worshiping, Kyle?"

"You're lying!" Kyle roared. "Enough! I'll break your legs and drag the truth out of you."

"Your idea of truth is damaged." Hammersmith scanned the balcony behind Kyle. There was little chance he could escape out the front door, but maybe . . . "Kyle, what is your power?"

"I punch hard. There's nothing else to it. It's just the same as yours."

Hammersmith fought off a grin. "The same, huh?"

"Why?" Stephanie asked, her voice cracking. "We were going to go to the city."

"We were never going to the city. You were just so easy, so stupid to lure out, unlike your bitch of a grandmother. I had to be the one to convince you to leave your ridiculously sheltered castle. And did you give me anything for it? So patient and pure. Oh well, you'll make a pretty corpse."

"She was right about you."

Kyle laughed. "And yet here we are."

Hammersmith pushed off the hardwood, his momentum increasing with every step. Instead of heading past Kyle he crashed into the enemy at top speed.

Kyle lifted off his feet as Hammersmith flew with him. They bashed against the wall, and the drywall and insulation sprayed out as the pair flew out into the night sky. Kyle drifted away from him, soaring off, but Hammersmith pulled him back by the wrist as he fell.

"You're not getting away," he whispered.

Hammersmith dragged Kyle with him down towards the ground, his momentum carrying them both with tremendous speed. The earth soon met them and broke apart under their weight.

SNAKE JAWS SNAPPED at Matthew's neck, going for as much flesh as it could. He misted away just as it touched, and the aggressive reptile escaped back into the holes in the wall in defeat once again.

These holes traveled down the length of the walls and up to the stairs. Catching up to Jason was the priority, but not letting these cultists escape was his own personal bugbear. He would have gone through the floor if he was convinced it wouldn't let this bastard escape.

Since getting out of that darkness and confronting Nieto not once, but twice, his head had been on the verge of connecting some sort of lost memory with his reality. Just like a puzzle missing a key piece, Matthew almost had the full picture. Castor's secret had almost entirely clicked in his head. The two were becoming one and the same.

"You're only going to get one chance, Snake. Come out, and I will put you under for a peaceful dream. Waste my time any longer, and I can promise a much longer hospital stay."

A pair of rattlers zipped out of the holes to his right. He leaned back, and they bit air. Matthew placed an ephemeral finger in one of their mouths. He held it still with his free hand and transformed his free finger into gas. A flurry of coughs came from the behind wall to his left. Matthew threw the snake, turned into mist, and glided through the wall towards it.

He reached a tiny groove just wide enough to fit a single person. There was enough space to walk the length of the floor. The snakes piled back into the shape of a human and gagged. The enemy fell against the wall, gasping. Matthew solidified and held his neck in a sleeper hold, squeezing tight.

The snake man thrashed. He tried becoming scaly and splitting into smaller nuisances, but he was too slow about it. Matthew had broken his concentration.

He turned parts of his skin into gas and expanded its hazy size, filling the narrow area, choking out all the small snakes, and forcing the enemy to reform into a human again.

Matthew reformed beside him. The wielder of Castor struck the snake man's face over and over until he fell over into a coughing lump and short breaths escaped him. He did not get up again.

This time Matthew became a puddle and dripped through the side back into the hall. He dropped the fallen enemy out in the hall. Finally, he could find Jason. Before wasting any more time, Matthew transformed into mist and smoked down through the cracks in the floor.

The building shook as he slowly sank downwards through thin fissures.

Multiple times he thought visions of Nieto popped into his head. But a shape beyond that dark silhouette assaulted his mind. A man made of intangible white flames walked the stars and soared between planets. He had never seen this being before, but he knew it was the Gemini Man.

The darkness that met him in that room jostled his mind free and allowed him to understand the constraints he had put on himself—those artificial limits. Castor was only as weak as he let himself become, and the Gemini Man was not weak. He could be the ultimate being.

Both Castor and Pollux *were* this thing once upon a time.

Castor called out to him. It was just out of reach. He couldn't quite make the final connection.

Matthew reached a giant metal door. It had been left wide open where flashes of light beamed out of it from the room inside. Inside, a long metal grating twisted and bent along the outer rim of the cocoon-like room. It had been knocked askew. Bodies lay about everywhere. At the front, a woman leaned against a pile of crates watching the floor through the grating below them. There at the base, Jason exchanged punches and heavy blows with a man made of black liquid. Bloodeater.

"Hey!" Matthew said to the woman by the door. She jumped at his voice. "Easy, I'm with Jason. You're Hammersmith's friend, right? Where is he?"

"Dead," she said. "But you see those cells over there? His partner's inside, along with others they took. I'd get them, but I can barely move: and I can't use my power. That villain stole it."

"Stole it? He can do that?"

"He works on blood. He was in my bloodstream for a day. Who knows how long he'll have my power for? Here, Bloodeater left the keys on me. Go get them out."

"Can you move? At this rate, this place won't be standing much longer."

"I can walk, barely. But they can't even get out. You better free them first. I'll help get 'em back out. Maybe I'll even let you two go free if we live."

"How kind of you. Hang tight."

He transmogrified into fog and wafted across the shaking scaffolding. Down below several of Bloodeater's men lay beaten and unmoving. An unconscious kid he had never seen before lay on an altar in the center of the room. Before Matthew could worry about that figure, he'd need to deal with the other prisoners. He counted the kids in the cells as he unlocked them. The boys and girls numbered more than the amount rumored missing. How long had this operation been going on for?

"Careful, everyone," he warned. "The scaffolding is very tricky."

The prisoners zipped from the cells toward the exit. Matthew helped guide them across to where the woman waited, leaning against the exit.

"You again," Roadbuster said to him.

"Sorry about your partner."

"Nothing to be done. You should worry about your own. He went down hard with Bloodeater's men, and I thought he was dead. But then the boy sprang up and punched the metal grating so hard that it quaked and threw just about everyone off. He's been attacking like a mad man since. You better get the kid off the altar before he brings this whole place down on top of us."

"I'll check him. Get the woman by the door. She knows the way out, I think. She was also the last person to see Hammersmith."

Roadbuster fell silent when they reached the woman. Her stare wavered at his approach, but he said nothing to her. Instead, he hoisted the wounded woman up onto his back. She tried several times to say something but came up short.

"It's alright," he said. "I understand. Once Bloodeater gets a hold of you, it's like you're just his skin. He doesn't care about the person inside and what it makes you feel like when you do things you wouldn't normally do. Whatever happened between you and Hammersmith doesn't matter."

"I'm the one who pushed him into the mirror. He fell through it, and he burned alive." She choked down her next words. "I killed him."

"That was Bloodeater. Not you. Hammersmith was a good kid. Wet around the ears, but there were few tougher. I doubt he suffered long."

"He might not be dead," Matthew interrupted. He didn't want to explain the artifacts or how Nieto's gates worked, but he had to give them something to go on. If Hammersmith held on to the earring Jason insisted on lending him, he could still be alive. "I've been through that mirror before, and I'm okay. He could be, too. Get to the surface and check. And be careful—the house at the top is not standing anymore."

Roadbuster cocked his head. "What exactly happened to you, White?"

"Long story. When I bring the kid on that altar up here, you guys run for it."

Matthew dissipated to the floor below, passing the crumpled bodies of Bloodeater's men, and reached the kid on the altar. He picked him up and realized the kid was conscious, but barely. He had tracts on his arms—they must have extracted blood. Matthew ignored it and took him in his arms. The tunnels shook as he misted back to the entrance. Two of the kids returned from the tunnels and carried the boy with them, Roadbuster and the woman at their side. The former prisoners disappeared down the tunnels as guttural yells burst from the battle below.

Roadbuster was right. Jason's face was locked in primal rage as he mindlessly bashed at the enemy. He screeched like a beast. What had set him off to that point?

Matthew misted back down to the bottom floor and slowly crossed it toward Jason. That memory of the Gemini Man drifted in the back of his head. It had meant something, somehow.

The oval space trembled violently as Matthew readied Castor and joined the battle. The Gemini Man whispered to him, increasing in volume with every stride. This would all be over in mere moments.

The earth quaked. The velocity at which the two falling fighters hit the ground surprised even Hammersmith. Dirt and grass indented under them into a small crater. Hammersmith had landed on top of Kyle, who took the brunt of the force. For once, Hammersmith's momentum power allowed him to avoid more harm than he received. But not entirely. Powers still had limits.

Hammersmith wobbled as he stood. Blood leaked from his broken nose. He tried steadying himself and snapped the nose back into place. A cry escaped him. That was only part of how bad the rest of him felt with cuts and scrapes all over.

"That was a very good shot, man," Kyle said.

The fallen enemy crawled out of the pit behind Hammersmith. His gashes leaked blood along his torn clothing. His arms and legs shook tremendously as he got up again.

Hammersmith swore. "I knew your power wasn't super strength."

"If I had any other power than this one, you might have gotten me."

"I still got you," Hammersmith said with a rasp. Even his voice hurt. "Cops are coming. Hear it?"

"Won't matter if you're dead."

Kyle lunged forward with both arms extended. Two pops filled the air, and bullets whizzed by. One struck Kyle in the shoulder. He weaved, his strike swinging past Hammersmith's head.

Hammersmith punched Kyle's chest with as much force as he could manage. Kyle gagged, blood and saliva leaking from his mouth. The attacker dropped to the dirt. He didn't rise again.

Cop cars shot around the block, siren lights breaking the night.

Hammersmith couldn't muster the energy to walk, but he needed to. He had to get going. Roadbuster was still out there in Albion, as were Matthew and Jason. He forced a step and felt the upturned earth meet his face.

"I don't have time for this crap," he mumbled into the dirt.

"It's fine. You've done enough."

Above him stood the woman from the apartment, holding a handgun he could barely make out through his darkening vision. She held out an earring in her right hand. Had he dropped it? It looked the same as the one he had used to get through the Mirror Gate.

"You dropped this upstairs," she said. "Where did you get it?"

"One of the guys who saved my rear. They're in trouble right now. I gotta get moving."

"You must not have seen it, but there were other police sirens out there tonight. I think your friends will be okay."

Sleep cast its spell over him like a fairy tale magician, and the pain began to numb. He caught the girl looking over the earring one more time.

"Saved me again, eh, Grandma?"

That was the last thing Ray Hammersmith remembered before his eyes closed. It was too bad he couldn't save anyone else.

CHAPTER 19
RISE OF THE GEMINI MAN

HE COULDN'T CONTROL his building anger, and it hurt even more than his open wounds. Jason had prided himself on being above this sort of thing. Sure he could be careless when it came time to act, but he always thought of himself as mature for his age. Fifteen-year-olds were reckless; he was sensible. Yet here he was swinging with unchecked rage at Bloodeater and wasting the energy Pollux had given him.

And he couldn't stop.

Bloodeater took a punch and spun backwards. Jason pivoted around and hooked the enemy's elbow in a hold before using his speed to throw him sideways. Bloodeater landed against the side of the room with such force that the remaining steel scaffolding above them jostled loose. It crashed down to the rocky terrain around them, clanging like dropped pots and pans by the barrel full. Loose ceiling stones from the impact came crashing down in a rain shower, some of which landed on downed cultists.

Bloodeater rolled in agony as metal and stone struck him mercilessly.

Jason should have felt some joy over a hit that had clearly hurt, but instead, his teeth tightened harder, digging into his lip and drawing blood. This suffering wasn't enough.

"Jason," Matthew said. The wielder of Castor came up behind him. "How's it going, man?"

"You look like you fell into a wheat thresher."

"You're one to talk. I expect you to do dumb things, not be like me."

"I saw *her*."

"Who? The woman Hammersmith talked about? I got her already. She's taking the prisoners out."

Jason spat blood from his lip. "My mom. When I was out like a light in that dark room, she came to me—maybe she was always there—hanging in the back of my mind. She was the one who led me to the Kharis Seed in Tyndarus, and she gave me the layout of this place. But I couldn't remember her whenever I woke up. I didn't know she was there, and now she's gone. I was such an idiot."

A sour mood crushed in on Jason. He tightened his fists. Few people knew his mother was a Prime because she barely used her powers. She could project her thoughts into others like a megaphone, but he didn't know it could continue after death. There she was clinging to him for life for so long, and he didn't even realize it. That must have been horrible. Jason couldn't make up for that. At the very least, he could stop this villain and end Nieto's little fan club. He could make her help count in some way.

His friend shook his head. "You may be an idiot, but so am I."

"Sure you are."

"I saw Nieto in the dark room. He tried to mess with my head, and my body was torn apart by the darkness as I tried to escape. At least, I thought I was being torn apart. But because of that, some pieces have begun connecting like pipes under the sink in my head. The water's flowing through again."

Across the room, Bloodeater still pushed heavy hunks of stone off of him. He shouted in anger as he threw aside a large piece of scaffolding. Within seconds he would be back.

"What do you mean, Matthew?"

"Normally, if we joined together now, I would be in charge because it's night. But that's only because we weren't complete. I'm one with Castor right now—its power is embedded in my mind and my bones. We're connected. We're one. If I merge with you now, I can force Pollux and Castor together. With my power, I can complete our true form."

Jason's fingers cracked under the weight of his squeezed fists. "I don't get it at all, but I don't care anymore. Just do it. He's going to send an army of lizardmen through those Mirror Gates just because we messed with Nieto's party. We need to do whatever it takes to stop him here."

"I'm not sure if we can separate after we do this. This might be permanent. Are you sure?"

"The town needs us, and I already said I don't care about myself. Do you?"

"Of course, I care, but I would rather end this soon before we bring the whole town down on top of us." He took a deep breath. "Are you ready?"

"Just do it, Matthew."

Matthew held Castor next to Pollux and narrowed his eyes. With a jerk, he slammed the two bracelets together and they melted into each other. A white light squeezed out like rays of sun through storm clouds. Matthew glowed before evaporating into smoke and zipped inside Pollux. Warmth exploded inside of Jason, buckling his knees.

Memories and ideas, notions and feelings, and an inexplicable thought, invaded his soul, twisting in and out like tied shoelaces. The light filled a foreign space inside that he never knew he had. Heat burned through his cells and caused him to cry out. But Jason held on to the oncoming rush as it forced its way inside of his muscles and bones.

Then his entire body exploded with white light, and Jason disappeared into his own mind.

BLOODEATER LIFTED a hunk of boulder-sized rubble and threw it. The boy dodged, and the stone and metal exploded with impact against the side of the altar room. The entranceway rumbled and caved in. He would have to dig his way out later.

Things were going quite well until these idiots showed up. He couldn't understand why the Master needed these two interlopers so badly despite never telling Bloodeater why they were so important. These punks had no value to anyone, rejecting the fires of purgatory the Master had offered and attempting to dismantle their operation. They needed to be destroyed.

Once he killed them, he could finally demolish this damn town. Seeing the sentinels—the lizardmen—up close had been a dream for ages. Finally, the Master would send some fire to Earth and cleanse it of these wastes. Bloodeater had wanted this for so long. Everyone else in the organization was counting on him. Even Suicide would finally be impressed.

A spasm rippled up his left arm again. Ever since eating that thug's heart back in New York, the one that gave him this super strength, involuntary thoughts twitched in his mind. The more he used the power, the more it irritated. Maybe it was more than simple super strength, but he didn't have the time to find out. He needed that one semi-permanent power to augment his temporary ones. He couldn't afford to swap it out. Not until he got that boy's super strength, anyway.

That was when the two idiots mixed and merged, as he knew they would. It wouldn't help them, but he was grateful for the option to kill them both at once. He crossed the rubble towards the flashing pair, the blood inside of his form rushing and boiling to peak levels. His hunger pangs would be satiated tonight.

"Why do you need them, Master?" he had asked. *"They could not withstand the fires of your limbo and ran with their tails behind their mangy legs back to Serenity City. We are the ones who will do whatever you ask. We are your true followers."*

The Master stared through the deep pits of Bloodeater's mind, silent as if he needn't bother answering his queries. Bloodeater had only ever met him through the mirrors and what light that came through them that doused his mind—that purple mist. His darkness that led to true light. Nonetheless, the Master's presence hit like a collapsing building crushing an infant. There was no man like him because he was no man. The Master was a god. Certainly, his physical form was dying, but he only needed a new shell to contain his power. He would rein over this pathetic galaxy forever once he had it.

"Why, Master?"

"Know your place, blood maggot. I require them, and that is all there is to it. You do not offer nearly enough to replace their full potential. They are mine. You will give them to me or die trying."

It wasn't rational, and the Master was always rational. He didn't need anything, and he asked for nothing aside from loyalty and sacrifices to the lizard sentinels. But everyone made sacrifices, so who was he to deny them? Living in blood and the darkness allowed Bloodeater to see what no one else could. Underneath the gloss and polish of this world lay only worm food and the abyss. The Master offered a world away from here, and it was the only logical choice to save everyone. Burn in the fires to save yourself!

What were a few corpses for immortality? Then these two came out of the cold to throw ice water on the fireplace. They were lucky even to be allowed to breathe. Bloodeater would be the one to fix that.

"You have nothing!" he said to the pair. "You do not deserve the fire."

White light burst from the duo, and he shielded his eyes. The brightness hammered at his mind. When it dimmed, he peered through the spots in his vision and found something he didn't expect.

There stood Pollux, his wrists both pitch white where the bracelets once were. His veins highlighted as if holy radiation filled them. His eyes shone as bright as his wrists had. An aura emanated from him that Bloodeater had never felt before.

"Lie down and die," the strange being said. "Don't even raise a fist."

Bloodeater cocked his head. That voice wasn't Pollux. It wasn't Castor either. The way this being carried himself reminded him of the Master.

That was it! That was why the Master wanted these two. They are the only ones that could destroy his dream, and their body would be the perfect replacement for his dying form. Only Bloodeater stood between these fools and their dream of destroying humanity. The Master would reward him with plenty of blood. He would stop them here.

"My Master wants what you have, but he won't ever meet you. Can't risk it. I'm afraid I can't let the two of you leave here alive."

"There is only one, fool. I am the Gemini Man, and you are in my way."

"I don't know what you think you are, Pollux, but I will show you what happens to those who besmirch the purging fire."

Bloodeater couldn't help but smile as the blood swam through his tightening hands. The super-strength pumped into his twitching form. All he needed to do is kill this pretender god. The Master would bathe him in fire for this.

CASTOR AND POLLUX swam through the Gemini Man's swirling thoughts. They were both him. The complete man knew what he must do next.

Nieto's altar and mirrors had to be destroyed first. The so-called Great Sorcerer King should never have another window into this world again. Then he had to get through Bloodeater. The quickest way to solve the problem was to bring this building down on them all.

Bloodeater morphed into his black liquid form and bolted towards him, cutting through the air in a flood of flying black liquid. It was useless. Apparently, he had no idea who he was attacking.

With one bound, the Gemini Man jumped forward and transformed into mist. He blew through the bloodstream and arrived out the other side. Bloodeater reformed and twisted around. The Gemini Man kicked him with such force that it lifted the enemy from the ground. In mid-flight, he caught the flying man and twisted his arm, whipping him downward.

Bloodeater slammed into the earth. The ground shook with the impact, and he spat out his own black blood.

Without pause, the Gemini Man stomped down on him.

But Bloodeater twisted arms into black blood and solidified them against his opponent's leg. The dark substance spread up his body, tightening with every passing second.

The enemy's strands of blood lifted the Gemini Man and slammed him back into the ground. Shattered stone crushed against his bones. Bloodeater whipped him up and down like a yo-yo.

The Gemini Man transformed, and the mist escaped his hold. He touched back down behind the enemy, his cuts throbbing unmercifully.

The blood wires shot towards him again, but he weaved through each strand far too easily.

He punched, sending teeth out of the blood man's cheek. But Bloodeater did not fall. He lashed his whips, slashing apart the Gemini Man's skin. Neither would give any ground. They exchanged blows, looking for the killing strike.

"What are you?" Bloodeater asked, his teeth somehow snapping effortlessly back into his mouth. "You aren't a Prime."

"No."

"If you would have joined the fires, I wouldn't need to do this. Do you understand? You're no god, just a freak. You are a mere meat-sack like everyone else! You cannot touch the Master!"

"My mother gave me this chance. I will use it. Then once I stop you, I can finally visit Cavern Cove like I always wanted and put this behind me. But your kind won't let me rest. So I'll just have to keep smashing you all to dust until you finally get the idea."

"You think we're evenly matched. But you're wrong. In case you haven't figured out who I am, I can show you right now."

Bloodeater transformed his body into a giant snake-like stream of blood and swam through the air in a torrent towards his opponent. The Gemini Man swung for him but hit air. Bloodeater had blitzed through and around the openings before bringing his fangs down into his foe. The blood torrent flooded into the freshly opened wound.

Lightning bolts of agony flashed inside the Gemini Man, doubling him over. Bloodeater had forced his way inside of his veins. Internal organs froze and broiled at the same time.

He wouldn't be able to get the enemy out now. Once attached to his insides, they were essentially a part of him. Neither of his powers would do much good, unless . . .

The Gemini Man did the only thing he could do—he transformed into the very air itself.

Atoms and molecules broke up in the atmosphere, but thoughts stirred inside him like a terrible mixing bowl experiment. Bloodeater had dug deep inside of his being, but the pain vanished. He wouldn't be able to follow the Gemini Man everywhere. It was time to show him how different they truly were.

The Gemini Man transformed into nothing. The void filled him for but that one instant before he reformed whole again. He sprang back into existence whole again and a long-forgotten warmth flooded through his very being.

Jason McCrae, now Jason Vermilion, was a teenage boy who had lost his family and ran away to find the ones responsible. He was given Pollux and now had the strength to achieve his goal.

Matthew White was a young man who had nothing and no one but fought to fade away from the world he had no love for. He was given Castor to go where he wanted.

So why were they here? Why was the Gemini Man here? None of it added up.

The Gemini Man screamed in agony as his subconscious was ripped asunder. Lights burst like heat rays inside of him. When he awoke, three figures stared down at each other in the void of his soul.

"I've been here before," Matthew said. "You don't want to be here, Bloodeater."

"Where are we?" Bloodeater asked. "I can't move."

"You're about to be crushed into dust."

"Last chance to escape," Jason said. "You better fight for it."

Instantly, the void vanished. The Gemini Man reformed, and his very being snapped into place as if it had never disassembled in the first place. His thoughts jumbled and rearranged, reminding him of just who he was and why he was there. Reality returned to its proper place. The light burned from Castor and Pollux, ejecting the poisonous black ink from his veins and organs.

A sizzling mess of dark blood reconstituted to a human in front of him. Bloodeater's dark form leaked life force, and he shifted on his feet as if his balance had not regained itself. Bloodeater grimaced as dark smoke billowed from his bent and broken body.

"You aren't human," Bloodeater said.

"You are one to talk."

"I cannot allow you near the Master. You die here."

"Wasting your last words on empty threats. Bad choice."

Bloodeater brought up both arms, and they bulged with blood and muscle, beefing up to five times the size of a normal bodybuilder. His bones creaked under the pressure. He slammed them down on the Gemini Man with a force that would have easily crushed a normal human.

The Gemini Man caught both limbs. The rocky ground buckled under the pressure of the attack, cracking open in a spider web. He threw the attacking arms backwards with a simple push and knocked Bloodeater off balance.

Reaching into the deepest pools he could imagine in his mind, the tension and heat built inside the Gemini Man's bones. He launched forward, and Bloodeater roared in response. The Gemini Man punched but once into his stomach, and the air split open with the vicious crack.

He grasped at Bloodeater's arms and spun around like a top. Wind whipped around them like a tornado.

After enough full spins, the Gemini Man let go of his foe.

Bloodeater soared upwards through the air over several hundred feet, black liquid spiraling out of his chest cavities. He struck the ceiling and the world rumbled with the force. His sagged rag-doll form limply twisted on its way back down as life force gushed out of his plentiful wounds.

On the way down, the Gemini Man punched up at the plummeting enemy. The hollow chest of Bloodeater burst open with the strike. The added force of his fall caused the Gemini Man's arm to tremble with the impact. Bloodeater convulsed and choked to dead silence. Blood shot out of every orifice and gash.

The cavern quaked around them. Stones dropped down around their still frames.

"I said you were dead," the Gemini Man said.

Bloodeater coughed out his namesake fluid. "Not human."

"Looks like we both have something in common."

The dead weight of Bloodeater dropped down in a hunk of dried dark goo and dirt. His remains rotted to nothing more than a blackened husk. He did not rise again. The dead expression of his face showed no emotion. After a moment, the corpse blew away into dust.

Boulder chunks dislodged from the ceiling and rained down everywhere. The altar and mirrors flattened and shattered, and the remains of the metal scaffolding, downed cultists, and jail cells were crushed in the debris. The Gemini Man spun and drifted through every rock, punching, and morphing to mist around each and every one on his way towards the exit. He would make it out.

Then his left arm throbbed. He had forgotten he was shot by the assistant earlier. Castor's power began to fade. Pollux would be left unbalanced.

The entire ceiling imploded, and he let out a flurry of strikes to shatter what he could. But the stones kept dropping regardless. Eventually, their sheer number buried him into crushing darkness.

The Gemini Man shouted as he fought back with the last of his strength. It was useless. The collapsing cavern soon swallowed him whole.

CHAPTER 20
SUNSHINE

THE VILLAGE WAS NOT MUCH like she expected. She had awoken inside the house on a bed made of straw and scratched the oncoming itch. Zelana changed into the borrowed farm dress and readied herself for breakfast in the home that had volunteered to shelter her for the night.

The children, a boy no older than ten years, and a girl only slightly younger, ran past her and outside. They had already eaten their lizard tails and began playing some game of knights and witches or some such. These mountain children were more fortunate than they realized. It made her slightly nostalgic, though not for reasons she understood. Not one memory of her childhood remained, and she doubted there were any memories of something like this.

It had been a full day since that strange man escaped back to Earth and the lizards on the ridge confronted Zelana's group. Her party slipped away from their pursuers and hid inside the mountain caves. Thankfully the two Vultures led their party to their village, where they were almost turned away. That is until they were told about the Mirror Gate the lot carried and Zelana being able to operate it.

Ever since that revelation, the group was confined to the village and among the people. Until the leaders discussed what to do about the gate, no one could leave.

After Zelana finished her lizard tail, Alain finally visited her. He sat at the table across from her as the rest of the family cleared out.

"Where have you been, Alain? Do you not think your sister is worried for you? I understand your old comrades are here, but that doesn't excuse you playing games like some child."

He rolled his eyes and pointed at her cheek. Sheepishly she wiped the crumbs away.

"Zelana, this past day has been one distress after another. I sent word via messenger bird back to Fortuna. They know we are here. But those two Earthwalkers in the lizard troop we took as prisoners refused to give us information. We do not even know if that man we saved survived his trek through to the other side. Understandably, the Vultures are attempting to comprehend what has happened and what they have here. You especially."

"Me? Oh, because I opened that Mirror Gate."

"Richter wants to see you. He's waiting outside. Be careful what you tell him. He's an ally, ostensibly. However, do not forget where you came from. Should the wrong party learn what you are capable of, you will be a target. You do not want what happened with your mother to happen again."

She pushed the remains of her bread aside. "I'm aware of where I come from, Alain. I just want the Mirror Gate. It is rightfully mine."

"Remember that when you speak to him. I will go see Dyne and Koa. They've been eager to leave as well. Perhaps I'll test the boy. It's been a dog's age since I thrashed another at swordplay, and he could use the practice."

"I would much prefer you find a florist in the village to speak with him. He is not quite as confident and cool as he appears."

Alain let a smile show through. "He's not the only one. Good luck, Zelana."

He exited the house bowing to the mother outside the door as he left. As soon as Alain left, a new figure entered the home and sat before her. He wore a light shirt and a leather hat on top of his smile. This was her first proper meeting with Richter.

"Young lady, it is good to see you looking so well. Slumber does well for a woman's skin."

"It does." He did not call Zelana a child, and that was enough to wrestle a grin from her. "I would have much preferred to do so back in Fortuna."

"I apologize for holding you here after you were good enough to rescue two of my men. Ravaging a cadre of lizardmen and catching Earthwalker traitors was also kind of you. There is another reason we kept you."

"The Mirror Gate, correct?"

"Smart girl. Let it be known that I do not consider you an enemy and will not use my position as leader of the Vultures to do any harm to your or your companions. Simply explain the fate of that other prisoner. Is he from the same world as Castor and Pollux? The messenger bird from Fortuna told me about them. How did they return? I take it you are the answer to that question."

"It is a long and complicated tale to say where I am from. But like Castor and Pollux I was endowed with special abilities from an artifact. I can counteract . . . *some* of Nieto's magic. One potent ability is the trick to open his Mirror Gates. That is how I was able to send that man back to Earth. I am not certain exactly of the process, but I will learn. I must. Now that I have one of his Mirror Gates, I plan to take advantage of my abilities."

"I can understand that," he said with a nod. "But what do you plan to *do* with the Mirror Gate?"

The laughter of children at play outside momentarily overtook her train of thought. It was a sound she enjoyed more than anything and lost none of its power out here in the mountains. Nieto would have this village destroyed and the people in chains, turned into mere automatons for his amusement. She wouldn't allow that to happen. Zelana had two worlds to protect now and someone to keep a promise to.

"I promised Pollux that I would retrieve it for him. He has a world of his own to protect."

Richter rubbed his chin and stifled a laugh. "Pollux, eh? He would be the one. I dueled with him. For an inexperienced whelp, he certainly had spirit and grit. I can see why one would be attracted by his fire. Do you have an interest in him, by chance?"

"Yes, he is fascinating. Castor is quite interesting, too."

He tilted his head. "That's not—never mind. What do you plan to do with that Mirror Gate? This is what I must know. We watch over these mountains to prevent Nieto's spread into Tyndarus. That mirror is the key to his infiltration of other worlds. It should be broken. What proof do I have that he can't still use it?"

She had little to offer. Her magic had a purifying agent thanks to the seed, but only in what she could touch herself. Zelana could purify the air around her and those she touched in the forest, but she couldn't stop the fog itself from being poisonous. There were limits to feats she could perform. She might use this Mirror Gate, but she could do nothing about the others out there. Not yet. She tried explaining as much to Richter, but he only shrugged in response. She still could not prove her powers.

"You plan to take the Mirror Gate back to Fortuna and do what with it? You might endanger the villagers if Nieto can send troops through it. We should destroy it, even if it might harm Pollux."

"Pollux has the other mirror." She did not know if they had retrieved it, but she believed in them. Jason and Matthew had never let her down yet. "Regardless, I can purify this gate so that Nieto can never use it again. Since Castor and Pollux have the other end, we can use it whenever they want. We can have a secret weapon who can help us if Nieto strikes again. Two, in fact."

Richter took a deep breath and locked his gaze on hers. His dark eyes were as pools of still water. "You have that much faith in them, do you?"

"I do," she said with more force than she intended. "I apologize for my bluntness."

"That's acceptable. I will give you the Mirror Gate, Zelana. On the condition that Kydil is given full ownership over it to watch in his village. It is not that I do not trust you, but if anything does go wrong, he will make the right decision to destroy it without hesitation. This Sorcerer King is no child's game."

"Do I look as if I play games, Richter? I am no child. Nieto runs afoul on Earth as well as Tyndarus. Castor and Pollux saved us. Do we not owe it to them to save their world as they saved ours?"

"Big words." He stood up and coughed into his fist. "But I believe them. Pollux is a lucky man."

"Castor, too. They will both be glad to have us as assets."

Richter laughed and slunk towards the doorway. He waved a hand dismissively. "I'll tell your friends, girl. You can leave whenever you want."

Zelana watched Richter as he patted the children on the head on his way towards the dirt road. He smiled as they went back to their play. Before he departed, he tipped his hat towards Zelana one last time. Richter was a strange man, but she had seen stranger.

But it was the idea of obtaining the Mirror Gate that gave her an unexpected thrill. She could finally see Jason and Matthew again. She might even see their world!

Once they got back to the village, she would get this to work. It might take time, but she had much time to spend. This quest might be over, but there were so many to come.

She found herself excited over seeing Ordopha's reaction to this discovery. Would Jason and Matthew be surprised? Whatever they were doing at that moment, they sure couldn't have been as excited as Zelana was.

When she finally fixed that mirror, both of their worlds would change.

DAYS PASSED around him like leaves in the wind. Cops and men in strange suits came to ask questions about just what he was doing underground to begin with. Of course, the truth remained off the table but he had to tell them something. The truth is that both Matthew and Jason had fought with a cult that worshiped a false god from another planet. He sat in the hospital room, his left arm in a cast, as the man he knew as Roadbuster finally reared his head again.

The older man had cleaned up from the last time they saw each other, but his fresh black suit and matching combed hair made him appear like a whole new person.

They sat across from each other outside the hospital room, an unspeakable tension between them.

"Hammersmith won't tell me what happened," Roadbuster said. "He says he was captured and brought underground like the rest of us but escaped through a tunnel and stumbled into the mess with that Carter girl. He's lying. None of the underground tunnels lead to her building."

"Maybe he just got lucky."

"Fat chance, buddy. Nonetheless, you did help us escape, so forfeiting the bounty will have to suffice instead of turning you in. I'll just have to turn down my employer and give back the half he gave us. I'll just say you got away."

"I appreciate it."

"No, you don't. There's more evidence right now that this cult is tied to the Williams' Tech building than there is that Matthew White and Jason McCrae were there. We've found contact lists and files in the mayor's blown office that list many high-profile staff members. Many were assigned to those upper floors. As far as everyone is concerned, you're both dead. We—*they* have no reason to haul you in."

"After everything that happened around here, it is the least you could do."

Roadbuster rolled the cigarette in his fingers and forced the smile forming at the corners of his mouth back into a grimace. "I still want to know what Hammersmith saw, but the dolt took my advice to heart about never telling secrets that weren't his. I'm not going to pursue this further. I suggest laying low someplace far from this town and making sure I never see you again."

"That sounds fair."

Roadbuster watched him sit up and saunter towards the door to the hospital room. His friend was waiting in the next room. Before he twisted the knob, the cigarette man called out.

"Don't worry about Jason. We know all about him and what happened to his family. He was never under suspicion regarding that crime, but he also has no living relatives that we could track down. They keep vanishing. Given the relationship between your powers, you're going to have a lot on your plate taking care of him."

Matthew didn't worry about that. Ever since he had awoken and Castor detached from his wrist, he didn't worry about what happened next. His powers were gone now, and what little he remembered about being the Gemini Man had already faded. Now it was back to business, and that meant no more running. He had to find a new place to settle in and start over. But Cavern Cove wouldn't be enough anymore. He needed somewhere the kid could call home.

"I have a place in mind," he said. "Mrs. Carter wired us some money as thanks. When Jason gets up, I'll tell him."

Of course, Jason had dropped his bracelet as well. His powers were also certainly gone. Not being Pollux anymore would certainly wound the boy, but it couldn't be helped. They lost their powers just as easily as they had gained them.

Unless the power came back, then Matthew would need to be by his side.

No more running.

"See Hammersmith before you leave. He's been waiting to tell you something." Roadbuster let his teeth show in his grin. "Thanks again."

Matthew stared back for a moment. "Let me know if you come in contact with that woman bounty hunter again."

"Why? It's not like we're a club."

Annette Kline vanished a day after escaping the tunnels and hadn't been seen since. Matthew didn't expect he would get to ask if she got her powers back, but he figured with the way Bloodeater was acting by the end of the fight, it had already run out for him. Confirmation would have been nice, but he wasn't going to lose sleep over it. He had his own powers to worry about.

"She was pretty hot," Matthew said. "I was thinking of asking her out."

"What a smooth talker. You ever think of growing up?"

"If I did that, then I wouldn't be the roaring success you see before you. Good day, sir."

Matthew entered the room with a weight pushing down in his gut. Jason slept undisturbed before him. The boy remained on an I.V. drip and was still out of it even a week after that mess. He was the one that harbored the physical form of the Gemini Man, so it made sense that it would affect him more, but the decision to become that thing remained Matthew's. His reckless choice caused this.

Birds chirped outside the window. Those would be Jason's only guests. No one else was left for the boy here on Earth. Matthew was the only one.

He reached into the bag beside the bed and ran fingers across Pollux and Castor. The familiar heat the trinkets once expelled had completely depleted. They were just jewelry now.

Or were they?

Even a call to Rachel Carter couldn't reveal anything. She had never used her power to the level that they had—it had only ever been used for Little Winter's protection. The users in her family always realized they didn't need the earrings anymore to use their abilities, but he couldn't tell if his situation was the same.

Only time could tell. For now, he would have to wait it out.

Matthew leaned back in his chair and his left arm spasmed when he accidentally struck it against the armrest. Everything still hurt a good deal. Though he wouldn't have to worry about that anymore.

His days of adventuring were over.

JASON DIDN'T DREAM about his mother again. It made sleeping far worse than it should have been. When he woke up and found Matthew sitting beside him in the hospital, the boy didn't even say anything—just trying to speak hurt him in a place he didn't understand.

He'd been out for over a week. It took a good spell before he could even look at his older friend.

Instead, Matthew pointed to his own left wrist. Castor was gone. Jason scrambled to check his wrist and found that Pollux was gone, too. All he had was that dumb white hospital gown.

Matthew held both bracelets in his hand.

"I can't transform," Matthew said.

A stone weight thumped inside Jason's stomach. That transformation into the Gemini Man had damaged them. He knew that Matthew was telling the truth and that it was true for him, too.

The Gemini Man took everything, and it might have taken it for good. Even more queasiness flowed through Jason. They might have lost their powers forever. How much more could he have screwed things up? How many people could he have saved with those abilities? Now they were gone. He covered his face with the crook of his elbow and felt his teeth clench.

"It's not that bad, Jason. Don't flip out."

"It's plenty bad. Do you know what we've done?"

"What we could. We leveled Nieto's entire operation of cronies and buried a few murderers. If we can't go on being Castor and Pollux we've at least got that under our belts."

"We killed him, right?"

"Are you really going to do this again?"

"That's not it. Did anyone see us become . . . *that*?" He couldn't say the name of the Gemini Man.

"No. The prisoners had all run by then." Matthew leaned back in his chair. "On the other hand, Hammersmith ended up in Tyndarus."

Jason finally sat up. "He what?"

Matthew explained how Hammersmith was lured by Bloodeater into the mirror as best he could. He had found a teenage girl and a band of warriors who saved him from man-sized lizards. If he didn't know it was true, Jason hardly would have believed it.

"Zelana found the other end of the Mirror Gate, then?"

"You got it!" Matthew said. "Looks like I was wrong. Destroying the mirror wasn't the way to go here. Now that she has it, we can send them whatever they need."

"We can't help them, though."

"Stop being a downer. That's my thing. Anyway, Zelana, Alain, and the others fought to get it. We can't let it go to waste for them. Stephanie currently has the Mirror Gate in her apartment. From what I hear, she's going to give it to us. Says it's the least she could do. So we're going to take it."

"We're going somewhere?"

"Yeah, I've got a place. No, it's not Cavern Cove. Going on vacation is out of the question now. The place I'm thinking about is out of the way. No one will find us there. And who knows? Maybe our powers will come back by the time we get there. Whatever happens, we are done with this life of wandering."

"They must have told you about my family. They're letting me go?"

"They've got nothing on you," Matthew said. "Roadbuster has some friends in high places that pulled some strings to get us through this. But I figured most of your situation out not long after we first came back to Earth. A man and a woman went out for a drive early in the morning out of the blue. Their car was found on a back-road miles away and burnt to a crisp. Their son later disappeared after their funeral." Matthew furrowed his brow. "The stranger part was that in the weeks before and after, several other extended family members suffered similar fates. It was as if the suspects were looking for something in particular. After the son disappeared, most assumed he died like the rest. I'm glad we ran into Roadbuster to clear things up for us and hide your real identity. No red tape to go through."

Jason couldn't help but not stare at Matthew. He did not expect him to bother with learning something like his past or agreeing to take him along despite knowing it. What happened to Cavern Cove and his permanent vacation?

"My mother was a Prime," Jason clarified. "She could send her thoughts into other people to speak with them. Others could also send thoughts to her. Her power was like a communicator hub. She couldn't read minds, but she didn't need to. She still always knew what I was thinking."

"Moms are like that."

"Right, but I learned something else. That woman I saw in my dreams? The one I couldn't remember? That was her. She guided me along this whole time, and I didn't even realize it. After everything she did for me, I can't even find out who killed her."

Matthew said nothing. He appeared to be waiting for Jason, so the boy continued.

"She died because I wasn't there to help. How many times has she saved me since? She even told us where the Kharis Seed and Zelana were when we were stuck in Tyndarus."

"She saved my skin, huh? I owe her a drink."

"The point is that I failed her, Matthew." Fire welled behind Jason's eyes. He tried to look away from his friend even as his voice cracked. "There's nothing I can do for her, and yet she's still helping me. I'm never there for her."

"You failed nothing. We stopped those guys; we did what we could. What else can we do? She gave you a second chance. You're going to use it. We still have things to do, places to be. You've got a long life ahead of you, God willing. She didn't do all that for you to sit here crying into your pillow. Get up and get back out there."

Jason felt his legs under the sheets. They were still numb. The cuts along his skin were scabbed over but had not healed yet. The lack of a bracelet left him oddly hollow. Pollux really was gone.

But he did remember the last dream where he saw his mother. Sparkling in the dark, she leaned in to kiss his forehead, but remained just out of reach—where she would be for the rest of his life. Instead, she made do watching from the shadows as he fought his enemies. She had stayed with him regardless of the fact she was alone in watching over him until her power ran out.

Now that she was gone, the anger and bitterness evaporated like rain puddles in the grooves of his soul. She did everything for him, and now it was his turn to do the rest.

"Once my legs wake up, I'll go anywhere you want to go, Matthew. Just promise me that we'll stay away from cults and crazy families."

"Don't worry. We're not going anywhere near that sort of stuff."

Jason leaned back in his bed and thought of home. That old two-story in the quiet neighborhood where the kids stayed out much too late playing ball in the streets and the block parties went on at interminable lengths. Those days were a far-off memory.

He turned in his bed towards the window. Sunlight splashed against his sore skin. He stifled a moan from his scabbed-over body. It was probably really hot out there in that summer weather.

"You do understand that we won't be powerless forever," Jason said.

"Give me a break," Matthew said with a laugh. "I'm not that lucky!"

EPILOGUE

HAMMERSMITH SAT on the steps of the apartment building, mindlessly flicking the lighter Roadbuster had given him. It had been an awkward week between the bounty chasing and discovering an entirely new world, but at least he was alive to appreciate it. On top of that, his partner had not told him everything about his past and that he knew people in high places.

Someone like Jason McCrae being discovered alive would normally cause a media sensation, but instead of that, many men in black suits showed up in town, and the matter was dropped. Roadbuster might have worked alone, but whoever his friends were swept it all under the rug for him. Perhaps he knew men in higher places like Sonlight or Aegis, but he refused to tell Hammersmith. As far as he was concerned, this matter was closed.

It wasn't as if Hammersmith could blame him. He was hiding something big, too.

"*Did something happen in that apartment?*" Roadbuster had asked.

"*Aside from our fight?*"

"*Yes. What did he do to stir you up so badly, and where were your clothes?*"

Hammersmith shrugged. "*You have your secrets, and I have mine. The case is closed, right?*"

"*I guess it is.*" Roadbuster laughed. "*Regardless, like you said, the case is closed. As for my friends, let's just say that our new pals will have a debt to pay sometime in the future. But that's got nothing to do with you. You might have what it takes to be a hunter, after all, Hammersmith.*"

They would be going back on the job, but things wouldn't quite be the same again. Not that it was particularly bothersome. Hunting scum never got old. There were always new places to be, and a whole world out there to see. As long as he never had to leave the planet again, all was good.

"Hey," Annette Kline said.

The bounty hunter stood before him in a frilly red summer dress that matched her hips and figure far too well. Both arms wrapped around her chest under her bosom. He tried not to stare and flicked the lighter again.

"Not collecting the bounty on those two, Ray?" she asked.

"We all got a share in busting the psychos here. Much as I wouldn't mind getting extra, they did save me. Besides, I didn't like the client."

"You and me both. I'm surprised you haven't left town yet."

"Still got people to thank, then I'm off."

Kline nodded to the door behind him. "How about her? She can't be sticking around."

"The Carter girl is going back home. We had a talk after I kicked the hell out of her boyfriend."

"Good going, stud! I would have loved to do the same, but my powers just came back. Freak probably would have enjoyed it, though."

"I'm still trying to piece this all together. Magic, another planet, aliens . . . it's quite a bit."

"That just means more players at the card table. We need to be smarter to read the others and play the right hand. It's just the way it goes. We're all against each other, but it wouldn't be as fun if it was just you and me, would it? You can only play the same person so many times before it gets dull."

He smirked. "So, you would be willing to play a hand with me?"

"In the right time and place," she said with a wink. "For now, I have to get back on the road. Can't keep wasting my time thinking about these things forever, right?"

"True enough."

He watched the way she gracefully slid with every step back to her rental car, a beat-up bug from a decade ago. She started her engine, waved, and tore off into the burning morning light. Annette Kline was not like the other members he'd met in his profession. Hunters were a much more varied bunch than he had originally thought.

Hammersmith sat back on the step and flipped the lighter around once again. Serenity City was going to take quite a drive, and they already had another client waiting for them for yet another job. When Roadbuster got back, they would probably take off, too.

He pocketed the lighter and laughed to himself.

Annette was right. As long as you're moving, things never get dull.

BOOK THREE

GEMINI OUTSIDER

MATTHEW WHITE

PROLOGUE

SUICIDE ALWAYS KEPT his tone casual when he spoke with the twelve Higher Ones. Some of the lesser men wore suits or dresses to look the part of being professional or proper, worthy of the purifying fires, but he would not look up to anyone and instead kept his head shaved and leather jacket close at hand. He wasn't like them. The Master was on his side —he didn't have to play to anyone. And today, these puppets declared Suicide the new prophet.

He stood alone in a semi-circle of stuffed shirts who sat in high chairs to look down at the lesser dregs they presided over. Despite his towering height, they didn't feel even the slightest bit off-kilter around him. Perhaps they still believed they had the Master's blessing. Why else would they call him here after two catastrophic failures and still have the gall to act superior?

Serenity City wasn't looking so hot these days, and the mess at Williams' Tech didn't help. The last thing the Hades Society needed was heroes on their tail, and yet that is what happened. Too many mistakes allowed this to happen. Forget formalities; Suicide could handle all this on his own.

He shuffled his scarred, meaty knuckles in his pockets. "First it was the Queen, and now it's Bloodeater. You've lost us two invaluable followers with your incompetence. Our targets are two moron brothers with nowhere to run. How have you not found them? The Hades Society has been around since the Primes first showed up on this planet—we've taken out tougher targets in record time. You've devalued the cause. If I was Nieto I'd be furious."

"Do not say the Great Sorcerer King's name," the greybeard in the center said. This clown had ties to some district attorney in the city, Suicide didn't know which. It didn't matter. None of this mattered. "And who're you to be speaking to us as such? We are the Council of Higher Ones. We outrank you."

"That must be why I'm here. You want to send me on a fruitless quest for Castor and Pollux. After failing to capture them twice, letting our Queen perish, and losing our forces in Albion and Serenity City in an embarrassing spectacle, you want me to do the sweeping for you. This never would have happened if you had recruited Thanatos."

"He hasn't been seen in years. We can't seek out ghosts, and he has been well known to detest groups, never mind causes such as ours. Forget him: will you go, or not? If you won't we have plenty of others far more loyal to the cause than you."

Suicide's teeth snarled like a wolf. "You know nothing of my loyalty, worm food."

"Be that as it may," the crone in the green dress said. Of the twelve she had been there the least amount of time: only seven years. Yet she acted as if she were some sort of expert. "Castor and Pollux have powers we do not quite understand, but the Master need not tell us everything. We ran into some unknown organization when chasing them down in Albion. We are still investigating the matter. Whoever it was, they will feel our reprisal as swiftly as the others who cross us. Castor and Pollux might be hiding, but we will flush them out."

Suicide rolled his eyes. "That organization probably handed them new identities and left them hiding out in some backwater berg. Fantastic job Bloodeater did. This is why you don't give zealots command of anything."

"He might have been too overzealous," the greybeard said. "But he was committed. We are certain the Great Sorcerer King embraced his essence into his bosom as he does all those who step through the True Path. Nonetheless, we have more where he came from."

"Oh, do you?"

"Yes, maggot, we do. Arrests and busts in Serenity City and Albion mean little if no one talks. The men captured are all disposable, and they will never talk."

"It isn't just Serenity City, you old idiot. As we speak, our posts in Miami, Washington, and Halo City are all being invaded by cops. By tomorrow, the Higher Ones will be all that remains of the Hades Society. That's how our enemies are hoping it'll go down, anyway. They think you're valuable."

The old man's face paled. "Your lying tongue is very close to being removed from your head."

"It doesn't matter if I am lying. Nieto no longer has use for you. Being unable to save his Queen, our most valuable Earth agent, and then fumbling extraction of our relics on top of it is unforgivable. You've failed too many times."

Suicide snapped his fingers and thirteen of his men flooded the council room with their blood-caked knives and loaded automatics trained on the twelve members of the council. The council stared agape at the force surrounding them. The complaints from the elders ceased as several rifles clicked.

"Hey, bro!" Elaine said. She wandered through the door with three other figures dressed in black. He had been waiting for her for far too long. The teenager had her red hair dyed black and wore a leather jacket not unlike his. Unlike the council, Suicide's crew had uses. "You need us?"

"No, this is fine. It'll be over fast."

None of their guards would come, having already met their end moments before. Suicide didn't mind the waste. Nieto's power went through him—he was to be the cleanser. He could always get new men instead of these fat cats hoping to make a few bucks on the way to salvation.

"*End them all*," the Master had said. "*I no longer require agents of this pathetic caliber. I can always make more mirrors. Once I awaken, any resistance by humans will become meaningless.*"

The Master was the only one who understood. Humanity was a collection of skin cells and hair follicles with slightly differing thought patterns that the mighty could manipulate. They shouldn't exist, and soon enough, they wouldn't. That had always been his goal.

"Traitor!" the greybeard said. "You have no right!"

"Rights don't exist, and neither does your will." Suicide spat on the carpet and rubbed his boot down against it. He snarled at the banners of coiled snakes strewn about this underground lair. Tacky place, this was. He leaned over their table and rubbed a thumb against the old man's suit, picking off a bit of lint. "You're pretty clean, old man. I can see why others consider you respectable. But what's inside that rotting head of yours?"

The old man locked eyes with Suicide and slowly he trembled. The two on either side watched him questioningly. He sweat and whimpered, clutching his skull. All Suicide had to do was touch him, and this was the result.

Whimpering turned to screams. The old man fumbled for his pocket, assuredly where his gun waited. But it wouldn't do him any good. Suicide was the one in charge now.

"Those thoughts in your brain are permanent," Suicide said, careful to emphasize every word. The old man looked at him, his eyes red and watering. There was only so much weight the mind could take. It wasn't like other muscles—it could never be trained to be tougher. All men were weak on the inside. "If you shoot me they stay forever. But I never choose to leave them forever. The mind is soft, but it adapts. Humans can conquer depression —it isn't easy, but it can be done. But it's not so easy to do if it comes and goes in spurts, is it? One day you'll be counting your money, and wham! Here come innocent thoughts of murdering your wife. And maybe those will go away if you act on it. Can't trust yourself if you can't think straight. I've seen it happen."

Greybeard pressed his face against the table and his arms down on his head. Sobs wracked his covered face. "I'll give you whatever you want. Just stop. Please."

"Shoot the bird on your right, and the geezer on your left, and I'll let you go."

The three members of the council glanced at each other, and several other members objected, but the old man only screamed further and longer before banging his head against the top of the table.

"Should I turn it up?" Suicide asked.

The piercing shouts of the man before Suicide could have broken windows. The old man scrambled for the gun in his pocket and aimed it at his tormentor. His right eye was shut, but the watering left remained focused on his enemy. Suicide watched the gun trained on him even as horrendous thoughts piled into the old man's mind's eye. The gun shook, but the trigger never budged.

After a full minute of shivering, the old man's walleyed stare found its way to Suicide.

He brought his piece to his own head. "For the fires of purgatory!"

Greybeard fired into his own head, sending what was left of his decrepit existence over his chair to the floor. The other members of the council watched the corpse in silence.

"That was disappointing," Suicide said. "It looks like he was more loyal to the cause than I thought. No matter, how about the rest of you? Would you like to die like him?"

The old woman in the dress shuddered as she looked down at what remained of her companion. She had to understand by now what her fate entailed.

"I only wished to save humanity."

"That was never going to happen. Nieto's going to win either way. Until he reaches full power, I'm going to make sure his path to Earth is clear. That means finding the relics and doing what you failed at. That means finding Castor and Pollux."

"But that is exactly what we were asking you to do! We also want to return them to the Great Sorcerer King. We're on the same side."

"Nieto wants results," Suicide said. "Societies function because there's a level of trust between those operating in them. Sowing mistrust inside of them is harder than you think, but sowing mistrust inside their heads instead? Break down the individual, and then you destroy the collective. It's an old fashion game of dominoes. You start with the inside and work your way outside."

She bit her lip and took a deep breath. "Do you know where they are?"

"I'll find out. Until then, they arrested some men in Albion, right? I don't think anyone will mind if a few fools go swan-diving off a billboard."

"But they were loyal to the Master!"

"Loyal to nothing. Like you, they're going to be nothing but a forgotten memory."

She screamed as he approached, but they always did when they knew what he could do. The world was nothing but a furnace for garbage, and he would enjoy every moment. As the woman sobbed and rubbed the gun on her neck, a small smile formed on Suicide's dry lips.

It was always nice when the trash burned itself.

CHAPTER 1
OUTSIDERS

THE SUMMER HEAT caused sweat to form through Jason's green t-shirt. At least here on the school rooftop, no one would see him. His sword in his grip, he practiced the stances Alain had taught him back in Tyndarus. The teenager huffed as he slashed his weapon at thin air, and spun around to deliver a killing blow to an opponent that wasn't there. Even if Jason was on Earth in the obscure town of Riverview, he would remain on guard. He would always be a warrior, even if he had no one to fight.

Summer school classes finished at the end of July, which meant no one was around by late August. Jason had come up here every day to train for the entire week since they'd moved to this town. All he had to do was sneak through the emergency exit, which was simple in the summer. Between this and how easy it was for Jason to move into Riverview unnoticed, he thought this town was too trusting for its own good.

The teenager carried his sword in a duffle bag, but that was only to prevent drawing attention to him as he walked around town. Even Matthew, his "brother" and caretaker, didn't know Jason was doing this.

It was August, and only weeks before the new school year started. Jason's interest in returning to school remained at an all-time low, but Matthew insisted on it. He had taken the right tests and would be put into ninth grade, just like his mom would have wanted. School always sucked and he had little doubt it would be any better here so far from Serenity City up in Canada.

Jason stabbed the blade forward, imagining he had run through a lizardman from the alien planet of Tyndarus, and circled to deflect a non-existent incoming blow. The next time he returned to that other world, he would be ready to take on anyone, even if his powers hadn't returned by then. This stop on Earth was temporary—he belonged on another planet far from here.

"Is that a sword?"

Jason froze and glanced over his shoulder. A tall, brown-haired kid with green eyes and short breath, and skin slightly pink from what must have been exercise watched him from the exit. The teenager slid onto the roof and let the door shut behind him. The boy gazed out over the roof into the nearby St. Laurence River several blocks away from their location. This school had been built at the top of a steep hill on the same street as the Anglican and Catholic Church, probably specifically for this view of the river. Jason never imagined other kids would go out of their way to come up here in the summer.

"I take a run by here every day," the boy said. "I kept thinking I saw someone up here dancing, but it's so hard to see. Since I had some time today, I thought I'd check it out. I'm Spencer. Spencer Richardson. You can call me Spence. I don't think I've seen you before."

"I'm new," Jason said. "Moved here this summer. I don't know anyone, so I just sort of do stuff like this on my own."

"But, wow! A sword!" Spencer's eyes brightened, and his smile broadened as he inspected the simple blade. "Where in the world did you get that? Your parents must be crazy."

"My parents . . . aren't around anymore. It's just my bro and me these days."

"Oh, sorry. I didn't mean to—"

"It's no problem. I just need someplace to vent, away from prying eyes. A school roof in summer is as good a place as any."

"What's your name, by the way?"

Jason placed the sword back in the sheath inside his duffle bag. "Luke. Luke Bartlett."

"Ah, okay, *Luke*. Good to meet ya! We don't get too many people moving to Riverview, at least from what I can see. Toronto is a lot more popular—more expensive, anyway. Say, are you going to be at that block party in a few days? Me and the guys are thinking of stopping by."

"Heard about it, yeah. Riverview has it every year, right? I dunno if I'm going. I've got a lot on my head."

"That's fine. I don't want to pry or whatever. It's not every day we get new faces in town. I'm starting ninth grade this year, so I've gotten used to everything Riverview can throw at me."

"Oh, yeah? I'm also starting ninth grade."

"Whoa," Spencer said. "Maybe that's a sign? We both play sports . . . kinda. We, I mean, my football team tends to practice early in the morning, just like you. So I might see you around town. Welcome to Riverview, by the way. The plainest town in all of Ontario . . . and probably all of Canada!"

Was this why Matthew had chosen to come here? He had failed to tell Jason anything about the place. All he said was he wanted to get the two of them as far out of the way of any potential pursuers as possible. After all, they were on the run from a mad magical god from another planet and his loyal cult. Who knew how far they would go to find the two of them?

"Nice meeting you, Spencer. Maybe I'll see you around town."

"Take it easy, Luke."

Spencer turned and exited, and Jason wasn't far after him. He locked up and left for the street below. Jason was lucky it was just someone like Spencer who found him and not a petty teacher trolling for excuses to hassle students. Serenity City, at least the school he went to, was crawling with those types. Sometimes Jason thought about those old friends of his that he left behind when *it* happened, but he couldn't dwell on those days. They wouldn't be coming back, and he didn't plan on going back, either.

Hard rays of yellow sun raked across the early morning streets of Riverview. This town wasn't too big or too small, hovering at around twenty thousand people in sixteen square kilometers: it was about as normal as you could get for a place outside of the big city. Jason wasn't one of them, and he wouldn't ever be. This world was waking up for their morning shifts, and he was on his way back home—if it could even be considered home.

He slipped down the sloping hill of Flutter St. between a throng of brick houses painted various hues of brown and yellow. The street was vacant, aside from the blue jays and the incessant barking of one Labrador retriever. Eventually Jason arrived out by the water where he could overlook the St. Laurence River, the body of water separating most of the provinces of Ontario and Quebec. It was quite the sight that the locals took for granted. He liked to look out over it and see the opposing side as a sort of distant world he could never step foot in. It was like a place he could always wonder about but never actually visit.

Jason took a hard turn left down a road that crawled into a tunnel of green summer brush that would lead him back to the house. No one ever seemed to come by this street, either, which made it nice to walk when he needed to think.

The slow rumble of an engine purred behind him, and the beat-up tiny black Volkswagen rolled up to his left. Jason instantly recognized the taxi sign on the roof as the windows opened and the car slowed down beside him. He kept walking regardless.

"I didn't tell you about this place so you could take off on me every morning," Matthew said. He pulled over and threw open the passenger door. "Come on, Jason. I have some free time before my second job this evening. Don't be your usual sulky self, and get in."

Matthew had a way of being a real pest if he didn't get his way, and Jason did not feel like dealing with that. Truth is he was feeling tired and just wanted to get back home to rest. Nonetheless, he climbed into the car and slipped on the seat belt. Matthew had already taken off before the door was even shut.

"Still hoping for your powers to come back?" Matthew asked.

"I feel a bit stronger, so maybe they are returning."

"It could also be that you're out there exercising all the time. You're naturally going to get in better shape."

"My strength is going to come back eventually, Matthew. Just like your transforming power will. I don't know why you keep acting like they won't."

Matthew sighed and tapped the steering wheel with his fingers. "It's not that they won't, but that I don't see how much it will matter if they do. We're not making ourselves targets for Nieto again. And heading back through the Mirror Gate to another planet is not something we should turn into a regular activity. It's more important that we blend into Riverview first. Got it, *Luke*?"

A sliver of uneasiness slithered through Jason when he heard his fake name again. It made sense to have secret identities when they were on the run, but he still didn't like it. He wanted to be Jason Vermilion, the wielder of Pollux. Just being plain old boring Luke Bartlett while there were villains out there in the universe that needed to be brought to justice would never sit right with him. But Matthew wanted it this way, and he always got what he wanted.

"Sure thing, *Scott*," Jason replied. "Don't worry; I won't blow your cover. You should know me better by now."

"Should I? One of the reasons I wanted as far away from Serenity City to begin with was to make sure you didn't go off on your own to deal with Nieto. You're very good at trying to be a lone wolf. It might even be noble if you weren't a dumb kid about it."

A flash of heat pierced Jason's grimace and sent it twitching. "That was in the past. All I can do is get ready for what's ahead. Unlike you, I'm not going to worry about where I've already been."

"And what's that future? Going to play hero in Tyndarus and forgetting all about Earth? When Roadbuster hooked us up with weapons to defend ourselves on this side of the border, I said nothing about you wanting a sword. I don't want to let Alain's lessons go to waste, after all. But you're becoming obsessed with it, Jason. You can't just run away your whole life."

Jason laughed. "From you, of all people."

"That's right. I've done some dumb things. I'm *here*, aren't I? That's how I know. The best thing to do is to sit tight and be quiet. We're no heroes. Sticking out our necks when there are psychos looking to cut it off is stupid."

They drove in quiet, though Matthew's attitude had visibly changed. He incessantly tapped his index fingers on the wheel. The lines under his eyes showed a man needing more rest than he got, which made it hard for Jason to really tear into him. He had never seen him this focused on being reserved before.

Even though they didn't really get along, Jason did not dislike his friend. Matthew had a few more years on him, and therefore more experience in the real world, and he also meant well. But he was also a hypocrite.

Matthew had no issue poking Jason about refusing to talk about his parents' deaths, but Matthew never spoke about his family at all.

Sure the two had been through insanity together and had come out more or less unscathed, and that was impressive enough. So why is it that it felt like they were still strangers to each other?

They drove in silence back through Riverview's small neighborhoods. Rows of brick and wood houses built many decades before he was born, and probably updated about the time he actually was, sat upon lush, cut grass, and smoothly paved driveways. The quiet in this place always struck Jason as eerie, though he had been used to the noise of the city and the relative peacefulness of this place was like walking on an alien planet. Being able to move around at sunrise without being assaulted with traffic sounds remained an odd experience.

A group of kids in t-shirts and summer shorts ran down a thin bike path past a young biking couple. That bike path sliced through the neighborhoods and led towards the shopping district further north from the park. These strange shortcuts made him think of trapdoors and hidden wall switches in those old Gothic-style castles. The suburbs could be weird like that.

The car blew past the college by the river, which was empty this time of year, as was the football field they soon rolled by. This place must have been where Spencer practiced with his team, though Jason had never seen them. Streets beyond that, they passed another Catholic Church, this one less classical-looking than the one by the school and built in what might have been way back in the 1970s with its boxy design and unflattering pale blue and brown color scheme. This part of town looked a bit older than the rest, as if Riverview was in the middle of a time warp transition. But at least they were getting closer to home.

Finally, the car reached a quiet road where duplex houses became a common occurrence. Jason had never seen so many before coming to Riverview. They looked about as old as that nearby church, with chipping paint and ancient shutters on the windows that definitely needed updating. The driveways had roots growing through them, and the roofs had shingles missing. Everything needed a good overhaul. But it was cheap, and that's what they needed right now. Besides, this was only a stopgap.

They got out of the car, and Matthew stretched. They lived on the right half of this duplex that looked as if it was cut in two and opposite half were smashed together. Each side had a black door covered in streaks of runny paint, which led into a tight corridor of a mudroom that opened up into a kitchen and living room before the backyard. The bathroom and two bedrooms were upstairs, and the basement—the only decent-sized room in the house—awaited downstairs. The place was too small for the two of them, though that might just be because they rarely got along.

A woman stepped out of the door beside their place with her arms folded. She had her brunette hair done in curls and leaned back against the wall as the two approached.

"Oh boy," Matthew whispered. "Here we go."

"Where did you go, Luke?" she asked Jason. "Made some friends already? Your brother has been looking for you all morning."

"Cool it, Lynn," Matthew said. "Don't ask him weird things like that out in the open."

"No one is listening, *Scott*. Whoever hasn't already gone to work is too busy cutting their lawn or cleaning inside. Our neighbors keep busy. I know my town. I've been living here a lot longer than you."

Lynn wore a light grey t-shirt that slid over her thin shoulders past the jean shorts that hugged her hips. She reached up to ruffle Jason's hair as he passed her on his way to the front door. He had only known her since they moved to Riverview, but he did like having her around. Especially because she annoyed Matthew. Jason smiled at her.

Matthew shrugged and unlocked their door. "We're your tenants, and you can't even act like we're strangers. Do you think your uncle would approve?"

"My uncle would have smacked you silly just for disappearing without saying a word for years. What's wrong with you? Couldn't send mail? You had my address—why didn't you use it?"

"What's it to you? I was unaware we were related."

"Funny. We've been friends since we were kids, and then you suddenly stop calling and coming up here, and I'm supposed to just forget?"

Matthew walked into the house, and Jason followed. The teenager noticed Lynn behind him in the doorway with her arms still folded. She closed the door behind her and leaned up against it.

"Jason, you still look tired. Get some rest."

"Leave the kid alone," Matthew said. "He knows what he's doing."

"I'm not a kid!" Jason stifled a yawn. "But anyway, shouldn't you hurry, Lynn? Doesn't the salon open early?"

"Yes, but it's my job to check on my tenants. Be careful leaving the basement door open. If you trip coming in the front door, it can send you quite a ways down. It might not hurt *his* thick head, but you always look tired, and the last thing I want to see is you lying at the bottom of those steps."

Jason didn't worry about the basement. He had been down there every night before bed, just staring into the lone Mirror Gate they had pilfered from Albion. Recently, there was a strange sheen about it that led Jason to wonder if it had activated. He almost thought someone was trying to come through from the other side. But that couldn't happen—they would be vaporized without having Great Sorcerer King Nieto's blood, or the power of the relics. Lynn didn't know about any of this, and Jason didn't blame Matthew for not telling her. How could anyone understand that a gate to a whole other planet lay in wake in their basement?

She sighed and grinned at Jason. "Are you looking forward to the block party this weekend, Jason? There might be some teenagers your age there."

He thought about Spencer. That kid didn't seem too bad. "Maybe."

"Stop saying our names!" Matthew whispered. "Do you want us to be found out?"

"Oh, please. We're inside now, and our neighbors don't care. And don't lecture me, Matthew. You disappeared for years and then suddenly show back up here, and don't expect me to ask any questions. I know something happened to you down in the states. Tell me what it is. I can help."

Matthew sat down in the stained leather couch he had gotten at the pawnshop on Monday. Jason joined him there. Lynn stood before him in front of the television, wiping the dust off the top of it. Jason hadn't seen his friend clean recently—probably because he was just too tired to bother these days.

Matthew stifled a yawn. "It's not about helping, Lynn. It's about keeping *him* safe. We've gone through the wringer, and barely came out the other side. You'd be better off not knowing."

"You don't have to be a tough guy. Why are you always hiding things from me? Ever since we were kids. Do you think I can't handle it? We've had a few problems of our own around here, I'll have you know. Some jacked-up loadies and roving gangs of Primes have caused plenty of issues for us over the years. But we stick together around here. We don't go off half-cocked like a lone wolf cowboy to who-knows-where to settle our problems."

Jason would have told them to cool it, but he had slunk back into the couch and allowed his heavy lids to close. In the back of his mind, he could hear them arguing, but he no longer cared. His consciousness had already left him.

As he slipped deeper into slumber, he thought he heard a woman's voice far away, as if echoing through the mountains of some forgotten snowy range. Jason tried to turn and twist, but he just could not make it out. She remained just out of his reach.

Down in the depths of his mind, where the power of Pollux once burned, he saw a face—a female speaking to him. Jason pushed through the void before him, just as he thought he recognized her.

"*They're coming*," she said.

Vibrations rattled the couch, and Jason stumbled out of his seat. He hit the floor with a dead weight and groaned. Streaks of orange sunset painted his skin as he squinted through his slumber. Had he slept all day? The floor underneath him rumbled again, jarring him awake.

Matthew leaped out of the kitchen. "What in the world was that?"

Lynn flew into the backdoor and asked a similar question. Of course their neighbor would be the first to notice it after the two of them did.

"Are you both okay?" she asked. "Did something blow up?"

"It's coming from downstairs," Jason said. "I can feel it."

The three of them made their way to the basement door with Jason out in front. He had already forgotten that face in the dream, but perhaps it didn't matter. Maybe this is what she was trying to warn him of. He flicked on the light switch and sidled with slow steps down the stairs with Matthew right behind him telling Lynn to stay out.

The walls rattled, as did the wooden basement steps under his feet. The lower layer of the house was barely seven feet tall and allowed just enough room to fit the Mirror Gate in when they moved it down there, but little else could squeeze in the limited space aside from boxes. Now, as he descended the stairs, the makeshift silver frame around the wall-length mirror shone bright gold before tinting white. The rumbling ceased soon after he reached the bottom of the stairs.

Matthew stood at his side, his left hand shielding his eyes from the light. "Who turned it on?"

The light then cut out. The Mirror Gate no longer looked like anything but a normal mirror again. Both Jason and Matthew breathed a sigh of relief.

"What is that?" Lynn asked from the top of the stairs. "I thought you said it was just a mirror."

Before Jason could say anything, the light pitched out in one overpowering beam, bathing the basement in brightness. The figure of a teenage girl stepped through the gate and landed on her knees on the basement floor before them. She wore a simple green dress and had her white hair done up in a bun. Her matching bright pale skin would have scared anyone if they didn't know what those who lived on the planet Tyndarus looked like.

Zelana scanned the two males and smiled at them. The gate behind her darkened, and she bowed to the pair.

"Jason!" she said. "Matthew! It is good to see you again."

CHAPTER 2
BURNING TOWN

LYNN STARED AT ZELANA open-mouthed as Jason struggled to find the words to explain all this to their neighbor. How could he sum up the events of the summer in a few minutes? How could he tell her that Zelana was an alien from a whole other planet far out in the distant void of space? How could he tell her he went to that world himself through another mirror just like the one the girl had just entered from? Even thinking about the madness he had gone through was enough to cause him to fall silent.

Jason's tongue might have dried up, but Matthew's didn't. He clapped Jason on the shoulder before climbing back up the stairs towards their neighbor.

"Lynn," Matthew said. "Let's go upstairs. I'll tell you all about it."

"You have a lot of explaining to do."

"Right, I will. It's been a crazy summer. I know I haven't been forthright with you."

"That's an understatement!"

Lynn continued to watch the girl by the Mirror Gate with a wide stare even as Matthew lightly pushed her back up to the first floor. She had no words. Matthew closed the door and left Jason alone with his friend.

"I—d", Jason stuttered. He still didn't know how to process this. "How?"

Zelana stared at him sideways. Her platinum locks flowed over her simple green dress as her hair bun broke loose. He hadn't seen her in person since the two males first escaped from the other world. She looked about the same as she always did, yet something was different about her, but he couldn't quite put a finger on what that was.

"Does that matter?" she asked. Zelana laughed as if she had just figured out a tough question on a test. "I am finally here!"

His mouth went dry. "Welcome to Earth?"

"It's good to see you!" she chirped.

Zelana jumped forward and hugged him. He rubbed the back of his head in confusion. His embarrassment slid away with his questions about her appearance as he squeezed her back. Right now, none of the details mattered as much as the fact that she was still alive and okay. After a moment, they let go, and she grinned up at him.

"I've been practicing with my magic," she said. "It is like training muscle. The more I use it, the more I understand how it is meant to be used."

"How so?"

"My father's magic created these Mirror Gates, and my own magic has roots in his. However, the Kharis Seed implanted in me has changed my magic to be the opposite. His force corrupts and twists, and mine purifies and enhances. Ever since your friend Hammersmith left our world, I have been training to use it without exhausting my energy. I've come a long way in mere weeks!"

"Clearly." He looked her up and down. She stood confidently with her hands on her hips and a laugh he missed more than he realized. Pure tranquility washed over him as the realization she was really here before him sunk in. "There's definitely something different about you."

She laughed and rubbed the back of her head to straighten her hair. "I suppose I am quite tired. My magic is not infinite. But I have finally achieved my main goal."

"That's all well and good, but you scared our landlord's niece quite badly."

"Oh, that is who was with you. She was quite beautiful. Shall you introduce me to her?"

Jason lightly tapped Zelana's forehead with the bottom of his fist. She looked up at him with confusion. He sighed. "Did you forget something, Zelana? You're an alien on a strange planet, and we're trying to hide from your dad's cult. Your skin and clothes alone are going to stand out. Did you not think of that?"

"Oh, please." She rolled her eyes. "Of course I have thought that far ahead. I am not some child."

Zelana lifted both hands, and a stream of yellow light like pools of water dripped from her palms and down her arms and into her body. Her skin glowed bright white just as the mirror did moments earlier.

Where once she had chalk-white skin and platinum hair, Caucasian skin and blonde locks now appeared, making her look like any other human. Any semblance of an Earthwalker from Tyndarus had been erased.

Zelana lifted her chin up in triumph. "Impressive, no?"

Jason blinked, trying to take in what he was seeing. She had changed her entire look in an instant. "You learned a lot. But it doesn't tell me the most important thing: why are you here?"

"Come on," she said, pulling him by the arm. "Introduce me to your lord's niece!"

"*Landlord*," he replied. "Wait a second!"

The two tore up the stairs and out into the hall. Zelana's excitement was palpable, though he still had problems accepting that she was here.

Lynn and Matthew were in the living room, hanging out by the back door and chatting by the tall windows and the orange sunset rays. Lynn's eyes looked ready to pop out of her eyes when she spotted the transformed Zelana. Matthew sighed and ran his palm across his forehead. The girl was not making any of this easier to digest.

Lynn pointed a trembling finger towards her, then looked back at Matthew. "How did she do that to her skin?"

"I told you," Matthew said. "She's from another planet. Where she's from, something like magic exists."

"You expect me to believe that? She has to be some kind of Prime."

"How many Primes can both walk through mirror portals and change the color of their skin? That's not a power set I'm aware of. Look, Lynn, I told you what happened when I applied to that job in Serenity City. They came from that planet in order to harvest people like Jason and I."

"Yes, Matthew, you told me. I can understand super-beings existing, because they do. I've met them. But imagining another planet where a magical alien rules over all is a different thing. Why would they want you, of all people? You're not even a Prime."

"Nonetheless, it happened, Lynn. They want to take over both worlds, and we have artifacts they can use to help do that. That's why we're hiding out here, far away from that mess. This girl was one of the people who helped us escape." Jason turned towards Zelana. "Why she's here *now*, however, is something I want to know."

The teenage girl strode to the center of the room and bowed to Lynn. The shaken woman took a step backwards at her approach. Matthew shook his head and rotated his wrist as if to tell her to hurry up.

Zelana frowned and pouted. "I merely wanted to see my friends again, Matthew. It has been quite lonely in Fortuna ever since Alain left for the capital to join the military."

"He did?" Matthew asked.

"Yes, mere days ago. While I was by myself, I wondered if I could counteract my father's magic and tried to experiment on our stolen Mirror Gate. It has taken me many attempts, but I finally broke through to this side. I have purified the mirror and banished my father's influence from it. Now anyone who wishes can go through without dying."

"You've tested this?" Jason asked, still doubtful. After all, how could she know it was now safe? "Wasn't this your first trip through?"

"It isn't perfect, I admit. I tried to bring a sword through with me, but it melted in the journey. My clothes survived due to imbuing it with enough of my magic, but even they are quite hot. They are a bit singed, too. My hair has also fallen loose. Does anyone have clothes I can wear?"

"Still impulsive as ever, I see," Matthew said. He gestured to Lynn. "Sorry, but can you help?"

"Are you crazy, Matthew? You just want me to trust this strange alien girl?"

"Yeah. I know it's asking a lot. If you can't trust her, then can you trust me?"

Lynn took a deep breath and closed her eyes. Her breathing techniques appeared to be working, as her breaths soon steadied. "You're just as irresponsible as ever, I see. I'll help, but you owe me a better explanation than the lies you've been feeding me. I want the full story."

Matthew nodded and looked to the wall clock. He swore under his breath. "I have to hurry to my second job. Can this wait until later? Jason can give you a better explanation in the meantime."

"I can do that," Jason said. He sounded more confident than he felt. Explaining what had happened since they were given powers was hard to talk about since even he himself hardly believed it was real at times, but Lynn did deserve something for her help. "You can leave it to me."

"Great, thanks." Matthew bolted towards the door and waved to Zelana on his way out. "Good to see you again, Zel."

He disappeared back out into the evening sun, leaving the three of them alone to face each other. Jason looked between the two girls, who were sheepishly scanning each other over. He scratched the back of his head once again. Now it was up to him to take over for Matthew and make sense of all this.

"So," Jason said. He cleared his throat. "This is going to be a long story."

MELLOW HOLMES PUNCHED the alley wall and cut off a curse slipping from the tip of his tongue. The teenager slumped down in the shade under the awning of the old pawn shop, wiping the sweat from his forehead. Old couples and kids already littered the sidewalks outside the alley, heading to whatever evening summer adventure they partook in. The local theater was playing some family movie from decades ago. Mellow didn't care so much about them but that the kid he was chasing got away again.

Burner had trusted Mellow to scope out the town and report strange happenings back to him. No other teenager would ever be lucky enough to get that sort of job, and Mellow had been watching that weird boy on the school roof for weeks now. Today would have been the perfect time to make his approach. If it wasn't for Spencer, that is. That moron jock got in the way again, just as always.

They'd known each other since kindergarten, but Spencer had always gotten under Mellow's skin. So self-righteous! Arrogant attitudes filled their school, but no one was as bad as Spencer. None of them quite understood what was going on outside their door, not like Mellow did. A better world was on the horizon. They would all get there eventually, but he would be the one to lead the charge.

Mellow rolled his eyes at some kids talking about a baseball game and took out the phone from his shorts. There was no sense waiting any longer. He called up Burner.

"*What is it this time, kid?*" the gruff voice mumbled on the other end. "*I thought you were spending the day indoors. It was a scorcher today.*"

"You know that new kid I was watching? He's making some friends around town. And not with reputable characters. I think we should look deeper into this guy and his brother."

"*I looked into them already, Mellow. They're just two brothers who moved into town after their parents died, looking for a place to stay. There are no records to indicate anything else.*"

"Burner!" Mellow growled. He slapped his mouth shut when he realized his tone. "Sorry for that. Listen, that kid not only plays with swords, but I checked out his place this afternoon, and there's this weird blonde-haired girl hanging out now. She wasn't there yesterday."

"*Maybe she's his girlfriend. Who cares? Listen, I've already got a guy following the older brother. If he sees anything funny, then we'll make a move, and not a second sooner. Understand? Drop it. This is no longer your concern. If you keep at it, it'll be you we visit next.*"

Mellow swallowed his fear and agreed. He hung up and leaned back into the alley shade away from the heat. The beams of sunlight reflecting off the grills of passing cars caused him to squint. Summers in Riverview were the worst.

Burner had been watching the town from the shadows for years now. Rumors said he came from Montreal, policing all along the St. Laurence River and robbing crooks and innocents between Quebec and Ontario alike. Nothing could be pinned to him or his men. The police hated him, as did the townsfolk, but Mellow knew better. Burner was a force of nature—he was a true hero. Heroes were needed today more than ever before.

Once Mellow finally got in with his gang this whole lousy town would finally see him for who he truly was. He would finally be seen as the hero they had overlooked. Mellow spun his phone through his fingers and thought a bit on his heroics.

He was destined to be a hero, and Burner's crew would get him there. He might not be a Prime, but that didn't matter—cops and soldiers could be heroes, too. Well, not the ones in *this* town, but probably the ones in the big cities. That was where the real action was.

Finally, an old beat-up black Volkswagen rolled down the street. The yellow-haired older brother sat in the seat, clenching the wheel, a frown on his face. He definitely looked a lot like that other kid. These were brothers, and they sure looked similar to each other.

Mellow called up the guys—they should know about this. Perhaps there was nothing to this investigation. Maybe they really were just two brothers and there was no smoke here. Very well. He could accept that.

But his sense of justice told him differently. These two were off, and he would drag the truth out into the light for all to see.

Because that's what heroes do.

MATTHEW HATED long days like these. After driving around for most of the morning and afternoon, taking townsfolk here and there in his taxi, it was time for his second job. He parked at the delivery center as the sun crested down the St. Laurence River, bathing the world in deep red and the warm breeze blew through the trees, rattling leaves. Even if the long day wasn't quite over for him, at least it felt like it was for a split second.

He pulled into the packing factory lot and stretched. The building was on the outskirts of town, closer to Pembroke than Riverview, with plenty of trees and dirt roads leading to rows of older homes and woods streets away. There were only about twelve other cars in the lot for this shift. Most didn't like working the weekend, never mind in the evening hours, but Matthew was different. He was already used to doing things nobody else wanted to do back in Serenity City.

After the sun departed into the oncoming night, he finally got out of the car and locked up. But this time he paused, scanning the bushes surrounding the fence around the lot. He couldn't see anybody, but he had an inkling he was being watched again. It wasn't his sixth sense —that still hadn't returned since the Albion event—but his head told him to be careful. It didn't make sense. No one should know who he was, never mind that he was in Canada instead of the US.

Matthew took a step over towards the warehouse, and his right leg smoldered with pain. He couldn't avoid cutting off his groan and kneeled down. The sharp feeling seared as if he were being branded. Matthew clutched it tight and bit down on his lip until the agony passed.

This aching had become more common in the last few weeks. The notion that it could be his powers returning was a possibility. But what could he even do about it? He lived a normal life now, and he finally got Jason out of that whole mess, too. It would be better to just ignore this entirely.

"You alright there, partner?"

Matthew looked up and saw Simon Barker staring down at him. He shot back to his feet and tried to play it off. "I thought my laces were untied."

"Oh, I thought you tripped. Never mind me, then. Ready for some fun times?"

"Fun? Is that what you call it?"

"Challenges are fun. Tedium is the ultimate challenge."

Simon Barker was in his late twenties, with a face like a triangle and a thin jaw to match. He wore t-shirts and jeans a lot, which went well with his beach-tanned skin and his well-toned body. He was married to a good-looking woman with a tan just like his, though their recent baby probably didn't have one. Matthew had only seen a few pictures, so he couldn't be sure. His co-worker slapped Matthew on the back.

"You are okay, right, Scott?"

"I'm always okay, Simon," Matthew said. He pretended to stretch his back. "I can work just fine."

"Good to hear, though why are you treating me like I'm your supervisor?"

"Sorry, it's been a long day."

The two slid into the building, where workers already began changing shifts. A dozen workers were both coming in and leaving, chatting away and filling the hallway. Matthew put his sack lunch in his locker and moved out onto the floor where someone turned on the radio to play some oldies. He ignored them and approached the packages on the line both for labeling and for packing the trucks. It would be best to get started ASAP before someone decided to make more small talk.

As his shift began, Matthew did what he always did. He sorted the packages, sending them towards the correct trucks for delivery. Nothing heavy today. They traveled both into Riverview and the surrounding towns, and he was always impressed with the hundreds of parcels he had to deal with every day. It made him appreciate just how connected everyone around here really was. He wasn't so used to that.

After about forty minutes, a presence arrived at his side. Simon began packing beside him, grinning the whole way. Unfortunately, he also decided to talk.

"I can't help but wonder," Simon said. He lifted a heavier package aside with a grunt. "You're still new here. Has anyone approached you yet? Any strange characters?"

"No," Matthew replied. "Unless you count my neighbor. She's a handful. Is this about the block party at the end of the week? Is some old granny going to ask me to bring bean dip?"

Simon smirked. "Hardly. I'm asking because we have some bad seeds hanging around town causing trouble. They like to mess with newcomers. I thought you might have been hurt from running into them. I guess not."

Matthew thought back to his days in Serenity City and his time running from Nieto's cultists and his acolytes from another world. For someone who had prided himself on staying out of trouble, Matthew sure ended up in a lot of it. In comparison, some two-bit thugs from an out-of-the-way town like this wouldn't be anything to worry about.

"I have enough problems back home without worrying about local toughs."

"I'll bet," Simon said. He waved to someone across the floor before returning to the conversation. "Lynn still giving you trouble?"

The rest of the shift went on about the same as it always did. The strange aches he felt before failed to re-materialize, and he was glad for it. Instead, Simon treated him with stories of past block parties that took place in Matthew's neighborhood. Music, local food, book fairs, games, and even theater performances, were all common. Lynn had mentioned something about the subject multiple times, but Matthew hadn't given it a second thought. He had his mind focused on financial stability and safety before any pleasure. The party was at the end of the week, so maybe he would look it over when the celebration came around. Jason could use the distraction, especially with Zelana showing up. Some normality would be nice for them all, for once.

It was pitch dark when it was time to clock out and go home. Crickets chirped, and a random owl hooted somewhere out in the abyss of brush outside the warehouse. Matthew stumbled out into the night with his shoulders burning. He might never get used to that feeling. It wasn't so bad, though.

Once he reached his car, he woke up real quick. Large gashes had been run across the back tires. He perked up and gazed around into the hard black of night. Several of the other workers came running.

"What happened?" Simon asked.

"Someone slashed my tires."

Matthew gazed out into the dark and thought he saw two figures moving through the black of the trees. If he wasn't so exhausted he might have gone after them. Instead, he just cursed and leaned against his car. There were traces of flames alongside the gashes. They were burnt. The culprit was definitely a Prime.

Matthew pounded his roof with a tired fist. So much for normality.

MELLOW SAT in the alley for hours. Night had fallen, and the crowds had all dispersed. Every now and then, a jogger or a dog walker passed, but the streets were otherwise barren. That was the way he liked it.

Burner told him to sit tight and wait until he had more information, and that is what he would do. Even if Mellow's parents told him to stay away from Burner, he just couldn't do it. He'd rather sleep out here in the alley then deal with those morons again. It was summer, anyway. There was nowhere he had to be except where he *wanted* to be.

A flash of white light filled the alley. He squinted as he always did when the brightness overtook his senses and waited for Bernard to finally teleport in beside him. Soon enough, the Prime landed just above a stack of trash cans with his partner beside him. Bernard and Schwartz. The two men brushed the pebbles and loose bits of grime from their dark shirts and jeans.

"Do you always have to land like that?" Mellow asked. "Learn your power. You look ridiculous."

Bernard sneered, his crooked teeth flashing in his chubby face. "That only happens when I have to come to this stupid alley. My power won't let me teleport anywhere if there's no space to do it—it takes me to the nearest empty spot. These trash cans get in the way every time. It would be better if you would answer your phone or just find another place to hang around."

"Naw, I like it here. Besides, my battery's low."

Schwartz shook his head. The less dumpy figure straightened his jeans out. "This dump suits you. I used my knife and fire breath to mark Bartlett's tires. He won't be leaving town anytime soon, and it should send him a message to watch out. Satisfied?"

"Leaving?" Mellow said. "That's his taxi that they sometimes let him keep between shifts. He wasn't going to run away with it."

Schwartz walked past Mellow and stood out in the open street. Not another soul could be seen, but he spent some time looking around anyway. It didn't appear to matter to the Prime as he stretched his hams out in the middle of the sidewalk. "Check your messages. Burner thinks he might know who those two are—and there's a bounty on them down south. Or, there *was.*"

The idea of taking down potential Primes would give Mellow a name, even if he had to coast off Burner to do it. The teenager fumbled for his phone and called up Burner again. Thankfully there was still some battery left. "Hey, what did you find out?"

"*Don't you worry about what I found out.*" Burner's hard voice had lost none of its edge, despite the late hour. "*Stay away from their house tomorrow. That's all I'm going to say.*"

"That kid is going to meet with this jerk named Spencer tomorrow morning, though. He'll probably bring his girlfriend. How about I tail him while you follow the other one?"

"*You're very good at this, Mellow. I think I will let you in on what I've learned, after all.*"

Waves of excitement rushed through Mellow like a tidal wave. His chance had arrived. He pursed his lips as Burner finally spoke to him as an equal. The teenager hardly noticed what his superior was saying at first before calming himself down to listen.

The other two thugs in the alley shouldered past him into the night, eyeing the corner convenience store and movie theater. They threw stones from the sidewalk at store signs, and laughed as they stumbled down the road. Glorified messenger boys were all they were.

But Mellow Holmes was different. He always knew it, and soon would the world. What mattered was that his chance was here, and tomorrow would be his big shot to move up. No longer would he be a zero.

As Burner explained the plan, Mellow couldn't help but feel a rush of glee inside his gut. It was really happening! Tomorrow morning, everything would change. He could hardly wait.

CHAPTER 3
KNOW YOUR ENEMY

IT WAS ANOTHER bad night for Jason. He awoke several times in the dark, including when he overheard Matthew come home from his shift. His friend swore under his breath when he passed Jason's room, but quickly stumbled into his own bed. Jason didn't want to bother him since Matthew was always moving, but it was odd to hear him so angry so late.

As the morning sun shone through his blinds, Jason yawned and rolled out of bed. He glanced around his plain room, freshly painted white before they moved in; with nothing much aside from a dresser they got from a flea market to fill the twelve by eight foot room. It was a good size for him, but he had nothing else aside from the closet, dresser, and bed.

He dug around his room, searching for fresh clothes. He decided on a pair of blue shorts and a pale green shirt for this summer morning.

Before he could fully change, a small crash from out in the hall perked his ears. It sounded like dropped pans. He stepped out into the hall and spied Matthew in the room across from him sprawled across his bed, still in his clothes from yesterday. He was in a deep sleep. Another bang erupted from the kitchen. Someone was in the house.

Jason grabbed the baseball bat behind his door and slid down the hall. Sweat glistened on his forehead as he inched forward. A creak and a crack followed before a bowl hit the floor and shattered. He crossed through the living room towards the kitchen archway.

He leaned around the corner in time to see a female face staring back at him. Jason jumped backward, nearly tripping over the living room carpet.

"Jason!" Zelana said. "I thought you were sleeping."

Jason sighed and dropped the baseball bat on the couch. "I thought you were a thief."

"Do I look that shabby?" She spun around, looking herself over. Zelana was now wearing a light blue skirt and a matching floral blouse. "I thought these clothes looked good on me."

He wiped the sweat from his brow and nodded. "Too good. What are you doing here? I thought you were sleeping at Lynn's place?"

"I did, but I could hardly rest after yesterday. Miss Lynn found me these clothes and shoes in her closet, and I just had to see everything I could. What material are these dishes made of?"

"Glass. Look, I get that you're excited, but you just can't walk into people's houses like this, even if it's our place. That's a good way to get the neighbors to call the cops. What are you doing in the fridge?"

Zelana opened the door and exclaimed when she closed it. "Amazing! The light goes out!"

"This is a bit much so early in the morning." Jason rubbed his eyes. "How about we let Matthew sleep and find something else to do."

"Oh, was he sleeping? I apologize for my thoughtless behavior."

"It's fine." He tried to think of anything he could do to get her out of this place. Normally the boy would take his sword out and get some training done, but the last thing he needed was to draw attention to Zelana. "I met this guy named Spencer yesterday. I think he said he's practicing football this morning. Want to see a new sport? It would sure beat hanging out here."

She clapped her hands together and laughed. "That sounds lovely. Can we see the river?"

"Sure. Now, how about we head out before sourpuss wakes up?"

"Shouldn't you eat breakfast first?"

As if on cue, his stomach growled. He tried not to blush. "I suppose, but let's hurry up."

Jason swept and cleaned the floor with Zelana's help, and the two of them each poured a bowl of cereal. The girl couldn't help but ask all sorts of questions, from what the light in the fridge was to what those metal objects rolling through the streets at high speed were. She kept going, even after they tidied up and left the house. All this before his brain had even woken up.

But he didn't mind. Just her being there was enough to take his thoughts off everything getting under his skin. With her here, he felt oddly at ease. Her safety was one less thing he no longer had to worry about.

Jason guided Zelana through the morning hour of Riverview. He headed back along the water towards the school, walking along sloping banks. Zelana trailed him, glancing at each thing she spotted along the way from house, to stop sign, to paved roads.

"What are these gardens?" Zelana asked. She stared at a large flower with a round head and plentiful orange petals. "You have Field Flowers on Earth?"

"We call them sunflowers here. I was unaware you liked these things."

"Now that I think about it . . . yes, I do. How about yourself?"

He glanced over his shoulder, hoping no one had seen the two of them watching their neighbors' gardens. "No, they're okay, but not my thing. I'll take you to the florist later. I'm sure she'd love to have a curious customer like you."

And yet, as they moved, he couldn't get over the feeling that he was being followed. Had a neighbor gotten curious, or was it someone else? Jason made quick tracks up the street. When Zelana finally caught up, he told her as much.

"Remember," Jason whispered. "My name in this town is Luke Bartlett. Matthew is Scott."

"Oh, I understood. Miss Lynn told me much last night. My father's men might track you here. I hope he never discovers this town because it is quite beautiful." She turned towards the river, her eyes sparkling like the water itself. "This river—what is it called?"

"That's the St. Laurence." He continued forward, and she trailed after as he spoke. "It connects to the Atlantic Ocean and through the province of Quebec. It splits through the country and the eastern provinces a bit. Mat—I mean, *Scott* would know more about it. He grew up in the next town over."

"Delightful!" She smiled at him and then glanced out over the water. It was strange seeing her so excited. "What a fascinating place. You live across the river from a whole other kingdom? And they are not threats to you? I can see why your brother wanted to return to this place so desperately. It is quite breathtaking!"

Jason had to admit that she had a point. He hadn't really paid much attention to Riverview since landing here weeks ago. The weather was nice, the town had enough going on, and the people didn't seem so bad overall. All the better if Nieto's men never found this place.

"We should get to the school before it gets packed out on the water."

The pair hurried back up the hill towards the location he had gone almost every morning since he first moved to Riverview. The two-story school with Gothic arches and pillars and beige and brown coloring loomed over the pair of them. Roger B. McKinney High School had an intimidating feel for a building meant to house six grades of students. It was weird not having a middle school in Ontario, but Jason had seen stranger. If he could get used to life on other planets, he could get used to one high school to house every grade.

A chain-link fence traveled around the length of the school, blocking it off from the surrounding houses and the neighboring field. The parking lot in front of the school had at least a dozen cars and vans parked around the locked entranceway. While this neighborhood usually had little in the way of morning activity, the chatter of adolescents nearby broke the quiet. Jason followed the noise to an open gate in the fence behind the school. It led into the field where a football team was practicing.

There he found at least twenty students in grey gear and practice uniforms running around the field with some parents and family watching from the stands. A group of players tackled dummies, others kicked footballs, and yet more threw the balls to each other in pairs. Judging by the perspiration and panting, they looked to have already been going for quite a while.

"What training is this?" Zelana asked. She stared quizzically as a coach with a bushy beard and chubby gut shouted at one student to hustle up. "His fierceness is not to Alain's level."

Jason chuckled, despite himself. "I would hope not. The bleachers have some spots free. We can watch from there."

The stands were laid out in rows of four on each side of the football field. A smattering of parents and siblings or friends sat in smatterings around the seats. Jason chose the one closest to him, on the bottom bench.

"What is the aim of this game?" Zelana asked. "The name is straightforward enough. Does it involve kicking?"

"A little. One team kicks to the receiving team to begin the game. Then they run plays to get through the opposition and score a touchdown on the other's end zone. There's more throwing and catching than there is kicking." He scratched his ear as a thought came to him. "Though I guess there are field goals."

She stared blankly at the field for a moment before turning to him. "I'm not sure I understand, but that was a satisfactory description. You sound as if you know the game."

"I watched games with my dad. It's pretty easy to get after you see a few plays."

They fell silent as the practice went on. Spencer was among the group, a left tackle that kept his quarterback in one piece. No matter how many plays they practiced, only one receiver could get around him. Jason couldn't help but whistle to himself at the teenager's performance. He was good, and the team's plays reflected his thoughts in how they relied on his blocking. Others in the stands even cheered a few times, including two other teenagers in the neighboring bleachers.

Finally, Zelana spoke again. "Are you close with him?"

"I just met Spencer yesterday. He looks like a decent guy."

"I meant your father."

"Oh." He winced. Jason tried not to think about his parents. It hurt a bit less to imagine they were still out there somewhere, maybe on vacation. "Yes, we were."

She kept her attention on the game as she spoke. "What was that like, being close?"

"Just father and son stuff, I guess. You know."

"Ah." She smiled slightly and fell silent again.

Embarrassment hit him like a truck, and his cheeks reddened. Jason had forgotten about Zelana's volatile relationship with her parents. She had been imprisoned in that tree for countless years, her magic harvested for Nieto. Here he was acting like she knew anything about what he was saying. He had a tendency to forget how good he actually had it.

"My dad taught me how to throw a punch," Jason said. "He told me how to clean up after myself, and how to build a tree-house and ride a bike. He loved watching sports, and going on dates with my mom. He was going to teach me how to fish this summer. Those plans changed. I miss him."

Zelana still didn't say anything, only nodded along in response. A receiver fumbled the ball, and one father in the stands groaned. The mood shifted a bit for a reason Jason couldn't comprehend, and it made him think of his dad's reaction to the last Superbowl where a similar mistake occurred. It allowed him to laugh. Zelana soon joined him.

"Feel better?" she asked. "You have been awfully stiff since I arrived on Earth. Are you worried about your abilities returning?"

"I can't be Pollux without it."

"You still are Pollux, Jason. Just as I have the Kharis Seed's power, you have Pollux. The relic's power will not leave you for another until you die."

"Then where is it? I haven't felt it since the fight in Albion."

"Perhaps it's waiting for the right moment. I do not know. These artifacts have ways of their own. Did that player just kick that ball through those two posts? Is that allowed?"

He grinned. "That would be a field goal. That's three points instead of the usual six."

"Ah, okay," she said with another nod. Zelana continued to stare blankly at the game before her. "I am very lost."

A teenager sat down on the bench behind him. This boy wore a black shirt and skinny jeans. Greasy long hair and bangs fell over his eyes. He gave a half-smile that made the hair on Jason's neck stand up.

"Hey," the newcomer said. "Name's Mellow Holmes. Some people call me Mel. I've been seeing you around town. Don't think I've seen her, though."

"We're new." Jason pushed the knot in his stomach down. "I'm Luke. This is . . . Jennifer."

Zelana glanced at Jason but quickly focused on the game. She didn't acknowledge the boy behind her.

"Is she your sister or cousin?" Mellow asked.

"No," Jason replied, and instantly regretted it. The fewer questions this guy asked would be better. "She's my neighbor's cousin from out of town. She's staying here for a few days."

Mellow put out his pale white hand, and Jason shook it. The oddly cold and sweaty grip unsettled him further. Zelana also took his hand and slipped an awkward smile out. Mellow grinned and offered a clearly fake good-natured laugh.

"How about you, Luke?" he asked. "What are you doing in Riverview?"

"My brother wanted to move away from the bustle of the city. I can't blame him; it was hard to be there."

"I can imagine." There was a pause before Mellow fell silent. The practice went on. It appeared he had finally given up asking questions until he suddenly spoke randomly. "Did you ever hear about Murphy and Janine White?"

A cold ripple ran across Jason's spine. Why was this guy mentioning Matthew's real last name? Jason swallowed his unsteady feeling and flatly responded. "Are they townspeople? I've never lived here before; why would I know them?"

"They died about ten years back, I think. Their son and his wife moved down to the States to live in Serenity City. That was a long time ago. They got caught up when that Achilles guy went mad and leveled a chunk of the city. After that, they would visit their parents up here every now and then, but they were never the same again. All the liveliness was gone. They died before old Murphy and Janine did, though. Cancer."

"That isn't uncommon ever since Primes showed up." Jason sighed. This guy was talking about Matthew's family. Jason tried to keep cool. "Sad story."

"I just thought the two of you reminded me of the old couple's kids. My parents used to talk about them all the time and about how the poor folks rarely got to see their grand-kid. They're buried in the graveyard down on Gerard Street. It's just a block west from here —you can find a shortcut through the back gate over there. No one visits them. It's such a shame."

"Why are you telling me this?"

"Because I've seen your brother out there before." Mellow winked at Jason. "I think he relates to these poor geezers. Maybe he's over there right now. Either way, I'll let you be. Sorry for interrupting your date."

Mellow laughed to himself and leaped off the side of the bleachers. He shuffled stiffly away towards the front gate by the high school. No one on the field paid him any mind as he vanished out into the parking lot. Jason couldn't help but watch him go, hoping he would never see the shifty teenager again.

"What's a date?" Zelana asked.

"That's not important." Jason finally looked away from the gate. "We need to check out that graveyard."

"That boy is not to be trusted. I could hardly contain myself as he spoke so knowledgeably about that which he knew nothing. He has never met Matthew: that much is certain."

"I don't know anything about that Mellow character, but I don't think he was entirely lying. He's paranoid and full of himself, and that's why he was testing me. I knew kids like that. They're the type that volunteers to be a hallway monitor just so they can get a rush out of punishing kids." Jason let out a relieved breath. This was the guy following him? It could have been far worse. "I want to know if that guy did anything to the graveyard. He looks like the type to hang out in places like that."

"We might miss the rest of this game."

"It's just practice; they don't usually have games this early in the day."

Jason didn't want to trust Mellow Holmes, but he didn't want to imagine what would happen if Matthew's grandparents really were buried there and this jerk did something to their graves. The dead should have the chance to rest after going through so much in this life. There were few things that got under Jason's skin more than disrespect for those no longer here among the living. Mellow was clearly too full of himself to have respect for anything other than his own ego.

Spencer waved to him as the two went out the field's back exit behind the players. Jason nodded back to him. They didn't have much of a chance to talk, but at least the teenager seemed like a decent guy. Contrasting him with Mellow was as different as the sun and the moon. The team continued their practice even as Jason and Zelana walked out into the street.

Yet still, even while they moved in the quiet morning light, something seemed off. That feeling only strengthened as the pair crossed the empty streets and stepped through the cemetery gates. Jason might not have Matthew's sixth sense, but a rough prickling jabbed at the back of his neck anyway.

Someone was following them.

"Stick close to me, Zel."

Zelana held her hands behind her back as she walked beside him. The clouds appeared to be distracting her. She didn't look over at his words. "Is it my father's men? Did they find us?"

"I think we walked into Mellow's trap. Whatever that may be."

"Should we flee?"

"I don't even know where they are. For now, let's look for the grave, then go. If they don't think we're aware of their presence, they might underestimate us."

Thankfully, this graveyard wasn't difficult to explore. The road sloped up to the field of gravestones. It was empty aside from the sea of dead and random trees dotting the old place. This Catholic cemetery had names going back to the nineteenth century, which spanned the length of the block length graveyard. He walked the small paths between clusters of buried families, scanning each moniker as he went.

And yet the longer he checked the names on the graves, the more he came to the conclusion that he was lied to.

There was no one in the graveyard with the names Mellow Holmes gave him. This was a trap.

Zelana tapped Jason on the shoulder, and pointed back towards the steel gate they entered from. It had been shut when they weren't paying attention. Thankfully, he didn't see anyone else in the graveyard with them, but a sharp feeling nipped at the back of his neck regardless.

A pair of voices in the wind told him that someone was coming.

FINALLY, the knocking on the door ceased and allowed Matthew to go back to sleep. His headache dulled and allowed him to slip back into his deep slumber.

He had some words with his boss and the cops last night before he even got home. They let him go, and his boss even got him the day off, but it did little to settle Matthew's nerves. Someone was targeting him. Jason should probably know what happened, but he would surely still be sleeping. That was all he did these days when he wasn't training. It could wait a few hours. Right now Matthew could barely even think.

A creaking floorboard caused his eyes to involuntarily snap open. White beams of light pierced through his blinds to reignite Matthew's headache as he turned over. Jason must have gotten up. It wasn't like him to sneak around, but it didn't matter. The noise was nothing.

Matthew buried his face back in the pillow and tried to return to the world of sleep. Despite his aching skull, a dull hammering broke through even that. It told him to get up. Even if he didn't want to, he needed to awaken. Was that his sixth sense?

"*Oh, come on,*" he whispered into his pillow.

Matthew moaned and rubbed his forehead and the bridge of his nose. No rest today.

He slunk out of bed and realized he still wore his clothes from last night. He didn't even get a chance to change after coming home before falling asleep here. When did he become so off-kilter? Nevertheless, he stretched and shook himself awake. By the door he heard another floorboard creak.

Before he could say anything, a voice whispered to another out in the hallway.

"*You sure this is the place?*" a surly man said. "*Which room is he in?*"

A second voice shushed him, this one higher-pitched "*Quiet! He has to be here. Burner said so.*"

Matthew found the aluminum baseball bat leaning against his garbage can by the door. What was it dong there? Had someone moved it here? What was going on in this house?

He froze up. Where was Jason? Did these burglars do something to him?

Matthew scooped up the weapon, and slowly peeked through the crack in his door. The two voices went silent, but creaking told him they were nearby.

Holding his breath, Matthew moved out into the hall, the bat tight in his hands. Sweat rolled down his neck as he kept his breathing steady. For the first time in ages, he really wished he still had his powers.

CHAPTER 4
WELCOME TO RIVERVIEW

ZELANA LOOKED at Jason as if he had turned into an elephant. He couldn't blame her for that reaction. They were in a graveyard, and yet they couldn't find the graves they were seeking, after all. Before he could apologize for wasting her time, she pointed behind him. Jason twisted in time to see a fist swing for his face.

Jason jumped backwards, and tripped. He rolled to the ground. The paved walkway burned with the heat of the sun. His palms ached as he pushed back up to face his opponent. However, no one was behind him.

A white light caught the corner of his eye. He turned to see another fist blitzing for his chin. Jason put up his left arm and prevented the fist from cracking his jaw. His arm sang with the hit.

Jason spaced himself back a few paces and finally spotted his attacker. A wiry man in black pants and a matching pair of heavy boots with a grey bowling shirt stood across from him. The attacker ran a palm across his crew-cut. The tiny scars around his sharp cheeks moved up when he smirked at Jason. This psycho was clearly a Prime.

"What are you doing?" Jason asked.

"It's always better when they fight back," he replied. "I've got a message for you."

"Then use your lips instead of your fists."

"Don't talk so high and mighty, as if you have the high ground. You've been so busy with me you didn't even notice your girlfriend over there."

Fear washed over Jason. He glanced over his shoulder and saw that Zelana was no longer standing there. Another man, this time a larger figure in a sleeveless shirt and jeans, had the girl pinned down to the pavement with her right arm behind her back. Jason clenched his jaw. He was so busy with the Prime in front of him that he didn't think there could be another one.

"Jason!" Zelana squeaked out. Her face was pressed against the hot pavement, yet nothing held her head there. This man was another Prime. She winced. "I cannot move."

Jason growled. "Get off of her!"

The teleporter gave the fallen girl a thumbs up. "Thank you for confirming the name, girl. Jason McCrae, officially killed in the Williams' Tech Corps building disaster earlier this summer. It looks like Burner's hunch was right. We really should give our informant a cut of the bounty."

"Easy, Bernard," the man holding Zelana said. "Don't want to give away the game just yet. Just state our case before someone notices the closed gate."

"Don't boss me around, Cartwright. I'm having too much fun here."

"Hey!" Jason shouted. "Who exactly are you guys? What do you want?"

Bernard cocked his eyebrows. "*Want?* Want doesn't have anything to do with it. You're in our town, and now you have to pay the toll. Luckily for you, there's someone else willing to cover it for you. Now, get down on your knees where you belong."

Despite the fact Bernard was some sort of teleporter, it appeared he had limits. Nothing stopped him from leaping over and forcing Jason to go wherever he chose—unless his power didn't work that way. It was a small advantage, but one the boy would need. Without Pollux or his sword he didn't have much else to fight with.

Zelana struggled against whatever invisible force held her down, wincing the entire time. Fury flooded through Jason's insides. A rush of anger tightened his guts and sharpened his thoughts. He would be the one to put them both down.

MATTHEW INCHED down the hallway of his duplex. A voice whispered ahead of him in the kitchen—a male voice, and it wasn't Jason's. The deep tone betrayed the intruder as being older. It really was a burglar.

Hairs on the back of Matthew's neck stood up. His sixth sense was warning him but it was too muted to be of any use. Before he knew it the sensation had already vanished. He bit his lip to avoid cursing. The one time he would have loved to have his powers back, and it disappears on him again.

The voice in the kitchen called again. "Where are you, Boon?"

"*Here,*" someone said from behind Matthew.

Matthew twisted at the voice. A fist punched his mouth.

Sharp pain rang through Matthew's skull and sent him reeling forward. He spun around and swung the bat in a single motion. It blitzed towards the face of the man standing behind him. The weapon struck the air, an unseen force holding it still. With an invisible jerk, the bat was thrown down the hall, slamming against a chair in the living room. Matthew blinked and rubbed his sore cheek.

The attacker was about as tall as he was, standing over six feet and wearing a polo shirt and slacks. If it wasn't for the gashes across his neck, he might be mistaken for just another neighbor. But his cold, grey eyes showed a hardened man used to much worse scuffles than the one he was currently engaged in.

"You must be Matthew White," Boon said. The bat drifted around the attacker's head like a satellite. "Or are you going by Scott Bartlett now?"

"Get out of my house before I throw you out."

"Your threats are as empty as your apartment in Serenity City. Tell me: why did you leave?"

Matthew sneered. "You've got the wrong guy."

"Burner will be the judge of that. Make it easier on yourself and put up both hands. We're going on a little trip." Boon turned his attention beyond Matthew. "Hey, Page. Help me over here."

At the end of the hall, the other man showed his ugly face from the kitchen. He was a shorter guy, around average height, who would never stand out in a crowd. He wouldn't stand out, that is, if his nose wasn't crooked and his hair badly combed. As it is, he looked like an escaped circus freak in his jeans and button shirt. Page sighed when he saw Matthew.

"Is he going to fight back?" Page asked. "It's too early for fighting. I still wanted to get my Eggs Benedict at the diner. It's not like they allow me into Canada Drive-In these days, you know?"

"I heard about you," Matthew said. "You're that group that goes around harassing out-of-towners. I might not have anything worth stealing, but I will send you out of here with bruises instead. Consider it a free gift."

Page shook his head and blocked the edge of the hallway by spreading both arms across its length. Trickles of red light flickered from his half-open mouth, and fire pooled on his tongue.

"Give it up, White," he said. "You can't run anymore, so you might as well come quietly."

"I don't even know who you are."

"Stop playing dumb."

Matthew considered his options, as limited as they were. The thin hall allowed little movement, only being barely wide enough to fit two of him, and with one attacker on each end, it didn't allow him room to escape. He would have to push through both Primes on his own.

Boon nodded and the floating bat flew towards Matthew's head. He pivoted, but still the aluminum object struck him dead on the right shoulder. It spun upwards in the air, and he caught the weapon with his left hand. His shoulder surged with pain as he did so.

A flash of orange erupted out of the corner of his eye. Matthew crouched, and fire burst over his head like a flamethrower, crisping the edges of his hair. He hit the floor in time to see the geyser of red shoot past him towards Boon. The thug ducked back a few steps as the flames trickled to a dead stop before the burglar.

"Get the point?" Boon said. He grimaced at his partner before looking back at the fallen opponent. "That was a warning shot on both our ends. He could burn you to ashes, and I could cave your skull in with a gesture. Come with us, and everything's copacetic."

Behind Matthew, Page licked his lips and an orange blaze leapt off of his tongue like spittle. Page watched the fallen victim climb back to his feet with an impatient roll of the eyes. "Hurry up, White. We don't have all day. Your little friend is already with us, so just make it easy."

Matthew's knuckles tightened around his bat. It wouldn't be enough for these two. He sighed to himself. There was only one way out of this.

"Oh ho," Boon said. "Are you planning to rush me? Dumb move."

Without his powers, he had little choice. Matthew bolted forward, his bat lifted. Even as he moved, the heat pressed against him —flames growing on his back. He had nowhere left to dodge, but he couldn't worry about it. There was no way forward except through these punks.

Still, the warmth on his back inched closer. Within seconds, the flames would burn him alive.

BERNARD TELEPORTED to his left and threw out a punch. Jason instantly raised an arm in defense. The blow deflected, Bernard spun like a top, his leg sweeping outward towards his opponent. The back of his foot struck Jason's temple, and sent the teenager reeling towards the hot pavement below. He held his sore head, and flipped sideways to his feet. However, Bernard had already vanished.

Behind him, the husky voice of Cartwright spoke. "I'm not sure what we're going to do with you, McCrae. Even though you're officially dead, there's no telling what you're worth."

"That's not my name," Jason said. Whether Luke Bartlett or Jason Vermilion, he was no longer that kid from Serenity City. He could never be that person again. Jason scanned the graves for any sign of Bernard, but found no one. "You've made a big mistake."

"Burner doesn't make mistakes," Cartwright said. "We're going to take you in, as well as your *brother*, if that's what you wanna call him. The only question is what to do with the chick." He tapped the back of Zelana's head with his knuckle. Grabbing her hair, he pulled her neck back. She refused to speak despite the grimace of pain across her dirtied face. "She's not bad. Maybe we can get a few bucks from her parents. What's her name?"

White heat split through the headache forming in Jason's mind. His desire to break every bone in Cartwright's body was only surpassed by his hatred for Pollux's absence. The sweat poured down his brow with his tightening muscles. That familiar stone feeling hardened in his gut, and he knew the time for fooling around was over.

Bernard was a coward, but he was swift. He knew how to strike, and how to move into Jason's blindside to do it again. The thug controlled the flow of this brawl. The only way to change it was to force Bernard into facing Jason on his terms. The boy watched Cartwright holding Zelana down, and knew how he would force Bernard to come to him. Jason would make him defend his ally.

Jason dashed towards Cartwright. He kept his head low, but his eyes on either side of him. Yet, as the boy moved, he felt his body become somewhat lighter. Had Pollux returned to him?

Bernard popped into existence to his right. The thug punched downward at Jason's skull. Unfortunately for the teleporter, his wild strike whiffed into the air, and left him swinging off balance. Jason pivoted so fast from the attack he nearly fell over himself. The teenager grabbed the collar of his opponent and slammed a hard fist into his chest. Bernard gagged, spittle flowing free from his lips, but did not teleport away. Jason struck again and again, but still the enemy didn't attempt any form of resistance from the assault.

It dawned on Jason that Bernard's power did not work on anything but himself, and possibly those who wished it to work on them. This villain needed to knock both Jason and Zelana out for it to work, and with Cartwright holding them down it would be made much easier. Jason growled as the connections clicked in his brain like a circuit. These probably weren't Nieto's men—they were too sloppy—but they were scum nonetheless.

Cartwright swore and lifted from his knee, but Jason saw him coming. The teenager spun and flung Bernard into his ally, and the two tumbled backwards to the pavement behind Zelana. She was still groaning as the two struggled to get up.

The pair stood to face Jason as he approached them. He wouldn't give them a chance at a reprisal. Fortunately for him, he didn't have to.

"I can't move," Bernard said. He tried to move his legs but remained standing in place.

Both Cartwright and Bernard froze as if caught in mud. A hard white glow flowed over their bodies like an outline. They watched their skin with dawning realization that something was wrong, though it wasn't until Zelana spoke that they understood the source of their confusion.

"Precisely," she said. The girl still laid flat on her stomach, each hand gripping a leg of her enemies. Her fingers pulsated in a heavy white light as she held on tight. "Now choke on your own powers."

Before the two attackers could do anything, they lifted off the ground as if Cartwright's power had been used backwards, and then the pair blinked from existence. They did not return to the graveyard again. Just like that, the battle had concluded.

Zelana panted hard and coughed, clutching her chest. Jason made a beeline towards her. He flipped her over onto her back and checked her over. Despite the girl's fatigued state, she had no wounds aside from a bruise on the back of her head where Cartwright had struck her earlier. Soon enough, she gathered enough of her breath to wave him off.

"Thank you, Jason," she said. "But I'm fine. I simply used magic I shouldn't have."

He let out a sigh of relief and slumped down to a sitting position beside her on the pavement. She sat on her knees, brushing pebbles from her bare arms and legs. Eventually, her breaths steadied once more. Despite her safety, he still had one question on the tip of his tongue.

"What did you do to them?" he asked.

Zelana winced as she straightened her hair. That bruise must have stung. "I reversed one power and forcibly activated another. I don't quite know where I sent them, but I saw a picture in one of their minds and used that for bearing. There was a body of water, perhaps the river. They should not be returning quickly. That's just as well since I cannot stand."

A tiny trickle of blood pooled under her nose. Jason fished for a pocket tissue and handed it to her. She held it under her nose and closed her eyes as if in concentration.

"Your power is in purification and enhancement," Jason said. "Maybe you shouldn't use it for things like fighting. It doesn't agree with you."

"The seed has changed my constitution, yes. But I could not sit by while they hurt someone I care about, just as you wouldn't."

He stared at her before nodding. "Fair enough."

"Your strength is returning. I saw how you hit that Bernard brigand." She beamed up at him. "It was magnificent when he grunted."

He couldn't help but laugh. "Thanks, Zel."

Jason shouldered her up, and the two moved back towards the gate. She limped a few steps, but slowly her legs straightened out. He didn't mind so much, she was rather soft and light, not to mention that he did owe her. However, her strange silence at his side did throw him off a bit.

Those two attackers hadn't come for *her*, though. They didn't recognize Zelana, yet they did know *his* old name. But Jason McCrae was dead, so why were they still looking for him? If this wasn't about Nieto, then who was it that sent these guys?

His eyes widened when it dawned on him. What about Matthew?

Jason found himself moving faster, weaving through graves. Zelana quickened her pace as if she realized it, too.

Matthew was in trouble.

THE FLAMES PRESSED against Matthew's back, and still, Boon awaited his approach ahead of him. Matthew spun around and threw his aluminum bat through the wall of fire, sending it spinning into the blaze. His weapon cracked against something solid on the other end of the orange wave, and someone yelled. Despite that cry, Matthew continued his charge forward into Boon, his shoulder digging into the villain's chest and sending them both sprawling down to the floor.

The pair rolled into the wall, their limbs flailing. Matthew's head struck the basement door, and speckles of red pain sprinkled over his vision. Rough fingers slid over his throat and squeezed.

"Now I know you're who we're looking for," Boon said. "Forget about taking you anywhere, I think I'm just going to put you in traction instead."

Down the hall, Page groaned, but Matthew could focus on nothing but the man digging his skull into the basement door and choking him. He gasped for air, but still, the pressure on his mind strengthened. No matter how he thrashed, the hold couldn't be broken. Black midnight encroached on his thoughts.

"*Castor,*" he whispered. Heat burned somewhere down in his gut. "*Castor . . .*"

Why did he say that? Castor was gone, and never coming back. Matthew was a normal man again. No, that was what he had hoped. Matthew could put this whole thing behind him and finally set up a life for him away from the chaos of this Prime-filled world. Escape from this madness was an impossibility, and he had to finally accept it. He wasn't just Matthew White anymore, but Castor—one half of the Gemini Man.

But the power wouldn't come to him. He bit his lip and felt at the fringes of his very being, searching for a scrap of intangibility to escape this hold. Embers of fear tickled the hairs on his arms. However, try as he might, Castor never arrived.

"Stop talking to yourself," Boon said. "You're going to be doing enough chatting when we get you to Burner."

Pounding at the front door caused both of the grapplers to look up from the floor. Someone was knocking.

"Are you okay in there, Matthew?" Lynn asked. "Did something happen?"

Boon sneered. "Who's that bitch?"

Matthew used the moment to kick forward. His attack struck Boon's chest and sent him rolling across the floor. He banged into the opposite wall.

"Call the cops!" Matthew shouted. "I've got two burglars in here."

"Damn," Boon muttered. He rubbed his chest and tore off towards the back door. "Get up, Page. We're going!"

Matthew stumbled up again to see his two attackers flee out the back door and into his yard. The pair leaped over the fence and disappeared into the morning light of the neighborhood. He rubbed his sore throat and the pressure relieved itself.

At that point, it dawned on him. Where was Jason?

He jumped up and ran into Jason's room but found no one. The kid was out. Matthew punched the wall and shuffled back out into the hall.

Lynn threw open the front door and held her phone up high. "The police are on their way! Are you okay, Matthew?"

"I'm fine," he said. Matthew met her at the threshold. "But you told them my name. Now they know I'm who they're looking for."

She blushed and ran a palm across her face. "Sorry. The cops will be here soon enough. I'm not going to tell *them* your names."

"That doesn't matter. What does matter is that Jason is out there, and they're after him, too."

"*Who* is after you, Matthew?"

He felt the back of his head, which was still warm from the earlier burst of fire. His skull and throat ached. He would definitely need Castor to deal with this group, or else he was done.

"I don't know who it is, but they're going to get what they want. It's war now."

THE WARM WIND licked his face like the best summer memories of his youth, but still Burner stood on the docks, staring out into the morning sun. His slacks and white golf shirt were as uncomfortable as ever, but this was who he needed to be now. No longer was he that idealistic kid who was going to change the world —now he was a nomad king, living out the rest of his years in silence. Sure, he was still relatively young in his late thirties, but he already felt like he was ancient. As long as he could have everything the way he needed to be, he would be happy.

Burner wasn't happy. He hadn't been for a long time. But at least when he stood by the St. Laurence he could still smell the water and imagine all the places it connected and flowed through, just like he did. They were one and the same, destined to roll on forever without a moment's peace, because that's what they were made to do. Burner had it figured out. He even kept a hunting knife under his bed, but that was just for paranoia's sake. Deep down he knew no one would ever come for him. He wasn't that lucky.

His fingers ran along the ring on his right hand, caressing the green stone. He hated the thing, constantly reminding him of past failures, but that is why he kept it. The guys always asked if they could have it since he disliked it so much, but Burner could never part with the trinket. He would only get rid of it if he retired and let someone else worry about the business. In other words, he would rather die with it around his finger. This weight was his, no one else's.

He hadn't heard from the four idiots since last night. Not one of his guys called to reconfirm the plan before this morning. They had gotten sloppy over the years, though it wasn't as if he could fully blame them. The group was small, at only two dozen spread across four towns, yet it had gotten away with so much for so long. Sooner or later, they'd hit the wall, but it wouldn't be now. He wouldn't let these clowns ruin a good thing.

A sound like air gushing from a tire brought him back to attention. He searched around the dock for the mysterious disturbance but found nothing. That is until he looked up.

Two bodies appeared twenty feet above the water, flashing white. They tumbled out of thin air and splashed down into the river like stones. They quickly floated to the surface, gasping for air.

He swore to himself as he recognized the forms of Bernard and Cartwright thrashing about and spitting out water.

"Lost, boys?" he asked them. "I don't see the kid with you."

The two coughed as they approached the dock, kicking the whole way. They climbed aboard before they finally had the spare breaths.

"There was a teenage girl with him," Cartwright said. He spat water out before he continued. "She used our powers against us."

"Girl? I don't recall anything about a girl from the report. It's just supposed to be two fugitives."

Bernard shook his head and rubbed his bruises. "The kid can pack a punch, but I didn't notice any kind of super-strength. I think your reporting is off. That girl is far more dangerous."

"Ridiculous." Burner fished for his phone from his pocket and called up Dobbs. His tips on bounties have never steered him wrong before. "I'm going to settle this right now."

"Do what you want, Burner," Cartwright barked. He threw off his shoes and lay flat on the docks, breathing hard as water soaked the wood around him. "I'm telling you, something's not right."

The phone rang far too many times for Dobbs. He usually picked up on the second ring, eager to talk business. This time, it took a full minute before someone picked up.

"*Yes,*" the voice on the other end said. It wasn't a question.

"Finally," Burner said. "Tell me about the Williams' Tech fugitives, Dobbs. You said they had powers, but you didn't mention any Prime girl. You aren't feeding me the whole story."

"*Don't say it's true,*" the voice said. "*Are you telling me the Master's daughter is there with them? That complicates things, though not by much.*"

Burner could not be certain at first, but a realization hit him as the speaker went on in his flat tone. That was not Dobbs. He kept his tone steady and professional as he replied to the foreign voice.

"Where's Dobbs?"

"*He's around. Listen up, friend, I have a few errands to run, but I'll be up there by tonight. If you want some help catching those little fish, then you're getting a primo net."*

"Who is this?"

"It's bright and sunny today, isn't it? Must be so nice up there. That'll change."

The phone clicked, and the call ended. Burner threw his phone down by his foot. It took every bit of restraint he had to avoid stepping on it. Who was Dobbs hanging out with now?

Burner looked over the water, his mood ruined. He hadn't spent the last seven years running up and down the St. Laurence River for some low-class thug to come in and push him out. This wart would be burned off, and then they would keep the entire bounty to themselves.

"What's the problem, Burner?" Bernard asked. "Issue with the bounty?"

"Get the guys together. Some pimple from the states is on the way to Riverview. Sounds like he wants a piece of the bounty."

"I want to get that kid back, though."

"That can wait. For now, we got a genuine tough guy coming into town. Let's give him a real good welcome and show him what Riverview is all about."

CHAPTER 5
THE HARBINGER APPROACHES

IT DIDN'T TAKE LONG for Jason to get back home. On his way through the streets, Spencer drove by with his older brother. Zelana told them the local gang had attacked them. Oddly enough, neither Spencer nor his brother appeared shocked to hear the news. Instead, they offered to drive them back home.

The van had to be at least a decade old, a slightly faded dark green color. In the front the older brother sat next to a teenage boy Jason recognized from the practice, and in the backseats were Spencer and his girlfriend. Spencer introduced them as Kevin and Shannon. Jason sat in the rear seats with Zelana, glancing out into the passing streets.

"That sounds like Burner," Spencer said. His brother sighed, but the teenager ignored him. "He's a punk who used to be some hero's sidekick a long time ago, I think. Don't know why, but he went rogue and ran off. He's never been caught since his friends all have powers that help him with actual robbery. They're not killers, just crooks. Who knows how much he swiped to get that boat of his."

"Shut up, Spence," the brother said. "These two don't need to hear about that. Just steer clear of Burner and his goons, and you'll be okay. Now that they've tested you, they should keep their distance."

"If you ask me," Kevin interrupted, "you should have put those guys in the hospital. You're lucky you fought them off without powers. Someone needs to teach those scumbags a lesson."

Jason blandly nodded. He disagreed with the assessment, but he couldn't quite say so. Somehow Burner learned who Jason and Matthew were, and now he was coming for some sort of bounty. But *what* bounty? After the Albion incident, Hammersmith told them they were no longer being looked for. Jason McCrae was legally declared dead. So, who gave them the hint as to who they might be?

Shannon glanced over the seat at them. "Before you left the field, I saw you two with Mellow Holmes."

"Are you serious?" Kevin laughed to no one in particular. "You guys really drew the short straws today!"

"Yes," Zelana said. "He seemed very interested in the graveyard."

"That's because he's a creep," Shannon said. "I've been in a class with him since kindergarten, and I'm telling you he's just not right. He mutters to himself, cusses out anyone who gets close and is generally a jerk. I don't know why he spoke to you, but you should be careful."

Spencer interrupted. "I don't think he's that bad. He just prefers being alone."

"You can say that, Spence," she replied. "But I know him better than you. Every now and then I see him looking at me and I just feel the pure hate coming off of him. He's unbalanced. I wouldn't be surprised if he's partnered up with Burner."

Kevin shook his head. "He's one of those guys that need a solid punch in the face. You know the type? One solid uppercut will set him right."

They soon turned down the street towards the house with three cop cars parked along the curbside. At the front door, Matthew and Lynn stood talking to several officers in uniform and one fatter plainclothes detective. When the van pulled up, Jason wasted no time getting out.

"Cops are here fast today," Spencer said. "How did they know what happened to you?"

Jason waved to him. "Who knows? Thanks for the ride, Spencer."

"Give me a call later. We'll hang out. I think you could use some fun, especially after today."

"Thank you for your assistance," Zelana said. She was about to curtsy when Jason tapped her shoulder. Instead, she waved. "Hopefully, the next we meet will be under better circumstances."

As the van took off, both Matthew and Lynn noticed the pair's arrival and called out to Jason and Zelana. The two dashed across the lawn over towards them.

"Is this your brother, monsieur?" the plainclothes detective asked. He wore a slightly too tight suit with a brown overcoat and trilby draped over his balding rust-colored hair. "I am Detective Leclerc, sir. Two lowlifes appeared to have attacked your brother this morning."

"What a coincidence," Jason said. "We met two of them out by the graveyard."

Matthew blinked. "What do you mean you met two of them?"

"Easy, monsieur," Detective Leclerc said. "I'll take the boy's statement, but I'm going to tell you one thing. Without any evidence, it's going to be next to impossible to prosecute your attackers. Primes with mobility abilities make alibis and timelines difficult to establish. This would be much easier if you filmed any of it."

"I don't have a phone yet," Jason said, the pit in his stomach growing.

"We just moved here, Detective." Matthew's bared teeth betrayed his barely concealed annoyance. "Don't tell me you're fine with hooligans policing your city."

Detective Leclerc paused, his hard brown eyes boring into Matthew's. "I understand if you're upset, monsieur, but it isn't as if I *like* this. This group has been running up and down the river for years now. We haven't gotten the support to bring them down because all they do is pilfer and steal, leaving no evidence behind. Worst is assaults that can't be proven as assaults. They probably thought you had money, and now that they know better they will leave you alone. Mark my words. Still, we will do everything we can to catch these rats."

The detective took Jason aside and asked for his story. As Jason divulged what had happened in the graveyard, he found his hurried tone slowing and eventually flattening out. The realization that the police wouldn't be able to do anything hit him dead on, draining his energy. These lawbreakers would get away with it.

But it wasn't just Burner's men that worried him. If they really were being backed by Nieto, then much worse was on the way than a few petty thieves. Beating them back would only solve the problem temporarily. As the events in Albion showed, these guys would do anything to get what they desired. They would never stop coming.

Even as the detective asked him feeble questions, Jason's stomach tightened. Nieto would be back again, and he knew where they lived. No one was safe—not Matthew and not Zelana. Could innocents like Lynn, Spencer, or Shannon, be spared in this war? He already knew the answer to that one.

These thoughts swirled in his mind as the detective prodded him for info he didn't have. They wouldn't be able to help him. He was alone again.

That was fine—Jason was used to being by himself. He would stop these guys on his own. Riverview's very existence depended on him, and he would not let it down. He would never let anyone down, not ever again.

"Are you okay?" Zelana asked him. She looked the boy over with a crinkled brow. Her worry made him more uncomfortable than he liked. "Do you need to sit?"

"I'll be fine," Jason lied. He hadn't been fine in a long time.

WHEN THEY FINALLY got inside, Matthew could breathe easy. He watched the cop cars slowly pull out of his yard and down the street. Several of the neighbors both across the street and beside his duplex watching from their windows returned to their lives. Matthew could only be glad it was over, though his plans for not sticking out in Riverview had been thwarted.

Jason threw open the basement door and bolted down the stairs. Matthew followed him, as did the two women. The boy flicked on the lights and approached the Mirror Gate, its surface reflecting off the overhead bulb.

"Okay Zelana," Jason said. "Open it up. You're heading back."

She winced and took a step back, visibly shaken by his words. Jason didn't even look at her, his attention on the colorless Mirror Gate. Before she could say anything, Lynn stepped between the two of them.

"Before we discuss any of this," Lynn said. "You need to tell us where you went this morning."

Jason glanced between the two adults. When Matthew didn't say anything, the kid sighed. "The guy I met yesterday invited me to see his team's practice. We went over there, met some creepy kid in the bleachers, and then visited the graveyard. I'm not sure what else you want from me. There's nothing exciting about it."

"Why do you want me to leave, Jason?" Zelana gripped his elbow, and leaned forward. He still didn't meet her eyes. "Do you think I am a burden? That I cannot carry my own weight?"

"They knew who I was," Jason said. "They knew who Matthew was. After your performance, now they're going to know who *you* are. The next time they show up they're going to be ready, and my powers still aren't back yet. How about yours, Matthew?"

Matthew didn't have to reply, so he didn't. Jason wasn't looking for him to agree, either way. The kid was always like this.

As Jason described their trip to the graveyard, Matthew tried to piece all this together. Zelana drifted away from the group towards the Mirror Gate, and Lynn was too absorbed in the story to question the boy, but Matthew remained silent in thought over it.

Whoever this Burner guy was, he had clearly found some sort of bounty for the two of them. The one back in Serenity City was canceled, the two of them declared dead, which meant nobody should still be after them.

Nobody that is, unless Nieto was involved. At this point, Matthew couldn't think of another reason they were being targeted. Neither of the two attackers appeared to know who Nieto was, which meant they probably in the dark. If that were the case, then trouble was on the way.

"Anyway," Jason said. "If they find out who Zelana actually is, she's going to be the prime target. She needs go back through the gate."

Lynn sighed. "That isn't going to help either of *you*, though. They know where you live. They're going to come back. What are you going to do the next time they sneak through your door?"

"We could run again." Jason blanched at his own words. "We might have to."

"No more running," Matthew said. The force of his own tone took him by surprise. "We can't spend our whole lives on the run. We don't have the means to do that, and they'll never stop. Besides, if we leave now, they might go after our neighbors to find out where we went."

"You just don't want to leave." Jason pointed a finger at Matthew. "If we went back into Tyndarus it would be a lot harder for them to find us. No technology, and a whole race specifically opposed to Nieto, gives us the edge. Why don't we just go there? Why do you want to stay on Earth? What has it ever done for you?"

Nothing, of course. Matthew didn't have much in the way of good memories on Earth, and there was no doubt there would be many more bad ones to make. Now, with enemies out to end him he had even less chance to settle down. Perhaps a life where he could be left alone would forever be out of his reach.

He watched Zelana run a palm across the Mirror Gate. The girl went out of her way to come here, just to see them. Despite having no family, and nowhere left to go, she had done nothing but help the two of them. How could he abandon her now? "I could ask the same thing of you, Jason. Do you want to keep allowing Nieto to run roughshod over Zelana's world as well as ours? That's two different planets where he commands psychos and monsters to hurt people like her, or even those like Lynn who have nothing to do with him at all. Even if we run from him forever, nothing will change. He's going to keep doing this."

"So what do you suppose we do, Matthew? Plan a raid on Tyndarus when we can't even find his base? And without our powers? We can't even find him in his own world, so what chance do we have defending ourselves from him here? The only reason I was fine with coming to Earth is because I thought it would be harder for him to find us, but here he once again has the upper hand."

Matthew rolled his eyes and sighed. "Did you forget about how easily he found us when we were actually *on* Tyndarus? We put just as many innocent people at risk, and we still didn't stop him. Face it, Jason. We can't avoid Nieto by running. We're going to need to hit back."

"That's easy for you to say. You're not the innocent people getting caught in the crossfire."

"Wait," Matthew said. He paused as the thought came to him. Jason's tantrum began to make sense: he was scared. "Is the reason you want to go to Tyndarus because you think you could hide there? And you have the gall to insinuate *I'm* a coward for staying on Earth?"

Jason clenched his fists, and was about to reply when a bright white flash filled the basement. The three of them shielded their eyes before the light finally faded. There at the edge of the basement the Mirror Gate pulsated its bright tint. Zelana had activated the gate.

She turned to face them. "I am not certain how long I can keep it open, so I will make haste. Thank you for having me in your home. I appreciate your hospitality more than you will ever know."

"No, wait!" Lynn shouted. "Can everyone please calm down? Zelana, no one wants you to go, okay? Don't overreact. Jason, tell her you don't want her to leave."

But Jason didn't reply. Instead he folded his arms and stared at the floor. He always could be a totally brat when he wanted to be.

Matthew groaned. "It isn't going to change anything at this point. Those thugs were after us, and you look just like another normal girl to anyone who wouldn't know any better. This doesn't have anything to do with you, Zel."

"The hell it doesn't!" Jason roared. "Nieto is after her too, remember? If they find out she's here then they will stop at nothing to get her."

"But they don't know she can travel through the Mirror's Gate, do they? Listen, I agree she shouldn't stay here forever, but to throw her out like this is overreacting. We don't even know anything about where that bounty came from. Your friends even told you these guys hassle newcomers to Riverview. First, let's learn about this guy, and then we can make a decision, okay?"

"Matthew, you're such a—"

Before Jason could finish his thought, a body stumbled through the Mirror Gate. Zelana let out a small squeak as she looked down at the woman who landed at her feet. The strange woman slowly pushed herself up to her elbows and stood up. Ordopha wore a simple beige dress that had blackened and was already beginning to smoke.

Matthew found his tongue was tied as Ordopha glanced around the basement before catching a glimpse of him. She let out a relieved breath when she saw her old friend.

"Matthew! You're alive!"

She shouldn't have been here, but then neither should Zelana. What was it with Tyndarus continuing to intrude on his world? Matthew had separated the two places in his mind, and yet here they were colliding again. Nonetheless, Ordopha stared up at him, her radiant smile flashing through the dirt covering her.

He moved to her side with Zelana and helped her up. They patted down her smoking dress.

"Ord?" he asked. "How did you get through there?"

"I have been attempting to get through since Zelana charged in yesterday. We were worried until we heard voices. The villagers assumed she would come back, but I needed to be more certain. When I heard yelling through the gate moments ago, and the mirror turned white, I thought this would be my chance to get to the other side."

He wanted to ask so many questions, and yet his greater concern lay with her smoking dress. Lynn offered to find her new clothes. But his neighbor still appeared confused.

"Matthew, what the heck happened to you in that other world?"

"Apparently more than I realized."

The lot traveled back upstairs, but not before Zelana made sure the Mirror Gate was no longer activated. Matthew appreciated that—the last thing they needed was even more unexpected visitors.

Lynn had a lot of questions, and it was time he answered them. Whether they ran from Riverview, or stayed and fought, the end result would be the same. The past would never stop coming back to bite him. He needed to strike back.

No more hiding. Matthew White was dead; he was Castor now. The Gemini Man was no coward, and neither would he be any longer.

"MELLOW!" the old man shouted. "Where did you go?"

Mellow Holmes charged through the front door of his house, nearly running into both his father and mother. He wheeled around them out of the mudroom and into the hallway through to the kitchen. Thankfully, the folks had left the air-conditioning on.

The teenager poured himself a bowl of instant oatmeal and heated some water from the kettle. It was a busy morning, and now it was time to relax.

"Mellow?" his father repeated. "It isn't like you to get up so early, especially on the weekends. Did you go for a run?"

"I guess you could say that."

"Very good!" his mother said. "Get yourself cleaned up, and we'll all go to the summer festival together. It's been a long time since we've all gone to Church together."

Both his father and mother were dressed up far too decently for a Saturday morning. His father wore clean slacks and a matching polo shirt, and his mother wore a floral sunflower dress. Mellow was certain the other boring adults at the Church festival would look much like them. He never understood their need to impress others. Didn't they have any sense of originality?

His father smiled. "What do you say, Mel?"

Mellow dug a bowl out of the cabinet and fetched a matching spoon from a drawer. "No, thanks. Don't feel like being around other people."

"Don't be a child," Mr. Holmes said. "You're fifteen now. It's time to stop playing around every day lost in your own sandbox. When are you going to act like an adult?"

"I am an adult." Mellow swallowed the flickers of anger burning in his throat. "Anyways, it's summer. It's not like I've got anywhere else to be."

Mr. Holmes sighed and put both hands on the kitchen counter. "You aren't a Prime, Mel. You have no powers, and you never will. There's nothing wrong with being like the rest of us."

"I've accepted what I am." The rage nearly caused him to gag. Thankfully, the kettle whistled and allowed him a distraction from the conversation. "If everyone else would, then things would be a lot easier."

"Mrs. Ames called me last night," Mrs. Holmes said. "Her son was walking Muffy and saw you sitting around in the alleyways by the theater again. Some suspicious characters were there talking with you. What exactly are you doing after dark, Mellow?"

"Those are just my friends."

"The hell they are." Mr. Holmes took a deep calming breath. "What happened to Joshua, Paul, or Spencer? Didn't you use to hang around with them? You're better than a thug."

"What does it matter?" Mellow could no longer muster the motivation to get upset. Just hearing those names hardened his resolve. "I'm not taking drugs, I'm not drinking, and I'm not hurting anyone. That should be enough for you, for anyone."

His father watched him sit at the table with his bowl of oatmeal before he finally replied. "Why should the bare minimum be enough?"

"Maybe I'll show up later," Mellow said. "Can I just get some breakfast for now?"

"Alright, Mel." Mr. Holmes looked to his wife and then to his son. "Just don't take too long."

"I won't."

Finally, his parents departed for their silly festival and left him in peace. Once the door shut he breathed a sigh of relief. He preferred being alone over hearing them prattle about things he didn't care about.

Mellow tossed his empty bowl and spoon in the dishwasher and called up Burner.

The teenager hadn't heard anything about the plan since he left those two morons at the field that morning. Perhaps that was a good thing. If that kid wasn't actually that Jason McCrae guy and his "brother" wasn't Matthew White then the kid would have seen him as crazy and wouldn't go check out that graveyard. He would just be another ignorant kid like the rest of them, not knowing people like Mellow were around to keep them safe. The plan was foolproof, unless Luke Bartlett was an idiot and checked out a grave that had nothing to do with him. Then he would deserve whatever came to him. Mellow's hands would be clean either way.

No one understood anything in Riverview, which is why Mellow hated this town so much. They all went about their lives oblivious to those that kept them safe and warm. He could only see them as ungrateful brats and outdated elderly people who all thought they could live their mediocre lives ignoring the injustice around them. The cops only went after safe targets, the ones that weren't themselves scum, that is. Primes ruled the cities with an iron fist and steered clear of nowhere bergs like Riverview. Everyone kept to their own little corners and lived in their own worlds. They didn't deserve salvation.

So instead, Mellow would crush them all. They would understand how weak they all were, and how they needed a strong hand to lead them.

He fell onto the couch and threw his feet over the armrest. Queasiness punched his gut, and bile licked at the back of his throat. While he waited for Burner to answer, Mellow could only grit his teeth and wait for the pain to pass. What was he so worried about?

Sure, he didn't have a power, but it wasn't as if he would be any different with them. Some days, however, he thought it wouldn't be so bad if he were a Prime just to get rid of the stress. Surely no one else had to go through the pain he did just to do the right thing constantly? Maybe he just needed to toughen up like Burner said. Justice doesn't dispense itself, after all.

"*There you are, Mellow,*" Burner said. His voice crackled on the other end. "*I was expecting you to call sooner.*"

"I went for a walk after I left the field. The summer wind feels good against my headache. At least it's gone now."

"*You stress too easy. Consider toughening up, boy.*"

"Yeah, yeah," Mellow said. He coughed through his sore throat. "Forget about me. What happened with the two nitwits? Are they who you thought they were?"

"*There's been a small change in plans.*" Burner trailed off as someone else interrupted. The mystery man had a small back and forth with the boss before Burner returned to the phone. "*The source who gave us the information might have been compromised. We're not actually sure if those two are who we were told they were, but they are suspicious. That girl with them is a Prime, for sure. But we have no information on her. However, it seems like our source will be coming by tonight. We should have a clearer picture by then.*"

"Very nice." Mellow couldn't help but grin. So many wheels were in motion. "What time?"

"*Around ten tonight, and at the old warehouse. I'm bringing the crew in case my source is stickier than he sounds. Either way, you did good work today. You should be proud, Holmes.*"

"I know."

Mellow put his phone away and stretched across the couch. The wall clock told him it was near ten. In twelve hours, the meeting would begin, and he would be there with everyone else. Once they bagged these scofflaws, everyone in Riverview would know his name. Then he could move on to bigger and better things. It was all coming together. The pit in his stomach would be filled with five-star meals and beautiful women as far the eye could see. The tickle in the back of his throat caused him to laugh. Summer really was the best season.

The bright white glow of the sun slipped through the giant window in the living room. He winced as he turned over to meet it. Couldn't his parents have at least closed the curtains? Mellow pulled them over the overwhelming sunlight, bringing a pleasant darkness to the home.

"Twelve hours," he said to himself. What to do for twelve hours?

For now, he would take a break. Perhaps some video games? Whatever. He could do anything.

The teenager took a deep breath and pushed the pit in his gut down deep inside of himself. Mellow Holmes had earned his rest.

"WHERE DID JASON GO?" Matthew asked. The kid just couldn't stop being a pain. "We come upstairs, have some breakfast, and he disappears. He better not have gone back out."

Only Zelana sat at the kitchen table with him. Lynn had taken Ord to get a change of clothes next door, and the boy was nowhere to be seen. Matthew wanted to yell at somebody, but instead, he settled on getting annoyed at himself. He still had no clue what to do next.

Zelana spoke up. "Jason departed to his room to sleep. He complained about his bones hurting him."

"You said something about how he knocked back one of those losers who attacked you. His strength might be returning."

"I suppose it is," she said at length. Zelana stared down at the kitchen table as if engrossed in conversation with one of the small gashes in the wood. "He has still not returned to full strength, however."

"Are you still bothered about him telling you to go back to Tyndarus? He was trying to think of your safety. I'm sure he would prefer you stick around."

"Perhaps."

Matthew scratched the back of his head and felt at his newly shaved hair. What else could he say to her? He'd never been good with girls. Zelana still intently watching the table when he suddenly stood up. Matthew paced the kitchen floor, thinking of his next move.

"What were you two doing at the graveyard? I'm sure it wasn't sightseeing."

"It is difficult to explain."

She told him about that strange teenager named Mellow who regaled the pair with a story about two elderly neighbors. Somehow, this punk implied he knew Matthew's grandparents when they were still alive, even though such a thing was impossible.

"He couldn't have known them. My grandparents are buried in Pembroke. That's where they lived most of their lives. That kid was lying."

This Burner bastard even had teenagers working for him. Matthew needed to think of a plan, and think of one fast.

But something else still bothered him. Jason remained as evasive as ever. He shouldn't have taken this Mellow kid so seriously.

"You could have just asked me about my grandparents if you two wanted to know."

"Jason believed this boy might be threatening to vandalize the graves, so he wanted to check as soon as possible. Why he didn't know they weren't buried here in the first place is beyond me."

Matthew tried a different track. "You know what happened to his parents, don't you? You did read his mind back on Tyndarus."

"Most of those memories have faded, but I do remember some. Did he not tell you about it? I don't believe I should be the one to tell you."

"That's up to him. I want to know *why* he won't tell me, not what actually happened." He watched confusion breaking out on the girl's face, and interrupted her questioning stare. "I'm going to be frank. I know Jason better than he thinks. The whole reason he went to the graveyard was because he thought I was hiding something about my past. We both know that."

She nodded, slowly. "He doesn't trust anyone, not really."

"Now isn't that time for this childish crap from him. We've been stuck together all summer, and now we're bound together by a power neither of us can understand. We've even been the Gemini Man. If he wants to ask me a question, he can ask me the stupid question. If I need to know something, he should tell me. I might not remember any of his memories when we were combined, but I know what happened to his parents bother him a lot. Why won't he tell me?"

"I don't know, Matthew. He was on the streets of Serenity City for over half a year after they died, and then he met my mother. You know what happened after that. Perhaps it isn't that he doesn't want to tell you and more that he doesn't want to think about it. Jason does not like to discuss what he cannot control."

"And that's why he's still a kid. We need to be on the same page if we're fighting together. If you want to know about my family, I can tell you. There's no secret. But what happened today is not something that should happen again. We're a team. We need to act like one."

"I agree," Ord said. She stepped through the back door with Lynn at her side. "You two are far more formidable together than apart."

Matthew did a double-take when he noticed Ordopha dressed like Lynn. They were both rather slim and shapely, but seeing Ord's new Caucasian skin color and blonde hair in a bun made her look like Zelana's older sister. That girl's powers were something else. Ordopha smiled at him, and it took a moment for him to remember what he was going to say.

"You're very lucky," he said to her. "That Mirror Gate has killed countless others before you. Why did you just blindly charge through?"

"I thought you or Zelana might be in trouble. Ever since she traveled over here I have heard all manner of voices from the mirror in Fortuna. But the way through was sealed until Zelana finally opened it earlier." She turned to face the girl. "Why didn't you return? We were waiting to hear word from you."

"Voices can be heard through even a deactivated Mirror Gate," she said. "What would I say?"

"You know very well that isn't what I mean." Ord furrowed her brow. "Alain and some of the men have gone off to the capital, and the rest of the villagers are on edge. We don't know if Nieto is close to discovering our location or not. Yet here you are hiding on Earth with Castor and Pollux. Are you attempting to run away from Tyndarus?"

"Oh, please," Zelana said. She folded her arms and rolled her eyes. "You two sound so much alike."

Ord looked from Zelana to Matthew. "We do?"

"*Anyway*," Lynn said. Her rough voice betrayed one who hadn't had enough sleep recently. Matthew couldn't help but feel some guilt over that. "I'm wondering if your whole village is planning to stay in these apartments. We're going to have to start building more rooms for them. That's going to cost extra, Matthew."

"I am not planning on staying," Ordopha said. "I came to make certain everyone in this home was still breathing. That being the case, we should return, Zelana. The villagers are worried about you."

"You can tell them I am all right." Zelana crinkled her lip as if a bad smell had crawled up her nostrils. "I am fitting in fine, and we are planning to visit the neighborhood block party in a couple of days, though I'm still not certain what that is. More importantly, there are men after Castor and Pollux, and I intend to help my friends."

Ord breathed hard. "I thought I heard Matthew in trouble earlier in the morning. Loud shouting and clatter erupted on the other side of the Mirror Gate. Is that what this was about?"

Matthew interrupted in order to bring clarity to the situation. Things were getting more and more complicated, and he was beginning to think they would never get back to normal. Not only was he no good with women, he now had to deal with three of them simultaneously. Silently, he wished he had another work shift to attend: anything to avoid more of this. A familiar headache was growing in the back of his head. Ord nodded as he finally got her up to date.

"Should Nieto be involved," she said. "We will be ready. Do you have a bow and some arrows I could use? It would be best to seek them out before they make their next move."

Lynn stuttered. "B-bow and arrows? Are you all insane? You can't just turn Riverview into a war-zone. I don't know anything about this Tyndarus you all are from, but we don't settle things here by spilling blood."

"Right," Matthew replied. "We just roll over and let the law take care of it. The detective from Quebec sure seemed *real* concerned about catching the guys who attacked me. But you are right about one thing, Lynn. We can't just go in guns blazing. Heck, I don't even have a gun. Never had the time to deal with the permits, and Hammersmith wouldn't go through the hassle of supplying me with them. But he did find me a pair of swords and a bow with some arrows. I figured that anything could happen around here, so it would be best to be prepared."

"You actually *do* have a bow?" Lynn paused, letting this all sink in. Finally, she sighed. "I'm sorry, I'm still trying to get used to all this."

"It's fine," he said. "We'll get ourselves armed, and then tonight I'll go hunting for

Burner. I'm sure there are plenty of people who know where he can be found. I'll confront him face to face."

"After dark," Zelana said with a nod. "That is the best time to strike an opponent unaware."

Lynn slapped the table with her palm. "Be real. What are you planning to do with him, Matthew?"

"I'm going to ask questions he will gladly field the answers for. It's going to go swimmingly; it'll be like we're the best of friends."

Matthew paced into the living room. He couldn't deal with any more of these silly questions, and a strange fatigue had begun to overtake him. This day would just never end. He walked into the living room in an attempt to shake it off.

Ordopha was the first one behind him. "While I understand your rage, Matthew, I do feel you should rest. Your face is an odd shade of green. Please, sit."

It wasn't his intent to obey her, but still Matthew stumbled into the couch. When did he get so exhausted? Matthew rubbed the bridge of his nose, and Ordopha sat beside him.

"Is this because your powers are returning?" she asked.

"It's been happening more and more recently. I guess this is why Jason is sleeping. Those scuffles we had today didn't help. Maybe they did, I don't know." He cupped his head in his hands and leaned back into the couch. "This is such a pain in the neck."

"You do not have to handle it alone. Even without Jason you have Zelana, Miss Lynn . . . and myself. You have many allies on Tyndarus, did you know? Your story has spread far since you've left. That is a good portion of the reason as to why Alain left for the capital. You should come and visit again. There are many who would like to see the legendary Castor and Pollux."

He hadn't thought about ever returning to Tyndarus. It wasn't for any particular reason. Perhaps he had put it to the back of his head subconsciously as if it were a dream that ended. Things came and went in life, and that was the way it always was. You move on, and you adapt.

But he never considered the past refusing to leave him be. Just like a bleeding man in the ocean, the sharks never stopped attacking. How long would he have to swim before he saw dry land again?

"How about this?" His words slurred, but he forced his tongue through anyway. "After we finish with this, you come to the block party with us, then the two of us will go back to Tyndarus for a few days. I could use a vacation, anyway."

Her eyes widened as if she hadn't expected that response. "I suppose now that Zelana has altered the Mirror Gate such a thing is possible. I am fine with staying around here a bit longer. Since Alain left to visit the capital it has been a rather lonely in the village. The villagers mean well, but we are still considered outsiders. It will take some time to adjust to living outside the mountains."

"I'll bet." Matthew's lids pulled down on him like a heavy weight. "Making a home isn't so easy. Why did Alain go to the capital, if you don't mind? What's the real reason?"

"Village life is not for him. So he went off with some men to join the battle against the tiger-men across the sea and spread the news of Castor and Pollux. He felt his talents were best suited somewhere else."

Though Matthew understood, something made him want to change the subject. "*You . . . know.*"

"Matthew?"

The last thing he heard was Ordopha's voice as he fell forward into her, sleep swallowing his consciousness whole. While it was the last thing he wanted, he accepted his fate with open arms. Just a few minutes of rest and he would be ready to roll.

Shocks of pain thundered in his marrow, causing him to shoot back up. But he no longer saw Ordopha, nor did he even see his living room. Warm summer wind wrapped him tight. Somehow Matthew was outside.

The warm road under his knees burned through his jeans. He forced himself up and stumbled forward on sore legs. The sun screamed down on the empty back road surrounded by endless rows of pine trees. The road ahead rolled on into a tall hill miles away on the horizon. Wherever he was, it was no longer in Riverview.

Smoke slipped over his shoulder from behind him. He sniffed and thought he smelled a fire. He twisted around to find his hunch was correct.

An overturned, aflame car lay in the center of the road. No other traffic could be seen for miles around, and neither were there any pedestrians nearby. Whatever had caused this accident had long since left this area abandoned. That is if it was an accident at all.

Matthew rushed over to the vehicle and cried out for help. No voice came from his mouth, but still, he yelled. The heat on the door scorched his fingertips, pushing him back from the blaze. Instead, he crouched down and peered through the shattered passenger window.

There he found two bodies in the front seats, burned to a near crisp. They had been dead for some time. Nothing could be done for them now.

His weakened knees failed him, leaving Matthew to tumble down onto his rear end. He stared blankly into the burning vehicle. What could have happened? How did he even get here, anyway?

"*Matthew*," a female voice said. It sounded like it was coming from the passenger seat, but no lips moved on either corpse. "*Jason is in danger. You must keep him safe.*"

Matthew attempted a reply, but once again no voice sounded from his mouth. It didn't appear to matter as she continued on.

"*I have no time left. The harbinger is approaching. Only the Gemini Man can face what is coming. Matthew! Please look after Jason.*"

His vision blurred and shattered like glass, returning him to sudden darkness. Before Matthew could even process what had happened to him, screams reverberated into the void like a megaphone at a suicide jumper. He couldn't avoid covering his ears to escape the cacophony.

"Matthew!" Zelana shouted.

He threw himself awake and fell sideways. Matthew slammed against the carpet in the living room, where sparks of pain fluttered in his eyes. That was the same carpet he bought at the flea market with the old living room TV. He had made it home again. Slowly he sat up.

"Are you well?" Zelana stood over him, offering her hand. He took it, and she helped steady his balance. "You have been asleep for the entire day."

Sure enough, traces of moonlight slipped in through the living room window, washing the house in pale white mixed with the light yellow tint of outdoor streetlights. He glanced at the clock to reveal it was past seven at night.

"Dang," he muttered through a yawn. "I really was out of it. What's wrong?"

"I have been checking up on Jason all day, but I last looked several hours ago because Miss Lynn was teaching us how to use her stove. When I came back to look just now, he was gone."

Matthew leaped up and flew down the hallway. That idiot couldn't have been so stupid as to go out now. Not after what had just happened today. Could he? Matthew flew open the bedroom door and scanned Jason's bed in the dark. He threw back the covers to find nothing but piles of clothes and a pillow underneath. The house phone sat in the middle of the bed. Jason was gone.

The dream played back in Matthew's mind, and the woman's warning caused sweat to form on his brow. Enemies were hiding in Riverview, and something even worse than these punks was on the way.

Jason was out there somewhere in town, playing around like a fool. The kid could be oblivious, but this was a whole new level of dumb.

The woman's words played back in Matthew's mind again as he searched every room in the house for his friend. "*The Harbinger is approaching.*"

That idiot kid was in danger, and he didn't even know it.

CHAPTER 6
NIGHT STALKERS

THE FEVER BROKE, and Jason awoke with a sweat-soaked pillow under his face. A conga drum thumped mercilessly inside his skull, beating his consciousness awake. He sat up and wiped his brow clean.

Jason checked the clock—it was half-past four in the afternoon. Low orange light bathed his room, bringing a sharp pain to his headache. He drew the blinds shut and fell back on his bed. The dark at least gave his thoughts some breathing room.

He quickly changed his clothes for fresh shorts and a clean blue shirt and allowed his thoughts to center. He hadn't had any time to process anything that had happened recently.

Jason remembered that Mellow geek from earlier that day. He seemingly knew a lot about Matthew and his family, even if he was lying about knowing his grandparents. However, that didn't explain how he not only found Jason on the field but appeared to know the teenager was related to Matthew in some way. Who was Mellow Holmes? He had to know something about those men that were pursuing them.

The clothes Jason had worn yesterday sat in a pile on the floor. He shuffled through them and found the note with the phone number Spencer had given him. The football player knew Mellow, and had to have at least some information they could use. Jason decided to call him up.

The exhausted teenager leaned out into the hall to find dead silence meeting him. Everyone had disappeared. Not that he blamed them—they had their own lives to live. He crossed the hallway into the living room, where the home phone was. On the couch, he spotted Matthew in deep slumber. A pillow had been placed under his head, as well as a thin sheet over him. He was biting his lip, and his eyes twitched as if he were in one heck of a battle. Jason tried to shake him awake, but it was no use. He must have been exhausted, too.

Jason found the phone beside the couch and took it for himself. He departed back to his room and left Matthew to sleep.

After shutting his door, Jason called Spencer and waited for his new acquaintance to pick up. It didn't take very long.

"*How are you feeling?*" Spencer asked. "*Everything alright at the homestead?*"

Jason cleared his throat. "As alright as it can be. Listen, I want to talk to that Mellow guy. Can you tell me where he might be?"

"*You don't actually think he had anything to do with the graveyard, do you? I've known him forever. I know he's annoying, but he would never hurt anyone.*"

"He might not," Jason admitted. There was always a chance he was being used by Burner's gang. Jason just didn't know. "That's why I need to talk to him. I want to clear the air and make sure there are no hard feelings. I think it would make my big bro feel better if he knew, too."

"*Ah, I getcha. This town isn't that big so having enemies just isn't something anyone wants. I'd still be careful if I were you. Burner's gang doesn't usually go after anyone more than once, but it has happened before. Tell your bro to watch his back. You too.*"

"I'm not scared of him." Jason didn't need to bluff on that account. There were worse things in this world than a wannabe gangster in a small Canadian town. "Where does Mellow hang out?"

"*He doesn't stick around at home much, but he does hang near the main drag in town where all the stores are. I've seen him in the alley near the movie theater and pharmacy playing with his phone or watching people. He might even be seeing a movie. Around here, we have a showing every night around six and at nine during summer. The six o'clock showing is his favorite.*"

Jason couldn't help but be impressed. "You know a lot about this guy."

"*We were friends.*" Spencer's voice went flat before it perked up again. "*Anyway, I gotta go! I'm heading out-of-town tonight to visit relatives. Good luck, man. When you finally get your own phone, be sure to add my number.*"

After hanging up, Jason made his bed. He put his pillow and a clothes pile under the sheets, just in case Matthew awoke while he was gone. There was no sense worrying him, and Jason would be back shortly. He just needed to ask that punk a few questions.

Jason slipped out the front door and locked it behind him. It was already five in the afternoon, and he had less than an hour to catch Mellow at the movie theater. Thankfully, he had nothing in his way but his own lack of energy.

The main street lay about nine blocks to the west, and he only had to slip through some otherwise empty neighborhoods along the river. It was a bit too humid for most folks to bother going out, and sure enough adults appeared to either be driving in air-conditioned cars or peddling their bicycles quickly to their destination. Only the clusters of kids playing around in the nearby park and on the bike paths didn't act phased by the weather, but kids were always more resilient than given credit for. He knew that well enough.

Jason couldn't help but glance over his shoulder with every unsteady step he made. No one was following him that he could see. Spencer's hunch was right—that gang probably had better things to do than harass him again. It was too humid today for that sort of thing, anyway.

There was plenty of traffic along the drag, but only a handful of people browsing storefronts along the sidewalks. Jason shuffled forward, peering into every alley along the way. There was no one to be found on the side paths. Spencer apparently knew Mellow as well as he said he did.

A couple of blocks later, he found a movie marquee straight out of some 20th century picture book. It had the title of Riverview Theater in tacky bold letters with big red doors and a box office waiting by the door. It was awkward approaching the living artifact. No one from where he was from ever went to movie theaters. They were for old people. However, he had also never been in a theater of this type. He was used to these places being big grey boxes with nothing inside by janky seats and bad stereo sound. His dad had always told him old movie theaters were a different experience—in fact he had always said he would bring Jason to one when he was older. But that could never happen now.

The boy grunted. Now was not the time to think about the past. Jason rubbed the aching muscles on his right arm and approached the box office. The teenager inside took his money for the surprisingly cheap ticket price which allowed him inside through the large doors. The cool, stale air of an air conditioner blasted Jason in the face, but that was the only modern convenience around. The rest of it reminded him of those old black and white photos of these places he saw online.

Thick red carpets ran across hardwood floors towards a glass case convenience station ahead of the entrance. Two sweeping staircases, also with red carpeting, wrapped around on either side to the second story where both the balcony and a metal door awaited. The bathroom trailed off to the side, and a pair of ancient arcade games he had never seen entitled *Sunset Riders* and *Violent Storm* played ancient sprite graphics on their screens. He wasn't much for video games, but they did look exciting enough. Two sets of double doors were set on either side of the glass concession stand, leading to the lone theater in the building. The area inside this place wasn't big, but it used its space wisely.

Behind the cash stood a single teenage boy who looked to be around Jason's age. The kid wore a checkered shirt and a small matching hat that covered his golden hair. He smiled simply at Jason as he approached the casing.

"Good evening," the employee said. "New in town?"

Jason blinked. "How do you know that?"

"I've seen you around Riverview looking quite lost over the last few weeks. Where's your girlfriend?" The teenager winked. "Hope you don't mind if I say she's pretty hot."

Jason forced a smile. "She's with her family today. By the way, do you happen to have a phone I can use? I forgot mine at home."

"Sure." The clerk gestured to a small phone he had behind the counter. "There's always someone who forgets to charge, you know. Though it isn't like we've had many people today."

"That's weird." A sudden sharp ache sliced through Jason's inside. He avoided clutching his stomach. "In fact, I was expecting more people because of the heat."

"Well, there is the block party in a few days, and moving around in humid weather isn't fun for anybody. Oh, and I almost forgot that there's a festival today at the Lutheran Church. Though I'm Anglican, so whatever." He shrugged. "Anyway, sorry for that. Did you want something? There's not much popcorn left."

"Does a guy named Mellow come here often?"

The employee grimaced. "Mellow Holmes? Yeah, he's already inside. Always comes to the showing at six, usually on Wednesdays or Fridays, orders popcorn and a coke, and keeps to himself. Rude guy. What could you possibly want with him?"

"Just need to ask him some questions. Anyway, can I use the phone for a few seconds?"

The employee handed Jason the phone, and he took advantage of the generosity. Jason called his home, hoping that Matthew might answer. The least he could do was to tell his friend where he might have gone. But Matthew didn't answer. Neither did any of the girls. Instead he had to leave a message.

"Hey, bro," Jason said, in case someone overheard him. "I'm at the theater for the six 'o clock showing. I should be back by . . . eight, I think. Don't worry about me. I'm fine."

Jason hung up and handed it back to the employee. The teenager behind the counter nodded as the speakers screeched through the theater entrance. The movie was starting. Jason bid the clerk goodbye, thanking him for the phone, and entered the actual theater.

The inside was quite impressive; especially considering it was the only screen in the building. There were three rows, the ones on the sides being about six seats wide compared to the row in the center being about eight. A few hundred could fit in this cavernous space. The balcony, too, was rather large, able to seat at least several dozen more bodies. He couldn't imagine a movie theater ever really needing this much space.

However, when he saw the screen it all began to make sense. It looked as if it were propped up above a large flat stage that stood behind it. This establishment must have doubled as a play house for the community. They probably used it for neighborhood meetings, too.

The lights were down, and he squinted to see through the dark. Old trailers played on the movie screen as the handful of people inside settled down. Jason scanned them for Mellow Holmes.

In the back right corner, he saw a younger couple embraced with a popcorn bucket between them. Aside from those two, a handful of older middle-aged couples with a kid or two sat in the center, a trio of three young guys munched loudly a few rows beside them, and one teenager lay huddled in the center of the back row in silence. Jason couldn't help but grin—he'd found his target.

Jason approached the boy in the back row and swung over the seats to land next to him. It was Mellow Holmes all right, but he didn't so much as twitch when Jason sat beside him. He merely munched his popcorn and stared dead ahead.

"Find another seat," Mellow said. He still didn't look over. "There's plenty of space."

Jason sighed and slumped into the chair. The cool air-conditioning actually felt good for once. "No, I think I like it here."

The teenager finally stopped munching his popcorn and watched Jason from the corner of his vision. "Well, look who it is. What can I do for you, *Luke*?"

"Drop the act. Why did those guys attack me in the graveyard?"

"You're nuts, Bartlett. Sorry if someone jumped you, but that's none of my business. I just thought I would tell the new kid a cool story to welcome him to our lovely town. Excuse me for trying to be friendly."

Jason balled his fist, and red pain rushed through his lower arm. He bit his lip and stifled his voice. Violence wasn't going to get him through this. Pollux wasn't ready to come out, either.

"Okay, fine," Jason said. "Thanks for your help. So what movie are we watching?"

"You came here without even knowing what's playing?"

"I just wanted to get out of the house, and I've never been to a theater like this." Jason fell back into his seat, putting his hands behind his head. "Thought it would be fun."

"Tonight's cult night. They pick old movies that are voted on by community members. You can vote online or ask the ticket taker to put a slip in the box. You get four choices and have to pick the best one."

"That sounds wholesome. What did you vote for?"

"I don't vote. It's a waste of time. I just watch whatever they put on, and tonight it's *Deep Kick* from 1986. Not a bad year for these kinds of things. Michael Dudikoff plays an ex-US Marine who ends up fighting in an underground fighting tournament. But he doesn't know the hand-picked favorites are all mutants created by the villain to give him an edge in the betting. It's quite a violent flick."

Jason shrugged. "I'm used to violence."

"After today, I guess you would be. Now, would you kindly shut up and let me enjoy the movie. This is my break time."

"Break time from what? You got a late night job or something?"

"I'm always working, buddy."

Fatigue threatened to swallow Jason whole again. The seat was too comfortable, and the cool air blowing through the cavernous cinema made him want to curl up and sleep. Instead, he kept one eye on the movie and the other on Mellow. He couldn't let this chance escape him.

The movie was fine for what it was, but as it played, Jason kept trying to find a way to approach his neighbor. Mellow jumped, laughed, and cheered, any time the hero won against an opponent. For some reason, he took to this movie like a cat in a room of mice. After a scene where the main character kicked a hole through a mutant's chest, an idea dawned in Jason's mind. This kid was no fighter—he was a poseur.

"Are you a Prime, Mellow?"

The boy instantly stopped chewing popcorn and let his hands fall to his sides. Mellow didn't answer right away, instead deciding to ignore Jason.

"You're not one, are you?" Jason said. "That's okay because neither am I. But sometimes it's frustrating not being able to do cool things. We can't all be heroes, you know."

Mellow's lip stiffened. "You have no idea what this is like."

"I do, though. I'm not a Prime."

"Yes, you are. I know you have powers. You are nothing like me, but I'll fix that. Pieces of garbage like you will be put in their place."

"Do you think hanging out with guys like Burner will give you power? Do you think attacking people makes you good man? Which one of us is the piece of garbage?"

Mellow stood straight up in his seat. "You don't know a single thing about him! You're just filth, hiding from justice. But you won't be free forever. I'll be the one to put you away!"

"Keep it down!" the young woman sitting in the corner said. Her date nodded with her words. He looked as annoyed as she did. "Take it outside if you're going to argue. You're disturbing the customer, kid."

"Shut up, Kat," Mellow said. The punk's face had turned red. "This doesn't concern you."

She leaned across her seat and over her boyfriend. "This is my theater, kid. My dad gave this place to me. If you don't like it, then leave. Every single time you come here you make a scene, and no one enjoys it. I only put up with it because your folks donate so much. But you? You're nothing but a pain in everyone's neck. Just look around—you're bothering all my customers. Why don't you and your friend here find some other place to have a discussion?"

The small number of customers stared at the two teenagers in the back, distracted from the scene of Michael Dudikoff climbing the underground tower and blowing mutants away with his bazooka. Somehow they found this loud scene in real life more exciting.

Finally, Mellow threw up his hands in defeat, and jumped over the seats. "I don't need this," he said. "This town is such a waste of my time."

Jason followed him out into the lobby where the employee from before still sat in wait behind the counter. Mellow ignored the clerks and charged out the front door with Jason at his heels.

Outside, night had already dawned on Riverview. It looked like it was past seven, though Jason had no watch or phone in order to check. Instead he followed Mellow down alleyways heading towards the river. The fuming teenager was so distracted he didn't appear to notice he was being followed.

After about five minutes of mindless mumbling, Mellow stopped in the middle of an alley between a box-shaped store and a friend chicken restaurant. He gathered his breaths, and leaned against the wall. Jason waited behind him, bracing for impact.

Finally, Mellow turned around. "You ruined my night, moron. Are you happy?"

"Hey, I was enjoying the movie, too. You're the one who blew up at the owner—at least; she said she was the owner. What's your damage, Mellow? First, you approach me at the football field with smiles then you blow up when I approach *you*. You can dish it out but can't take it? Do you do this to everyone who moves to Riverview, or is this reserved for those that Burner points you towards? Are you a dog?"

"You know what?" Mellow's bright red face and wild, wide eyes almost took Jason aback. The rage inside this kid was barely contained. "Do you want to meet Burner so badly, *Luke*? I'll introduce you. Then you'll understand why I tried to warn you to back off. Well?"

Jason couldn't help but stare at his aggressor. This anger was totally out of proportion to what had just happened mere moments earlier. "Cool it, man. You're going to have a heart attack at this rate. All I want to know is why you sent Burner after me. I never did anything to you."

"You're a damn criminal!" he roared. "They might have legally declared you dead and dropped the charges, but you're still the same Jason McCrae that was suspected of both blowing up a building down south and also killing his parents. You've got a lot of nerve coming to my town."

"I didn't blow up any building. In case you haven't heard, I'm not a Prime, nor do I have access to explosives. As for my parents? I don't even know who killed them. I've been trying to find that out since last year. All I've ever done is look for the truth."

Mellow scoffed and spat on the ground. "They wouldn't be after you if you weren't involved in something shady."

"You're one to talk! You're running around with *actual* criminals."

"No, stupid, I'm not." Mellow's anger drained from his expression. He leveled one finger at the opposing teenager. "Burner is the only thing protecting this town from outsiders like you coming in to upset the balance. He doesn't hurt anyone who doesn't ask for it."

"Then why does he need to hide? Let me talk to him man to man, and we can get this all settled."

"You want to settle this?" A grin spread across Mellow's face. "Then come with me."

Mellow Holmes stomped down the alley and into the street. Jason followed him out of the narrow space and onto the sidewalk. The streetlights brightened with the darkening sky. Jason's bones still ached, but he marched on regardless. A little exercise should shake that off. Hopefully this wouldn't take long, and he could get back home. All he needed to do was talk with Burner, and this could all be straightened out.

Matthew could rest easy; Jason would solve this issue on his own.

THE PHONE BURNED in Matthew's hand. He had heard the message Jason had left him, but a call to the cinema proved the teenager had already left. Not only did he leave, but he had left with another boy his age.

Zelana paced Jason's room as Matthew sat on the bed trying to think. "I really am sorry, Matthew. If I would have come back earlier I would have noticed he disappeared."

"Forget about that dimwit. You said you were with some other teenagers earlier today. Do you have any names? He's probably with one of them."

She put a finger to her temple as if trying to think of an answer. "He wrote down a series of numbers Spencer told him when we were in that car. I think that is called a phone number?"

That had to be it. Under Jason's covers were some clothes. Perhaps he had left the number in there. Matthew sorted through the rags. "Want to help me out here?"

Zelana blushed. "I'd rather not."

"Can't blame you. This isn't very pleasant for me, either." Matthew found the shorts Jason was wearing earlier. Inside the pocket, he discovered a slip of paper with a phone number. "Bingo."

"Oh, you found it!" She let out a relieved breath. "Thank goodness."

Matthew called the number and waited for someone to pick up. It rang a few too many times for a teenager—didn't they love phones? Not that he would know. He last used one for work ages ago, but that was in a whole other life.

A female voice picked up the other end. It took him a moment to process that this couldn't be Spencer, but before he could voice his opinion she was about ready to hang up.

"This is Luke Bartlett's brother Scott," Matthew said. "Is this Spencer? I was under the impression he was a boy."

"*I'd hope so,*" the girl responded. "*He is my boyfriend, and the goof left his phone in my bag again. I'm Shannon.*"

"Shannon?"

Zelana interrupted. "Let me speak with her."

"Do you even know how to use a phone?" he rasped. "Wait, I'll just hit the speaker."

Once he turned on the speaker, Shannon's voice projected across the room. Zelana expressed her disbelief and exclaimed. Matthew begged her to be silent, but thankfully the girl on the other end chuckled instead.

"*Is that Jennifer?*" Shannon asked. "*I had the impression she was a country girl, but I'm starting to wonder what country. Anyway, what's up? Are you both looking for Luke?*"

"He is out hanging around some boy his age at the theater." Zelana looked up and down the phone as if confused where she should be talking into. "Do you know who they might be?"

"*Spencer and the guys are in Pembroke tonight. It's some team thing, I think. The only one I can think of that would be at the movie theater is Mellow Holmes. You really don't want to look for that creep. He isn't worth finding.*" She mumbled to herself, and the sound of light tapping emerged in the background. *"From what I know he usually hangs out around the main drag, but . . ."*

The silence after the last word bore into Matthew's thoughts. "But what?"

"*One sec, I'm doing a search. Why does your brother want to hang around with him, anyway? He's not going to beat him up is he? Mellow has been spotted with some unsavory types after dark before. It's not a good idea to mess with him.*"

There was no doubt in Matthew's mind that it was a bad idea, especially considering Jason's powers still hadn't returned. But that never stopped the boy from being stupid before. Why would it stop him now? The kid preferred doing things alone. How was Matthew supposed to keep him safe when the nitwit continued trying to throw his life away?

That dream flashed before his eyes again. Those charred corpses on the abandoned back roads left to their agonizing deaths. Who would do such a thing, and were they on the way to Riverview now? What if they were already here?

He put it out of his mind. Either way, the last thing anyone needed was Jason running off on his own.

"You needn't worry about him," Zelana said. Matthew wasn't sure if her words were directed at him or the other girl. "He might be reckless, but he is aware of his limits. He wouldn't fraternize with this Mellow brute without a valid reason."

"*Oh, okay,*" Shannon replied. "*So, check this. Debra says she's seen him walking around the trails outside of town, and near the warehouses by the river. If he's out, and it's not on the main drag then he's probably around one of those two places. That sounds about right for that creeper. Spencer might know more, but none of his dumb friends are picking up. Sorry.*"

That was enough for Matthew. "Thanks for your help, Shannon. I'll see if I can find him."

He hung up, and let out a breath. Now they had to look all over town for Jason and that other dumb kid. Thankfully his headache had subsided, but he could have done without more of Jason's foolishness.

"It was good to speak to you, Shannon!" Zelana said into the phone.

"I already hung up, Zel."

"What does that mean?"

"Communication is severed." She blushed, but he ignored it. "Enough of that: where are Lynn and Ord? We need to tell them about Jason."

"They are still in Miss Lynn's home. I never had the chance to tell them about him missing."

"At least they're still there. Get yourself together, Zel. We're going hunting."

IT HAD TO HAVE been near eight when Jason stepped into the wooded park with Mellow. The playground equipment was all rusted and overgrown trees blocked all view of the surrounding neighborhood. The town had given up on this place long ago.

Mellow sat on a park bench and dug out his phone. He mumbled into it before hanging up.

"We have an important meeting in two hours," Mellow said. "So we don't have a lot of time. Burner still said he'd come talk to you before then. Be grateful."

Jason folded his arms and leaned against a tree. "I'll be grateful when he says he'll leave me alone."

"Yeah, yeah, whatever. Play me another tune." Mellow pocketed his phone, sat back, and draped his arms over the back of the bench. "Whether Burner clears you or not, I don't care. I don't want you in my town. You've gotta go. You don't belong here."

"Judging by what I saw in that theater, it's you who doesn't belong here. No one in this town likes you very much, Mel."

"The feeling is mutual, let me tell you. But that doesn't matter. None of this does. Once the town's clean they'll all change their tune. No one worth anything is appreciated in his own time. Just the way it is. And don't call me *Mel*. Only my friends call me that."

Jason couldn't help but crack a smile and let a laugh slip out. Even though he was sore all over, something about Mellow's sincerity when he delivered his spiel made it even funnier. The dour teenager eyeballed Jason as if he were the scum on the bottom of his shoes.

"You're not serious, are you?" Jason asked.

"You wouldn't understand." Mellow's face reddened. "I've spent my whole life in this town. It's nice, and the people are friendly, and every day starts with a brand new sunrise where everything goes great. At least, that's what we're taught. Really the world is just a bunch of cowards pretending everything is perfect, doing everything in their power to ignore the truth."

"That's deep for a kid who has never left his backyard."

"Burner will show you, and I'll be enjoying it when he does."

At the edge of the park, a man stepped through the brightening streetlights and into the untamed brush. The tall and muscular figure with a shaved head and snow white skin tinged with a sickly green hue took steady and confident steps towards them. His dead eyes barely focused on anything. What really stuck out to Jason was the behemoth's heavy leather jacket, black pants and matching safety boots. The hands were covered in old cuts but were as meaty as the rest of his muscular form. The mystery man had no expression of joy, sadness, or anger, on his face.

Jason wanted to make a quip not unlike one Matthew would say, but something about the giant brought an unease deep in his mind. His legs wanted him to run, but fatigue held him in place.

"Boys," the imposing man said. "You're wanted back at the base."

"Who are you?" Mellow asked before Jason could. His voice wavered like he had been trapped in a freezer for several hours. Did he have the same feeling Jason did? "Burner was supposed to be coming here."

"I volunteered to come in his place. You see, I wanted to meet the great Pollux for myself, or are you no longer going by that name? The old lady's files said you were calling yourself Jason Vermilion now. At least they did before they were wiped out. Then there's that other cover you got from whatever alphabet soup agency sent you here. It's been quite a ride, Pollux, but it's time to go back. The Master is waiting."

Mellow froze, staring at the towering thug. The boy's mouth fell open as his tongue made silent syllables. He reminded Jason of a mouse surrounded by cats.

The stranger's hard eyes locked onto Jason. "Would you like to show me what you've got? I want to see Pollux up close. Give it a try, Vermilion."

"Are you the Harbinger?" Jason found his lips saying. Where had he heard that name before?

The giant's brow lifted almost imperceptibly. "I'm surprised you know that name. Most in the underworld call me Suicide. It's a bit much, but what are you going to do. No one chooses their own names there. Not like it matters—you're going to be out like a light in a second."

"I don't know why you're butting in here," Jason said. "I want to talk to Burner, not some bulky hooligan with a death wish babbling nonsense."

"Don't!" Mellow said. His voice warbled so much it sounded like he was sitting on a washing machine. "This guy is bad news."

"You know him?"

"No, I don't. I just . . . *have a feeling*."

Matthew wanted to call him crazy, but he felt the same way. It could have been some kind of Prime power giving Suicide this dark aura, but Jason doubted it. The odd feeling came from a presence deep beyond the unfocused brown eyes on his specter-like face. Something was missing inside Suicide, and Jason did not want to find out what it was.

"Feelings are just crossed wiring in your brain, boys." Suicide stretched his arms and cracked his knuckles. "Don't disappoint me. Energy is about the only thing children have going for them."

Jason hardly remembered making the decision to charge forward—he just did it. His instincts begged him to flee, yet here he was moving towards Suicide instead. Traces of Pollux floated deep in the void of his mind, and desperately Jason clung to them. He could win. A surge of agony spiked through Jason's bones, but still he dove in.

His fist cracked into the side of the thug's cheek. Suicide reeled back a step. It might not have been his most powerful punch, but it would send a message. Anything was worth not having to hear him say another word.

Suicide stroked his cheek and let out a small breath. "You're not even trying. That's a disappointment. I was hoping for more, but that's typical in life. This is as far as you go, Vermilion."

Ripples of red pain like a knife cut through Jason's being. He gagged, choking on air, and dropped down to his knees. A torrent of black thoughts and intense anger flooded his mind, screaming wildly. Sweat dribbled into his eyes and saliva spurted from his throat. It was like drowning in a whirlpool of black tar.

Visions of mutilated corpses, violent death, and bloody physical abuse of innocents, clouded his consciousness. He couldn't think about anything besides darkness, the dead, and his inevitable demise just like them. Jason was doomed to die, as was everyone else he knew. Nieto would crush everything into paste. The Earth would be nothing but a dust-covered globe, and all Jason's struggles would be in vain. He watched his friends and family butchered over and over again like a video on constant loop inside his mind. His brain remained locked on this mindless carnage, unable to move on.

A crushing pressure squeezed Jason's soul. The black vice dug into his thoughts and clenched his muscles. Before he knew it, Jason was lying on the ground of the park.

He blinked and the pain was gone. As soon as it came, the feeling of death left him. It took him a second to realize he lay on the pavement with drool pooling in the corner of his mouth and tears in his eyes. His muscles twitched involuntarily. Was he dead? Jason's body refused to move an inch.

Suicide stared down at his crumpled victim. "I haven't even hit you yet."

"What did you do?" Mellow asked. Jason could barely see the teenager still cowering on the bench. "Don't touch me!"

"Relax, Mel," Suicide replied. "Ready for the meeting? You don't want to be late."

"No, I don't." Mellow wouldn't look down at Jason, instead, he stared beyond him. "No way."

"Good kid."

Suicide stepped past Jason, his heavy boots crunching down into loose gravel. The muscular man didn't even glance down at his victim.

Jason lashed out and gripped Suicide's boot as he passed by. He held tight and squeezed, attempting to call on Pollux for power. However, he could barely think or concentrate, his thoughts a swirling dark void of despair. It wanted to pull him back in. He acted only on instinct now.

"Not done yet?" Suicide said. "That's a rarity."

Jason could do little but rasp through clenched teeth and slit eyes. "Stop!"

The shadow of Suicide filled Jason's fading vision as the thug kneeled down to meet the fallen teenager. The boy could barely see his enemy anymore.

"Time to grow up," Suicide whispered.

The shadow of a man descended on Jason. He grabbed a fistful of the teenager's blond hair and pulled his head up a few inches from the ground. The rest of Jason's body remained prone and unmoving. Suicide punched Jason dead in the face. The boy's brain rattled as spurts of warm blood ran down his forehead and cheeks. The heavy weight constantly beat against his face, sending splashes of red blood out. Jason's arms couldn't even move to defend himself; they remained twitching at his sides. A parade of agony marched through him. Nonetheless, every hit sent his mind deeper into the shadows.

Finally, Suicide let Jason's head fall limp to the pavement. The teenager tasted the blood filling his mouth, and let the eyes roll back in his head.

"What are you doing?" Mellow hissed. "The trees might block the view from the neighbors, but it's not foolproof. What if someone sees?"

"Then I'll kill them."

A hard boot slammed against Jason's skull, and the world went black. The last thing he heard was his own body jerking against the ground. The constant kicks from Suicide faded to a light thumping as his brain turned off.

But in the black abyss, an odd outline of a distant road Jason had never seen before appeared. A burning car lay flipped on its surface. There Suicide stood staring down at the wreckage. He didn't smile, he didn't laugh, and he didn't say a word. He watched the fire burn brightly.

Then the flames disappeared, like everything in Jason's mind. It all returned to the void Suicide loved so much.

Eventually, everything would return there, or so the whisper in the back of Jason's thoughts said over and over like a demonic mantra. It needed him to know defeat was inevitable—and running only delayed what was coming. This pit was where he belonged, and it was where he would stay for the rest of his meager existence.

There Jason silently shouted into the darkness swallowing him whole. Soon he was no more.

CHAPTER 7
AT THE WATER'S EDGE

"WHY DID YOU CHOOSE ME to come with you?" Ordopha asked Matthew. "Wouldn't you prefer Zelana?"

Despite it being near nine at night, the darkness had already consumed Riverview. Matthew wouldn't get any extra light for his search, though it probably wouldn't have helped much in the woods. Matthew and Ord had driven around the river watching the docks and the warehouses along the way to Pembroke, but saw no sign that anyone had been there recently. No one out of the ordinary, anyway. Normal folks still took their boats out of the water and drove away from the docks, giving the impression Matthew was in the wrong area.

He hoped Lynn and Zel were having better luck on the trails down on the west end of town, but they hadn't called his cheap, disposable phone yet to tell him anything. At least he could trust Lynn to keep an eye on Zelana. Someone needed to. He would have to repay her if this madness could subside for even a minute.

Matthew turned down a dirt road and gripped the wheel tighter with his sweaty palms. That stupid kid was going to get it when Matthew found him.

"Matthew?" Ordopha asked.

"Sorry. You wanted to know why I chose you to come with me? Zelana panics too easily, and I can never calm her down. Lynn's a lot better at that sort of thing than I am."

"Is that all?"

"You took the bow with you, right?"

She smiled. "Yes, and arrows, too."

"I don't think Lynn could handle that, on top of everything else. She just discovered the existence of a whole other world, met two people from it, and learned about magic and Mirror Gates. That's more than enough for one person. I would rather not lead her into trouble. When I find that kid he's going to get a punch in the face."

"You will always be you, Matthew." She laughed.

He cocked a brow. "What does that mean?"

"Nothing. I hope we find him soon."

"I hope he's doing stupid teenager stuff, and not involved in anything worse."

The longer they drove through the trees the more Ordopha watched the passing brush. Matthew couldn't quite look away—there was something different about her since she arrived here. He couldn't put his finger on it. Even her face, skin tone changed as it was, contained a slight green tint. Ordopha had to be tired, but she didn't show it. She never did.

As they drove he tried to make small talk. She didn't divulge much of anything except to tell him that her brother Alain had gone to the capital to join the military. Matthew could imagine what it was like there for her to be in an isolated village like Fortuna and not know anyone, especially since he still hadn't gotten used to Riverview yet. Perhaps they had more in common than he first thought.

"I know you're worried about Jason," he said. "But you really should rest. We're close to Pembroke now, the next town over. I don't know how much longer we'll be going for."

"No, I can endure. Living under Nieto's heel was worse than this."

Before he could reply, a car honked. Three black vehicles passed him on the inside, crossing the opposite side of the thin road. Where would anyone be going so late at night on these roads?

One of the passengers in the first car, a mustached man in a suit wearing glasses, winked at him. Matthew wasn't sure what it was about the guy, but his skin crawled. Whether it was his sixth sense or not, a sickly prickling ran up Matthew's arms. He pretended to look away from the car.

The trio of cars tore off into the night ahead, but Matthew wouldn't let them get too far. His fingers tightened on the steering wheel, and he sped up. Whatever happened, he was going to keep on these guys, but he wouldn't risk being spotted.

"Did you recognize them?" Ordopha asked. Her eyes were near closed as she slid back into the seat. "Are they friend or foe?"

"We're about to find out."

A rush of pain shimmered through his bones, but still he drove on. Matthew drove off into the dark, and turned down his headlights. A buzzing in the back of his mind told him to tear off after these cars. It might have been a hunch, but it was the best lead he had.

However, he couldn't help but remember his dream as he drove in the dark woods. The images of those burnt corpses remained in his thoughts. All he could do was hope it wasn't premonition.

"Steel yourself, Matthew," Ord said. She watched him from her prone position in her seat. "You will find him soon."

Even though he wasn't so certain of her words, he decided to believe her. "I know."

The two drove off into the dark. Trees whipped by them on either side as even the moonlight disappeared behind the thick brush, leaving them alone in the void. Only the sound of the motor kept them company as they sunk deeper and deeper into the dark of night.

JASON'S MIND swirled back to consciousness when the moonlight washed him over. His cheek ached, distracting him from even doing so much as coughing. The back of his head hurt worse. He rubbed his skull, but that made it throb harder. He rolled over to his knees and crawled to his hands. His balance refused to steady and his stomach stirred. Before Jason could understand it, he vomited.

The boy wiped his chin off and managed to stand up. He barely recognized the warehouse behind him, but the water beside it couldn't have been anything other than the St. Laurence River. Heavy clumps of forest awaited on every side of the stream, blocking the view of everything but the moon above. Jason had no idea where he was otherwise. He might not even have been in Riverview anymore.

The large forty-foot warehouse with boarded-up windows loomed over his bent body. Cracks in the foundation and the surrounding dock made it seem as if it had been abandoned years ago.

The man behind Jason broke the silence. "He's up, Boon."

At the end of the dock, around fifteen men of various sizes approached, every one of them wearing black shirts, slacks, hats, and jeans. The one called Boon slowly crossed the dock towards Jason. He had black bags under his eyes, and his expression looked as if he had just wrestled a bear.

"You've been a real pain in the neck, boy," Boon said. The rest of the men followed him. "You and your big bro."

Jason clutched his sore head. The swirling sensation was not unlike his brains were being boiled into stew. When the feeling finally passed, he found his voice again. "Where is Mellow?"

"Everything that happened, and you're wondering about that loser? What kind of an idiot are you?"

He grit his teeth. "The worst kind."

"Time for the meeting," Boon said. "Hope your stomach's settled. Last thing we need is for it to get even messier inside."

Two men seized Jason's arms and locked him in a hold. He didn't struggle against the pressure. It wasn't as if he could fight the gang off, especially with bubbling sickness broiling his mind.

A pair of black-dressed punks slid open the large rusted warehouse doors. The gaggle flooded inside with Jason in tow. They closed the hunk of metal behind them, trapping the group in the dark. However, a line of six artificial lamps lined the floor on each side of the spacious warehouse. In the dead center of it all stood a cluster of men in black, some of which held lamps of their own. Jason found himself being pushed towards them.

Seeing anything aside from outlines of people tinged purple from the moonlight sticking through the cracks was difficult, but Jason preferred it that way. The less he had to look at the less likely he was to vomit again. His brain still spun with faded memories of death and gore.

Someone spoke ahead of him. "So, who are you supposed to be, Suicide?"

Jason squinted through his mind fog. Two groups of men stood apart from him in the dusty warehouse, facing each other. He counted at least eight members in either crowd.

"Me?" the one called Suicide asked. Jason recognized that voice, but from where? He traced the speaker to the group on the right side. "That's not really any of your business. But you did some good work catching the runaway puppy, so some kudos is in order. Good job, Burner."

"Don't patronize me," Burner replied with a higher-pitched voice. He was in the left group. "How did you get my number? Where's my comrade? I thought he was with you."

"He's never been with me." Jason made out the source of the deep voice as a tall man, probably closer to seven feet tall than six, in front of the right cluster of bodies. Suicide stood among an odd group, including a man in a green suit and a teenage girl in a leather jacket of her own. Suicide gestured his shoulder, and green suit man stepped out of the vast space with a bag in hand. The big figure took it from the shorter man's hands. "Though I did take something from him."

Suicide threw the bag on the ground between the two groups. He fell silent as if he expected Burner to pick it up. Eventually, a man to Burner's right did.

Burner pried open the bag, and stared blankly into it for a length of time that felt like a century. Finally, he reached in and pulled something out.

"Where did you get this watch?" Burner asked. He threw the bag down, and brandished the object in his hand. It glinted faintly in the moonlight. "Why is it stained with blood?"

"That was his fault. He declined to join the cause. If it wasn't for the girl here, I would have brought his hand. Enjoy that watch because it's the only thing of his you'll ever find again."

Another voice Jason recognized audibly gasped from the dark. "You killed him?"

"He was already dead," Suicide said. "And now you have a free watch. Life might be fleeting, but it doesn't mean you can't go out in style."

Burner went for the back of his pants and drew a handgun. He aimed it directly at Suicide's face. The big man didn't move, even when the weapon clicked. Burner's men went for their own weapons, as did the thugs beside Suicide. Only the giant and the girl refused to draw a gun.

"Speaking of fleeting life," Burner said. "Any last words?"

"I thought you wanted to know why we were seeking this kid. Don't tell me emotion for your criminal buddy set you off. No wonder you never made it out of the minor leagues. You're all kids playing grownup. Put the gun away and let's discuss this like adults."

"Bro," the girl said. "I've got enough of them. Let's just take the prize and split."

"Not yet, Erin. No one needs to get emotional."

As Jason watched the argument, his mind pieced all the parts together again. This Suicide was the one who brought him here. He'd scrambled Jason's brain, and crossed his wires, but the longer Jason was awake the more it all came back again.

This Burner might have been a scumbag criminal. He might even have been worth putting away for the rest of his life. Jason didn't know enough about him to speculate.

However, Suicide was on a whole other level. Even through the dark open warehouse, everyone with guns trained on each other, he hoped someone shot the giant. Someone, *anyone*, needed to stop him now.

Every time Jason attempted to speak his tongue tied up and his mind remembered the images of decay and hyper-violence. A ten ton weight crushed down on his mind, causing his legs to wobble. If the men on either side weren't holding him, he would have fallen over.

Suicide was a monster. This insane villain would murder everyone in the warehouse. But all Jason could do was gag on his own spittle as visions of his own personal hell crushed in on him. He would die here, forgotten and alone. Suicide stood close by, waiting for a moment of weakness to butcher anything he could get his hands on.

"Let's talk rationally," Suicide said. "Or someone is going to die. And no one wants that. Right?"

"You're either immensely confident or a fool to come here after killing one of my allies. Give me a good reason not to blow you away."

A dry laugh poured out of the dark space where Suicide stood in the yawning space. No one else reacted, so it might have been Jason's imagination, or maybe they were as stunned as he was that someone like him could make a sound like that. The boy just knew that death was on its way.

"There's no point getting upset," Suicide said. "We're all going to be dead soon enough as it is."

AT LEAST a little bit of relief settled on Matthew as he left Ordopha to sleep it off in the car. She had fallen into slumber and refused to awaken, so he could do little but leave her someplace safe. He had parked in some heavy brush away from the docks and covered the car in branches. When he was certain she was covered, he crept into the woods towards the docks.

Thankfully he managed to get through to Lynn and Zelana to tell them where he was, but they were already following a lead of their own. He hoped they were chasing a dead-end, and the closer he trudged towards the water the more he became certain he was the one who would find something.

The moonlight beat down into his splitting migraine. Matthew's bumbling legs caused him to tackle a tree trunk three or four times. The night was not doing any favors for the creaking muscles under his bruised skin.

At the edge of the water he spotted a relatively small dock. This one was in the middle of an inlet. The arm of the wooden dock stretched out fifty yards or so into a warehouse at least forty or fifty feet tall. He assumed it was some sort of boat storage once a long time ago. Now it was an abandoned hovel in the center of the inlet's indent, surrounded by wild growth. The moss and gravel-covered shore proved no one had used this place in a while. This made the three black cars parked by the dirt road look even more suspicious. These night owls did not want to be seen.

Though he peered across the way towards the warehouse, he didn't see anything in the way of lookouts. Nonetheless, Matthew removed his shoes, put them on his head, and slowly crossed the water towards the old building. The water level inside the inlet only went up around waste deep, but he wouldn't rush it. Matthew kept low and refused to walk too fast.

He pulled himself up on the dock and allowed his clothes to drip harmlessly in the water. He couldn't sneak in if he was dripping water everywhere, so instead, he waited for the worst of it to taper off. The warehouse was bigger up close, about the size of a smaller supermarket store. At the rear was a little dock that led to a motorboat.

Finally, Matthew put his shoes back on and sidled up to the side of the warehouse. Voices inside chatted back and forth amongst each other. This gave him the opportunity to check the boat.

Unfortunately, it was just a typical motorboat, the same sort he'd seen moving up and down the river since coming to Riverview. There were no clues out here. He would have to check inside.

He peeked through the rear sliding door, and a familiar feeling trickled down his spine. He could hardly see anything aside from a small hallway covered in dust. Matthew slid through the door, careful not to make any noise, and lightly stepped down the hall.

Low voices up ahead broke the quiet. Matthew entered a yawning black space with artificial lights lining the length of the enormous, near fifty foot room. A lamp had been placed in between two groups at the center of the room with some other lights around the perimeter, though they were much weaker. The parties consisted of near a dozen men on each side. Matthew could barely make the people out, aside from the one on the left side looking the giant who fell from the beanstalk. They were already talking amongst each other when Matthew slid behind a metal pillar in the dark.

"Who are you really, Burner?" the enormous figure said. "Everyone in this town thinks you're a retired bank robber that commits petty crimes to sustain your reputation. After all, you have hideouts on both sides of the river, don't you? It's impressive you've carved out a niche for yourself. No one would know you're a failed sidekick. Not without the rumors."

"Do you want me to shoot you, Suicide?" the man opposite the big one said. "Did you come all the way up north just to die like this?"

"You don't have to act with me, sidekick. I remember Killer Angel, a hero with the ability to fly and throw piercing feathers that could do everything from poison to burn its targets. It was a wonderful ability. Shame your power couldn't stack up. Acid secretion is good for short range, but not much else."

Burner fired his gun. The bullet screeched past Suicide and struck the metal wall behind him. Suicide's men appeared ready to fire back until the big man put up an arm to stop them. Burner's weapon pointed back at his enemy's head again.

"Get to the point, Suicide."

"Sorry, I don't usually talk his much. I find pathetic people interesting. You desire to know why I wanted this kid and his brother badly enough to kill your friend and come up to leaf territory to threaten you. It's fairly obvious. In this world, there are those who accept the truth and those who hide from it. I recruit the former, and I dispose of the latter."

"What *truth* are you babbling about?"

Suicide said nothing for a long time. The eerie quiet lasted so long Matthew thought he might have been spotted. He looked down to the floor for a weapon, but found nothing aside from dust. However, six feet from him, he made out a body propped against the pillar. The corpse had blood leaking from his ears and lay slumped against the metal. Matthew checked the dead man and found only a pocketknife on him. He took it in hand.

That was when his eyes finally focused on the dark, allowing him to see into the group by the lights. Jason was among their numbers, being held by two thugs. The boy was out of it, looking as if he had been beaten within an inch of his life.

Burner gestured, and the two men carried Jason past the group towards the back of the warehouse. They moved slowly, though the kid shambling around contributed to that.

"Stay away from the back," Suicide said. "We're talking business now."

The girl behind Suicide tripped, and the green-suited man caught her. She laughed to herself before her giggles turned to angry swears.

"Get off me, Jace," she said. "Did you think I was going to faint like some weak little girl? I'm no lilting flower."

"Then you shouldn't have fallen. Get it together, Erin. Pull your own weight."

"Shut up! My bro knows no one works harder for him than me. No one is tougher."

Suicide swore at them. "The both of you morons shut up. We're having a discussion."

Burner sighed. "Until you tell me what you want, the deal is off. The kid isn't worth anything, so I'm going to take him back to town."

"There is another world aside from this one." Suicide's words froze everyone in the room, including the men carrying Jason. They all stared at the speaker. "The one I work for rules that planet. He wants those two fugitives because they stole something precious from him, and he needs it back."

"I should have shot you."

"Small brains always resort to violence to get their way." Suicide pulled a small shining object from his pocket and showed it to Burner. The mirror piece glowed purple. "You can see it all through that."

Burner watched the solid surface, his tongue tied with the rest of his men.

"This is another planet in a far-off solar system," Suicide said. "It's called Tyndarus and it is located at an insane distance from Earth that I couldn't possibly calculate. We couldn't get there via spacecraft unless our technology jumped a thousand years or so. You're touching a piece of a gate that can take you there instantly—but only with the Master's power. Without it the trip would kill you. The Master is fascinated with humans, for some inexplicable reason, and is working his way to come here. He will eventually do so. It's inevitable."

"Even if I believed you," Burner said. His mouth remained agape. "Why would I help some alien trying to take over Earth? Maybe I like it here."

"You don't. No one does. But I'm not asking you to join—I'm not even threatening you. I'm reporting an inevitability as certain as death and disease. You can either join the winning team, or you can die. You're not getting the choice later, so I'll give it to you right now. That watch is what happens when you make the wrong decision, so make the right one. If you love your place in this world, then this is your chance to keep it. Do the smart thing for once, Burner. Reject your natural cowardice, and embrace the future."

Burner and his men said nothing, possibly taking in what the sociopath had just said. However, before anyone could reply, a gunshot rang outside.

The front door slid open and three men appeared at the opening, panting heavily. One had an arrow in his shoulder.

"Burner!" one said. "Someone started firing arrows at us. While we were escaping, I found Arnold and Phil hidden in the trees. They're dead."

Several of the men chattered amongst themselves. Matthew's fingers tightened on the found pocketknife. Ordopha was out in the woods, but not one of these thugs had seen her yet. He would have to make a move before they did.

Guns barked in the dark, and the men by the door dropped. Both parties of men in the warehouse spun and shot at each other. Screams and shots echoed in the building, causing lights to shatter and bodies to tumble down and roll out of the way. Men hid behind pillars and returned fire.

In the chaos, a bullet struck one of the men carrying Jason, sending the other two beside him spinning to the floor. Suicide stood over them, and stomped down on the head of the second thug. Jason scratched against the floor in an attempt to rise.

Suicide crouched beside the boy, and whispered down into the fallen teenager's ear. Matthew could just barely make it out what he said through the chaos, but it was something he wouldn't forget anytime soon.

"What do you know, Jason? This reminds of the time I killed your parents."

Suicide dashed off towards the rear of the warehouse, leaving Jason in the dust as bullets launched across the warehouse. Stray shots kept Matthew in place. This madness would end with everyone dead, and he had no doubt that was what Suicide wanted.

IT WASN'T until Suicide whispered those words to him that Jason could focus again. He turned over onto his stomach as shots careened overhead and men bellowed around him. Suicide ran out the back, but Jason still couldn't muster the energy to go after the bastard. He climbed to his knees, careful to keep low. Nearby, Burner bolted towards the back of the warehouse. The thug tore through the dark, ignoring the gunfire in pursuit of Suicide.

After two attempts to rise, Jason pushed forward and tripped across his own feet. Embers of rage burned in his gut and seeped down to his legs—the soul of Pollux flowed inside of him now. It wasn't quite as powerful as he remembered, but at least he could finally feel its presence again. Jason tumbled out into the night where that familiar white moonlight met him through the warm summer air.

Jason leaned against the back of the warehouse, his legs taking him sideways along the wall. His breath slowly caught up with him as he looked out towards the rear dock. Darkness ruled the night.

Burner was facing down Suicide on the small thirty-foot dock. The shorter man bled from his right arm and crouched on his knee but still kept his gun trained on Suicide.

"You can barely hold that sidearm," Suicide said. "Can you even squeeze the trigger?"

"Enough!" Burner said through clenched teeth. "You can tell your master to go to hell. Sorry to say, but that'll be difficult to do since I'm sending you there in five seconds."

"You're already dead, Burner. That's just the way the dice rolls."

Burner slumped down to the dock. Steam sprayed up from underneath where his blood leaked out. Jason couldn't see the source of the wound, only the moonlight reflecting off the stone on his ring. He instead focused on the subject of his rage.

Suicide looked up at the teenager with a blank expression. "What are you doing out here? I thought our first round would have taught you your lesson."

"Why?" Jason asked, choking back his rage. Warm water rolled from his eyes and down his cheek. "Why did you kill them?"

"It was a job, kid. Burner was just in the way."

"Not *them*—my parents!"

"Oh, right." Suicide nodded to himself in thought. "I didn't have any beef with your folks. Martin and Virginia McCrae were upstanding citizens, as far as that goes. The Master wanted Primes with certain abilities to grow his influence across Earth. He really began pushing this forward about two years ago. I'm not sure why; I think it had something to do with his power fading without a suitable host. It doesn't matter. He wanted strong men by his side. Those with psychic-style powers are his favorites, hence why he sought me out. I approached your parents with an offer from him, and they accepted."

All rationality left Jason's mind. The blazing bonfire of Pollux burned deep in the abyss of his soul, surpassing the sickness playing whack-a-mole with his stomach. Jason only saw a pile of skin and bones wrapped in a leather casing standing before him at the end of the dock. One hit and the meat bag would be obliterated into dust. All he needed was a single punch from Pollux.

"Calm down, Jason," Matthew said from behind him. "You've done enough tonight."

Jason paid him no mind. "I'm not going to kill you, Suicide. I'm going to shatter your bones and organs so you'll spend the rest of your days howling in pain. Every inch of your existence will be spent in misery, and every time you think about it, you will remember why you're like this."

For reasons Jason could only speculate on, Suicide actually laughed. His face never broke out into a smile, and his volume never rose beyond a low din, but it was a meaty, emotionless laugh that went well with his dead, staring eyes.

"That's good!" Suicide said. "I like that feeling you're giving me. That's the sort of thing that keeps me going. Deliver on your promise!"

The gunshots continued firing in the warehouse behind him, but they were slowing. It would only be a matter of time before the surviving criminals returned to help their superiors. Jason wouldn't let that happen. This murderer would never get out of this town.

Suicide cocked his head. "You look sick. Still thinking about how I cooked your Mommy?"

"Jason!" Matthew shouted. But he was too late.

Jason launched across the docks, a hidden flame inside egging him on. His sudden speed took him by surprise, and he stumbled in his first few steps. He leaped over Burner's steaming body and the ground cracked under his landing weight. The dock wood split as if it had been eaten through. Jason made up for his unsure footing by leaping again. He jumped much too high and bolted down towards Suicide in an arc. Despite his balance Jason brought his fists down like an ax handle at the source of his ire.

Suicide simply sidestepped, and Jason's full weight landed on the dock, shaking the entire structure. The enemy backhanded the boy and flashes of gutted bodies and broken bones flooded the Jason's mind. Familiar faces were shot, stabbed, suffocated, and burned alive. In the midst of them he watched Suicide looking over his mother's corpse. The dock caved in.

"This is how it ends, Jason," Suicide said.

The teenager roared a primal scream. In his rage, Jason mindlessly pounded both fists down again and again on the crumbling wood. The entire length of the wooden platform collapsed. All three of the figures dropped through the scattered planks and slapped down into the river.

Jason kicked against the water, pulling him deep under, but his mind refused to allow him concentration. Visions sliced at his thoughts, causing him to gag, and water rushed inside his lungs.

The last thing Jason remembered before going under was the figure of Suicide slipping away into the dark waters, leaving him to sink. The boy tried to kick after him, but his limbs refused to move.

Dreams of the dead and mutilated attacked Jason, and the realization he would soon join them filled his sinking thoughts with terror. The darkness obliged his fears and consumed him whole.

CHAPTER 8
DARK STARS OF TWILIGHT

MATTHEW DIDN'T think twice. When the deck went under, and all three bodies splashed into the river, he swam after Jason. The cold water instantaneously cleared his headache. He couldn't feel anything at all aside from the burst of adrenaline as he pushed downward towards the flailing form of Jason.

The kid kicked about like he was being strangled even though nothing touched him. Had he been hit by a stray shot? Matthew reached for him and found the boy pushing back against his hold.

However, Jason wouldn't be budged. Matthew wrapped his arms around the boy's waist, but he couldn't move him. Somehow it felt as if Jason had gained several hundred pounds out of nowhere. Bubble streams of lost air leaked out of the teenager's gaping maw.

Deeper the two sank, and fear clung to Matthew tighter than he held on to Jason. He couldn't lift the kid. Jason was going to drown.

Matthew felt for Castor in his mind, begging for any help he might get from the power deep inside. Water forced its way in his lungs as he closed his eyes tight, and screamed into the dark corners of his thoughts. Just a scrap—one single fraction—of Castor would be enough.

Just as the lights went out in Matthew's mind, a spark erupted in the water before his eyes. A shock rippled through his body and spread out into the river.

The vision of his first transformations passed before him—the time he escaped from the mountains and when he became a puddle to sneak into that mist village. It all returned to him. He became water and swam across the ground like a moving body of liquid. Just like that his body remembered what his head knew. Matthew was Castor and Castor was the wind and water, and everything in between. He swam and flew through the world and anything that passed his way. Such was the power of Castor. Cool memories and hot sensations washed over his numb body.

Matthew awoke, coughing violently. He found himself pulling his sore body up an embankment and out of the river. A limp teenager was tucked under his right arm. Matthew threw Jason onto the grass and the boy gagged up water. Matthew dragged his own numb body out of the river and allowed his lungs to catch up with the rest of him.

How did he get here? Was he dreaming, or did Castor actually work? Perhaps someone else had aided them, but he doubted that. Matthew rubbed the blurriness from his eyes and searched around. The two of them were downriver, still in the forest, but now in the middle of a long grass field. The field went on several dozen yards up to a sharp and short rock base which led to the very road he traveled to come down here in the dark. The car was at least a mile to the west from their position.

Sirens lit up the night, and the gunfire to the west of their position died off. There was no chance he'd get back to the car from here. Matthew checked the disposable phone in his pocket, but it was beaten and bashed up. It might still work, but he didn't have the time to test it out. They had to escape before the cops arrived.

Matthew put Jason's arm around his neck, and hoisted him forward. He brought the boy towards the embankment leading to the road. The boy mumbled to himself incoherently, but refused to wake. Whatever Suicide had done to Jason had really taken its toll.

Finally, they reached the rock embankment and Matthew propped Jason down against it. He removed the phone from his pocket and called Lynn's number.

A sudden pressure spiked at Matthew's back. He turned at the odd feeling and met the source moving towards him. A giant man drenched in river water shambled across the grass field in the dark, illuminated only by the harsh moonlight giving the impression of a moving shadow. Before Matthew could do anything, the figure leaped upon him and seized his shirt collar.

"Castor," Suicide said. "I was told you were the slippery one."

"What does it take to get rid of you?"

"I wish I knew."

Suicide leaned back and the pair tumbled over. The two rolled in the grass until Matthew whipped his opponent off of him. Suicide rolled back up as Matthew retreated a few steps to regain balance.

The phone had gotten lost in the brush, and Jason had fallen forward to the dirt, but that was the least of his worries. Suicide's jacket was missing but his soaked and ripped up black shirt displayed his corded arm muscles. His trim figure under the torn shirt revealed plenty of badly healed cuts and scars. Matthew leaned forward, readying for another assault.

"You are supposed to be the rational one, not the strong one." Suicide's tone sounded strangely disappointed. "How are you better at fighting than the boy is?"

The attacker clearly had no idea Jason could barely use Pollux right now. Matthew used this chance to fool Suicide. "I'm older. Have you never stopped to consider that maybe your Master lied about what we are and what we have? All we're trying to do is live normal lives."

"Normal lives?" For the second time that night Suicide laughed, and it sounded no better than the first. The hollow chuckle burned in Matthew's ears like a buzz saw on a steel pipe. No smile appeared on Suicide's face. "You know how you get a normal life? You run away. It's so very sad. You aren't normal, Castor. You will never be normal. How can you not understand this? Delusional people annoy me more than the ignorant ones, because at least the latter has an excuse. You are deliberately ignoring truth for fantasy. That's the mark of a coward."

"Keeping others safe is not cowardice."

"Worrying about dead weight is the mark of a weak mind. *Vermilion* can take care of himself. He did well against me tonight—twice, even! Meanwhile, you crept around in the shadows waiting for an opportune time to strike and run. What kind of man are you supposed to be?"

"Come any closer, and you'll find out."

Suicide tore off what remained of his tattered shirt. "I didn't hit you with my power yet because I wanted you conscious. I had some questions I wanted to ask. Simply stop this and come with me to the Master, or I will shatter you to pieces where you stand. Then I will sweep up the shards of your mind and cart your remains over to him regardless. Take the rational route. You only live once."

"I've never been lucky at the tables." Matthew raised his fists. Spikes of pain stabbed into his biceps and he winced. He needed to make this quick. "But I got by pretty good in the alleys."

"You asked for this."

Matthew jabbed, and his opponent dodged. He threw a few more punches, but Suicide batted his fists away. The enemy rushed in and elbowed his chest, and a sharp flash of agony rattled his brain. Matthew pushed on and delivered an uppercut, cracking Suicide's nose. The impact of the hit drew blood and caused Suicide to swerve sideways. The large man pivoted, dodging Matthew's attack, and backhanded his lunging opponent on the nose which sent sparks of pain, and something else, surging through Matthew's brain like lightning. One strike after another collided against Matthew as his mind scrambled with visions of death and destruction of people he knew quite well—bashed corpses and bleeding bodies littered the battlefield of his mind and sent him down to his knees. Death squeezed his soul, and brought him to wretch.

Suicide stood tall over his crumpled body. "I told you."

Visions filled Matthew's mind like a miasma mist, preventing him from hearing anything else Suicide might have said. The nightmares crushed into his brain, and what he saw made him ill.

Ordopha and Lynn lay dead in the corner of Matthew's mind, arcs of their sprayed blood staining his hallway walls, with their lifeless, vacant stares gazing at nothing. Their faces in open-mouthed terror, he saw the murderer standing above them with a sword held tight in his hands and a mad grin on his mad visage. It was Matthew White, dressed in the same leather armor he wore in Tyndarus, the people's supposed hero. The vision smiled at Matthew as he kneeled on the grass in the real world, his mind swirling with these vile thoughts.

Suicide kicked Matthew across the face, and the sick man landed in the tall grass. More evil thoughts played in his head like a forgotten memory running on a movie screen. Matthew hardly even noticed the blood dripping down his lips as his body twitched mercilessly.

With a final push of strength, Matthew climbed up to one knee, his mind tilting. He balanced himself with both hands against the grass, even as his vision spun.

"This is why you deserve everything you get," Suicide said. "You were told it was futile, and you attacked anyway. The end result was never going to be different. Why did you even bother?"

A mirage of Jason being stabbed by Matthew caused the injured man to wince. He held his bile down in his gut. "Because I don't have a choice. I've seen what your Master can do."

"But you've never seen what he *will* do. Scorched earth, shallow graves for the hopelessly irrational, and true happiness, await all of us. That's a future I can fight for. What are you fighting for? Comfort? Stability? That's nothing but the dream of a child refusing to grow up. I'm doing you a favor, Castor."

"You've never done anything for another person in your entire life."

Suicide thought to himself. He shrugged. "You're probably right."

"I'll put you down."

The big man brought up his fist. "You'll make a good corpse."

Wind whistled and a small shaft whipped through the night air. The thin arrow pierced Suicide's raised fist, sticking through to his palm. Suicide swore and clutched his wounded right hand. He turned in time for another to strike his right shoulder.

Suicide sprinted forward into the brush, and another arrow whipped by him, landing in the tall grass. A fourth shaft whistled through the air, and struck Suicide's left shoulder. The retreating man grunted as he disappeared into the trees.

Matthew searched around in the dark for his savior. Standing on the road above the rock base he spotted the night-camouflaged figure of Ordopha aiming her bow towards the trees. When it appeared obvious Suicide wouldn't return, she descended down the incline towards Matthew.

His body tilted sideways, and she caught him under her smaller shoulder. They swirled, off balance, but he didn't fall, instead finding his footing. The pair leaned against the tall rocks.

"Can you stand?" she asked, her voice wavering. "What did he do?"

Though he appreciated her more than he could say, Matthew couldn't look his savior in the face. Whenever he tried, those visions returned stronger than ever. Instead, he kept watching the trees where Suicide had fled to. The brute never returned.

"Jason," Matthew said. "Where is he?"

She whispered. "He is in the grass to your left. Sleeping. What happened in that fort?"

"It wasn't a fort. They were hiding out in an old warehouse, recruiting more faces to join Nieto's insane cult. Negotiations broke down when you attacked."

"I didn't attack! When you left me in that steel carriage, I awoke to a loud beating sound like a drum. I thought you were in danger, so I followed it to a group of bodies being buried in the woods. The grave diggers walked like mindless dolls as if they were unaware of what they were doing. I saw other men being attacked from behind, which made it clear this was some assassination plot. I fired on the guards near the base in hopes they would run in to warn whoever was inside. Some fired on me, so I had to stop them. Not long later did I hear a series of small explosions like fireworks from inside."

"Suicide was always planning on slaughtering Burner's men." Matthew swore. How did Nieto always manage to find these guys? "He made certain no one was in his way. All this to get us. That rotten—"

He winced in pain.

"I fled towards the building and heard the dock collapse," she continued. "That giant of a man swam downstream, screaming about Jason and you, and I pursued. Unfortunately, those men were littering the woods attacking each other, and sneaking by took more time than I wanted."

"It's fine." Matthew bit his lip. Black thoughts rushed in again. "We need to get out of here."

"You don't look fine. Are you hurt? Why won't you look at me?"

"I can't. Every time I do a horrible vision flashes in my head. Suicide is a Prime with some kind of mental power."

She paused, seemingly unable to come up with a response to the ridiculous thing he said. Suddenly, she stood up. Matthew risked watching her and paled when she died a gruesome death in his mind yet again.

"Do you hear that?" she said. "Someone is coming. It sounds not unlike one of those motorized vehicles like the one you use."

The two of them carried Jason and sidled up the rocks to peer onto the road. Coming from the opposite direction Suicide had fled in was a small, rusted purple car. Matthew thought he recognized it but didn't want to risk leaning closer to check. The small vehicle pulled over to the side of the road, and the passenger door opened. Matthew and Ord leaned lower against the stone. Matthew put his arm across her shoulders and pushed her down further below any potential sight-line. She clutched her bow.

"Jason?!" the voice cried. "Ordopha?! Matthew?!"

The familiar female voice caused Matthew's heart to leap into his throat. He jumped out of his hiding place and called out.

"We're over here, Zelana!"

The figure of the teenage girl sprinted down the road towards them, masked by headlights. The car followed after her, and pulled over in front of the two. Lynn stepped out of the car and crouched down to peer at them. Zelana slid down the rock base towards Jason.

Ordopha looked back and forth between the two new arrivals. "How did you find us?"

"Jason called us," Lynn said. She appeared to be watching Matthew as she spoke, though he avoided her gaze and looked in the general direction of Jason. "Is he okay?"

Matthew checked the boy and found he had the formerly fallen phone clutched in his right hand. He must have regained consciousness during the scuffle with Suicide and called before he went under again. Zelana checked the boy over for wounds.

"We need to get out of here," Matthew said. "Those police sirens are heading to the warehouse upriver. We don't want them to find us just down the road from it."

The three young women helped him hoist Jason up the rocks and into the car. Sparks of pain flashed in his head when he saw the unconscious kid's face. He gritted his teeth and avoided looking too close at him. They loaded Jason inside the backseat and climbed in. The car turned around and drove back the way it first came.

Only once did Matthew glance out the window. He let the warm wind of the summer night wash over him and his dangerous thoughts. The girls asked all sorts of questions, but he couldn't concentrate enough to answer any of them.

Instead he fell into slumber. There he met the evil visions that choked him alive as the pressure beat down on his soul. Somewhere in that deep abyss, he heard that cold, empty laugh of Suicide egging him on to end it all. That vapid glee stuck in Matthew's mind like crazy glue.

Somewhere out there Suicide certainly was laughing. The giant had won the night, and made everything a mess. Riverview wouldn't last another day in his presence.

CHAPTER 9
SUICIDE

MELLOW'S STEPS carried him through the night with a power he never knew his legs contained. Guns fired indiscriminately, and familiar voices shouted, their throats full of gargled blood. He couldn't block the chaos from his thoughts as he blitzed through the trees.

Andy and the boys had run into the warehouse to tell them someone was firing arrows outside. Then that Suicide psycho's men gunned them down. Why did they even have guns? Burner never used them . . . but then why did Burner's men fire back? Where even was Burner? The shots rang around the warehouse and sent Mellow running out the front entrance. No arrows ever hit him on his run through the trees, and he was beyond thankful for it. All he wanted was to live.

Branches and brush banged against his panicked frame. Mellow Holmes didn't even know where he was going anymore; he just hoped he was going the right way. Nothing made any sense, and both shots and sirens rattled around his head with his endlessly beating heart.

Was everyone dead? He wouldn't imagine it. If he closed his eyes, he would wake up back home playing video games. There, Mom would scold him for shouting too loud and Dad would chastise him for staying out too late. Once Mellow got back there, everything would be like it always was again. Then he could go about his day just like always, protecting the people from themselves. They needed him—he couldn't die here.

Thoughts of Suicide rushed into him as he pushed past tree trunks. He was there when that behemoth beat Luke Bartlett—no, what did he call him? Vermilion? Either way, Mellow was there when he pounded that kid into the dirt. There was no expression in Suicide's dead eyes as the blood from his striking fist splashed on his face. Psychopath. Evil.

When the victim had stopped moving, the giant wiped his fists off with the handkerchief in his pocket. His hollow gaze caught Mellow next, and the boy froze, his lip trembling. Suicide stared at him blankly as he cleaned his own knuckles.

"*Pick Vermilion up and bring him to the car. It's on the other side of the bushes.*"

Mellow's knees knocked together as he slowly sunk to meet the boy on the ground. The victim was unconscious and unmoving, with shallow breaths. Mellow let out a squeak in his throat.

"*Stop shaking, kid,*" Suicide said. "*I'm not going to do that to you. We're on the same side. I'm here to take him, remember? If I was going to attack you, you would know. I don't like to lean on my power too much or else it loses potency. Now, get this kid to the car.*"

Of course Mellow listened to the monster. What else could he do? Against a force that powerful, the teenager's only choice was to bow and grovel. A few of Burner's men, like Page, ran out into the park to help the boy lift Vermilion up. The four men carried him into the black car.

"*Don't worry,*" he told Mellow. "*We were going to have to beat this moron down either way. That guy just made it easier. Come on, Burner is waiting for us.*"

But Page was now lying in the middle of the warehouse as a ragged corpse. Bullets made short work of him. Mellow's ally wouldn't be coming to help him out of this jam or any ever again. It all happened in an instant.

Now, Mellow Holmes was alone.

As if he were running on automatic, the teenager turned down a familiar alley. Warm tears leaked down his face. He collapsed on all fours, gasping hard. Vomit trickled out of his mouth, but Mellow choked it back. He spun to his back against the wall and into a sitting position. Hours could have passed and he wouldn't have known it—time just seemed to stand still. All he could focus on were the dead bodies in that warehouse.

Sirens whistled off in another world while Mellow stared blankly into the main drag. No cars, no people, nothing at all walked the streets. Just hours ago, he was here enjoying his time at the movies—before that kid showed up.

A light rustle made Mellow tilt his head. Did he hear someone approaching? Blown newspaper scraped the pavement and the shuffle of kicked gravel played a small symphony underneath the distant blaring of sirens. It crept closer. Did they find him? His fingers dug into his knees.

Something tapped his thigh, and Mellow shouted. He jumped straight up to his feet and fell against the opposite alley wall. He spun around to meet his attacker. No one was there.

His head pounded with the blood rushing inside of him. Were his enemies invisible? Who were those men with Suicide? They killed everyone. Mellow was next. They would end him here.

But the force rumbled again in his pocket. He reached down and felt the vibrating phone. Mellow let out a breath and his knees went out from under him. He dropped into a sitting position, thankful that his reaction was just his imagination. They hadn't come for him, after all.

Mellow checked his phone, and instantly his heart leaped back into his throat once again.

Page's number was calling. Someone was using the dead man's phone to find Mellow. The boy turned off his own phone, and hugged his knees. He needed to get out of here, and fast, but his legs still wouldn't allow him. Instead, he sat there in the dark alley trying to think about better things like what it would be like when he finally ruled this town. Nothing like this would ever happen to anyone under his watch. He would make sure of it. But Page's lifeless face twisted in pain nudged itself into his thoughts. Who had his dead ally's phone?

Mellow shook his head. This was all nothing. It meant nothing. It would all disappear if he ignored it. This night was a bad dream, and when he went home and pulled the covers over his head it would all be over. In the morning Riverview would be the same dump as always, and he would be ready to protect it. The future awaited him.

Flashes of light split the alleyway's air, and Mellow's stomach sank back into his spine. That was Bernard's teleport when he brought multiple parties through. Did he escape? Mellow tucked his face into his knees. He just wanted it all to go away. Why couldn't they leave him alone?

"It's me, Mellow," Bernard said. "I knew you were here. You're always here."

The teleporter brought three people with him. Mellow didn't look to see who they were. It didn't matter. He dug his head back into his knees. Hopefully, Bernard would just go away.

"We meet again," Suicide said.

The boy threw his head backwards. His skull cracked against the brick, sending stars across his tear-stained vision. When it cleared, he saw the roughed-up figure of Suicide crouched right in front of him. Bernard and that girl with the leather jacket from the warehouse stood behind Suicide with a green-suited man. For some reason Bernard stared blankly ahead.

"Bernard!" Mellow said, his voice rasping. "Why did you bring them here? They killed Page!"

"We're with them now." No emotion broke through Bernard's flat tone. It was as if this was someone wearing a Bernard skin-suit and moving him like a puppet. "You should calm down."

The girl waggled her fingers at Mellow. Her skin looked oddly bruised around her eyes—the boy was sure she didn't have those in the warehouse. "It was good you escaped. We don't need any more blood to be spilled tonight."

Mellow couldn't manage the words to reply to any of them. They were all insane.

"You look like hell," Suicide said. Blood dripped from the cuts on his face. "I'd know."

Mellow's voice quivered. "Go away."

"I heard from your friend over there that you know where Castor and Vermilion are hiding. He says that Burner only told a small handful of you guys. Unfortunately, those fellows are dead."

"I had nothing to do with it." It was a partial truth, which allowed the boy to show more confidence than he felt. "You should have asked Boon or Page about it. They went there."

"That's unfortunate."

Mellow remembered Page's corpse, and a shiver tickled his spine. If only he could forget. He didn't want to imagine what happened to the others. "I don't want anything to do with this."

"Sure, you do. Bernard told me you live a pretty good life with your folks. They were at that church festival today, right?"

The man in the green suit waved his hand, and the air split open, just as it did when Bernard used his power. They had the same Prime ability? Who were these guys?

Hairs stood up on Mellow's arms. He stared over at Bernard. Burner's former friend remained completely emotionless as he was led through green suit's portal. Bruises coated Bernard, and a black eye showed him as someone who had been through a real grinder. But he still looked at Mellow Holmes no differently than he would a stranger.

"We're going to be friends, Holmes," Suicide said. "I'll show you what it's like to strike fear into the hearts of the wicked and the righteous alike. It's a lot easier than you think."

THE SLAP REVERBERATED through the house, leaving Jason stunned. He tumbled backwards into the couch and rubbed his cheek. It didn't hurt so much as it took him by surprise. Ordopha stood above him, breathing hard, her false Caucasian skin reddening in her rage.

Jason had only regained consciousness mere moments ago and was still trying to remember what happened when Ord hit him. Matthew sat outside on the backyard porch with Lynn by his side talking about something or another. Neither of them had said anything to Jason since he woke up. Zelana waited in the hallway behind Ordopha looking away from him. What was going on tonight?

"Why are you so tenacious at being a silly child?" Ord asked. Her breaths stiffened as she fought for a calming tone. An odd green hue formed on her cheeks. "You put us all at great risk tonight, and almost cost Matthew his life. Is your desire for action so grave that you would risk everyone?"

"I don't—" Jason began. He clutched his head as a migraine attempted to push its way through his thoughts. The memories of the night flooded back into him. "I don't . . ."

"You don't think," she finished for him.

"There's nothing else I can say." His mind played him footage of the dead bodies in the warehouse. "I screwed up. I'm sorry, Ord."

"Your regret is a cheap prize after facing death."

Jason had gone out earlier simply to ask some questions around town, and it had somehow spun out from that into this madness. He wanted to know more and more, and eventually he had no longer remembered why he started in the first place. Following Mellow Holmes to that park was a near-fatal mistake and almost cost everyone here their lives.

In the case of Burner and his men, it *did* cost them their lives. Though Jason had nothing to do with that group, he should have treated this threat more seriously. After all he had been through on Tyndarus and during the disaster in Albion, he should have known better than to charge into trouble. Why was he like this?

Ordopha stopped talking. She sat on the couch beside him. Before he could say anything she pulled him into a hug. He blinked, confused as to what was happening. His friend whispered a few words of gratitude for him being alive and then let him go. He couldn't help but notice the growing odd green shade of her skin and that she was still breathing awkwardly.

"What's wrong, Ord?" he asked.

Zelana answered for him from across the room. She still didn't look at him. "She isn't adjusting to Earth as I did. Our people simply aren't meant to live here. Perhaps my father's reshaping of Tyndarus changed the atmosphere. I don't know. I'm going to send her back tomorrow morning."

"But you don't look sick," he said. "The change in atmosphere doesn't affect you?"

She said nothing for a moment. "I'm not normal, Jason. You know that. I don't know what I am. I don't belong anywhere."

Her words didn't shock Jason as much as they should have, but his brain was having trouble catching up to the events of the night. Somewhere in that mess, he glimpsed the mangled form of another dead body and shook it off. Maybe not everything needed to be remembered.

"Suicide," Jason said. "He had a piece of a Mirror Gate, and showed it to Burner before everything went off the rails. That means Nieto really did send him here from Serenity City. Maybe it is a good thing if you go back to Fortuna, Ord. Maybe you should go with her, Zelana. The last thing he needs to know is that you're here."

"You would like that, wouldn't you?!" Zelana shouted. She stormed past the two on the couch and out into the backyard where Matthew and Lynn were.

"I did it again, didn't I?" Jason could only stare after her with his mouth agape in confusion. He really should have learned how to shut up. No one knew how to dig a grave better than Jason Vermilion did.

"Jason," Ordopha said. She rubbed her eyes. "I don't think I've ever met another with a harder head than you. Other than my brother, that is. You two could easily exchange advice on how to best say the most inappropriate things and the worst moment."

"I only wanted to keep her safe, for crying out loud. What's so wrong with that?"

In any other situation he would have begged Zel to stay. He liked having her around more than anyone. Matthew might have been his friend, but he had a strong connection with Zelana he couldn't describe. Perhaps it was because he was the one to save her from that tree. Her father wanted to use her as a tool, which was why he sealed her in that tree back on Tyndarus to begin with. Nieto wanted his daughter's power in order to boost his own waning abilities.

The last thing anyone on either Earth or Tyndarus needed was a god-being threatening their very way of life, and there was no way Jason would lose her to him.

"She risked her life coming to this world," Ord continued, "and you keep attempting to send her away. You would do well to learn how to use the brain in your head."

He couldn't help but slump in his seat. What a disaster of a night.

Ordopha stood once more and moved towards the center of the living room. She thought to herself in quiet, no longer facing Jason.

"Go to sleep, Jason. We could all use some rest."

His friend walked out the backdoor and into the yard without a further word. She slipped behind the two sitting on the porch and disappeared into Lynn's home. Jason sat alone on the couch.

A black lump boiled in the pit of his stomach. Memories of this disaster of a night attached themselves to his brain, threatening him with yet more queasiness. There was nothing more he could do here tonight when he couldn't even think straight. As much as Jason wanted to apologize to Matthew and Lynn, opening his mouth to speak was far too risky. Bile rose up in his throat.

Jason lurched down the hall, his thoughts weighing him down with every passing second. All he could imagine was resting his aching skull on that soft pillow and drifting off to a world where the lingering pain was only his imagination. This would all wash away in dream land.

In the middle of the hall, a scene tore into his reality, taking him to a whole new place. Out on a back road far away, he watched a car spin over onto its side. Another car pulled up behind it and stopped in the middle of the road. Suicide walked out of the car beside the wreckage and turned to look at Jason. There was no smile on his face—nothing but the same empty eyes he had seen so clearly earlier in the night.

"*The Harbinger comes for all*," Suicide said.

Then as soon as the vision appeared, it faded away again. Jason had at some point ended up on his mattress and with his face buried in the pillow. His fatigue soon consumed him.

However, what came to him in his slumber was anything but comfort or rest.

MATTHEW DIDN'T say a word to Ordopha as she disappeared back into Lynn's place. She had been through enough tonight, and none of it was her fault. Nothing that happened on Earth was her business, and she would be better off living a normal life on Tyndarus. She could still find someone and start a family of her own, putting all of this behind her forever. Going back home in the morning was the best thing for her health and her future.

Secretly, he was relieved she wouldn't be able to stay. Though he couldn't tell anyone *he* would rather leave, too. Matthew did find himself pining more and more for that strange world of Tyndarus since this whole mess started. What wonders could be seen out on that mysterious planet away from this madness?

Then there was the poisonous elephant in the room: the one who had sent all these people after him from Marguerite Stohl, to Bloodeater, to Suicide, with certainly more to come. Nieto would never stop. Playing on the defensive like Matthew was doing would lead to more deaths in the long run. Every individual who was hurt tonight was injured because he refused to take Nieto on himself. Would he hide away for the rest of his life, or would he strike back against the monster that had caused so much grief to so many people? His solution here was becoming clear.

But first, something had to be done about this Suicide character. He was dangerous, much too deadly, to be allowed to walk free.

"I wanted to thank you for everything you've done for us, Lynn," Matthew said. "There is no way for me to repay you. After this is settled we'll be getting out your hair. Sorry for everything."

He made up his mind. He would go to Tyndarus and wage war on Nieto until this ended. Lynn was talking, but he was no longer listening. She wouldn't understand. She couldn't.

His unfocused eyes locked on to a single blade of dry grass at his feet. The more he focused on it the more the heat in his brain lessened, and the more sweat pooled on his neck.

He should get up and step on it. His teeth clenched, and he stood to rise . . .

"*Matthew!*" Lynn shouted.

He nearly jumped out of his skin, and twisted to face her. "What?"

"You were zoning out on me there. Why do you always do that? Ever since we were kids."

"I'm just thinking about things."

"It's always about plans within plans with you. You can't read a room to save your life, but you can think your way out of any situation. Just act for once, Matthew. Like tonight when you went after Jason into the water. There was no hesitation—you just did it."

"You weren't there. And it isn't like I was going to sit by and let a friend drown. Sometimes you have to act without thinking, but not always. Sometimes you need to weigh your options."

"Weighing options?" She sighed and rubbed the sleep from her eyes. "You took a strange alien woman out alone into a dark corner of a world she has no idea about. Then you left her alone in a vehicle she had just discovered existed for the first time only hours earlier. She told me how scared she was when she noticed you were gone. How long did it take to weigh that one out?"

He stood up and stretched. Ord saved him tonight, and Lynn just wouldn't get it. "Ordopha is a lot stronger than she might look. I know her better than you."

"You know her? You met her once on a strange planet months ago. How well could you know her?"

"You don't know what we went through, Lynn. Don't act like you were there."

Lynn scrunched up her fists, and stood up to meet him. She looked ready to go for round two. However, instead of yelling, she took a calming breath and stared him dead in the eye.

"Maybe you wouldn't have been *there* if you never left *here*."

His old friend quietly disappeared back into her home. He looked after her for a moment, unsure of what to even do next.

"Women," he whispered, scratching his head.

Matthew took one step back towards the house, and his legs gave. He tilted sideways, and rammed his shoulder into the side of the open doorway. Fortunately he didn't feel anything aside from the fatigue washing over his thoughts.

Sleep had so consumed him that he didn't even realize he had fallen into his bed until exhaustion overwhelmed his senses. The hot humid summer air wrapped him like a blanket in his pitch black room. Dreams soon overtook reality, pulling him from his worries and cares into bliss.

Sweat soaked his forehead as he tossed and turned. It wasn't long until those dreams he knew so well turned into nightmares, and then spoke to him.

"*I'm coming for you,*" the nightmare said. "*Once I have you I will drag you down to hell. You will never see the sun again.*"

Deep in Matthew's bones he knew the voice was serious, but he was much too late to do anything about it. Sleep dragged him down into the dark where he would never escape again.

"*It is very nice to meet you, Castor. Please, relax. Let us get to know each other.*"

CHAPTER 10
NEW DAWN

THE HUMIDITY pressed against Jason, choking him in and out of sleep. Aches and relief twisted into a raging whirlwind inside his mind. He blinked one time and woke in his bed, and another he opened his eyes and found himself being chased through an alley. One time he saw his own parents shot to death in a drive-by on the beach. Nothing was real, and yet everything was.

The dead body of Mellow Holmes lay propped up in front of the movie theater. His neck was bent at a wrong angle, and bullet holes pierced his forehead and lungs. The bloody teenager still clung to life, staring at Jason Vermilion through a space neither could see.

What Jason couldn't understand was how the face of the dead boy wavered and flickered like ocean water at the surf, showing different pained expressions, and eventually transformed into other people. In the bloody mess Jason glimpsed Matthew, Marguerite, Alain, Ordopha, Spencer, Jason's own Mom and Dad, his old friends, and lastly, Zelana.

"It doesn't hurt," the corpse said. "*Not for long.*"

Heavy pressure squeezed Jason's mind, pressing malevolent thoughts into his head. He threw himself across the bed, shoving his face into the sweat-slicked sheets and gritting his teeth. The visions beat every other thought out of his mind, leaving him with nothing but death and agony. All he could do was throw himself around his bed in his limbo between sleep and the waking world. Jason turned over and was treated with the vision of Zelana being beaten, crushed, shot, stabbed, and strangled. He was allowed to see her die in every imaginable way while he could do nothing but watch.

"It doesn't hurt," the corpse said. "*Not for long.*"

"*Jason?*"

The boy turned around. Alleys rolled on into the horizon behind and ahead of him, graffiti staining the walls, and broken concrete and old buildings tumbled on as far as the eye could see. Was this Serenity City? He hadn't been there in so long he hardly recognized it, just as he barely remembered the figure in front of him.

The middle-aged woman with curled blonde hair beckoned him to come closer. She wore the same green blouse and silver necklace around her neck the last day he saw her alive. Jason's mother smiled up at him with the same knowing look he had seen so many times before.

"*What's wrong, Jason? Why aren't you coming closer?*"

He tried to remember what he was supposed to feel looking at her, but all he had was a hollow beat in his heart and a constant buzzing in the back of his brain. He couldn't feel any emotion.

"*Jason,*" she said. "*Why do you keep forgetting me? I meet you in your dreams and every morning you forget. Did I mean so little to you?*"

What was she talking about? She told him that she was going away—that they would probably not meet in this life again. He'd spent many nights awake in his bed unable to sleep, thinking about how she was gone. The only distraction he had was getting up early to train. She knew all this, so why was she acting like she didn't?

Jason opened his mouth to speak, but nothing came out.

"*What's wrong with you, Jason?*"

A spark of pain flickered in his jaw. When he clutched it, a flood of stray thoughts poured through his mind and caught on his tongue. The universe wanted him to speak, but his jaw refused to let him. Thoughts, all uncontrolled and unfocused rushed their way through him. Drool ejected out of his trembling mouth and tears pushed their way from his widening eyes. Every thought he had ever had stirred in his brain like a piping hot stew. Jason tried to scream, but he still had no voice in the void.

He saw his mother from the corner of his mind watching as he slept. She smiled down at him, that familiar white tooth grin slipping through her curled lips. The lips twisted to a familiar leather snake-skin and her teeth sharpened to fangs. What were once bright blue eyes became black spots like dark, glassy marbles. She approached his prone form, her figure lengthening and twisting until it was nothing but a snake with dark green and red scales. The monster slithered on its belly and dashed out into the depths of Serenity City, leaving Jason alone once again.

His voice choked as she barreled away from sight. The realization hit him again and again until his stupid mind would finally accept it. No matter what he did, she wouldn't come back.

Jason bellowed into the depths of the city until a voice echoed back at him. As the stranger returned his cry the world around him brightened as if it were set ablaze and he was looking in on hell. The high voice soon knocked him back to consciousness.

"*Wake up!*"

Jason turned over to find Zelana staring back at him, her familiar blonde hair draped over her face and her arms lying on his bedside with her face right before his. She said nothing, since she wasn't alive. The teenage girl lay there dead, staring back at him. Blood rolled down from he top of her head.

"It doesn't hurt," the corpse said. "*Not for long.*"

The last thing Jason remembered were his frantic cries being absorbed into the unending nightmare around him. Unable to move, he could only look on as death pushed in on his mind, eager to devour him whole.

"*Jason!*" Zelana shouted. "*Get up this instant!*"

A cold feeling like sub-zero ice water dripped from Jason's brain down his spine and to his feet as he jerked awake. Instantly a slamming weight not unlike a sitting elephant pressed down on his skull. He twisted out of bed and landed on the floor.

"*Jason!*"

The fog in his mind dissipated from his eyes and allowed him to see again. Jason saw Zelana crouched over him, shaking him by the shoulders. His breaths softened as he looked her up and down.

"Are you Zelana?" he asked.

"What sort of nightmare did you have?" She helped him sit up beside her on the floor.

"It's over?" Beams of red light through his blinds—it was the sun fighting to bring sunrise to Riverview. Birds couldn't even be heard outside yet, it was so early. Jason couldn't help but laugh at his meaningless victory. "It's over."

"What is over? You were throwing yourself about and shouting all night. We heard you next door. I came to see you several times and each visit was worse than the last. This was no mere nightmare. Miss Lynn helped me attempt to awaken Matthew but he also keeps sleeping. Is this about Castor and Pollux? Are their powers returning finally?"

Jason's sweaty palm grabbed at his bedpost. He hoisted himself to his feet, even though his head still swam like it was hit by truck and flattened by the giant spinning wheels. He fumbled through his drawers for fresh clothes. No way would he be going back to sleep again, or staying in these sweat-soaked rags from yesterday.

"I'm awake now," he said. "That's all that matters."

"Stop moving! Sit down."

"No," Jason said through chattering teeth. He decided to forgo the new clothes. "I have to head into town."

"The sun hasn't even risen yet. Where are you going, Jason? Please tell me what happened."

Jason turned towards the door. Zelana pushed him backwards into the room, and his body was so exhausted it couldn't resist even that light force. He tripped over his own shaking legs back into his bed again. His limbs seized and locked as he landed, refusing to let him rise again.

She put a hand against his forehead, and then put her own forehead against his. He attempted to push her back, but his head swirled too much for him to even see straight. Zelana sighed and stood back up.

"You have a fever, Jason. Stop getting up. Your health comes before fruitless endeavors."

"I'm not sick," he said. Pain flared in his tendons and muscles. He bit his lip. "Let me up."

Where did this agony come from? He hardly remembered, but embers of memories from the night before burned when he attempted to think back to everything that happened.

The crushing feeling started when that Suicide punk first hit him back in the park. He was a Prime, and not a typical one. Whatever it was his power did, it stuck around long after contact, and attacked the mind relentlessly. It had brought him low and wouldn't let him shake it off.

Slowly the realization of who Suicide was returned to him. How did he forget such an important thing? Suicide murdered his parents. He slaughtered them both, and he was still out there.

Jason pushed himself up, but Zelana stopped him. She placed her palm on his forehead, and that familiar warm light bathed his vision in a soft white glow. His mind split, cracked, and sealed back in an instant as if quick-dry cement had been poured into his very thoughts. His muscles fell lax, losing all their tension. All of his fears, joys, and thoughts, emptied from Jason's thoughts.

"I can't find the source," she said from some space he could no longer perceive. "Who did this to you, Jason? Was it that one called Suicide? No matter. For now it is enough that you rest and let your wounds heal. You will be fine. Please, trust me."

Jason barely heard a word as he fell back into the white space and away from reality again. A warm waterfall washed his thoughts into slumber.

It could have been a century that he lay in that void, or it might have been a few seconds. Time didn't matter as long as he drifted in emptiness and separated from the pain held off by that invisible wall she had put up. He felt nothing as his mind basked in the sunlight shining like a heat lamp over his soul.

Then Jason sat up, his eyes glazed and sore as if he had been staring at the sun for hours. He rubbed his eyelids in time to see hard white light beaming through his blinds. He had to have been asleep for at least a few hours. His back and shoulders ached as he rotated them.

"You're finally awake!" Lynn said from out in the hall. "How are you doing?"

She had her brunette hair tied back behind her neck and an apron on. In one hand she held a broom and in the other a dustpan. This sight was not what he expected and his lack of response to her question appeared to annoy her.

"Oh, come on," Lynn said. "I don't look that weird. This is my family's building after all. I am responsible for it."

"That's not it." Jason's voice rasped worse than he expected. He tried to clear it with a hard cough. "I almost forgot who you were. You clean early."

"It's noon, Jason. You don't look like you've slept for a second."

"The last thing I remember was hitting the bed. Shouldn't you be at work?"

"I took the day off. Luckily I rarely take sick days, and you guys need the help. Zelana is picking up some aspirin at the pharmacy for me. She's starting to get the hang of this place."

"Where's Ord?"

"Zelana brought her back through the mirror earlier this morning." She sighed. "Matthew wasn't too happy about it, but it's not like he said anything. He never does."

"Thanks for cleaning, but I can do that." Jason rolled over onto his feet and attempted to stand. His knees cracked and forced him to sit back down. Muscles still ached, and he still felt no more refreshed than he did when he woke up before. "I'm surprised Matthew lets you do this."

"Matthew isn't here. I always have to work around that idiot and—" She paused as if debating to say what she really wanted to say. "Never mind that. A detective from the station came by: the one who was here after the home invasion. He wanted to ask you and Matthew some questions, but since you were sleeping Matthew went alone."

Jason's tongue ran across his dry lips. It took a few seconds for him to absorb what she said.

"Is he in trouble?" he asked.

She gave him a small, reassuring smile. "He didn't do anything, so he should be fine."

"If you say so. You know this town better than I do. Clearly."

"Go back to sleep, Jason. Matthew still wants to talk to you when he gets back."

"Sure."

Lynn disappeared back into the hallway, and the loud whine of a vacuum cleaner filled the silence. Thankfully she was kind enough to close the door first.

Jason bent over with his feet on the floor, his hands on his head, and his elbows on his knees. He rubbed his temples with his palms trying to understand what he should do to make up for this. The teenager had instigated the conflict with Suicide. But it was difficult for him to remember how he did it, and the longer he sat there, the more a dark fog filled his mind.

The boy fell backwards and hit the mattress flat. His muscles seized again, allowing him to slip back into slumber. That familiar black fog swallowed his thoughts and brought him back to the world of nightmares. Somewhere in the haze he could hear low laughter as the world imploded around him.

"YOU CAN SEE why I brought you here," the detective said. He sat back in his chair and sighed while he scanned Matthew. "The last few days since Burner's gang first antagonized you have been quite the show. Wouldn't you say, Monsieur Bartlett?"

Matthew rubbed his back. The chair wasn't doing any favors to his spine. Then again, neither was the room. He looked around the small grey space that contained nothing but a table and two of the most comfortable chairs in the world. He eyeballed the camera in the upper corner of the tiny sweltering space. Whatever these cops were hoping to get from him must have been worth this elaborate setup. He waved at the camera and leaned into the table towards the officer.

"It hasn't been fun for me, Detective," Matthew said. He fought off a yawn but it broke through regardless. Sleep never arrived last night. Not even for a single second. Yet somehow Lynn said she couldn't wake him up. It didn't make any sense, but he didn't bother to question it. Just because his body slept didn't mean the rest of him did. "I'm thankful you found the car. My boss can only take so much craziness."

"You look like you've been beaten with a hammer, Monsieur." The detective sat back in his seat and stretched. His brown suit's buttons stretched over his bulbous gut. "But that's nothing compared to what we found by the old picnic grounds. They stole your car and brought it into the forest, covering it in all sorts of crud. The nearby warehouse was nothing but ashes when we got there, and not a single soul to be seen. It doesn't appear like any bodies were turned to ash—they were probably moved. We know one of Burner's gang has the ability to teleport. Since last night no one in his group has been spotted around town. There is one teenager rumored to be friendly with them, but he gave us nothing to work with. How about you, Monsieur Bartlett?"

"Me? I want to get home and ready for the block party tomorrow. I've been looking forward to that for a week. None of this business with Burner has anything to do with me."

"You must think I am dumb. This fire occurred mere hours after they first attacked you. Then they stole your car in the midst of this. I'm supposed to believe that is normal?"

Matthew shrugged, and wished he hadn't when the spikes of pine sliced through. He rubbed his shoulders. "I don't know what you want from me, Detective Leclerc. You must have looked into my past, my file, or whatever it is you do here. You then should know that I've never met this Burner or anyone in his group before yesterday. From what I can tell it seems like I was their new target before someone else interrupted their fun and sent them packing out of town."

"*C'est clair.* That sounds convenient. For you."

"Listen, Detective, all I want to do is be left alone. My brother's trying to fit into a new town, I'm getting in good with the guys at both of my jobs, and we finally feel like we can settle down. If these punks blew themselves up then it is of no concern to me."

Detective Leclerc removed a cigarette from his coat pocket and rolled it around in his fingers. He couldn't light it, for obvious reasons, but he inspected it all over as if he expected the cylinder to unveil some hidden mystery underneath its smooth skin. "From where I come from, someone who runs to a small town after living in a city like Serenity City has something to hide. That person is fleeing from a problem, and it is always something much worse than a couple of punks after loose change. I look at you and I see a man who has secrets. Just because it's not in a file doesn't mean they're not there. Do you understand, Monsieur *Bartlett*?"

"Can I go now? My brother isn't feeling well, and I've got the neighbor looking after him. Plus, I'd like to return the car to my boss before he really does fire me. It's enough that he lent it to me for as long as he did. Believe me; I'd like to know what happened. But it has nothing to do with me."

The detective watched the cigarette roll around in his hands for a few additional seconds before finally putting it back in his pocket. "Do you have a free hour?"

"After I bring the car back, sure."

"Do you mind coming with me? I would like to show you something."

Matthew fought off the urge to sigh or roll his eyes, not just out of his exhaustion in dealing with pesky cops, but because he got the impression that this one really wasn't after him for kicks. While he didn't want to leave Jason alone with Lynn for too long—she'd put up with a lot since they moved here already—he did find it curious that this detective appeared to know more than he was letting on. Matthew decided to go with him.

"Very good," Detective Leclerc said. He stood up and gestured to the door. "*Tasse-toi.* It's almost lunch and I've been going all day."

But the buzzing in the back of Matthew's mind pitched higher. Despite the lack of any real sleep last night, he still had fragments of those corpses flashing before his eyes. The truth was that talking to someone like the detective, someone he didn't know, allowed him to focus on anything else besides the crushing weight pressing down on his mind. That was the real reason he agreed to go with him.

He doubted this would ever subside—especially if it was Suicide's power. The notion caused a chill to bite at him. But if that was the case then why did Suicide use it on him? That punk wanted the pair of them alive, after all.

Before the day was out Matthew would find that bastard and put an end to him. No more would he hide from Nieto's stooges. However, he couldn't act just yet. Until his moment to strike arrived, he had to play the part of the hapless victim.

He forced a grin at the police officer. "Lead away, Detective."

MELLOW WOULD have felt so much better if that damn detective would have died instead of Burner. The cop came to his house to question Mellow that morning, bringing all sorts of queries from his already nosy parents. They wouldn't let up with grilling him about things that weren't their business.

"*Were you really hanging around with that gang like the rumors said?*" his mother had asked. "*I don't believe it. You're better than that.*"

"*You don't get it, Mom. Neither of you ever do. You don't know what I've seen.*"

His father remained stone-faced. "*You aren't leaving this house for the next week, at least until we discuss this entire debacle.*"

Emotion had welled in Mellow's gut. He didn't bother to even say so much as a good bye as he ran out into the early morning light. Both of his parents called after him, but he refused to even look back. Soon enough they were long gone, hopefully someplace far behind where he would never see them again.

They didn't understand anything. They didn't know true fear. They didn't meet a monster that destroyed with the touch of his hand. Adults ruined this world with their focus on safety and meaningless smiles. These out of touch fossils didn't understand what it was like to be hunted, to be prey. Death was knocking at their door.

His phone had vibrated every hour since last night, but he couldn't bring himself to answer it or turn it off. The number was unrecognizable, but he knew who it was. Suicide was still prowling.

Mellow passed the playground beside the main drag. This was the new one the adults had constructed to be more convenient to parents—they lived to shop. A couple of kids were out playing around, oblivious to the superiority of the old playground now covered in brush. They would soon tear down the old to make room for the new. The park he had spent so many days in as a child would soon be nothing but a memory.

He paused by the fence to watch the young runts. Mellow couldn't stop shivering. Thankfully the children ignored him, running around, jumping off monkey bars, swings, and chasing each other around like all dumb kids do. While he spied on them he saw through to the other end of the park where a familiar teenage girl walked past the opposite fence towards the main drag.

Bartlett's girlfriend wore a simple blue summer dress, and still had her blonde hair cut shoulder length, but she otherwise looked like the same teenage girl he had seen at the football practice. Since he didn't know what else to do, he followed her.

Mellow was too good at what he did, and he kept his distance, tailing her through the early morning with the rising heat. He still wore his same clothes from last night—that same pair of shorts and matching black top. They chaffed with all the recent heat and sweat, but he couldn't go home to change. This girl walking around clean and unshaken from what happened under her nose last night reminded Mellow just how stupid this whole town was. *They* didn't deserve the protection he offered them from the shadows. But then, as Burner said, heroes were never appreciated in their own time.

The reality of the situation built his rage. He had almost died last night—and Burner actually did—and no one noticed. Not one person in this shabby town had a clue how close they were to meeting certain tragedy. His anger boiled to new levels. Sweat glistened on his already reddened arms. Nonetheless he would soldier on: that was what heroes did.

His phone rang. Mellow recognized the number. The girl was too far ahead to hear him, and thankfully she had turned into the drug store. He used the moment to duck into his familiar alley, and pick up his phone.

He didn't get to say anything when the familiar hard voice of Suicide burst in his ear. "*Where have you been? I thought you were serious about protecting this town.*"

Try as he might, Mellow's lips struggled to form words. "I am," he managed.

"*Oh? Enlighten me. Where are you and what are you doing?*"

"I'm at the drug store, tailing the freak girl who hangs around with the guy you're looking for. Despite everything you did to me, I'm still doing my job."

"*You're a good boy, Holmes. But I've already guessed one of them would go to the pharmacy. They're both sick. Go inside and distract her for a few minutes, and chase anyone else out of the store. The man inside will help you. We'll meet you out back when you finish up.*"

The phone went dead, but Mellow had no answers. Finish up? What was he supposed to finish up, and why did Suicide think Dr. Taylor, the owner of the pharmacy, would help him? That middle-aged guy was nice to everyone in town, except Mellow and actual delinquents. There was no way he would understand what was going on. However, it wasn't as if Mellow had any other lead, so he strode into the drug store with his hands in his pockets.

Cool air from the air conditioner made him choke a bit. He had been in the sweltering heat all night, and his skin had forgotten the feeling of anything less than the boiling summer weather. He rubbed the sweat from his bare arms onto his shorts and shirt.

The cramped store didn't help. Three eight foot shelves lined up from left to right filled with bottles of aspirin, creams and ointments, and basic care products like shampoo and soap. Mellow scanned the empty store and found the girl talking with Dr. Taylor at the cash register. The boy approached, keeping sure the store really was vacant. No one would see anything happening inside.

"I've never seen you around," Dr. Taylor said. "We rarely get young ladies such as yourself visiting Riverview."

"I am staying with a relative," she said. "But our neighbor is having pains and has no way to go out and get . . . *aspirin* . . . so I was asked to get it for him. I have the currency in hand." She flashed a large bill. "Could you please sell me wares?"

Dr. Taylor laughed, his jowls shaking with his large stomach. "You really are from out of town."

The tubby guy was balding, and his mustache grey, but he wasn't small. He had to be just under six foot, slightly taller than Mellow. No one aside from people he hated tended to notice how intimidating the doctor could be, since he rarely showed his angry side except to delinquents—and Mellow. Dr. Orson Taylor's popularity around Riverview was undeserved.

"I am getting accustomed to it," the girl said. Her cheeks reddened as she glanced helplessly around the shelves. "Where would I find the medicine I require?"

"Aspirin is in the second row to your left. Choose the one you want and I'll ring you up."

The girl looked down at the bill in her hand and then towards the shelf where he was pointing. Finally, she nodded. "If you say so."

"Take your time, Miss. Most everyone else is getting ready for the block party tomorrow over near Sparrow Row. I don't think it will get busy today." A phone rang in his pocket. He glanced down at it. "Sorry, I have to take this."

He turned around, and answered his phone. She wandered over to the aisle, ignoring the old man talking to his wife or whoever would call the fat lump.

Mellow crept behind the shelves. He sidled towards her, making sure to block the direct route to the exit. The last thing he wanted was to scare her away. She looked fragile enough, despite clearly being slow-witted on top of it. Heroes shouldn't pick on the weak.

She rummaged through bottles on the shelf, eyes straining as if she couldn't read the simple words written before her. How dumb was this girl?

He tapped her on the shoulder. "Hey. That one says *aspirin*."

The girl spun around, and pushed him back. He wobbled, and regained balance, making sure to block the way out of the drugstore. She stared at him with palpable disgust, her lip upturned and eyebrows scrunched.

"You," she said. "You are the one that attacked Jason."

"I didn't attack anybody! That guy ambushed us and your boyfriend fought him. He got manhandled, too."

"He said you were in the warehouse afterwards. You were with that vicious dog and his litter."

"*Liar!*" Mellow whispered, harshly. He clenched his teeth, and swallowed what he really wanted to say down his raw throat. "None of us are on his side. We were there for a meeting, and then he turned on us. All my friends are dead, stupid! Why would I team up with that monster?"

She blanched. "Then why are you here?"

That was a question he didn't have an answer for. He wanted to tell the truth—that he was following her because he was scared of what would happen if he didn't, but he could never say that. All he wanted to do was keep the town safe, and it had been up to now. That is, it *had been* safe until she arrived. Her and those two brothers. Yes, it was *her* fault all this was happening. She deserved whatever fate awaited her. He had no guilt for whatever happened to this villain.

"I wanted to know if Bartlett was okay. It was a crazy mess last night, and several friends didn't make it." He choked up at the last two words, but muscled past it. He couldn't show weakness, especially not in front of her. "The cops questioned me and said that kid and his brother were alive. I didn't tell the police they were at the scene, though. That wouldn't do anyone any good."

"As it happens," she said, hands on hips. "Neither of them is healthy. That is why I am here. Go away, Mellow Holmes. You are not a friend and I have no desire to speak to you."

Mellow thought he heard a scuffle around the corner of the shelf and shook it off. It was probably just a mouse. The old guy's teenage employees never came in on time during the summer, which left the place unkempt more often than not. Mellow was focused instead on the villain standing before him.

"As if I'd ever be friends with a dimwit," he said. "I'm only here to confirm that they're still alive. Now the lot of you can get out of town before something bad happens."

"Don't threaten me, *boy*. I do not listen to the words of brigands and liars."

"Don't call me a boy, *girl*, and stop talking like you're from another planet. You're going to meet someone worse than me if you stick around. This is a warning, kid."

The girl bared her teeth. "Treating me like a child? How dare you!"

Before Mellow could reply, the bulky figure of Dr. Orson Taylor swooped around the aisle behind the girl. The massive man clapped both his hands on her ears, and he dug his palms in. The girl's mouth opened as if she were screaming, but no voice came out of her anguished expression. That odd doctor's face was also scrunched up as if in agony as he held her tight.

Then, he let go. The girl fell listlessly to the floor. Dr. Taylor tipped backwards and also tumbled against the shelf before landing beside her. Mellow was left looking at two unconscious figures at his feet.

Somewhere nearby, the radio played an old country song. His brain held him there, locked in stasis. He couldn't process what had just happened.

On the floor, the doctor's pocket rumbled. It was his phone. Mellow considered ignoring it, until his own pocket quivered at the same time. Could it be the same person calling? The coincidence would be too much. Mellow answered his phone, with his eyes still on the two at his feet.

"Yeah," he said, blandly.

"*Did the good doctor do his job?*" Suicide asked.

Mellow nodded, not realizing no one could see him doing it. "The girl is down, and so is he."

"*That's very good. Go lock the front door, then grab the girl and come around the back. A car is on the way. Someone else will take care of cleaning before the old man recovers.*"

"You're out of your damn mind," Mellow said, his mouth dry. He swallowed, his raw throat aching. "You can't attack people in broad daylight."

"*Do your job.*"

Suicide hung up. Mellow dropped his arm to his side. The queasiness built in his stomach as he locked the front door. His fists tightened, and his eyes watered. Mellow Holmes was no one's punching bag.

Suddenly he froze as memories of that Bartlett kid getting beaten into the ground chilled his mood. His lip trembled, and he swore. They were all destroying *his* town. Mellow crouched down to pick the girl up, just as he was told. There was no choice, but to do what he had to.

However, he would remember this. Suicide would get his comeuppance, and Mellow would be the one to do it. His name would become a legend, and everyone would know it.

That dream made him smile; allowing him to lifted the unconscious girl off the ground without any guilt or strain. There was no hero in this world quite like Mellow Holmes.

CHAPTER 11
SUMMER STORM

THE DETECTIVE'S CAR was quite an uncomfortable place to ride. Matthew made sure to not tell him anything, but the Quebecer kept talking regardless. The air conditioning was busted, and both men were sweating more than was healthy—the humidity had crept up since the early morning's dry warmth. Thunder squealed in the clouds, but still the detective continued to chatter. It didn't do much to aid the red nails of pain banging inside Matthew's brain.

It also didn't take long to figure out where the detective was going. The dark red Oldsmobile slipped down those familiar dirt roads covered in overstretched branches and thick brush. The humidity strengthened they got into the forest the more sweat pooled on Matthew's neck. This detective was taking him to the warehouse from last night.

"Thanks for letting me bring the car back to my boss," Matthew said. "The guy has the patience of a saint, even after being screwed with so much by these guys."

"People who live in Riverview are used to Burner's nonsense. Or, more accurately, they *were*."

"So, Burner's dead then?"

"*C'est complique*. We do not know." The detective sighed. He rubbed the bridge of his nose. "There are no remains of people in the ashes. We've found some blood in the forest, and half-dug graves, but not one corpse we've found."

"In other words, you don't know anything, but you think I do."

"Actually, I thought Mellow Holmes might have, but he clammed up. I want you to see this."

The car pulled up to the side of the forest trail, blocked by police caution tape as well as other vehicles and wandering cops. It was about as busy as Matthew figured it would be, though there weren't as many officers as he thought. Matthew unbuckled his seat-belt when the detective stopped him from moving.

"What's wrong?" Matthew asked.

"You don't hear that?"

As if the weather were waiting for his word, a heavy downpour pounded down onto the world. Streaks of hard rain blocked the forest view in a haze of meaty drops. Matthew leaned back into his seat, and waited for detective to say something. The air in the car grew heavy.

A sudden prickling in the back of his neck brought Matthew's attention to the forest outside his window. Though he couldn't see anything, a harsh buzz like a fat bee floated in his thoughts. Matthew squinted through the water-streaked window into the storm. Nothing but rain and trees waited out there. His sixth sense was warning him. What it was trying to warn him *of* was unclear.

The light tapping of rain doused the world for only a mere five seconds before it tapered off. Once it finished, the two got out of the car. Thunder roared in the distance.

"That, I did not see coming," the detective said. He removed a cigarette from his pocket, and lit it up. "I thought the storm would pass over. The humidity was already making it hard to breathe."

Matthew glanced out into the trees. He couldn't see anything out of the ordinary, but a feeling told him that he was being watched. He needed to ditch the detective to see for himself. "Detective Leclerc, I already told you I don't know anything about Burner or his gang. Why do you insist on dragging me into this?"

"I'm not dragging you into anything." The detective took a long drag. "Luke and Scott Bartlett are squeaky clean nobodies from the south. They don't have so much as a parking ticket to their name and they have no relatives. An interesting *famille*, these Bartletts."

Did the detective figure it out? Matthew didn't let his nerves show. "My family really isn't that interesting, Frenchman. You're really begging the question of who we are, here."

"You've misunderstood me, Monsieur Bartlett." He flicked aside, and stared after it wistfully. "I come from Montreal. Not sure if you've ever been. Construction unions have caused problems going back decades. When Primes appeared that made it worse. Reconstruction was a business, as was hiring mercenaries and the like to invent problems, and to fix them. The madness went on and on. Those unions especially had it out for Detective Serge Leclerc. I was transferred many times, even suspended. But I kept arresting them. *Je suis fatigué*. Tiring work."

"Cities are never going to change, I guess," Matthew said. "Is that why you're in Riverview?"

"Precisely, my friend. I am here because I dig where they don't want me to dig, so I know a thing or two about secrets. I also know a thing or two about witness protection."

The tingling in the back of Matthew's brain returned. Was it being caused by this guy, or was it from whatever was out there? "Could you get to the point, Detective? I don't want to be out here all day."

"These people who came to *my* town —are they related to you? Do you know them?"

"I don't know who they are."

The portly figure of Detective Serge Leclerc nodded. He didn't ask why Matthew didn't answer the first question. "Are my people in danger?"

"From what I can guess, these new guys wanted something Burner had, so they came and took it from him and salted the ground. This was a Prime thing, I'd guess."

"I don't suppose we will find any corpses elsewhere then." It wasn't a question. The Detective stroked his uncombed hair. "Burner's men were scum, but this event has left me uneasy. I'm going to find who did this, and they're all going behind bars. They will tell me everything. Is that okay with you, Monsieur *Bartlett*?"

"Do what you have to, Detective. I don't know anything about them, except that if they took down Burner and his guys they must be strong Primes."

"Primes think they are all invincible, but they are nothing but bluster once you get under the surface. Glass cannons."

"Have you ever heard of a Prime named Suicide, Detective?"

He paused. "That's a rumor in the underworld. One touch and he can destroy your mind. From what I recall he disappeared years ago. I haven't heard the name since I left Montreal."

"Maybe he didn't disappear."

The Detective opened his mouth as if to say something when his radio blasted out a sharp stab of static. He climbed back into his car to answer the incoming call.

Matthew took in the view of the dock from last night, at least what he could see through the trees. Everything that wasn't black ash or charred tree trunks was being combed through by dark garbed cops slapping mosquitoes off themselves. Some officers slipped on the banks. The humidity hadn't broken yet, the rain just made the terrain difficult to traverse. None of them would find anything.

Matthew wanted to tell the detective about Suicide, but the truth was that he knew almost nothing about him. He only knew about Nieto, and the type of men that would follow him wouldn't be the type that would care about icing competition. Burner just got in Suicide's way.

A swirl of nausea gripped him, and his vision tilted. Matthew gripped the side of the cop car and felt his insides begging to be outside.

"Hey!" the Detective said. Matthew turned to meet him. "Your face is green."

"It's fine." Matthew choked back what was pushing itself out. The Detective was pale white. "You look worse than I feel. What's up?"

"Someone attacked Docteur Taylor at the pharmacy, and I bet I know who. This might be the lead I need. Get in. I will take you home."

The car spun around and blazed back in the direction it came. Matthew's stomach flipped, and he held his mouth as they whipped through the green. Detective Leclerc went on about something, but he could hardly concentrate on any of it. Visions of rotting flesh returned to his mind.

When they approached the river where Matthew was rescued last night, he finally had enough. He pestered the detective to pull over.

"What's wrong?" Detective Leclerc asked. He parked on the side of the road and let Matthew out. "Don't get sick in the car!"

Matthew fell out of the vehicle and to his knees. His stomach churned and he bent over, allowing himself to vomit. Pictures of the dead flashed inside his mind. Thunder cracked above him. Matthew's fingers bore into the dirt with the pain.

"Are you alright?" the Detective yelled from behind him.

He wasn't, but Matthew couldn't tell this cop the truth. He watched Ordopha, Jason, Lynn, and Zelana, all die before him—however, now they were being murdered by *his* hands. Matthew watched himself stalk them with mad glee in his eyes as he crushed them beneath his boot heel. The dreams were now invading his waking hours. He tried to stand up, but his legs just weren't having it.

"Go on without me, Detective," Matthew said. He wiped his mouth, and fought of a gag. "If I stay with you I can't promise I won't throw up in your car."

"I have to get to the pharmacy. It's going to rain again. Are you sure you will be okay, Monsieur?"

"I'll be as fine as I can be. Good luck, Detective."

Finally, the car spun off down the road towards town. Within seconds the Detective disappeared into the trees and the sound of the engine was a distant memory, its rumble replaced with the oncoming storm. It was a two minute drive for him to get back to town—that translated for a lot longer of a walk for Matthew, but he would put up with it. His stomach growled, and he winced.

He turned around and more sickness rose in his throat. He braced himself on his knees.

When the queasiness subsided, Matthew stood tall. It could have been fifteen minutes, or it could have been an hour, but he couldn't tell. Nonetheless, the clouds in his mind broke. Thunder growled closer. Matthew took a deep breath and stretched. Now for the long walk home. He lamented not taking an umbrella with him.

The buzzing returned in his mind, this time drifting to the front of his brain. He looked up towards the river, at the same spot where he pulled Jason out. There, a giant man wearing a large blue robe overlooked the water. The noise in his head pitched louder as Matthew approached. This had to be the man following him.

Matthew stopped a good thirty feet behind the cloaked man. The hum in his head died out as he opened his mouth to speak. "That's a lot of clothing to be wearing in this weather. The rain isn't over yet and the mosquitoes are really biting. Need directions to town?"

"I'm exactly where I need to be, Castor." The robed man turned around to meet Matthew. "You look ill. Did my servant injure you badly?"

The face of the mystery man appeared through the hood of the robe. The familiar grey skin and short platinum hair gave way to an empty smile Matthew hadn't seen since he was last on Tyndarus. It was Rantan, one of Nieto's children, and one of the men who had hunted Matthew and Jason down.

"Is seeing me so disturbing, Castor? You must have thought me dead."

Jason had been the one to fight Rantan. The Earthwalker used his Prime power to change into animals and he became a giant earthen golem. The boy smashed him into pieces and left him as nothing more than dust in the wind. He was dead.

But as Matthew looked him up and down he realized that he wasn't quite the same Rantan they had defeated. This man had a spider web of black cracks across his chalk white face leading to his right eye. That red eye shone like stain glass with an unsettling mixture of red, green, black, and blue, in the iris. It was as if he had been plastered together from scraps.

"You're supposed to be dead," Matthew said. "You and your brother."

"Do not speak of *him*. Tell me where my sister Zelana is. I wish to pay her my respects."

"We left her on Tyndarus, where you should be. How did you get here? Are your other siblings here, too? Escape from certain death must run in the family."

Rantan bared his teeth and the fissures on his face deepened, the black lines looking more like markings matching his popping veins. Matthew involuntarily took a step backwards. He had never seen the hedonist pig show any expression other than a grin before.

"Don't ever mention them in my presence, worm. I am here to set things right. You, Pollux, and the girl, will be returning with me to Tyndarus. You have this one opportunity to set things right again peacefully. Face your fate, and come with me back into the Mirror Gate."

The sky flashed with lightning and grumbled, and sweat dripped down Matthew's legs. The queasiness and unending headache thumped in the back of his brain. This wasn't the time for a scuffle, but if he had to knock this monster out, he would do it.

"I already rejected that fate once before."

"Yes, when you killed my mother. My father's hold has weakened tremendously on this world due to your interference. His puppets are tearing each other apart and declaring themselves his new prophets. It's all juvenile, but I have decided to step in and put order to it. Your meddling ends now. The Harbinger will not wait for you to cease being a coward, Castor."

"Who is a coward? You attacked me and brought me to an alien planet off in some distant galaxy. I never asked for that."

"You made the contract; therefore your options are forfeit."

"Is legalism your argument? No court would take the word of mad alien with a god complex."

"Whether you were deceived or not is irrelevant to the point. You came to our world, learned your place in the grand scheme of my father's future, and fled. It is laughable! I stand by my assessment: you are a coward. You didn't stand and fight, *boy*."

Matthew growled. Normally that word wouldn't bother him, but coming from a ponce like Rantan made it sting twice as hard. Droplets of rain pattered against his shoulders.

"This is why your moron troop keeps following me," Matthew said. "Is that right? You won't stop until you drag me back to your hell world and turn me into a meal for your master. Well, that won't happen, Rantan. I'm never going back there."

The downpour burst from the clouds above, dousing them as they watched each other. Rantan threw back his robes and presented his grey bare arms underneath. Cracks filled his skin as much as his face. Matthew assumed he must have received these back when he pulled himself together after Jason killed him. It looked like Matthew would have to be the one to finish what that kid started.

Matthew brought his hands up into a fighting stance.

Rantan shook his head. "As I said, you are a coward."

The rain made his movement heavy and sluggish, but still Matthew's leg muscles pumped for all they were worth. Mud slid under his shoes as he jammed his fist forward. The water-soaked smile of Rantan twisted as Matthew fell upon him.

Matthew cracked Rantan's jaw, sending the bigger man spinning. They exchanged punches, but neither fighter would give an inch even as blood trickled from their lips. Rantan jumped forward with a head-butt that struck against Matthew's right eye. The fading pain in Matthew's mind flared up again, causing an ear-splitting ringing in his brain. Matthew clutched his head as those familiar visions of death and destruction returned, and his stomach bubbled again. Rantan took advantage of Matthew's blurred vision, his punches throwing him down to the ground. A weight slammed down on the back of Matthew's head—it felt like Rantan's boot. Try as Matthew might, he could not rise.

The hard weight of the rain plastered him down like cement blocks tied around his limbs. His head beat like a snare drum.

In his mind he threw Ordopha to the ground and brought his fist down on her. The terrified look she gave him twisted like a dagger in his soul. Vomit pushed its way out of his mouth in the real world.

Rantan's boot shoved Matthew's face down into the mud where water pooled in the rain and shot up his nostrils. "Suicide's power reveals the true you, Castor. What exactly are you seeing?"

"*Liar*," Matthew said. That couldn't be the truth. There was no way Matthew could ever do this to anyone, especially Ordopha. "You're lying again."

"As if a coward would know anything about that which I speak. Who are you killing, Castor? I hope it is that woman from Tyndarus—the one that shot my sister with the arrow. She wasn't my type, if I recall correctly—too small and thin. But I'm glad I didn't kill her if only for this moment."

The power down inside of Matthew pulsated, but he couldn't quite touch it. His mind shook—his lack of concentration wouldn't allow him to reach out to anything. So instead he pleaded.

"*Please, give it to me*," Mathew whispered.

A ripple of heat swam through his bones. The water beating into his skin no longer pushed him down but merged into his thoughts and body, becoming one with him. Matthew darted forward to his knees, and shoved Rantan off of him. Castor spoke to him through the haze of mutilation and gore playing inside his mind. He glared at Rantan who merely grinned back at him. Castor would wipe that freak's smile off his broken face.

Matthew took one step forward, and a heavy weight struck the back of his skull. The world flipped upside down, and he landed in the mud. A paralyzing sting of genocidal thoughts crippled his mind from thinking of anything else.

"That took too long," Suicide said.

Rantan laughed, still staring at the prone form of Matthew. "It was much too fun to stop. Speaking of fun, what are you doing here?"

"We have the girl. Pretty sure she's your sister—Erin's having problems holding her."

"Excellent. Then there is only one fool left."

Matthew would have objected if he had stayed awake long enough to do so. Instead his mind drifted off to slumber as the rain washed the world around him. Eventually even the cracks of thunder melted into the void inside his mind where he killed Lynn for the four hundredth and thirty-third time.

Suicide whispered into his ear. "Have you gotten used to the screams yet? Listen to them long enough and they go from being foreign, to being a part of your very being. Soon enough, you will learn to love it. This *is* joy, Castor."

The horrified wails of the dead carried Matthew into hell. Their moans became as indistinguishable as his own cries in the dark. They all swirled together in a tornado of damned souls screaming for relief that would never come. Nothing remained but constant agony and a future of infected thoughts with no hope of escape. Only the never-ending death and pain remained.

Somewhere the rain circled the drain, and left him alone in the dark with nothing but his own thoughts to drag him further into the pit. His misery left him nothing but a shell.

The dreadful reality of damnation was all he had left. He would never escape from his prison of blood and bone. There was nothing left but death.

CHAPTER 12
MIDNIGHT LIGHTNING

THE THUNDER broke Jason's trance. He opened his eyes in time to see bright lightning flashing outside his bedroom blinds. Heavy droplets struck the glass with such a force that he could hear them rumbling the house itself. The storm growled in the dark of the night, momentarily knocking his thoughts away from the carnage inside his waking brain.

The first thing that amazed him was that he could stand without issue. The crushing pressure on his head had been released, and his bones no longer ached when he moved. Had the sickness finally departed? He checked to find he was still wearing the clothes he put on earlier that morning. Apparently he hadn't dreamed those moments with Lynn or Zelana.

How long had he slept? His mind spun in wheels, struggling to understand what had happened. That was when he remembered it was the night before. Had he really been out for a whole day?

Jason went for the light switch, but it flicked uselessly into the on position. The room remained dark. He tried it a few more times to no avail. The power had been knocked out.

He stretched, unable to understand where the pain had gone aside from his stiff bones. Jason moved out into the hallway, lightning casting white flashes and black shadows across the narrow hallway. The house remained dead quiet aside from the endless splashing of rain.

Matthew's room was empty, but it did allow Jason to check the clock. It was only seven at night. How heavy were the clouds outside to make it this dark? He headed for the kitchen.

The thick rain made visibility outside the blinds impossible, but Jason still couldn't make out anything in their small backyard. This storm didn't want anyone outside.

The kitchen was as vacant as the rest of the house. Matthew had not left him anything to indicate where he went. Jason sat at the table. He listened to the endless beating of heavy water outside the walls as he strained his half-asleep brain to think of his next move.

Out of the corner of his eye he became vaguely aware of a red flashing light in the nearby living room. The phone! Why hadn't he noticed it before? Jason scratched his head. Everything was moving so slow inside his creaking brain.

It was an old school answering machine. A small ancient cassette sat in a small brown box with a playback button on the front. Nobody used these anymore, but Matthew insisted on it for convenience sake, especially since their address was unlisted. He was convinced they wouldn't get many calls, so what was the point of getting anything more high-tech than this? The pawnshop owner agreed, of course. At least this thing ran off batteries, which meant Jason could still check it in this weather.

Jason crouched over the answering machine, trying to remember how it was used. Finally, his brain pointed him to the rewind and play button. He sighed at his own incompetence before clicking at the answering machine.

"*Good morning, Vermilion.*" Jason bit his lip at Suicide's voice. How long ago had this been sent? "*You've been sleeping for over twenty-four hours by this point. I hope you don't mind the interruption. Your number was unlisted, but your great friend Mellow found it for me. He's a good boy despite his . . . deficiencies. How are you feeling? Tired of the constant images of slaughter rolling around in your little head? Don't worry; I've lightened those up so you can get a few more winks. I can be a nice guy, you know.*"

It took a second to understand what this psycho was saying. Suicide had been the one screwing with his brain. If he could do this much damage to him, what could he have done with Matthew?

"*Your girlfriend has also come over to play. The guest room is getting packed. I suppose it's not so bad since we cleared out the former residents, but still.*" There was a good ten-second pause where Jason waited with bated breath. "*Just you, Vermilion. No friends, no wannabe heroes, and no cops. Come to the docks in Riverview this time—the ones south from the high school. I'll give you until noon because I don't think your body will be up to moving until then. Sorry, my powers can be a little rough. At least I can vaguely guess how tired they make others.*"

Jason clenched his fists. His body appeared to have already recovered ahead of time. Did Suicide not know this, or was there something else at play? Had Pollux finally returned? Did it hasten his recovery? Jason's mind couldn't quite process anything right now, which led him to allow Suicide to finish his message while the storm raged on outside.

"*Remember, only you have the invite. Zelana and Castor are waiting. It's been interesting dealing with you, but we have greater plans to tend to. See you in a few hours.*"

The message ended, and the machine clicked. Jason sat at the kitchen table and thought about what had been going on while he was asleep. The wheels in his brain finally turned as if the rust had been peeled off. Clarity returned to his mind.

Suicide appeared convinced Jason would be out until at least the morning. If that monster's power was so strong it must mean he had control over its intensity. The range and focus of it was so fine-tuned that it had put Jason out of commission for over a day. If it attached to multiple people like Matthew too, then it was an even worse ability than Jason imagined.

Wait, what about Lynn? Suicide didn't mention her. Jason's jumbled thoughts slowly centered. He would call her and wake her up. He had no clue what else he could do.

Jason found Lynn's number and rang her up. He waited for anyone to pick up, but it kept ringing. The rain cascaded harder as he stood there like an idiot.

The phone clicked. "*Matthew?*" Lynn asked.

"No," Jason said. "It's the shorter one. Where did you guys go? The last time I spoke to you everything was normal."

"*I thought it was, too.*" She said something else he couldn't make out. He thought he heard someone else's voice in the background. "*It's been a crazy day.*"

"You aren't at home, are you? Is Zelana there? I'm so lost."

"*Listen, Jason. Zelana and Matthew are missing. They went out this morning and never came back. I went out to look for them but got caught in the storm. I think I was being watched, too.*"

"I know," he said. "I got a message on the phone from Suicide. He has them. Where are you? We'll meet and talk. The power's out here. I can't see lights outside. Is it out all over town?"

She disappeared from the other end of the line. Very faintly, he heard whispers underneath the hard rain and static. Who was she with?

"*Go into my place and find my rain poncho in the closet by the front door. Put that on and be careful outside. We're at the movie theater. Come as soon as you can.*"

"Did you say *we're*?"

"*Not now.*"

"Alright, hang tight."

Jason hung up. The sharp prickling inside his mind had subsided for the first time in over a day. Suicide's hold really was loosening. The villain thought the teenager was out of the game. This was Jason's chance to act.

He slipped on his running shoes, lamenting that he never had the chance to buy better clothes for this sort of weather. Thankfully, the back porch had a roof that allowed him to walk outside unmolested by the rain. Too many of the more modern homes forsook porch roofs, if they even managed to have porches at all. Lynn's uncle was clearly someone who put a lot into his craft. Jason realized he didn't know that much about her. When he saw his neighbor again he would have to talk to her more. He had shrugged off too many people since coming here.

Lynn had fortunately left the backdoor unlocked, something she rarely did, which meant she must have exited in a hurry. He stepped inside, and that first impression only strengthened.

Unlike Jason's place, which was rather bare and hardly decorated, Lynn kept her home in order. She spent most of the daylight on the weekend cleaning, dusting, and washing her floors. Every time he had visited her, the family photos in the main hallway and the kitchen cabinets almost blinded him with the light reflecting from them. Jason associated Lynn's home with the scent of lemon cleaning products, because it always smelled fresh. It was no wonder she was agitated in their place.

But when Jason entered through the back, he found the opposite. Her kitchen drawers had been thrown across the room, and the cabinets left open with plates spilling out onto the counters. The kitchen table was actually upside down. Instantly Jason tensed as he stepped through the dark home with the rain masking his steps. An intruder had been through here.

The living room was no better. He inspected overturned furniture and shattered picture frames strewn across the floor. On the opposite wall, someone had used spray paint to spell out a crude message for her to find. It said, "*NO QUESTIONS. UNDERSTAND?*" in sloppy markings.

Jason stared at it for a minute, trying to process where this came from. Mellow had been following Jason for a while now, so why would Suicide's men not know where they lived? Why were they harassing Lynn? Perhaps Mellow kept some information close to his chest. That had to have been why they didn't bother going into the place next door to find Jason. Either way, Jason decided not to exit out her front door. The last thing he needed right now was to be recognized.

He stumbled his way to the closet by the front door. The flashes of lightning made visibility at least possible. He peeked into her bedroom and saw that it was also disheveled. A bit of crimson red marker stained the wall inside her room with small letters. He leaned in to get a closer look.

The graffiti read, "*M.R.P's pad. No tim.*"

These letters appeared to be written by someone other than the first set. Unlike the earlier threat, this looked like a clue. The author must have rushed it due to the missing last letter, though Jason had no idea what the initials represented. Difficult as it was to see in the dark, the message stuck in his mind. He just could not puzzle out its meaning.

The boy threw up his hands and went back for the raincoat. He could worry about all of this later. For now, he had to find his friends.

THE ROARING THUNDER snapped Matthew awake. The small humid room didn't let him see anything but grey walls, though his wrists being bound behind his back to a metal hook in the ground was the more pressing matter. This forced Matthew into an awkward bent pose with his face rubbing the floor. He sat backwards and his back cracked, sending out small waves of pleasure from his cramped position. It didn't distract from the handcuffs around his wrists. Constant sharp pain flowed through them as if tiny nails had been driven into his skin.

A lamp dangled above his head, casting hard orange beams across the small space. The heat sent sweat down his back and through his shirt. As if the humidity wasn't enough. The floor slightly tilted underneath him, and distant rumbling told him that the rainstorm still raged. Where had he been taken?

"You're awake," a female voice said.

To his left, leaning in the corner of the room, was a teenage girl. He recognized her from the warehouse as Suicide's lackey. She wore a damp white shirt and jeans, with her head against the wall. Her skin was an odd shade of green bordering on yellow, and her eyes were glazed over. Still, she had a slight grin on her face.

"I wanted to see your face when you woke up," she croaked.

The ropes behind Matthew made a grinding noise as he forced himself forward. It was only when they clanked that he understood they weren't ropes—they were chains. His captors didn't want him to leave.

"Your name is Erin, right? What are you doing with Suicide? You do understand what he is, right? He's going to kill you when he has no more use for you."

"Not my bro. He knows I have value —no one can do what I can. You, though, you're just a weapon. He's gonna beat you into shape until you know your place."

"He's already killed enough people, Erin. You're responsible for helping him do this."

"Don't lecture me. I tried. I tried so many times to stop people like you from hurting yourselves. You all want to kill each other, and I'm going to let you. There's nothing left but the end. It's only a matter of when, and I'm making sure it isn't anytime soon."

The girl was babbling at this point. He couldn't talk sense into her. Matthew instead tried to focus on Castor, his one ace in the hole, but reaching that latent power was tough with the constant agony running through his wrists. His eyes shut; he waded through the deep pit in his soul, searching for anything resembling that hidden strength. Embers of Castor waited at the bottom of the well, but remained just out of reach. Nonetheless, he leaned forward as if hoping to touch it.

That was when the door flew open. The wood slab narrowly avoided striking his head and instead bashed against the wall before Erin. She didn't move at the overly energetic entrance. Hard white light beams from the hallway filled the room. A dark figure masked in the brightness stepped into the room, shutting the door behind him. Matthew could not see who it was.

"Where did you take me?" he asked the figure.

In response, the shadow kicked Matthew in the chest. The prisoner gagged and fell backwards; his bonds prevented him from fully falling to the floor. Erin giggled. Matthew hung sideways, attempting to sit back up. Another kick sent him down once more.

The figure yawned. "That was a pretty good nap. Don't spoil it for me, Castor."

"Suicide," Matthew said between breaths. "What is your game in all this? Don't you understand what Nieto is going to do when he comes to Earth? That's why we left Tyndarus. He can't get the power of the Gemini Man."

"I allow myself forty winks and let my hold over you and your friend slacken, and this is all you have to offer me?" Suicide kicked

Matthew again. It was hard to see, but Matthew was certain the creep was smiling. "We barely know each other, but I was sure you'd have gotten it by now. The Master was right. You are a coward."

Matthew spat saliva across the floor. "Rantan is your Master? I thought it was Nieto."

"You can serve two masters, especially when one offers more than the other. It isn't as if their goals are different. But since one has lost communication with me, I've leaned harder on the other. It doesn't matter. None of this does. Erin, get back to your room."

The teenage girl wobbled as she stood and pushed her way back out into the hall. Matthew tried to imagine what hold he had over her, but it made no sense. This punk valued nothing and no one.

"Are you trying to get Earth destroyed?" Matthew asked. "Are you *that* much of a psycho?"

Suicide punched Matthew across the face. He reeled with the strike. "Are you done asking stupid questions?"

"There's nothing stupid about asking why someone wants to wipe out their own planet. Do you want Nieto to win? Why? What do you have to gain?"

"I only live for one thing, Castor. Moments like this." Suicide punched him again, and warm blood trickled from Matthew's nose. "That border between misery and oblivion is exciting and oh-so-very thin."

"If you let Nieto have us, it's going to be a whole lot worse than misery that takes Earth."

"I hope so!" Suicide roared. His voice was coated in poison, holding back either a laugh or a horrified yell. Matthew still couldn't see his attacker through the bright light shining directly over his head. Suicide kicked him again and again. "Get under the boot, worm. That's all you're good for!"

Matthew choked out more saliva. "You *are* crazy."

"No, I'm not. I understand humanity's fate better than you. All the Master is going to do is speed up the process of decay, then he can travel to other worlds to do it again and again. Forever and ever. There are entire alien worlds out there that can use the crushing despair we can deliver them—places like the planet that Zelana girl comes from. We have her, too. She's also going to the Master."

Matthew shook the pain from his thoughts. They found Zelana, but Suicide didn't say anything about Jason. What had happened while he was out? "She's here?"

"That's not what I said. We're keeping the two of you separate until Vermilion gets the message I left him. He should be up around six in the morning if my calculations are right. We would have just gone to pick him up, but we can't find your address and we obviously can't use Burner's connections to find it. Our one lead appears to have run away. No matter, Vermilion will have no choice but to come here on his own."

"I guess I can't talk any sense into you, Suicide. I've already dealt with a bunch of Nieto's cronies before, but you're on a whole other level of delusion. I don't want to kill you."

The shadowy form of Suicide bent down until his face was right before Matthew's, bathed in orange light. Suicide's eyes looked like black pools masked by the heavy light above him. "I hope you do."

Before Matthew could question the insanity, Suicide's right hand fastened around his throat. Waves of green sickness flooded Matthew's mind, casting visions of mutilated innocents and horrific death and disease into his brain. He watched Suicide stomp Lynn dead in her own house. She called out for help, but no one ever came. Ordopha's entire planet burned to ash. Matthew felt the bile rise to his throat at the same moment that familiar weight crushed into his head.

Matthew fell forward, the chains holding him still. Suicide backed up into the darkness as the void pulled the prisoner back into sleep. The hold fastened stronger around his mind.

"*I hope you do,*" Suicide repeated.

That was the last thing Matthew remembered before he plunged into the pool of despair once more. He could do nothing but watch his loved ones murdered as a voice at the back of his thoughts reassured him that this was the way it should be.

The hollow laugh of Suicide filled the small, humid space. It pierced into Matthew as he sunk back into his slumber, certain he would never find his way out again.

JASON DIDN'T think anyone was following, but that didn't stop him from glancing over his shoulder in the rain soaked night multiple times. Despite the yellow raincoat and the umbrella, the boy still felt the weight of the water beating down upon him. Not only that, but his lack of boots meant the rain bouncing half a foot of the sidewalk still soaked his feet and shins. At least the humidity appeared to have been blown out by the storm, but that was of little comfort. Little was visible in the downpour as he walked the main roads.

The teenager trudged through the night, unaware of how long any of this was taking him. For the first time Jason wished he had begged Matthew for a phone, or perhaps a part-time job to get one himself. Anything would have been better than walking through this storm alone and without a clue. The buzzing of the rain in his ears didn't help the irritation that was setting in. The streets might have been empty, but it still felt as if he were taking hours to get anywhere.

Despite the endless slog, a voice inside the cracks of his mind told him he was going the right way. Jason didn't have Matthew's sixth sense, but he didn't believe that had anything to do with his sure footing. The teenager had walked these streets so many times despite only being in Riverview for a few of weeks that it had become second nature. Had he adjusted to the town, or had it spoken to him on another level? As absurd as it sounded, Jason didn't feel like a simple tourist at that moment. He belonged on these streets.

Eventually, his feet carried him by familiar brick buildings on his left and right. Though details were hard to make it in the blur of falling water, Jason soon traced his path to the movie theater. He recognized the shut box office where days ago he had bought a ticket. Jason tried the door to find it locked. He didn't expect a different result but he would need to find an alternate way inside.

The boy ran his fingers along the rain soaked building. He vaguely remembered the alleyway on the side of the theater. Jason soon found the gap and slipped through it towards the back.

However, even though it was just an alley, he could barely see. Slowly Jason moved until he found the back of the building. He swung around into yet more downpour and an open space he figured had to be the parking lot.

His fingers found a metal railing and some stairs on his left. This could only be the rear entrance. He huffed up the steps, pushing through the beating rainfall.

At the top, he found a solid door. He tried the knob to find it locked, and then knocked. A sinking pit in his stomach questioned what he would do if he couldn't get in here, but he didn't have to ponder long. The door opened, and a woman stood there holding a battery-powered lamp.

"Get in!" she said.

Jason launched himself through the opening, and it shut tight behind him. He wiped his eyes and shook his head as the stranger he could barely see removed his rain poncho for him. The boy let her take it and he removed his soaked shoes and socks.

"Go get yourself cleaned up in the bathroom," the familiar voice said from behind him. "I'll take care of your clothes. Don't want you getting sick."

"Thanks," Jason said. He thought he recognized her—she was the woman who owned the theater. This was the same woman Mellow yelled at the night Jason met Suicide. The young woman wore jeans and a white shirt, and her glasses sat on top of her brunette hair. "You're Kat, right? Where is Lynn? Is she alright?"

"I'm surprised you know my name. She's in the living room with the others. We've been expecting you. First, focus on yourself. You don't want to get sick, do you? Leave your clothes outside the bathroom and I'll wash them. When you're done getting clean, I'll put them out for you, fresh as ever." She directed him down the hall. "My full name is Katrina, by the way."

Jason stumbled into the bathroom, barely able to see anything. He felt around and found a battery-powered lamp by the sink and turned it on. The light broke the small migraine forming in his mind. He removed his sticky clothes and bent around the door-frame, where someone took them from his hands. The door closed, he turned on the shower.

In the mirror above the sink he saw something odd—his skin was covered in bright red welts as if he had been pelted with heavy and sharp rocks. The crimson bruises dotted him all over, but they didn't hurt. He'd felt worse before.

Jason climbed into the shower to forget about all of it. The hot water instantly beat down upon his skin, and allowed his mind a sense of relief as steam cooked him lightly. The longer he stood there and allowed the shower water to strike him the more the heavy weight lightened. Slowly he scrubbed himself clean as the deepest parts of his mind thanked him for the dousing.

The shell in his mind peeled like a crust breaking apart around a scab. Cool waves of relief stirred with the raw thumping of a headache in his numb body. The sensation in his skin and muscles returned as he cleaned himself, but as he did so he remembered other unpleasant things.

"*Goodbye, Jason,*" his mother had said.

She had spoken to him so many times since her death last summer. Had it already been a year? So many times he had woken up and forgot she was there in his dreams with him. But now she was gone. The powers that kept her tied to this plain had run out.

He let the water crash down on him as his mind worked. What did she say? Why couldn't he remember most of his dreams? Zelana and Matthew were at risk, and he was the only one who could do anything, yet here he was being useless. Thoughts, doubts, and fears, twisted like a tornado. He had screwed up so many times over the past year. How could one teenager be so clueless?

Jason lightly pounded the wall with his fist, and the whole room shook.

"Easy in there!" Kat said from outside the door. "Just turn it down if it's too hot! My husband isn't going to want to patch this place so soon after we got it the way we wanted."

That was the moment Jason noticed his skin pruning. He had been in there for too long.

Finally he turned off the shower and dried up. Outside the door he peeked and found a set of clothes lying in plain view by the threshold. It was a pair of black slacks and matching polo shirt. Kat's husband's clothes, no doubt.

They were slightly too big for him width-wise, but at least they fit. Jason cleaned up after himself and traversed the darkened hall towards the living room. Voices were already chattering when he got there.

"It's about time, kid," Burner said. "We can't wait all night."

Jason's heart nearly jumped out of his chest. Sitting on the couch was the very gang leader he thought dead. Burner wore jeans and a slightly wrinkled black t-shirt with a bandage wrapped around his right arm. Next to him was another man with black jeans and a blue muscle shirt. He looked like the man that Matthew described when he was attacked in their home.

"Burner!" Jason said. He put up his fists. "I've been waiting for this."

"It's too late for your posturing. Sit down and shut up."

"Big talk for someone who went into hiding."

"I couldn't even get my clothes at the hideout, kid. No shirts, not even my best shoes. I don't even have my lucky pocket knife. All I've got are the clothes we swiped off a clothesline."

"Always a thief, I see."

"Easy!" Lynn stepped out of the kitchen, holding a mug of what smelled like orange juice. "Burner and Boon are on our side. Though Boon still owes me an apology."

"I do?" the man with the sandy hair and scarred face said. "For what?"

"You called me a bitch."

"I don't even remember seeing you before tonight, lady."

Kat sat in the seat opposite the pair in the corner of the room. Lynn had a chair from the kitchen she used, though she did not look too comfortable as she glared at Boon.

"Fine, be that way." Lynn sighed. "Anyway, Jason, you better listen to this. Burner is the one who approached me today when he saw me around town asking questions."

Jason remained by the hall's archway, and folded his arms. "You're the one who brought Suicide to Riverview. Don't think I didn't know it was you."

"Spare me the headstrong bravado, boy." Burner didn't bother to look at Jason. He continued to stare at the cup before him on the coffee table. "The important part in all of this is that they're all dead. Page, Schwartz, Ronnie, Gill, and Michaels . . . all my men."

"The police said there were no bodies near the forest," Lynn said. "I asked. No proof that anything happened. They wouldn't even search for Matthew because they couldn't find any motive for his disappearance or clue that he was in trouble."

"There are two Primes with Suicide," Burner said. He still refused to look at anyone as he spoke. "One takes control of others by touch. The other is a tree-hugger with some sort of earth powers. He's the enforcer. The first one took control of Cartwright. Between the two of them you're never going to find the people they killed. All fourteen of my guys are gone, except for Boon. We only made it out because Boon has sharp eyes—the rest were stabbed in the back. That's how Suicide works."

"Start from the beginning," Jason said. "Who is Suicide, and what does he have to do with you? You are the one who called him here, aren't you?"

"No." Burner's sturdy tone left no doubt in what he meant. "He invited himself in."

Burner went on to describe his connection in the underworld of Serenity City, a man named Dobbs. This information broker had always let them know about scores and fugitives that found their way outside the city limits and up north. Even though the bounty for Matthew White and Jason McCrae was canceled due to their supposed deaths in the Williams' Tech Corp. disaster, Dobbs received a tip that they might still have value if found alive. Unfortunately, someone else with good ears was listening in to Dobbs' racket. That was the man named Suicide.

"I don't know what Suicide wants with two worthless dead fugitives," Burner continued. "It's not just money. He has some sort of grudge that goes beyond taking you in. Maybe he knew someone in Williams' Tech when it went down? I don't know, but I hear Williams himself woke up from his coma, and they are in the process of dealing with a government investigation. The casualties, as far as I know, were all higher-level types in the upper floors."

Jason was starting to get it. "Williams' Tech was a cover for Suicide's boss and his wife. Without control over it, the place is useless to them."

"Be that as it may, this guy still has it out for you. Whatever you did in that building, perhaps it involved killing someone he cared about. Either way, this feels like a personal grudge."

Jason knew Suicide had no such noble intentions of revenge. Nieto had zoomed in on someone scrounging for loose change like Dobbs, and used the guy to find the pair. Given that Suicide silenced everyone along the way, he must be keeping Castor and Pollux a secret. Nieto wanted the world to think they were dead. Suicide would take out anyone in his way from Mellow Holmes to Burner if his Master willed it. He was no different than Bloodeater in that respect.

The realization sent an icy chill dripping down Jason's back. Everyone in Riverview was at risk. He couldn't just hide out in town hoping the problem would go away. Jason had a small window to stop Suicide, and he needed to do it before the monster realized Jason was awake.

"Whoever Suicide is doesn't matter," Jason said. Thunder cracked outside, but only Kat flinched. Jason rubbed his sore ears. "This is our chance to strike before he knows what hit him. He has two people important to me, and I'm going to get them back. Do you know where he's hiding?"

"I can guess." Burner took a sip of his coffee. "I have a yacht under Bernard's real name at the large harbor. He probably ripped that info out of Cartwright's head. Obviously, we can't get there in this weather, but when the rain lightens up, I'm going to move in."

"That's not bad, but I'm not sure it's right," Jason said.

Boon sneered. "You doubting Burner's word? He didn't have to tell you any of that, brat."

"It has nothing to do with doubt. You guys must not know what they did to Lynn's place."

Jason went on to describe his trip into his neighbor's house. She visibly paled as he described the upturned state of the place, and even Kat had to reassure her that the assailants left hours ago. But all four of them perked up when Jason mentioned the odd message scrawled in her room.

Burner spoke first. "That's an address. It's Cartwright's uncle's place on Fuller Avenue. He has a place in Riverview several blocks away from here."

"It's only streets away from our house, Jason!" Lynn said. "It's going to be right in the center of the block party tomorrow. That is, if it hasn't been canceled due to this weather."

"Yes!" Boon cracked his knuckles. "We've got an address. I've been dying to get some licks on them punks."

"Whoa!" Kat interrupted. "There's going to be a lot of people out there tomorrow. It's a big day for Riverview. Think carefully here. You don't want innocents getting hurt."

Burner cleared his throat. "The other side of it is that it could be a trap. They might have been trying to lure Lynn to the address. They were threatening her with those other messages."

Jason let out a hard breath. They were both right, but he still had to make a decision. There were two different locations of interest, and just as many missing people. Suicide was a tricky piece of garbage, and not one that would make this easy. With the storm raging on, they would have to wait until the morning to even make their move regardless of what they chose to do. Jason needed a plan that could help them all move without being put in too much danger. After careful consideration, he thought one up.

"We can move easier in a crowd," he said. "The block party officially starts at six, right? How long does it take to get busy?"

Lynn furrowed her brow. "Around nine. The streets get filled fast about then. Not to mention that carnival rides by the Ultramart mini-mall start up. The little kids make it very noisy quickly. I think the O'Rourke family is planning some sort of stage-based trivia game on St. Hubert Street, so that's going to get noisy, too. Fuller Avenue is the street right before it. This is all assuming the weather clears by the morning. Are you planning something, Jason?"

"Always." He grinned. Now he knew how to act. "We're going to slip into the crowd and casually inspect the address we were given. If we see anything suspicious, then we can consider acting on it. If not, then we can check out the yacht. I take it the harbor gets busy, too."

Kat nodded. "They have a big race planned for tomorrow afternoon. Riverview has really been leaning into August in the last few years as their big summer month. That's where Dale, my husband, has been—doing a last sweep of the racecourse. Hopefully, the storm didn't do too much damage. He'll be out there all day tomorrow."

"Dale's a sturdy guy," Lynn said. "You can depend on him."

Kat rolled her eyes. "You'd know."

"What do you mean?" Jason asked.

"I, well, used to go out with Dale." Lynn blushed. "It was a few years ago."

"It's not every day that your sister tries to steal your man," Kat said. "You'd be surprised how popular Lynn is with the guys. They called her a tease in high school. She never went far, though."

"Kat!"

"Wait," Jason interrupted. "You're sisters?"

The two women stared at Jason, then each other. They let out a small shared laugh.

"I'm the stable one," Kat said. "Lynn's never been reliable. She's the one that liked to go out and party, while I would stay home. That's why this whole situation has been odd. It's not like her."

Lynn's cheeks reddened again. She waved it off. "Shut up. He doesn't need to hear this."

"Anyway," Boon said. "We'll wait for the rain to lighten. Once the people start showing up for their little fair, we'll sneak in. I'll take the park area with Burner. We can watch from cover since we're supposed to be dead. You lot can take the busier area with all the houses where all this silly family nonsense is going on. You're less likely to stand out than we are."

Burner interrupted as if he didn't hear his ally. "Listen up, kid. I have a score to settle with Suicide, so I'm only going to go wherever he is. Don't expect me to help you if you get in a tight spot."

"I didn't expect anything from you, anyway." Jason stared into the deep pits that were Burner's eyes. It looked as if he stared through the boy into some other dimension. "I want to stop him, too, but my goal is to save my friends. Keep in mind that if I have the option to save them over stopping him, I'm going to take it."

The two watched each other in silence as if expecting their opponent to grow a third head out of their necks. Boon shook his head and stared out the window into the downpour while Lynn kept track of their back and forth.

Kat interrupted the standoff. "How about you two tough guys go to your separate corners? We've got a ways to go before we can do anything, and the last thing I want is a fight. It took forever for Dale to remodel this place. The power being out doesn't help, either. I hope those trucks I heard earlier were out to fix the problem. Lynn, take Jason to the kitchen. I'll make sure these two stay put."

Lynn followed her sister's advice and led Jason out of the room. A small table awaited ahead, masked with the dancing black shadows of rainwater reflecting from the nearby window. The pair sat across from each other, Jason with his back to the wall.

The storm lightened at least slightly, though that might have been Jason's hope. He never minded rain much even when he was younger—there was a relaxing serenity to silence he couldn't fully appreciate when running to school functions or the community center. And right now Jason needed this silence more than ever.

Unfortunately, Lynn soon broke it.

"Can you do me a favor?" she asked. For some reason, she avoided looking directly at him. "We don't know each other that well, but I'd like to think we can trust each other."

He enjoyed the dance of rain for a few seconds before he responded. "What do you need?"

"Don't tell Matthew about what my sister said. She can be obnoxious, but she has a mouth."

"I don't think he'd care. Does he even know you have a sister? I didn't."

"We all grew up over in Pembroke. The next town over, if you didn't know. Matthew left with his parents when he was a kid. We moved here when my dad started to get sick and needed help running his apartments with my uncle. Don't think Matthew knew we were living here when he chose to move to Riverview. He probably wanted to avoid all of us." She ran a finger along the cracks in the table, still refusing to meet Jason's eyes. "He's such a clueless idiot."

"No, I'm the dumb one. Matthew takes things so seriously he develops tunnel vision. Like he has to carry the whole world on his shoulders all the time. It's pretty aggravating. Though I shouldn't talk since I'm the one who steered us into Suicide to begin with."

"You are a lot more alike than either of you would admit." She didn't say anything for a long time. "Matthew used to come back every summer, you know. I missed him and his parents, at first, but they always came back telling us stories of heroes and villains and the crazy things that happened in the big city. He was always smiling in those days. That was a long time ago. But then he stopped smiling, and then he stopped coming."

"That doesn't sound like him."

"His parents were obsessed with Primes, even after Achilles went on that rampage almost twenty years ago. But the more they got into it, the less Matthew did. They would come back every summer to visit the grandparents. By the time he was thirteen, Matthew had all but lost all interest in heroes. He never said why. But that wasn't the worst of it. Next summer he came alone—to his parents' funeral. They had both died of cancer, seemingly overnight. I tried to talk to him but he never opened up. At fourteen, he just disappeared back into the streets of Serenity City. I never saw him again. That was eight years ago."

"You never saw him again? But he contacted you when we came here."

"Well," Lynn said. She paused before continuing. "He sent me letters over the years. Very outdated way of operating, sure, but I appreciated it. I wrote back, but every time I talked about visiting he just never addressed the subject. I can't explain it, but it felt like he exiled himself from reality. I couldn't really tell you why. When he came back with you, that was when I saw something was different. He wasn't that same quiet kid I knew years ago. Though I couldn't have imagined he would have gotten involved in all this craziness."

"Trouble sticks to us like glue. Suicide, especially, is a whole other level of crazy." Jason remembered the psycho's words, still ringing in his ears. "He killed my parents, you know."

Lynn didn't reply. She simply reached over and put a hand over Jason's trembling fist.

"If Suicide thinks he's going to take my friends after he took my family, he's got another thing coming. All we ever do is run from these monsters. In the morning, that stops."

"Easy," Lynn whispered. "Remember Zelana and Matthew. We need to help them first. Suicide is not the first thing you need to think about. According to Burner, all of his men were killed by this man. We don't really know what he can do."

Jason let out a breath, and the shaking stopped. The morning would be hard to wait for. He had already lost everything once before—heck, so had both Matthew and Zelana—but he would not lose it again. And neither would they. Pollux had chosen him, and Jason would make it matter.

She smiled at him, and he just knew his cheeks reddened. He had only known her a short time, but he was beginning to like her. She reminded him of a big sister he never had. There wasn't much in the way of family left as it was. This whole time she threw herself into helping them and all she got for it was her life upturned. The rest of this mess was his to clean up.

"Was Kat telling the truth?" he asked. "Do you really go out partying all the time?"

"Oh, come on. Don't say it like that. I let guys take me out on dates because I like going out. Kat's implying things I would never do in a million years when she says things the way she does. All because I went out with Dale once when we were in tenth grade. She's always been spiteful."

He stifled a laugh. "Sounds like how you argue with Matthew."

"Maybe I'm more like Kat than I thought."

"You're not too bad, Lynn."

"Right. I'm worse."

They sat in the dark staring out into the storm for a long time. He couldn't see a clock, nor did he ask the time, but he didn't need to. His consciousness dipped in and out of slumber many times. Eventually the rain lightened and the sun peeked out through the blinds from the clouded horizon. The downpour dried up as sunrise pushed out the dying night. The power came back on and jarred him back awake. Lynn cheered and put coffee on, but Jason remained seated and thinking about what he needed to do next.

The clearing weather meant the block party was on after all. Now he was ready to go hunting.

CHAPTER 13
MORNING THUNDER

THE CROWD GATHERED earlier this year than last, at least according to Lynn, filling the streets of Riverview with hundreds of people. Some residents had already opened tables by the streets and stands by their houses, including flea markets, yard sales, and places to grab breakfast. For a mid-size town like this, it was quite busy.

Lynn whispered some random bits of trivia to him as the pair walked through the burgeoning morning crowd. The town had only been doing the block party for three years, and yet it already felt like a big event. It was only ten in the morning and yet dozens of families and younger guys with their girls perused the sidewalks. The crowds glanced at the wares on each table and the chatter grew louder with every passing moment. It really was a large-scale block party, the first Jason had ever seen. That would have been exciting in any other situation, but he had to push it to the back of his mind.

Lynn led Jason through the hundreds filling the streets. By noon there would be some sort of concert on Leacock Drive, the street running between Fuller Avenue and St. Hubert Street. Things would blow up soon enough. Until the scheduled time Suicide had given him, the group agreed to search the streets for any clues before sneaking into the house. Jason didn't like that. He had never been good at a stealth approach.

"Burner just went off on his own, huh?" Jason said. "Hope he doesn't screw everything up."

"I didn't think he'd help us, but he won't get in our way." Lynn tilted her over-sized straw hat over the exposed shoulders of the sundress she borrowed from her sister. "I didn't expect the storm to blow out the humidity so quickly. I feel like I'm dressed too light. How about you?"

Jason wore a red cap low over his eyes and, unfortunately, had to wear one of Kat's husband's muscle shirts with ugly horizontal green stripes on pale yellow. It ran past his waistband over his long black shorts. Other than his shoes and underwear he wore someone else's clothing, and might as well be someone else. At least he didn't look like Jason Vermilion.

"I smell something good," he said. "Is that barbecue?"

"The Frenettes cook a mean burger. I guess they're starting early this year. Hang on, my phone's going nuts."

Jason scanned the crowd. His jaw involuntarily gaped at the mass of people. Kids chasing each other, teenagers joking about, and adults gathering in groups to chat about trivial things. It all combined with the overwhelming murmur of the crowd, the scent of both prepared and cooked food, and the hundreds of bodies swerving through the streets both towards tables of goods for sale and for old friends and family members. Every passing moment was a new sight. What would his parents have thought about this? While his mind wandered, a finger tapped him on the shoulder.

"Are you okay?" Lynn asked. "I don't think it's too cold, but maybe you would have been better wearing an actual shirt."

He rolled his eyes. "I'm fine. Who was that on your phone?"

"It was Boon. He found your new friend Spencer. The kid was talking with his friends and just sort of ran off awkwardly. Boon thinks he might have seen something."

"Where is he? I'll go check."

"No, you won't." She sighed, breathing through her nostrils. "No one needs to know you're here, Jason. No diverting from the plan until we find Matthew or Zelana. Let's get to the house."

She had a point. As much as he was curious about what Spencer's deal was, it could very well be unrelated to all this. Jason and Lynn couldn't risk exposure yet, not when they were so close to the house.

Jason followed her through the crowds, his mind now focused on the path ahead, though a sharp regret held onto his mood. He wished his Mom and Dad could see this, and if it wasn't for Suicide, they would have.

The boy balled his fists and marched on. No one in this crowd would ever lose someone like he had. Jason Vermilion—Pollux—would make sure of it.

THE LONG NIGHT almost killed Mellow Holmes and he wished it had. Not only could he not go home, but hiding out in places Burner's men knew about was also not an option. Mellow could only stay in the old park—the abandoned place he had hung out in so many times when he was a stupid kid. He slept under the over-sized slide which allowed him plenty of room in the underneath gravel pit. He used his shirt as a pillow, and he couldn't help but toss and turn, praying not to be found.

Mellow marveled at the cooler weather. Puddles splotched around the empty park almost made him think he'd awoken in a swamp. He stretched, and climbed out towards the top of the slide. The rising murmur of voices streets away, beyond the thick tree line and unkempt greenery interrupted the singing of birds. It took a moment for him to remember today was the day of the block party.

He wouldn't be attending, not today and not ever again. Mellow Holmes had instead kept awake most of the night, considering places to run away to. His relatives were not on good terms with him, and they would most likely tell his parents where he was. He rubbed sleep from his aching eyes. Why did people have to be so petty?

Mellow sat at the top of the slide and glanced around the park. Water puddles, rusted monkey bars, overgrown trees and bushes, and those old creaking swings blowing in the breeze reminded him how old this place was. This park had been abandoned despite being so close to the center of town, and hadn't been cleaned properly in ages. No one could even see here from the surrounding houses, both because the brush was too thick and because the idiots were all at the block party. The last thing any of these chumps were doing was thinking about what this place meant to people like Mellow Holmes. Nobody ever thought, though. That is why they needed his protection: whether they understood it or not. Everything gets thrown away once it outlives usefulness, and that would never be him.

A breeze blew through his sore spine. He bent over, cupped both elbows in each hand, and winced. Sleeping outside in a storm certainly wasn't the smartest thing he'd ever done. The stuffiness of the air caused him to constantly cough. At least he was alive.

"*Hey!*" someone called.

Mellow peered through the treeline at an approaching figure. He lifted his legs to attempt a get away, but the stiffness refused him in his efforts. The figure left the shade of the brush and the shadows fell from him to reveal a familiar acquaintance.

"Spencer," Mellow said. He cleared his scratchy throat. "What are you doing out here?"

Spencer sprinted forward, dodging puddles, towards Mellow. The more muscular teenager wore his usual red shorts and matching t-shirt with his grey sneakers. He always looked ridiculous, and he didn't look any better today as he waved down Mellow. Spencer should have been at the block party with his gaggle of idiots, away from here. The last person Mellow wanted to see was this moron.

"Are you crazy?" Spencer asked. He stopped at the bottom of the slide to look up at his former friend. "I got a call from your parents. They were all kinds of freaked out because you disappeared on them. I said I'd try to find you. Did you really run away? Why?"

"Go back to the block party, Spencer. This has nothing to do with you. It hasn't in a long time."

"I've never had beef with you until you started insulting my friends and got in with those criminals. Everyone thinks you're part of that gang, but I always defended you. Did something happen with them? Some kind of inner feud?"

Mellow pinched the bridge of his nose in an attempt to chase off a growing migraine. "This has nothing to do with you, Spencer. Go home before you get hurt."

"Don't threaten me, Mellow."

"That wasn't a threat. That was a warning. Just go back and lie. Tell my folks I'll be home tonight after the fireworks. That should be simple enough for your slow brain, shouldn't it?"

"I'm not going to lie. Get off the slide. I'll bring you back myself."

A stab of rage caused Mellow to leap up to his feet. He looked down at Spencer, his teeth grinding. "Don't you do this now! Don't you pretend like you have any idea what's going on, you slow-witted troglodyte. When we were kids, we were going to change the world—fix the villains and put the heroes at the top. You ran away like a coward towards girls and sports and whatever other idiocy your stupid hormones dragged you into. Now that I'm so close to achieving what you abandoned you want to stop me? Who the hell do you think you are?"

Spencer simply stared back with his brow crinkled in obvious disbelief. "You're not a Prime, Mellow. There's nothing you can do about villains or criminals. Grow up."

The last two words caused the hairs on the back of Mellow's neck to stand up. He launched himself down the slide, skidding on both feet and balancing with his arms. Spencer watched Mellow blankly even as his old friend ran into him at full speed. The two tumbled to the ground in a pile of flailing limbs.

Mellow's fist found Spencer's face, and a geyser of joy erupted in his brain. He punched down again and again. It was caught short when Spencer gripped his wrists and spun him sideways. The two rolled along the ground until Mellow ended up underneath, pinned to the wet dirt. He roared and thrashed against Spencer's hold, but his enemy refused to let go.

"Get off me!" Mellow spat in Spencer's eye, but the bigger boy simply held tight. "This has nothing to do with you!"

"Stop saying that!" Spencer shouted. "Why does it have to have something to do with my life in order for me to do something about it? You tell me, stupid. Did this have anything to do with those Bartlett brothers? Did your friend Burner attack them? What happened at that warehouse?"

"Shut up!" A fit of rage allowed Mellow to free an arm. He elbowed Spencer in the face and the bigger boy rolled off of him. Mellow jumped up and put a short six foot distance between them. "You gave up on this a long time ago. We each made our choices, and that's that. You go back to your life, and I'll go back to mine."

"That's not how it works." Spencer rubbed his bruised cheek. "I'm the idiot? You're the one acting like it's all or nothing. We're just teenagers, Mellow. We still have years to be dumb. Just because you made a bad call it doesn't mean it's over. Sure, I screwed up. I didn't see how far down this rabbit hole you tumbled down. But we can fix it together. Let's go back to your parents and put this behind us. You don't need to play this game anymore."

"It's too late," Mellow said, more out of reflex than any belief. His emotions dared him to leap at Spencer again and pound him into the dirt, even if it ended with him hurt worse. This is who Mellow Holmes was now, and it was time for the world to accept it. "You're in my way Spencer. Move."

"Isn't this adorable," someone said. "A bunch of little kids play-fighting."

A dozen men stepped through the surrounding trees, all dressed in every manner of summer wear from straw hats to sun glasses and even bathing trunks, vests, and sandals. They encircled the two teenagers, brandishing long knives from behind their backs. Mellow recognized some of these men from the warehouse the night Burner and the others were killed. Bile leaped up his throat and he choked it down, shivering involuntarily as he took a step back.

Mellow and Spencer backed into each other. The dozen men closed in, but stopped a good twenty feet away. The man at the front, a scruffy man wearing a green suit gestured to them with his hunting knife. Mellow knew him as the man with Suicide the night Burner and his men were killed. The green-suited man didn't smile, though his voice sounded as if he were laughing.

"Enough games, kid," the leader in the suit said. "Suicide wants you at the docks."

"Did they follow me?" Spencer whispered. "But how did they know I was looking for you?"

Mellow's fists whitened as he trembled with rage. "Shut up."

"Wondering where we came from?" the same man asked. "All we had to do was prod Mr. and Mrs. Holmes so they contacted little Mellow's best friend and then follow him here. It wasn't too complex. This is what it's like to deal with children."

Suicide's henchmen slowly encircled Mellow and Spencer, approaching with careful steps. Mellow wanted to run, even collapse, hoping to escape. But still all he could think about was the boy standing behind him who wouldn't leave him be.

"My name is Jace Reeves," the green suit man said. "I'd like to show you what a real Prime can do."

IT WAS NEAR ELEVEN when Jason noticed a flock of men fleeing the house the two of them were watching. Three cars were parked in the driveway, and each filled with at least half a dozen men. They tore off towards the west, leaving the house seemingly unguarded. The crowds made sure the cars could only go slowly, jerking their brakes through the mass of people.

The house was fairly impressive for this area. It was a two-story home with light yellow paint and brown shudders on each window, including the jutting tall window on the left end that had to be the living room area. There were no sounds coming from inside, and all the windows had blinds over them. Burner's men must have been making good scratch to afford places like this. Just what was he paying them, and where would he even get the money?

Jason and Lynn hid by a large oak tree's thick trunk from across the street from the house. They waited for the crowd to thicken, which it had, before they moved in. Now that those cars had left this was their chance.

That didn't mean it couldn't be some kind of trap. Burner and Boon weren't picking up the phone which meant Jason and Lynn were on their own.

"Lynn," Jason said. "I think you should follow the cars. They might be going somewhere important. You should be able to tail them without issue."

"You're going in there alone, aren't you?"

"I'm just gonna scope it out. If I see anything, I'll call the cops."

"As if I believe that." She put a hand on her hip, and scanned the packed street. "But I don't like the sound of those cars rushing off, so I'll follow them. Do anything dumb, and I will slap you. Understood? I'm pretty sure I hit harder than Ordopha."

He forced a small laugh that came easier than he expected. "I've got this."

Lynn patted Jason once on the shoulder before slipping into the crowd. She kept her straw hat low over her face. Within a few seconds she disappeared. Now it was only Jason and the hopefully empty house.

He hesitated. The last time Jason slipped into a home unwelcome was in Albion, and that house ended up a pile of rubble. Though that was technically Matthew's fault, Jason still bore responsibility, just as he did here.

The teenager rounded the groups of people slipping through the street. Bushes and tall grass hid his advance into the yard. He moved towards the backyard between the houses when a sudden voice caused him to stop in his tracks. Zelana! It came from inside the window. Jason slid up to the house and peered inside.

Through the crack in the curtain, he could only make out the edges of subtlety moving shadows beyond what he thought was a desk. The hum of voices could be heard. He tried to cock his cars to listen in, but Pollux still wasn't quite giving him the power that he needed. Despite that, a faint voice spoke from the other side of the wall.

A male voice came through. "The boys found the mice?"

"Is Vermilion with them?" Zelana asked. "Big bro is asking."

"I was just told that his little friend Spencer was with Holmes. I'm sure at least one of them knows where Pollux is."

"Good," Zelana continued. "This whole mess is exhausting. I just want to go home."

Grass shuffled, and Jason leaned back. Did someone see him? Not a soul approached, but the crowd was getting louder on the street. A burst of amplifier feedback caused him to cringe. They were setting up for a concert. The noise could help him move silently.

They had found Mellow somewhere out there. That had to be where those cars were going. Lynn was heading in that direction. She would call the cops to deal with that. Jason could only act here, to find out just what was going on with Zel.

The teenager slowly stepped around the back of the house when the ground under his feet rumbled. It quaked, tossing him back and forth. He dropped to one knee and braced his hands on the ground. And then, just as soon as it started, the earthquake ended. A drum snare sang out over the continued crowd murmur. Whatever had just happened had hardly affected their party.

Jason turned the knob to the backdoor and slipped into the house.

The teenager found himself impressed with the place. Clean white walls and the shining wood cabinets in the kitchen welcomed him inside. He smelled something like rot nearby. Jason stepped out of the kitchen into the living room.

At least, he could only assume it was the living room because it was far larger than the kitchen, but it otherwise looked nothing like a lounge area, never mind a finished room in a house. Bare beams with patches of drywall loomed above him. This cavernous space was all this first floor consisted of. If there was supposed to be a mudroom or extra room by the front entrance, it hadn't been built yet. Along his left, stairs went up to the second floor and a shut door underneath that was either a bathroom or a basement.

This house had not been finished. Despite that there were desks and cabinets leaning against the windows and walls. Whoever had been constructing this house simply stopped near the end of the job. Considering what happened to Burner and his men, it would never be completed now.

In the center of the empty room, Zelana sat in a wooden chair, still wearing the same sundress she had worn the last time he saw her. Her legs were folded and her hands lay lightly across her knee. She turned at his approach, not even so much as smiling at him.

"Jason Vermilion." Her voice lilted when she spoke, twisting into a higher pitch that hardly sounded like Zelana. Her eyes scanned him up and down as dispassionately as if he were in the bread aisle at the supermarket. "Who told you about this place?"

Beside her, a large man turned when she said Jason's name. He wore a heavy black cloak and thick matching garb underneath that went down to his boots. Jason recognized the broad pale grey face and wild platinum hair. However, the black fissures across his face like cracks in the sidewalk were new. They led to the large man's multicolored right eye which looked like a smashed marble. That wild eye locked onto Jason like a bear eyeing fresh salmon.

"The boy who killed me," Rantan said. "I am honored you have allowed me the opportunity to take my revenge. What luck! I am truly grateful to the Master for all. Retribution is mine."

"You survived, Rantan," Jason said. "Your father sent you here, did he?"

"The Great Sorcerer King has nothing to do with my being here. This entire undertaking is mine. After pulling myself from the grave and learning what you had done to my only family, it is only natural I should take vengeance. Unfortunately, *your* kin had already been killed before we even met. So I'll take what you have now, and I will take my sister back, as well." He patted Zelana's shoulder. She didn't flinch. "The last thing you will see is her smile as I remove your head from your shoulders."

Rantan crossed the floor to the dresser at his left. While he did so, Jason gestured for Zelana to come over to him, but instead she sat perfectly still. Her brother returned holding two swords.

"She isn't going to listen to you, Pollux. She's under my control now, and will be until we return back to Tyndarus. My father will be glad to see her before he melts her down and consumes her essence to regain his power. You, however, will be nothing but a mangled corpse smashed into dust. Father will just have to try again to find the Gemini Man. Unfortunate for you."

Jason took a step back. He had nowhere to run. Zelana stared blankly towards him, out of sorts, as if she were a wall ornament. Rantan crossed in front of his sister, blocking Jason's line of sight.

Jason readied himself for an attack. Instead, a sword clanked at Jason's feet.

"Pick it up, Pollux. We will finish what we began in the forest. No powers. Just strength."

The boy looked down at the sword and then at Rantan. The big man didn't flinch, didn't laugh, and didn't so much as crack a smile. Even though Jason wanted nothing more than to just grab Zelana and run, the glint in Rantan's usually laughing eyes showed maniacal glee hiding under the surface. An uncontrollable urge to crush it sparked in Jason's mind. He went for the sword.

Rantan drew his blade as well. Still, no smile dawned on his visage.

However, low breathing panted from somewhere close by. Pollux wouldn't quite tell him what it was, though the source had to be in the house, possibly in the yard. Some of Suicide's men? But then why didn't they come out to greet him?

Jason didn't care. The man he thought he had killed stood right before him and hoped to return the favor. The teenager recalled the lessons he had received from Alain and attacked first.

Their swords clashed and a familiar ripple ran along Jason's bones. That familiar excitement returned. It had been so long since he last duel to the death. Familiar aches and pains ran along his body, preventing Pollux from giving him power. Rantan easily beat him back. A slash drew blood on Jason's cheek.

"What's wrong, Pollux? Is this all you have ? You were mightier in our previous bout."

Zelana stared blankly back at Jason. He wiped the blood from his cheek with his thumb. "You haven't seen anything yet," he said.

Jason roared and beat back the approaching blade. He wouldn't die here. Too many people waited for him.

The floor rumbled with another earthquake, but the two kept fighting regardless. They ducked and sidestepped even as they stumbled around. At this rate the town would be torn apart by these tremors. Nonetheless he kept to his duel. The world would have to wait.

A sword strike caused Rantan's arm to tremble and he took a step back.

"What's wrong?" Jason said. "I'm just getting started."

Rantan bared his teeth and returned the blow, their swords dancing off each other.

Somewhere deep in Jason's gut, heat grew. Pollux was coming. He only had to survive long enough for it to return.

Despite that, Zelana's stare unsettled him. As he fought, Jason couldn't help but call to her in an attempt to wake her up. But she only stared back.

The enemy cut his arm, sending a thin line of blood dripping to the floor. Jason shook his head. This was no time to be distracted. Zelana would have to wait. He had a fight to the death to concern himself with.

CHAPTER 14
THE GIANTS ATTACK

WHEN JACE REEVES knelt down, the earth quaked uncontrollably, throwing Mellow off his feet. Spencer hit the dirt beside him, narrowly missing dunking his face in a rain puddle. The other eleven men in the enemy's party bent and weaved but remained standing. Clearly they had been through this before.

Reeves, the green suit man, plunged both fists into the earth and his body twisted and morphed as the dirt consumed him like quicksand. He dropped into the very ground itself. Then the earth stopped shaking. Despite the tremor's intensity, it was over as quickly as it arrived.

"What was that?" Spencer asked Mellow. "What did he do?"

"Don't ask stupid questions. He must have teleported underground somehow."

"Wrong," one of the men said. "Not even close."

"I saw what I saw!" Mellow said with a frantic tone he could no longer hide. "He went into the dirt! What else could it be?"

"You are one noisy brat," the thug said. "We should have drowned you with the others. Pay attention, boy. You're about to see who Reeves is."

Spencer took Mellow by the shoulder. "They're just blowing smoke. They don't—"

The ground burst open like a geyser, sending stone everywhere. Mellow cowered as he spotted the dark behemoth emerging from the hole in the earth. The over-sized thirty-foot hulk stood out of the pit, its bulky body and wide frame constructed of stone and the very dirt it had come from. Empty black ash eyes watched him even though the boy saw nothing in the sockets. The voice from the golem creature howled down at him.

"Master called this a Golem, from the Burning World," the thing that was once Jace Reeves said. It voice grumbled and growled with every word. "He lent me his power so I could experience his strength for myself."

Mellow's knees knocked out from under him and sent him back down to his rear end. He stared, open-mouthed, and his lip trembled. He could swear he saw Reeves use a different power on the night Burner died. So what was this?

"Wait," Mellow whispered. He understood. "You're a mimic. You copy powers."

"Perceptive runt," the Golem said with a rumble. "That won't help you when I crush your body and consume the remains into my flesh. Hold them, men. Run them through if they struggle."

The eleven men moved in on Mellow and Spencer, but only Spencer swung at them. Mellow couldn't even stand up. None of this made sense. All Mellow did was stare at the golem creature and remember his dead allies, including the twisted face of Page in the warehouse, almost assuredly since eaten by this monster.

"Get up, Mellow!" Spencer shouted. A knife pierced his forearm and he shouted. Blood trickled from the wound as Spencer backed up. "At least fight back!"

"*No*," he whispered blandly. It wasn't supposed to end this way, not for Mellow Holmes, the great hero. He still had mountains to conquer and villains to slay. But here he was looking down this mountain of a monster, and he couldn't even get up. "Damn it!"

Spencer seized Mellow's arm and lifted him. It was a useless effort. They were still surrounded and had no way out. As Mellow tried to think, Spencer was shouting in his ear.

"Stop babbling, you ox," Mellow said.

"I said that something is wrong, Mellow. Look!"

The men surrounding the teenagers suddenly shouted and dropped back. They had their knives held out awkwardly before them. The blades twisted in towards their guts and the eleven men dropped to their sides struggling against their own weapons. It was as if the tools grew brains and decided to attack their own users.

"I just made it," Boon said.

Burner's henchman emerged from the brush with his hands outstretched as if holding an invisible force before him. Telekinesis! That's right, Boon had a telekinesis ability! At least six of the men surrounding Mellow and Spencer let out gurgling cries as blood seeped from newly made gashes on their guts. Boon ignored them and moved towards the teenagers.

"You're lucky I'm here, Mellow. They would have done you like they did the other guys. Now, get out of here. I have some business to attend to." Boon jerked his arms and three of the enemies gagged, wheezed, and let their head drop lifelessly to the dirt. "Getting going, punk."

"Are you blind, Boon?" Mellow asked. Was everyone here an idiot? "Don't you see that giant golem right there?"

"I see him. That's why I'm telling you to go. This whole park is about to be torn apart. Unless you want to be put in the grave with the rest of us, I suggest you run. Now."

"Come on, Mellow," Spencer interrupted. "He's a Prime. He can handle it."

The golem charged forward. Its giant arm swiped at Boon. The defender dodged, but the hit cracked against Spencer, sending the teenager sprawling across the ground. He rolled into a puddle. The golem took a step towards him when a cavalcade of metal blades slammed into its back. Every one of the eleven knives broke on impact. The monster momentarily lost its balance before it pivoted to face its attacker. Boon swore at his ineffective assault.

Mellow used the chance to scramble up again. The golem had lost interest in the teenagers and was now instead focused on Boon. Mellow slowly backed away from them towards the brush.

"My men," the thing said. "You handled them all quite ably."

The eleven men were all strewn about in the dirt. They all had deep stomach wounds, and none were fighting to get up again. Boon didn't appear to notice any of them.

He laughed. "You guys are paper tigers without an ambush, aren't you?"

"Isn't that what you just did?"

"Eye for an eye, mud man. Do you think your little mimic power can help you out against me? Underestimate your enemies, do you? That's going to cost you big."

Despite Boon's words, the golem did not cease attacking. His large punches were dodged and defended, but not altogether avoided. He struck Boon, and cuts to erupted on his skin. Blood dripped from his nose and lip. Burner's henchman could not land a single hit on the monster, and only dodged, but he displayed no fear.

Mellow noticed Boon's oddly confident behavior was also at odds with his usual careful demeanor. He never attacked unless he was certain of victory. But the strangest part of him was the ring with the green gem stone on his ring finger. Burner never let that ring out of his sight. Mellow swallowed the fear in his throat. Burner didn't make it, after all.

"Look out, Mellow!" Spencer shouted. He wobbled as he stood up. "Beside you!"

Mellow looked to his left in time to see one of the wounded thugs dive for him. Despite his bloody stomach he still bared his teeth in a frothing rage. Mellow put his arms up as the enemy fell upon him—and then was tackled out of the way.

Burner stood over the struggling attacker and placed his hand over the enemy's face. The punk screamed as steam came off his face and a horrible hissing sound brought the punk to dreamland. Burner stood up over the unmoving opponent and left him there in the dirt.

"Time to go, Mellow. You too, kid." Burner gestured behind him. "We've got a boat to catch. Boon can deal with this on his own."

Over his shoulder Mellow could vaguely see the outline of a car through the trees as they moved through the growth. His escape!

"Your man can't handle this," Spencer said. He clutched his bruised and bleeding right arm as he limped towards Burner. "Just call the cops."

"We can't risk the giant following us, and we have a limited window before Suicide knows what happened here. You want the cops? Go get them yourself."

Spencer crinkled his nose in disgust. He looked at Mellow with an inscrutable expression before he tore off into the brush and out of the park. He removed his phone from his pocket as he ran. Mellow took a step after him, a strange urge pulling at him. Why shouldn't he go with him?

"Not you," Burner said. He put a hand on Mellow's shoulder and shook his head.

"You're going to come with me and spill everything Suicide told you."

Mellow's tongue dried up, leaving him unable to reply. Why couldn't this madness end?

"Good job, Boon," Burner called out.

Boon didn't turn around to face him. "You can always count on me."

"Ridiculous," the Golem roared. "You haven't landed a single meaningful blow on me, and you won't. I'll prove it by ending this with one strike. I'll crush your fat head."

"That's going to be hard without touching me."

Boon put out both arms and yelled as the ground beneath him cracked, split, and fractured. Playground equipment shattered and rusted pipes and old branches spun around. His psychic telekinesis ability was going all out. Earth itself was thrown up with large stones from underground as the golem fell over in the resulting earthquake.

During this storm of Prime energy, Burner grabbed Mellow's wrist and dragged him out of the park. Before Mellow could think, he was in the passenger seat, and the two were driving off towards the center of Riverview.

"Where are we going?" Mellow asked blandly. "Home?"

Burner's flat expression didn't change. "You could say that."

HIS ELBOW CRACKING into Rantan's ugly face was the most satisfying feeling Jason had experienced in days. The enemy's sword pierced his shoulder, but it was worth the look of shock Rantan gave him when he spat saliva. Jason's right shoulder surged with white-hot agony as the blade jerked free from his flesh.

Rantan receded a step. Jason did the same, his trembling right limb at his side.

Stray slashes and stabs had cut up the wood and plaster of the half-finished floor. The entire house creaked. And yet, Zelana still stared blankly ahead of her.

"Whatever you did to her," Jason said, "you better undo it now."

Rantan smiled through his bruised cheek. He slid up beside her and tapped the stained sword on the girl's shoulder. "It wasn't my power that left her this way, Pollux. It was your carelessness that led her here."

"I'm not here for your ridiculous speeches. Give her back, and tell me where Matthew is."

"Castor is already preparing for his trip as we speak. We planned to send you both to Tyndarus at the same time while holding my sister as hostage here. It is a shame you came to the wrong location. Now Suicide will send Castor through alone instead."

They hadn't yet noticed Burner was still alive. Though Jason couldn't trust that scumbag, at least that hooligan would throw a monkey wrench into the works of this monster. Hopefully, Burner would reach the boat in time to stop anything from happening to Matthew. Zelana was another matter.

Jason held tight to his trickling shoulder wound. "She's your sister, isn't she? Are you such a zealot for your dad you'll turn her into a battery?"

"You stupid whelp," the enemy said. Rantan's fingers clasped tighter on Zelana's shoulder. His nails dug in and small splotches of blood appeared on her skin. She didn't flinch. "You really have no idea how little we matter, do you? We only exist because he *allows* us to. Whether I want to be fuel for the Great Sorcerer King is irrelevant. That is what I will be. That is what this one will be. That is what you and this whole world will be. That you can't accept this, that you continue to fight against reality is your biggest failing. Just look at how much misery you have caused by not fulfilling your destiny. Williams' Tech, Albion, and Riverview . . . all that suffering is due to your stubborn will."

"My destiny is not to die."

"Everyone dies, boy."

"After we've finished what we were meant to accomplish. No one exists to be trampled on by killers like you. I saw your mansion in that thieves' forest. You looked like you were at home there. Is all that meaningless?"

Rantan's nostrils flared as he threw his sister aside. Zelana hit the floor, and Jason went for her. He was intercepted by Rantan diving in on him. Their swords clashed in a whirlwind of slashes. The bigger man's attacks grew in fierceness, sending Jason back. They attacked, moving in and out of each other's range. Their battle rocked across the house. Before Jason knew it, he was back in the kitchen again.

The boy blocked a wild swing and lost balance. Rantan's sword slid through Jason's stomach. Jason saw red. Rantan seized his throat, and squeezed. Jason choked for air.

"Without Pollux," Rantan said. "You are nothing."

Red streaks of blood speckled in Jason's eyes. An intense acid-like burning in his stomach prevented him from concentrating on the insane strength crushing his throat. Where did this psycho get this power from?

"You thought you understood my abilities," Rantan whispered. "My blood allows me to be nothing better than the best, even as a Prime." A subtle bitterness coated his words. "My entire body can be remodeled to match any living creature I wish. This is how I survived your assault on Tyndarus. Golems are notoriously hard to kill, and I inherited their properties. It is not mere mimicry: my very muscles and bones can surpass those of the mightiest mammal. To think it would even surpass you—the legendary Pollux. *Disgusting.*"

Rantan whipped his arm, releasing Jason from his hold. The boy flew across the kitchen, and slammed into the back door. The solid surface gave under his impact and allowed him to roll across the grass into the backyard. Jason's body let out a spasm as he attempted to breathe again. He lay unmoving on his back, staring into the sky with what little vision he could still muster.

Rantan's babble continued in the background. Jason thought the ground quaked under him again but couldn't be certain it wasn't his brain hemorrhaging. Saliva ejected out of his mouth before his vision blurred and dimmed.

"My blood is stronger than yours, Pollux. It appears your bracelet chose the wrong wielder."

The boy's voice refused to respond to his demands of speech. All he could think of was the agony gripping his bones like a crab claw crushing an enemy.

"Where are you going?" Rantan said to someone Jason couldn't see.

A woman's scream opened Jason's eyes and brought his attention to the rear window of the kitchen. He saw the fence before him, the sky's horizon below it from his upside down position. A large object plummeted down into the blue through the clouds—but it wasn't falling, it was flying upwards. Jason flipped over to his elbows to see just what this thing in the distance actually was.

The object was a golem—the same one Rantan had transformed into back on Tyndarus. How did this one get on Earth? It continued to lift several hundred feet in the air as he puzzled over its appearance. Was it flying out of the old park?

But before he could wonder further, the golem dropped down as if gravity had remembered to work. The creature plummeted at high speed, and disappeared down into Riverview blocks away from Jason's location. The ground then quaked as if a bomb had gone off underground.

A burst of adrenaline allowed Jason to move his arms underneath him and he bounded back up. The boy pivoted to face down Rantan, but instead found Zelana kneeling beside her brother and staring out into the town where the golem had just been. For a reason Jason couldn't understand she was crying.

"Jace!" she sobbed. "That was Jace!"

"Get a hold of yourself, girl," Rantan said. "It appears Pollux has more allies than we first thought. What are you doing, whelp? Get up!"

Zelana clutched her temples with both of her palms. "I can't! She's pushing against me. It's too unstable. She's going to break out!"

"Damn it all," Rantan said. He kept his sword trained on Jason while he spoke to her. "Call the fool in the basement to send us back. We can't risk her breaking free now."

"I've already called him. Help me back inside."

Zelana leaned on her brother. Blood dripped from her nose and ears. Rantan pushed her back, and she fell against the house.

There was nothing Jason wanted to do more than leap forward and strangle the bastard, but it took all of his focus and energy just to stand up. Only a warm heat in his stomach kept his consciousness afloat. This growing feeling numbed his pain with each passing moment. Pollux must have been trying to save his life.

Out of the door emerged one of the thugs that had attacked Jason and Zelana in the graveyard. He was covered in dirt and soot, his eyes sunken in and black. Despite his disgusting state, he trudged out into the sun and blandly waved his hand.

A portal opened up—the same one he had used to attack Jason days ago. Zelana leaped into it, and Rantan followed. But before he jumped into the void, he ran his sword through the teleporter's stomach.

"Thank you," he said. The teleporter dropped listlessly to the ground. "You can rest easy."

Rantan vanished into the portal, and the floating void pulsed and faded. The man on the grass groaned as his power was dying with him.

Jason pushed forward on his weak legs, his left dragging slightly behind him. He had little time to act before the ability died with its user. Despite himself, he tore a piece of his shirt off and threw it to the gasping man.

"Put pressure on the wound," Jason said. "I'll try to come back for you."

Just as the portal faded away into the ether, Jason bounded inside of it. The world flashed and went dark as he spun through whatever madness this was. Did he make it, or did that Prime die already? He wouldn't know until he hit the bottom.

Wherever that was.

MELLOW WANTED to stop shaking. That giant quake a second ago: he knew what that was. Boon had sent that golem-thing down into the earth after lifting it into the sky with his power. With that impact there was little hope that either of them would still be alive. But then why was Burner still keeping him here in his car, and why were they still going to his boat? Why couldn't this nightmare just end? He had suffered enough.

But Burner apparently didn't think so. While the car slid through the packed crowd mulling through the street, Burner kept his focus on the path ahead of him. Mellow considered darting out of the car, but where would he go? Everyone wanted him dead.

"Mellow Holmes," Burner said. "I'm far too trusting, and so are you. It's the one thing we both have in common. I should have let you be a stupid teenager."

Despite his usual brazen attitude, Burner's tone held a tinge of melancholy. Mellow had never seen him as anything but the confident and misunderstood guardian of Riverview. He didn't like what he was seeing.

"Boon had your ring," Mellow said. "Did you give it to him?"

Burner continued on without answering the question. "It was all bound to catch up to me eventually. Fate's always had me by the throat. I fooled myself into thinking I was free."

"They rejected you because you were just a sidekick, but they didn't know your true worth. I know, Burner. I've seen it. No one cares about this town more than you."

"You're wrong, Mellow. I don't care about this town. Never have. I was trying to carve out territory for myself. A place to belong. As long as you've got a home to lay your head, you have a place to protect. I threw all that away in another life. I just wanted to survive, not live."

No, none of this was true. Mellow wouldn't believe Burner was anything but what he showed himself as being. He had to be lying, probably shaken from all the recent craziness.

"Hey, Burner, what do you think about Suicide?"

"Quiet!" Burner blurted. He gestured to the crowd passing around the car. In the midst of it one man had pushed his way through the cluster towards the vehicle. "Put on your good citizen mask, Mellow. Don't run out on me now."

Piping red anger flushed across Mellow's face. Why did everyone think he was a coward? None of them had to go through any of the things he did—they all thought he had it so easy. He would show them what he was made of. Today he would become the hero he always knew he was; the man Burner had seen when he first hired him. Mellow puffed his chest and smiled at his boss.

"I never run," he said.

"You've never had to. Now be quiet. I think I know this guy."

The tanned man leaned down towards Burner's window and lightly knocked on it. Mellow felt his stomach shrink back. He couldn't afford to blow it now. This was his chance. Burner complied with the newcomer's request and opened his window.

"Burner?" the man said. His face reminded Mellow of an isosceles triangle. His thin cheeks made it seem as if he hadn't eaten for ages. "My name is Simon, you probably don't remember me. I couldn't help but notice you've got the Holmes boy with you. I hope you don't mind me asking, but what is he doing there?"

"That's not your business," Mellow replied. "We have something important to do."

"I met another teenage boy who was injured—a woman named Lynn showed up. She's the neighbor to those Bartlett brothers who were attacked. She brought the boy to the hospital, but he kept saying something about the park. Now I see you coming from there. What are you up to now? Nobody asked you to police our town for us."

Burner kept his eyes on the road ahead as he waited in the traffic. "Speaking of which . . . you might want to call the cops, Simon. That earthquake was caused by a Prime, and they might still be in the park. You can stand there and lecture me all you want, but there are more important things to do."

Finally, the traffic budged, and the car moved slowly down the street through the masses. However, this Simon do-gooder wouldn't let it go. He followed along the side of the car.

"So the rumors were true," he said. "Outsiders did attack the warehouse in the woods last night. If that wasn't you, then who are the ones after the Bartlett brothers? Is it some of your shady criminal friends?"

The more Simon spoke, the more irritated Mellow got. These idiot brothers had only been in town for mere weeks, and somehow they managed to have people like this nobody worry about them. Meanwhile Mellow had lived here his whole life, and was consistently treated like trash. They would all understand their mistake in underestimating him.

"Your friends are in trouble right now," Mellow said. He gave Simon both the park and the house address he had given through the graffiti last night. "Send some police to check in on them. We're going to deal with the culprit right now."

Simon looked at him as if he had grown a second head. "Are you brain-dead? Why don't you just send the police there, too?"

"Because this is my fault," Burner interrupted.

The traffic broke, and Burner tore out through the new opening. Several bystanders wheeled out of his way, but the boss sped onward down the streets of Riverview towards the water.

Mellow looked out the back window. "I hope he calls the cops."

"He will," Burner said. "I know him. He'll definitely do it."

"That guy didn't act like you knew him, though."

"He doesn't. But I made it my goal to learn a lot about my town. It's part of the job. Simon Barker is your typical blue-collar nobody, but he isn't above getting in the way of people like me. You don't get to be where I am without having some understanding of people."

Burner felt at the finger that had once housed his ring. Mellow swore that his boss smiled, if only for a split second. "You told me you were almost married once. What happened?"

"She got caught in the crossfire. That's how most people go in my line of work. You better not shed a tear for Boon, Schwartz, Page, or any of the others who Suicide butchered. They wouldn't want it. Instead, make their killers regret their mistakes. That's what we're doing here. You understand that, right? This is your last chance, Mellow. I need your assistance, but I will give you a choice. Get out of the car now, or go all the way. There are only two paths."

Mellow swallowed hard. Not a single part of him didn't want to hightail it out of this car. He could always run back home, beg for forgiveness from Mom and Dad, and hide in his room until this all blew over. Maybe it would all just go away. None of this had anything to do with him, and he wished he could keep it that way.

Instead, Mellow said nothing as Burner slipped down the streets towards the water. This would all be over soon. At least then he might have a story to tell about the legend of Mellow Holmes—a real hero. A small tinge of happiness crept through his fear. This might work out after all!

CHAPTER 15
PANIC ON THE WATER

THE DARKNESS soon gave way to sunlight as the portal broke around Jason. He stumbled out onto his knees in the dirt, his energy fluctuating as Pollux concentrated on preventing his gashes and stomach wound from opening further. He found the bleeding had already slowed. There was no way to know how long this would last, so he immediately stood and took stock of his surroundings.

He had landed on the edge of a treeline beside the river. A good hundred feet away was a warehouse with a yacht docked beside the concrete building. He had been taken far from the town center to somewhere on the fringes.

Up ahead, Rantan threw open the large doors of the warehouse with Zelana at his side. Not once did he even look back as he charged inside. Jason wasted no time following after them.

Every step hurt as Pollux buckled under his forceful movements. The boy limped as he ran, swerving through thin birches and hopping over the plentiful rocks peppered along the way. All he could think of was that warehouse ahead.

Outside of the still open doors sauntered out two men in dark suits. Jason recognized them from the other night—Suicide's thugs. They removed handguns from the holsters under their jackets and leveled them at the approaching boy. Jason was too close to run away now.

The guns barked, and Jason received every bit of their bite.

A SCREAM AROSE Matthew from his slumber. The chains around his body kept him bound as they had when he first fell unconscious, but a renewed strength brought his attention back to his predicament. Someone was injured, and it sounded serious. He couldn't tell if it was a male or female, his brain didn't allow the distinction in its fatigued state, but it was close by. Matthew bit his lip and closed his eyes—he would need to push his way through the pain.

His mind slipped through the red mists of agony and dove down into the sea of his soul. He submerged so deep his breaths left him and he gagged, but the pain fell far behind him in his plunge. Lungs burned and thoughts pounded the deeper he swam, but he couldn't stop now. His body reeled and his face reddened. His bones knew what his mind wouldn't accept—Castor waited ahead.

Gunshots went off nearby, but he ignored them. He couldn't afford to lose his focus now.

Scraps of white light buried deep inside him brightened the depths of this pit. He kicked and dove further, past the insecurities and doubts assailing him. The torrent pushed him back, but Matthew refused to quit. He knew this light—it was a part of him. They were one and the same.

Foam spewed out of his mouth and his face paled blue, but Matthew drew closer regardless. *Twenty feet, fifteen feet* . . . his body trembled . . . *ten, nine, eight* . . . spasms caught his muscles . . . *five, four, three* . . . he fainted against his bindings.

But his inner self swam on. It touched the light and a surge of warmth flashed through Matthew's soul. Every part of him numbed, and then all feeling returned in one explosive moment.

Matthew gasped as pain and pleasure shot into to his body all at once. He leaned against his chain bindings for support as the spasms fought for control. Matthew coughed and gagged as the color slowly returned to him—or at least as far as he could figure in this dark room. Despite his watering eyes and heavy breaths, and the agony swimming underneath his tired bones, a new feeling had overtaken it all. It was the knowledge that a piece of him had finally returned.

He leaned forward into his bondages and a single thought allowed him to surpass every injury and do what came second nature to him. Castor had returned. Matthew transformed into mist.

Everything was as it should be as the pain was momentarily forgotten. Wholeness transcended all agony. Matthew was who he was always meant to be again.

The mist puffed up over his former chains and soared towards the crack in the metal door. He slipped through it as easily as he always had and came out the other side. A thin hallway with light coming from the left and up some stairs awaited outside his prison. Two guards stood at attention with automatics on either side of his door. They didn't notice the growing fog below them.

He formed into a man again between the two guards. They both jumped at his appearance. The duo each turned and fired directly at Matthew, and their bullets pierced him. However, their shots each struck through Castor's mist form, each striking the other guard. Both men shouted as they dropped dead.

Matthew's sixth sense flared—more threats waited nearby. Whether it was below or above was hard to tell. His power told him danger lay in every direction.

While he wasn't physically injured, the pain of the shots passing through Matthew remained. He reformed into a human again and stumbled against the opposite wall. Stabbing, searing heat peppered inside his bones. The wielder of Castor pushed forward with his hand against the wall to brace him. Daylight shimmered ahead.

Faint groans caught his attention. He traced it to one room ahead. Matthew listened close—it was a girl. Was it the same one from last night? What day was it, at this point? He had no idea how long he'd been out for. Matthew used his mist to slip under the door.

On the other side he found the same teenage girl from the warehouse. She wore the same beaten up shirt and jeans she had on when he first saw her, and here she was lying on top of the lone bed. She was alone and sleeping, but had her brow furrowed as if in deep concentration. Her teeth were bared and eyes shut tight, with her skin white pale as a snow-capped mountain.

Matthew shook her shoulder, but she wouldn't awaken. Then he remembered—she was a member of Suicide's gang. A Prime! Whatever power she had must be in use right now. Instead of letting her rest, he picked her up and brought her back into the hall. He would deal with whatever she was doing later, but he wouldn't leave her here to roam free. First he had to escape and find Zelana.

Slowly he remembered everything that had happened to him. The assault by Suicide—and Rantan! That piece of work had come to Earth. At some point they had also found Zelana. He needed to get out of here and warn Jason. There wasn't any time to dawdle.

As Matthew carried the mumbling girl towards the sunlight he questioned just what she was doing here. He tried talking to her, but she still didn't respond. How would he break whatever power she was using? What was she even trying to do? He couldn't just kill her, any number of things could happen if he did. Matthew climbed the stairs with her in his grip.

"*Mom,*" she mumbled. She grabbed at his arms, and her nails dug into his skin. He winced, but she didn't appear to know what she was doing. "*She's pushing me out. Help, Mom.*"

Matthew tried to speak, but a cough came out instead. His throat still burned. He would have to just leave her to talk to herself.

"*You're mine now!*" the girl whispered. "*Stop fighting me!*"

At the top of the stairs Matthew came out onto the deck of a yacht. He didn't know too much about boats except that this one appeared to be two stories tall and wide enough for a semi-truck. Behind him were small stairs towards the deck which led into the pilot's chamber. Before him was the river itself surrounded by brush, though across the way were rolling hills that lead into a smattering trail of farmhouses. It reminded him of the north side of Riverview. Was that where he was?

The wide forty-foot dock beside the boat stretched towards land where a refurbished warehouse sat like some overgrown two-story house. There had to be some sort of phone inside. Matthew needed to contact someone fast.

A boot kicked him across the face. Matthew dropped sideways and landed against the wooden deck. Stars dotted his vision and his right temple sang. The girl tumbled out of his arms and landed across the wooden floor beside him, splayed out.

Suicide landed hard against the deck in his heavy boots. He must have jumped from the roof to the pilot's chamber. Was he waiting for Matthew to show up? The giant of a man brushed himself off and reached behind his belt.

"I guess I just have to do it myself," Suicide said.

"Where's Zel—"

Suicide drew his gun and fired into Matthew. The shot struck his inner thigh. Matthew bit his lip as he choked off a cry. The pain was unbearable, but still, he tried to concentrate. Whatever happened next he couldn't afford to be shot again.

The thug aimed the weapon at Matthew, and fired. Speckles of red pain filled Matthew's very being—and then it disappeared again. Suicide shot again, no trace of joy on his visage.

"No more talking," Suicide said. "Just die."

THE GUNSHOTS didn't work against Jason like he thought they would. When most Primes with super strength were shot, the bullets would deflect off of them as if they were made of tough steel. But these shots sunk into Jason's skin as if flies caught in a trap. The pain sizzled in his flesh as he charged forward, but the bullets stopped dead as if running into wall.

Both men guarding the warehouse swore as he barreled on into them. Jason punched the first man so hard in the gut that he lifted off the ground and vomited blood before landing flat on his face in a heap. Jason grabbed the second shooter by the collar and whipped him downward. The earth dented underneath the thug's face with the impact. Jason's attackers fell limp.

His nerves and muscles forced the bullets in Jason's skin out, as if his body had a will of its own. The small slabs tumbled out of his flesh and clinked against the dirt. No blood poured from his wounds, but he was worried they would start gushing again if Pollux gave out on him. He had no way of knowing if his injuries would heal on their own with his power. He could only pray his body would hold together after his energy ran out.

Inside the warehouse he found a refurbished loft not unlike the ones back in the city. A rolling grey shag carpet and matching dark furniture covered the flat space ahead of him. The second floor had little more than a ladder leading to a small bedroom overlooking the water. This place looked oddly cheap to be owned by these criminals.

At the opposite end of this hundred foot cave of modernity he found the wall beaten in, revealing the insulation and a six foot tall mirror placed against the tattered back wall. The Mirror Gate glowed faint purple and smoked ever so slightly.

"How many of these do I have to smash?" he whispered.

In front of the Mirror Gate he found Rantan, this time with his sister. Zelana had fallen to her knees and was clutching her head and making low murmuring noises. She was crying.

"What is the matter?" Rantan said. "Do your job, wench."

She spoke between sobs. "I can't! They killed Jace. You saw him fall!"

"Yes, he's dead, but so what? He went up against a mightier foe and was slain. Were he not weak he'd still be alive. Now, get up and put my sister into the mirror. It is time to end this ridiculous game."

"She's pushing back," Zelana said. "What sort of power does she have? I had to relinquish control of all the others just to focus on her, and it's still slipping."

"It was bound to happen. She has the blood of the Great Sorcerer King in her veins, and you are just a common peasant a girl. Now, hurry. Do the one job you have."

The girl whined. "*. . . I can't hold on.*"

"Wait, Rantan," Jason said. He kicked aside the furniture in his way, shattering it with his strikes. "You won't be leaving here."

Rantan sighed and pushed the girl over to the floor. "More of this pointless fighting."

Pollux numbed Jason's pain as he moved, allowing him a modicum of maneuverability as he blitzed across the floor. The searing cuts, bullet holes, and bruises, mattered less than defeating the man before him. Rantan roared as he swung his sword towards Jason's neck.

The boy ducked, and the sword slashed a few hairs from his head. Rantan swooped in for another swing.

But Jason saw the blade coming. Rantan moved much quicker than a usual swordsman but the boy was even faster. And he was getting nimbler with each dodged attack. The sword viciously cut the air as Jason weaved around the slashes. Despite that, Rantan never stopped swinging.

"This is your family, Rantan," Jason said. "Don't you understand what your own father is making you do?"

"He doesn't make me *do* anything." Jason jumped back to avoid a wide slash. "After you killed my brother and I, we rose from the ground. He walked away from all that we fought for. No one will say what happened to my sister, but I am certain she is gone, too. The Great Sorcerer King did not take them from me, maggot. *You* did."

"Don't act like your sins are justified." Jason's muscles surged with power as his anger grew in his squeezed fists. "Your father killed my parents!"

Jason punched Rantan in the chest. The supercharged impact lifted the mammoth-sized man from his feet. Rantan soared backwards, crashing into the ground in a roll before stopping in front of the Mirror Gate. He coughed up saliva and blood and stood again. He looked down at his fallen sister, who lay prone on the floor.

"Get up," Rantan said to her. "I've had enough incompetence from you, little girl."

At those words, Zelana—or whoever controlled her—crawled to her hands and knees. She breathed hard, and her arms trembled, but she still fought her way back up.

Rantan put a meaty hand on her cut shoulder and squeezed. The girl let out a squeak. Her brother swooped around behind Zelana and put his blade to her throat. She didn't appear to notice as her breaths remained ragged and her eyes shut. Jason stopped his approach and raised both hands in surrender.

"You're not going to kill her, Rantan."

"Why shouldn't I? She is a major cause of my misfortune. My other siblings knew their place, but she could not be what she was made to be. Did you know she is older than we are? The Queen declared she should be sealed away until the time her magic grew to the level where the Great Sorcerer King could use her. But you freed her and gave the wench the Kharis Seed, infecting her. It is only natural she should pay the price for being allowed to live. The rest of us have."

"She's all you have left. Don't give her to the man who doesn't care whether you live or die."

"Shut your filthy mouth, wretch! I only live for one purpose. I can never be what the Great Sorcerer King needs—I am one of the failed children. But at least if I kill her, I will make my mark. Make no mistake: I will cut her faster than you can move to strike me."

Jason kept his expression flat to mask the anxiety attacking him. Should he risk rushing Rantan and put Zelana at risk? He might even make it in time, but Zelana could still get severely injured. Rantan slowly backed up to the mirror as Jason thought up how he should act.

"You will do nothing, Pollux." Rantan put one hand on the Mirror Gate behind him. Purple smoke plumed out of the surface. "You cannot save her."

"Yes, he can," Zelana said.

Suddenly, the entire surface of the Mirror Gate turned bright white, as if metal heated too hot. Rantan bellowed in pain, loosening his grip on the girl. Zelana had placed her palm against the Mirror Gate without her brother's notice. She shouted for Jason to move.

"Damn girl!" Rantan shouted. He backhanded the girl through his pain.

Jason lunged forward in time to catch Rantan's blade jabbing into his chest. A shot of agony ricocheted through his insides, but only for a moment. The sword broke under his forward force. Jason tackled Rantan, and the two flew backwards, away from the fallen Zelana.

Heat assailed them as they tumbled into the Mirror Gate. Jason could do nothing as he fell downwards into the endless pit.

MATTHEW'S BREATHS fell much too hard. He lay on his back on the yacht's deck, a bullet in his inner thigh, one in his left forearm, and one in his chest. Six feet before him stood Suicide looking down at him, most likely wondering why only three of his twelve shots managed to hit someone sitting right before him. But Matthew's sixth sense was still going crazy, warning him of another threat on this boat. What was it? Either way, Castor had saved Matthew's life by allowing him a transparent form, but it wouldn't matter if this psycho hit him again.

"Now, I see," Suicide said. He exaggerated his head shakes not unlike a child nodding to a teacher while repeating knowledge he already understood. "So that's why the Master wants you. Touching you is a real chore. I can relate to that. However, it's not going to matter if you bleed out, is it?"

Castor allowed Matthew to solidify, but the bullet wounds and excessive use ground on his insides. He couldn't do this forever. Matthew readied himself in case Suicide lifted the weapon again.

"They call you Castor," Suicide said. He ejected the magazine from his handgun. Slowly he shuffled through his pockets, looking for another. "Is that a hero name? Are you a hero, Castor?"

Matthew debated rushing him, but his injuries held him back. Instead, he slid backwards to the edge of the yacht. The girl remained unconscious on the deck, but she was fine: Suicide wouldn't kill his own sister. All Matthew could do was worry about how to get out of here and find Zelana—wherever she was.

"Heroes are deluded do-gooders unaware of how they waste every second they breathe on nothing. Your struggling is just as pathetic, so you'd fit right in."

"I don't get why you're with Nieto," Matthew said. "No matter what you say, the two of you are not looking for the same thing. He might be cracked, but you're broken."

"We're nothing but tools to the other. Mutual benefits."

"You would know all about tools."

The unconscious girl on the deck suddenly screamed. Both Matthew and Suicide jumped at the sound. She rolled around clutching her face.

"She's free!" Suicide's sister shouted. "She's free!"

"Then get her back, stupid!"

Matthew used the moment to push himself backwards. He flipped over the side of the yacht just as Suicide looked his way. A bullet ricocheted off the railing.

When he hit the water, Matthew's wounds sang. It was as if railroad spikes had been driven into each of his injuries. They pulled him down into the deep. Shots sunk into the water above, but they were too off the mark. Matthew was more worried about what the girl had said.

Was she talking about Zelana? Had she broken free of them? But where was she? He would have to escape this place to find out. In order to move quicker through the river, he needed to transform into water.

Matthew's body warped into the liquid and he instantly thought his entire being was being torn apart. Not unlike being drawn and quarter, his soul torn into pieces. Everything flared at once—and then was silenced.

His very being drifted into a dark void. There was no more agony and no more joy. Matthew White was no more.

CHAPTER 16
RIVER MASSACRE

THE CONSTANT GUNFIRE did worry Mellow, he had to admit. When Burner pulled up to the dock it was already pure chaos. Two men lay unmoving in front of the warehouse, and shots were going off on the yacht. Burner removed a small pistol from his glove compartment and checked the magazine for bullets. A chill ran down Mellow's back.

"Why didn't you use that in the park?" he asked his boss.

"The same reason they didn't bring guns. You bring the cops into this, and it gets crazy quick. Not to mention that it wouldn't have helped. That guy Boon killed was a giant stone monstrosity. But now? I've about had it. No other choice."

"I see."

"Stay behind me," Burner said. "If you find either of those brothers, try to get them out. I'll cover you."

Mellow smiled through chattering teeth, "I'm surprised you're doing this. Suicide's crazy."

"I've lost enough today, I think. There's no turning back. Come on, kid. Time to be a hero."

Burner led him out towards the yacht, but Mellow didn't feel like a hero. As they ran up the dock he could only feel every instinct telling him to turn around. When they reached the top of the ramp they found a teenage girl lying against the wall by the stairs into the yacht. She was unconscious and breathing short. Mellow recognized her from the warehouse.

"Check her out, Mellow. I'm going to look around the inside. Suicide has to be somewhere."

"S-sure," Mellow said. He crouched in front of the girl and checked her forehead. It was hot. A fever? "This is weird, Burner."

Burner looked over from the stairs. "What is?"

The girl's hands smacked against Mellow's ears, and a sudden spike of red burning set itself into his brain. He went for her arms, but it was as if they were glued against his head. Her eyes snapped pen at his yell.

"It's just you?" she whispered. "Better than nothing. You're all killers, anyway."

"Mellow!" Burner yelled.

The air popped. Burner's body jerked sideways as bullets struck his chest and shoulder from down the open stairs into the yacht. His gun slid from his hands as he dropped backwards.

Suicide emerged from the bowels of the ship. He fired another bullet into Burner before picking up his victim's weapon and throwing it overboard. After scanning the area for more intruders, Suicide lifted Burner up by the collar and dragged him over to the railing.

"I've never met so many rats eager for drowning," Suicide said. "Never mind killing the same person twice. What a day."

The agony in Mellow's brain twisted into an unbearable scream. All he could see was the face of this girl forcing her way inside, just as what happened to that other teenage girl back in the pharmacy. He remembered what happened to her and an icy chill froze his pain for the second he needed to act.

Mellow's arms shot out and his hands tightened around the girl's throat. He squeezed for all he was worth, trying to force her out of his mind. In the haze before him her face faded in and out of his vision. Her grip wasn't as tight as the doctor's was yesterday. Was something off with her? He couldn't worry about that. For now, he just needed to get her off.

"What's this?" Suicide said. "Finally doing something, Mellow Holmes? Shame it involves hurting little girls. Aren't you being too rough with her?"

An unexpected shout brought the hairs on Mellow's neck up. A familiar sizzling noise gave him the jolt he needed to force his attacker off. Burner had grabbed Suicide's face with his right hand and punched the enemy's chest with his left.

Mellow threw the girl down, and she finally let go of his ears. His ragged breaths caused his vision to sparkle. He looked upon the girl, gasping and pleading with her eyes wide and hands up. The anger in is brain wouldn't be quenched. His teeth clenched tight. These monsters had done enough. Mellow lifted a fist at the fallen girl, who didn't react how he expected. She looked up at him with an expression of shock before she whimpered. Her eyes rolled back in her head and she fell back, unmoving. She had fainted.

A gunshot rang out behind Mellow. He pivoted towards the noise and saw the source.

Suicide held Burner by the throat, steam wafting off the large man's face and chest. His clothes were melting off the top half of his body where streaks of red burning flesh were strewn across his reddened muscles. His eyes bored down at the crumpled man in his hands.

Burner forced a grin through his bloody lips. "How's that for rough?"

"You son of a bitch!"

"Mellow!" Burner said. He coughed. "Good job. I knew you had it in you!"

Suicide tightened his hold and lifted Burner up. The smaller man tried to grab at his wrists, but he didn't seem to have the strength. Suicide's bloodshot eyes narrowed. "Stay dead this time."

Suicide flung Burner's body over the side of the yacht. It splashed down, and the big man stumbled backwards, dropping his gun from his trembling, and scarred, wrist.

Fear threw Mellow forward without a second thought towards the firearm. It was his ticket out of here. No more of this madness. He slid across the deck and touched the pistol.

The kick crunched against the side of Mellow's neck. Sparks of black filled his vision as he gagged. His body spun sideways with a second strike, sending him rolling. More kicks crashed against his chest and head, repeating like an endless drum. Mellow coughed, blood spraying out of his mouth, as he landed on his arms and knees. He involuntarily shook when he saw his own life force staining the ship deck.

"Oh, *that hurt*," Suicide said.

Mellow peered over his shoulder at the hulking behemoth behind him. A cold feeling like death struck him when he saw that Suicide wasn't angry. He was smiling through his hard breathing. His right eye was half closed, and the flesh Burner had touched was mangled and gnarled, but still, he grinned down at Mellow. Despite the joviality he displayed, there wasn't a trace of joy in his tone.

"You wouldn't know anything about that, would you?" Suicide asked. He pointed his gun at the blood on Mellow's lip. "This is probably the first time you've ever bled, so you probably don't appreciate the feeling of teetering on oblivion. This is what it's like, Mellow Holmes. A stupid teenager pretending he's a hero in a world of actors pretending to be heroes. The only difference is that *they* have the skills to back up their lies. That girl you knocked out was the first person you've ever beaten, isn't she? Pathetic. Very pathetic."

That girl still lay unmoving on the deck, but Mellow couldn't focus on her, nor could he think about Burner or anything else. The only thing he could think about was the gun barrel pointed at his head. He trembled on his hands and knees.

"How about a gift?" Suicide asked. The joy returned to his voice. "Have one on me, hero."

Suicide fired—but into the boy's stomach. Mellow screamed like he never had before. This pain overtook even the fear. Ripples of anguish whipped by like a flash flood through his muscles and bones. All he could think about was how the next bullet would end his entire life.

"But because of everything you and you friends have done to me and the Master, I have another gift for you, Mellow Holmes." Suicide bent down beside his victim. "I want you to remember this feeling as the last one you will ever know."

Mellow was going to die. This was it. He almost threw up from the pain, but instead focused all the energy he had into his legs. Run! He could run! He would escape no matter what.

The weight of a meaty leg crushed him back down into the deck. Mellow struggled as Suicide wrapped his giant hand around his face. Suicide squeezed, holding him in place.

"Relax, Mellow Holmes," he said. "It won't hurt for much longer."

As the fingers dug into Mellow's brain, a feeling like burrowing drill bits jabbed into his consciousness and he screamed as loud as his lungs would allow him to. Inside his mind played pictures of mutilated bodies, explosions, and blades, dissecting and pulverizing everything he had ever known. Over and over, strangers, acquaintances, family, and everyone over the world suffered a fate of eternal death—then he saw worse things, things that he never imagined a human being could do to another. Death, destruction, corruption, and utter hopeless despair, assailed him. His place in the universe became clear while he was unable to move as the innocent were abused by the guilty and sex and drugs were potent enough to destroy others for. The wicked could have whatever they wanted with the force they displayed, and the meek could only be crushed by mindless urges that superseded their own lives and dignity. Mellow Holmes watched hundreds, thousands of deaths on fast forward and on a loop, where reality held him down and forced him to watch it all unfold. Somewhere above the dizzying sights, sounds, and smells, the harsh mumble of Suicide continued to speak to him.

"I told you," Suicide said.

Then, as suddenly as it attacked him, it ended.

Mellow's body twitched and his eyes rolled back in his head. An impulse in his stomach told him to throw up, but he couldn't do anything but lie on the deck as reverberations of horror remained transfixed in his head. All the spinning thoughts in his brain prevented him from doing anything at all.

"Hey, boy," Suicide said. "Look here."

With all his strength, Mellow lifted his head towards his attacker. He saw the gun pointed at him, but couldn't muster even a squeak of fear. It wasn't anything like bravery—his brain didn't know how to react. He couldn't feel anything despite the brain soup stirring in his head. He could only look at Suicide with a blank expression.

The gun blasted and Mellow jerked. The bullet sunk into his chest and blood rushed from the wound. But Mellow only looked impassively at it—he felt no pain, no reaction to the shot.

Suicide put his gun away. "And that's my gift to you. Enjoy your last minutes on Earth as a vegetable. No more whining like a kicked puppy or crying like a little girl. Now you just get to be what you actually are when your emotions are out of the way—an empty husk. This is what you are, Hero. I hope you appreciate seeing the real you."

Mellow wanted to get angry, to spit in the villain's face and show him he wouldn't be defeated. He needed to show that Suicide was wrong about the hero of Riverview, that he had no idea who he really was, and that Mellow was beyond whatever trickery had just assailed him.

But the boy felt nothing. There was no rage, no fear, no joy, and no pain. He looked at the man who had killed him as blankly as if he was the neighbor's dog barking at him. Mellow's body soon numbed, and his head hit the deck again. He couldn't muster any emotion.

"Enjoy oblivion, Mellow Holmes," Suicide said. "You'll have a few others joining you shortly."

Mellow's body must have been cold because he shivered as the darkness overtook him. Soon enough he knew nothing but the night covering him in the midst of this summer day. Chill numbed his bones.

He thought he heard a gunshot, but that no longer concerned him. Mellow Holmes let his head roll back, and the silence embraced him.

THE WARM white light of the tunnel didn't burn like Jason expected it to. Unlike the previous time there was no purple mist, and no spinning tornado of blackness awaiting him around the sides of the funnel. Instead, he felt the beating heart of some powerful heat pushing him upward and onward through the forty foot tall and wide space. This time, the Mirror Gate was on Jason's side.

Rantan spun through the air like a rag-doll thrown through a fire tornado. His clothes and skin burned, steaming and letting streams of smoke gush from all over his flailing limbs and sizzling skin. His chalk white skin heated to a hard red pitch, and his screaming voice caused Jason's own skin to crawl.

The pair twisted forward in a zig-zag pattern. It was as if Jason were caught in a wild river flow, being thrown towards the shining opening at the end of the tunnel. He flew into the exit and instantly the bright lights departed when he went through it.

Jason landed on his hands and knees, the warm stone tiles remarkably hot to the touch. He checked his clothes and both his shirt and pants were still in one piece. Thin streams of black smoke drifted from his garb, but it was nothing compared to the last time he went through a Mirror Gate and they were incinerated instantly. Here he could move normally. The teenager looked up to find Rantan and instead found a familiar location.

He had arrived in a stone castle with familiar arched doorways and torches hanging on the walls. A large open window showed him a clouded sky overlooking a misty mountain range. There he spied a castle tower perched amidst a labyrinth of smaller rock fortresses far below. A glow of hard purple mist encircled the tall tower like a demonic halo.

Jason was not only in Tyndarus—he was in the mountains again, and the same place their enemy resided. In that black tower was the Great Sorcerer King Nieto; Jason could feel his presence, even without Matthew's sixth sense.

"Pollux!" Rantan screamed.

At the edge of the chamber, Jason spotted his enemy holding an odd oblong horn. He put it to his mouth and blew, and within moments a chorus of matching instruments sounded throughout the ragged mountain range. The alarm had been sounded.

After a brief pause, a flood of lizardmen in leather armor and carrying short swords poured into the room from doors on either side of him. Some held arrows with their bows, and before he knew it near twenty warriors blocked both exits out of the chamber.

"Thank you for making this easier for me," Rantan said. He snapped his fingers, and the lizards slowly pushed towards Jason. "Come quietly or lose your head."

"How about I just take yours?"

"Enough of this childishness. Seize him!"

The lizardmen hissed before charging towards their target. Jason met them in the center of the room with the full strength of Pollux. Arrows flew, but they didn't seem to hit him.

Jason punched the first in the chest so hard the armor rippled against his fist before crunching. The lizard squealed and dropped to the floor, but more fell upon the teenager. As he punched and dodged with the aid of Pollux he noticed something odd. The arrows weren't hitting him. Instead, they flew over his head. As he fought off the crowd encircling him, his eyes traced the arc of the projectiles.

The shafts struck the Mirror Gate—the archers were not aiming for him. Their shots cracked and splintered the frame around the gate. Some arrows flew harmlessly into the open Mirror Gate, but the ones that hit the fringes caused the portal to ripple and spark like a torn electrical cable.

It hit him: they were attempting to break the Mirror Gate and trap him here!

"Figured it out?" Rantan asked, his tall frame still sticking out over the crowd. "It's not going to do you any good. You should have stayed home, boy."

Jason threw off the enemies dog-piling him and pushed for the Mirror Gate. As he reached the portal, the glass shattered and crumbled to the stone tiles. The white light of the gate dissipated. All that remained was an empty black frame against the interior castle wall. The shards bounced as they leaped from the broken mirror. It had been completely wrecked.

The Mirror Gate was destroyed—he was trapped in the alien world of Tyndarus.

"I'll repeat myself," Rantan said from behind him. "Come quietly, or lose your head."

The teenager turned, his focus still on the floor. Slowly the realization dawned on him that he wouldn't be able to return to Earth. However, instead of fear or anger, a strange sensation of relief washed over him. No Zelana, no Matthew, no Lynn, and no one at all could hold him back. Now it was Jason Vermilion alone against Nieto's forces. This was his chance to end this entire hidden war.

"You shouldn't have done that," Jason said. He could feel the smile burning on his lips. Pollux flowed through his veins with incredible power, no longer suffering his doubts or sense of justice. "I apologize for what's about to happen to you."

The alarms didn't cease despite the chaos going on around him. More of Nieto's forces were on there way from all over those lonely mountains and the hidden fortress complex.

But they were the ones who should have been worried. If Jason was going to die, he would take them all out with him.

The castle rumbled as the roar of footsteps sounded from nearby hallways. Jason roared with them and plunged into the enemy forces. Swords flashed and arrows flew, but he fought on as he tore into their numbers.

Death would be coming for them all.

CHAPTER 17
MASS SUICIDE

"DEATH AWAITS YOU!" Rantan shouted to Jason. "There is no way out of this, Pollux. Face your fate like a man."

Instead of his enemy, Jason focused more on the shattered mirror behind him. His only escape from this hell had been taken from him, and now he had nothing but Pollux and the sword he picked from a fallen lizardman. His sizzling clothes also wouldn't last much longer as the heat only grew hotter on his threads the longer he fought. Pollux wouldn't hold out forever, and eventually these endless hoards would overtake him.

No matter how many he cut down, lizards still charged into the fortress chamber, keeping it constantly filled with at least a couple dozen of enemies at a time. Slashes ripped across his arms and legs in the skirmish. A spear thrust into his chest, and it tore along his stomach as he pivoted. His fingers trembled, and he knew Pollux was already fading.

"Why do you reject your inevitable destiny, Pollux?" Rantan called out. Though it was difficult to see him, Jason noticed Rantan's skin had been singed near black, and his clothes were little more than charred rags. "This is where you—where all of us—were meant to be."

Jason tried to speak, but the odd warmth on his back distracted him. All that was there was the broken Mirror Gate, so what could it be? He turned and felt the heat grow even hotter.

"Impossible!" Rantan said.

A bright white light poured out from the broken mirror and filled the room, causing his enemies to fall back from their approach. A voice whispered from the light and caused him to forget his injuries for a moment.

"*Hurry!*" Zelana said. "*I cannot hold it forever!*"

The pieces of the Mirror Gate lifted from the floor and pulled themselves back in place along the frame, but their cracks remained. The light poured in from the other side, and the white heat returned. She had somehow fixed the gate.

"*You!*" Rantan screamed from somewhere in the blinding white room. "You're just a battery! You aren't capable of anything else!"

"Still haven't figured it out?" Jason asked. "This is why your dad can never rule anything but this empty place. You look at us like we're bugs, and yet we sting you into submission over and over. But next time? That's when I'll be the one to sting both of you. Count on it."

Jason leaped into the Mirror Gate and the light died as he fell inside. Behind him the world he left disappeared as if a shut door slammed tight. The light died in the funnel around him as he shot forward, not unlike a rolling blackout. Soon enough, only the exit several hundred feet before him kept any light shining into the void.

Then it was gone.

The exit blacked out and vanished, leaving nothing but endless dark surrounding Jason. He was flying blind in the emptiness.

"*It's okay, Jason,*" someone said.

A vague circle of light surrounded him in the blackness, but before him, a presence formed into a person inside his thoughts. He couldn't believe what he was seeing—or was he seeing it all?

"Mom?"

THE WARMTH of the summer sun caressed Burner's cheek as he opened his eyes. He stared blankly into the slow moving clouds high above, reminding him of younger days when he used to sit under them with the guys. That was so long ago. They knew how it would go. The group of them would take over the world and make things better for everyone. Heroes were new, and they would fix the mistakes of the past. No longer would they live in a world as broken as the one humans had created before them. The boys and Burner would make sure of it themselves. He tried to remember their faces, but they had all faded, leaving him alone under the summer sun. They always faded when he woke up.

The former gang boss moved his fingers and a spasm ran up his arms. He coughed blood.

"I can't stay here."

He sat up and a burning sensation instantly prickled in his muscles. One second—all he needed was a single moment and he could recover. He always did. That's why he was the leader.

The gang had always done what he asked with no questions, and he had always steered them right. But now they had left him behind, just like those heroes he used to admire as a brat. Burner never wanted to become a villain, but what choice did he have? Would he play politics like those frauds in Montreal, Toronto, or even down south in New York or Serenity City? Would he get rich off brand endorsement deals and tax loopholes while pretending to be a good guy like the other so-called heroes? No, it made more sense to cut to the chase and stop pretending. He was unsalvageable, a villain, and that was all he would ever be.

That was what he thought until those two drifters came into town, anyway. Bringing trouble he never thought he'd see. In only a few days his insignificant empire had been smashed into dust. Burner would never be able to rebuild from this, but that didn't really bother him much. Things change and in this world where monsters do battle every day, life is very fleeting. At least he had fun.

"*You sure you want to trust these guys?*" Boon had asked last night. "*That kid is a fugitive. We might make a few bucks ditching town and handing him in over in the states.*"

"I owe it to the other guys to put Suicide away. They'd never rest if I ran away from a new player flaunting his hand." Burner looked around the small apartment. He could faintly hear that Jason kid talking with Lynn in the kitchen through the outside rain. They were already planning to stop Suicide on their own. Why shouldn't he join in? *"Besides, he's just a kid. He can't do it alone."*

"So he needs criminals to help him?"

"How many drug dealers did we chase out of here? We're thieves, not killers."

"Whatever you say."

Burner handed his ring to Boon. *"I'm leaving this to you. After tomorrow, you're going to be the one in charge of the operation."*

"Why?" Boon inspected the ring as if he expected it to turn into a bird and fly away. He rubbed it between his hands. *"Didn't that hero you worked with give you this? Before he died? Why give it to me? I don't even know why you kept the thing."*

"Nostalgia, that's all." The rain soon tapered off, and the two fell quiet for a long time. Burner could only worry about the day ahead of them. The other guys would have their revenge. *"The two of us will finish this. First chance you get, ditch the kid and the woman."*

"You're the boss. Just don't do anything rash. The guys would hate you if you got killed now."

As he now found himself lying on the ground by the river in a bloody heap, Burner could only laugh. God's sense of humor was unmatched. The fire that rippled through Burner's stomach gave him the opportunity to flip over to his hands and knees. With a jolt of energy he stood up, allowing some of his acidic blood to drip and sizzle against the dirt. He braced himself against a nearby tree and attempted to regain his bearings. A gunshot went off in the distance.

Slowly it returned to him. He didn't crawl out of the river on his own. That man dragged him out—the one called Matthew. A gun had fired somewhere out in the forest and took Matthew's attention from the wounded man. He told Burner to hold still and that he would be right back. Matthew disappeared, but Burner didn't get to thank him—though he wasn't sure if he would have done it. Wouldn't dying there in the water have been better? Not to mention that gratitude wasn't his style.

He couldn't see anything other than the fuzzy blur of light brown and grey tree trunks and bark, but the echo of gunshots was one he was used to. He traced it and pushed himself forward.

As Burner shambled forward he remembered his last days in the city when those so-called heroes showed him the door. He was nothing but a low-level sidekick, someone who would never amount to anything, so why pretend otherwise? It wasn't as if they were wrong with their assertions of his character. He was *here*, wasn't he?

However, the years did go by, and he did get richer, he might have been richer than any of those fakers, but he never did anything with it. What was the point? Why was he even doing this? If there was a reason to it all, he could never figure it out. He was a greedy dragon protecting his treasure horde. That was all he ever would be.

It took a moment to realize he was lying on the ground again, his breaths coming heavier and heavier. He couldn't forget about that Holmes boy and that he had dragged him into this. Burner only hoped Matthew White would be able to save him.

No—Burner would do that. It was his responsibility. He pushed himself up again, but hit the dirt once more instead.

Burner's breathing stopped and he rolled over to his side. The last thing he saw was the forest trail fading from his vision as he reminded himself that he still wasn't done yet. He could still be a hero. The path before him was clearer than ever before. The former sidekick closed his eyes and never opened them again.

JASON FLOATED in the void between portals in disbelief. The faint outline of a woman painted the emptiness before him. How was anyone here in the dark? How did she get here? More importantly: this figure had the voice of his mother.

"Who are you?" he asked it. "Did Nieto send you? How did you break the mirror?"

"*Her power gave out,*" his mother's voice said. She echoed around him. "*Zelana is trying her best to open it again. People will die unless you return to Earth. Tyndarus can wait.*"

Something about the way she spoke comforted a deeper part of him, one he had thought long lost. He didn't want to admit it, but he wanted this being to really be his mother. "Would staying in Tyndarus be so bad? I might be able to kill Nieto if I stayed."

He didn't believe his words, but he needed to hear her response. This was a test. He desired to know if she was who she sounded like.

"*Look.*" Inside her shadowed shape, Jason could see a picture forming in the intangible dark. "*She's waiting for you.*"

The void parted to reveal the warehouse Jason had just escaped from. The place was still as battered and broken as he left it. By the broken Mirror Gate he saw a familiar teenage girl kneeling down in front of it.

Zelana's eyes were closed and her forehead was against the Mirror Gate. She was shaking, but remained unmoving as a white light faintly shone from her skin and through her small balled fists. Her demeanor unsettled Jason, but she remained concentrated on whatever it was that she was doing. Had she been the one to break through the void to reach him here? Did she send this woman, or was this really his mother? He couldn't decide on what the truth could be.

"*You can't stay here.*"

"What about you?" he asked, his voice quivering with anger. He didn't know whether it was Zelana, or the shape before him that disturbed him more. "Are you coming with me?"

"*This is all I have left. I'm using it to keep you focused in this place. There are others in danger right now. Go to the boat as soon as you return. You don't have much time.*"

He choked back the words hanging in the rear of his throat. "I'm sorry I've screwed up so many times. I won't let you down again."

Something familiar and comforting like the heat of a blanket in the coldest winter embraced him through the darkness. The voice whispered words in his ear and vanished, leaving him alone again. He called out for her, but there was no reply. Only the infinite dark stared back at him.

White light split the emptiness apart. The swirling heated funnel of the Mirror Gate returned, and the pathway ahead of him lit up again and dragged him forward. Jason flew through the new opening and slammed down on the warehouse floor again. The Mirror Gate sparked and cracked behind him before finally shattering into pieces.

Jason rubbed his sore head and slowly sat up. Every muscle fiber felt as if it had been run through a meat grinder. Pollux had run him dry, and he was feeling every inch of it now. He attempted to stand, but fell back down to into a sitting position.

"Jason!" Zelana said. She grabbed him by the shoulder. "I'm so sorry! My power left me for a single instance and I lost you in the Mirror Gate. I thought you were gone forever. I'm sorry!"

She spoke in such a blur he could barely make out her words. The dizziness didn't help. In that moment he saw she choked back sobs. Tears streamed down her face.

Jason faced her and mouthed any platitude he could think of to settle her down. She rubbed her tears away with her knuckles and didn't notice him move closer. She was shaking far too much for that. Jason embraced her in a hug, squeezing her tight against his chest. Her shaking slowly faded as he held her in his arms.

"You're okay," he said. "I'm okay. That's all that matters. It's over."

Zelana was quiet for a few moments before finally nodding against his chest. "Thank you."

Finally he let her go and she looked away, rubbing at her red eyes. Jason found some energy return and forced himself back up. He moved towards the entrance of the warehouse.

"Where are you going?" she asked.

"There's a boat outside, right? I have to go there. I made a promise."

She rushed up behind him and put both hands on his back. A rush of white energy pooled into his spine and flooded throughout his aching bones. Zelana had done this once before, but it felt different here—this time the energy was clean, clear, and strong. He felt it pulsating within him. Pollux was supercharged and he could do anything again.

"This should give you enough to get there. I'm sorry, I can't do much else."

"You've done enough," he said. He couldn't bring himself to turn around and look at her. The embarrassment was too much, not to mention if he did he might not want to leave. "Matthew needs my help, so does this town. You sit here and wait. I'll be right back."

Jason dashed out of the warehouse towards the dock, bounding with every step. His energy had been renewed and doubled. He could take on the world now.

However, his mother's final words stuck in his mind. They were the last things she would ever say to him, and he would remember them as long as he lived in this life. One day he would learn just what they truly meant.

"*You've got a long road ahead of you*," she had said. "*Make it count.*"

He would, and Suicide would regret ever coming into his life in the first place.

SUMMER HAD ALWAYS been the worst season. Suicide had to wear lighter clothes, deal with jubilant children, and listen to happy couples chatting amidst crowds. Of all the seasons, it led to humanity's stupider inclinations. Hope, joy, and, love—meaningless words that didn't mean anything to one with a brain. Hiding from the cold, crushing, emptiness of the universe was the one thing humanity was good at, and it was the one thing Suicide wished to show to others more than anything.

Unexpectedly, this summer had been one of his favorites. It wasn't the dead men that thrilled him; no, they were the lucky ones. It was the pure terror on their faces before their life was snuffed out by him. The moment they met the truth and learned their pathetic fate: that is what Suicide lived for. This summer allowed him to see their fear more than he had in years.

And it wasn't even over yet!

That Mellow kid lay unmoving on the deck, as did that stupid girl, Suicide's sister. They both looked as if they had been through the ringer, which brought a warm feeling to his chest. But it was the empty eyes of Mellow Holmes that really sold him. It wasn't every day Suicide could use his powers to utterly destroy another, but then again, this was the best summer he'd ever had. The boy hadn't even closed his mouth since Suicide dropped him. For all intents and purposes he was dead. He would be atoms when Suicide blew the boat after his escape down the river. Then this whole mess could be blamed on Burner and his personal squabbles with the town. Poor Mellow would be another victim in this senseless violence. Suicide had already found that hunting knife Burner hid under his bed. All he had to do was use it on the corpse and plant it at the scene. This was really going too well.

Suicide leaned back against the yacht railing and the cool summer breeze of the river embraced him. He lifted his gun towards the boy's prone position. He'd already shot him in the gut, but the kid didn't scream—how could he with no feeling inside? Suicide scanned the boy over for someplace to shoot that wouldn't kill him right away. This day was going too well to end it now.

The hard breeze kicking up behind Suicide's back sent a rough chill across his shoulders. A cold front? He turned to face it and found a moving mist launching itself towards him.

"Castor?" he asked the fog.

An arm leaped out of the mist and seized his throat. It pulled him forwards, and Suicide flew over the railing and fell down into the water.

He hardly understood what was happening. The water rushed by him as he shot through it like a bullet. He didn't have time to think about it before the force suddenly let him go.

Suicide whipped forward, and shot out onto land, rolling into the gravel by the shore. He ached as if he had been run through a knife drawer as he spun to a stop. Suicide climbed to his knees, despite shaky balance and choked water out from his burning lungs. He rubbed his blurred eyes.

Through his clearing vision, he glimpsed a young man step out of the river and towards the shore. Castor—Matthew White—approached Suicide with a limp in his step. But there was something strange about him. Underneath his torn and stained clothes Suicide could only see bare skin: no bruises or blood. His bullet wounds were missing.

A spark of fear popped inside of Suicide's brain like a firecracker. He had shot this guy. He saw the holes himself. And yet there

Castor was, marching towards him, breathing hard and moving sluggishly, but without any of those bullet wounds in his body. Whatever power the Master gave him must have been much greater than Suicide was told.

He laughed despite his sore jaw. "Bullets don't work, huh?" Castor continued in his direction, ignoring his words. "I guess you forgot what else I can do, Castor."

Suicide punched his target and his fist struck air—despite his attack not missing its mark. Castor had turned into pure mist. When Suicide's hand passed completely through, his enemy became whole again. Suicide was still off balance from the swing when his opponent punched him in the nose. The big man's brain jumbled with the hit.

Strike after strike beat against Suicide's chest and face, Castor's body somehow slipping between every single one of his reprisals. Normally, Suicide would just use his power on his attacker when he hit him, but Castor's movements were too unpredictable to concentrate on, never mind touch skin that kept transforming into air. His brain rattling in his head didn't help.

One last punch sent Suicide backwards. He splashed down into the ankle deep water, his back scraping against the rocks. He coughed a mixture of water, spittle, and blood out as he sat up to face his aggressor.

"You've learned some new tricks. I didn't think you'd be the type to hold out."

Castor winced as his breaths arrived harder and harder with every passing minute. His raised arms trembled and his legs shook. Whatever energy he had tapped into was running low. All Suicide had to do to win was wait this out. Perhaps using his trump card would be enough to shake his opponent off. This was much too fun! He only needed a few extra seconds to set it up.

"So this is why the Master wanted you. Although, I do have a few questions. How is it that both you and the boy have powers that are the exact opposite? You aren't related, and from what I could learn, you were never Primes. So where did this ability come from? What is the Master hiding?"

"Now you care?" Castor said, at length. His ragged breaths caused his speech to stilt. "I told you what Nieto wants goes beyond your cheap kicks. You don't understand the first thing about him."

"I don't need to." Suicide stood up. His legs nearly gave out on him but he smiled anyway. "I'm going to give you one last chance to give yourself up, or else someone is going to die in the next few minutes. You know I make good on my word, Castor."

"No more talk. I'm going to break your damn neck and drown you in the river."

The prospect of that thrilled Suicide, but he had something else in mind. He removed his phone from his pocket. Thankfully, it still worked. He showed the flat, thin slab to Castor. The bombs on the yacht would do their work a bit earlier than he wanted, but it would be worth this moment. He would use the phone to blow the boat now. Every single one of these vermin would meet their end today, and, hopefully, so would he.

"Too late," Suicide said. "Now listen as they die."

CHAPTER 18
END OF THE OUTSIDERS

FOR SOME UNFATHOMABLE REASON, both Mellow Holmes and that girl from the warehouse were lying alone and unconscious on the deck of the yacht. Jason found only those two teenagers. Neither Suicide nor Matthew were there.

Jason peered out over the water and thought he saw two people on the opposite shore across the St. Laurence River. There he spotted the two he was looking for with his enhanced vision. Suicide was holding a phone to Matthew and looking rather haggard. What were they doing over there? The two of them would have to wait. Jason had another job to do before dealing with that.

The boy picked up both the fallen teenagers under his arms. At that moment he heard a click issue from somewhere deep in the bowels of the yacht. Jason paused in thought. He remembered Suicide's phone and his tired mind made the connection quick.

"*A bomb!*" he whispered.

The teenager sprinted towards dock, but from the subtle rumbling underneath the deck he knew he wouldn't make it to the shore in time, even with Pollux's supercharge. He needed to leave the ship now with the two teenagers in his grip.

Before even thinking about it, Jason crouched, sent Pollux's force down hard into his legs and leaped. The yacht exploded as he soared upwards into the sky.

The air ripped apart, and heat pushed up under the boy as he launched vertically. He soared easily over a hundred feet in the sky, his legs thrashing madly underneath him. Boards and hunks of metal gushed out across the river, the dock, and the shore as he overlooked it all. The force of the explosion tore the yacht into pieces, leaving it a giant fireball wreck. The updraft, however, tossed him off course of his original jump. He ended up gliding towards the forest trees behind the warehouse.

The wind blew up under his drop as the treeline approached closer and closer. What scraps of Pollux that remained inside pooled into his frame and would allow a steady landing—if he could only judge his distance.

Jason crashed through tree branches. He angled both the girl and Mellow away from the brush as he fell, careful to watch his drop at the same time. Cracking and crunching arrived underneath him as the blitz of black and brown tree brush blinded him. He couldn't see how close the ground was, but he still attempted to slow his descent by kicking against any tree trunk he could see. Greenery slapped him across the face.

Then he saw the earth rush up to meet him.

The ground trembled underneath his weight as he landed on his feet. It pushed down under him and threw him forward and off balance. His legs gave out and both teenagers tumbled out of his arms and listlessly to the dirt. Jason dropped in a dead weight and landed on his face, arms outstretched. Pollux left him to slumber.

Zelana's voice cried out from somewhere nearby, but he didn't get to see her before he met the darkness.

THE LOOK on Castor's face was worth blowing up Burner's yacht earlier than planned and enduring the pain of those acid attacks on his sore flesh. The fireball consumed the boat whole and the remaining scrap flew out into the river and along the shoreline. Everyone on that wreck was dead, and Suicide couldn't help but feel a little jealous. Castor, in contrast, fell silent.

As the draft blew across Suicide's cut-up cheek, he fought off a wince. Instead, he grinned through the agony. This summer kept improving. The rage on Castor's face told him what was coming next. He crushed the phone and threw the remains into the water. The void awaited him. It was time!

"You probably should have saved those children first, Castor." Suicide held his joy in check, but his body trembled with happiness regardless. Just a little prodding and he could get what he'd always desired. He'd won! "It's all because of your failure. How does it feel to be a murderer?"

"This is all you are." Castor's flat tone unnerved Suicide. He turned to face the criminal before him with no change of expression, despite what had just happened. "That boy was a harmless kid, and that girl was your sister. You killed them without even thinking about it. No hesitation at all. There is nothing inside of you."

"The last horse finally crosses the finish line. You've got to take me in, so come do it, you stupid bastard. But I'm not going to let you." Suicide removed the hunting knife from behind his back. He didn't get to use it yet, which made this the best time to give it a workout. "Unless you kill me here, I'm going to gut you, Castor. You know I'll do it."

"The only thing you're going to do is drown."

Castor rushed across the knee deep water. His fists poured down on Suicide like hard rain. The knife flashed as Suicide swung, but the blade wouldn't meet its mark. Castor slipped between every slash and punched at his victim. Suicide reeled as the hits scrambled his brains and drew blood.

The killer grinned, his crimson-stained teeth flashing despite the lack of a successful reprisal. This was what he had waited for! Pain exploded inside like a Molotov cocktail, spreading agony all over his insides. This man was going to kill him. The void was just ahead. Finally!

All the slaughter in the world couldn't prepare him for this. So many twinkling lights extinguished from vacant stares while he stood over their corpses. What was the feeling he would experience? Would it be euphoria? Agony? Nothing? They were the same to him. Joy and pain were two sides of the same coin, and the default state of emptiness.

He didn't want to laugh as his acid-scarred face split open, but it also didn't matter. Through the chaos of battle, he ran his knife along Castor's thigh. The attacker grunted, and more ecstasy pumped into Suicide's brain. Dying and slashing apart his killer at the same time! He couldn't imagine a more perfect way to die.

"Come on, Castor!" he yelled. "Don't run out on me now!"

Castor shoved Suicide down into the river. Instantly, water rushed in to choke at his lungs. Suicide shoved his knife above the water, hit something solid, and twisted. A cry of pain echoed somewhere in the muffled world over him. The knife slipped out of his hand, and a pressure squeezed on his insides. Despite his gasping, and the rushing darkness closing in on him, he still had energy to spare.

His head was brought above water again, and he coughed the liquid from his lungs. Castor held him by the lapels.

"Stop laughing!" Castor shouted. "Do you really want to die here? Like this?"

Suicide spat in his face. "You've killed better men then me, I'm sure."

"I won't kill you."

"You have no choice. I'll kill you like those kids on the boat if you don't. Then I'll find that bitch that hit me with the arrows, and I'll blast her to pieces, too. They'll die if I don't."

A fog-like cloud passed Castor's visage. Instead of the anger and rage that had bubbled over into this slaughter of a fight, the young man had now become someone entirely different. He smiled his teeth like razors at Suicide.

"I'll give you something better!"

Castor wrapped his left hand around Suicide's throat, but his right appeared to vanish. It twisted in bent in the wind like it was made of air—or was that fog? Castor shoved it forward into Suicide's mouth, and the gust flooded through his nose. He couldn't quite make it out at first, but he soon realized he was breathing in a potent gas. His brain rippled and bent with the strange stench filling his nostrils.

Suicide writhed and kicked as the strange sensation numbed his entire convulsing body. An invisible force beat against his thoughts, turning his nervous system off like a spigot. Everything numbed, and his mind slipped away. His eyes rolled back in his head as he twitched.

The world left Suicide behind and he slumped down into the water.

He tumbled deep into an abyss somewhere far from this world. Everything he knew fell away. Suicide landed face first on solid ground he couldn't feel and breathed in air he couldn't breathe. Not only had the world vanished, but so had Castor. Suicide was all alone in this impossible place.

His muscles wouldn't so much as twitch. He couldn't think, he couldn't speak, and he couldn't move. Somewhere above him, the faint rushing of water and the chatter of someone talking slowly faded away with the rest of his senses.

Was this death? No, he hadn't felt anything like pain. He was sleeping, or something close to it.

As the silence overtook his last remaining thoughts, his mind softened like a dumb vegetable in the empty space. It wasn't long before he could think of nothing. The final words coming to his scrambled brains cursed the man who had robbed him of his victory.

Somewhere he thought he heard the Master laughing, but by that time, it didn't matter. The killer named Suicide was no more.

THE POLICE BOATS took far too long to come down the river. It had to have been because they were busy dealing with the madness at the block party, but they still were too late to do anything here. The detective Matthew had met days ago stood on one boat waving at him on the shore. Matthew waved back, hoping they wouldn't take too long.

The wielder of Castor looked at the unconscious form of Suicide beside him. He thought the villain might find his way back up, but he knew better. Matthew pumped enough gas into his brain to mess him up forever. He didn't want it to go down that way, but there was little choice. He couldn't give a psycho like this license to hurt others, nor did he want to give him the release of death like he wanted. Trash like Suicide didn't deserve anything resembling an escape. There he would lie, trapped in his own diseased mind until he rotted with it.

But Matthew didn't consider that monster. The last thing he cared about was Suicide. Jason was still out there, as were Lynn and Zelana. Thankfully the detective told him about Jason after the boat landed on the shore. That stupid kid had managed to rescue the teenagers from the boat while Matthew was busy with this psycho. He owed that kid again.

It was a crazy day. There was chaos in the center of town, and that was where the majority of the police were. A bunch of outsiders were stabbed to death in the old park where a giant boulder had somehow shattered the ground, destroying the entire site. No innocents were harmed, but the strangers in the park weren't so lucky. The only survivor in that mess was Boon, one of Burner's men.

Oh, and there was Burner to think about. How was he making out?

Matthew climbed on the boat with Detective Leclerc and they headed for the opposite shore. It was hard enough to believe it was all over until he saw both Jason and Zelana standing side by side next to the destroyed deck and the scrap on the shore, waving towards them. They both looked like they'd been through hell, charred black and covered in cuts and bruises, but they were both alive.

For the first time in a long time, Matthew laughed long and loud.

The cops on the boat looked at him like he was crazy, but it didn't matter. Nieto wouldn't chase off the two of them ever again. He knew the boy would agree with him on this one, too.

The pair had made their stand. No more running, no more hiding, and no more capitulating with the being that wanted to destroy them and their world. It was all over. That hard fought battle across two worlds and two countries was finished.

Finally, they were home.

EPILOGUE

THE LEAVES were beginning to turn. Late August showed its hand to the oncoming September weather. Fall was around the corner and the cool breeze of the early morning didn't disguise this shift. That long, chaotic summer had finally ended.

Matthew leaned against the window by the front door, watching Jason board the morning bus for the first time in Riverview. Matthew admired how easy the kid made it look to accept such a difficult change he had never asked for. Despite it being his first day of school in a new town, the boy didn't display any jangled nerves. He had been through worse, or so he said.

After the mess on the river, Jason's wounds had healed within the week. Matthew had been almost as fast. They hid the recovery from the townsfolk as best they could, but Matthew suspected Jason's new friends might have noticed something was wrong, especially that Spencer kid. Thankfully that boy wasn't too seriously injured, though he didn't like to talk about what happened. Matthew didn't blame him.

Zelana had gone back to Tyndarus, but neither she nor Jason was upset to see the other go. In fact, they had been smiling the entire time she was leaving. Matthew wondered if something had happened between them, but since they were better off he didn't push it. He still needed to return to Tyndarus and apologize to Ordopha as it was. He owed her more than anyone. After everything they went through, Ord deserved some gratitude.

As the bus drove off, Matthew turned his attention towards the grey van passing the house for the second time that day. It would certainly follow Jason to school, but Matthew wasn't worried about that. His sixth sense had told them the pair was being watched, but the ones watching them were keeping their distance. This meant not using his powers and hoping that eventually they would eventually lose interest.

Matthew figured these were the same people that Roadbuster contacted to help them out of Albion and got them across the border. These guys were probably more interested in who was after the two of them than the two former fugitives themselves at this point. That was fine—if Nieto wanted to risk exposure, he could send another agent. It would end worse for him this time.

The only survivors in the enemy camp numbered three, technically four. Suicide had been in a coma since Matthew put him there, and was shipped back to Serenity City to a heavily guarded cell. The other survivor included Boon, the man with telekinesis abilities, and Suicide's "sister" Erin—which wasn't her real name, and she wasn't his sister. No one knew who she was. Either way, both were still healing and would be shipped to Ottawa for trial shortly. Neither showed much interest in escape, choosing instead to remain quiet in their cells.

Mellow Holmes was another story. The boy was a mess and had to be brought in for emergency surgery. A day later after clinging to life, he made it out by the skin of his teeth. However, something changed in him. The teenager no longer felt anything, no joy, no anger, and no sadness. He just stared blankly ahead with no particular reaction. Suicide's power had done tremendous damage to him, possibly permanently removing a piece of him. Matthew hoped if he returned to school today that Jason would try to talk to him. Ever since the incident, Mellow Holmes had refused to speak to a single soul, but he did allow Jason and Spencer to visit. That was something, at least.

And, most importantly, he was alive.

Throughout this whole ordeal that was the major thought that Matthew couldn't help but appreciate. He had wanted to run, to hide, from the world desiring to crush him into dust, but he soon found he wasn't running anymore. He didn't want to, didn't need to. The two of them had come so far from where they started, but they made it regardless. There was still more to do, too.

Once those watching them finally left, and once Zelana returned, they would plan their next move. Nieto would not keep getting away. The next time Matthew returned to Tyndarus, it would be to permanently end the being who desired to destroy their world. Nieto's whole operation would be stopped at its source. The Gemini Man was unstoppable.

As he thought to himself, Lynn came through the back door. She carried her vacuum cleaner and wore old overalls with her hair tied back. She jumped when she saw him watching her. He laughed and she blushed. Lynn hated being seen wearing stuff like that. Matthew beckoned her towards the window, and she joined him, puzzled.

Finally, he broke the silence. "I never really thanked you for everything, Lynn."

"That's—" she cleared her throat. "That's okay. It's what I do."

"You do a lot. I have tonight off. Want to see a movie? Jason started working part-time at the theater and told me there's a classic playing tonight. Interested?"

She smirked. "Sure you can handle me?"

That familiar van drove away into the early morning sunlight, and Matthew smiled as the nuisance left. They would be back, but for now he could breathe easy. This is just the way it was. A long day waited ahead of them, just like any other.

And that was fine with him.

"Sure. We can handle anything."

BOOK FOUR

CODA

GEMINI DREAMER
&
GEMINI DESTROYER

GEMINI DREAMER

CHAPTER 1
EVERY NIGHT

THE DREAMS HIT HIM hard a year ago, and they never stopped coming. Every night, he was reminded of it all. They always made him remember what he never wanted to think about.

Boon was fourteen years old the first time he killed a man, though he wasn't named Boon at the time. The bullet glided through the gangster's heart, knocking him back out of the apartment and tumbling over the building. The body crashed into the roof of a car, setting off the alarm, but the psycho never got up again. Neither did Boon ever return to that hole he once called a home after he walked away from the bloodshed and debauchery.

Then the dream ended.

He woke up in a cold sweat, the memory passing by like a speeding train in the night. These days, the memories were coming faster and even more furious, as if he were losing a race with his own mind. Then, there was that voice, getting louder and louder every single night. Boon sat up in his bed and rubbed his eyes.

The midnight hour sent moonbeams across the concrete basement floor, shining a pale spotlight on the pile of firewood lying in the dusty corner next to the ancient insulation. It took a moment of staring open-mouthed before he finally remembered where he was—on the run.

Boon ran a hand through his hair and felt the unshaven dark locks in his pale, trembling palms. How long had it been since he had gotten a haircut, anyway? Months? This endless purgatory would never end. He felt at his sunken cheeks and realized he hadn't eaten in a few days. Perhaps this time, his stomach could keep something down.

Boon threw on the nearest grey tank top and pulled his jogging shorts back on. His gut growled as he slid across the basement floor on bare feet.

"You awake, Amy?" he asked.

The young woman didn't move. He looked over the slight figure of the teenage girl lying under the sheets, her pale white face facing the ceiling with eyes shut tight. The imprint of her arms lying on her chest from under the covers was clearly visible from his perspective. He grumbled and scratched at his bedraggled hair. She was out again.

"Do you have any idea what time it is?" he asked her. She didn't stir, though he hardly expected her to. "You can do anything, and you choose to do this. It's late. Rest already. You're going to get us killed."

"Oh, shut up, Nathan," a male answered.

The figure of the middle-aged heavyset man descending the stairs caused Boon to flinch, but any fear soon passed when he realized who it was. "Don't call me that, Amy."

"Cute," the big man said. He dropped six plastic bags full of what looked like groceries on the cement floor. "We've been here for like a year. We might as well use our real names."

Boon leaned back against the wall. "I threw that name away a long time ago. Nathan Baxter wasn't a killer. At least, he wasn't supposed to be. But I guess that doesn't matter much now when we're hiding from a psychotic cult. We'll be here for a long time, hopefully not forever. At least we look enough alike that people think we're siblings when they see us. Last thing we need is more suspicion following us. Wait, what's that?"

He leaned down towards the pile on the floor, pushing through the dried meat and vegetables and found a thin book at the bottom. He flipped through the old paperback, sighed, and glanced back at the old man.

The large figure shrugged. "I don't know. When I possess someone for long enough our thoughts sometimes mix into each other. He must have thought I'd like that book, I guess. Anyway, I'm going to take him back home now. You might as well go back to sleep, Nathan."

Boon stood up and tossed the book at the sleeping girl. "If your thoughts mix, then it's dangerous to keep using him like this. You don't need to do this anyway. I can lift wallets, remember?" Boon directed his thoughts to the back pocket of the big man and pulled the wallet out with only his mind. He caught the floating slab in one hand and waved it in his victim's face. "It's just that easy."

"Give it back," Amy said through the large man. She used his body to put the wallet back in his pocket as she continued to sleep in the bed beside them. "This guy runs the grocery store so it's easy to get him to do things without raising suspicion. You look like a hobo and would give us away instantly. When are you planning on cutting that mane, anyway? You look better without it. Maybe we could even get you a date. There are some cute girls at the market, you know."

They had only been here for a year, but she seemed far more adjusted to this life than he was. Considering what she had been through, he didn't blame her. Nonetheless, teenagers should not be so used to risking lives or living on the run. He remembered the look his own mother gave him after shooting that dealer, and he shivered. No more of that. This limbo of an existence needed to end.

"Give it a rest, Amy. Just take him back home already. I'm sure someone is going to miss him."

The old man paused as if he were going to argue then grumbled instead. He spun around and marched back up the stairs. "At least, take that book off my face."

The basement door shut as the large man disappeared into the night. Boon obliged Amy's request and picked the book he threw aside off of her nose and glanced over it. Fairy tales. Kids loved these, right? He placed it next to her and walked back to his bed. Hopefully, that would be the last disturbance for tonight.

A thought passed through Boon's tired mind as he sat down on his bed again. Those dreams he'd been having more and more over the year were only becoming more and more clear. The source had to have been a Prime, someone with powers.

But who? Was it that cult that paid for his bail as well as the girl's last year? But that was so long ago now. Certainly they couldn't have found them? Didn't they have better things to do than just hunt a pair of ex-criminals?

Boon laid down on his creaking bed and rubbed his eyes with his palms. What had that guy said back then? It had been a year now. He thought back, and slowly, the memory returned.

"*Walk away now, and I can't guarantee a second chance,*" the man in the suit said. He tapped the hood of his white van and pointed to the tinted windows. "*Come back with us to the base, and we will give you a second chance. You owe us as much after murdering our followers and getting off with it.*"

The wide man wore a lime green suit and had his greying locks combed back, the smile of a serial killer adorning his lips. Amy glanced between Boon and this very imposing figure who thought he was doing them a favor. Even though they were in the middle of the rear parking lot during the summer day, there was not a soul around to watch their conversation between the cars. Boon wiped sweat from his forehead, cursing the heat, before he finally addressed the piranha before him.

"*You are the reason I'm here,*" Boon said. "*You came to my town, killed my boss and my friends, destroyed everything you could get your hands on, and you think I'm going to join your gang? I can understand if the girl here hates me since she was on your side, but I have no loyalty to you at all, even if you used connections to get me out of this pickle. It's the least you owe me. Now, I'll be leaving. If I ever see you again, you'll join your pals in the morgue.*"

"*You're going to regret this, Baxter,*" the suit barked. He continued shouting even as Boon walked away from him out of the parking lot. "*Don't have any second thoughts! Hey, where are you going?*"

The girl sidled up behind Boon as he strode down the ramp towards the street. "*Are you really going back to that town? Even after everything we—I did there?*"

"*No. I ain't got no place there anymore. Why do you care?*"

She shrugged. "*I don't. But I'm coming with you.*"

"*I don't exactly need a weird teenager tagging around with me. If you're hoping to find that Gemini Man I keep hearing about, forget it. I don't know him.*"

"*We were sent to your town to find him—a man too dangerous to be allowed to live. At least, that's what they said. They said a lot of things, Boon. I don't even know if he exists. But I do know that you helped wipe out Suicide's group when they scoured Riverview looking for him. You and me? We're targets now. They're going to treat us just like that so-called Gemini Man. Ironic, isn't it?"*

"*Hysterical. But I don't want to look after some kid.*"

"*Well, too bad. You're the only one left that can take responsibility for the Riverview incident.*"

And Amy had been with him in the year since leaving that lot. She never told him the real reason she decided to follow him, but he had always secretly hoped it was for revenge. He did, after all, kill one of her friends in that madness. After losing everything in Riverview, he'd welcome death.

But that never happened. Instead, she not only divulged her real name wasn't Erin, like everyone in Riverview thought it was, but she also her true nature. The fierce fighter who was a zealous follower of Suicide's cult was in reality a scared little girl puffing her chest up: a glass cannon. On top of that, she insisted that she harbored no ill will towards Boon for helping to stop her group. Why was this? She wouldn't say.

As Boon turned over into his bed, he remembered that book the man she possessed had given her. A book on fairy tales? Had her victim seen something in her that even Boon missed? He slipped back into slumber as the questions piled up again.

"*No*," the voice said in his head. "*That girl almost died. Death changes people. By the way, what would Burner say about you living with one of the people who killed him?*"

The name of his old boss echoed in Boon's head with his thumping headache. Who was this voice, and how did he know so much about them? It was too high-pitched to be his own, yet too low to be Amy. He almost wished that if this mystery voice was a killer that he would just strike already and end this endless cycle of nothing.

"*You're running out of time, Boon. They're on their way to you. There isn't much time remaining.*"

Boon's eyes snapped open the same moment an explosion went off in the distance. He sat up, perfectly aware that whatever caused that was closer than he would want. He knew exactly who they had to be.

Their pursuers were here.

AMY ALWAYS FELT OFF when she drove a car in someone else's body. Though her power allowed her complete control by sending energy into her target's brain, she always felt like she would merge with her victim when it happened. It used to be easier to not have their consciousness spill over into hers, but that changed on the last job, when she attacked that girl. Her power had knocked the wind out of Amy. Now, her mind wandered even when she was not inhabiting someone else. What was it about that girl that changed Amy so much? She even found herself joining up with one of the men responsible for killing her allies and sending her to jail. But were they even on her side in the first place? Doubts attacked the teenager more and more as the days in hiding went on. Her impulse control had weakened since possessing that teenage girl in Riverview, and now she found she was more willing to listen into the voices she used to suppress in order to more easily control their shells. She *had* to start listening to them. How else would she be able to drive?

Nevertheless, this man she held in her power now did not put up much of a fight when she took control. In fact, he seemed to be letting her drive while lightly guiding his movements under her control to do simple things like hit turn signals and tap the brakes.

"*I know how to drive, Davis,*" she said through his mouth. "*Just go to sleep until I get you home. It'll be easier that way.*"

There weren't much in the way of even lampposts out here in the country. They were several miles away from the town of Huntingdon in Quebec. The empty roads with farms on either side and endless fields in the dark made everything seem even more lonely as she guided him down the vacant streets toward his home. She could just leave his head and let him control himself again, but he might lose control or flip out if she did. It would be easier for everyone if she took him home.

"You remind me of her, you know," Davis suddenly said with his own voice.

She didn't have to ask who he meant, though she also wasn't supposed to know who that was. A kaleidoscope of old memories spun through her mind more and more as she possessed Davis these days. She almost wished she didn't take him over, but he was always the safer target.

There were birthday parties, fairs, and picnics, all of which flashed through her like a particularly violent flood. They all danced to music, chanted at the local sports events, even visited the library together. The visions came so fast that she almost lost control of the steering wheel.

"*Davis, stop.*"

"I can't."

"*What's that sound?*"

A car leaped out of the forest to her right, slamming into them with incredible speed. Their vehicle spun with the hit, rolling over with the strike and sending Davis reeling against his seat belt. It continued to spin for what felt like a solid minute before landing directly on its roof.

Amy undid the seat belt and dizziness nearly overtook her. She shoved open the door and tripped out into the night air.

"A bit late for you to be out, old man," the criminal in the attacking car said. He crossed the road, his profile masked by moonlight. "Could it be you were visiting someone you shouldn't have been?"

"No," Davis said. How did he keep breaking free of her control? He breathed heavy as he slumped against the spinning wheel of his upside down vehicle. "Just going out for a night drive. Here, take my wallet."

The stranger didn't move as Davis tossed the small wallet before him onto the pavement. Instead, he turned back towards the woods he had just barreled out of. "Let us hurry now. Tell me where the criminals are hiding."

Davis coughed and blood ejected from his lips. "They're not criminals."

"You are not the law; you do not get to decide. Only the Master decides."

"They're just kids."

Amy tried to struggle against Davis' will, to try and put him back under her control. She couldn't make him shut up. Her consciousness slid further out of grasp as she yelled in the void that was overtaking her. Davis was dying.

"Whoever they were before doesn't matter anymore," Davis said. His breath rattled between words. "Whoever you are, you need to let it go. We don't have a long time in this world. It's best to forgive and move on. Why not just let them go?"

The stranger glanced back into the woods once more. "What is it? Who is there?"

Out of the trees stepped a line of about seven men in trench coats and hats, marching across the street towards the accident site. Each of them looked exactly the same, all moving in a jerking fashion and carrying medieval-like battleaxes.

The man before Davis drew a gun and fired. Two of the approaching figures dropped to the ground, but the rest swarmed over the attacker like a pack of wolves, hacking away. The screams of Davis' killer filled the night as Amy fell away from the scene, her consciousness spent. The last thing she remembered were the words of the man she possessed as the entire world fell away.

Her eyes jerked awake, and she was back in bed again, in that same basement. Amy leaped up and threw on her skirt, shoes, and a shirt before sprinting over towards Boon. She shook him awake, the events of what had just occurred spouting from her lips like a machine gun. It took a moment for him to process everything before he rolled out of his bed, changed, and directed her to the stairs. They had to get out.

As they tore up the stairs and towards the car, she realized she was holding that book in her hand—the same one Davis had given her. The pair slid into the car, and, while Boon revved the engine and tore off into the night, she looked it over. A book of fairy tales?

The old rust bucket bolted down the road as she stared blandly at the book. Why did he give her this book? A bookmark lay in the story *The Three Princesses in Whiteland*. She flipped through it as Boon yelled at her.

"Look alive! They found us."

Out of the forest behind them, two cars tore out of the trees and screeched after them. Boon twisted and turned the wheel, but no matter how many roads he spun down, the pursuers kept after them. He could not seem to shake them.

A concrete spike pierced through the bottom of the car, tearing the vehicle in two. Both Boon and Amy were thrown sideways as the metal split. She rolled into the brush as a series of spikes stuck up through the pavement, beating against the scrap. One bore through the engine, and the car exploded.

Scrap flew everywhere, the fireball blinding her. Amy forced herself up and around a nearby tree as the remains soared across the dark woods, sending small flames everywhere.

The girl's breath refused to catch up with her as she lay in dark of the woods, screams breaking the night behind her. She thought of Davis, lying there in the middle of the road dying, unsure of why he had given himself up to die for someone he didn't even know. The earth behind her rumbled.

She leaped up, and a hand seized her throat, shoving her back into the dirt. Red spots matching the flames crossed her vision. But there was no arm attached to the hand. In fact, the appendage was oddly cold.

A man stood over her, his figure blocked by the shadow of the dancing blaze. He wore a long coat, and his left hand appeared to be missing. "It's time to come home, Erin."

Amy gagged. "That's not my name."

"You took it when you made the pact. That girl is no more. You traded that life away when you took on your chosen name. The Master will welcome you back."

"No!"

The girl tried to cry out, but the hand lifted her vertically as if it were attached to a much larger man. A heavy weight struck the back of her head, and she slumped into darkness. Before she lost all sight and sound, her mind raced to the dying body of Davis out on the road. Another ally dead. How many more would she kill before this was all over?

"Don't worry, girl," the aggressor said. "You're safe now. I will take you to the Dreaming City."

CHAPTER 2
MAN OF STONE

BOON WINCED as the rocks scraped his back. Fire cooked the world around the former criminal, sweat blinding his eyes while his breaths caught up with the rest of him. He flipped back onto his feet at the same moment a crowd of men in long black jackets flooded the road to his right. Their silhouettes were difficult to make out in the dark of the woods, aside from a man standing by the concrete pillar where the scrapped car burned endlessly.

"Nathan Baxter," the figure said. "We've been searching for you."

Boon's power grabbed at the shards of glass and burning remains of the vehicle scattered about. His mind wrapped them like a boxer's fist in tape. He lifted them, allowing the hundreds of scrap pieces hover about like floating satellites, and threw the junk forward with all his strength through the burning brush. The projectiles glided through the cooked air like a fastball throw across a baseball diamond pitch.

The road itself tore up and lifted around some of the attacks, defending the targets not unlike a shield blocking arrows. But not all of the enemies were so lucky. The glass and metal riddled at least a dozen of the men, sending them spinning with the pelting and dropping the victims to the road. Boon used the moment to find cover behind a row of thick birches and caught his breath. He took solace in the fact that he at least took a chunk of his pursuers down with that blow.

That is, until they got up again.

The bodies lurched back up, jerking awkwardly as the metal and glass stuck from their heavily jacketed forms. They still could not be fully made out in the dark, but he was beginning to doubt they were human. The cement fell from the unharmed attackers, and the one in the center spoke out.

"Is this how you killed the men in Riverview, Baxter?"

Boon stayed silent, instead scanning the brush for Amy. Where did she land? Was she even still alive?

"All that talent and you waste it being a petty thief and pointlessly defying the Master like this. You have no reason to be so obstinate. We've seen your files."

Files? Who cared about files? Yes, Boon had killed before, and he still remembered the look on his mother's face when he blew away that dealer, sending him off the balcony and into the parking lot. That freak deserved it, no one denied it—but the way she watched him when he turned around to see her . . . that was not a look of pride. Those wide eyes never looked at him the same. He left home not long after that. There was no place for him there anymore.

"You ran with Burner's gang, yes? Running up and down the St. Laurence River, stealing and pillaging like some wannabe Robin Hood and his merry morons. How did that end up, if you don't mind me asking? They're all dead now after daring to defy us, and only you remain. But that's just fine. After all, you and yours did the same to ours. Too much needless death. This isn't about revenge, Baxter. We see your talents, and we want to make use of them. What else do you even have left?"

Boon couldn't spot the girl anywhere within their number. Did she run? Was she still out there? He used the moment to grab even more scrap with his mind, including the pieces still embedded in some of the killers. Perhaps, he could get something out of them before they lost patience with him. Boon wiped the building sweat from his forehead and leaned out from the trees. He wouldn't have another chance after this.

The trash embedded in the men wobbled, thanks to the power in his mind's eye. Boon kept his hold on it as he faced his enemies.

"I don't have anywhere left to go, correct. But neither do any of you. I might be a screw-up, someone who made every stupid mistake a fool can make, but I will always be more than a killer. I can hold my head a little bit higher that at least I'm not like you."

The leader in the center laughed. None of the others moved. "Is this really all that this world has? Scurrying rats and dead mice rotting in the maze? I have been to this world multiple times, but I still do not see what the Master sees in humans. You have nothing to offer the universe, nothing to offer him. And yet he insists on giving you chance after chance. What is your hold on him?"

"So now you're aliens?"

"Now I'm going to put an end to this game."

"Something is definitely ending here."

Boon thrust both his arms forward with his thoughts, and the shards inside the bodies lifted their victims off the ground. With a simple gesture, the dozen or so men flew backwards into the brush. He heard the crunching of bark and bone as the flames burned on, but not a single cry from the victims was let out. Before he could question any of it, one of the men appeared beside him.

A fist cracked against Boon's face, and sent him twisting backwards into a birch tree. His shoulder struck the trunk and shook leaves and roasting flames down into grass. For a moment, Boon thought the attacker's arm looked somewhat dislocated.

He moved in, swinging wildly. Boon's fists found their mark, and his victim reeled with the hits. Flesh bruised, and his knuckles cracked against anything that came close. He'd been in too many fights to know that letting your opponent any breathing room was suicide.

But the attacker didn't react quite like Boon expected. The victim wavered with each hit but never cried in pain or really made any expression on his still face that he felt any thing at all. Boon kicked him down when another goon grabbed him from behind. The sore fighter felt the full nelson tighten on him as he struggled in his enemy's grip.

"See?" the leader said from the burning road. "This is as far as humans can go. Once you join us, you will see and feel things you never thought possible as a human. All we have to do is break you to atoms before building you up again."

"I won't break anymore." Boon ground his teeth as he shook against the man behind him. "But I will break you."

"Say farewell to your pathetic life and welcome eternity. It is time to visit the Dreaming City."

A loud crunch erupted from behind Boon. The two arms holding him loosened their hold and spiraled into the grass, dismembered. The corpse behind Boon flopped forward as if it had been sliced in two, falling over in halves. There stood his rescuer, a man with a battleaxe and a similar long coat to the men currently trying to do him and Amy in.

"Run," he said. "Head north to my left and up the road. You'll know when to stop."

"You can't handle this alone."

From the road, Boon spotted the men from earlier, emerging out of the brush again as if his attack had only mildly inconvenienced them. They moved no differently from earlier. What were these guys made of? Perhaps they really weren't human, after all. How could he hope to take them on if they wouldn't stay dead? Boon was but one man.

As if they heard his thoughts, more men arrived out of the brush around him, a dozen men who looked just like the one who saved him seconds earlier. The two armies of strange warriors faced each other with Boon lingering behind the group of clones. Before he could question any of it, the opposing parties collided with each other, a brawl breaking out. Boon used the chance to run.

He blitzed through the trees, following the direction his savior had told him to go. Questions littered his mind. Why were all these parties converging on him and the girl now after a year in the wilderness, and what did they really want with them? There was clearly more to this than mere gang recruitment. Boon had been through that song and dance before. This was different.

At his side, he spotted the man who saved him—or one of his clones. The weird man held Amy in his arms, the girl was out like a light and covered in soot and small lacerations. Boon breathed a bit easier. Perhaps this guy really was on his side.

"They called me the Cutter, once," his rescuer said. The two ran side by side for what seemed like forever through the woods. "I have since taken on the name Percival Locke. You are both in greater danger than you think."

Before Boon could ask anything, a burning tree branch tumbled down for his head. He dodged and rolled into yet more endlessly burning flames. As he sprang up and continued his run, he noticed both Amy and the stranger had vanished. Boon ran onward, certain he'd find them again if he kept going.

He soon came out of the trees and into a clearing—or what was supposed to be a clearing. Instead, only old brick and concrete buildings lay ahead of him. Lamp lights shone bright in the midnight hour. The town was couched in the middle of what was a river. Boon couldn't speak and state that he had been here hundreds of times before. There was never any town in this part of the woods.

"Nathan?" his mother said. "You're finally here."

To his left out of an alley emerged the woman Boon hadn't seen in near two decades from the trees. She looked older, a bit greyer hair and some extra weight, but her round cheeks and red hair were the same as they ever were. That wide-eyed stare was one he'd never forgotten.

"You're just in time, Nathan. Welcome to the Dreaming City! We are on the way to paradise."

Boon bit his lip, his serious expression never wavering. He said nothing as he followed the old woman into the dark of the town. No words would come from his parched throat.

The town was dead for the late hour, and it sure looked normal enough with plenty of expected buildings for so far out in the country from supermarkets to a library to even car dealerships, a park even awaited ahead. This place was undoubtedly real.

And yet he knew this town was not right. A familiar feeling filled his thoughts the deeper he strode into the unknown.

"*The Dreaming City isn't as it seems.*"

That voice was trying to speak with him again. Who was it? However, it soon faded away into the night.

Despite that, he felt a strange form of relief as he looked upon his own mother walking before him. For the first time in ages, he knew it was going to be okay.

He was home.

CHAPTER 3
THE DREAMING CITY

AMY REMEMBERED STARING at her mother's gravestone for what felt like hours. The rain poured on, her umbrella buckling under the pressure pressing down from above. Everyone else had long since left—it wasn't like her mom was particularly loved in life or anything. Nonetheless, Amy couldn't help but watch the grave. Reality just didn't feel real.

"*There's no turning back now,*" Suicide had said. "*You get that, right?*"

All she could do was nod at her new boss's words. Had she done this? Was it her decision that led to all this? They said they found her body after she had killed herself alone in a motel room, but that didn't feel like Amy's mother. She had never been afraid of anything, least of all life.

"*But you have plenty to be afraid of, Erin. That's your new name now. You earned it. A bit of fear is good for the mind—keeps it sharp. When the Master finally arrives, we will all have plenty to be scared of.*"

"*What do I have to do?*" She swallowed hard, the pit in her stomach hardening.

"*This is real life. Wake up and enjoy it. There is no place in it for those who refuse to face the truth. You are a monster, just like me. Our powers are proof of that. Time to show the world.*"

The storm faded away into the darkness of her mind, and the past left her stranded behind. All that remained before her were those police photos of her mother taken after she was found in that motel room. Amy swore she could hear her whispering to her in the void.

"*I'm still watching, waiting.*"

The girl dry-heaved as her eyes snapped open. It was all just a dream. Sweat glistened on her forehead as the tears welled in her eyes.

Amy's headache was only matched by her fatigue as she awoke in the hotel bed. She rubbed her stiff shoulders as she rolled over and felt the slumber leave her. The striped green and white wallpaper and the sun shining through the blinds told her she was no longer in that basement anymore. It took a moment for her brain to catch up with the realization.

She leaned forward when she realized the clothes lying on the corner of the mattress. No one else was here, so who brought her to this place? Wasn't she in an accident? The girl rubbed her temples, but more memories refused to return. She just couldn't remember.

After showering and changing, Amy made note of her bruises and cuts. How many times had she been through the ringer since joining the Cause? She couldn't keep count, but the pain had never gotten easier to accept. Suicide told her it never would. She sat on the bed, her beige shawl and matching dress oddly comfortable. Why did these look so medieval? New matching shoes even waited by the door. Where was she?

The hotel door jiggled and opened, revealing a man on the other side. The young-looking man wore a light blue suit, had his platinum hair combed back, and locked eyes with her as he walked in. His ashen skin reminded her of death, but she would never tell him that. He approached with a blank look on his face.

"I am Percival Locke," he said. "Do you yet remember anything from last night's entanglement with the mob?"

As his voice trickled through her eardrums, memories slipped out of the gate of her mind. A slight migraine caused her to wince, and she rubbed her forehead. There she saw that monster in the coat attack her in the woods before she was rescued by . . . the man standing before her. But what had happened to Boon? She stood up and jabbed her forefinger into Locke's chest.

"You brought me here." She glanced around the hotel room before glaring at him one more. "This doesn't look like Huntingdon. I don't see Boon, either. How did we get here? Who are you, Locke?"

"A friend."

"As opposed to those killers from last night? What have you done with Boon?"

"He was brought here, too. You should worry more about what this place *is*."

"And that is?"

Locke stared down at her, his expression unchanging. He opened his mouth to say something but then appeared to think better of it. Instead, he gestured to the window behind her.

She obliged him and looked out into the daylight. It didn't take long for her to see why he could not tell her what he meant.

The sky's bright blue hue reminded her of arctic ice, far too dark and shining to be the color of summer, never mind in this part of the world. The buildings themselves were simultaneously ancient in their structure, reminding her of that Art Deco style she'd seen in those old movies her mother used to bug her to watch, and also new in that none of them had any wear and tear on them whatsoever. They were also all white like marble, making her think this had to be some diorama or art project.

But it was the people that were the strangest. All of them dressed like weird peasants in some middle age play, tunics and rags abound, just like what she was given to wear. The entire thing was a mishmash of modern and ancient, an impossibility that made her think this had to be a dream.

This definitely wasn't Huntingdon. It might not even have been Earth for all she knew. Primes had to be at work here . . . but what possible power could create a world like this?

"This is not the work of a mortal man," Locke said.

She watched him from over her shoulder. "Are you crazy?"

"My sanity has little to do with your reality, Amy."

"You know my name."

"You were the target of my brother, of course I know who you are. Before you ask any further questions, you should know that this is the Dreaming City, a creation of Primes such as yourself and Boon, as well as something beyond that."

"So I *am* a prisoner!"

"No," he replied. Locke gestured to the people down on the street. "Not yet, anyway. Once you are put to sleep by the Dreamer himself, you will join the others here—a preparation for the world our father hopes to create. Thanks to the efforts of the Gemini Man, his presence has been greatly diminished on Earth. I led you both here because I believe with your abilities we can destroy this place and the last vestiges of my father's influence on this world."

She bit her lip. "So the Gemini Man is real. We really were sent to find him in Riverview."

"He is very real, the one man that can put a stop to our father's plans; a man who can both shatter reality itself, as well as slip between its cracks. Only one such as that can hope to battle the Great Sorcerer King. Thankfully, the plan to send your group to stop him failed. However, our father weakens and the Gemini Man grows stronger. This Dreaming City is one of the last vestiges of his power on your world. You humans are still very much in danger unless it is destroyed."

She took a step away from him. "Are you implying you're not human? If not, then what are you, and where do you come from?"

"Have you never questioned why *you* were sent to Riverview a year ago? Have you never wondered why your leader so badly wanted a pair of inconsequential drifters hiding out in a small Canadian town? Why those like Boon's friends had to die to keep their presence quiet? You were mere pawns—the last desperate attack of a dying god."

"If this so-called immortal Gemini Man is so scary, why did they think a bunch of weak Primes like us could stop him?"

"There is nothing weak about those who can see through dreams, Amy. There is more to this world than what you can see—you know that better than anyone. This place is but one such example."

A jagged thought stabbed its way into her brain. This man was trying to poison her thoughts! The Great Sorcerer King had been the leader of their movement, yes, but he had always steered them correctly. She had been one of those that had seen through the holy mirror into the Real World, after all. Even now she remembered the flying ships, the lizardmen, and the purple mist adorning the alien mountains. This world wasn't all there was! There was much more.

But that is the moment it clicked inside her head. What if this city was part of that world she was shown?

Amy pushed past Locke and ran out the hotel door and down the hallway. Those far away and distant hills of the Real World filled her imagination as they always had before. The Great Sorcerer King had always told them that he would take them from their false home and bring them where they belonged, but only after the work had been properly done. After the evil had been purged. No more like her mother would have to die. She had been gone a full year: perhaps things had changed!

Joy filled her very being, and Amy smiled as she leaped steps to the bottom floor in her run. The nightmare of Earth was finally over.

The girl threw open the lobby door and met the summer sun. A heavy cool air struck her like the world after a rainstorm. The smell of sunflowers and sewage hit her, as did they sounds of traffic screeching blocks away. It was a normal town; but it was *off*, and she couldn't figure out why that was. The girl leaned against a lamp post outside the hotel and stared open-mouthed at the traffic.

"It's not Tyndarus," Locke said. He stepped beside her, his hands in his pockets. "This isn't the world on the other side of the Mirror Gate. You'd burn to death if you followed my father into Tyndarus. He always knew you would."

Amy bit her lip as the tears formed, blurring her vision. She didn't want to believe it, but it was clear this man wasn't lying to her. This wasn't the paradise they were promised for carrying out the Master's dirty work. She wiped at her eyes with the crook of her elbow. "Are you saying the Master really did lie?"

"You already know he lied, but it was a partial truth he told. There are spaces out there, hidden from sight, sound, and the human mind—other worlds. Planets, realms, whatever you can imagine and then some. My father, however, plans on ruling them all. He just needs agents clearing the way for him to make it easier. That is what this very place is meant to help do. The last of his agents on Earth are here, and they are planning a kamikaze move to open the gates to the world of Tyndarus. This is their last play."

She cleaned her face and allowed her sobbing to finally die off. Nothing he said should have been a surprise, but something about waking up here brought her back to another state of mind—a place she had seen in her dreams far away from Earth. "What do you mean by a kamikaze move?"

"The Dreaming City is a construct of several Primes, his last agents. It is in a place between your world and mine, opened by a man who gave far too much to a cause that isn't his. They mean to sacrifice all their captives here, and themselves, and use the resulting blood to open the portal permanently. The only thing stopping them is you."

"Me?"

Was that why those madmen sought them out? Suicide had fallen in Riverview, the place she had also been apprehended, but had he really cleaned out the majority of their numbers like he said they had? If so, what was the Great Sorcerer King's goal in the first place? Were they always meant to be fodder for his portal?

"I know you have a lot of questions," Locke said. "However, I don't have much time to answer them. Your friend's life is in danger. He is being targeted as much as you are."

For the first time since waking up, Amy felt her senses sharpen at his words. That was right—it was Boon who carried her over the past year, when her former friends merely wanted to conscript her as a tool again. He had not once ever forced her to use her powers, though she could never figure out why he let her tag along with him in the first place. Now it was her turn to save her new brother.

Memories of old man Davis dying in the wreck on the road that she caused returned to her. She had puppeteered him with her own power as if he were a mere tool: and he let her. A cold chill caused her to bite her lip. He didn't deserve any of this—but she would pay every one of his killers back for what they did. This cursed power of hers had to be good for something.

"Point me in the right direction, Locke. I refuse to let anyone else die."

"That's a shame," he said. "Because we're about to kill a god."

HE OVERLOOKED THE WATERFALL with a sense of peace he hadn't felt in ages. As Boon sat on the park bench by the railing overlooking the river that ran through town, he could only question why it had taken him so long to come here. This city wasn't one he had seen on any map before, not one he had encountered when he traveled to the next province to escape anyone who might be following him. And yet every time he tried to remember the name, it just slipped from his mind. Despite the swirling and bustling activity of the town, he had the impression this couldn't be real.

But she was here, right beside him. Aside from her Caucasian skin tinting an odd yellow, she looked as she should. Where else could this be, unless it was Hell itself. There was no chance of that being true. Hell couldn't possibly look this nice.

"You never came home," his mother said. "I thought you died in a gutter somewhere."

"Might as well have. Everyone else is dead. Now I'm just waiting out the clock."

"You were always over-dramatic, Nathan. All I wanted was my usual amount. You didn't have to kill Freddy. It isn't like another dealer didn't just take his place. Was reform school worth it?"

"That's where I met Burner, after all. See this? This ring was his final gift to me. It's all I have left of the guys. There's no one left. Now what do I do?"

"What do you think? Start over here with the rest of us."

"It's too late for me."

"Remember what I told you: you can do anything. It's never too late. Don't forget that!"

For the first time in years, Boon looked at his mother. Her torn jeans and dirty shirt were replaced with slacks and a short-sleeved green top. No wrinkles or grey hair adorned her small face and her smoke colored eyes were clearer than he had ever seen them before. She could have even been younger than he was. If it wasn't for her voice, he might have never known her identity. Did coming to this place change her so much?

"Did you lead me here, Ma?"

"They told me you were here. Do you truly know what lies on the other side, Nathan? I've seen it."

"So Suicide's cronies got to you."

"Nothing gets to me, Nathan. You know that. Not even when you killed my man. It didn't take long to find another one." Her smile wavered for a moment. "But I couldn't find another son."

"That kid is dead. I changed my name to Boon because I wanted to start over. It was the only way I could put all that behind me. Being a thief was much better than being a killer . . . or a junkie."

"Despite everything, we're both here now. Do you have anywhere else to be? Perhaps we can put all that behind us and move on."

Boon shifted in his seat and winced. He had lost an entire year of his life running from the group that created this very place. Was it all in vain? There was nowhere else for him to go, nothing to do except resume a career of pilfering with his telekinesis power. But everyone was gone now. Would he form another gang and do the same thing again? Did Burner really throw his life away and give him his ring just for that? But Boon's old boss didn't know about this place. Perhaps that changed everything.

"Who made this place, Ma?"

"I already told you."

"No, you didn't. I asked you the name of the Prime in charge of building this artificial city. I know there's more than one. Give me names."

She blinked at him before cocking her head. "Why do you need to know that? Just throw it all away, all your cares and worries, and we can move on together into the Real World. There is nothing to be gained from knowing anything more than you already do. The Master has shown us the way forward. Why do you need to be this way, Nathan?"

"You're not my mom," Boon said. A knot tightened in his stomach, and he clenched his fists. "Who are you, really?"

Her head cocked again, and her smile widened until a laugh jerked its way out of her mouth. It wasn't a simple giggle, her entire body rocking as she clutched her gut with both arms. The longer she laughed, the more her voice warped into a mechanical facsimile of a real one, almost as if her cackling was being lost in the static. "Whoever I want to be."

A bang exploded behind him, and Boon threw himself off the bench. A bullet bore through the plastic seat and shards littered the concrete. His mother looked up at him and winked before her head rolled off her neck. Before he could see if she had been hit, her remains crumbled into dust, slipping through the slits in the bench and forming a pile on the ground. She was dead?

"*You had your chance, Nathan. We invited you in, and you rejected us. You chose to run yet again.*"

"Ma?"

Another shot rang off in the distance, striking the ground beside him.

Boon tumbled over to his elbows and pushed himself up. He passed the dust by the bench and sprinted into the street. Another bullet careened off the lamp post beside him. Where in the world was he being sniped from?

However, as he ran down the road towards the closest building, he noticed one particular thing—not a single person reacted to the shots going off. All the adults continued looking at their phones or their path forward, almost as if they not only didn't hear the bullets but also didn't see him running. The children went on playing with their friends and running around even as the gunfire crunched stone and brick. That didn't even go into their weird Middle Ages garb. He had reservations about this town before, but now he was almost certain they were justified.

"*Into the pool hall,*" a boy's voice said. Boon quickly recognized him. That was the voice from his dreams. "*I will bring you back.*"

Boon shoved the door open and caught his breath as the gunfire quieted down outside. The shooter obviously could no longer get a bead on him. He followed the invisible boy's direction through the crowd, not one noticing them as they continued watching the screen playing some ballgame. That strange humid wind slipped through him again. Not a single one of the patrons so much as shivered at the sudden air change—a change that should not have been able to happen indoors.

"This place isn't real," Boon said. He elbowed past a pool player who didn't so much as react to the strike. "Where am I?"

The boy almost whispered into his ear. "*The Dreaming City. I choose who awakens here, and you are one such man, Nathan Baxter. Come through the tunnel and meet me in the hospital, if you wish to end this.*"

"You think I'm going to trust the kid that was tormenting my dreams for a year?"

"*I am the only chance you have of waking up.*"

Boon swore as he pushed open the janitor's closet. He shoved over the brooms and cleaning instruments and found a hidden panel at the back. Inside was a set of stairs that led down into the dark. A palpable heat pushed through it.

Glass shattered outside the pool hall. The windows of the pool hall blew in, throwing shards all over the floor. Customers walked across it as if they saw nothing. Nathan Baxter sighed and forced himself into the basement opening.

Maybe this really was Hell, after all.

CHAPTER 4
GLASS ASSASSIN

"WHY WERE WE BROUGHT HERE, LOCKE?" Amy asked. She followed him to a nearby chip-stand where some kids lingered around. The crowd paid no attention to the pair's approach. "Are we invisible or something?"

"You have not yet been absorbed into the dream."

"What does that mean?"

Gunshots went off a block away, and she ducked down. None of the other people, including Locke, appeared to budge at the sound. Instead, he directed her into the alley behind the stand where the sun did not reach. More bullets fired as she asked him to explain himself and this place.

Locke closed his eyes in concentration before he spoke. "The sniper is in the bell-tower one block east. You're going to need to storm the building and take him down."

"*Me?*" she asked. Her mouth went dry. "How can I do that? My power is possession! Anyone I possess will just get shot dead."

"Your power isn't needed; I just need a part of you." Locke gripped her shoulder and pulled back as if he were ripping off flesh. However, there was no pain. Instead, it looked like a person was dragged out of her body to stand beside her: an identical twin! The other Amy looked as puzzled as she was to be there. "A gaggle of you are going to storm the tower and possess *him*. Do not worry, you will not be going alone."

A strange lightheaded feeling overtook Amy, her words slurring. Locke grabbed at her, creating half a dozen exact clones of the girl. The teenager's doppelgangers all glanced among each other in confusion.

"It's my power," he said. "Do you feel any different?"

She did, though she couldn't say why that was. Her anger had dissipated as had the aches and pain she had retained from the previous night. None of the other clones appeared to have noticed anything different as they continued to stare at the man before them. Were these her exact doubles or was there something more to his power? They did not feel apart from her own flesh.

"What did you do to me?"

"I ripped pieces out of you and made them material. All of this is you."

"I don't get it."

"You don't need to. I've got a plan, but we need that sniper for it to work. He is basically the prison camp guard, for lack of a better term, and he is currently distracted. Unless we act now, there is no other way out of this city. Are you ready?"

She put aside her confusion and nodded. Though there were exact doubles of her standing around, they didn't feel like separate people, and if she squinted, she thought she could even see from their perspective. They all moved in different ways she herself had considered as if each were an extension of her own thoughts. A strange peace washed over Amy, and her eyes watered. She wiped them away as Locke explained his plan.

"I'll help you until we save Boon." She tried not to look him in the eye. Pangs of guilt hit her somewhere a million miles away from her current position. What had his power done to her? "Then you put me back to normal. I don't want a piece of any more of these so-called paradises from all you monsters."

Locke looked over the crowd before him and laughed. "You really are just a child. There is so much more to this world than your silly fears and desires, girl. You'll see, once we escape this dream."

More shots went off, and any lingering doubts she had about helping this Prime before her completely evaporated. There was a killer out there, and this time she would be the one to stop him.

WILSON SCANNED THE BUILDINGS, following the target that dashed into the bar. The sniper's x-ray vision allowed him to pierce the brick of the building itself, seeing the prey as he ducked inside. The shooter's bullet from his rifle shattered the entrance glass. There was no chance Baxter would be escaping through there now.

The assassin sat back from his perch on the edge of the bell-tower and used the moment to reload to the next cartridge. He checked the scope and sighed. It would have been nice to have a challenge for once. Baxter would be dead in the next fifteen minutes, even if Wilson wasn't the one to do it.

The drones of the Dreaming City went on about their lives, shuffling from meaningless location to location, oblivious to the truth of the matter: none of this was real. This entire construct existed to train them into being complacent for when the Master finally arrived to consume their world. Even if his physical form was fading these days, his overwhelming power remained. Even if his body weakened, he still would own it all. The path merely needed to be cleared for him.

And now, with Baxter and the girl finally retrieved, there were no more loose ends remaining. Dead or alive, they would be joining the Master's forces. Just like Wilson had.

As he steadied the rifle, the shooter glanced down at the park below. A line of figures formed by the edge—they all dressed in the same garb and wore hoods over their heads. There were at least two dozen of these females, dashing across the greens, swerving through oblivious civilians towards the bell-tower. The assassin wasted no time aiming down his sights and firing away.

Gargled screams of agony cried out as he gunned down as many as he could. Wilson reloaded even as several of these enemies found cover behind trees, cars, and anything else they could find. He swore. This had to have been the work of that traitor.

When he lifted his rifle again, a body collided against his back. Arms wrapped his neck and dragged him backwards. Wilson tumbled down the steps of the bell-tower with his aggressor at his back. Flesh slapped against concrete as they rolled downwards. Grunts filled the bell-tower. He lost his weapon as they fell.

Wilson reached back and grabbed at the attacker. He hooked his neck with one arm and punched back with the other. The enemy groaned and struggled, eventually letting go. The pair twisted on the steps to face each other, unsteady on their feet. Wilson put up a hand at the bloodied and bruised man before him.

"You know you cannot beat me, Cutter," the assassin said.

"My name is now Locke, brother."

"You have forfeited all right to call me your kin, coward. Only a weakling runs when the Master is so close to the end. We are nearly there!"

The traitor jumped forward, and Wilson kicked at him. The enemy cried out as he soared back into the stone wall. The assassin leaned in and delivered a punch, his fists crunching endlessly into his flesh. Relief washed over him as he unleashed his violent urges on the one who deserved them the most. His strikes bloodied the one called Locke, sending him down at his feet in a mangled heap. This coward had always been the weaker brother. Nothing had changed.

"I'll kill your other doppelganger monstrosities just as easily, traitor. It is time to end our quarrel, once and for all."

The enemy wiped blood from his nose, panting madly. He sat back against the wall and smiled bloody teeth up at Wilson. "You never wanted to understand, did you?"

"There is nothing to understand. We exist but for one purpose, and that purpose is closer to being achieved than ever before. Your interference is but a minor stumbling block to the Master's goal."

"He is your *father*, brother. Why do you never address him as such?"

The assassin's rage took hold of any sense he had left remaining. Wilson lunged forward, his cold and scarred hands crushing the traitor's throat. He squeezed with every drop of anger he had, causing his enemy to gag and thrash. It would be an honor to obliterate all of these living blockades. Only then would the Master finally have a clear path towards paradise, and then . . . *and then* . . .

"We have no family," Wilson said through stiff lips. "We are extensions of the new divine—mere arms and legs for the true body. You speak in a stained tongue."

"You are wrong, brother." The coward breathed heavy as he clutched his bloody skull. "We can be much more than tools for a monster."

"Monsters go against the natural law, traitor. You are the beast here. Not I."

"Let us be straight with one another. Neither of us is in our true form. Right now we are each biding time for others to do the real tasks for us. Perhaps, we are not so different."

"Biding time?" Wilson wiped blood from his temple. "For your clones to catch me?"

"They're not my clones."

A flood of steps cascaded up the stairs. Wilson blinked at the sound, and the traitor rushed him. The pair grabbed and bit at each other as they spun down further down the staircase. Before he could even gain his bearings, a pair of hands clamped on Wilson's ears. It felt like a woman? It had to be his target!

A burning sensation slipped into the assassin's brain. At least, that's what he thought it was. Sparks rattled around inside like spare beans in a coffee tin. He couldn't struggle as invisible hooks sunk into his soul's back and dragged him backwards out of Wilson's body.

The killer cried out, flashes of red pain stabbing throughout. There he saw Wilson's final moments of life again, walking through the night streets of the far-off city. The thick summer night wasn't dissimilar from this place. It was as if he were watching Wilson's last moments from a sky-hook high above the world itself.

At night, in the humidity-choked streets, a large man teleported above Wilson and brought the knife down into his neck. The death was quick and practically without pain, and the target hadn't realized he died before his corpse hit the ground. Not even his power would have been able to prevent a killer like that one.

Wilson was soon forgotten as another lowlife in a scum-filled brand of work, just as his murderer was when *he* died mere weeks later. It was as unceremonious as he had expected it would be. Guns for hire rarely end up any other way. He was erased within a month, so much so that he wasn't even missed when his corpse was taken over by another. Made whole again, Wilson would have been thankful had his soul not long departed this vessel back then, though there were still traces of the dead man in this thing. Even now as he was dragged away, torn cruelly from his savior by the wretch behind him, he wondered if he would finally stay dead this time.

As Wilson died again, the assassin felt himself fall away from his host body. He glanced at the cavalcade of clones encircling his corpse again and growled.

"This is but one shell, traitor!" he shouted through Wilson's dying breaths. "I still live."

Even now, he felt his power ripple through the Dreaming City as more of his shells like Wilson poured out of the buildings and through the streets towards the bell-tower. At least one of them would end these intruders for good—all for the Master. Even as Wilson's body drew his last breath again, the assassin smiled as the clones of the woman circling his body all twisted to face his own personal army of the former dead.

Paradise would not be stopped so easily!

CHAPTER 5
THE DREAMER'S PRISON

"YOU'VE MADE YOUR DECISION THEN?"

Boon's ears perked, and he stopped in his tracks. The dark of the basement stretched on forever in every direction around him, visibility all but impossible. Ever since he had slipped into the bar and ran down here, he had felt eyes upon him, but little existed aside from the dark void that appeared to spin on into infinity. It took him far too long to remember that he wasn't in any normal place but in the Dreaming City.

"You're not the voice," Boon said. No, it wasn't the same boy that spoke into his mind. This tone was much deeper, and more acidic. "Are you the sniper?"

"I am all, in essence."

"You're a murderer. The girl told me what you did to the old man. And then there was my mother. Who was responsible for that illusion?"

"There are no illusions here, Nathan Baxter."

The floor itself rumbled like a volcano going off mere feet away. Boon could hardly keep himself standing as he wobbled about the concrete floor. It might have helped if his power allowed him to lift himself in the air, but he wasn't that lucky. He dropped to all fours in an attempt to steady himself.

On either side of him, walls of concrete sprang up as if pulled from the ground itself. They went on forever in both directions. The slabs skidded across the floor not unlike bulldozers moving at a quick pace.

Boon put up his hands and tried to grab at the cement with his power, but it proved too difficult. The large and wide object was hard for his mind to grasp. His approaching death edged closer, squeezing tighter with each passing moment. Sweat poured down his forehead.

"You could have had it all but chose death instead."

"I've never been much of a gambler." He thought on Burner again, the two of them riding one of the boss's boats down the St. Laurence River years ago. The guys were there, hooting and hollering like he remembered. A grin formed on his twitching lips. "I should have died long ago."

The walls crushed in on either side of him, their impossible length far too wide for him to escape. Boon planted his fingers against the concrete, his muscles straining as it squeezed in on him. Bones creaked as he uttered under his breath, his power searching for anything at all to grab on to—even a crack would have been enough. Boon pressed his hands against the solid wall as the enemy continued jabbering.

"I built a whole city for those who needed a home," a man said.

A figure of a man in a long coat sauntered across the top of the wall towards Boon. He kept perfect balance as his voice echoed through the cement itself. This was the man who took out their car in the woods.

"I don't need a home," Boon said through his grunts.

"All men need a place to lay their heads down, Baxter. Even men who wasted their lives on petty gain and vice instead of Higher Things."

Boon cried out as the slabs pressed in on his arms. "Higher Things? Like God?"

"The only god that matters. Your new one. Why do you insist on struggling over everything? You are no fool. I know; we've looked into you. So why do you insist on self-destruction?"

The walls pressed against Boon's back and chest as his breaths rattled in his lungs. He pushed his fingers into the concrete, unable to find any way inside. His Prime powers just weren't enough.

A surge of pain caused him to scream, and his consciousness nearly left him. For a moment, he thought he saw his mother's face again.

She stood above him from atop the walls looking down at his writhing form. His enemy did not react to her appearance. The dying man's mother strode across the cement towards him, and he thought of the last time he saw her.

Boon's mother was not the person he met on that park bench. The most recent time he met her, she had black marks under her eyes and bruises across her face. She had found a new man, and Boon had reached his limit.

"*Simon's willing to take you up the ladder, Nathan,*" she had said. "*Why are you so lazy? Don't you want anything?*"

Boon stared around her trashed apartment and suddenly felt gratitude he had escaped this place for juvie when he did. That was not a feeling he ever expected to have. "*I don't have any plans, Ma. But one thing I'm not going to be is the man on top looking down on the ants as he steps on them.*"

"*You can do anything, and you choose to run.*"

"*That's right.*"

"*If you leave, Nathan, you better never come back. The last thing I ever wanted as a son was a loser.*"

He remembered the boyfriends, the beatings, and even the hangers-on that clung to those around her for even scrap of credibility among those she aligned herself with. Even the kids he went to school with were scared of him purely because of the rumors—not anything he had ever done. That was years and years ago, but it had also never changed. Nathan Baxter was the son of a dead man and a coward, and no matter what route he took in life, he would end up as one of them. Boon had never ingratiated himself well with clout-chasers and the barnacles of society, and the last thing he would ever do was become one of them. He looked at the rage on his mother's face and waved his goodbye. There was no home for him anymore.

"*Why do you always run away?*" she asked as he threw open the door.

"*Because I'm looking for a place I can stay.*"

Boon's eyes forced themselves open, and he remembered where he was. His mother was right above him now, the marks on her face a distant memory, much younger in appearance, and her clothes a radiant white dress he had never seen her in before. The cement grinded into him, and blood slipped onto his lips as he smiled at her. She kneeled down, and her warm hands pressed against his eyes.

It was then that he remembered that she had no idea what became of him after he left home. But as he felt the life leave his body, he must have said something about her, because the man standing on the wall answered him.

"She was your sacrifice to be here, Baxter." Boon's slits of eyes traveled up towards him. "We ingratiated you to the Order ahead of time, you see. Everyone needs to shed blood beyond themselves for the Master. That girl you are traveling with lost her own mother, so it only seems fair that you would suffer the same. It is a shame you rejected us. She was essentially sacrificed for nothing. Oh well, another whore dead."

But she wasn't.

Boon had looked her up, even if he didn't speak with her. He knew that she had finally thrown away her old life after he had left. His mother had found a new husband and built a family. She had found her place. And now, because of him, she had lost it all. Even now, he was a thorn in her side.

"Don't worry, we made it look like an accident. Mortals would beg for such a generous death. Her new family sobbed long at the funeral, unaware of who she really was. But you knew, right, *Boon*?"

His mother vanished again, leaving him alone in the dark. For the first time in ages, a sob wracked on Boon's chest. Rage smashed against sorrow as he soundlessly screamed through the searing agony crushing him in. His fingers pressed into the cement as he gripped at the atoms itself and bit his lip. He felt his face redden as blood streamed down his chin. His mind rotated in his skull, finding new paths he could not perceive with just his five senses. He would tear it all apart.

As if it were sand, the cement pooled around his fingers. Boon's mind slammed against the particles themselves and dragged him down inside the inner workings of existence itself. The Dreaming City was material even if it was held up by those who stood just outside physical space itself. He could still use it.

"*You've run a lot,*" the boy said into his mind. "*But I need you now. Break the Dreaming City, while we have the opportunity. This is our chance!*"

Boon tore at the cement before him as if it were tissue, his rage egging him on. Chunks of the walls blew apart not unlike a bomb had exploded them into bits and the air slipping back into his lungs gave him a second wind. The dark filled with thousands of cement chunks, spinning around him like a shallow tornado.

The cement man rolled backwards across the floor, landing on his knees. His wild expression and frazzled hair showed more fear than he probably wanted to show.

"You can't do this!" the killer shouted at Boon.

"I can do anything."

Boon gestured with his hands, and the spiraling wind of debris arched downward into his enemy. Stone and rock rubble pelted the victim as he tried to defend himself with his arms. Clothes and skin tore apart in the attack as the clatter filled the emptiness of the unending basement. Blood and crooked bones and ripped skin shook and rattled under the weight of the endless stone cyclone, beating the attacker into the dust. The parade of destruction went on for what felt like hours before there was nothing left of his foe but torn bits of clothes. The remnants of rubble that hadn't yet been smashed to pebbles fell to the floor as Boon released them.

The telekinetic fell to his knees, panting heavily. That had been the strongest usage of his power that he had ever activated before. Boon wiped debris from his hands.

"*Tell me your name, kid,*" Boon said in his head. "*You're in this city, aren't you?*"

"*I'm Ed. In the hospital. Hurry before* he *finds you again.*"

Boon steadied his breaths and waited for his energy to catch up with the rest of him. His knees shook as he forced himself up and to look at the remains of the man he had killed. Should guilt have attacked him in that moment? He didn't know. Instead, Nathan Baxter decided to focus that energy towards finding the source of this Dreaming City and shutting it down.

He ran through the remains of the basement, heading towards the opposite end from where he first entered. This Dreaming City would soon wake up. That so-called Master awaited him.

CHAPTER 6
SECOND SON

THE CHAOS IN THE PARK wasn't noticed by any of the civilians. Amy felt gratitude for that. Clones of the teenager and Locke pounced upon the dozens of figures in trench coats and hats surrounding the bell-tower while normal people went about their day as if nothing was going on.

Her possession power carried over to the doubles that Locke made of her. As she took them over, it allowed her to sever the connection these automatons had with their enemy. Locke was right—one monster was controlling this entire enemy force. And they were also all dead.

Locke guided her through the streets as bodies of clones and corpses were tossed here and there, even as normal civilians walked blissfully by them in the summer heat. Her breaths arrived hard as she struggled to chase after him and stumbled through the streets.

"What did your power tell you about our enemy?" Locke asked. "Do you know where in the city he is hiding?"

"It was like I was cutting the strings of a puppet master." She coughed and cleared her throat as she ran. "I can't control the dead, so all I can do is break his hold over them—whoever *he* is."

"Our enemy is no normal Prime, at least not anymore. His body has been infused with an extreme dose of magic, and it has turned him into a monster beyond humans. Did you learn where he is?"

"At the hospital. But there was something else there—some sort of presence I couldn't touch or communicate with. Who is this enemy, Locke?"

The ground rumbled as if answering for him. The pair tripped and tumbled in the street while the pavement cracked and crunched. Amy landed on her elbows and let the dizziness wash over her.

For a moment, the memories of Wilson returned. Assassinated targets dropped to the ground and carnage ruled in the eye of her mind. In between the cracks of the dead man's psyche, she spotted another man hiding from sight as if in a game of hide and seek. His large form ducked into the crevices of a dark castle somewhere out in the mountains of some far off land. He stared back at her through infinity, his teeth grinding and anger building, before letting out a primal scream that caused her to jump.

"Get up, Amy," Locke said. He took her by the arm and forced her to her feet. "The enemy is just ahead. Once we shatter this dream, its prisoners will be freed to the places they were pulled from. Only *he* stands in the way."

Blocks before them, the hospital grew and warped, as if being rebuilt in real time and at hyper speed. The glass in the windows tumbled about as they bent and twisted into Gothic-style arches and the beige brick reformed to black stone. The entire building restructured itself, growing taller and looming over the rest of the Dreaming City. The ground continued to quake long after the small hospital was but a memory.

The pair rushed forth towards the new hospital without another word.

"*Hurry,*" the boy's voice said. "*You are so very close.*"

Amy tried to ignore the voice, but it looked as if Locke flinched at it as he ran alongside her. Their true enemy aside, who was this boy? Was this the voice Boon had talked about hearing before?

She remembered the dying old man who had given her that book. Davis had no reason to be kind to her. All these people had been trying to help, and she had done little in her life but run and hide from the world. The girl thought to her own mother's funeral—how long was she expected to go on this way?

Amy and Locke dashed up the street towards the old hospital where her answers awaited her. This dream needed to end. They all had to wake up.

☠

THERE WASN'T ANY HEAT AT ALL when Boon left the basement and climbed to the next floor. He passed up the stone stairs that morphed with each step; he made into a more modern plastic substance. Abandoned gurneys and deactivated machines lay strewn about the faded yellow hallways. Not a sound aside from his own footsteps played back as he entered what had to be the hospital. Although judging from its vacant state, he questioned if this was another trick of the Dreaming City. The lack of sunlight and the smell of dew after a morning rain told him this place wasn't normal.

Surely enough, the window showed nothing outside its frame. The only sight was of fog hundreds of feet below and an infinite void of clouds rolling on ahead. But how did he get so high in the sky, and where were all the people? Not even the sun lay in the sky—only a vague light like an overhead lamp just out of view shone down weak rays upon this nonliving world. Boon balled his fists and punched them together just like he did before most jobs. No turning back.

In the distance, a faint beeping whispered into his ears. Was that an EKG machine? The lone electronic bleeping cut through the silence and into his insides. The target had to be just ahead.

Boon slipped down the hall, his steps as quiet as he could manage, but still no other sound or clatter disrupted him. No patients lay in any of the rooms, no doctors or nurses stood at any of the abandoned desks. The constant beeping only grew louder the faster he ran down the hall to the north.

At the end of the hall were two comically large swinging doors made of what he thought were metal. He would have thought they didn't belong if this were not part of the Dreaming City. Everything here was just wrong enough to feel unreal. Boon pushed the heavy doors open, his muscles twisting against him. He fought off a groan and wiped the sweat from his eyes as he finally muscled his way inside.

"*You made it,*" Ed said into his mind.

Boon approached the bed. "It was you."

"Come no closer," he replied. The boy sat straight up in the bed, the wires and needles still plunged into his skin, and turned towards Boon. "Your lot has done enough damage to our city."

"You're not Ed." Boon scanned the kid up and down—this was a boy, but the older voice was of a man. The child's empty stare looked walleyed. "But you're in his body. This is why he asked for help."

"*His* body? You appear to have no idea of the situation you are in, Baxter. Young Ed rests in the bosom of the Highest King, where magic flows through veins just as freely as life force. That is because the Master *is* life force itself. We prepare the way for the Great Sorcerer King, the one who will lead all in this dead existence into the paradise none deserve but all will attain. He is your only hope for salvation."

Regardless of what the enemy said through the boy's lips, an impression could not be escaped from his demeanor. The child's bloodshot eyes remained half open, and an unnaturally bent hand raked itself across his wild mane of sandy hair. The boy's chalk-like skin gave the impression he hadn't seen sunlight in years. Dry lips attempted to form words as he glanced Boon over once more.

"*He's hidden my older sister,*" Ed said into his mind. "*Her name is Laura. Ask him where she is.*"

Boon didn't have any better ideas to get information out of this guy. "Listen, whoever you are, I want two things. First, shut down this nightmare town. Second, tell me where Laura is."

The boy cocked a heavy lid. "How did you learn that name? No one else should know of her but the child, and said boy is currently indisposed. He rests in paradise as we speak, you know. I occupy this vessel to properly guide others to the true world he resides in."

"True nothing. You have some sort of possession power. You're just another Prime with a God complex. I've seen this hundreds of times before. You all end up the same."

The enemy chuckled, the boy's body shaking awkwardly as if he were about to pass out. "You truly believe I am a mere Prime, do you?"

"Of course. It makes perfect sense. You took control of all those foot soldiers, as well as the boy, to create this whole town. That monster I took out in the basement was clearly your head in construction. Without him, you're left without any way to maintain this place."

"I am impressed." The boy did not cease his strange grinning, which turned to laughter. "But your understanding remains very limited. Mortals always are *so very* limited in understanding."

"Like I said," Boon replied. "Just another mental patient with delusions of grandeur. Just what I would expect from the man behind Suicide and his pack of dogs. No wonder you roped them in."

"That is very rude, Nathan. Suicide was a soldier, much like that girl you are with was. Do you know why we gave her the name Erin?"

"I'd rather know why you dragged my mother here."

"Oh that is a simple query to answer."

The boy waved a hand and a strange coldness filled the air.

Boon's mother morphed through the floor itself as if emerging from water. Beside her emerged the same man he had killed in the basement, both wearing the same mangled clothes they wore when he met them. They lined up on either side of the boy, expressionless.

"*It isn't just possession,*" the boy said in Boon's head. The voice faded in and out. Was it taking effort for him to speak this way? "*I can't hold him back much longer.*"

"Who are you really?" Boon asked.

"He's my brother." The man from back in the forest slid into the hallway behind Boon. Amy shortly joined him. The Prime reintroduced himself properly as Percival Locke. "He isn't human. Neither am I."

Amy nodded. "Locke cloned me, and I used my power on members of his army. I saw things—their lives, their deaths, their hopes, their highs, and their lows. Our enemy isn't really possessing them—he's reforming corpses from the grave and using what remains inside them to puppet their bodies. It's much stronger than just a Prime ability."

Boon glanced back at the enemy before him. "So you did kill my mother."

"It was a necessary sacrifice, Nathan," his mother said. "All for the Master."

Wrath swelled inside. He bit his cheek in an attempt to regain composure. "Did you kill the boy's sister, too? All for your delusion of a paradise?"

"We all lose those important to us." The boy's smile flickered. "Those who are there for us will sometimes turn on you. But with paradise? Such a thing is impossible. I'll show it to you right now."

A psychic wave of sickness whipped through Boon's organs in an instant. Both he and Amy fell to their knees. The universe around him barrel rolled and a high pitch whistle danced through his skull. He vomited as he tried to speak.

"*I do not need the dead to seize control of you.*" The enemy spoke those words through the boy, but it was not him who moved. Was it not his power? Was someone else here? "*You are just another automaton.*"

"Enough, brother!" Locke said. "Let us solve our squabble ourselves. Do not involve *him.*"

The boy blinked, and that foreign voice disappeared once more. "Lets."

The floor gave out under Boon, and he tumbled downwards. The ground hit him so fast that it took a moment to realize what had occurred. He rubbed at his bruised cheek. The cement man from the basement skirmish floated down from above, pieces of the tiles forming steps for him to descend. He trembled as he faced Boon, no expression on his face, and his eyes almost rolled back in his head. Control must have been lax with the host's concentration spread so thin.

"Don't think I won't have the energy to kill you, Baxter," the enemy said, his mouth moving at odd angles. "You are still a mere mortal."

Boon took note of his position. Amy, Locke, and the boy, were still upstairs, and now he had a new problem to deal with. With the ceiling above him caved in, rubble had fallen and smashed the monitors, beds, and equipment in the hospital room, leaving piles of stone, metal, and plastics, everywhere. He grabbed at them with his mind and lifted the avalanche of debris into the air.

"I'll die one day," he said. "but not today and not here."

The two forces each ran in on the other, concrete and flying junk smashing about the room. Boon would kill this immortal cement man right now, even if he had to destroy the entire Dreaming City to do it.

CHAPTER 7
TOMORROW'S KINGDOM

THERE WERE SO MANY INSECTS in this building that it could be mistaken for a roach nest instead of the gateway to the True Kingdom. Rantan swore with the boy's tongue. The Great Sorcerer King might have been gracious when need be, but the loss of so many useful tools would not be so lightly ignored, and especially not forgiven.

"Rantan," the traitor said to him. "It is enough. Let the boy go."

"You dare use my name, Cutter?" he replied through the boy's mouth. "Perhaps you have forgotten your station."

"That is no longer my moniker. I have come here to finally end this game."

Rantan sneered through the boy's lip. "Game? I have created a new world for the Master, all I need is that girl behind you, and I will have collected all the tools I need to open the path towards the Kingdom for all. The Master will have his throne returned to him. You have no seat at our table. You are obsolete."

"Father's body is dying. He imbued you with enough of his essence to increase your power and abilities in hopes that you would find a suitable vessel to tide him over before his life span runs out. The problem with this thinking is that he does not know you and your insatiable appetites as I do. His time is short, and he has relied on a fool that cannot control his passions. Father is doomed to face his end against a force only growing stronger as he fades away."

"Fades away?" Rantan laughed. "You really do have little idea about what I am now."

Though he inhabited Ed's body, this child was just one of many puppets his newfound power allowed him to take the strings of. Once the Master had imbued Rantan with magic, he had discovered how to make his very essence intangible. He soon found a promising Prime with mind control abilities and consumed the fool whole before building his army through the resulting psychic link, including through the dead. Corpses could be reconstructed, their minds scanned and thought patterns before they died analyzed. On top of it, Rantan now resided in a target who could control dreams. There was no stopping the Master now.

The boy sat up, and the wires and needles fell from his skin. He was much too weak to escape Rantan's grasp now. There was nothing for him to do but cede control like all the rest had. Now Rantan would seize control of the entire Dreaming City for the Master. There was no soldier as loyal as the first son.

"We were born for this, Cutter," he said. "We exist only as his left and right hands, and nothing more. Do you know what use a severed limb has? All it does is flail around before rotting in the dirt. Change your name if you wish; you are still the same traitor that denied his fate for a lie."

"I never had a name before. I called myself the Cutter, and the lizardmen called me Oronidamus, their name for *Legion*. I existed as tool to mince all in my path while swarming the land like a plague. My death at the hands of the Gemini Man and the loss of our sister, Camille, was enough to show me that even our lives are not endless. I cannot break everything apart forever. We will die like all the rest. We are mortals, Rantan."

"You dare mention our sister. She chased the Gemini Man through the Mirror Gate after we fell in battle and was never seen again, presumably lost forever to the darkness. While you ran away, I searched endlessly for any trace of her. She had always fought, unlike you. She was loyal to the end, always understanding of what it meant to be the first son, even from her position."

"You didn't look far enough for her. What if I told you that I know how to find our sister?"

"I would call you a liar as well as a traitor."

"Aren't you tired of this endless back forth, Rantan? Isn't it time to stop fighting?"

Rantan gestured to the woman behind him, and she mindlessly stumbled forward, her eyes darting in different directions. The chaos exploding on the floor underneath, and the leading of his troops through the hallways to this location was taking too much of his attention and time. He needed to end the traitor before Rantan was dragged into a fight in this weak body. The Cutter had always been his worst match up, and it was a risk allowing him get this close. The young woman behind the traitor backed up a few steps and looked to the ongoing battle, seemingly more interested in the scuffle below than the two squabbling brothers.

The older woman stood by his side, and Rantan looked up at her from the boy's body. "She reminds you of Mother, does she not, Cutter? Just like ours, she was abandoned by a son when she was needed the most. Our sister, too, is gone. You say I am the delusional one, and yet you spout obvious delusion yourself. I have always been there for our family, even when they have not been there for me."

"I know where Camille is, Rantan. You simply need to trust me."

"Trust?! I have always been alone because of traitors and cowards like yourself abandoning the cause." The boy waved his right arm and once more the woman beside him crumbled. Her body broke into dirt and clay clumps before smashing against the floor. "Trust?! You have not earned any such thing, traitor!"

"Father gave the gift to you, did he not? The ability to create Mirror Gates? You stink of his essence, his rot. Show me one, and I will reveal the truth of who we are and what we are capable of."

For but an instant, the old rage Rantan once reveled in bubbled to the surface. He clenched his fists and felt the blood seep out of the boy's palms. There was no pain, at least, none for Rantan. Then, as quickly as the anger arrived, it disappeared, and that cold, clammy reality enveloped his brain and crushed his stomach once more. The Master's essence flooded his senses. He felt nothing again.

First, it was when his sister vanished, then when his brother lost his nerve, then learning his mother was truly dead, killed by that infernal Gemini Man that they had failed to capture, he had slowly lost the zest that had defined him so well. No booze tasted as delicious; no meat satiated; no woman satisfied his desire; and no battle quenched his desire for victory. It was just cold hollowness, all the time at every moment. The only thing that would ever fill the gap would be fulfilling the purpose of his birth. What else could do so? Camille would have known what to say, but she was dead. She had always been there when he was lost and alone. She had always been there when he awoke from the night terrors he could never quite escape.

But Rantan was so very close to enlightenment now. All he needed to do was kill off the last remnant of his past—his own kin. Rantan stared up with the boy's eyes as his brother took a stride forward.

"Halt," he said. "No closer. I will show you a Mirror Gate regardless, since I do need to return your corpse to the Master. But you will gain nothing from this."

"You can call him Father. He is not your master."

"Still your filthy tongue, worm of a jackal's corpse!"

Rantan presented his left palm, and a thin shaft of light pushed its way out of the center. It shone white for an instant before turning dark purple and pumping smoke out. He dragged it free with his right hand, almost like unsheathing a blade, and the piece grew at least six feet long. As it came into existence, the piece expanded as if the atmosphere itself were pulling it into shape. The large mirror slammed its back against the ground, facing up as it rattled. A spark of pain caused Rantan to wince as he watched it glow.

"Satisfied?" he asked his brother. The Mirror Gate pumped purple smoke. "You wanted this."

A sad smile spread on the traitor's face. "This satisfies no one, brother."

"Wait." A thought had just occurred to Rantan. The girl was no longer behind him. A shout of pain screamed from below. Had she gone down there? "Where is the wench?"

Hands clapped against the sides of his head, and a searing pain ripped its way into his brain. He had felt this before in the body of Wilson—it was that accursed girl again! She was trying to pry into their minds. Rantan bellowed in pain from the boy's body and shook like a leaf in an updraft.

"I went around the hallway while you two were talking," she said. "This is for Davis."

Rantan's mind bent and morphed as if being molded like clay, wrung out by the girl's power. In the haze of agony, he saw it all: death, slaughter, execution, all the faces of those he willingly butchered to not end up like one of his father's failed experiments. He ran so far, but it was all to die here. His brother was right: escape was impossible, and somehow he always knew that. Rantan wailed and reached back, elbowing the girl in the stomach. The pressure lessened, and she gagged.

Rantan seized the girl by the collar and whipped her backwards. She grunted as the wall indented with her body's force, and she tumbled into the rubble. His mind swirled like a whirlpool as he attempted to keep his balance. Illness churned inside his organs.

The second he thought he was free, he turned to see his own brother staring him in the face. Locke placed a hand on Rantan's head and pulled back as if trying to rip his spine from his body.

However, instead, Rantan felt himself dragged out of space itself, landing on floor beside the boy's body. The child he had inhabited twitched in the dirt behind him. Rantan looked back and then up at his brother who stood over him.

"When did you gain the ability to do such a thing? I inhabited that boy's heart, just as I did to all by targets, including the dead. You never used to be able to use your power so precisely."

"Would you like to see, brother?" Locke asked. He smiled down at the fallen warrior. "It is time to face our destiny."

A whiplash of past, present, and future, both of his and those Rantan had embedded himself inside, echoed into his soul like a vibration the size of the galaxy itself. The warrior screamed even as he felt himself being lifted up to the sky and then dropped.

Locke brought him down into the Mirror Gate, and the two fell through the solid surface. The frame lit up in a bright white light as he tumbled into the cavernous drop underneath the pair. The tunnel's dark purple light was consumed by this impossible glare that sliced into him with the memories of mutilation that dashed around his mind. His insides broiled as he fell into the endless deep.

"This is it, Rantan," Locke shouted into his ear. "This is where we bring it to an end!"

The end of the tunnel widened as the pair fell, opening up and swallowing them whole. A loud crack sounded from behind them, and glass shattered, certainly being the Mirror Gate itself. Regardless, he rolled out into the foreign sky, choking on the air around him.

Locke smiled at him as the pair plummeted to the earth far below them.

"This won't end me, brother!" Rantan exclaimed.

"No, that's for what we find on the ground."

The duo dropped down towards the distant forest underneath, the wind whipping against them. Rantan's insides twisted furiously as he gagged and saliva poured from his mouth, but still he thought of seeing his brother walk away from him kept his anger palpable. That memory would always remain.

It didn't matter if they both survived this drop. Rantan would remove his head and return to his father as his greatest creation. He was, after all, the first son. Nothing could take that away from him, not even his own brother.

Locke was correct. This would be the final time they would meet on the field of battle, even if it killed them both.

CHAPTER 8
DREAM'S END

THE BROKEN PEBBLES rolled out of Amy's hair as she shook herself awake. The building quaked, sending more rubble off the ceiling and breaking against the ground. Up ahead, the strange glowing mirror lying on the floor let out a large crack and shattered into pieces. She forced herself up with a wince and approached the unconscious boy lying on the floor next to the broken device.

Amy shook the child awake. "Hey. You're Ed, aren't you? You created this place."

The boy groaned, and she hoisted him onto her back. It didn't look like he would wake up so easily. Amy sidled over to the hole in the floor and glanced down at the pair below.

Boon dodged a large slab of thrown concrete slamming into the swinging hospital door behind him and knocking it from its hinges. He rolled and skidded across the floor, ramming into the opposite wall. Her friend kicked off and regained his balance in time to throw a giant hunk of stone back at his opponent.

His enemy, however, no longer seemed cognoscente of where he was. Rantan's agent moved in jerking motions, limbs twisting awkwardly in the wrong direction. Despite the fact that the corpse looked quite dead, he still continued to attack, tossing chunks of rock at Boon in an attempt to kill him. But why was he still attacking? Should not Rantan getting thrown into the Mirror Gate have broken their connection?

"That man is dead," Ed said. He rubbed at his eyes as he spoke from Amy's back. "All of the men in those coats are just puppets. You're going to have to use your power on him, like you did to me."

"Get close to *that?* How?"

"Mr. Baxter can help you. Hurry. We need to break *his* connection with this world before he finds a way to take control again. He always finds a way back in."

The boy passed out once again and left her alone. Amy searched around for stairs to the floor below when she saw it.

The world outside the window turned into a sheet of grey clouds whipping through white skies where hard red stars shone in the distance of whatever underworld this was a part of. As she gazed out into the abyss, a warm feeling fell over her swirling mind along with a slowly rising pitch like a scream in the rear of her thoughts. Whatever was out there was forcing its way here. Whoever this was, it was more than just the killer Locke took through that mirror.

Amy ran down the stairs towards the chaos and the unconscious boy held to her tight. Even if they escaped this place, would they even be able to get to Earth?

There was only one way she could get the answer to that question. They had to put this insanity behind them now and for good, before that presence got here.

"WHAT IS THIS MADNESS?" Rantan choked out. It was all he could manage to say through his choppy breaths. "Where have you taken us?"

The large man was in his normal body again, muscular and thick, far away from his prison in that child. That form broke up in the

Mirror Gate, like most organic material did, leaving him as his original pale person once more. He looked upon his brother as the pair stood in the empty field of some alien world, waist-length purple grass and light yellow skies greeting them. The only other sound was the distant hum of some mechanical contraption or another. He couldn't discern were he was not that he cared. Rantan was more interested in learning just what his brother's game was.

"I wanted to show you this, brother." Locke's clothes smoked lightly, but they didn't burn away. Did it have something to do with the purified light in the now-shattered Mirror Gate? Did he create that? "You might as well see this, as you will never return to Earth again."

"A weak threat."

"It is not a threat. It's reality."

"What reality? You have simply taken me to an uninhabited world. There is nothing to show me here." Rantan flexed his muscles and stone formed around his sore skin. He pointed a crooked finger at his brother and swallowed his rage back. "Did you think taking me from the Dreaming City would disturb the plan? All I need do is return, and all your work will be reversed."

Locke sighed and scratched at his head. He glanced off into the trees as he spoke. "You very well know that the two of us cannot kill the other. Our abilities forbid it, as does our blood. We are destined to run like machines until our father tires of us, or until another frees us from the curse."

"You believe in *freedom?*" Rantan's smile cracked and fell into full laughter. "I never took you one to fall for the honeyed words of the damned. You well know such a thing does not exist."

"Are we truly destined to continue this slaving away forever?"

Rantan edged a step towards his brother, then chanced another. Locke did not budge at his approach. "All we are destined for is to be one with the Master."

"You believe such? So be it."

"I do not need to believe in reality for it to be true!"

Stone knuckles formed on his fists, and Rantan leaped upon his brother. The pair exchanged blows, but a hollowness stung the larger attacker's chest. Locke ripped stone out of Rantan's hide, sending duplicate corpses of the bigger man's body crumbling in the wind with every strike. As a consequence, the mangled flesh of his brother became replaced with a new Locke in his place. This was how their duels always went. Neither would either truly fall at the other's hand.

But it was inconsequential. Rantan had no reason to stop now, and his brother's spilled blood only gave his fists more reason to keep striking. Someone would die today, and he was satiated with the idea that it would be the both of them. Not everyone gets to die on the battlefield, murdering a traitor and strangling the life out of his corpse. Only rare heroes get such an honor.

Rantan bounded up into the air, his massive girth soaring over forty feet up. He landed down in the earth with a crunch, his brother tripping backwards onto his rear. The planet itself shook with his full weight touching down. Rantan dashed for Locke's throat, his giant digits twitching for flesh to tear.

However, the ground of this alien planet did not cease trembling. For a moment, he thought the earth underneath was just that weak. That is, until it opened up under his feet.

The planet itself gripped at Rantan's stone body, squeezing and digging into his flesh. It pulled him downwards as if devouring him. The darkness swallowed the large man whole and left him scrambling for any way out. A face slipped out of the black emptiness—a woman watching him from the void.

"*It is over, Rantan.*"

He choked out only one word. "Camille?"

The planet devoured Rantan and took him into its bosom. All that remained were his soundless screams.

BOON'S CHEEK SLASHED OPEN and spilled blood across the broken stone of the hospital. He spun on his arms and threw a slab of concrete with his mind at the enemy. His opponent took the rubble dead on in his face, and his neck bent at an awkward angle.

But the dead man still kept moving.

Boon's telekinesis kept him alive, blocking chunks of concrete from caving in his head. He backed up, keeping his distance from the dead man before him.

"How many times do I have to kill you?" Boon asked.

"*He is already dead, as you will be soon.*" The lips on the corpse moved but the voice projected in Boon's mind. "*You will all die and be reborn in my image.*"

"Your Master is dead. I saw him go into that mirror, and the light went off. Just give it up."

Purple mist billowed out of the dead man's ears and mouth, squeezing through the pore's in his skin. Whatever was controlling the body went far beyond natural means. He stumbled against the stone as he attempted to walk.

"*I have no Master. This is the paradise that my servants have built for me, worm. I will not allow it to end, even if these worthless fools allow themselves to fall to the likes of you. My influence will never wane.*"

"It's already fading. Don't you see?"

Boon hardly noticed it himself before, but the walls themselves and the windows dripped as if they were melting. The longer their brawl went on, the more it intensified. Streaks of white water poured from the ceiling, and the glass washed away. Warm wind flowed through the outside gaps. This place was fading.

"*I see nothing but the void for you.*"

The enemy lifted an arm, but the floor did not budge, as if ignoring his calls. In fact, no more concrete or stone arose at his command. It was as if there were no more material for his power to grab onto. Perhaps because the Dreaming City had already begun to fade.

It was the same with Boon. Try as he might, even the rubble lying on the ground could no longer be touched with his power. The Dreaming City was waking up.

"You should have stayed out of Riverview," Boon said. "You should have left the guys alone."

"*I go where I please. I will not be denied my paradise by trivialities such as yourself.*"

Behind the dead man, Amy slowly slid out of a hole in the wall. She carefully stepped over towards him, moving slowly. Boon decided to give her the time she needed to do whatever she was planning. He still had words to impart on this monster regardless.

"This is our world, not yours." Boon jabbed a thumb towards the melting window beside him. "You might be able to mimic it, but you'll never have the real thing. You do not understand anything about it."

"*I decide what is real.*"

"All that remains of your dream world is a memory. And soon, wherever you are, I bet the Gemini Man will do the same to you. You never did manage to find him, did you? Too bad. There's nothing left but for you to be wiped away, like a bad dream."

Before the dead enemy could react, Amy pounced on him, her hands fastened around the corpse's ears. The pair thrashed, but the body was too broken to put up a fight. It flopped onto the floor, limbs bending and snapping in incorrect directions. The lips puckered like a parched salmon caught by a river bear.

Amy dug her hands in deeper and the voice bellowed in reaction, shaking the entire world itself. Purple smoke gushed out of the corpse and spun upwards, disintegrating into the sky where the ceiling had once been. Within a moment, it was all gone, leaving a single phrase burned into Boon's mind.

"*The dream will never end, as long as I live.*"

Strength left Boon, and he dropped to his knees. He wiped at the gash on the side of his head and found the blood had already dried up. Amy kneeled before him and looked all over, informing him that all his cuts and bruises were the same. They had disappeared.

"Our bodies are returning," Ed said. He slipped through the same hole in the wall Amy arrived from. "The bad guys have lost their connection. Now I can wake us up and send us home."

Amy put his arm over her shoulder as he wavered. "Where are we going to wake up?"

"The same place we first entered from. I need you both to find my sister when you wake up. She should be close to me, but I don't know how bad off I am. Please find us."

Boon and Amy glanced at each other, then nodded to the kid. It had been a year since they went on the run, and they had spent so much time avoiding the world that was out to get them. He couldn't escape the awkward feeling that they were now willingly throwing themselves into danger instead. Wasn't this the exact thing he told the girl he wanted to avoid back when they were bailed out?

The former criminal rubbed at his dry wounds and remembered his mother's words. "We can do anything, kid. It'll be simple."

The world filled with haze and melted away into nothing. When the hospital remains vanished, and the white skies faded, Boon found himself standing in the woods again. Birds chirped and squirrels rushed through leaves and branches to escape his sudden reappearance in the world again. Boon rubbed his temple and allowed himself to regain his breaths.

From his blindside, Amy dashed through the trees calling his name. She still wore those weird medieval rags as she had in the Dreaming City. He waved her down before the two made their way back towards the old abandoned house through the trees.

They wouldn't be staying, however. He made that kid a promise, and, like he told Burner before he died, Boon would never run from a promise again. The guys might be gone, but he was still alive. There was still a part for him to play in this crazy mess of a world of heroes and villains.

And from now on he would play it right.

THE PAIN WAS UNLIKE ANY Rantan had felt before in his life. Every inch of his flesh and skin ached, as did the bones grinding underneath it all. Sweat slipped into his eyes as he forced them open and found he was in some dark room. The large man flipped over to his trembling hands and knees and vomited bile he didn't even know he had left in him. Lights flicked on from somewhere he couldn't discern and lit up the cage he had awoken inside.

Rantan had been indeed left in a cell, though of what sort he couldn't determine. The material of the floor and bars of the vast room looked foreign to him—not like any steel he had glimpsed or felt before. Not that it would stop him. Such imprisonment had never held him back before.

"Don't bother, Rantan," Locke said. "You are not escaping this time."

The prisoner followed the voice to the edge of his cell. There Rantan found both Locke and a woman standing alone on the opposite side watching him. The anger returned, and he felt for his power once more. He would absorb this strange steel and attain freedom once more. And yet, as he kneeled down and put a palm on the floor, he found nothing happening. Rantan was the same over-sized wounded brute he always was.

"What is this?" he asked. "What did you do to me?"

The woman spoke up. "You are very far from home, brother."

"Camille?" Rantan squinted to get a better look at her. Truly, it was his sister, the same platinum hair and thin face he knew so well—the same woman that spoke to him on the nights he could not sleep, telling him of possibilities beyond the empty mountains. A lump formed in his throat that he instantly choked back. Had she truly lived? But why was she not standing by his side? She had always stood by him, and with their Master, before. She didn't look any older, though her dress of head to toe black garb and a matching over-sized hat on her head made her appear as if she were a part of some other military force. "What happened to you, sister?"

"I fell from the Mirror Gate into this world where I lay weakened for some time." She presented her bare arms. Scars adorned her skin. "I wandered the land, the earth as my only guide for so long. I lived off the plants and what animals that did not poison me. The longer I lived among the wilds, the less I thought of our ridiculous war on Tyndarus. Our father's influence soon faded as I struggled to survive. Then I met *him*."

Rantan cocked his head. "Who?"

Camille called a strange name from behind her. Out of the shadows stepped a muscular purple-faced man with a baby in his arms. He kept his distance from the cell and handed Rantan's sister the child.

"This is my husband and daughter, brother. They rescued me from the fate you are currently trapped in. We live far beyond

Tyndarus. I have found more to life than fighting to find a place to die."

"You lie!" Rantan bit his lip and pounded a fist against the foreign bars. Why could he not absorb them? He sneered at Locke. "This is your doing, traitor. You turned her against us!"

"He turned nothing, Rantan. You have been living a lie, a nightmare of our father's creation, and you will no longer live it again. Outside of our father's influence, you will slowly change, and become like the two of us. You will forcibly atone for all your deeds."

"Not if I escape."

Locke folded his arms. "Then do so. But you cannot, can you? Do you know why? Your body has been covered with a special plastic film designed by the scientists of this world. Your power cannot work without direct physical contact, just like mine. However, should you escape that layer, you can also not transform into a mineral or solid unless it has already pierced your flesh before. We know your true Prime ability. The alloy this cell is made of is exclusive to this planet. You will be here for a very long time, brother."

Rantan's stomach cartwheeled around in his gut and sweat pooled on his forehead. No matter how much he poured his power out, it would not release. The Master's voice had departed and left him alone, stranded him among his foes. He was alone and abandoned once again. The warrior yelled and shouldered the cell bars as the rage overtook him. They refused to so much as shake.

"The Master will kill you all!"

"He's dying, Rantan," Camille said. "That is why we sought the Gemini Man to begin with. Father's flesh is dying, and without you, he now has no more large pawns to carry on his bidding. His dream is dead."

"And what do you get out of robbing us of our destiny? A planet of fools? A husband and child? You have betrayed royalty to live as a peasant! All I wanted was for Father—"

Rantan paused. His two siblings merely stared at him, and for the first time in Rantan's entire existence, helplessness consumed him. There was no reasoning with their madness; they were no longer his comrades in arms but traitors looking on at a mere lowly clown. But he did not sense any hatred or pity from them. There was something else hiding underneath their frowns that he could not quite understand. His energy drained, Rantan sighed and slid to the floor, the cell bars against his back.

"What is it you want from me? I have nothing. My strength is all I have, and it is useless."

"Let us talk, brother," Camille said. "What do you have to lose? When was the last time we ever spoke among each other about anything other than our duty? Do you even remember our youth any longer?"

"Some of it."

It had been ages. Rantan didn't like to think about it, but his rage had only built and built over the decades serving his father—the Master, as he called him. That dark anger billowed as events constantly went wrong—the Gemini Man escaping their hold, his sister disappearing, the disaster in Riverview, and especially the brother before him turning away from the cause. Everything was in his control—until it wasn't anymore. If he wasn't a tool to conquer the weak, then what even was he?

The large warrior had been given so much power from his father, but all of it had led to nothing but a city of corpses, automatons, and false dreams, which washed away into the night. All it took were two stray criminals and his own brother to destroy that utopia and lead Rantan here, abandoned and forgotten, destined to fade away to nothing. What was all this for? What dream could he ever have? Why did his body suddenly begin feeling so light after he awoke in this place?

"I have nothing to offer you or anyone," he said. The pit in his gut grew to a chasm. He swallowed air and felt the tension release. "My dream is dead."

"You never really had one," his sister said. She rocked the baby before her gently in her arms. It giggled a little. "No one has ever given you a choice before, have they? All we existed as were extensions of someone else's dream—a dream that is over. Will you just roll over and die then? Is that what a warrior like you does?"

Rantan stared at the baby before him for a long time. He remembered his other sister, Zelana, and how he did nothing as his own mother took her away to be nothing but fertilizer—fuel for his father's own magical energy. It took the Gemini Man rescuing her for him to question his own usefulness. Was glorified compost not what they were destined to be? He could not even save the girl: it was the Gemini Man that did that. And yet as he stared at his sister's child he couldn't help but wonder just what might have occurred differently if his siblings had the same chances Zelana had when she escaped, exploring Tyndarus and Earth as if they were wonders beyond basic mortal comprehension. How could he ever hope to understand any of that?

Rantan winced at the sudden migraine attacking him. "Though I would much prefer my mansion in the forest, I suppose I had better get used to this place. Shouldn't I?"

"You? Get used to it?" Locke balked at what his brother had just said. "I believe that is the first time you have ever done such a thing. Usually the world bends to Rantan the Mighty!"

"Tell me, Camille," Rantan said. The oldest sibling folded his arms in his cell and looked away from the family before him. "How did you end up with that brat? How did you forget our father, our duty?"

His younger siblings smiled at each other before Camille finally answered. "It's a long story."

The mighty warrior shrugged. "We have all the time in the universe."

CHAPTER 9
GEMINI DREAMER

THE CAR ROLLED DOWN THE HILL towards Birch Lane, quicker than Amy had anticipated. Boon took the wheel of the old Toyota truck and steered it along the dirt road, gravel crunching underneath. Birch Lane was thin and full of dust and pebbles, but what else did one expect from the countryside? They had to drive past Huntingdon to get here and avoid the cops, but it took little time at all for the pair to get here.

The summer sun screamed down at them, the AC refusing to even work. She wiped the sweat from her forehead as Boon drove onward. Soon, they would reach the place they had been searching for.

It had been a long time since she left home, and everyone she knew from back then was long gone. Even her replacement "family" turned out to be little more than a cult for insane monsters from another world. She was never anything more than a tool for them. Amy looked up at Boon and wondered why exactly she chose to follow him when they were bailed out of police custody a year ago.

She had invaded his town with her "family" and wiped out his gang, and yet he did not look upon her with hatred. It might have been pity, but when he sat there in court hearing about her past his demeanor had changed. The first thing he asked her was about her mother and how she was killed by the very people who claimed to support her. He never looked at her in anger again.

This world was a mess: heroes, villains, superpowers, and even magic, ruled the hearts and minds of the populace and guided every aspect of them. Sometimes, it was easy to forget that there was more to it all than rooting for the home team. Even now, as they sought out the child who saved their lives, she could only think about how much more they were capable of doing instead of mindlessly fighting over scraps and pieces of each other's dead dreams. Maybe if she had woken up sooner, her mother would still be alive.

Amy rubbed the tears from her eyes and wiped her cheeks. She had been given the code name of Erin for the old group because it was her mother's name—the very person she was responsible for killing. Could she ever truly make up for that? She had no right to cry over it.

"After we meet up with Ed, we'll head back to Riverview," Boon said. He didn't look away from the road. Her friend cleared his throat. Did he see her tears? "I want to know more about these Mirror Gates and this other world. I also want to make sure our pals won't be coming back again."

She shrugged. "You think that's a good idea? Maybe we should keep lying low like before. In case that monster takes over Ed again, and the Dreaming City comes back."

"All the more reason we should do this." He finally looked over at her. "How else are we going to make it up to those caught in the crossfire?"

There wasn't any other way forward, she knew as much. The only options were to pretend none of this happened, like it was all a bad nightmare, or admit what went down and prevent it from happening again. She knew what the correct choice was.

And the only way to move on was to bury the past for good. "You're right, Nathan."

"You don't have to call me that."

"It's your name, isn't it?"

"Yeah, it is. But I threw it away so long ago because I didn't think I had the right to use it again. The woman who named me died because of what I did."

"After all we've been through, I think you've earned it." She smiled and patted him on the head. "You know, I didn't think you'd be such a goody-goody. You always had this bad boy energy about you."

He lightly batted her hand away and smiled out of the corner of his mouth. "Yeah, yeah. And I bet you thought you were a tough chick, too. Life's full of surprises. We're about to see one."

The Toyota pulled into the dirt-covered driveway. The small house was clearly old, white design with black trimmings, and a dark red tool-shed to the right where heavy brush lay. It had not been taken care of in a while, clearly needing maintenance. The two parked the truck in time to see the front door of the home open.

Ed limped out of the front door, leaning on a young woman beside him. That had to have been his sister. In fact, when they later questioned him they learned she was left here to take care of his body under threat of death if either of them ran off and abandoned the other. It was easy to monitor them with that monster hiding in his heart. Ed had searched endlessly for the right people to wake them up from the dream and didn't even realize she was at his side. Now they were free.

But at that moment, Amy was more than happy to see the two of them alive, proof that sometimes blood could be thicker than water when she had failed living that old phrase so many times. The two siblings embraced her in a hug and invited the visitors inside. They obliged, more than happy to be able to rest a spell.

"I'm sorry I made you see those horrible nightmares for so long," Ed said. "It was hard enough sending messages without being caught, but I really didn't know if you were good people or just criminals."

Boon waved him off. "Don't worry about. We probably deserve worse. At least now we've got a chance."

The siblings invited the two inside where they rested, ate dinner, and talked long into the night. Ed's older sister even showed quite an interest in Boon's boring stories, something Amy could never imagine. She must have just been looking for any excitement, being trapped out in the sticks for so long.

But Boon was right; they did deserve worse. They had made so many mistakes. And yet she couldn't help but be grateful for the chance to be more than a series of repeating errors forever.

As the night came on, fatigue took over. The other three were still talking while she fell asleep sitting on the couch, exhaustion gripping her hard.

There in the dreams she saw her mother one last time waving to her from across a crowded street the daughter could dare not approach. There were others in the mass, too, including some she recognized. Davis gave her a big grin from the group, and the girl woke up in a flash.

She had been laid on the couch with a blanket over her as the rest of the house slept. That was when she went for her bag. Some of the trinkets survived their car going up in flames, including the book Davis had given her. Amy removed the fairy tale book and searched for the bookmark under *The Three Princesses of Whiteland*.

As the night barreled on and sleep pulled her under again, she read it through. There she fell into a world where justice was true, and love actually did conquer all. There, truth would always win out. Amy read the last line just as she fell into slumber.

The girl laughed as pleasant thoughts filled her dreams and carried her away. It was a good story.

GEMINI DESTROYER

PROLOGUE

THE GREAT SORCERER KING SAT on his bloodstained throne attempting to remember the memory buried deep in his mind. How long ago was it that he traveled the stars plundering abandoned ships and scanning graves for treasures thought lost to every manner of civilization? What were the names of his crew-mates? What did they even look like? That past life had not just faded but became locked out of his mind as if it were a restricted area he simply could never again enter without the right clearance.

They were all dead now anyway.

He coughed out blood, splattering against his heavy boots on the stained floor. The entire mountain palace shook, telling him that the enemy army wouldn't be far off now. However, he didn't pay much attention to their approach—they would not change anything he had to do. What he was more concerned about was his life force pouring from his mouth. Since when did the Great Sorcerer King Nieto bleed? Since when was he just another mortal?

Piles of his dead lizardmen lay around the throne-room, some even eating the corpses of their fallen allies, but the only figure he could bother to give attention to was the man kneeling before his throne. The Gemini Man glanced up at him with hatred in his flashing eyes, his white pulsating form barely human himself. Normally, he would be the King's greatest enemy—if the fool wasn't surrendering to him here and now.

"Free Zelana," the Gemini Man said, his voice booming through the crumbling halls and causing a few lizardmen to scamper out of the room. "She is not your tool. She only returned to you because she thought she could bargain with a monster. We both know she was wrong."

The King remembered the girl arriving at his throne, pleading for a semblance of what she considered sanity—that she knew her father was dying and wanted to save him and the rest of Tyndarus before it was too late. She was a fool.

Then again, all mortals were.

"She is my daughter," the King replied. "I will do with her as I please. If you desire her back, then you should surrender to me. Our battle will only succeed in destroying more of my Kingdom otherwise. Are you not here to save Tyndarus and your wretched planet Earth? Join me now and I will leave them both in peace."

The Gemini Man stood tall, his eyes flashing white with some light beyond what the King could perceive. The chimera being paused, apparently considering the Great Sorcerer King's words, and then slowly nodded.

Their battle had been raging for hours, and neither would give. The Gemini Man had to know he had little way to win against an immortal sorcerer and was destined to lose as so many others had before him. This pest had been a thorn in the King's eye for years now, refusing to bow to his superiors, but now he was left with no other choice. All for a girl destined to be consumed like all the rest.

"Are you sure you want that, Nieto?" the Gemini Man asked. "You might live to regret it."

The Great Sorcerer King stood up. "I regret nothing."

"Precisely. You don't."

The victorious warrior seized the Gemini Man by the throat, his gauntlet still smoking from the previous encounter. He dug his fingers in as the Gemini Man stared blankly back at him. There was no reaction—no writhing in pain. The King drained the essence of the enemy before him, his energy growing with every passing moment. A youthful vigor filled his very being, the first he'd felt in thousands of years.

And yet the Gemini Man did not so much as blink. It was as if he felt nothing at his impending death.

A flash of light filled the room, and the Gemini Man disappeared. However, the King was still standing. The forgotten memories nipping at the corners of his mind finally rusted away and allowed him to focus on the one true reason he had lived for so long—to make the universe itself a part of him, no different than his arm or leg. It would no longer be anything but a mere toy box for the mighty and strong. And now the only strong being remaining was the Great Sorcerer King himself. The game board had been cleared.

He turned towards the stairs behind the throne, and some lizardmen scampered away from him. He ignored the cowards and called to his last remaining elite force through his mind.

"*It is over. Commence total destruction now. Not a single enemy is to reach the fortress in the next twenty-four hours. If they do so, it will be your heads.*"

They responded like a chorus of thunder in the depths of the midnight hour. "*Yes, Master.*"

The Great Sorcerer King laughed a laugh he hadn't in hundreds of years as he crushed the skull of one particularly craven lizard. The creature still had the blood of its brother on its tongue as it screeched its last.

The King hardly minded. It was finally finished, the war on Tyndarus was over. He had won it all.

Now it was time for the universe itself.

CHAPTER 1
DEAD & ALIVE

THE BOY SAT ALONE on the bleachers as the ceremony played on the football field down below. It was graduation day, and now, his class was busy at the celebration, dancing and chatting it up in the crowd. He dressed as nicely as they did, wearing the nice grey suit his mother gave him, but he still didn't feel like a part of their group. They had all graduated together, and it should have been one of the happiest moments in his life. He wished he could feel some semblance of happiness over his accomplishment, but he had lost that ability years ago. Now all he could do was wait for it to finally end.

It had been years since the incident in Riverview, and yet some residents still felt its effects. Mellow Holmes, however, could only live with it. Sensation had been robbed from him, and he knew he would never get it back.

"Mellow," his friend said, sitting beside him. "Why aren't you mingling with everyone else?"

The boy shrugged. "I dunno, Spencer. Why aren't you?"

"I already did. Wish I could've seen Jason, though. Oh, should I have said his real name?"

"It doesn't matter anymore," Mellow said. Jason was another friend who had been through so much. "He left after exams for Tyndarus, saying he and Matthew were going to finish the fight or whatever. Said something about that sorcerer king guy who ruled over the punks who attacked Riverview way back when. I don't think he's coming back. I don't think I would."

"Don't be dramatic."

"I'm not. I still can't feel anything thanks to that bastard's powers." Mellow stared at his hands as he balled them into numb fists. "I want to be happy about graduating and scared my friend might die out in another world, but I can't. Couldn't even force myself to cry. It's like I'm just an empty cup that can't be filled."

Spencer leaned forward and squinted at his friend. "You look sick. Still having those dreams?"

Mellow groaned and sat back in his seat. Ever since the beginning of their last year of high school, he had been seeing that girl watching him out of the corner of his eye. Whether he was visiting the hospital, or sword training on his own thanks to Jason's lessons, he would see her looking. However, any time he tried to point her out or meet her, she would vanish as if a mirage. Nobody believed she existed.

"I saw that girl you were talking about," Spencer said.

It took a moment for Mellow to process his words. He leaned forward again. "You what?"

"Pale skin, slim, and fire red hair, right? Wearing a silver hairpin? She approached me in my backyard this morning and apologized for following you. I asked why she didn't want to tell you herself, and she said something about it being too late now. Before I could ask anything, she vanished into a whirlpool of fire. Figures she'd be a Prime; those folks with powers are always kooky, but what did she want from you? Is she related to Suicide?"

That name caused Mellow to shake involuntarily, even if the fear could not arrive. It had been years since that killer came to town and caused mayhem, murdering many, but he still remembered that behemoth for using his power to deaden Mellow's emotions, leaving him incapable of feeling anything at all. Jason and Matthew, two halves of the Gemini Man, fought him and his gang off, putting Suicide into a coma, but it had been too late for Mellow Holmes. As an empty vessel the boy now just sort of floated through life, unable to live or die. It was a permanent limbo of emotion that left him hollow.

"Suicide is still in that coma, I think," Mellow said. "I haven't heard anything about that group he was in since they carted him away years ago. Not even Jason or Matthew have said anything even though they've been going to Tyndarus regularly since then. That summer changed a lot."

"Who is that young woman you spoke of?" a man asked. Both teenagers almost jumped out of their skins when they saw the pale-skinned figure of Percival Locke standing above them on the bleachers. He was wearing a classy grey suit not too dissimilar from Mellow's. "You've never told me of her."

"We all thought he was going bonkers," Spencer replied. "Sorry."

"It seems as if she left you a warning." Locke scratched his platinum hair. "Though I do not know what her game is. How long have you been seeing her, Mellow?"

"Recently? More and more. Is what she was talking about why you're here?"

"You once told me you didn't care if you lived or died. Is that still true?"

Mellow shifted uncomfortably in his seat. He had an idea of what was coming and didn't want to think about it. Before he could say anything, Locke spoke first.

"I need you to come to Tyndarus with me, Mellow. The mission I need you for has a very low chance of success. Think carefully before you make a decision."

"Me?" Mellow asked. "I don't have any powers."

Spencer glanced between them, a nervous smile on his face. "You guys kidding?"

"No," Locke said. "This is quite a dire situation we are in."

"Need my help?"

Locke shook his head. "Just Mellow."

Spencer stood up and rubbed his hands together. "Okay, I guess that's a sign for me to get going. I don't really understand any of this Tyndarus stuff, and it's pretty far out of my comfort zone. But if you're heading there, then please tell Jason to come back at least one more time. The guys want to hang out soon. Summer won't last forever." He nodded to Locke and then took a step down the bleachers before turning back towards Mellow. "Same with Zelana. We kind of miss them, you know? They made a good couple. Take care, Mellow."

Zelana was a name Mellow hadn't thought of in awhile. She had clung to Jason almost as long as Mellow had known them, and she was also there to help them all get back on their feet after the Riverview incident. She had forgiven Mellow, despite how he had mistreated her back then, and he deeply regretted that he couldn't feel the guilt he should have experienced over it. Now, she was also missing. What had been going on in Tyndarus these days?

Spencer descended the bleachers and rejoined the party below. Shannon jumped into his arms and gave him a peck on the cheek, her dress swaying in the summer breeze. Spencer's girl really did seem to think the world of him. Even now, she didn't think much of Mellow, but he did deserve the treatment. He might have changed in the years since the Suicide incident, but a lot of the folks around town still didn't trust him. They would probably always think of him as the idiot who nearly got himself killed by criminals and tried to run away like a coward at the first sign of trouble.

Such a thing might have unnerved most people, but not him. When Mellow Holmes awoke from his coma without much in the way of feeling, he couldn't even manage to drudge up enough depression to brood over his mistakes. It was like waking up as a blank slate every day, his emotions allowing no control over him. However, it also allowed him the ability to think more clearly.

"What could you possibly need on another planet with someone like me, Locke? I'm not a Prime; I have no powers. Not only that, I'm barely a human anymore. I'm just a hollow shell."

"That's exactly why we need you, Mellow. Come with me, and you'll see. But I repeat—this is almost certain death. We need you, but you must be aware of the likelihood of success first."

Mellow glanced down at the field and then back at Locke once more. "I have said that life or death makes no difference to me anymore. Are you sure it's that hopeless?"

"Didn't you always want to be a hero? This might be your only chance."

That cursed word caused Mellow's to wince. Heroes were those like the Gemini Man —people who put themselves out there for others. Mellow had never done anything for someone else, not really. Though he did consider how he supported the gang that terrorized Riverview because he was frightened for his own pathetic life. And he still ended up like this—a void of humanity watching a celebration he could never indulge in. What did he have to lose, at this point?

"Okay, Locke. I'll go. Tell me what's going on."

Locke lead him to the car as he watched the party over his shoulder. He didn't feel anything except useless, and that was the one thing he could allow allow himself to be again. That is partially why he let Jason teach him how to use a sword. He would never be backed into a corner again. Next time, he would be the one to defend his home instead of cowering away in fear. Mellow Holmes would never be that piece of garbage he once was again.

The drive to Locke's place didn't take very long, and in the ten minute ride along the shore, he explained everything that had happened in the last few days. Mellow listened as he watched the boats along the water.

This summer was to be the final march of the Earthwalkers of Tyndarus against their enemies in the magic city of Mageuopolis. Matthew White and Jason Vermilion, the two halves of the Gemini Man, learned that the Great Sorcerer King had somehow kidnapped Zelana, who was apparently his daughter. They traveled to his mountain fortress in a rage, breaking the barrier of miasma itself. Victory appeared to be at hand. However, they never returned, and the poison air reformed, stronger than it had ever been before. Now, they need someone to slip in and put it down for good. They would not get another chance, especially if the Gemini Man had fallen.

As Locke explained this, Mellow stared out the car window into the approaching forest. Bad memories of that summer returned to him, pushing in doubts over his abilities, and he tried to forget it. When Locke had finished his story, Mellow thought he caught a figure in the treeline ahead. Was that blue hair?

"Stop the car!" he shouted.

Locke complied, slamming on the brakes, just as a twelve foot wave of blue flames plumed out of the treeline and scorched the very road before them. The car swerved, nearly tipping over on two wheels. The fire burned the edge of the woods beside them, and both Locke and Mellow exited the car to see just what had caused it.

"Blue fire?" Locke asked. "Who made this?"

Harsh blue flames licked at the trees and road as a young woman stepped out of the shade. Her pale skin matched the alien tint that Locke had, but her unnaturally bright ice-colored eyes caught Mellow's attention as she stepped through the brush. She wore tight leather clothing, her arms and legs exposed but blazing endlessly. Her long hair flowing behind her like a river, its color not too dissimilar. She reminded him of the teenage girl he had seen around town before. What was a Prime like her doing here?

"Mother?" Locke whispered.

Mellow cocked an eyebrow. "What?"

"No," the woman said. "But you will soon meet her."

She raised her arms skyward, and the flames burst out forward like a bonfire doused with heavy gasoline. They touched fifty feet into the sky, emphasizing the barrenness of this old back road. It was absolutely an ambush, and they were meant to die here.

"Now then." She slowly stepped forward, the heat pressing down into the pavement as she strode towards the pair. "Who wishes to burn first?"

Chapter 2
The Girl in the Mirror

It wasn't long before Locke leaped over to Mellow and put his hand on his shoulder. The older male jerked his arm back, and a clone of the teenage boy stood before him. Locke replicated the process five more times in succession and left Mellow with six of himself in the middle of the road. The woman watched the doppelgangers as Locke cloned himself as well. Twelve men faced down this strange Prime.

The clones did not feel like separate versions of himself, but Mellow had seen the effects of Locke's power before. All six versions were like extensions of the boy, moving wherever he willed. It was clearly their best bet to fight against a Prime that scorched her targets to cinders.

"You look just like Queen Shaula," Locke said. "But she is dead. How can that be?"

"We are all one with the Master, as you well know." She pointed a blue flaming finger at Locke. "Come now, the time for games is over. Your pathetic army will no longer be able to face the full power of the Great Sorcerer King. This is your only chance to lay down your arms, traitor."

She raised her arm, and a line of fire shot along the ground. The blaze scorched towards Mellow, and he dived sideways. All of his clones did the same, one nearly getting his suit burnt. He patted his back as the flames spun out into the forest across the road, ripping into the bark. Three trees by the pavement exploded into fire and crumbled to the ground.

"I hear you call yourself Locke now, Cutter. I apologize for not letting your grave be on the world that birthed you, but I am in a hurry. I need to be there for when the Master reaches full strength. It should be in as little as a day at this rate."

"So it's true," Locke replied. "He did absorb the Gemini Man."

"Yes! Now he has power over reality and unreality, all and one. You are an automaton, an extension of his being, and nothing more. Do you understand that now? You could never escape him."

As she slowly approached, savoring her haughty words, Locke whispered in Mellow's ear to run. The boy tried not to react at the idea. It sounded more than crazy. First of all, he didn't even know where they were going. Secondly, this woman would burn them all to death, clones or not, before they got anywhere.

A sense of relief broke through the tension in Mellow as he realized his impending death. The flames danced from the smiling woman as she stepped closer. Whatever lack of feeling he had in his bones was superseded by an instinct he had deeper down inside that screamed for mercy and wanted him to run. Truth be told, he did consider listening to it.

However, that was the Mellow Holmes that existed years ago—the coward that thought of himself as a hero above others instead of the gnat he really was. That scumbag deserved death, not escape, but now he had a mission to complete first. He wouldn't die before seeing it through.

Mellow bolted towards the woods, and all of the different Locke clones followed Mellow and his group. It would be harder to torch so many potential targets. However, one of Mellow's doppelgangers remained behind and faced the woman. She threw flames past him, striking the road and hitting a couple of duplicates. They lit ablaze and slowly cooked as they fell to the pavement. Locke's doubles shouted in pain as they burned, but none of Mellow's did. Unfortunately for Locke, the clones all shared pain between them. Mellow's deficiency in this case was actually a blessing.

"Do you not fear death, little man?" she asked the Mellow before her. "Is this the reason that traitor sought you out? It is a shame. I will have to scorch you and the rest to cinders right away."

"No, you will not," another woman said.

Behind Mellow, a teenage girl with fire red hair emerged from the forest. She was dressed the same as the murderer before him, with the same leather clothing and flowing hair. Their faces betrayed that these were definitely sisters, twins at that. The only difference between them was their hair color and that the redhead wore a silver hairpin. Mellow crouched into a ready position, waiting for one on either side to strike.

"Oriane," the blue haired woman replied. "Now, why are you here?"

The red haired woman glanced at Mellow. She looked to be around his age, definitely a teenager like her sister, though her stiff posture indicated one much more mature than the would-be killer. Oriane drew deep crimson flame in her right hand. "No, Celeste. You will cease this assault immediately. We have no business on Earth."

"Oh please. Yes, we very much do. We

must be the harbingers for the kingdom to come. Has your mission here made you as soft as these fools?"

"My business on this world is irrelevant to you, sister. I am warning you one last time to depart from here. This world is not for you, or anyone, to soil."

Celeste grimaced at her words. "Another traitor. Why is it so many of you turn away when the road to the final victory has finally been found? Are you blind? Regardless . . ."

The blue-haired girl threw her flames out, and they struck Mellow dead on. His bones twitched and bent under the heat, and his flesh melted. Smoke strangled his breaths. Whatever sensation he had in this body was dying out—he would be turned to ash in seconds.

"No!" Oriane shouted. "Stop this, sister!"

Celeste scoffed. "Now for the rest."

However, she did not expect the burning Mellow to instead lunge for her. He clung to Oriane's sister, sizzling Celeste with her own flames. The blue-haired woman cried out in pain and screamed for him to release her. Mellow's body fell apart in the blaze. His legs, torso, and eventually his head burned away.

The last thing Mellow saw of Celeste were the fresh burns on her face as he vaporized.

"You caused this, sister," she said. Mellow only heard one more thing before he disappeared. "You will pay double for his transgressions."

But that was only one of Mellow's bodies. He continued to run through the forest, his three remaining bodies, with four Locke duplicates beside him. The teenager didn't know all the ins and outs of the pale man's powers, but he did not really create separate bodies detached from the original—they were all connected as if one flesh. While Locke sweat and panted heavily, the teenage boy felt little different than usual. For once, he was glad to be so numbed.

"She killed one of me," he said to Locke. "But there's another woman there now."

Locke looked back. "I can tell."

Sure enough, a pluming geyser of tall blue and red flames shot up into the air over the tree tops. The blaze whipped around like two clashing tornadoes, licking at each other in the distance. The sisters still battled on.

"Wait, was that the woman Spencer was talking about?" Mellow asked. Now, that he realized it, she did remind him of the red-haired girl that watched him sometimes. She appeared so different dressed like that and covered in flames. "She looked just like the blue-haired girl. Who is she?"

"Their appearance seems to be like that of my mother, but younger. But that can't be, because she died in the Williams' Tech building explosion years ago. She is no longer among the living. It seems my father was hiding something from the rest of us."

"The redhead called herself Oriane. Recognize the name?"

Locke shook his head. "No, not at all."

They didn't have to run far before they came out into a clearing where a large house lay. Even still, the dueling fires clashed endlessly behind them. It probably wouldn't be long before one of them won over the other. Locke directed the remaining clones to go back and distract them, and they complied. Regardless, the original Locke and Mellow tumbled into the house and locked it behind them. The pair moved so fast that the teenager could barely take note of the immaculate wood floors and stone walls. The framed pictures on the wall showed scenery that looked somewhat like Earth, but different in a way Mellow couldn't pin down.

Down into the basement they fled, into a tunnel of carved rock. Locke flipped on a nearby switch to turn on the lights above. The tunnel let out into a room where a large wall length mirror sat against the wall, its frame a harsh gold tint.

Locke placed his hand on the surface and it glowed white, nearly blinding Mellow. When the brightness dulled, the mirror now contained nothing but a simple light, no reflection at all.

"This is the last one," Locke said. "Unfortunately, I can't make these Mirror Gates myself anymore. We lost Zelana, and our magic is fading. So this will have to do. Last chance to turn back, Mellow."

Before waiting for an answer, Locke leaped into the Mirror Gate and disappeared as if it were some sort of doorway. An earthquake rumbled, and Mellow nearly fell over. His clones were scorched away. Those girls had to be getting close.

Mellow ran forward and leaped into the

Mirror, white light consuming him whole. It soon gave way to a funnel of bright lights that sucked him down like a drain.

The teenager spun through the infinity before him, soon losing sight of Locke entirely. Not that he could have seen him at all—he could no longer even see his hands before his face. Even sound fell away around him until nothing left was silence in this impossible space.

A patchwork vision speckled into the spaces between reality. There were no faces, but he recognized voices he had never heard and names he never knew, all talking about some sort of journey ahead of them.

"*It's only a legend, boy,*" some voice said in another language. The words translated themselves inside Mellow's brain. "*You won't find anything out here but broken planetoids and dead stars. I don't care what legends you think are out here. We're only in his place because the Emperor's fortune teller told him something lay in this direction. If we find anything it will be a miracle.*"

"*Miracles are everything,*" someone replied from Mellow's perspective. "*The Emperor took our system with nothing but magic and miracles at his side. Surely, there will be more to find out here in the deep darkness. We are but mere extensions of his will, after all.*"

A glimpse of some broken old castle faded into existence before it vanished again, and Mellow fell back into the light. Before it completely dissipated, the person he had inhabited exclaimed one last thing.

"*These are what we have been seeking! The Gemini Bracelets will break the boundaries of mortality!*"

Mellow Holmes tumbled out of existence and into the end of the tunnel of light. Whatever past he had glimpsed had long since departed and left him in the present again.

He kissed sky and landed hard on rocky ground, his body trembling with an agony he didn't feel as he tried to stand up again. The annoyance could sometimes be too much—the pain still affected his body even if the sensation never came. Locke hoisted him up and quickly assessed that they were in the middle of a battlefield.

Though they had come out of a tent, scores of warriors fought in the middle of this narrow mountain range, men with platinum hair like Locke against a force wearing similar leather armor consisting of lizardmen. Their swords, spears, and arrows battered against each other as war cries of hundreds filled the air. Mellow looked upon this madness with his mouth agape. Jason's stories really were true, as was the world he had been told about from Zelana.

Tyndarus existed.

And now he was in the middle of a war zone.

CHAPTER 3
THE FALL OF MAGEUOPOLIS

"LOCKE!" a woman shouted from somewhere nearby. "You've returned! Come quick."

In one of the large tents lay many injured warriors, wrapped in bandages and blankets. The men were being attended to by women wearing white robes. The one who called to Locke was a remarkably beautiful one that caught Mellow's attention as soon as he saw her. She was wrapping an arrow wound on one of the injured fighters as she called out to the two of them.

"This is Mellow Holmes," Locke said. "I'm taking him to the tunnel."

"That name sounds familiar." The young woman looked Mellow up and down. "He's too young."

"He does not feel pain, Ordopha. We have no one else. He is our last chance."

Ordopha finished up with the arrow wound and approached the two of them. She squinted at Mellow before realization dawned on her. "Matthew told me about you. Is it true that your sense of pain is gone?"

Mellow nodded. "Thanks to a Prime. But why am I here? I have no powers or magic."

"We have no time to spare. The lizardmen have redoubled their efforts ever since the miasma arose rose again. We will not hold out at this rate. Locke will explain what needs to be done. I must return to aid the wounded; so please get yourselves equipped."

She handed Mellow and Locke leather armor and some swords. They changed and she went back to her job. Mellow found the practice of sliding on armor awkward, but thankfully Locke helped explain the entire process to him. The boy couldn't get over how unreal this all was, even if he needed to accept it as reality. Was he really fighting in a war? The two males discussed the properties of their equipment as Ordopha worked on and explained what had happened over the last day.

Apparently, the Gemini Man stormed the mountain fortress city of Mageuopolis, attacking just as it seemed the enemy was in retreat. But then the atmosphere changed, and the barrier of dark miasma that had once protected the city reformed once more. The Gemini Man never returned.

The lizardmen that poured out of the mountain miasma were howling like rabid monkeys with saliva dripping out of their mouths. Despite their losses, there were still enough of them to clash against the hundreds of men that he could spot in this narrow mountain range.

"What makes you think I can pass through there unharmed? That's definitely poison." Mellow wiped his forehead clean of sweat. Was that fear he was beginning to feel? No, such a sensation was impossible. "And I'm not much of a sword fighter. I learned from Jason after we made up, but I'm no expert."

"There is another way," Locke said. "Not just anyone will be able to traverse this path."

He led the teenager towards a different tent where horses lay inside. Except, of course, that they weren't horses. These were the same size but were instead over-sized wild cats. One of them purred as Locke scratched its chin. He handed Mellow the reins to a second one. The boy looked at him as if he had gone mad.

"It is a lot to get used to, I know." Locke laughed, a nervous smile growing. "Have a seat on the cat-tral and follow me. That one before you is quite friendly, I assure you."

Mellow, of course, did what he was told, though there wasn't much else he could do. Once he grabbed the reins and called for the cat-tral to move, it was already off and following Locke's ride. The beast was rather steady as Mellow clung tight, leaping rocks and scurrying along cliff edges. Before he knew it, they were already in the mountains, and the sounds of battle fell behind them.

Jason and Matthew had both told him stories about Tyndarus many times, but he hadn't fully believed them despite their pretty words. Who would have imagined a whole other world existed just on the other side of a mirror, and who possibly could have guessed that it would contain wondrous sights and creations such as these? All this, and the existence of a force like magic, lay hidden in the corners of the universe. Well, it was not apparently hidden *that* well, it seemed.

The more he rode the cat-tral and the more the wind hit him, a familiar warm sensation grew inside the teenager's chest. He could hardly remember the last time he felt so alive. An experience like this back home was not anything he could imagine—not even in the big cities crawling with heroes and villains. A smile dawned on his lips despite his inability to feel anything. Was this the sort of thing that lay out there in the universe so far outside of his home?

The pair eventually stopped in front of a cave entrance. Locke checked his cat-tral's pack and removed a small sack. He handed it to Mellow, and the two disembarked from their rides.

"This is it, Mellow. This is the path that leads to Mageuopolis. Your pack has enough food to last you the full day's journey through there to the other side. Do you think you have what it takes to make it?"

"Hang on." Mellow put up a hand. "Are you loopy? I'm no fighter, even if you hand me a sword and supplies. What makes you think I can travel alone in a cave to some weird magic city in the mountains that I've never even seen before? What am I even supposed to do there? On top of it, why didn't you show this to the others. They might have been able to sneak in through here."

"They would not have survived. But you will. You are the only one who can right now."

Mellow looked at him askew. "What makes you figure that? I'm just a coward who has done nothing but run his whole life. What's in there?"

"Well, you have not run so far. And as for being alone . . ." Locke leaned in and grabbed Mellow's shoulder. He pulled back several times and created eleven clones of the teenage boy. "It should also help dilute the fog's effect on you. The path itself has a bit of history, which is the very reason no one else can take it."

"Meaning?"

"It is complicated."

Locke went into it. As it turned out, this was the pathway he had used a long time ago when he was but a child. The tunnel burrowed deep into the earth where some strange kind of high pitch whistle would bury itself into the target's brain. It would induce agony inside thoughts and refuse to let up until the victim escaped, or died. Even one of the Great Sorcerer King's blood could not sustain themselves in there for too long. The only one who would be able to traverse it would be one who can overcome the agony involved.

"So that's me," Mellow said. "Is that what you're saying?"

Locke nodded. "There is no one else who could do this. Not even the Gemini Man. Of course, you are free to decline, but it is why I sought you out to begin with. Once Jason reminded me of your predicament, a few nights ago, I thought you might be the perfect candidate. Regardless, you are our only hope in surpassing the miasma and slipping through that barrier. It could be certain death, however. What say you, Mellow Holmes?"

Mellow gazed into the abyss of the cave before him and let out a hard breath. Whether he wanted to go or not, he did not think he had the skills to survive out in an alien world. Fighting monster lizardmen, dodging poison gas, and scaling a mountain city was not quite anything he ever expected that he would do.

However, his clear thinking allowed him to be rational about it. This was one of the few bonuses he had from that predicament a few years ago that left him emotionally deadened. This was his last chance to do anything remotely like those heroes he admired so much as a child, from before he destroyed himself pretending to be one. After this, it was college or whatever, then a normal job and life, or at least as normal as it could get in Riverview. He had never actually been needed before, either, and it was clear that there was no other person that could fulfill this task. Mellow Holmes was no longer the loser he was back then. Now, he could finally prove it.

"Okay, Locke," he said. "I'll do it. But you better tell me exactly what I gotta do."

After Locke informed Mellow of the answers to his inquiries, he pointed him towards the cave entrance and let him travel in of his own accord. His eleven doppelgangers followed in a file through the darkness. The dank air chilled him through his leather armor, though he only knew it because the hairs on his neck stood up. Even the wind itself seemed to want him to turn back.

The strangest part of the journey deep into the cave was that it did not get darker as he walked the narrow path. No, it only got brighter, despite no light source. In addition to the brightness pressing in on him, a buzz slowly rose in the back of his head. It hummed louder and louder, long after he had forgotten how long he had been underground for. His bones even trembled as if a frequency beyond him rattled his insides. Regardless, he felt none of it, and neither did his clones. Whatever was out there distracted him more than anything.

Eventually, his stomach growled, and he sat down to eat some of the food Locke had given him—simple bread and water, probably meant to avoid a queasy gut. He had vomited before in his deadened state, despite not even knowing he was ill, so it was definitely a good call. As Mellow ate, his clones became fed as well. He didn't quite know how Locke's powers worked, but none of his doppelgangers were separate from him or had individual thoughts—every one was an extension of Mellow Holmes. Once he finished up, the party of him moved on, rested and energized.

Hours he went on, walking without ceasing, all sense of time lost. His legs only got heavier, sweat dripped down his back, and his breaths fell harder, though he dragged himself on anyway. At the same time, that incessant buzzing and brightness refused to go away. It was easy to see why no one would have been able to stand this place for long. The only reason Mellow knew he had been there for too long was when his body gave up and brought him down to slumber with the rest of his clones.

He couldn't even see the cavern any longer, nor could he hear his own steps, but consciousness left him to the darkness, pulling him under.

At first, the teenager figured it was mere exhaustion, but soon any memory of the tunnel left him behind, as did the brightness and the squealing pitch. In fact, so too did any trace of Tyndarus leave his presence. He blinked awake in a place far beyond any he had seen before.

Mellow Holmes had awoken in space.

CHAPTER 4
GEMINI HARBINGER

"*IT'S HERE, I KNOW IT,*" someone said. "*It's the bracelets!*"

There were no people to be seen. In fact, there was no life at all. Mellow had woken up on what he had assumed the moon would look like back home. Endless space and stars stared at him from above, and the rocky grey ground told him this wasn't just any planet. The voices without bodies spoke on, talking about some world that must have been here long ago.

A golden castle had once been here. Actually, it would be more accurate to say that *remnants* of a golden castle littered this dead place, coins and jewels floated about as if gravity had died with the rest of it. Smashed stone and upturned dirt were strewn about everywhere. Mellow's mind drifted into the ruins of this long dead kingdom as the voices continued speaking to each other.

"*Nieto,*" one of them said. "*What are you doing?*"

"*Preforming the ritual.*"

The loudest scream Mellow had ever heard in his life nearly deafened him. He instinctively winced as the shouts of agony echoed throughout the eternity of this impossible space. Who were these beings? Were they even people? No matter what sounds of chaos and bloodshed he thought he heard in this place, he still could not see anyone at all. Then a voice spoke again.

"*It is time for a new king, my friends. Do not worry. My mercy extends to the living.*"

The universe quaked and growled like it was being torn apart. This madness of invisible violence and life-ending death cries replayed in his mind as if stuck on loop. Mellow had an inkling that his body wanted to be sick, but he ignored the instinct. He couldn't afford to waste time.

That was the instant he realized that he didn't quite know where he himself was. The teenager reached around but could not even see or feel where his arms were. It was as if his consciousness had been ripped clean of his bones and tossed into the emptiness of space. Perhaps, that was the point of this whole trap in the first place. Thankfully, his deadened emotions allowed him to keep his breaths calm under his sweating muscles and the cyclone of insanity spinning around him.

He imagined where his arms were and used them to push up underneath him and gave him the impression he was rising from the ground. As he struggled to fight for his own soul, visions of this dead world continued playing without any faces, locations, or people to see. Mere ideas and an onslaught of memories flooded inside while he fought to regain his balance.

There was a *thing* called Nieto—there was no other description the boy could think to give this creature. A long time ago, he lived and thrived in some kingdom. Time went on, and he rose up to become one of the most trusted sorcerers for his world. As he studied for ways to build the kingdom and extend the royalty's reach he found a legend—a story of a long-extinguished civilization that attempted to crack reality itself by controlling every element of the physical plane to reach beyond it. In the process, he learned how to grow the energy inside of him to become a life force of his own—he became a living relic himself. It would go without saying that a legendary weapon had no need to bow to others.

This is where the being called Nieto found the first relics in his search—the Gemini Bracelets, and began his experiments to activate them.

"*No good,*" Nieto said, discarding another of his former allies to the corpse pile. "*My own race is insufficient in imbuing the physical properties needed to house a god. But there is always the stars!*"

And sure enough he took to space, world to world, until he found the planet of Tyndarus and created a whole race of people he called Earthwalkers to embody the cause. Even as his own corrupted life force made him seemingly immortal, he knew he needed the relics to truly reach the godhood he so desired. With a whole world made to worship him, it would only be a matter of time before he would make that a reality.

Nieto looked up from his throne towards Mellow, watching as the boy crawled forward in the cave tunnel. Mellow could still see no discernible face in the purple fog surrounding that armored body, but he did glimpse the red eyes questioning his very plight.

"*My kingdom has no need of bio waste, boy. I suggest you flee as you always have. I will not be as lenient on you as Suicide was if you do not turn back now.*"

But Mellow closed his eyes, his body seizing under him while he forced himself onward. The world fell away as he concentrated, the weird magic of this place unable to grasp at him, as he thought of home.

Riverview felt so far away at that moment, but he knew it all too well. The river itself, the old park that was long gone now, and the school he had graduated from. What was coming next in his life now that those days were over? He focused on that, and soon, his thoughts turned to the young woman with the red hair.

How many times had he come across her but never had the chance to talk to the girl. Even without the ability to feel anything, he did think something was different about her They had locked eyes more than a few times, but never was he able to interact. Why had she saved him?

Oriane was her name. Mellow pictured her in his mind's eye, and her face became clearer and clearer as the world fell away again. Eventually, he could see her red lips mouthing something as he drew closer. Just as he reached the young woman, her voice broke in.

"How in the world are you alive?"

Mellow opened his eyes and found he was back in the cave again, crawling in the middle of the tunnel. Just before him crouched Oriane, staring at him. Her silver hairpin glared light into his eyes.

He tried shrugging but nearly lost his balance. "I guess I'm made of tougher stuff."

"You might be. At least, some of you."

Behind Mellow, two of his clones suffered from seizures. They flopped around in the dirt, kicking up rocks, with saliva dripping from their mouths. After a few minutes, the pair stilled. Their lifeless bodies faded away like a mist lifting in an updraft.

Had those doubles felt something? That should not have been possible since Mellow himself hadn't been able to feel anything in years. Nonetheless, the sweat dripped down his trembling skin. Would his lack of sensation be enough to save him from this place? He might end up dead like the clones.

The boy turned to the young woman. "You saved me back in Riverview. Why would you do that?"

"Not now. We cannot linger here. This is where the memories were buried and stored."

She lead him forward down the tunnel and introduced herself formally. The further they traveled and the more she spoke, the further away the cacophony in his mind got. By the time they reached a neighboring complex of purple stone caves, the sound had fallen to the back of his mind. None of the other clones had fallen, either. He breathed a sigh of relief.

"I thought you had lost all sensation?" she asked. "You truly are made of steel, Mellow Holmes."

"You've been following me this long, and you really believe that?"

"Monitoring your actions has shown me your true character. Most anyone else who had lost the ability to feel happiness, sadness, anger, or general joy, would have given up long ago. Yet you have survived years."

"There wasn't really any other choice. All that quiet made me realize just how much of a scumbag I was. I couldn't even get a high out of it anymore. If I regained feeling tomorrow, I would just revert to being that same person that hurt so many long ago. Cowards never change. I didn't have any reason to turn away those who asked me to come here. Even after all I did, they still forgave me. It's more than I ever deserved."

"I do not think you can be anyone apart from who you are, Mellow Holmes. That is why I monitored you for so long. I could not understand how you lived as freely as you did while missing such an important part of yourself. Envy consumed me. Despite that, once I was told to destroy you and all others who had opposed the Great Sorcerer King, I could not bring myself to do so—I could not destroy a world of one who had lived so strongly, nor the world that allowed it to happen. I could not let you become me."

He fell silent as they traveled onward. Though he didn't quite believe he was anywhere near as strong as she thought, he did agree with her views on Earth, especially Riverview. Mellow had allowed his worry over his hometown in a world of heroes and villains to sour into poisonous hatred, and it almost killed them both. There is no way he would ever be able to make up for such evil, ignorance or not, so it was all he could do here to try what he could. As long as he followed Locke's instructions, he would make it through just fine.

"We are not alone," she said.

Sure enough, out of the corner of the cavern emerged a pair of lizardmen. They lurched towards the two intruders, their blades flashing. Five more followed them, hissing away.

Mellow and his clones drew their blades. A tinge of fear momentarily stopped him. Why did he feel that? The sensation quickly passed, and he took the fight to the lizards.

The battle echoed throughout the cavern, and two of Mellow's doppelgangers were quickly slain. He fumbled as he tried moving in on his opponent, but the lizardman botched his swing for the boy's neck, and Mellow ran the enemy through. The lizardman gagged on its blood as it died, but Mellow felt nothing at the death. Sometimes, his curse was a blessing.

As the battle went on, he moved from opponent to opponent, a fire kindling inside of him. He heated up until all that remained was himself and one lizardman. Their swords slashed at the air, looking for a killing blow. After one too many attacks, a feeling of joy pushed his way through him, and he froze. Was that happiness?

The lizardman tackled Mellow to the ground in his confusion. They rolled about, unable to get a decisive strike, screaming bloody murder at each other. The boy punched and thrashed, but the lizard refused to budge. It had reclaimed its grip on its sword and brought it down on Mellow.

It then gagged as Oriane removed her dagger from its throat. The beast stumbled off of him, and Mellow ran it through for the final kill. Finally, all that was left was the two of them in the cavern. All of the clones were now dead and gone.

Mellow's breaths arrived heavy as he stared up at the young woman. He had almost died, true, but it was thanks to her that he was still in one piece at all. She put out a hand and helped him stand back up, her face as inscrutable as ever.

"You didn't use your fire," Mellow said.

Oriane nodded at his words. "My powers are not quite like those of the Queen, and neither are my sister's like her. Our flames need rest before they can be rekindled."

"Did you kill Celeste?" he asked. "I can't see how else you'd be here if you didn't."

She removed a grey orb from out of her leather outfit. Mist appeared to be swimming inside it.

"She is in here."

"She's what?! Is that magic?"

"The orb runs off the King's magic. He fashioned it to capture those of his own blood, should they run astray. But enough dawdling. We must hurry, Mellow Holmes. The Great Sorcerer King will not wait for you to invade."

"Fine," the teenage boy said. "But call me Mellow. My full name sounds awkward."

She smiled. "As you wish. I am Oriane, as you know. We will talk more once we survive."

"It's a date."

"Yes, it is a date." She looked at him like he was speaking a dead language. "What else would it be?"

He shook his head. "Never mind."

The pair moved on down the narrow pathway through the shadows of the darkened space towards torchlight and stone steps leading up. He soon reached old damp stone stained with dried blood and the purple mist filling the halls. This had to be the fortress. Heavy steps echoed through the halls ahead of them.

"This way," Oriane said. "I know a hidden path that leads up."

Mellow followed the teenage girl through the musty hall into one of the rooms. She pulled loose a slab in the wall to open up a new passage and lead him inside. The entrance sealed shut behind them, leaving the pair in the dark. There, a new spiraling staircase awaited them with daylight shining in from small cracks in the walls above. Without pause, the pair sprinted up the stone steps.

The worst part of his trek was that he had no idea how long he was in that underground cavern for, nor did he remember what he was supposed to do here in this place. As they wasted no time bolting towards their destination, he tried to think back to his discussion with Locke. What was it he said at the entrance?

"You don't need to defeat the Great Sorcerer King, Mellow. You only need to reach the throne-room where his crystal resides. Smash that, and you will destroy the source of the miasma."

"You want me to sneak in alone?"

"I know it's dangerous. If you make the wrong move, you will die, but we have few options as it is. Your chance of success is low, true. This is your last chance to turn back. What do you say?"

As Mellow ran up the steps, he thought about how lucky he had been in making it this far. He might not return from this quest, but it didn't bother him as much as he thought it might. Why had he been so eager to go on a suicide mission like this anyway?

Oriane lead him so far up that windows were now becoming a common sight to his right. The purple-stained sky covered in miasma allowed the mountain city of Mageuopolis to come into view. Scores of warriors stormed the structures on the opposite side of the large range, and they were getting closer. It really did look as if they had fought long and hard to reach this far in. A strange warmth lit inside of him.

A long-forgotten memory returned to Mellow Holmes in that moment. Back when he was in kindergarten, he used to play in the old park with the other kids. One time, he recalled playing heroes with his old friend Spencer, chasing those super-villains down to stop their plot of overthrowing the government. Spencer was his sidekick and said boy's future girlfriend was the villain. Mellow was the one who flew in and used his super-strength to destroy the bomb and take down the evil woman. As she fell in defeat, the entire playground roared in triumph, and he let out the loudest victory shout of his life. This was how it should have been. In that moment, he knew how a hero should be.

Even before the passing years and mundanity and disappointments of modern life poisoned his thinking into resentment, he still believed in the way a hero should be—strong and reliable. Even a coward like him knew it would never be that easy.

Even now as he ran to his certain death with those doubts nibbling at the back of his thoughts, and the memories of fear telling him how he could escape this, all of it fell away into the haze. Those poisonous thoughts and doubts that had been continually chewing at him, dragging his hopes down, he decided to push them aside. Though they would never fully go away, at least he could do something to show that he wasn't what he used to be. Whatever he was now he had no idea, but this was the chance to be something more, and he would take it.

Oriane led him out of the stairs into a new hallway lit with the muted hue of the outside mist. The pair approached a large wooden door ahead of them. At that very moment, Mellow Holmes knew he was going to die. Despite that, a smile dawned on his face.

"Here we are," she said. The teenage girl blinked at him. "Are you smiling?"

"Yeah, I guess I am."

CHAPTER 5
THE GREAT SORCERER KING

THOUGH MELLOW FELT NOTHING due to his condition, he could still tell when sensations wanted to force their way into his body. As he crossed the threshold into the chamber ahead of him, his very flesh rippled as if it were trying to escape him. The smell of blood and gore caused him to gag, and his eyes to water. That was when he knew he had reached the source of all the madness in this fortress.

In the center of the chamber sat a large oval crystal with jagged edges, its purple color almost blending into the miasma pumping out of it into the rest of the room. The object was at least seven feet tall and about half as wide, floating two feet off the floor over a small stone plateau. Dark whispers and incomprehensible humming slipped out of it, bringing sickness to Mellow that he couldn't feel but knew existed because his stomach questioned why he wasn't vomiting.

Even with the pure malice and disgust radiating out of the crystal, the more sickening sight were the scores of lizardman corpses and bloodstains strewn about the large chamber.

Disemboweled, dissected, decapitated, and dismembered, the man-shaped lizard bodies were battered nearly beyond recognition as the man on the throne at the rear of the room watched Mellow and Oriane approach the wicked crystal.

"So I wasn't mistaken," the large man said. "All of this for a mere child? Not even an Earthwalker, a Prime, or one of my children, but a boy. How did one such as you manage to slip so far inside Mageuopolis?"

"I guided him," Oriane replied.

He waved a large gauntlet towards her. "You would. There is something degenerate in the blood of Earthwalkers. No matter how I bring you to life, you always end up betraying me—all except for *one*."

The Great Sorcerer King wore heavy black armor covered in purple mist and stood at over seven feet tall, but his very face was masked by the helmet he wore, coated by the same miasma this crystal swam in. Surely, breaking it would do a lot of damage to his operation. But how could Mellow hope to even crack something so big? He was no Prime. Mellow was only a powerless teenager with a sword.

"You had more freedom under my rule than without," the enemy said. "All men toil under the very systems they create, scouring it for cracks and holes they can slip through and get a foothold over the dregs. True leaders reach for the top at all cost, while even the village fool looks for a way to climb over his fellow riffraff. I offer a world where there is no ladder to climb, no gain to slashing your compatriot's throat for extra coin, and all of you would rather make me your villain instead. You see, all you want is an excuse for your own evil. You are just a lesser form of me—a sad imitation."

"My Lord," Oriane said. She kneeled in front of the throne before the king. "You sent me to Earth to spy on Jason Vermilion and Matthew White as you gathered strength here for your invasion, and I listened. I did as I was told."

"Yet you returned here at a crucial moment for your cause and brought in a powerless whelp to be slaughtered like a pig. On top of that, you defeated your own sister while stopping her from doing my bidding. Tell me, Oriane, why have you betrayed me like this?"

As they spoke, Mellow found himself drawn to the giant crystal, his mind captivated by the dancing miasma and the whispers beckoning him. Somewhere, deep inside, his sixth sense was bubbling, trying to say something he couldn't process. Whatever had happened to him in that cavern had weakened the power over him that wrecked his inability to feel, and he had the inkling that it might give at any point. But then he remembered Locke's words, and knew that it would be the worst case scenario for that to happen here.

"*Your weakness is the only advantage we have now,*" he had said.

"*My lack of feelings is an advantage?*"

"*My father's magic poisons everything. It eats at your insides, preventing much in the way of resistance. Unless you are the Gemini Man and able to transcend all sensation, you will be killed before you can get close enough to so much as harm him. Even I as his son cannot approach him at this stage. Our only chance is for one who can circumvent his ability and get at the heart of his madness. But your odds of success even then, are slim. This is why I keep warning you, Mellow. Are you sure you want to do this?*"

Mellow had gazed into the cave where no man had returned from before and let out a sigh. He didn't want to throw his life away, who would? Even still, he did owe Matthew and Jason for saving his town when he had betrayed it to villains so long ago. His emotionless state was his own fault, but now it could be a weapon? The only answer was obvious.

Now, as he thought back on the words of Locke, he could only involuntarily tremble as he approached the crystal. All he had to do, apparently, was touch it. Such a thing was easier said than done as a force like a hard intangible wind pushed back against him. Even as he forced his way towards certain death, Nieto and Oriane continued their discussion before him.

"My Lord," she said. "You are capable of such greatness. You have reshaped this world and created a race of living beings, even fashioned a way of transportation that transcends the rules of nature, and yet still, you are holed away here all alone in the deep mountains, living among the only natives of the world that have not betrayed you."

"Yes, both the Earthwalkers and the tigermen will meet their deaths once I am complete. What is your point?"

"Why do you waste it all in slaughter? I know you were the one who murdered these lizardmen, even as their brothers fight for you down below. Why do you insist on such carnage?"

"Shut your mouth, you ungrateful trollop." His matter-of-fact tone caused even Mellow to flinch. The king finally stood up from his throne. "I am not your equal. That pathetic boy over there is not your equal either. Do you know what you even are? You and the sister you have with you are imperfect versions of my beloved wife. I reconstructed her, my only loyal subject, cleansing her of any potential human-like traits she might have had. My queen shed them for me, but there was always a chance you would gain them back again, so I created you younger, more impressionable for my ends. It seemed to have worked. How many missions have you carried out without complaint? And now you feel like you have morals or a conscience? You do not. I *know* you do not. I tore it out of you myself. For all your talk, you still led that boy to his death. What do you hope to accomplish, Oriane? What will be your final words before I absorb you again and wipe the slate clean once more?"

Oriane trembled in her kneeling position, unable to move or say much of anything. She had been on Earth for a long time, Mellow had remembered seeing her for months, but he had only seen her as the weird girl who didn't know how to socialize. That was common enough. Yet now, here she was on one knee, pleading with her own master to spare the very planet she was assigned to help destroy. Finally, she looked up at her king and squeaked out her answer.

"It doesn't have to be this way."

Great Sorcerer King Nieto lunged forward so fast that Mellow barely saw him move. His fist slammed into Oriane's stomach and knocked her backwards. She rolled against the stone floor, sprawling out onto the ground itself. She gagged and coughed.

Mellow took one step towards her, but she shouted at him to stop. Oriane pushed herself up to all fours as she gasped.

"You have a task yet to complete."

"A task?" Nieto said. He laughed from under his helmet. "I would like to see this so-called *task*."

The boy bit his tongue. He knew running out to help the girl was pointless when he was just another mortal. But Locke had assigned him his mission, and now there was little choice but to complete it. Mellow turned back and ran towards the crystal.

"This is your plan?" Nieto asked. "You will die before touching it."

Mellow reached out, and the invisible force pushed him back. His arms forward, he dug in his heels. A loud crack ripped the air, and it took a moment to notice a few of his fingers in his left hand flopping uselessly against the back of his palm. Long cuts loosed blood across his arms, and his legs cried out under him. The armor did little to protect him as even his chest leaked life-force out of his skin. Nieto continued to laugh, but Mellow did not recede even though he knew the pain, if he could have felt it, would have caused him to pass out. He still stomped onward, only a few feet from his destination. Finally, his entire left arm twisted and snapped, bending backwards behind him in the invisible wind. As his broken limb fell away, he pushed ahead and slammed his head against the crystal. Instantly, the force stopped pushing him away—instead, it pulled him inward. His body crashed against the purple surface.

"Oh, did you believe merely reaching it would cause you to win, boy? No, now it will eat you whole instead. Humans truly are stupid creatures. You are no less idiotic than your Gemini Man."

A tornado of blackened energy thrashed inside Mellow's bones. His very organs trembled and shook as if they were being diced apart. Blood trickled out of his mouth and nose as the boy clung to the crystal with his one free arm. It was killing him, but still, he held on tight, closing his eyes in concentration.

There in the void, he saw everyone currently in the throne room. Nieto, a being of this poisonous energy, stood alone in a flat plain, a smoking crater behind him where his shattered and wrecked ship had landed. Out of the ground emerged a woman before him, beautiful and striking, her breasts and hips as perfect as her eyes and the smile emerging on her lips. The pale-skinned lady kneeled before the being in front of her and plead her allegiance to him.

"*You are the first,*" he said. "*You are to be my Queen. Your name shall be Shaula.*"

Shaula nodded from her lower position. "*I will always be by your side, my Lord.*"

The world changed around Mellow again, and now, he awoke in this very fortress, still in the past. There was the man in the same set of armor as earlier, his face non-existent and still a wall of miasma. Here, two versions of the same woman kneeled before him. They were teenage girls, one with red hair and the other with blue. Both had the same face—the same as the woman he had first created ages prior.

"*You are not her,*" he said. "*She is still with me, but you will act in her stead. You will be the sword I need to slay the ones who defied me. Show me you are worthy of life, like she has. Otherwise, you will end up like all failures, like the other world that refuses to submit to me—like Earth.*"

"*Earth?*" Oriane looked up at him, slightly younger than Mellow remembered. "*What is that?*"

"*The world you shall inhabit, my little blade. Complete your mission and I might even allow you a territory to rule as Queen.*"

"No!" someone shouted. Mellow snapped awake again.

The crystal had now embedded itself in his very flesh, pumping miasma directly into his brain. Vomit poured out of his mouth as he struggled to regain consciousness. He still felt nothing, but none of his limbs would budge. Something else was filling his insides—something he couldn't process.

"You're just a human!" Nieto shouted. "You should be dead!"

The Great Sorcerer King raised an arm, and a purple spear formed in his hands. Without much in the way of pause, he flung it at the wounded teenager.

As the spear flew towards Mellow's unmoving body, another vision passed by him. He tried to keep his eyes open, but the world moved too slow and sluggish for him to be able to concentrate on it.

There he saw the red-haired girl hanging out in Riverview. She followed her targets for months, lurking in the shadows and disappearing from view into flames when needed. It was an easy job, even though these humans disgusted her a good deal. Why were they so happy, living such miserable lives? Didn't they know they could have freedom from all this nonsense?

And yet as time passed, she could do little but spend her days engaging in Earth's pastimes. At one point, she was even on a first name basis with the couple whose room she rented. How embarrassing.

She bumped into Mellow himself, a memory he did not even remember, at the fair as she was busy devouring cotton candy. Her face went red as she realized she screwed up. If he wasn't distracted with his own emptiness, he might have noticed. Nonetheless, before she could run, he offered his apologies and handed her a hairpin he had won in some game he no longer remembered. She stared at it and then him.

"*You might get more out of this than I would,*" he said. "*Have a good time, Miss.*"

"*You don't even know me.*"

He looked her up and down before running off to join his friends. His last words rang in her mind as he left. "*You look like you need a good time. Go have some fun, will you?*"

Another scream broke Mellow out his unconsciousness. The crystal was gone, but the purple mist remained encircling him. That was when he remembered Nieto's spear soaring towards him.

But then a body tackled into the boy. The spear stuck into Oriane's chest as he was knocked aside. She slumped over into the dirt and didn't stir again, her hairpin shining in the shadows of this chamber. Blood leaked out onto the fortress stone.

"Another failure," Nieto said. He fashioned another spear in his hand and sighed. "I will just have to make more, I suppose. So much waste. Divinity should be for higher things, no?"

Tears formed in Mellow's eyes, and everything hit him at once—all the fears, all the anger, all the happiness, all the joy, and all the despair, he was denied for so long. He shouted a war-cry that was so loud it deafened him and even caused Nieto to flinch. The purple mist pushed itself out of his body and flooded the chamber, filling every crevice in a typhoon of miasma that singed everything as if it were acidic.

The ceiling itself slashed apart and loosened blocks and stone, cracking the room apart in the process.

He remembered the deaths in Riverview, Suicide's face, and even the memories of Oriane, as well as how these lizardmen were slaughtered by their master in a fit of rage. Emotion crippled him, not allowing Mellow to move, as his whole body trembled and tears spewed from his eyes, saliva from his mouth, and mucous from his nose. It refused to stop despite the unending miasma raging out of his body.

The ceiling gave in, sending stone crashing into the ground and causing the floor to give in. Lizardman corpses slid into the crevices as the entire room gradually caved in. The unyielding emotions fueled his rage enough to allow him just the smallest bit of movement. Mellow ran towards the fallen Oriane as the entire room collapsed around them. He put himself over her at the very moment a large chunk of stone crushed down into his head.

There he saw a vision of the teenage girl walking into her rented room, dancing with herself, and leaping onto her bed. She played with the hairpin a bit before placing it on her with the mirror. She giggled a bit as the outside fireworks took her attention. They rumbled on as people hooted and hollered from the street below.

"*So this is Earth,*" she said.

That was the last thing Mellow Holmes thought about as the fortress caved in on top of him.

THE GREAT SORCERER KING FLOATED above the ruins of his throne room. He felt somewhat lighter, as if a large weight had been lifted from him—but not in a good way. It was as if he were missing internal organs or limbs, hollow. That human had somehow swallowed his crystal, the very artifact he created to hold his power source as his own body had begun to crumble ages ago. Not only that, but it was a mere boy who did it, and not even a Prime at that. What were these humans made of?

He considered searching for the corpses, but the rubble went floors down, and he did not have the time. With the crystal gone, the Earthwalker army would be at his gates soon enough. They would certainly think they had won this day.

But they had actually lost.

Nieto had not only the Gemini Man, but his own daughter, still. He would no longer need the miasma that had sustained him so long. A god he would always be.

As he flew upwards to the roof and the Golden Gate, he knew that this foolish war was almost over. All he needed was to wait.

"*Nieto, you would betray your blood?*"

He shook away the strands of ancient memories that still clung to him from those forgotten days. He had betrayed nothing and no one. Creating the ultimate state of existence had always been his only goal. All of this meat meant nothing, not even he did, not until the war had been won. And now, it was here. A new god was to be born, and the rest of creation would soon become one with him.

"*As long as you cling to your emptiness, you will never find fulfillment.*"

"Shut your mouth, old man," Nieto said, grumbling under his breath.

The king soared upwards to the roof, swearing to return to his world once he had conquered his own new body. That emptiness would seen be filled, and every inch of creation itself would bow to the Great Sorcerer King. They would all feel it—and the entire universe would tremble at his name.

And his salvation was only a stone-throw away!

CHAPTER 6
FINAL MEETINGS

THE WORLD ENDED, and Mellow felt every bit of it. His entire body, inside and out, and from head to toe, cried out in agony all at once, leaving him in a constant state of spasm. His mind wouldn't focus, and neither could he so much as open his eyes as existence itself stabbed at his very being. Was he even alive anymore? Was this his punishment for all that he had done wrong? Sweat blinded the boy as finally forced his eyes open again.

"He is awake!" Ordopha said. The woman sat beside him, her warm hands gripping hard on his left arm. He didn't even want to look at his limb—not that he could remember just what had happened to it. She wiped sweat from his forehead. A faint white light radiated off of her. "Mellow! It has only been a short time since we found you. Go back to sleep."

He attempted to speak, but only violent coughs escaped his sore throat. As he rocked in place with gags, he tried to steady himself, quickly realizing he was lying in a cot. Eventually, he found the energy to speak. "Oriane was buried in there."

"The girl?" Ordopha gestured to the cot beside him. "We found her underneath you."

There Oriane lay, asleep and still, her own chest patched over and glowing a faint white. She groaned in her sleep as several soldiers walked by her, inspecting the fortress halls. She was just another wounded among their numbers.

It returned to Mellow, why he was there. The boy had swallowed the crystal that powered this place at the same time the girl was taken down by Nieto. Mellow then exploded with emotion and brought the entire throne room down on them. But what had become of the Great Sorcerer King?

Mellow sat up and pain twisted at his insides. He cried out before falling back into his cot. Tears welled in his eyes. Had that crystal destroyed the effect of Suicide's power on him? This was not the time for his sense of feeling to return. Every inch of him screamed in agony. He closed his eyes tight as the pain pushed through.

"This is some bad timing," he said through gritted teeth. "Where is Nieto?"

"He has fled this world," Locke replied. His ally loomed over him. "And I have worse news."

"Can't be any worse than how I already feel."

"It is. That crystal will eat you from the inside unless we purge it from your body. Now that the miasma is gone and my father has left Tyndarus, we have limited time to act. You will not hold for much longer. Mortals cannot contain his essence indefinitely. Its unbridled power appears to have unlocked your sense of feeling again. That was not something I expected to happen."

"Neither did I." Mellow swallowed the pain and finally forced himself to sit up. "I think I can manage enough to get by."

"There is a reason you can." Locke gestured behind him. "Do you see that? It is the only reason you are sane right now."

On the floor lay a line of bodies, some still and others having seizures, none awake. It took a moment for Mellow to realize they were his clones. Unlike him, however, they were silent, choked by pain and tears as they thrashed about on the ground—the ones that weren't dead, that is. He counted at least twelve of them. The ones that expired soon faded away and Locke replaced them once more.

"Alain!" Ordopha said to one of the soldiers. "Restrain that one!"

A muscular soldier held fast to the most violent doppelganger and forced him down. "I am, Ord! I did not expect so much resistance from a mere child. Give me aid, Koa!"

Alain and a younger soldier held fast to one of Mellow's clones as the boy's double choked on its saliva, rocking back and forth. Soon enough, a seizure attacked the suffering clone, and he stretched out like an electric shock had zapped him before slumping still. Mellow watched himself die yet again. Soon enough, all the dead ones faded away again, leaving only the live ones still suffering. Alain and a few other soldiers forced the remaining clones still as Mellow watched on. There were only twelve he had seen, but he bet there had been more before he woke up. How much had that crystal affected him?

"It took many duplicates to dilute your pain, Mellow," Locke said. "As you slept, I pulled dozens on you out and even still, hours later, you have only finally managed to awaken. And as you see, I have only made the pain bearable enough for you to move. Eventually, that relief will fade." He watched another clone roll to its side and expire in silence. "At this rate, you have hours before even the clones will not be enough. Now that you are awake, the pain should be distributed more evenly."

Mellow bit his lip as he sat up. "If you knew this would happen, then why did you send me?"

"Taking my father's crystal away from him should have sapped his power—without a source, he would die and fade away, which would, in turn, leave the crystal powerless. In other words, they feed off each other. He should not have been able to live after you did that." Locke looked towards the ceiling. "Unless . . ."

"That's right," a woman said. "He no longer needs to the crystal."

Out of the crowd of soldiers standing around the room emerged a man and a woman wearing armor like the rest but with a similar face shape. The male was large, almost like a gorilla, and the woman was slim but moved gracefully like a cat. Something about them were very familiar to Mellow.

"Camille," Locke said. "You and Rantan had been allowed in Father's confidence more than I. Had he said anything more about the crystal's power?"

The woman shook her head. "Father never trusted any of his children enough to tell us deeper secrets. But Rantan was with him the longest. Did you learn anything from him, brother?"

The large man gripped his temples as if in thought. He then sighed. "All I can remember is Father's growing obsession with finding the Gemini Man. He did not appear to care about any of this, of us, until he controlled the ones behind the Gemini Bracelets."

"In other words," Locke said. "The reason why taking the crystal did not kill him is because he consumed the Gemini Man as his new source. It is as we feared. The crystal was our last hope."

"So he won?" Mellow asked. He scratched at the itches on his body. "Then we did all this for nothing."

Locke sucked at his teeth. "Not entirely. The fact is that he has no retreat option now. Once we save the Gemini Man, the Great Sorcerer King will have no more source to cling to. Like a parasite, he will die."

"What means do we have to approach him?" Ordopha asked. "The Gemini Man was the only one with the power needed. No other mortal can come close."

"There is one, Ordopha. We do know of one who could still oppose Father. That would be his daughter, Zelana."

Mellow remembered that teenage girl. She was the one who faced Suicide's gang back in Riverview years back, her abilities far beyond that of a Prime or anything the boy had seen before. But she had also disappeared from town around the same time Jason and Matthew had.

"Jason's girlfriend?" Mellow said. "But isn't she gone, too?"

"He needs to absorb her, as well." Locke looked to his siblings who all nodded. "She is our sister, but Zelana was made specifically as a battery for Father. Had she not swallowed the Kharis Seed, he would have already taken her by now. The seed purified the magic that he imbued in her, and he cursed that he would never be able to use her as he wanted. However, he no longer has the crystal as his source. Now nothing is stopping him from taking her back except time. He has that now. If he consumes her, then all is lost. She will not hold out alone."

"Then let's go." Mellow jumped to his feet. The one called Alain caught his arm before he fell. The boy blinked as streaks of red flashed across his vision. "How long have I been out?"

"Too long," Alain said. "I wish to save my friends as much as you, but mindlessly storming the Gate of Gold will lead you to an early end. Wait for the woman to awaken. She should be able to give us valuable information. Ordopha has healed her to the point that she should awaken soon. Just like you, most regain their senses soon after she is done with the healing ritual."

Not much could be added to that. As soon as Alain delivered his speech, the rest of the soldiers and children of Nieto gathered around in the nearby musty chamber to discuss what had happened. Despite how they had fought the lizardmen and chased the Great Sorcerer King off their world, few seemed very relieved or excited. It hit him that this wasn't yet over, and what came next would be scaling a far more impossible cliff.

Mellow left the cot despite Ordopha's protestations and found a window in a nearby room. This fortress still stood tall even with the battles in had been through, and he felt oddly safe in its walls. He stared out into the crimson red sunset over the mountain range. All semblance of the purple mist was long gone, and even birds sang outside. This world would eventually heal from Nieto—but would he?

The boy sat, his insides screaming, and remembered the last few years of his life. He used to think losing his emotions, his sense of feeling, was the worst thing he could experience. Even simple joys like eating a steak or beating some chump in an online match gave him nothing in return aside from the knowledge of accomplishment. Such a thing allowed him to concentrate, to get things done—if it wasn't for Jason showing him how to use a sword and his empty days practicing instead of thinking on his predicament, he'd be dead now. And that was no joke—Mellow Holmes had frequently considered how much his life was worth living.

But when he saw how happy his parents were when he came home with a good grade, or the joy on the football team's faces when they won a game, or when he attended a funeral and saw the tears, he reconsidered. There was too much to life that he didn't know or understand. To give up would be losing the chance to experience something new. And who knew what strangeness would arrive in the future? Even at his lowest, just as when Locke came to see him, he had secretly hoped for the best.

But never did Mellow Holmes imagine this.

His chest ached, causing him to shake. It was as if his engine were revving up. Whatever would happen to him could happen at any moment, and now his body wanted to react to all of these recovered sensations at once. If it wasn't for Locke using his power and muting its effect, he'd probably already be dead.

So what would he do with the time he had left? Mellow was still just a mortal. He had no powers.

Another person sat beside him in another chair. This man wore the same leather armor he did and removed his helmet before speaking to him. "If it isn't Mellow Holmes. I can't believe you're still alive."

"Boon?" Mellow's mouth fell agape. "What in the world are you of all people doing not only on another world, but here as well?"

"Repaying a debt," a girl said. In the doorway leaned a teenage girl wearing robes like Ordopha and her hair tied back. Another human? "But also because we want to be here."

"Wait." Mellow glanced back and forth between the two. It was bizarre seeing two beings dressed like that with Caucasian skin instead of chalk white. Not only that, weren't they enemies? "Isn't that the girl that was with Suicide? Didn't she help attack Riverview? Why are you with her?!"

Boon laughed. "Funny seeing humans beside yourself here, huh? You really never know where life will take you. I'll tell you what happened after this is all over, kid. For now, I think we have more pressing concerns. You need some backup crossing the gate?"

"Backup?" Mellow blinked at his old comrade. "I'm not even sure I can walk again, never mind storm a gate into some other mystery world. Definitely don't think bringing others is a good idea."

"Don't underestimate us," the girl said. "We've been through the ringer ourselves."

Mellow shrugged. "I don't doubt it. But I've got a ticking time bomb inside of me that is eventually going to go off and wipe everything out. The fewer people around me when it goes off, the less havoc it causes. Now, if only I could figure out how to use it against Nieto."

"You've changed." Boon looked the boy up and down, his eyes wide. "I almost didn't believe it when I saw you come through that Mirror Gate with Locke. Mellow Holmes charging into the unknown, and alone at that? If Burner could see you now . . ."

"I'm the reason Burner is dead, Boon."

"How do you figure?"

The memory returned, causing a sickness Mellow hadn't felt in years squeezing at his gut. Burner and Mellow soon found the boat where Suicide had hidden, hoping to put an end to the chaos unleashed on Riverview. But they were ambushed by their enemy as well as this girl currently in the room with them. Burner was shot, and Mellow knocked her unconscious despite his fear. That was when the boy felt the wrath of Suicide and was sent into a coma, losing his sense of feeling. Mellow shivered at the memory.

"My name is Amy," the girl said, waking him from his thoughts. "Mellow, I'm the one that got Burner killed, along with many others. That's why I'm here. It's all I can do, even after the cops let us go. I invaded your town and hurt many others, including you, and I can never take it back. But you are not to blame."

He smiled at her. "Cowards are always to blame."

Boon shifted his chair over and put an arm around Mellow's shoulder. He roughed his hair up as the boy struggled against him. Finally, he let the teenager go, laughing the whole way. "You are way too self-serious. Maybe you haven't changed that much. The past is the past, kid. It's over and gone. At some point, you got to move on and face the road ahead. Isn't that how you got this far?"

Before Mellow could reply, the young soldier named Koa appeared at the doorway. "The girl is awake!"

Mellow decided to put it aside and go to Oriane. Boon and Amy agreed, following him down the hall.

It was true that the past was over and done—he could never go back to that place again. But a part of who he was then would never fully leave him. Even now, that familiar putrid cowardly voice that caused his nerves to shrivel up when he was needed by others told him to run away. What was all this to him, anyway?

Life was full of partings and meetings, after all, but he would not be the one to make the call of who would be abandoned and who would be supported along the way. Not anymore. He might not be a hero, but he would not be a deserter either.

Before he let this thing kill him, Mellow had one last thing to do. It was time to face down death itself.

CHAPTER 7
LAST PIECE

THE LOT OF NEARBY SOLDIERS made a mad dash back down the hallway to where the cots lay. The men made a path for Mellow and the others as they reached the wounded once again. They kept their distance from the sitting woman, allowing him to move to the front.

Oriane held the smoking grey sphere from before. She gazed into it with a glassy stare.

"Oriane?" Mellow asked. "Isn't that—"

"Yes," she replied. The young woman slammed the orb on the ground, and it broke open, sending smoke across the floor. The crowd shielded their eyes. "I've made my choice. Now, it is your turn, Celeste."

The smoke soon cleared, and her blue haired sister stood before Oriane, her skin still stained with burns and injuries from their earlier battle. She raised her right hand towards Oriane, and blue flames sparked in her palm.

Every warrior grabbed at their swords, spears, axes, and bows, as shouts filled the hallway. Oriane, however, yelled at them all to be quiet and keep their distance. She stood up and met her sister face to face; both women held the same exhausted expression. Alain gestured to the others to be silent as the sisters stared each other down.

"You saw everything I did, Sister," Oriane said. "You experienced the Great Sorcerer King's madness firsthand. You now know exactly what he thinks of us."

Celeste's grimace flickered. "And what is that?"

"He has abandoned this world, and us. You were a tool, as was I, and we both wore out our usefulness. Put your flames away, Celeste. You have nothing to gain doing battle here. The fight is over—we have lost."

"Your arrogance is unending, Oriane. Do not think to lecture me!"

"Someone must. Your hard head is stronger than oak!"

The sisters went on arguing, but Mellow's attention was drawn elsewhere. He had just noticed an odd thing about the people who had rescued him—particularly the ones wearing robes. The women, like Ordopha, wore white cloth and tended to the wounded, a white light healing their injuries in a way he thought only Primes could. Though finding this many Primes with healing abilities of the same type was practically impossible, he didn't know what else to make of it. This wasn't from Nieto, like the magic he had swallowed, so what exactly was it? Had this world contained other types of magic, or was this something more?

However, it was the males in the darker robes with strange patterns that he really found himself drawn to. They reminded him of priests of some sort. These Earthwalkers were seeing lines of soldiers and talking in whispered tones about one thing or another. After speaking for a bit, the priest would jab his hand into the subject's chest and jerk out a mass of black substance that reminded him of rot or mud. There would be no blood or marking from where the priest's hand entered, but the soldier would look like he had just consumed a case of energy drinks before thanking the man in the robes and running back to join his allies. There was a weight lifted from them that Mellow felt even from his position.

That was when it hit him.

"This world outgrew Nieto a long time ago," he said.

Both sisters stopped their arguing to face him, more confusion than annoyance at his interruption. Ordopha smiled at him and urged him to continue.

"What I mean is that he is no god, no great king, or ruler. He's a mortal like everyone else. I saw it when I took the crystal. It's only now that I truly understand his game. But I'm sure you two sisters already know."

Oriane and Celeste glanced at each other and then at him. The blue haired woman shrugged and waved him off. "We are only told what we need to know. The Great Sorcerer King Nieto was here when the universe sprang from the abyss, and he will transcend it when all returns to it again. In the meantime, we were created to serve him. Our Lord cannot be defied. You should know that. His crystal contains his excess power, because he is overflowing with the life force of creation itself."

Mellow shook his head. "No, that is wrong. He is not that old."

The purple fog flowed through Mellow's soul like acid through a rain gutter, scorching his being. He flinched as he attempted to concentrate on what the crystal inside showed him. But try as he might, he could see no pictures, no visions, of what Nieto was or where he actually came from. All he could see was the being he was now, separated from his old power. It was the magic he merged with that made him the being that landed on Tyndarus so long ago—and that magic was now inside Mellow.

"He was a mortal, that is all I can determine," the boy said. "Nieto landed on this world long ago, his power a spoil of a conflict he had with his race. However, the force you call *magic* is poison on the living. It eats and eats until there is nothing left." Mellow swallowed, choking back a wave of pain as his eyes watered. He paused before he continued speaking again. "I don't know what he is, but I know it ate at him, just as it does all else. He created Earthwalkers to find a way to take the burden off himself, but they obtained sentience and rejected him. His own daughter Zelana was also created to be a siphon to take the burden off of him, and she also turned on that monster. The relics were his one source of escape from the magic eating him from the inside—in particular, the Gemini Bracelets. If he could create the perfect host for the relic and consume said victim, he could escape his fate."

Oriane folded her arms. "And now he has done just that."

"Yes." Mellow thought harder. The illness stirred inside of him, but still, he looked beyond it into the only solution staring him down. "So I have to give him back this crystal. It might not even do anything at this point, but there aren't any other options. Once I do that, you will see just how much of a mortal he is."

The two sisters watched each other again. None of the other soldiers in the area made any sort of sound as the pair fell silent. No one moved. The heaviness in the air was only matched by the weight pressing down on Mellow's insides.

Even still, he did see more than he wanted to through that blasted crystal. The two sisters birthed from a dark seed Nieto planted deep in his being ages ago, their personalities intentionally wiped, they were meant to be more mindless cogs in this infernal machine the Great Sorcerer King had made for himself. They were to correct the mistakes of the children that had left the dark for the light.

But try as he might, Nieto could not fully control what they were. Both sisters also became mortal, their souls slowly questioning the lives they were made to live—and Oriane was the first of the two to make that choice when given the chance. Would she be the last?

Celeste turned her attention from her sister to Mellow and then to the rest of the room. She clearly recognized she was outnumbered, should she decide to attack, but she did not seem to consider it. Instead, she let her flames die out and her arms drop. "I sometimes see it, you know?"

Oriane nodded. "Yes, I know."

"Memories that aren't mine. I see myself with a child, but the woman is not me, walking through the garden, picking the right blades of grass to whistle with my daughter. I throw her in the air and catch her as we dance to a song on the wind that no one can hear but us. But slowly the years pass, the girl ages, and my joy turns to wrath, then indifference, then obsession with a new project assigned by my master. I know this woman isn't me, but I still see her and that girl, lonely and cold, as she is locked away to be little more than compost. I shouldn't care." Celeste clenched her fists and spurts of blue flame burst out. "But I do."

"That is our sister," Locke interrupted. "Zelana."

Both sisters took their attention to the Earthwalker. Celeste cocked her head. "*Zelana.*"

"There is a reason Nieto wants her under his thumb," Mellow said. He closed his eyes in thought again. Memories that weren't his came to him of a girl who was to shoulder all of Nieto's burden, a girl left forgotten and alone. That is, until she was rescued—rescued by the very people he was to consume for himself. "If she was allowed to team up with the Gemini Man, and they were both at their full potential, then Nieto would most definitely lose. If we can free them somehow, we might be able to win."

Locke and his siblings approached the arguing sisters and stood beside Mellow. The man who had helped save the boy's life multiple times now patted him on the shoulder. "We can open the Gate of Gold for you, but once we do that . . . well, that's it. Very little of his magic remains in us. We will not be able to bring you back again. Are you certain you wish to do this, Mellow? I know I've asked you before, but this time we really will not be able to recover you. That gate was made for our father and mother only. Anyone else who enters will die. That might include you, even with his magic pumping into your very soul."

"No, it won't, Locke." Mellow knew that the magic inside of him burned against his very being, but it also protected him at the same time. It did not want its current host to die and leave it stranded in limbo. There really was no one else left to take this trip. A sudden spike in pain made his right arm spasm. "The crystal really wants me for itself. It won't let me die. My body will give out first. Let's get on with it."

Mellow gathered his equipment and met Nieto's children by the Gate of Gold in a chamber near the top of the fortress. Boon and Amy bid him good luck, as did Alain and the soldiers. Ordopha made him promise to come back alive, which he reluctantly agreed to. It wasn't as if he could be certain he could keep such a promise. With only a sword and shield and the magic flooding his mind, he hardly had much else to fight a so-called god with. When he reached the target room, he noticed the flame sisters were waiting for him.

He didn't have to ask why they were there—he knew. They had all figured out exactly what the two young women were by now, and there was little point beating around the bush. Judging from their powers and their memories, they were clearly fashioned from Queen Shaula, the wife of Nieto, someone who should have been killed years ago by the Gemini Man. And yet the sorcerer somehow drew her back out again in this strange set of sisters. They were the only two who could possibly help him now.

However, he still wondered about Celeste.

"I'm only going in order to find Zelana," the blue-haired sister said. "I don't know about you or the rest of these warriors and your goal, but I know if I find her, then I will discover that piece of me I've been missing—or maybe what the Queen inside of me has been missing."

Oriane patted her sister's arm. "Don't worry, Celeste, we'll find it together."

The two siblings shared a slight smile between them before following Mellow into the chamber. There they found the three children of Nieto standing before a gigantic wall length golden mirror shining light like a beacon out of the door and into the hallway. They met the approaching travelers with grins of their own.

"I hardly thought I would ever be standing here," the mountain named Rantan said. "But he must be stopped. Our home world can never reach its true potential under his boot-heel."

Camille nodded. "Not just here, but worlds all over count on you three. Once you make it back, I'll even introduce you to my children. You've never seen any child as adorable as they are."

"I look forward to it!" Oriane chirped.

Celeste folded her arms. "What do we do, anyway? Do we just run into it like it's a Mirror Gate?"

"That's right," Locke said. "Mirror Gates were based on this one, after all. Just watch yourselves in there. This is the last jump. I can't promise what you'll find on the other side. Father's certainly trapped the entrance somehow, as well. Steel yourself."

Mellow didn't say anything beyond goodbyes to the three children of Nieto that opened this gate for him. The two young women followed him as he jumped into the Gate of Gold and slipped out of existence. The hard light swallowed him whole.

The teenager tumbled into the brightness, spinning out of control as he was thrown about. It was only the energy in the crystal guiding him that helped him keep his bearings. Mellow didn't want to imagine how the girls were doing behind him.

As he fell into the light, a chasm of blackness opened up into the white ahead of him. A voice whispered out of the dark, calling out to him as he blitzed towards it.

"*This time, I break you, boy.*"

Mellow ignored his words and flew onward. They continued to pelt him, but he paid them no mind.

All remnants of fear in his nerves had been ironed out by his new resolve. This was the final battle. No way would he be intimidated out of it now. It was all about to end.

CHAPTER 8
GEMINI DESTROYER

A BURNING SENSATION engulfed Mellow as he flew out of the mirror. Touching down on solid ground did little to changed that as walls of flame crashed into him, scorching his flesh. The teenager couldn't even cry out as the fire lashed across his skin and burrowed deep into his bones. His breaths grew short as the blaze choked the air out of whatever space he had landed in.

The boy's armor melted under the intensity of the heavy blitz, and his flesh charred over. Mellow's helmet seeped into his skull as he fell over to whatever floor was under him.

It was there as he thrashed around that the purple mist forced its way out of him. It pooled around his body, pressing against the fire. Was it trying to heal him? Mellow's naked form fought with itself as he struggled to breath and see just what had attacked him.

Oriane and Celeste appeared at his side and threw out flames of their own, pushing back at the blaze attempting to cook them all. The two sisters threw off the fire, and Mellow choked his breaths free again.

His bare skin smoked, and the blackened patches healed over, returning his pinkish white hue again, though his armor did not return. He coughed, his flesh sore and thumping with pain, and rose back up again. When his eyes stopped watering, he managed to take in just where they had landed.

This wasn't quite a dungeon, but it also wasn't a castle. Blackened stone laid out what he thought was a cathedral with tall arches and stain glass perched everywhere between paintings of Nieto overlooking entire solar systems. Through the gaps in the windows were the endless sea of stars that might have been space, if there wasn't still plenty of air in this building. Chains and broken torture devices lay all over this tall chamber.

"We did not quite finish him off, Roseus," a teenage girl with purple hair said.

The second young woman with pink hair nodded. "It seems he was saved by our other sisters, Porfura."

The two women looked exactly as Mellow expected. Despite their different colored hair, they were just as Oriane and Celeste were—clones of Queen Shaula. How many of these had Nieto made?

Oriane gestured towards him to flee towards the stairs. Celeste outright told him to leave.

"We will hold them back," Oriane said. "You must hurry and find the lord of this place. Do not worry. We will find you when we win."

"Win?" Roseus said. She cackled as if the idea were as inane as Mellow's current nakedness. "You are in the belly of a god. There is no victory for you here."

Porfura nodded. "This war has already ended."

"Nothing has ended yet," Celeste said. "I will show you the folly of your so-called war."

Mellow struggled to gain his balance as he made a dash towards the stairs. A blast of heat flew towards him, but the flames were cut off by Oriane's own. The four young doppelgangers of Queen Shaula turned on each other and let their own powers loose. Spurts of multi-colored fire splashed all over the chamber. As they fought, the teenager slipped out of the lower level and closed the large metal door behind him.

Silence filled the fortress. His steps reverberated in his head, carrying him forward as if a mind of their own. There, he could swear the entire fortress, or whatever it was, rotated around him like a corkscrew as he ran. His gut cartwheeled and choked his thoughts as the smell of incense mixed with embalming fluid tickled his nose. He let the bile leak out of his lip as he forced himself to move through this sickness.

There weren't even any sort of pathway or hall, but an endless stream of identical chambers that were the size of the auditorium at school, only without the rows of seats and the stage housing all those goofy props and costumes. A voice whispered in his ear and beckoned him forward, sliding through the silence, and guided him into one spot in particular. He clutched his knees as every hard breath jerked out of him. The boy bit back at the vomit demanding to be let loose on the world and swallowed it back.

It was then that he noticed where he was. Two grand sweeping staircases on either side of this gigantic chamber of red carpeting and black stone led up to a second floor where an altar lay in wait. This platform was surrounded by glass like a tube and filled with purple mist. Mellow didn't have to guess to know that someone was in there—someone who wanted out.

He sprinted up the stairs, the crystal in his bones supercharging his movement. Puffs of purple smoke somehow forced its way out of his skin like car exhaust, even as his whole body rumbled with excitement. It soon covered his naked form like a coat of armor, replacing the clothes that had been scorched away into ash moments ago. That sickness inside did not waver, preventing Mellow from appreciating any of it.

Halfway up the left staircase he was interrupted by a presence slipping into the chamber on the opposite steps. He turned to see the Great Sorcerer King himself watching him as if he were there the whole time. The enemy no longer held a barely tangible shape, wearing heavy dark armor and a helmet that masked his non-existent features. Instead of the purple energy gathering around him, fissures of white light littered his body randomly. It was as if an energy desired to burst forth from within.

"This girl can't help you now, whelp," Nieto said. "She sacrificed herself to save the same fools who gave themselves up to save her. And now here you are to throw your own life away for those you also have no relation to. You humans are all so very ridiculous, you know. Without your silly sentimentality and attachments, you might have bested me. Instead you have given me the very tools I need to destroy you with. I don't think I will rule your Earth, after all. It would probably best to just destroy it, as Suicide requested. You are all far too inept to be allowed to live."

Mellow wiped the corners of his mouth. The voice in the tube spoke louder and louder to him. If he could absorb that miasma in there, he could wake up the prisoner. The boy inched up the stairs as he spoke. "All I did was run and destroy the things I wanted to protect most. I poisoned myself into being the worst thing I could be. I'm not that creep anymore. You won't stop me."

"Exactly, you are a perfect example of my point. All your effort was completely worthless. Just like you thinking that freeing my presence will make a difference."

"No. Despite my failures, and despite the fact I didn't deserve it, after your follower robbed me of my emotions, I wanted to die. I almost did. Even before your son approached me to come here I thought I would miss out on life and become nothing but a passenger, staring in from the outside. But it was people like Jason Vermilion, Matthew White, and your daughter Zelana, who helped me through it. There was more to all this than taking what I want. Without others, it's all worth nothing. *She* told you that, too. Didn't she?"

"*She* is nothing but fuel, and you are

nothing but a corpse that has not yet been buried. I shall rectify that mistake."

Nieto leaped forward off the steps with a blazing speed Mellow had never seen before. His hands sharp like claws, the sorcerer king slashed the boy's throat. Mellow backed up and dodged a follow-up as he clung to his bloody neck. Waves of anguish flooded through him. Thankfully, the wound healed up, allowing him to breathe, even as Nieto moved in again for another volley of strikes.

Mellow hopped up the steps, the stone shattering behind him. The boy bounded upwards even as the stairs burst apart from the enemy's attacks. However, the stone would repair itself instantly after being broken, almost as if Nieto were cutting through pure air. Mellow reached the top of the steps and turned about to face the approaching sorcerer.

Nieto rushed forward, and Mellow intercepted. Both of Nieto's claws sunk into Mellow's chest, and the boy let out a cry. Warm blood trickled out of his flesh as he gripped both hands of his attacker. Purple miasma plumed from the open wounds and dizziness momentarily consumed him before he snapped himself back awake again. Mellow used the jolt of energy to squeeze Nieto's hands, and the large attacker laughed.

"You truly are a child," the Great Sorcerer King said. "And what exactly do you hope to do against a being you cannot harm?"

"I don't have to hurt you. I just have to push back hard enough."

The boy jerked Nieto's wrists, and a crack sounded from the king's hands. He slipped the gauntlets loose and fitted them on himself as the Great Sorcerer King reeled painlessly from the attack. Mellow shoved his enemy back before leaping towards the tube behind him. He punched the tough gauntlets against the glass—once, twice, and broke it with a third strike.

Miasma flowed out of the broken tube and flooded into Mellow, causing him to vomit this time. He fell to all fours and gagged again as the enemy cackled behind him. Nieto kicked the boy and send him rolling sideways. Mellow gripped his stinging ribs and attempted to focus through his blurring vision. All he could see were Nieto's wrists moving normally again.

And he also had normal hands. Caucasian skin presented itself where the gauntlets had been.

"Surprised?" Nieto asked. "I already told you that I no longer need my magic to sustain myself. I am whole once more."

"You were never whole, Father," Zelana said. "There has always been a piece of you missing."

The beautiful girl Mellow remembered quite well stood behind him, her white robes still smoking, and her blonde hair tied in a ponytail. He had almost forgotten she had used her own magic to become human years ago, something her father could never do. As she looked upon the two fighters before her, the young woman's hands lit up in with a bright white light. It was the polar opposite of the miasma currently flowing through Mellow's very being.

She sprang forward, her fists flashing with light. She lashed the beam outwards, and it cracked against Nieto's armor, piercing like a spear. The light left a smoking hole in the enemy's flesh, causing him to look down at the wound in surprise.

Within a minute, the opening reformed as if it had ceased being intangible, showing bare Caucasian skin. The armor was clearly superfluous—his flesh could not be harmed regardless of what struck him.

"Zelana," Nieto said. "Ever the disappointment. I know you heard and saw all in there—I very much wanted you to. Did you get a good look at his face when I stole it from him?"

Rage encompassed every part of Zelana. Her balled fists and tight lips could melt steel. "I will kill you, Father. You know I will."

"You will do nothing, whelp. I know you too well." Nieto removed the helmet from his head, and Mellow's stomach churned when he saw the face emerge from under it. No longer was it a formless mass of miasma, but a human being. "Not when I look like *him*."

Nieto threw his helmet aside, apparently no longer interested in hiding his visage. The face he wore was now that of Jason Vermilion, or his unrelated twin, Matthew White. Whichever one was difficult to tell with the cracks adorning it. He smiled at his daughter, who only breathed harder the longer she looked at him.

"Zelana," Mellow said. "He *is* the Gemini Man now. What are we supposed to do?"

"There is only one thing left." She stood at his side and presented her hands. "We combine both my magic and yours, and we take the fight from the physical realm."

Mellow cocked his head. "We do what?"

The teenage girl gestured for him to match her movements, and he complied. Both of them lifted their right hands, and their magic glowed bright. Their energies mixed and matched, swirling around each other, but like water and oil never quite becoming one. The queasiness in Mellow lifted slightly as an uncomfortable warmth filled his organs. At the same time, Zelana winced and cried out as if something were striking her from the inside. They clasped hands; their energies were becoming one and flowing through each of them.

"You really truly believe you can beat me now," Nieto said. "I am a master of the material and immaterial, just like the Gemini Man. In fact, I *am* him now. I also do not harbor his weaknesses. I will not sacrifice my life for any lesser creature. How do you suppose mortals overwhelm an immortal?"

"We attack the mortal in you," she replied.

Mellow reacted by an instinct he didn't know he had in him and moved with Zelana. The two teenagers ran screaming into Nieto who only laughed at their approach. He punched at them both, but the pair swirled around his attacks, their very being spinning like a drill through the Great Sorcerer King's armor. His stunned look was momentarily overtaken by what Mellow thought was fear.

The boy punctured the bare flesh with the gauntlet and tore it open. Nieto's fist slammed into his face and sent him stumbling as the girl flew in from behind, bringing down a bolt of magic.

Nieto turned in time to eat her energy straight on in his face. Teeth and lips tore open as the beam flowed down his throat and spurts of blood swirled about his body as if he swallowed a tornado. The Great Sorcerer King spun around in time to meet Mellow face to face.

The two teenagers unleashed a flurry of magic, slashing open flesh and breaking bones with overwhelming power. Nieto punched out and beat against flesh, sending both Mellow and Zelana bloody and reeling.

Nonetheless, the fortress filled with light and darkness, sickness and health, joy and anger, as screams of every sort of voice one could imagine cried out as the assault continued. Pain and euphoria split the universe, and reality bent as all three figures were blown out of existence itself. Nieto, Zelana, and Mellow, all collided together at once, and a lightning bolt of impossible light flashed with the sudden thunder.

Within a nanosecond, the impossible fortress, and reality itself, was gone.

CHAPTER 9
THE ENDLESS PLAINS

EVERY SINGLE BIT of the Great Sorcerer King burned as if he had been doused in scorching magma and dragged into the core of the planet itself. Flesh parted and reformed over and over again. He awoke in what he thought was outside, but not in any place he had seen before. This new space was a flat plain that went on forever in every direction with only a light warm wind to remind him that the interior world of the fortress had been left behind. Clear blue skies and a heavens' piercing sun shined down from above.

That was when he heard the groaning. Several feet away in the knee-length grass lay a moaning figure overflowing with purple miasma. His whole body was rotting away as his low voice turned to screams of pain. Mellow Holmes was dying.

"It was a good attempt," Nieto said to the boy in the dirt. The enemy lay struggling for breath as the Great Sorcerer King approached. "But a mortal will never defeat a god."

Nieto brought his boot down on Mellow Holmes again and again until the boy himself was nothing but a memory, like the remainder of the purple mist fading away into the plains. Finally, he was rid of that child and the remnants of his old self. All that was left was to finish the girl.

"Father," Zelana said.

The Great Sorcerer King followed the

voice of his failed daughter to where she lay. The girl's pale skin was charred purple and bleeding the red blood of a human. Her dirty face and crumpled bones showed another who didn't quite make the jump to wherever this was. Her breaths arrived hard through squinted eyes.

"This is your last chance, Father," she rasped out. The girl's swollen eyes gazed up at him, not with fear but with something much worse—pity. "You have lost. Make it easy on yourself."

"I see you truly have gone mad, Daughter." Nieto gestured to where he crushed Mellow Holmes to death. "One of you is already dead. Once I rid myself of your failure, I will no longer have anyone left to oppose me."

Her expression turned to one of puzzlement. "Do you truly not see where you are? Do you not truly understand what you've become? Father, you have already lost. It is done."

"I am the one standing, not you."

"You are not standing anywhere. Has your perspective been so warped and poisoned that all perception has been lost? It is already finished for you. The so-called Great Sorcerer King is no longer any sort of sorcerer or king, and what is great about you was lost long before I was conceived."

"Enough!"

"I'm sorry I couldn't do more for you, Father. I suppose we will have to part here. Goodbye."

"I said that is enough!"

Nieto felt his entire being surge with a blind rage that flowed harder than any of the magic he once housed inside. Just as he did before, he jumped forward and brought his weight down on the girl, matching what he had done to the boy moments earlier. His anger brought an end to her prattling. Soon enough, she was also dead, leaving the Great Sorcerer King as the lone victor in this war.

Finally, he had become the god he had always known he would be.

"Master?"

Behind him appeared Shaula—but it wasn't Shaula. There were four of her, each with different colored hair, all scorched with flame and cuts. They had all been fighting amongst each other, for reasons he could no longer remember. The confusion inside of him slowly turned to wrath the more he looked them over. These were young fakes, pale imitations of someone much grander than they. They all stared back at him with a gaze of fear and confusion that reminded him that they would never be her, no matter how much he desired to bring her back. The one with red hair said something to him that he didn't bother listening to before he took a step forward.

The quartet all instinctively receded at his approach. They clearly had enough of the Queen in them to realize he would kill them like the rest. They had to die, after all. They were mere forgeries.

He punched the blue haired one in the stomach and she fell. Nieto then grabbed the two nearest and lifted them before slamming the pair into the earth. They both pleaded for him to stop as he repeated his attack over and over. A blast of red flame caused him to lose his grip and stumble backwards a step. The lone remaining fake stood alone before him.

"We have done all you have ever asked," she said. "Why do you insist on destruction?"

"You cannot destroy what is not real."

"I am real."

"You are spare parts cobbled together through the void. You have no purpose. You and these living puppets thought you could take your own strings and dance. Where has that gotten you? Nowhere but an early death."

"You may have brought us to life, but you will not put us to death."

The other three rats hid behind the red-headed forgery, catching their breaths. Their leader merely stared at him, again, just like the dead ones, not with fear, but pity. His wrath only grew the more he looked upon these living mistakes.

"There is more out in the universe than your petty whims," she said. "I am going to see it all."

Every time they spoke, every time they moved, they reminded him of *her*—his queen. Of course, that is partially why he created them in the first place, but they could never understand that. Even his own children had been allowed to live for as long as they had because they contained something of her that he could never quite find again, no matter how deep he dug into the magic that was once his. Now, they were just a reminder of that piece he could never find again.

"There is nothing to see except the void," he replied.

Nieto threw out a simple thought, that these forgeries would just die, and all four of them flew backwards as if hit by his very command. They rolled across the grass several feet before stopping on their knees and elbows. He stared after them for a second before the realization of what had happened finally hit him. He had truly transcended time and space. Nothing could stand to the Great Sorcerer King any longer. They were all little more than ants to be crushed by his perfectly polished boots.

His long and painful journey was finally over; Nieto had won.

"*That's about enough now,*" Shaula said. "*It's time to come home, my love.*"

Nieto spun around towards the voice. She was here! She lived! He was instead met with the empty plain. The Great Sorcerer King turned back, and no one else, including his victims, remained. Only that endless blue skin and knee-length grass awaited him. Where had they all escaped to? Nieto turned one last time and found two familiar men staring at him: the two halves of the Gemini Man.

Jason Vermilion shook his head. "You didn't just bite off more than you could chew—you tried to swallow it whole in one bite."

"And now you're choking," Matthew White added.

The nearly identical males stood before him, dressed normally in their garb from Earth, not even a bruise or scratch on their bodies. That shouldn't have been possible, but then neither should his victims have disappeared. Perhaps, he truly wasn't in control here? The pair watched the Great Sorcerer King as if he were a monkey in a cage, pity on their faces. These fools had no right—they should have been dead.

"You!" Nieto exclaimed. "You should not be here!"

Jason Vermilion shook his head. "We never left."

"You dug too greedily, Nieto." Matthew White gestured to his own forehead. "Doesn't it hurt?"

At the exact moment White said that, Nieto's vision spider-webbed and fractured as if it were a mere sheet of glass. Red splotched his sight, and his throat seized. Breaths fell heavy, and his limbs involuntarily twitched into a spasm. Blood ejected out of his skin as if he were being squeezed by an invisible force. The Great Sorcerer King was dying.

"What?!" Nieto choked out. "How?!"

"You are just a mortal," both said at the same time. They faded away, and a new figure emerged in their place—a singular man. This impossible figure of pure white energy stood before Nieto, the heat radiating off of him scorching the Great Sorcerer King's very being. "You just hid it well. But you couldn't stop consuming, could you?"

As the Great Sorcerer King's very soul twisted and turned inside and out, he threw himself upward and flew into the air. It was this infernal place—it was attacking him somehow. If he could get off-world he could start over again just as he did when he first landed on Tyndarus so long ago. He was immortal, after all! He would live forever.

The plain disappeared around him, as did the sky, tearing apart into nothing as he flew upwards. When the stars and emptiness of space appeared in its place, he understood just what had happened.

That Gemini Man allowed himself to be consumed, the being comprised of Matthew White and Jason Vermilion had tricked him. They found a way around his defenses. Their powers were far beyond what even a god like Nieto could consume and that allowed them the foothold to tear him up from the inside out. All the times they crossed swords and brawled for supremacy, and it was his own weakening body taking on another that proved to be too much. And now, without his magic, taken by that Mellow Holmes child, he had nothing remaining to defend himself with.

"*All those people,*" Zelana said. "*Was it worth betraying them?*"

"The dead don't talk!"

"*Yes, they do, Father. All the time. You can even hear them now.*"

Once more, Nieto stood in the ruins of a long dead kingdom, the forbidden magic pluming from his perfected body as he looked to the stars. His mad grin widened as reality set in on him. No one remained to stop him—now he would rule all he could find. World after world would fall to the Great Sorcerer King!

But that was all in the past. His home was gone, scorched out of existence. They were all dead and gone, a consequence of his new found powers. His heresy would become truth and he would leave them behind.

Centuries fell by him as he soared through space, his very essence splitting apart. Memories he thought forgotten returned to him —his conquests, his subjects, his children . . . *her*. All leading to his death out in the void of space. And still the voices of the dead spoke to him as if he were one of them.

"*I'm right here,*" Shaula said. "*Just reach out and touch me, my love.*"

The day they all turned on him, Earthwalkers and lizardmen slaying each other and spilling blood across the land, was a disaster, but still he remembered her face when the betrayal occurred. She watched him, unable to look away, her eyes never once turning from him. She grasped his ephemeral hand all the tighter. Queen Shaula would always be there, just as she was right now.

There, in the deep darkness of the void, he found her again. Her platinum flowing hair and perfect features naked in the scorching sun. Shaula stretched out her hand through eternity itself, and he, in turn, grabbed greedily at her. That long-forgotten smile radiated into his very being, and for a moment, he remembered the first time he found that magic so long ago. This is what he had been waiting for. She dragged him forward, her lips touching his.

And then he was gone.

SHE STOOD BEFORE HIM, naked in the sun. He awoke alone and naked in the wild, his arms and legs as broken as his spirit. His bones shattered, his skin scorched, and every piece of him numb from everything except the pain; he could only stare at the tree branches shielding him from the sun.

His Queen stayed alone with him in this new world, bringing him broth that he drank as he lay broken on the makeshift mattress in a hidden hovel. He could no longer even speak, his voice torn from him with the rest of his body.

"*You kept me alive inside of you, my love,*" she had said. "*Now I will do the same for you.*"

There they remained, alone and forgotten by time and the universe itself for the remainder of their short lives. He had only his sight and his hearing, guided by his Queen as he was forced to live on, broken and dumb in an abandoned corner of existence. The agony of his rotting flesh rarely seemed to subside, but her being there allowed him to bear it more as they learned to survive. And there they lived on in the wilds.

The King was dead, but he was not. He would carry the weight of his mistakes for the rest of his short life. And for once that reality did not scare him. All mortals were meant to suffer the same fate, after all.

As he lay crippled in the desert world, a smile escaped his numbed lips. It was all over now. At least, he would be with her until that moment of truth arrived.

She clasped his hand once more, the warmth bringing a tear to his dry eyes. Thunder rolled on in the distance.

"The storm grows close," she said. "Do not worry, my love. I will be with you until it is done."

And she spoke the truth.

CHAPTER 10
END OF THE GEMINI MAN

REALITY WARPED AND ROLLED around like a lone sock in the dryer as Mellow Holmes opened his eyes. It took a moment for him to notice the glowing white being floating beside him surrounded by an orb of piercing light breaking space and time itself. He wasn't alone with the Gemini Man—nearby were also Oriane and her three sisters, drifting slowly through the planet's atmosphere beside another young woman hugging their savior tight. Nieto was nowhere to be seen.

The aches and pains inside of Mellow had disappeared. He flexed his hands, and they cracked, a nice bit of pain he had almost forgotten. It looked as if the crystal had not consumed him.

"It's gone," the Gemini Man said. "The crystal broke and killed you when you and Zelana were absorbed into Nieto. It's a miracle you are breathing now. He had no idea what that plain truly was."

Mellow scrunched his nose. "A miracle, huh?"

Far below, the ground itself slowly approached. It was Tyndarus, the mountains he had left behind were now coming back into focus again. There, he could faintly hear voices cheering from what felt like were miles away. Exhaustion gripped hold of him as the Gemini Man slowly took them down.

"Oriane," Mellow said to one of the girls. "You're still in one piece."

She grinned. "Yes, however, I feel worse than you look."

"You must be feeling pretty awful then." He groaned as he stretched. "What was that plain, anyway?"

"It's better you don't know," the Gemini Man said. He squeezed Zelana a little tighter, and she reciprocated. "Let's just say, no one can truly die there because it is beyond the physical realm."

"Then Nieto is—"

"No, he left it of his own accord with his last bit of power. He won't be coming back. It is done."

Mellow's sore bones told him he would be feeling it for weeks, maybe months, but it hardly affected him at that moment. Never did he think he would ever feel again, never mind that he would have survived this whole ordeal to begin with. That much was certainly a miracle.

Eventually, he would touch down on the earth again, and he would see the others, from Ordopha and Alain, to Boon and Amy, and to the rest of the soldiers, all celebrating the end to a conflict older than he was. That would be nice. For the first time in a dog's age, he smiled out of happiness. It was a nice feeling to have.

The bright light of the Gemini Man faded the closer they got to the ground, and he could swear the body itself was breaking up. His savior seemed to notice his concern and winked at him.

"Don't worry," the Gemini Man said. "It will last long enough to get you back home."

"Then what happens to you?"

"Me?" The Gemini Man paused for a moment as if thinking it over. "I get to go back home, too."

The boy fell silent at those words. For the first time in perhaps his whole life, Mellow Holmes thought of his home and smiled. That world felt like a whole new adventure to him now, ready to be explored for the first time ever. Riverview would be there waiting for him, and for once, he was excited for it.

Tomorrow, Mellow Holmes would wake up in his old bed again, and he was just fine with that.

EPILOGUE

MATTHEW WHITE SAT ON THE BENCH beside Mellow Holmes as the fireworks went off by the maddening crowd across the street. Men and women hollered away as kids ran through the night chasing each other and hollering.

Riverview really knew how to celebrate summer, something Matthew had learned years ago at this point. Had he really been here that long? It felt like he had just arrived with Jason yesterday, and now their whole quest was finally over.

Across the street, Jason and Zelana sat side by side and chatted excitedly with the other recent high school graduates. It was a long journey for them, too, and it was good to see them relax together. They earned their alone time.

"The two of them are leaving, right?" Mellow asked.

Matthew nodded. "They're heading out into the stars. They want to see what's out there."

"Together, huh?"

"Yeah." Matthew laughed, remembering how those two kids still pretended nothing was going on between them. "Together. Hopefully, they send an invite back here when they finally get hitched."

"You're not going with him?"

Of course, Matthew had considered traveling with Jason again, since they had been tied together with their powers for years at this point, but after considering the recent happenings, there would be little point. They were no longer the Gemini Man, after all.

"Our powers are gone," Matthew replied. "It's happened before, but this time it feels different. I might regain the ability to be intangible again. That might come back someday. But the Gemini Man is gone. I think we hit the limit when we broke reality itself to destroy Nieto from the inside out. I can't even remember any of the details of that plain we were in—all the Gemini Man stuff has faded from both of us. It's not coming back. Jason and I have no reason to stick together anymore, and it's time for him to move on and live his own life. It's a big universe. He should see it for himself."

Mellow watched the fireworks a little longer before responding. "I'm going to Tyndarus. Oriane invited me to see it with her, and she's still trying to help her sisters adjust to life outside of the mountains. Celeste is a bit grumpy, but she's getting there. Roseus and Porfura, though? Yeah, they're still struggling. They've never left that inside space Nieto kept them in before. Everything is new to them."

"That's a good mentality to have in general."

"Maybe, but Oriane says she can't do it alone. She keeps asking for my help for some reason."

"I figured she would. A bunch of our pals are heading out to the stars. Boon hit the road again, but Amy decided to follow Locke and his siblings off-world to see Camille's family on a whole other planet. Really is amazing how much is out there we don't know about. It makes sense you kids would want to see it all."

"Not you?"

Matthew shrugged. "No, I've spent my whole time running here and there and all over the place. It's time I finally stayed in one place and put my roots in. Of course, I'll still head to Tyndarus thanks to those personal Mirror Gates that Zelana made some of us; there are still some important people I need to see, but I'm going to stick with Riverview long term. It just feels like home, and I can't see myself anywhere else."

"Home, huh," Mellow said. He pursed his lips as if considering Matthew's words about his own hometown. "Yeah, it is. No matter where I go out there, I guess this will always be my home. And for once, it doesn't bother me to say that. Anyway, got to go. Good luck, Matthew."

Matthew winked at him. "Have fun out there."

Mellow joined Oriane amidst the crowd as a cavalcade of fireworks exploded above in the night sky. His friend Spencer soon slapped him on the shoulder, and the group let out a laugh together. They all mingled together until it was hard to see who was who in the giant mass of celebrants.

It had been a long time since their journey began, and Matthew White hardly remembered what his life was before he went on the road ages ago. What he did remember was the crushing feeling of futility that he lived in a world of heroes and villains that could roll over and flatten him at any moment. For a while, he had thought that being the Gemini Man might reverse that fear, make him the one with control instead. But that was always a fleeting hope, one destroyed with the obvious realization that he was just a mortal like everyone else. Matthew could either build or destroy, grow or waste away. There was nothing else but to finally make that choice and take the step he needed to take. He, like everyone else, had a limited time in this short life, and now, it was time to do it right.

Out in the crowd, his childhood friend Lynn gestured for him to join her along with the many summer celebrants. She wore her hair back, and was as warm as ever in her love of life. The young woman had always been there, and he owed her more than he could give back. She called out again, and so did the others hovering around her in their group. Life went on, and so would he.

Matthew White sat up from the bench and joined the people he cared about. The celebration went on all night, and he was a part of it until the very end. He wouldn't be alone anymore, no matter what happened next.

And that is all there was to it.

The End

Afterword

I WANTED TO THANK EVERYONE involved at Silver Empire and Heroes Unleashed, especially Russell and Morgon Newquist for allowing me the opportunity to write the story of Gemini Man that you have just read through. Without them, none of this would exist.

Special thanks go to Manuel Guzman and L. Jagi Lamplighter for helping me get the extras together for this edition. I could not have done it alone!

At the same time, I need to thank every backer of the crowdfund campaign who helped not only fund this omnibus you are currently holding in your hand, but also the two bonus stories that allowed me to put the final bow on the story of the Gemini Man.

Thank you all for allowing me this opportunity to tell you this tale of a pair of lost heroes on their way to being found.

It's been a long journey since I began writing this series back around 2018. Many events both personal and otherwise conspired to make quite a rocky road. Finally, five years later, I was able to deliver on the promises I set out to make with the initial launch of Book One way back then. Whatever I pursue next will only be possible because of the lessons learned writing the Gemini Man and the support every backer and reader has given me along the way.

Once again, thank you all for your support. None of this would have been possible without all of you.

God willing, however, this is just the beginning! The Gemini Man series might be over, but I have many more projects on the way.

Until the next we meet, keep on moving. You never know what tomorrow holds.

~JD Cowan

About the Author

JD Cowan is a writer with an obsession for stories and Truth. He takes pleasure in looking for Light in the places where darkness grips the tightest. His works include *Grey Cat Blues, The Pulp Mindset, Someone is Aiming for You & Other Adventures, The Last Fanatics,* and short stories in Cirsova, Storyhack, the PulpRev Sampler, and the Planetary Anthology Series. His works can found at Amazon.

He blogs at wastelandandsky.blogspot.ca and can be found on Twitter @wastelandJD for those interested.

Works

Books

Brutal Dreams
Someone is Aiming for You & Other Adventures
Grey Cat Blues
Knights of the End
Y Signal

Gemini Man Series

Gemini Warrior
Gemini Drifter
Gemini Outsider
Gemini Destroyer

Non-Fiction

The Pulp Mindset: A NewPub Survival Guide
Generation Y: The New Lost Generation *[with Brian Niemeier and David V. Stewart]*
The Last Fanatics

Anthologies

The PulpRev Sampler
Corona-Chan: Spreading the Love
Pulp Rock
Sidearm & Sorcery, Volume One
Sidearm & Sorcery, Volume Two
Pulp On Pulp: Tips & Tricks for Writing Pulp Fiction
Swords & Maidens

www.ingramcontent.com/pod-product-compliance
Lightning Source LLC
Chambersburg PA
CBHW080723020726
47503CB00010B/2771

* 9 7 8 1 9 9 0 3 2 0 1 6 3 *